P9-CQY-397

GREEN MARS

Books by Kim Stanley Robinson

FICTION

The Mars Trilogy
Red Mars
Green Mars
Blue Mars (forthcoming)

The California Trilogy
The Wild Shore
The Gold Coast
Pacific Edge

Escape from Kathmandu
A Short Sharp Shock
Green Mars (novella)
The Blind Geometer
The Memory of Whiteness
Icehenge
The Planet on the Table
Remaking History

NONFICTION

The Novels of Philip K. Dick

Green Mars

Kim Stanley Robinson

BANTAM BOOKS
NEW YORK · TORONTO · LONDON · SYDNEY · AUCKLAND

SPECTRA and the portrayal of a boxed "s" are trademarks of
Bantam Books, a division of Bantam Doubleday Dell Publishing Group, Inc.

All rights reserved.
Copyright © 1994 by Kim Stanley Robinson.

BOOK DESIGN BY MARIA CARELLA

No part of this book may be reproduced or transmitted
in any form or by any means, electronic or mechanical,
including photocopying, recording, or by any information
storage and retrieval system, without permission in
writing from the publisher.
For information address: Bantam Books.

ISBN 0-553-09640-0 (HC)

Published simultaneously in the United States and Canada

Bantam Books are published by Bantam Books, a division of Bantam Doubleday Dell Publishing
Group, Inc. Its trademark, consisting of the words "Bantam Books" and the portrayal of a rooster,
is Registered in U.S. Patent and Trademark Office and in other countries. Marca Registrada. Bantam
Books, 1540 Broadway, New York, New York 10036.

PRINTED IN THE UNITED STATES OF AMERICA

for Lisa and David

CONTENTS

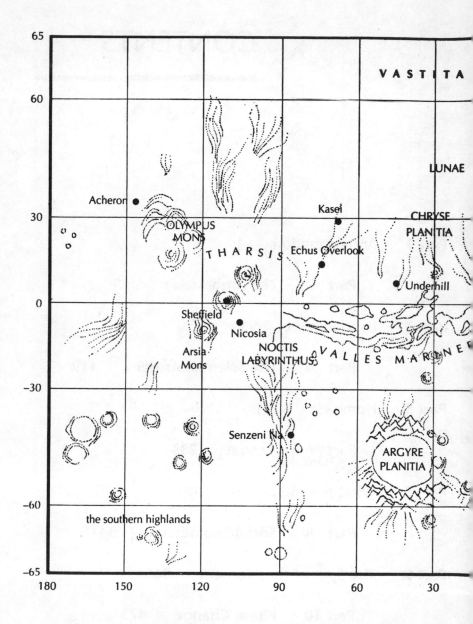

65

60

VASTITA

LUNAE

Acheron ●

30

Kasei

CHRYSE
PLANITIA

OLYMPUS
MONS

THARSIS

Echus Overlook

Underhill

0

Sheffield

Nicosia

Arsia
Mons

NOCTIS
LABYRINTHUS

VALLES MARINER

-30

Senzeni Na ●

ARGYRE
PLANITIA

-60

the southern highlands

-65

180   150   120   90   60   30

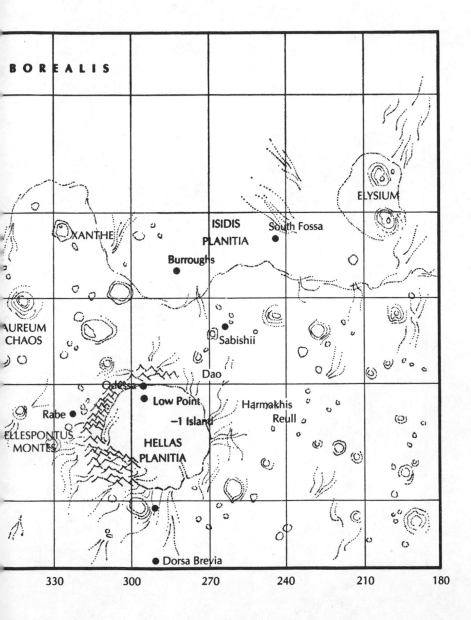

BOREALIS

ELYSIUM

XANTHE

ISIDIS
PLANITIA

South Fossa

Burroughs

AUREUM
CHAOS

Sabishii

Dao

Odessa

Rabe

Low Point

−1 Island

Harmakhis
Reull

ELLESPONTUS
MONTES

HELLAS
PLANITIA

Dorsa Brevia

330   300   270   240   210   180

PART 1

Areoformation

The point is not to make another Earth. Not another Alaska or Tibet, not a Vermont nor a Venice, not even an Antarctica. The point is to make something new and strange, something Martian.

In a sense our intentions don't even matter. Even if we try to make another Siberia or Sahara, it won't work. Evolution won't allow it, and at its heart this is an evolutionary process, an endeavor driven at a level below intention, as when life made its first miracle leap out of matter, or when it crawled out of sea onto land.

Again we struggle in the matrix of a new world, this time truly alien. Despite the great long glaciers left by the giant floods of 2061, it is a very arid world; despite the beginnings of atmosphere creation, the air is still very thin; despite all the applications of heat, the average temperature is still well below freezing. All these conditions make survival for living things difficult in the extreme. But life is tough and adaptable, it is the green force viriditas, pushing into the universe. In the decade following the catastrophes of 2061, people struggled in the cracked domes and torn tents, patching things up and getting by; and in our hidden refuges, the work of building a new society went on. And out on the cold surface new plants spread over the flanks of the glaciers, and down into the warm low basins, in a slow inexorable surge.

Of course all the genetic templates for our new biota are Terran; the minds designing them are Terran; but the terrain is Martian. And terrain is a powerful genetic engineer, determining what flourishes and what doesn't, pushing along progressive differentiation, and thus the evolution of new species. And as the generations pass, all the members of a biosphere evolve together, adapting to *their terrain in a complex communal response, a creative self-designing ability. This process, no matter how much we intervene in it, is essentially out of our control. Genes mutate, creatures evolve: a new biosphere emerges, and with it a new noosphere. And eventually the designers' minds, along with everything else, have been forever changed.*

This is the process of areoformation.

One day the sky fell. Plates of ice crashed into the lake, and then started thumping on the beach. The children scattered like frightened sandpipers. Nirgal ran over the dunes to the village and burst into the greenhouse, shouting, "The sky is falling, the sky is falling!" Peter sprinted out the doors and across the dunes faster than Nirgal could follow.

Back on the beach great panes of ice stabbed the sand, and some chunks of dry ice fizzed in the water of the lake. When the children were all clumped around him Peter stood with his head craned back, staring at the dome so far above. "Back to the village," he said in his no-nonsense tone. On the way there he laughed. "The sky is falling!" he squeaked, tousling Nirgal's hair. Nirgal blushed and Harmakhis and Jackie laughed, their frosted breath shooting out in quick white plumes.

Peter was one of those who climbed the side of the dome to repair it. He and Kasei and Michel spidered over the village in sight of all, over the beach and then the lake until they were smaller than children, hanging in slings from ropes attached to icehooks. They sprayed the flaw in the dome with water until it froze into a new clear layer, coating the white dry ice. When they came down they talked of the warming world outside. Hiroko had come out of her little bamboo stand by the lake to watch, and Nirgal said to her, "Will we have to leave?"

"We will always have to leave," Hiroko said. "Nothing on Mars will last."

But Nirgal liked it under the dome. In the morning he woke in his own round bamboo room, high in Creche Crescent, and ran down to the frosty dunes with Jackie and Rachel and Frantz and the other early risers.

He saw Hiroko on the far shore, walking the beach like a dancer, floating over her own wet reflection. He wanted to go to her but it was time for school.

They went back to the village and crowded into the schoolhouse coatroom, hanging up their down jackets and standing with their blue hands stretched over the heating grate, waiting for the day's teacher. It could be Dr. Robot and they would be bored senseless, counting his blinks like the seconds on the clock. It could be the Good Witch, old and ugly, and then they would be back outside building all day, exuberant with the joy of tools. Or it could be the Bad Witch, old and beautiful, and they would be stuck before their lecterns all morning trying to think in Russian, in danger of a rap on the hand if they giggled or fell asleep. The Bad Witch had silver hair and a fierce glare and a hooked nose, like the ospreys that lived in the pines by the lake. Nirgal was afraid of her.

So like the others he concealed his dismay as the school door opened and the Bad Witch walked in. But on this day she seemed tired, and let them out on time even though they had done poorly at arithmetic. Nirgal followed Jackie and Harmakhis out of the schoolhouse and around the corner, into the alley between Creche Crescent and the back of the kitchen. Harmakhis peed against the wall and Jackie pulled down her pants to show she could too, and just then the Bad Witch came around the corner. She pulled them all out of the alley by the arm, Nirgal and Jackie clutched together in one of her talons, and right out in the plaza she spanked Jackie while shouting furiously at the boys. "You two stay away from her! She's your sister!" Jackie, crying and twisting to pull up her pants, saw Nirgal looking at her, and she tried to hit him and Maya with the same furious swing, and fell over bare-bottomed and howled.

It wasn't true that Jackie was their sister. There were twelve sansei or third-generation children in Zygote, and they knew each other like brothers and sisters and many of them were, but not all. It was confusing and seldom discussed. Jackie and Harmakhis were the oldest, Nirgal a season younger, the rest bunched a season after that: Rachel, Emily, Reull, Steve, Simud, Nanedi, Tiu, Frantz, and Huo Hsing. Hiroko was mother to everyone in Zygote, but not really—only to Nirgal and Harmakhis and six other of the sansei, and several of the nisei grownups as well. Children of the mother goddess.

But Jackie was Esther's daughter. Esther had moved away after a fight with Kasei, who was Jackie's father. Not many of them knew who their fathers were. Once Nirgal had been crawling over a dune after a crab when Esther and Kasei had loomed overhead, Esther crying and Kasei shouting, "If you're going to leave me then leave!" He had been crying too. He had a pink stone eyetooth. He too was a child of Hiroko's; so Jackie was Hiroko's granddaughter. That was how it worked. Jackie had long black hair and was the fastest runner in Zygote, except for Peter. Nirgal could run the longest, and sometimes ran around the lake three or four times in a row, just to do it, but Jackie was faster in the sprints. She laughed all the time. If Nirgal ever argued with her she would say, "All right Uncle Nirgie," and laugh at him. She was his niece, although a season older. But not his sister.

The school door crashed open and there was Coyote, teacher for the day. Coyote traveled all over the world, and spent very little time in Zygote. It was a big day when he taught them. He led them around the village finding odd things to do, but all the time he made one of them read aloud, from books impossible to understand, written by philosophers, who were dead people. Bakunin, Nietzsche, Mao, Bookchin—these people's comprehensible thoughts lay like unexpected pebbles on a long beach of gibberish. The stories Coyote had them read from the *Odyssey* or the Bible were easier to understand, though unsettling, as the people in them killed each other a lot and Hiroko said it was wrong. Coyote laughed at Hiroko and he often howled for no obvious reason as they read these gruesome tales, and asked them hard questions about what they had heard, and argued with them as if they knew what they were talking about, which was disconcerting. "What would *you* do? Why would you do *that*?" All the while teaching them how the Rickover's fuel recycler worked, or making them check the plunger hydraulics on the lake's wave machine, until their hands went from blue to white, and their teeth chattered so much they couldn't talk clearly. "You kids sure get cold easy," he said. "All but Nirgal."

Nirgal was good with cold. He knew intimately all its many stages, and he did not dislike the feel of it. People who disliked cold did not understand that one could adjust to it, that its bad effects could all be dealt with by a sufficient push from within. Nirgal was very familiar with heat as well. If you pushed heat out hard enough, then cold only became a sort of vivid shocking envelope in which you moved. And so cold's ultimate effect was as a stimulant, making you want to run.

"Hey Nirgal, what's the air temperature?"

"Two seventy-one."

Coyote's laugh was scary, an animal cackle that included all the noises anything could make. Different every time too. "Here, let's stop the wave machine and see what the lake looks like flat."

The water of the lake was always liquid, while the water ice coating the underside of the dome had to stay frozen. This explained most of their mesocosmic weather, as Sax put it, giving them their mists and sudden winds, their rain and fog and occasional snow. On this day the weather machine was almost silent, the big hemisphere of space under the dome nearly windless. With the wave machine turned off, the lake soon settled down to a round flat plate. The surface of the water became the same white color as the dome, but the lake bottom, covered by green algae, was still visible through the white sheen. So the lake was simultaneously pure white and dark green. On the far shore the dunes and scrub pines were reflected upside down in this two-toned water, as perfectly as in any mirror. Nirgal stared at the sight, entranced, everything falling away, nothing there but this pulsing green/white vision. He saw: there were two worlds, not one—two worlds in the same space, both visible, separate and different but collapsed together, so that they were visible as two only at certain angles. Push at vision's envelope, push like one pushed against the envelope of cold: *push!* Such colors! . . .

"Mars to Nirgal, Mars to Nirgal!"

They laughed at him. He was always doing that, they told him. Going off. His friends were fond of him, he saw that in their faces. Coyote broke chips of flat ice from the strand, then skipped them across the lake. All of them did the same, until the intersecting white-green ripples made the upside-down world shiver and dance. "Look at that!" Coyote shouted. Between throws he chanted, in his bouncing English that was like a perpetual song: "You kids are living the best lives in history, most people just fluid in the great world machine, and here you're in on the birth of a world! *Un*believable! But it's pure luck you know, no credit to you, not until you do something with it, you could have been born in a mansion, a jail, a shantytown in Port of Spain, but here you are in Zygote, the secret heart of Mars! Course just now you're down here like moles in a hole, with vultures above all ready to eat you, but the day it's coming when you walk this planet free of every bond. You remember what I'm telling you, it's prophecy my children! And meanwhile look how fine it is, this little ice paradise."

He threw a chip straight at the dome, and they all chanted Ice Paradise! Ice Paradise! Ice Paradise! until they were helpless with laughter.

But that night Coyote spoke to Hiroko, when he thought no one was listening. "Roko you got to take those kids outside and show them the world. Even if it's only under the fog hood. They're like moles in a hole down here, for Christ's sake." Then he was gone again, who knew where, off on one of his mysterious journeys into that other world folded over them.

Some days Hiroko came into the village to teach them. These to Nirgal were the best days of all. She always took them down to the beach; and going to the beach with Hiroko was like being touched by a god. It was her world—the green world inside the white—and she knew everything about it, and when she was there the subtle pearly colors of sand and dome pulsed with both worlds' colors at once, pulsed as if trying to break free of what held them.

They sat on the dunes, watching the shore birds skitter and peep as they charged together up and down the strand. Gulls wheeled overhead and Hiroko asked them questions, her black eyes twinkling merrily. She lived by the lake with a small group of her intimates, Iwao, Rya, Gene, Evgenia, all in a little bamboo stand in the dunes. And she spent a lot of time visiting other hidden sanctuaries around the South Pole. So she always needed catching up on the village news. She was a slender woman, tall for one of the issei, as neat as the shore birds in her dress and her movement. She was old, of course, impossibly ancient like all the issei, but with something in her manner which made her seem younger than even Peter or Kasei—just a little bit older than the kids, in fact, with everything in the world new before her, pushing to break into all its colors.

"Look at the pattern this seashell makes. The dappled whorl, curving inward to infinity. That's the shape of the universe itself. There's a constant pressure, pushing toward pattern. A tendency in matter to evolve into ever more complex forms. It's a kind of pattern gravity, a holy greening power we call viriditas, and it is the driving force in the cosmos. Life, you see. Like these sand fleas and limpets and krill—although these krill in particular are dead, and helping the fleas. Like all of us," waving a hand like a dancer. "And because we are alive, the universe must be said to be alive. We are its consciousness as well as our own. We rise out of the cosmos and we see its mesh of patterns, and it strikes us as beautiful. And that feeling is the most important thing in all the universe—its culmination, like the color of the flower at first bloom on a wet morning. It's a holy feeling, and our task in this world is to do everything we can to foster it. And one way to do that is to spread life everywhere. To aid it into existence where it was not before, as here on Mars."

This to her was the supreme act of love, and when she talked about it, even if they didn't fully understand, they felt the love. Another push, another kind of warmth in the envelope of cold. She touched them as she talked, and they dug for shells as they listened. "Mud clam! Antarctic limpet. Glass sponge, watch out, it can cut you." It made Nirgal happy just to look at her.

And one morning, as they stood from their dig to do more beachcombing, she returned his gaze, and he recognized her expression—it was precisely the expression on his face when he looked at her, he could feel it in his muscles. So he made her happy too! Which was intoxicating.

He held her hand as they walked the beach. "It's a simple ecology in some ways," she said as they knelt to inspect another clam shell. "Not many species, and the food chains are short. But so rich. So beautiful." She tested the temperature of the lake with her hand. "See the mist? The water must be warm today."

By this time she and Nirgal were alone, the other kids running around the dunes or up and down the strand. Nirgal bent down to touch a wave as it stalled out next to their feet, leaving behind a white lace of foam. "It's two seventy-five and a little over."

"You're so sure."

"I can always tell."

"Here," she said, "do I have a fever?"

He reached up and held her neck. "No, you're cool."

"That's right. I'm always about half a degree low. Vlad and Ursula can't figure out why."

"It's because you're happy."

Hiroko laughed, looking just like Jackie, suffused with joy. "I love you, Nirgal."

Inside he warmed as if a heating grate were in there. Half a degree at least. "And I love you."

And they walked down the beach hand in hand, silently following the sandpipers.

Coyote returned, and Hiroko said to him, "Okay. Let's take them outside."

And so the next morning when they met for school, Hiroko and Coyote and Peter led them through the locks and down the long white tunnel that connected the dome to the outside world. At its far end were located the hangar and the cliff gallery above it. They had run the gallery with Peter in the past, looking out the little polarized windows at the icy sand and the pink sky, trying to see the great wall of dry ice that they stood in—the south polar cap, the bottom of the world, which they lived in to escape the notice of people who would put them in jail.

Because of that they had always stayed inside the gallery. But on this day they went into the hangar locks and put on tight elastic jumpers, rolling up sleeves and legs; then heavy boots, and tight gloves, and last helmets, with bubble windows on their front side. Getting more excited every moment, until the excitement became something very like fright, especially when Simud started crying and insisting she didn't want to go. Hiroko calmed her with a long touch. "Come on. I'll be there with you."

They huddled together speechlessly as the adults herded them into the lock. There was a hissing noise, and then the outer door opened. Clutching the adults, they walked cautiously outside, bumping together as they moved.

It was too bright to see. They were in a swirling white mist. The ground was dotted with intricate ice flowers, all aglint in the bath of light. Nirgal was holding Hiroko and Coyote by the hand, and they propelled him forward and let go of his hands. He staggered in the onslaught of white glare.

"This is the fog hood," Hiroko's voice said over an intercom in his ear. "It lasts through the winter. But now it's Ls 205, springtime, when the green force pushes hardest through the world, fueled by the sun's light. See it!"

He could see nothing but it: a white coalescing fireball. Sudden sunlight pierced this ball, transforming it into a spray of color, turning the frosty sand to shaved magnesium, the ice flowers to incandescent jewels. The wind pushed at his side and rent the fog; gaps in it appeared, and the land gaped off into the distance, making him reel. So big! So big—everything was so big—he went to one knee on the sand, put his hands on his other leg to keep his balance. The rocks and ice flowers around his boots glowed as if under a microscope. The rocks were dotted with round scales of black and green lichen.

Out on the horizon was a low flat-topped hill. A crater. There in the gravel was a rover track, nearly filled with frost, as if it had been there a million years. Pattern pulsing in the chaos of light and rock, green lichen pushing into the white. . . .

Everyone was talking at once. The other children were beginning to race around giddily, shrieking with delight as the fog opened up and gave them a glimpse of the dark pink sky. Coyote was laughing hard. "They're like winter calves let out of the barn in spring, look at them tripping, oh you poor dear things, ah ha ha, Roko this no way to make them live," cackling as he lifted kids off the sand and set them on their feet again.

Nirgal stood, bounced experimentally. He felt he might float away, he was glad the boots were so heavy. There was a long mound, shoulder high, snaking away from the ice cliff. Jackie was walking its crest and he ran to join her, staggering at the incline, at the jumbled rock on the ground. He got onto the ridge and got into his running rhythm, and it felt as if he were flying, as if he could run forever.

He stood by her side. They looked back at the ice cliff, and shouted with a fearful joy; it rose up forever into the fog. A shaft of morning light poured over them like molten water. They turned away, unable to face it. Blinking away floods of tears, Nirgal saw his shadow cast against the fog scraping over the rocks below them. The shadow was surrounded by a bright circular band of rainbow light. He shouted loudly and Coyote raced up to them, his voice in Nirgal's ear crying, "What's wrong! What is it?"

He stopped when he saw the shadow. "Hey, it's a glory! That's called a glory. It's like the Spectre of the Brocken. Wave your arms up and down! Look at the colors! Christ almighty, aren't you the lucky ones."

On an impulse Nirgal moved to Jackie's side, and their glories merged, becoming a single nimbus of glowing rainbow colors, surrounding their blue double shadow. Jackie laughed with delight and went off to try it with Peter.

About a year later Nirgal and the other children began to figure out how to deal with the days when they were taught by Sax. He would start at the blackboard, sounding like a particularly characterless AI, and behind his back they would roll their eyes and make faces as he droned on about partial pressures or infrared rays. Then one of them would see an opening and begin the game. He was helpless before it. He would say something like, "In nonshivering thermogenesis the body produces heat using futile cycles," and one of them would raise a hand and say, "But why, Sax?" and everyone would stare hard at their lectern and not look at each other, while Sax would frown as if this had never happened before, and say, "Well, it creates heat without using as much energy as shivering does. The muscle proteins contract, but instead of grabbing they just slide over each other, and that creates the heat."

Jackie, so sincerely the whole class nearly lost it: "But how?"

He was blinking now, so fast they almost exploded watching him. "Well, the amino acids in the proteins have broken covalent bonds, and the breaks release what is called bond dissociation energy."

"But why?"

Blinking ever harder: "Well, that's just a matter of physics." He diagrammed vigorously on the blackboard: "Covalent bonds are formed when two atomic orbitals merge to form a single bond orbital, occupied by electrons from both atoms. Breaking the bond releases thirty to a hundred kcals of stored energy."

Several of them asked, in chorus, "But *why*?"

This got him into subatomic physics, where the chain of whys and becauses could go on for a half hour without him ever once saying something they could understand. Finally they would sense they were near the end game. "But why?"

"Well," going cross-eyed as he tried to backtrack, "atoms want to get to their stable number of electrons, and they'll share electrons when they have to."

"*But why?*"

Now he was looking trapped. "That's just the way atoms bond. One of the ways."

"But *WHY?*"

A shrug. "That's how the atomic force works. That's how things came out—"

And they all would shout, "*in the Big Bang.*"

They would howl with glee, and Sax's forehead would knot up as he realized that they had done it to him again. He would sigh, and go back to where he had been when the game began. But every time they started it again, he never seemed to remember, as long as the initial why was plausible enough. And even when he did recognize what was happening, he seemed helpless to stop it. His only defense was to say, with a little frown, "Why *what?*" That slowed the game for a while; but then Nirgal and Jackie got clever at guessing what in any statement most deserved a why, and as long as they could do that, Sax seemed to feel it was his job to continue answering, right on up the chains of because to the Big Bang, or, every once in a while, to a muttered "We don't know."

"We don't know!" the class would exclaim in mock dismay. "Why *not?*"

"It's not explained," he would say, frowning. "Not yet."

And so the good mornings with Sax would pass; and both he and the kids seemed to agree that these were better than the bad mornings, when he would drone on uninterrupted, and protest "This is really a very important matter" as he turned from the blackboard and saw a crop of heads laid out snoring on the desktops.

One morning, thinking about Sax's frown, Nirgal stayed behind in the school until he and Sax were the only ones left, and then he said, "Why don't you like it when you can't say why?"

The frown returned. After a long silence Sax said slowly, "I try to understand. I pay attention to things, you see, very closely. As closely as I can. Concentrating on the specificity of every moment. And I want to understand why it happens the way it does. I'm curious. And I think that everything happens for a reason. Everything. So, we should be able to tease these reasons out. When we can't . . . well. I don't like it. It vexes me. Sometimes I call it"—he glanced at Nirgal shyly, and Nirgal saw that he had never told this to anyone before—"I call it the great unexplainable."

It was the white world, Nirgal saw suddenly. The white world inside the green, the opposite of Hiroko's green world inside the white. And they had opposite feelings about them. Looking from the green side, when Hiroko confronted something mysterious, she loved it and it made her happy—it was viriditas, a holy power. Looking from the white side, when Sax confronted something mysterious, it was the Great Unexplainable, dangerous and awful. He was interested in the true, while Hiroko was interested in the real. Or perhaps it was the other way around—those words were tricky. Better to say she loved the green world, he the white.

"But yes!" Michel said when Nirgal mentioned this observation to him. "Very good, Nirgal. Your sight has such insight. In archetypal terminologies we might call green and white the Mystic and the Scientist. Both extremely powerful figures, as you see. But what we need, if you ask me, is a combination of the two, which we call the *Alchemist.*"

The green and the white.

Afternoons the children were free to do what they wanted, and sometimes they stayed with the day's teacher, but more often they ran on the beach or played in the village, which lay nestled in its cluster of low hills, halfway between the lake and the tunnel entrance. They climbed the spiraling staircases of the big bamboo treehouses, and played hide and seek among the stacked rooms and the daughter shoots and the hanging bridges connecting them. The bamboo dorms made a crescent which held most of the rest of the village inside it; each of the big shoots was five or seven segments high, each segment a room, getting smaller as they got higher. The children each had a room of their own in the top segments of the shoots—windowed vertical cylinders that were four or five steps across, like the towers of the castles in their stories. Below them in the middle segments the adults had their rooms, mostly alone but sometimes in couples; and the bottom segments were living rooms. From the windows of their top rooms they looked down on the village rooftops, clustered in the circle of hills and bamboo and greenhouses like mussels in the lake shallows.

On the beach they hunted shells or played German dodgeball, or shot arrows across the dunes into blocks of foam. Usually Jackie and Harmakhis chose the games, and led the teams if there were teams. Nirgal and the younger ones followed them, cycling through their various friendships and hierarchies, which were honed endlessly in the daily play. As little Frantz once crudely explained it to Nadia, "Harmakhis hits Nirgal; Nirgal hits me; I hit the girls." Often Nirgal got tired of that game, which Harmakhis always won, and for better fun he would take off running around the lake, slowly and steadily, falling into a rhythm which seemed to encompass everything in the world. He could circle the lake for as long as the day lasted when he got in that rhythm. It was a joy, an exhilaration, just to run and run and run and run. . . .

Under the dome it was always cold, but the light was perpetually changing. In summer the dome glowed bluish white all the time, and pencils of lit air stood under the skylight shafts. In winter it was dark, and the dome flared with reflected lamplight, like the inside of a mussel shell. In spring and fall the light would dim in the afternoon to a gray and ghostly dusk, the colors only suggested by the many shades of gray, the bamboo leaves and pine needles all ink strokes against the faint white of the dome. In those hours the greenhouses were like big fairy lamps on the hills, and the kids would wander home crisscrossing like gulls, and head for the bathhouse. There in the long building beside the kitchen they would pull off their clothes and run into the steamy clangor of the big main bath, sliding around on the bottom tiles feeling heat buzz back into their hands and feet and faces, as they splashed friskily around the soaking ancients with their turtle faces and their wrinkled hairy bodies.

After that warm wet hour they dressed, and trooped into the kitchen, damp and pink-skinned, queueing up and filling their plates, sitting at the long tables scattered among the adults. There were 124 permanent residents, but usually about 200 people there at any given time. When everyone was seated they took up the water pitchers and poured each other's water, and then they tore into the hot food with gusto, downing potatoes, tortillas, pasta, tabouli, bread, a hundred kinds of vegetables, occasionally fish or chicken. After the meal the adults would talk about crops or their Rickover, an old integral fast reactor they were very fond of, or about Earth—while the kids cleaned up and then played music for an hour and then games, as everyone began the slow process of falling asleep.

One day before dinner a group of twenty-two people arrived from around the polar cap. Their little dome had lost its ecosystem to what Hiroko called spiraling complex disequilibrium, and their reserves had run out. They needed sanctuary.

Hiroko put them in three of the newly mature treehouses. They climbed the staircases spiraling up the outsides of the fat round shoots, exclaiming at the cylindrical segments with their doors and windows cut into them. Hiroko put them to work finishing construction on new rooms, and building a new greenhouse at the edge of the village. It was obvious to all that Zygote was not growing as much food as they now needed. The kids ate as modestly as they could, imitating the adults. "Should have called the place Gamete," Coyote said to Hiroko on his next time through, laughing harshly.

She only waved him away. But perhaps worry accounted for Hiroko's more distant air. She spent all her days in the greenhouses at work, and seldom taught the children anymore. When she did they only followed her around and worked for her, harvesting or turning compost or weeding. "She *doesn't* care about us," Harmakhis said angrily one afternoon as they walked down the beach. He directed his complaint at Nirgal. "She isn't really our mother anyway." He led them all to the labs by the tunnel hill greenhouse, chivvying them along as he could so well.

Inside he pointed to a row of fat magnesium tanks, something like refrigerators. "Those are our mothers. That's what we were grown inside. Kasei told me, and I asked Hiroko and it's true. We're ectogenes. We weren't born, we were *decanted*." He glared triumphantly at his frightened, fascinated little band; then he struck Nirgal full on the chest with his fist, knocking Nirgal clear across the lab, and left with a curse. "We don't have parents."

Extra visitors were a burden now, but still when they came there was a lot of excitement, and many people stayed up most of the first night of a visit, talking, getting all the news they could of the other sanctuaries. There was a whole network of these in the south polar region; Nirgal had a map in his lectern, with red dots to show all thirty-four. And Nadia and Hiroko guessed that there were more, in other networks to the north, or in complete isolation. But as they all kept radio silence, there was no way to be sure. So news was at a premium—it was usually the most precious thing that visitors had, even if they came laden with gifts, which they usually did, giving out whatever they had managed to make or obtain that their hosts would find useful.

During these visits Nirgal would listen hard to the nights' long animated conversations, sitting on the floor or wandering and refilling people's teacups. He felt acutely that he did not understand the rules of the world; it was inexplicable to him why people acted as they did. Of course he did understand the basic fact of the situation—that there were two sides, locked in a contest for control of Mars—that Zygote was the leader for the side that was right—and that eventually the areophany would triumph. It was a tremendous feeling to be involved in that struggle, to be a crucial part of the story, and it often left him sleepless when he dragged off to bed, his mind dancing through to dawn with visions of all he would contribute to this great drama, amazing Jackie and everyone else in Zygote.

Sometimes, in his desire to learn more, he even eavesdropped. He did it by lying on a couch in the corner and staring at a lectern, doodling or pretending to read. Quite often people elsewhere in the room didn't realize he was listening, and sometimes they would even talk about the children of Zygote—mostly when he was actually skulking out in the hall.

"Have you noticed most of them are left-handed?"

"Hiroko tweaked their genes, I swear."

"She says not."

"They're already almost as tall as I am."

"That's just the gravity. I mean look at Peter and the rest of the nisei. They're natural-born, and they're mostly tall. But the left-handedness, that's got to be genetic."

"Once she told me there was a simple transgenic insertion that would increase the size of the corpus callosum. Maybe she fooled with that and got the left-handedness as a side effect."

"I thought left-handedness was caused by brain damage."

"No one knows. I think even Hiroko is mystified by it."

"I can't believe she would mess with the chromosomes for brain development."

"Ectogenes, remember—better access."

"Their bone density is poor, I hear."

"That's right. They'd be in trouble on Earth. They're on supplements to help."

"That's the g again. It's trouble for all of us, really."

"Tell me about it. I broke my forearm swinging a tennis racket."

"Left-handed giant bird-people, that's what we're growing down here. It's bizarre, if you ask me. You see them running across the dunes and expect them to just take off and fly."

That night Nirgal had the usual trouble sleeping. Ectogenes, transgenic . . . it made him feel odd. White and green in their double helix. . . . For hours he tossed, wondering what the uneasiness twisting through him meant, wondering what he *should* feel.

Finally, exhausted, he fell asleep. And in his sleep he had a dream. All his dreams before that night had been about Zygote, but now he dreamed that he flew in the air, over the surface of Mars. Vast red canyons cut the land, and volcanoes reared nearly to his unimaginable height. But something was after him, something much bigger and faster than him, with wings that flapped loudly as the creature dropped out of the sun, with huge talons that extended toward him. He pointed at this flying creature and bolts of lightning shot out of his fingertips, causing it to bank away. It was soaring up for another attack when he struggled awake, his fingers pulsing and his heart thumping like the wave machine, ka-*thunk,* ka-*thunk,* ka-*thunk.*

The very next afternoon the wave machine was waving too well, as Jackie put it. They were playing on the beach, and thought they had the big breakers gauged, but then a really big one surged over the ice filigree and knocked Nirgal to his knees, and pulled him back down the strand with an irresistible sucking. He struggled, gasping for air as he tumbled in the shockingly icy water, but he couldn't escape and was pulled under, then rolled hard in the rush of the next incoming wave.

Jackie grabbed him by the arm and hair, pulled him back up the strand with her. Harmakhis helped them to their feet, crying "Are you okay are you okay?" If they got wet the rule was to run for the village as fast as they could, so Nirgal and Jackie struggled to their feet and raced over the dunes and up the village path, the rest of the children trailing far behind. The wind cut to the bone. They ran straight to the bathhouse and burst through the doors and stripped off their stiff garments with shaking hands, helped by Nadia and Sax and Michel and Rya, who had been in there bathing.

As they were being hustled into the shallows of the big communal bath, Nirgal remembered his dream. He said, "Wait, wait."

The others stopped, confused. He closed his eyes, held his breath. He clutched Jackie's cold upper arm. He saw himself back into the dream, felt himself swimming through the sky. Heat from the fingertips. The white world in the green.

He searched for the spot in his middle that was always warm, even now when he was so cold. As long as he was alive it would be there. He found it, and with every breath he pushed it outward through his flesh. It was hard but he could feel it working, the warmth traveling out into his ribs like a fire, down his arms, down his legs, into his hands and feet. It was his left hand holding on to Jackie, and he glanced at her bare body with its white goose-pimpled skin, and concentrated on sending the heat into her. He was shivering slightly now, but not from the cold.

"You're warm," Jackie exclaimed.

"Feel it," he said to her, and for a few moments she leaned into his grip. Then with an alarmed look she pulled free, and stepped down into the bath. Nirgal stood on the edge until his shivering stopped.

"Wow," Nadia said. "That's some kind of metabolic burn. I've heard of it, but I've never seen it."

"Do you know how you do it?" Sax asked him. He and Nadia and Michel and Rya were staring at Nirgal with a curious expression, which he did not want to meet.

Nirgal shook his head. He sat down on the concrete coping of the bath, suddenly exhausted. He stuck his feet in the water, which felt like liquid flame. Fish in water, sloshing free, out in the air, the fire within, white in the green, alchemy, soaring with eagles . . . thunderbolts from his fingertips!

People looked at him. Even the Zygotes gave him sidelong looks, when he laughed or said something unusual, when they thought he wouldn't see. It was easiest just to pretend he didn't notice. But that was hard with the occasional visitors, who were more direct. "Oh, you're Nirgal," one short red-haired woman said. "I've heard you're bright." Nirgal, who was constantly crashing against the limits of his understanding, blushed and shook his head while the woman calmly surveyed him. She made her judgment and smiled and shook his hand. "I'm glad to meet you."

One day when they were five Jackie brought an old lectern to school with her, on a day when Maya was teaching. Ignoring Maya's glare, she showed it to the others. "This is my grandfather's AI. It has a lot of what he said in it. Kasei gave it to me." Kasei was leaving Zygote to move to one of the other sanctuaries. But not the one where Esther lived.

Jackie turned the lectern on. "Pauline, play back something my grandfather said."

"Well, here we are," said a man's voice.

"No, something different. Play back something he said about the hidden colony."

The man's voice said, "The hidden colony must still have contacts with surface settlements. There's too many things they can't manufacture while hiding. Nuclear fuel rods for one, I should think. Those are controlled pretty well, and it could be that records would show where they've been disappearing."

The voice stopped. Maya told Jackie to put the lectern away, and she started another history lesson, the nineteenth century told in Russian sentences so short and harsh that her voice shook. And then more algebra. Maya was very insistent that they learn their math well. "You're getting a horrible education," she would say, shaking her head darkly. "But if you learn your math you can catch up later." And she would glare at them and demand the next answer.

Nirgal stared at her, remembering when she had been their Bad Witch. It would be strange to be her, so fierce sometimes and so cheerful others. With most of the people in Zygote, he could look at them and feel what it would be like to be them. He could see it in their faces, just as he could see the second color inside the first; it was that kind of gift, something like his hyperacute sense of temperature. But he didn't understand Maya.

In the winter they made forays onto the surface, to the nearby crater where Nadia was building a shelter, and the dark ice-spangled dunes beyond. But when the fog hood lifted they had to stay under the dome, or at most go out to the window gallery. They weren't to be seen from above. No one was sure if the police were still watching from space or not, but it was best to be safe. Or so the issei said. Peter was often away, and his travels had led him to believe that the hunt for hidden colonies must be over. And that the hunt was hopeless in any case. "There are resistance settlements that aren't hiding at all. And there's so much noise now thermally and visually, and even over the radio," he said. "They could never check all the signals they're getting."

But Sax only said, "Algorithmic search programs are very effective," and Maya insisted on keeping out of sight, and hardening their electronics, and sending all their excess heat deep into the heart of the polar cap. Hiroko agreed with Maya on this, and so they all complied. "It's different for us," Maya said to Peter, looking haunted.

There was a mohole, Sax told them one morning at school, about two hundred kilometers to the northwest. The cloud they sometimes saw in that direction was its plume—big and still on some days, on others whipping off east in thin tatters. The next time Coyote came through they asked him at dinner if he had visited it, and he told them that he had, and that the great shaft of the mohole penetrated to very near the center of Mars, and that its bottom was nothing but bubbling molten fiery lava.

"That's not true," Maya said dismissively. "They only go down ten or fifteen kilometers. Their floors are hard rock."

"But hot rock," Hiroko said. "And twenty kilometers now, I hear."

"And so they do our work for us," Maya complained to Hiroko. "Don't you think we are parasites on the surface settlements? Your viriditas wouldn't get far without their engineering."

"It will prove to be a symbiosis," Hiroko said calmly. She stared at Maya until Maya got up and walked away. Hiroko was the only one in Zygote who could stare Maya down.

Hiroko, Nirgal thought as he regarded his mother after this

exchange, was very strange. She talked to him and to everyone else as an equal, and clearly to her everyone *was* an equal; but no one was special. He remembered very keenly when it had been different, when the two of them had been like two parts of a whole. But now she only took the same interest in him that she took in everyone else, her concern impersonal and distant. She would be the same no matter what happened to him, he thought. Nadia, or even Maya, cared for him more. And yet Hiroko was mother to them all. And Nirgal, like most of the rest of the regulars in Zygote, still went down to her little stand of bamboo when he was in need of something he couldn't find from ordinary people—some solace, or advice. . . .

But as often as not, when he did that he would find her and her little inner group "being silent," and if he wanted to stay he would have to stop talking. Sometimes this lasted for days at a time, until he stopped dropping by. Then again he might arrive during the areophany, and be swept up in the ecstatic chanting of the names of Mars, becoming an integral part of that tight little band, right in the heart of the world, with Hiroko herself at his side, her arm around him, squeezing hard.

That was love of a sort, and he cherished it; but it was not as it had been in the old days, when they had walked the beach together.

One morning he went into the school and came on Jackie and Harmakhis in the coatroom. They jumped as he entered, and by the time he had gotten his coat off and gone into the schoolroom he knew they had been kissing.

After school he circled the lake in the blue-white glow of a summer afternoon, watching the wave machine rise and pulse down, like the clamping sensations in his chest. Pain curved through him like the swells moving over the water. He couldn't help it, even though it was ridiculous and he knew it. There was a lot of kissing going on among them these days in the bathhouse, as they splashed and tugged and pushed and tickled. The girls kissed each other and said it was "practice kissing" that didn't count, and sometimes they turned this practice on the boys; Nirgal had been kissed by Rachel many times, and also by Emily and Tiu and Nanedi, and once the latter two had held him and kissed his ears in an attempt to embarrass him in the public bath with an erection; and once Jackie had pulled them away from him and knocked him into the deep end, and bit his shoulder as they wrestled; and these were just the most memorable of the hundreds of slippery wet warm naked contacts which were making the baths such a high point of the day.

But outside the bathhouse, as if to try to contain such volatile forces, they had become extremely formal with each other, with the boys and girls bunched in gangs that played separately more often than not. So kissing in the coatroom represented something new, and serious—and the look Nirgal had seen on Jackie and Harmakhis's faces was so superior, as if they knew something he didn't—which was true. And it was that which hurt, that exclusion, that knowledge. Especially since he wasn't that ignorant; he was sure they were lying together, making each other come. They were lovers, their look said it. His laughing beautiful Jackie was no longer his. And in fact never had been.

He slept poorly in the following nights. Jackie's room was in the shoot beside his, and Harmakhis's was two in the opposite direction, and every creak of the hanging bridges sounded like footsteps; and sometimes her curved window glowed with flickering orange lamplight. Instead of remaining in his room to be tortured he began to stay up late every night in the common rooms, reading and eavesdropping on the adults.

So he was there when they started talking about Simon's illness. Simon was Peter's father, a quiet man who was usually away, on expeditions with Peter's mother, Ann. Now it appeared that he had something they called resistant leukemia. Vlad and Ursula noticed Nirgal listening, and they tried to reassure him, but Nirgal could see that they weren't telling him everything. In fact they were regarding him with a strange speculative look. Later he climbed to his high room and got in bed and turned on his lectern, and looked up "Leukemia," and read the abstract at the start of the entry. A potentially fatal disease, now usually amenable to treatment. Potentially fatal disease—a shocking concept. He tossed uneasily that night, plagued by dreams through the gray bird-chirp dawn. Plants died, animals died, but not people. But they were animals.

The next night he stayed up with the adults again, feeling exhausted and strange. Vlad and Ursula sat down on the floor beside him. They told him that Simon would be helped by a bone marrow transplant, and that he and Nirgal shared a rare type of blood. Neither Ann nor Peter had it, nor any of Nirgal's brothers or sisters or halves. He had gotten it through his father, but even his father didn't have it, not exactly. Just him and Simon, in all the sanctuaries. There were only five thousand people in all of the sanctuaries together, and Simon and Nirgal's blood type was one in a million. Would he donate some of his bone marrow, they asked.

Hiroko was there in the commons, watching him. She rarely spent evenings in the village, and he didn't need to look at her to know what she was thinking. They were made to give, she had always said, and this would be the ultimate gift. An act of pure viriditas. "Of course," he said, happy at the opportunity.

•   •   •

The hospital was next to the bathhouse and the school. It was smaller than the school, and had five beds. They laid Simon on one, and Nirgal on another.

The old man smiled at him. He didn't look sick, only old. Just like all the rest of the ancients, in fact. He had seldom said much, and now he said only, "Thanks, Nirgal."

Nirgal nodded. Then to his surprise Simon went on: "I appreciate you doing this. The extraction will hurt afterward for a week or two, right down in the bone. That's quite a thing to do for someone else."

"But not if they really need it," Nirgal said.

"Well, it's a gift that I'll try to repay, of course."

Vlad and Ursula anesthetized Nirgal's arm with a shot. "It isn't really necessary to do both operations now, but it's a good idea to have you two together for it. It will help the healing if you are friends."

So they became friends. After school Nirgal would go by the hospital, and Simon would step slowly out the door, and they would walk the path over the dunes to the beach. There they watched the waves ripple across the white surface and rise and crumple on the strand. Simon was a lot less talkative than anyone Nirgal had ever spent time with; it was like being silent with Hiroko's group, only it never ended. At first it made him uncomfortable. But after a while he found it left time to really look at things: the gulls wheeling under the dome, the sandcrab bubbles in the sand, the circles in the sand surrounding each tuft of dune grass. Peter was back in Zygote a lot now, and many days he would come with them. Occasionally even Ann would interrupt her perpetual traveling, and visit Zygote and join them. Peter and Nirgal would race around playing tag, or hide and seek, while Ann and Simon strolled the beach arm in arm.

But Simon was still weak, and he got weaker. It was hard not to see this as some kind of moral failing; Nirgal had never been sick, and he found the concept disgusting. It could only happen to the old ones. And even they were supposed to have been saved by their aging treatment, which everyone got when they were old, and so never died. Only plants and animals died. But people were animals. But they had invented the treatment. At night, worrying about these discrepancies, Nirgal read his lectern's whole entry on leukemia, even though it was as long as a book. Cancer of the blood. White cells proliferated out of the bone marrow and flooded the system, attacking healthy systems. They were giving Simon chemicals and irradiation and pseudoviruses to kill the white blood cells, and trying to replace the sick marrow in him with new marrow from Nirgal. They had also given him the aging treatment three times now. Nirgal read about this too. It was a matter of genomic mismatch scanning, which found broken chromosomes and repaired them so that cell division error did not occur. But it was hard to penetrate bone with the array of introduced auto repair cells, and apparently in Simon's case little pockets of cancerous marrow had remained behind every time. Children had a better chance of recovery than adults, as the leukemia entry made clear. But with the aging treatments and the marrow transfusions he was sure to get well. It was just a matter of time and of giving. The treatments cured everything in the end.

"We need a bioreactor," Ursula said to Vlad. They were working on converting one of the ectogene tanks into one, packing it with spongy animal collagen and inoculating it with cells from Nirgal's marrow, hoping to generate an array of lymphocytes, macrophages, and granulocytes. But they didn't have the circulatory system working right, or perhaps it was the matrix, they weren't sure. Nirgal remained their living bioreactor.

Sax was teaching them soil chemistry during the mornings when he was teacher, and he even took them out of the schoolroom occasionally to work in the soil labs, introducing biomass to the sand and then wheelbarrowing it to the greenhouses or the beach. It was fun work, but it tended to pass through Nirgal as if he were asleep. He would catch sight of Simon outside, stubbornly taking a walk, and he would forget whatever they were doing.

Despite the treatments Simon's steps were slow and stiff. He walked bowlegged, in fact, his legs swinging forward with very little bend to them. Once Nirgal caught up to him and stood beside him on the last dune before the beach. Sandpipers were charging up and down the wet strand, chased by white tapestries of foaming water. Simon pointed at the herd of black sheep, cropping grass between dunes. His arm rose like a bamboo crossbar. The sheep's frosted breath poured onto the grass.

Simon said something that Nirgal didn't catch; his lips were stiff now, and some words he was finding hard to pronounce. Perhaps it was this that was making him quieter than ever. Now he tried again, and then again, but no matter how hard he tried, Nirgal couldn't guess what he was saying. Finally Simon gave up trying and shrugged, and they were left looking at each other, mute and helpless.

When Nirgal played with the other kids, they both took him in and kept their distance, so that he moved in a kind of circle. Sax admonished him mildly for his absentmindedness in class. "Concentrate on the moment," he would say, forcing Nirgal to recite the loops of the nitrogen cycle, or to shove his hands deep into the wet black soil they were working on, instructing him to knead it, to break up the long strings of diatom blooms, and the fungi and lichen and algae and all the invisible microbacteria they had grown, to distribute them through the rusty clods of grit. "Get it distributed as regularly as possible. Pay attention, that's it. Nothing but this. Thisness is a very important quality. Look at the structures on the microscope screen. That clear one like a rice grain is a chemolithotroph, *Thiobacillus denitrificans*. And there's a chunk of sulphides. Now what will result when the former eats the latter?"

"It oxidizes the sulphur."

"And?"

"And denitrifies."

"Which is?"

"Nitrates into nitrogen. From the ground into the air."

"Very good. A very useful microbe, that."

So Sax forced him to pay attention to the moment, but the price was high. He found himself exhausted at midday when school was over, it was hard to do things in the afternoon. Then they asked him to give more marrow for Simon, who lay in the hospital mute and embarrassed, his eyes apologizing to Nirgal, who steeled himself to smile, to put his fingers around Simon's bamboo forearm. "It's all right," he said cheerily, and lay down. Although surely Simon was doing something wrong, was weak or lazy or somehow wanted to be sick. There was no other way to explain it. They stuck the needle in Nirgal's arm and it went numb. Stuck the IV needle in the back of his hand and after a while it too went numb. He lay back, part of the fabric of the hospital, trying to go as numb as he could. Part of him could feel the big marrow needle, pushing against his upper arm bone. No pain, no feeling in his flesh at all, just a pressure on the bone. Then it let up, and he knew the needle had penetrated to the soft inside of his bone.

This time the process did not help at all. Simon was useless, he stayed in the hospital continually. Nirgal visited him there from time to time, and they played a weather game on Simon's screen, tapping buttons for dice rolls, and exclaiming when the roll of one or twelve cast them abruptly onto another quadrant of Mars, one with a whole new climate. Simon's laugh, never more than a chuckle, had diminished now to just a little smile.

Nirgal's arm hurt, and he slept poorly, tossing through the nights and waking hot and sweaty, and frightened for no reason. Then one night Hiroko woke him from the depths of slumber, and led him down the winding staircase and over to the hospital. He leaned groggily against her, unable to wake fully. She was as impassive as ever, but had her arm around his shoulders, holding him with surprising strength. When they passed Ann sitting in the hospital's outer room something in the slope of Ann's shoulders caused Nirgal to wonder why Hiroko was here in the village at night, and he struggled to wake fully, touched by dread.

The hospital's bedroom was overlit, sharp-edged, pulsing as if glories were trying to burst out of everything. Simon lay with his head on a white pillow. His skin was pale and waxy. He looked a thousand years old.

He turned his head and saw Nirgal. His dark eyes searched Nirgal's face with a hungry look, as if he were trying to find a way into Nirgal—a way to jump across into him. Nirgal shivered and held the dark intense gaze, thinking. Okay, come into me. Do it if you want. Do it.

But there was no way across. They both saw that. They both relaxed. A little smile passed over Simon's face, and he reached over with an effort and held Nirgal's hand. Now his eyes darted back and forth, searching Nirgal's face with a completely different expression, as if he were trying to find words that would help Nirgal in the years to come, that would pass across whatever it was that Simon had learned.

But that too was impossible. Again they both saw it. Simon would have to give Nirgal to his fate, whatever it was. There was no way to help. "Be good," he whispered finally, and Hiroko led Nirgal out of the room. She took him through the dark back up to his room, and he fell into a deep sleep. Simon died sometime during the night.

It was the first funeral in Zygote, and the first for all the children. But the adults knew what to do. They met in one of the greenhouses, among the workbenches, and they sat in a circle around the long box holding Simon's body. They passed around a flask of rice liquor, and everyone filled their neighbor's cup. They drank the fiery stuff down, and the old ones walked around the box holding hands, and then they sat in a knot around Ann and Peter. Maya and Nadia sat by Ann with their arms around her shoulders. Ann appeared stunned, Peter disconsolate. Jurgen and Maya told stories about Simon's legendary taciturnity. "One time," Maya said, "we were in a rover and an oxygen canister blew out and knocked a hole in the cabin roof, and we were all running around screaming and Simon had been outside and he picked up a rock just the right size and jumped up and dropped it in the hole, and plugged it. And afterward we were all talking like crazy people, and working to make a real plug, and suddenly we realized Simon still hadn't *said* anything, and we all stopped working and looked at him, and he said, 'That was close.' "

They laughed. Vlad said, "Or remember the time we gave out mock awards in Underhill, and Simon got one for best video, and he went up to accept the award and said, 'Thank you,' and started to return to his seat, and then he stopped and went back up to the podium, as if something had occurred to him to say, you know, which got our attention naturally, and he cleared his throat and said, 'Thank you *very much.*' "

Ann almost laughed at that, and stood, and led them out into the frigid air. The old ones carried the box down to the beach, and everyone else followed. It was snowing through mist when they took his body out and buried it deep in the sand, just above the wave's high-water mark. They slid the board out of the top of the long box and burned Simon's name onto it with Nadia's soldering iron, and stuck the board in the first dune. Now Simon would be part of the carbon cycle, food for bacteria and crabs and then sandpipers and gulls, thus slowly melting into the biomass under the dome. This was how one was buried. And sure, part of it was comforting; to spread out into one's world, to disperse into it. But to end as a self, to go away. . . .

They all were walking under the dim dome, having buried Simon in sand, trying to behave as if reality had not suddenly ripped apart and snatched one of them away. Nirgal couldn't believe it. They straggled back into the village blowing on their hands, talking in subdued voices. Nirgal drew near Vlad and Ursula, longing for reassurance of some kind. Ursula was sad, and Vlad was trying to cheer her up. "He lived more than a hundred years, we can't go around thinking his death was premature, or it makes a mockery of all those poor people who died at fifty, or twenty, or one."

"But it was still premature," Ursula said stubbornly. "With the treatments, who knows? He might have lived a thousand years."

"I'm not so sure. It looks to me like the treatments are not in fact penetrating to every part of our bodies. And with all the radiation we've taken on, we may have more troubles than we thought at first."

"Maybe. But if we had been at Acheron, with the whole crew, and a bioreactor, and all our facilities, I bet we would have saved him. And then you can't say how many more years he might have had. I call that premature."

She went off to be by herself.

That night Nirgal could not sleep at all. He kept feeling the transfusions, seeing every moment of them and imagining that there had been some kind of backwash in the system, so that he had been infected with the disease. Or contaminated by touch alone, why not? Or just by that last look in Simon's eye! So that he had caught the disease they could not stop, and would die. Stiffen up, go mute, stop and go away. That was death. His heart pounded and a sweat broke through his skin, and he cried with the fear of it. There was no avoiding it; and it was horrible. Horrible no matter when it happened. Horrible that the cycle itself should work the way it did—that it should go around and around and around, while they lived only once and then died forever. Why live at all? It was too strange, too horrible. And so he shivered through the long night, his mind gone cyclonic with the fear of death.

After that he found it extremely hard to concentrate. He felt as if he was always at a remove from things, as if he had slipped into the white world and could not quite touch the green one.

Hiroko noticed this problem, and suggested he go with Coyote on one of his trips out. Nirgal was shocked by the idea, having never been more than a walk away from Zygote. But Hiroko insisted. He was seven years old, she said, and about to become a man. Time he saw a bit of the surface world.

A few weeks later Coyote dropped by, and when he left again Nirgal was with him, seated in the copilot's seat of his boulder car, and goggling out the low windshield at the purple arch of evening sky. Coyote turned the car around to give him a view of the great glowing pink wall of the polar cap, which arced across the horizon like an enormous rising moon.

"It's hard to believe something that big could ever melt," Nirgal said.

"It will take a while."

They drove north at a sedate pace. The boulder car was stealthed, covered by a hollowed-out rock shell that was thermally regulated to stay the same temperature as its surroundings, and it had a no-track device on the front axle to read the terrain and pass the information to the back axle, where scraper-shapers plowed their wheel tracks, returning the sand and rock to whatever shape they had had before their passing. So they could not race along.

For a long time they traveled in silence, though Coyote's silence was not the same as Simon's had been. He hummed, he muttered, he talked in a low singsong voice to his AI, in a language that sounded like English but was not comprehensible. Nirgal tried to concentrate on the limited view out the window, feeling awkward and shy. The region around the south polar cap was a series of broad flat terraces, and they descended from one to the next by routes that seemed programmed into the car, down terrace after terrace until it seemed the polar cap must be sitting on a kind of huge pedestal. Nirgal stared into the dark, impressed by the size of the things, but happy too that it was not absolutely overwhelming, as his first walk out had been. That had happened a long time ago, but he could still remember the staggering astonishment of it perfectly.

This was not like that. "It doesn't seem as big as I thought it would," he said. "I guess it's the curvature of the land, it being such a small planet and all." As the lectern said. "The horizon isn't any farther away than one side of Zygote to the other!"

"Uh huh," Coyote said, giving him a look. "You better not let Big Man hear you say such a thing, he kick your ass for that." Then— "Who's your father, boy?"

"I don't know. Hiroko is my mother."

Coyote snorted. "Hiroko takes the matriarchy too far, if you ask me."

"Have you told her that?"

"You bet I have, but Hiroko only listens to me when I say things she wants to hear." He cackled. "Same as with everyone, right?"

Nirgal nodded, a grin splitting his attempt to be impassive.

"You want to find out who your father is?"

"Sure." Actually he was not sure. The concept of father meant little to him; and he was afraid it would turn out to be Simon. Peter was like an older brother to him, after all.

"They've got the equipment in Vishniac. We can try there if you want." Coyote shook his head. "Hiroko is so strange. When I met her you would never have guessed it would come to this. Of course we were young then—almost as young as you are, though you will find that hard to credit."

Which was true.

"When I met her she was just a young eco-engineering student, smart as a whip and sexy as a cat. None of this mother goddess of the world stuff. But by and by she started to read books that were not her technical manuals, and it went on and on and by the time she got to Mars she was crazy. Before, actually. Which is lucky for me as that is why I'm here. But Hiroko, oh my. She was convinced that all human history had gone wrong at the start. At the dawn of civilization, she would say to me very seriously, there was Crete and Sumeria, and Crete had a peaceful trading culture, run by women and filled with art and beauty—a utopia in fact, where the men were acrobats who jumped bulls all day, and women all night, and got the women pregnant and worshipped them, and everyone was happy. It sounds good except for the bulls. While Sumeria on the other hand was ruled by men, who invented war and conquered everything in sight and started all the slave empires that have come since. And no one knew, Hiroko said, what might have happened if these two civilizations had had a chance to contest the rule of the world, because a volcano blew Crete to kingdom come, and the world passed into Sumeria's hands and has never left it to this day. If only that volcano had been in Sumeria, she used to tell me, everything would be different. And maybe it's true. Because history could hardly get any blacker than it has been."

Nirgal was surprised at this characterization. "But now," he ventured, "we're starting again."

"That's right, boy! We are the primitives of an unknown civilization. Living in our own little techno-Minoan matriarchy. Ha! I like it fine, myself. Seems to me the power that our women have taken on was never that interesting to begin with. Power is one half of the yoke, don't you remember that from the stuff I made you kids read? Master and slave wear the yoke together. Anarchy is the only true freedom. So, well, whatever women do, it seems to go against them. If they're men's cows, then they work till they drop. But if they're our queens and goddesses then they only work the harder, because they still have to do the cow work and then the paperwork too! No way. Just be thankful you're a man, and as free as the sky."

It was a peculiar way to think of things, Nirgal thought. But clearly it was one way to deal with the fact of Jackie's beauty, of her immense power over his mind. And so Nirgal ducked low in his seat and stared out the window at the white stars in the black, thinking Free as the sky! Free as the sky!

It was Ls 4, 2 March the 22nd, M-year 32, and the southern days were getting shorter. Coyote drove their car hard every night, over intricate and invisible paths, through terrain that got more and more rugged the farther they got from the polar cap. They stopped to rest during the daylight, and drove the rest of the time. Nirgal tried to stay awake, but inevitably slept through part of every drive, and through part of every day's stop as well, until he became thoroughly confused in both time and space.

But when he was awake he was almost always looking out the window, at the ever-changing surface of Mars. He couldn't get enough of it. In the layered terrain there was an infinite array of patterns, the stratified stacks of sand fluted by the wind until each dune was cut like a bird's wing. When the layered terrain finally ran out onto exposed bedrock, the laminate dunes became individual sand islands, scattered over a jumbled plain of outcroppings and clusters of rock. It was redrock everywhere he looked, rock sized from gravel to immense boulders that sat like buildings on the land. The sand islands were tucked into every dip and hollow in this rockscape, and they also clustered around the feet of big knots of boulders, and on the lee sides of low scarps, and in the interiors of craters.

And there were craters everywhere. They first appeared as two bumps rolling over the skysill, which quickly proved to be the connected outer points of a low ridge. They passed scores of these flat-topped hills, some steep and sharp, others low and nearly buried, still others with their rims broken by smaller later impacts, so that one could see right in to the sand drifts filling them.

One night just before dawn Coyote stopped the car.

"Something wrong?"

"No. We've reached Ray's Lookout, and I want you to see it. Sun'll be up in an hour."

So they sat in the pilots' seats and watched the dawn.

"How old are you, boy?"

"Seven."

"What's that, thirteen Earth years? Fourteen?"

"I guess."

"Wow. You're already taller than me."

"Uh huh." Nirgal refrained from pointing out that this did not imply any great height. "How old are you?"

"One hundred and nine. Ah ha ha! You best shut your eyes or they'll pop out of your head. Don't you look at me like that. I was old the day I was born and I'll be young the day I die."

They drowsed as the sky on the eastern skyline turned a deep purply

Mars South Polar Region

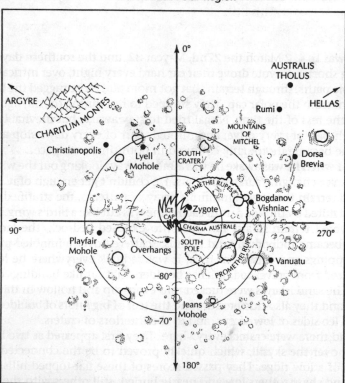

blue. Coyote hummed a little tune to himself, sounding as if he had eaten a tab of omegendorph, as he often did in the evenings at Zygote. Gradually it became clear that the skysill was very far away, and also very high; Nirgal had never seen land so far away, and it seemed to curve around them as well, a black curving wall that lay an immense distance off, over a black rocky plain. "Hey, Coyote!" he exclaimed. "What *is* this?"

"Ha!" Coyote said, sounding deeply satisfied.

The sky lightened and the sun suddenly cracked the upper edge of the distant wall, blasting Nirgal's vision for a while. But as the sun rose the shadows on the huge semicircular cliff gave way in wedges of light that revealed sharp ragged embayments, scalloping the larger curve of the wall, which was so big that Nirgal simply gasped, his nose pressed right against the windshield—it was almost frightening, it was so big! "Coyote, what *is* it?"

Coyote let out one of his alarming laughs, the animal cackle filling the car. "So you see it isn't such a small world after all, eh, boy? This is the floor of Promethei Basin. It's an impact basin, one of the biggest on Mars, almost as big as Argyre, but it hit down here near the South Pole, so about half of its rim has since been buried under the polar cap and the layered terrain. The other half is this curved escarpment here." He waved a hand expansively. "Kind of like a super-big caldera, but only half there, so you can drive right into it. This little rise is the best place I know for seeing it." He called up a map of the region, and pointed. "We're on the apron of this little crater here, Vt, and looking northwest. The cliff is Promethei Rupes, there. It's about a kilometer high. Of course the Echus cliff is three kilometers high, and the Olympus Mons cliff is *six* kilometers high, do you hear that Mister Small Planet? But this baby will have to do for this morning."

The sun rose higher, illuminating the great curve of the cliff from above. It was deeply cut by ravines and smaller craters. "Prometheus Sanctuary is in the side of that big indentation there," Coyote said, and pointed to the left side of the curve. "Crater Wj."

As they waited through the long day Nirgal looked at the gigantic cliff almost continuously, and each time it looked different, as the shadows shortened and shifted, revealing new features and obscuring others. It would have taken years of looking to see it all, and he found he could not overcome the feeling that the wall was unnaturally or even impossibly huge. Coyote was right—the tight horizons had fooled him—he had not imagined the world could *be* so big.

That night they drove into Crater Wj, one of the biggest embayments in the giant wall. And then they reached the curving cliff of Promethei Rupes. The cliff towered over them like the vertical side of the universe itself; the polar cap was nothing compared to this rock mass. Which meant that the Olympus Mons cliff that Coyote had mentioned would have to be. . . . He didn't know how to think it.

Down at the foot of the cliff, at a spot where unbroken rock dropped almost vertically into flat sand, there was a recessed lock door. Inside was the sanctuary called Prometheus, a collection of wide chambers stacked like the rooms of a bamboo house, with incurving filtered windows overlooking Crater Wj and the larger basin beyond. The inhabitants of the sanctuary spoke French, and so did Coyote when talking to them. They were not as old as Coyote or the other issei, but they were pretty old, and of Terran height, which meant they mostly looked up to Nirgal, while speaking very hospitably to him, in fluent but accented English. "So you are Nirgal! *Enchanté!* We have heard of you, we are happy to meet you!"

A group of them showed him around while Coyote did other things. Their sanctuary was very unlike Zygote; it was, to put it plainly, nothing but rooms. There were several large ones stacked by the wall, with smaller ones at the back of these. Three of the window rooms were greenhouses, and all the rooms throughout the refuge were kept very warm, and filled with plants and wall hangings and statuary and fountains; to Nirgal it seemed confining, and much too hot, and utterly fascinating.

But they only stayed a day, and then they drove Coyote's car into a big elevator, and sat in it for an hour. When Coyote drove out the opposite door they were on top of the rugged plateau that lay behind Promethei Rupes. And here Nirgal was once again shocked. When they had been down at Ray's Lookout, the great cliff had formed a limit to what they could see, and he had been able to comprehend it. But on top of the cliff, looking back down, the distances were so great that Nirgal could not grasp what he saw. It was nothing but a blurry vertiginous mass of blobs and patches of color—white, purple, brown, tan, rust, white; it made him queasy. "Storm coming in," Coyote said, and suddenly Nirgal saw that the colors above them were a fleet of tall solid clouds, sailing through a violet sky with the sun well to the west—the clouds whitish above and infinitely lobed, but dark gray on their bottoms. These cloud bottoms were closer to their heads than the ground of the basin, and they were level, as if rolling over a transparent floor. The world below was nothing so even, mottled tan and chocolate—ah, those were the shadows of the clouds, visibly moving. And that white crescent out in the middle of things was the polar cap! They could see all the way home! Recognizing the ice gave him the final bit of perspective needed to make sense of things, and the blobs of color stabilized into a bumpy uneven ringed landscape, mottled by moving cloud shadows.

This dizzying act of cognition had only taken Nirgal a few seconds, but when he finished he saw that Coyote was watching him with a big grin.

"Just how far can we see, Coyote? How many kilometers?"

Coyote only cackled. "Ask Big Man, boy. Or figure it out for yourself! What, three hundred k? Something like that. A hop and a jump for the big one. A thousand empires for the little ones."

"I want to run it."

"I'm sure you do. Oh, look, look! There—from the clouds over the ice cap. Lightning, see it? Those little flickers are lightning."

And there they were, bright threads of light, appearing and disappearing soundlessly, one or two every few seconds, connecting black clouds with white ground. He was seeing lightning at last, with his own eyes. The white world sparkling into the green, jolting it. "There's nothing like a big storm," Coyote was saying. "Nothing like it. Oh to be out in the wind! We made that storm, boy. Although I think I could make an even bigger one."

But a bigger one was beyond Nirgal's ability to imagine; what lay below them was cosmically vast—electric, shot with color, windy with spaciousness. He was actually a bit relieved when Coyote turned their car around and drove off, and the blurry view disappeared, the edge of the cliff becoming a new skysill behind them.

"Just what is lightning again?"

"Well, lightning . . . shit. I must confess that lightning is one of the phenomena in this world that I cannot hold the explanation for in my head. People have told me, but it always slips away. Electricity, of course, something about electrons or ions, positive and negative, charges building up in thunderheads, discharging to the ground, or both up and down at once, I seem to recall. Who knows. Ka boom! That's lightning, eh?"

The white world and the green, rubbing together, snapping with the friction. Of course.

There were several sanctuaries on the plateau north of Promethei Rupes, some hidden in escarpment walls and crater rims, like Nadia's tunneling project outside Zygote; but others simply sitting in craters under clear tent domes, there for any sky police to see. The first time Coyote drove up to the rim of one of these and they looked down through the clear tent dome onto a village under the stars, Nirgal had been once again amazed, though it was amazement of a lesser order than that engendered by the landscape. Buildings like the school, and the bathhouse and the kitchen, trees, greenhouses—it was all basically familiar, but how could they get away with it, out in the open like this? It was disconcerting.

And so full of people, of strangers. Nirgal had known in theory that there were a lot of people in the southern sanctuaries, five thousand as they said, all defeated rebels of the 2061 war—but it was something else again to meet so many of them so fast, and see that it was really true. And staying in the unhidden settlements made him extremely nervous. "How can they do it?" he asked Coyote. "Why aren't they arrested and taken away?"

"You got me, boy. It's possible they could be. But they haven't been yet, and so they don't think it's worth the trouble to hide. You know it takes a tremendous effort to hide—you got to do all that thermal disposal engineering, and electronic hardening, and you got to keep out of sight all the time—it's a pain in the ass. And some people down here just don't want to do it. They call themselves the demimonde. They have plans for if they're ever investigated or invaded—most of them have escape tunnels like ours, and some even have some weapons stashed away. But they figure that if they're out on the surface, there's no reason to be checked out in the first place. The folks in Christianopolis just told the UN straight out that they came down here to get out of the net. But . . . I agree with Hiroko on this one. That some of us have to be a little more careful than that. The UN is out to get the First Hundred, if you ask me. And its family too, unfortunately for you kids. Anyway, now the resistance includes the underground and the demimonde, and having the open towns is a big help to the hidden sanctuaries, so I'm glad they're here. At this point we depend on them."

Coyote was welcomed effusively in this town as he was everywhere, whether the settlement was hidden or exposed. He settled into a corner of a big garage on the crater rim, and conducted a continuous brisk exchange of goods, including seed stocks, software, light bulbs, spare parts, and small machines. These he gave out after long consultations with their hosts, in bargaining sessions that Nirgal couldn't understand. And then, after a brief tour of the crater floor, where the village looked surprisingly like Zygote under a brilliant purple dome, they were off again.

On the drives between sanctuaries Coyote did not explain his bargaining sessions very effectively. "I'm saving these people from their own ridiculous notion of economics, that's what I'm doing! A gift economy is all very well, but it isn't organized enough for our situation. There are critical items that everyone has to have, so people *have* to give, which is a contradiction, right? So I am trying to work out a rational system. Actually Vlad and Marina are working it out, and I am trying to implement it, which means I get all the grief."

"And this system . . ."

"Well, it's a sort of two-track thing, where they can still give all they want, but the necessities are given values and distributed properly. And good God you wouldn't believe some of the arguments I get in. People can be such fools. I try to make sure it all adds up to a stable ecology, like one of Hiroko's systems, with every sanctuary filling its niche and providing its specialty, and what do I get for it? Abuse, that's what I get! *Radical* abuse. I try to stop potlatching and they call me a robber baron, I try to stop hoarding and they call me a fascist. The fools! What are they going to do, when none of them are self-sufficient, and half of them are crazy paranoid?" He sighed theatrically. "So, anyway. We're making progress. Christianopolis makes light bulbs, and Mauss Hyde grows new kinds of plants, as you saw, and Bogdanov Vishniac makes everything big and difficult, like reactor rods and stealth vehicles and most of the big robots, and your Zygote makes scientific instrumentation, and so on. And I spread them around."

"Are you the only one doing that?"

"Almost. They're mostly self-sufficient, actually, except for these few criticalities. They all got programs and seeds, that's the basic necessities. And besides, it's important that not too many people know where all the hidden sanctuaries are."

Nirgal digested the implications of this as they drove through the night. Coyote went on about the hydrogen peroxide standard and the nitrogen standard, a new system of Vlad and Marina's, and Nirgal did his best to follow but found it hard going, either because the concepts were difficult or else because Coyote spent most of his explanations fulminating over the difficulties he encountered in certain sanctuaries. Nirgal decided to ask Sax or Nadia about it when he got home, and stopped listening.

The land they were crossing now was dominated by crater rings, the newer ones overlapping and even burying older ones. "This is called saturation cratering. Very ancient ground." A lot of the craters had no raised rims at all, but were simply shallow flat-bottomed round holes in the ground. "What happened to the rims?"

"Worn away."

"By what?"

"Ann says ice, and wind. She says as much as a kilometer was stripped off the southern highlands over time."

"That would take away everything!"

"But then more came back. This is old land."

In between craters the land was covered with loose rock, and it was unbelievably uneven; there were dips, rises, hollows, knolls, trenches, grabens, uplifts, hills and dales; never even a moment's flatness, except on crater rims and occasional low ridges, both of which Coyote used as roads when he could. But the track he followed over this lumpy landscape was still tortuous, and Nirgal could not believe it was memorized. He said as much, and Coyote laughed. "What do you mean memorized? We're lost!"

But not really, or not for long. A mohole plume appeared over the horizon, and Coyote drove for it.

"Knew it all along," he muttered. "This is Vishniac mohole. It's a vertical shaft a kilometer across, dug straight down into the bedrock. There were four moholes started around the seventy-five-degree latitude line, and two of them are no longer occupied, even by robots. Vishniac is one of the two, and it's been taken over by a bunch of Bogdanovists who live down inside it." He laughed. "It's a wonderful idea, because they can dig into the side wall along the road to the bottom, and down there they can put out as much heat as they want and no one can tell that it's not just more mohole outgassing. So they can build anything they like, even process uranium for reactor fuel rods. It's an entire little industrial city now. Also one of my favorite places, very big on partying."

He drove them into one of the many small trenches cutting the land, then braked and tapped at his screen, and a big rock swung out from the side of the trench, revealing a black tunnel. Coyote drove into the tunnel and the rock door closed behind them. Nirgal had thought he was beyond surprise at this point, but he watched round-eyed as they drove down the tunnel, its rough rock walls just outside the edges of the boulder car. It seemed to go on forever. "They've dug a number of approach tunnels, so that the mohole itself can look completely unvisited. We have about twenty kilometers to go."

Eventually Coyote turned off the headlights. Their car rolled out into the dim eggplant black of night; they were on a steep road, apparently spiraling down the wall of the mohole. Their instrument-panel lights were like tiny lanterns, and looking through his reflected image Nirgal could see that the road was four or five times as wide as the car. The full extent of the mohole itself was impossible to see, but by the curve of the road he could tell that it was immense. "Are you sure we're turning at the right speed?" he said anxiously.

"I am trusting the automatic pilot," Coyote said, irritated. "It's bad luck to discuss it."

The car rolled down the road. After more than an hour's descent there was a beep from the instrument panel, and the car turned into the curving wall of rock to their left. And there was a garage tube, clanking against their outer lock door.

Inside the garage a group of twenty or so people greeted them, and took them past a line of tall rooms to a cavernlike chamber. The rooms that the Bogdanovists had excavated into the side of the mohole were big, much bigger than those at Prometheus. The back rooms were ten meters high as a rule, and in some cases two hundred meters deep; and the main cavern rivaled Zygote itself, with big windows facing out onto the hole. Looking sideways through the window, Nirgal saw that the glass seen from the outside looked like the rock face; the filtered coatings must have been clever indeed, because as the morning arrived, its light poured in very brightly. The windows' view was limited to the far wall of the mohole, and a gibbous patch of sky above—but they gave the rooms a wonderful sense of spaciousness and light, a feeling of being under the sky that Zygote could not match.

Through that first day Nirgal was taken in hand by a small dark-skinned man named Hilali, who led him through rooms and interrupted people at their work to introduce him. People were friendly—"You must be one of Hiroko's kids, eh? Oh, you're Nirgal! Very nice to meet you! Hey John, Coyote's here, party tonight!"—and they showed him what they were doing, leading him back into smaller rooms behind the ones fronting the mohole, where there were farms under bright light, and manufactories that seemed to extend back into the rock forever; and all of it very warm, as in a bathhouse, so that Nirgal was constantly sweating. "Where did you put all the excavated rock?" he asked Hilali, for one of the convenient things about cutting a dome under the polar cap, Hiroko had said, was that the excavated dry ice had simply been gassed off.

"It's lining the road near the bottom of the mohole," Hilali told him, pleased at the question. He seemed pleased with all Nirgal's questions, as did everyone else; people in Vishniac seemed happy in general, a rowdy crowd who always partied to celebrate Coyote's arrival—one excuse among many, Nirgal gathered.

Hilali took a call on the wrist from Coyote, and led Nirgal into a lab, where they took a bit of skin from his finger. Then they made their way slowly back to the big cavern, and joined the crowd lining up by the kitchen windows at the back.

After eating a big spicy meal of beans and potatoes, they began to party in the cavern room. A huge undisciplined steel-drum band with a fluctuating membership played rhythmic staccato melodies, and people danced to them for hours, pausing from time to time to drink an atrocious liquor called kavajava, or join a variety of games on one side of the room. After trying the kavajava, and swallowing a tab of an omegendorph given to him by Coyote, Nirgal ran in place while playing a bass drum with the band, then sat on top of a small grassy mound in the center of the chamber, feeling too drunk to stand. Coyote had been drinking steadily but had no such problem; he was dancing wildly, hopping high off his toes and laughing. "You'll never know the joy of your own g, boy!" he shouted at Nirgal. "You'll never know!"

People came by and introduced themselves, sometimes asking Nirgal to exhibit his warming touch—a group of girls his age put his hands to their cheeks, which they had chilled with their drinks, and when he warmed them up they laughed round-eyed, and invited him to warm other parts of them; he got up and danced with them instead, feeling loose and dizzy, running in little circles to discharge some of the energy in him. When he returned to the knoll, buzzing, Coyote came weaving over and sat heavily beside him. "*So* fine to dance in this g, I never get over it." He regarded Nirgal with a cross-eyed glare, his gray dreadlocks falling all over his head, and Nirgal noticed again that his face seemed to have cracked somehow, perhaps been broken at the jaw, so that one side was broader than the other. Something like that. Nirgal gulped at the sight.

Coyote took him by the shoulder and shook him hard. "It seems that I am your father, boy!" he exclaimed.

"You're kidding!" An electric flush ran down Nirgal's spine and out his face as the two of them stared at each other, and he marveled at how the white world could shock the green one so thoroughly, like lightning pulsing through flesh. They clutched each other.

"I am not kidding!" Coyote said.

They stared at each other. "No wonder you're so smart," Coyote said, and laughed hilariously. " Ah ha ha ha! Ka wow! I hope it's okay with you!"

"Sure," Nirgal said, grinning but uncomfortable. He didn't know Coyote well, and the concept of father was even vaguer to him than that of mother, so he wasn't really sure what he felt. Genetic inheritance, sure, but what was that? They all got their genes somewhere, and the genes of ectogenes were transgenic anyway, or so they said.

But Coyote, though he cursed Hiroko in a hundred different ways, seemed to be pleased. "That vixen, that tyrant! Matriarchy my ass—she's crazy! It amazes me the things she does! Although this has a certain justice to it. Yes it does, because Hiroko and I were an item back in the dawn of time, when we were young in England. That's the reason I'm here on Mars at all. A stowaway in her closet, my whole fucking life long." He laughed and clapped Nirgal on the shoulder again. "Well, boy, you will know better how you like the idea later on."

He went back out to dance, leaving Nirgal to think it over. Watching Coyote's gyrations, Nirgal could only shake his head; he didn't know what to think, and at the moment thinking anything at all was remarkably difficult. Better to dance, or seek out the baths.

But they had no public baths. He ran around in circles on the dance floor, making his running a kind of dance, and later he returned to the same mound, and a group of the locals gathered around him and Coyote. "Like being the father of the Dalai Lama, eh? Don't you get a name for that?"

"To hell with you, man! Like I was saying, Ann says they stopped digging these seventy-five-degree moholes because the lithosphere is thinner down here." Coyote nodded portentously. "I want to go to one of the decommissioned moholes and start up its robots again, and see if they dig down far enough to start a volcano."

Everyone laughed. But one woman shook her head. "If you do that they'll come down here to check it out. If you're going to do it, you should go north and hit one of the sixty-degree moholes. They're decommissioned too."

"But the lithosphere up there is thicker, Ann says."

"Sure, but the moholes are deeper too."

"Hmm," Coyote said.

And the conversation moved on to more serious matters, mostly the inevitable topics of shortages, and developments in the north. But at the end of that week, when they left Vishniac, by way of a different and longer tunnel, they headed north, and all Coyote's previous plans had been thrown out the window. "That's the story of my life, boy."

On the fifth night of driving over the jumbled highlands of the south, Coyote slowed the rover, and circled the edge of a big old crater, subdued almost to the level of the surrounding plain. From a defile in the ancient rim one could see that the sandy crater floor was marred by a giant round black hole. This, apparently, was what a mohole looked like from the surface. A plume of thin frost stood in the air a few hundred meters over the hole, appearing from nothing like a magician's trick. The edge of the mohole was beveled so that there was a band of concrete funneling down at about a forty-five-degree angle; it was hard to say how big this coping band was, because the mohole made it seem like no more than a strip. There was a high wire fence at its outer edge. "Hmm," Coyote said, staring out the windshield. He backed up in the defile and parked, then slipped into a walker. "Back soon," he said, and hopped into the lock.

It was a long, anxious night for Nirgal. He barely slept, and was in an intensifying agony of worry the next morning when he saw Coyote appear outside the boulder car lock, just before seven A.M. when the sun was about to rise. He was ready to complain about the length of this disappearance, but when Coyote got inside and got his helmet off it was obvious he was in a foul temper. While they sat out the day he tapped away at his AI in an absorbed conference, cursing vilely, oblivious to his hungry young charge. Nirgal went ahead and heated meals for them both, and then napped uneasily, and woke when the rover jerked forward. "I'm going to try going in through the gate," Coyote said. "That's quite the security they have on that hole. One more night should see it either way." He circled the crater and parked on the far rim, and at dusk once again left on foot.

Again he was gone all night, and again Nirgal found it very difficult to sleep. He wondered what he was supposed to do if Coyote didn't return.

And indeed he was not back by dawn. The day that followed was the longest of Nirgal's life without a question, and at the end of it he had no idea what he was going to do. Try to rescue Coyote; try to drive back to Zygote, or Vishniac; go down to the mohole, and give himself up to whatever mysterious security system had eaten up Coyote: all seemed impossible.

But an hour after sunset Coyote tapped the car with his *tik-tik-tik,* and then he was inside, his face a furious mask. He drank a liter of water and then most of another, and blew out his lips in disgust. "Let us get the fuck out of here," he said.

After a couple of hours of silent driving Nirgal thought to change the subject, or at least enlarge it, and he said, "Coyote, how long do you think we will have to stay hidden?"

"Don't call me Coyote! I'm not Coyote. Coyote is out there in the back of the hills, breathing the air already and doing what he wants, the bastard. Me my name is Desmond, you call me *Desmond,* understand?"

"Okay," Nirgal said, afraid.

"As for how long we will have to stay hiding, I think it will be forever."

They drove back south to Rayleigh mohole, where Coyote (he didn't seem to be a Desmond) had thought to go in the first place. This mohole was truly abandoned, an unlit hole in the highlands, its thermal plume standing over it like the ghost of a monument. They could drive right into the empty sand-covered parking lot and garage at its rim, between a small fleet of robot vehicles shrouded by tarpaulins and sand drifts. "This is more like it," Coyote muttered. "Here, we've got to take a look down inside it. Come on, get into your walker."

It was strange to be out in the wind, standing on the rim of such an enormous gap in things. They looked over a chest-high wall and saw the beveled concrete band that rimmed the hole, dropping at an angle for about two hundred meters. In order to see down the shaft proper, they had to walk about a kilometer down a curving road cut into the concrete band. There they could stop at last, and look over the road's edge, down into blackness. Coyote stood right on the edge, which made Nirgal nervous. He got on his hands and knees to look over. No sign of a bottom; they might as well have been looking into the center of the planet. "Twenty kilometers," Coyote said over the intercom. He held a hand out over the edge, and Nirgal did too. He could feel the updraft. "Okay, let's see if we can get the robots going." And they hiked back up the road.

Coyote had spent many of their daytime hours studying old programs on his AI, and now, with the hydrogen peroxide from their trailer pumped into two of the robot behemoths in the parking lot, he plugged into their control panels and went at it. When he was done he was satisfied they would perform as required at the bottom of the mohole, and they watched the two, with wheels four times as tall as Coyote's car, roll off down the curving road.

"All right," Coyote said, cheering up again. "They'll use their solar-panel power to process their own peroxide explosives, and their own fuel as well, and go at it slow and steady until maybe they hit something hot. We just may have started a volcano!"

"Is that good?"

Coyote laughed wildly. "I don't know! But no one's ever done it before, so it has that at least to recommend it."

They returned to their scheduled travel, among sanctuaries both hidden and open, and Coyote went around saying, "We started up Rayleigh mohole last week, have you seen a volcano yet?"

No one had seen it. Rayleigh seemed to be behaving much as before, its thermal plume undisturbed. "Well, maybe it didn't work," Coyote would say. "Maybe it will take some time. On the other hand if that mohole was now floored with molten lava, how would you be able to tell?"

"We could tell," people said. And some added: "Why would you do something as stupid as that? You might as well call up the Transitional Authority and tell them to come down here to look for us."

So Coyote stopped bringing it up. They rolled on from sanctuary to sanctuary: Mauss Hyde, Gramsci, Overhangs, Christianopolis. . . . At each stop Nirgal was made welcome, and often people knew of him in advance, by reputation. Nirgal was very surprised by the variety and number of sanctuaries, forming together their strange world, half secret and half exposed. And if this world was only a small part of Martian civilization as a whole, what must the surface cities of the north be like? It was beyond his grasp—although it did seem to him that as the marvels of the journey continued, one after the next, his grasp was getting a bit larger. You couldn't just explode from amazement, after all.

"Well," Coyote would say as they drove (he had taught Nirgal how), "we may have started a volcano and we may not have. But it was a new idea in any case. That's one of the greatest things about this, boy, this whole Martian project. It's all *new.*"

They headed south again, until the ghostly wall of the polar cap loomed over the horizon. Soon they would be home again.

Nirgal thought of all the sanctuaries they had visited. "Do you really think we'll have to hide forever, Desmond?"

"Desmond? Desmond? Who's this *Desmond?*" Coyote blew out his lips. "Oh, boy, I don't know. No one can know for sure. The people hiding out here were shoved out at a strange time, when their way of life was threatened, and I'm not so sure it's that way anymore in the surface cities they're building in the north. The bosses on Earth learned their lesson, maybe, and people up there are more comfortable. Or maybe it's just that the elevator hasn't been replaced yet."

"So there might not be another revolution?"

"I don't know."

"Or not until there's another space elevator?"

"I don't know! But the elevator's coming, and they're building some big new mirrors out there, you can see them shining at night sometimes, or right around the sun. So anything might happen, I guess. But revolution is a rare thing. And a lot of them are reactionary anyway. Peasants have their tradition, you see, the values and habits that allow them to get by. But they live so close to the edge that rapid change can push them over it, and in those times it's not politics, but survival. I saw that myself when I was your age. Now the people sent here were not poor, but they did have their own tradition, and like the poor they were powerless. And when the influx of the 2050s hit, their tradition was wiped out. So they fought for what they had. And the truth is, they lost. You can't fight the powers that be anymore, especially here, because the weapons are too strong and our shelters are too fragile. We'd have to arm ourselves pretty good, or something. So, you know. We're hiding, and they're flooding Mars with a new kind of crowd, people who were used to really tough conditions on Earth, so that things here don't strike them so bad. They get the treatment and they're happy. We're not seeing so many people trying to get out into the sanctuaries, like we did in the years before sixty-one. There's some, but not many. As long as people have their entertainments, their own little tradition, you know, they aren't going to lift a finger."

"But . . ." Nirgal said, and faltered.

Coyote saw the expression on his face and laughed. "Hey, who knows? Pretty soon now they'll have another elevator in place up on Pavonis Mons, and then very likely they'll start to screw things up all over again, those greedy bastards. And you young folks, maybe you won't want Earth calling the shots here. We'll see when the time comes. Meanwhile we're having fun, right? We're keeping the flame."

That night Coyote stopped the car, and told Nirgal to suit up. They went out and stood on the sand, and Coyote turned him around so that he was facing north. "Look at the sky."

Nirgal stood and watched; and saw a new star burst into existence, there over the northern horizon, growing in a matter of seconds to a long white-tailed comet, flying west to east. When it was about halfway across the sky the blazing head of the comet burst apart, and bright framents scattered in every direction, white into black.

"One of the ice asteroids!" Nirgal exclaimed.

Coyote snorted. "There's no surprising you, is there boy! Well, I'll tell you something you didn't know; that was ice asteroid 2089 C, and did you see how it blew up there at the end? That was a first. They did that on purpose. Blowing them up when they enter the atmosphere allows them to use bigger asteroids without endangering the surface. And that was my idea! I told them to do that myself, I put an anonymous suggestion in the AI at Greg's Place when I was in there messing with their comm system, and they jumped on it. They're going to do them that way all the time now. There'll be one or two every season like that, they're thickening the atmosphere pretty fast. Look at how the stars are trembling. They used to do that all the nights of Earth. Ah, boy . . . It'll happen here all the time too, someday. Air you can breathe like a bird in the sky. Maybe that will help us to change the order of things on this world. You can never tell about things like that."

Nirgal closed his eyes, and saw red afterimages of the ice meteor score his eyelids. Meteors like white fireworks, holes boring straight into the mantle, volcanoes. . . . He turned and saw the Coyote hopping over the plain, small and thin, his helmet strangely large on him as if he were a mutant or a shaman wearing a sacred animal head, doing a changeling dance over the sand. This was the Coyote, no doubt about it. His father!

.   .   .

Then they had circumnavigated the world, albeit high in the southern hemisphere. The polar cap rose over the horizon and grew, until they were under the overhang of ice, which did not seem as tall as it had at the start of the journey. They circled the ice to home, and drove into the hangar, and got out of the little boulder car that had become so well known to Nirgal in the previous two weeks, and walked stiffly through the locks and back down the long tunnel into the dome, and suddenly they were among all the familiar faces, being hugged and cosseted and questioned. Nirgal shrank shyly from the attention, but there was no need, Coyote told all their stories for him, and he only had to laugh, and deny responsibility for what they had done. Glancing past his kin, he saw how small his little world really was; the dome was less than 5 kilometers across, and 250 meters high out over the lake. A small world.

When the homecoming was over he walked out in the early-morning glow, feeling the happy nip of the air and looking closely at the buildings and bamboo stands of the village, in its nest of hills and trees. It all looked so strange and small. Then he was out on the dunes and walking out to Hiroko's place, with the gulls wheeling overhead, and he stopped frequently just to see things. He breathed in the chill kelp-and-salt scent of the beach; the intense familiarity of the scent triggered a million memories at once, and he knew he was home.

But home had changed. Or he had. Between the attempt to save Simon and the trip with Coyote, he had become a youth apart from the rest; the distinguishing adventures that he had so longed for had come, and their only result was to exile him from his friends. Jackie and Harmakhis hung together more tightly than ever, and acted like a shield between him and all the younger sansei. Quickly Nirgal realized that he hadn't really wanted to be different after all. He only wanted to melt back into the closeness of his little pack, and be one with his siblings.

But when he came among them they went silent, and Harmakhis would lead them off, after the most awkward encounters imaginable. And he was left to return to the adults, who began to keep him with them in the afternoons, as a matter of course. Perhaps they meant to spare him some of his pack's hard treatment, but it only had the effect of marking him even more. There was no cure for it. One day, walking the beach unhappily in the gray and pewter twilight of a fall afternoon, it occurred to him that his childhood was gone. That was what this feeling was; he was something else now, neither adult nor child, a solitary being, a foreigner in his own country. The melancholy realization had a peculiar pleasure to it.

One day after lunch Jackie stayed behind with him and Hiroko, who had come in for the day to teach, and demanded to be included in her afternoon lesson. "Why should you teach him and not me?"

"No reason," Hiroko said impassively. "Stay if you want. Get out your lectern and call up Thermal Engineering, page one oh five oh. We'll model

Zygote Dome for example. Tell me what is the warmest point under the dome?"

Nirgal and Jackie attacked the problem, competing and yet side by side. He was so happy she was there that he could hardly remember the problem, and Jackie raised a finger before he had even organized his thinking about it. And she laughed at him, a bit scornful but also pleased. Through all these enormous changes in them both there remained in Jackie that capacity for infectious joy, that laughter from which it was so painful to be exiled. . . .

"Here is a question for next time," Hiroko said to them. "All the names for Mars in the areophany are names given to it by Terrans. About half of them mean *fire star* in the languages they come from, but that is still a name from the outside. The question is, what is Mars's own name for itself?"

Several weeks later Coyote came through again, which made Nirgal both happy and nervous. Coyote took a morning teaching the children, but fortunately he treated Nirgal the same as all the rest. "Earth is in very bad shape," he told them as they worked on vacuum pumps from the liquid-sodium tanks in the Rickover, "and it will only get worse. That makes their control over Mars all the more dangerous to us. We'll have to hide until we can cut ourselves free of them entirely, and then stand safe to the side while they descend into madness and chaos. You remember my words here, this is a prophecy as true as truth."

"That isn't what John Boone said," Jackie declared. She spent many of her evening hours exploring John Boone's AI, and now she pulled out the box from her thigh pocket, and with only the briefest search for a passage, the friendly voice from the box was saying, "Mars will never be truly safe until Earth is too."

Coyote laughed raucously. "Yes, well, John Boone was like that, wasn't he. But you note he is dead, while I'm still here."

"Anyone can hide," Jackie said sharply. "But John Boone got out there and led. That's why I'm a Boonean."

"You're a Boone *and* a Boonean!" Coyote exclaimed, teasing her. "And Boonean algebra never did add up. But look here, girl, you have to understand your grandfather better than that if you want to call yourself a Boonean. You can't make John Boone into any kind of dogma and be true to what he was. I see other so-called Booneans out there doing just that, and it makes me laugh when it doesn't make me foam at the mouth. Why, if John Boone were to meet you and talk to you for even just an hour, then at the end of that time he would be a Jackie-ist. And if he met Harmakhis and talked to him, then he would become a Harmakhisist, maybe even a Maoist. That's just the way he was. And that was *good*, you see, because what it did was put the responsibility for thinking back onto us. It forced us to make a contribution, because without that Boone couldn't operate. His point was not just that everyone can do it, but that everyone should do it."

"Including all the people on Earth," Jackie replied.

"Not another quick one!" Coyote cried. "Oh you girl, why don't you leave these boys of yours and marry me now, I got a kiss like this vacuum pump, here, come on," and he waved the pump at her and Jackie knocked it aside and shoved him back and ran, just for the fun of the chase. She was now the fastest runner in Zygote bar none, even Nirgal with all his endurance could not sprint the way she did, and the kids laughed at Coyote as he skipped after her; he was pretty swift himself for an ancient, and he turned and jinked and went after them all, growling and ending up at the bottom of a pile-on, crying "Oh my leg, oh I'm going to get you for that, you boys are just jealous of me because I'm going to steal your girl away, oh! Stop! Oh!"

This kind of teasing made Nirgal uncomfortable, and Hiroko didn't like it either. She told Coyote to stop, but he just laughed at her. "You're the one that's gone and made yourself a little incest camp," he said. "What are you going to do, neuter them?" He laughed at Hiroko's dark expression. "You're going to have to farm them out soon, that's what you're going to have to do. And I might as well get some of them."

Hiroko dismissed him, and soon after that he was off on a trip again. And the next time Hiroko taught, she took all the kids to the bathhouse and they got in the bath after her and sat on the slick tiles in the shallow end, soaking in the hot steamy water while Hiroko spoke. Nirgal sat next to Jackie's long-limbed naked body which he knew so well, including all its dramatic changes of the past year, and he found that he was unable to look at her.

His ancient naked mother said, "You know how genetics works, I've taught you that myself. And you know that many of you are half brothers and sisters, uncles and nieces and cousins and so forth. I am mother or grandmother to many of you, and so you should not mate and have children together. It's as simple as that, a very simple genetic law." She held up a palm, as if to say, This is our shared body.

"But all living things are filled with viriditas," she went on, "the green force, patterning outward. And so it is normal that you will love each other, especially now that your bodies are blooming. There is nothing wrong with that, no matter what Coyote says. He is only joking in any case. And in one thing he is right; you will soon be meeting many other people your age, and they will eventually become mates and partners and coparents with you, closer to you even than your tribe kin, whom you know too well to ever love as an other. We here are all pieces of your self; and true love is always for the other."

Nirgal kept his eyes on his mother's, his gaze blank. Still he knew exactly when Jackie had brought her legs together, he had felt the minute change in temperature in the water swirling between them. And it seemed to him that his mother was wrong in some of what she had said. Although he knew Jackie's body so well, she was still in most ways as distant as any fiery star, bright and imperious in the sky. She was the queen of their little band, and could crush him with a glance if she cared to, and did fairly often even though he had been studying her moods all his life. That was as much otherness as he cared to handle. And he loved her, he knew he did. But she didn't love him back, not in the same way. Nor did she love Harmakhis in that way, he thought, at least not anymore; which was a small comfort. It was Peter she watched in the way that he watched her. But Peter was away most of the time. So she loved no one in Zygote the way Nirgal loved her. Perhaps for her it was already as Hiroko had said, and Harmakhis and Nirgal and the rest were simply too well known. Her brothers and sisters, no matter the genes involved.

Then one day the sky fell in earnest. The whole highest part of the water ice sheet cracked away from the CO_2, collapsing through the mesh and into the lake and all over the beach and the surrounding dunes. Luckily it happened in the early morning when no one was down there, but in the village the first booms and cracks were explosively loud, and everyone rushed to their windows and saw most of the fall: the giant white sections of ice dropping like bombs or spinning down like skipped plates, and then the whole surface of the lake exploding and spilling out over the dunes. People came charging out of their rooms, and in the noise and panic Hiroko and Maya herded the kids into the school, which had a discrete air system. When a few minutes had passed and it appeared that the dome itself was going to hold, Peter and Michel and Nadia ran off through the debris, dodging and jumping over the shattered white plates, around the lake to the Rickover to make sure it was all right. If it wasn't it would be a deadly mission for the three of them, and mortal danger to everyone else. From the school window Nirgal could see the far shore of the lake, which was cluttered with icebergs. The air was aswirl with screaming gulls. The three figures twisted along the narrow high path just under the edge of the dome, and disappeared into the Rickover. Jackie chewed her knuckles in fear. Soon they phoned back a report: all was well. The ice over the reactor was supported by a particularly close-meshed framework, and it had held.

So they were safe, for the moment. But over the next couple of days, spent in the village in an unhappy state of tension, an investigation into the cause of the fall revealed that the the whole mass of dry ice over them had sagged ever so slightly, cracking the layer of water ice and sending it down through the mesh. Sublimation on the surface of the cap was apparently speeding up to a remarkable degree, as the atmosphere thickened and the world warmed.

During the next week the icebergs in the lake slowly melted, but the plates scattered over the dunes were still there, melting ever so slowly. The youngsters weren't allowed on the beach anymore; it wasn't clear how stable the remainder of the ice layer was.

The tenth night after the collapse they had a village meeting in the dining hall, all two hundred of them. Nirgal looked around at them, at his little tribe; the sansei looked frightened, the nisei defiant, the issei stunned. The old ones had lived in Zygote for fourteen Martian years, and no doubt it was hard for them to remember any other life; impossible for the children, who had never known anything else.

It did not need saying that they would not surrender themselves to the surface world. And yet the dome was becoming untenable, and they were too large a group to impose themselves on any of the other hidden sanctuaries. Splitting up would solve that problem, but it wasn't a happy solution.

It took an hour's talk to lay all this out. "We could try Vishniac," Michel said. "It's big, and they'd welcome us."

But it was the Bogdanovists' home, not theirs. This was the message on the faces of the old ones. Suddenly it seemed to Nirgal that they were the most frightened of all.

He said, "You could move back farther under the ice."

Everyone stared at him.

"Melt a new dome, you mean," Hiroko said.

Nirgal shrugged. Having said it, he realized he disliked the idea.

But Nadia said, "The cap is thicker back there. It will be a long time before it sublimes enough to trouble us. By that time everything will have changed."

There was a silence, and then Hiroko said, "It's a good idea. We can hold on here while a new dome is being melted, and move things over as space becomes available. It should only take a few months."

"*Shikata ga nai*," Maya said sardonically. *There is no other choice.* Of course there were other choices. But she looked pleased at the prospect of a big new project, and so did Nadia. And the rest of them looked relieved that they had an option that kept them together, and hidden. The issei, Nirgal saw suddenly, were very frightened of exposure. He sat back, wondering at that, thinking of the open cities he had visited with Coyote.

They used steam hoses powered by the Rickover to melt another tunnel to the hangar, and then a long tunnel under the cap, until the ice above was three hundred meters deep. Back there they began subliming a new round domed cavern, and digging a shallow lakebed for a new lake. Most of the CO_2 gas was captured, refrigerated to the outside temperature, and released; the rest was broken down into oxygen and carbon, and stored for use.

While the excavation went on they dug up the shallow runner roots of the big snow bamboos, and cantilevered them out of the ground and hauled them on their largest truck down the tunnel to the new cave, scraping leaves all the way. They disassembled the village's buildings, and relocated them. The robot bulldozer and trucks ran all hours of the day and night, scooping up the battered sand of the old dunes and carting it back down into the new cave; there was too much biomass in it (including Simon) to leave behind. In essence they were taking everything inside the shell of Zygote dome along with them. When they were done, the old cave was nothing but an empty bubble at the bottom of the polar cap, sandy ice above, icy sand below, the air in it nothing but the ambient Martian atmosphere, 170 millibars of mostly CO_2 gas, at 240° Kelvin. Thin poison.

One day Nirgal went back with Peter to take a look at the old place. It was shocking to see the only home he had ever had reduced to such a shell—the ice all cracked above, the sand all torn up, the raw root holes of the village gaping like horrible wounds, the lakebed scraped clear even of its algae. It looked small and ramshackle, some desperate animal's den. Moles in a hole, Coyote had said. Hiding from vultures. "Let's get out of here," Peter said sadly, and they walked together down the long bare poorly lit tunnel to the new dome, stepping along the concrete road Nadia had built, now all ratcheted with treadmarks.

They laid out the new dome in a new pattern, with the village away from the tunnel lock, near an escape tunnel that ran far under the ice, to an exit in upper Chasma Australe. The greenhouses were set nearer the perimeter lights, and the dune crests were higher than before, and the weather equipment was set right next to the Rickover. There were any number of small improvements of that sort, which kept it from being a replica of their old home. And every day they were so busy with the work of constructing it that there was no time to think much about the change; morning classes in the schoolhouse had been canceled since the fall, and now the kids were merely a rotating work crew, assigned to whoever needed help the most on that particular day. Sometimes the adult overseeing them would try to make their work into a lesson—Hiroko and Nadia were especially good at this—but they had little time to spare, and only added an explanatory sentence to instructions that were too simple to need explanation in any case: tightening wall modules with Allen wrenches, carrying around planters and algae jars in the greenhouses, and so on. It was just work—they were part of the workforce, which was too small for the task even so, despite the versatile robots that looked like rovers stripped of their exteriors. And running around, doing the work, Nirgal was for the most part happy.

But once as he left the schoolhouse and saw the dining hall, rather than the big shoots of Creche Crescent, the sight brought him up short. His old familiar world was gone, gone forever. That was how time worked. It sent a pang through him that brought tears to his eyes, and he spent the rest of that day somewhat stunned and distant, as if always a step or two behind himself, watching everything that happened drained of emotion, detached as he had been after Simon's death, exiled to the white world one step outside the green. There was nothing to indicate that he would ever come out of such a melancholy state, and how could he know if he ever would? All those days of his childhood were gone, along with Zygote itself, and they would never come back, and this day too would pass and disappear, this dome too slowly sublime away and crash in on itself. Nothing would last. So what was the point? For hours at a time this question plagued him, taking the taste and color out of everything, and when Hiroko noticed how subdued he was, and inquired what was wrong, he simply asked her outright. There was that advantage to Hiroko; you could ask her anything, including the fundamental questions. "Why do we do all this, Hiroko? When it all goes white no matter what?"

She stared at him, birdlike, her head cocked to one side. He thought he could see her affection for him in that cock of the head, but he wasn't sure; as he got older he felt he understood her (along with everyone else) less and less.

She said, "It is sad the old dome is gone, isn't it. But we must focus on what is coming. This too is viriditas. To concentrate not on what we have created, but what we will create. The dome was like a flower which wilts and falls, but contains the seed of a new plant, which grows and then there are new flowers and new seeds. The past is gone. Thinking about it will only make you melancholy. Why, I was a girl in Japan once, on Hokkaido Island! Yes, as young as you! And I can't tell you how far gone that is. But here we are now, you and me, surrounded by these plants and these people, and if you pay attention to them, and how you can make them increase and prosper, then the life comes back into things. You feel the *kami* inside all things, and that is all you need. This moment itself is all we ever live in."

"And the old days?"

She laughed at that. "You're growing up. Well, you must remember the old days from time to time. They were good ones, weren't they? You had a happy childhood; that is a blessing. But so will these days be good. Take this moment right here, and ask yourself, What now is lacking? Hmmm? . . . Coyote says that he wants you and Peter to go along with him on another trip. Maybe you should go and get out under the sky again, what do you say?"

So preparations for another trip with Coyote were made, and they continued to work on the new Zygote, informally rechristened Gamete. At night in the relocated dining hall the adults talked for a long time about their situation. Sax and Vlad and Ursula, among others, wanted back into the surface world. They couldn't do their real work properly in the hidden sanctuaries; they wanted back into the full flood of medical science, terraforming, construction. "We'll never be able to disguise ourselves," Hiroko said. "No one can change their genomes."

"It's not our genomes we should change, but the records," Sax said. "That's what Spencer has done. He's gotten his physical characteristics into a new record identity."

"And we did cosmetic surgery on his face," Vlad said.

"Yes, but it was minimal because of our age, right? We none of us look the same. Anyway, if you do something like what he did, we could take on new identities."

Maya said, "Did Spencer really get into *all* the records?"

Sax shrugged. "He was left behind in Cairo, and had the chance to get into some of the ones being used now for security purposes. That has been enough. I'd like to try something similar. Let's see what Coyote says about it. He's not in any records at all, so he must know how he did it."

"He's been hidden from the beginning," Hiroko said. "That's different."

"Yes, but he might have some ideas."

"We could just move into the demimonde," Nadia pointed out, "and stay off the records entirely. I think I'd like to try that."

Maya nodded.

Night after night they talked these matters over. "Well, a little change of appearance might be in order. You know Phyllis is back, we have to remember that."

"I still can't believe they survived. She must have nine lives."

"In any case we were on too many news shows. We have to take care."

By day Gamete was slowly completed. But it never seemed right to Nirgal, no matter how much he tried to focus on the making of it. It wasn't his place.

News came from another traveler that Coyote would be by soon. Nirgal felt his pulse quicken; to get back under the starry sky again, wandering by night in Coyote's boulder car, from sanctuary to sanctuary. . . .

Jackie stared at him attentively as he talked about it to her. And that afternoon, after they were dismissed from the day's work, she led him down to the tall new dunes and kissed him. When he recovered his wits he kissed back, and then they were kissing passionately, hugging each other hard and steaming all over each other's faces. They knelt in the trough between two high dunes, under a pale thin fog, and then lay together in a cocoon made of their down coats, and kissed and touched each other, peeling down each other's pants and creating a little envelope of their own warmth, huffing out steam and crackling the frost on the sand underneath their coats. All this without a word, merging in one great hot electric circuit, in defiance of Hiroko and all the world. So this is what it feels like, Nirgal thought. Under the strands of Jackie's black hair grains of sand gleamed like jewels, as if minute ice flowers were contained within them. Glories inside everything.

When they were done they crawled up to glance over the dune crest, to make sure no one was coming their way, and then returned to their nest and pulled their clothes over them, for the warmth. They huddled together, kissing voluptuously and without haste. And Jackie prodded him in the chest with a finger and said, "Now we belong to each other."

Nirgal could only nod happily and kiss the long expanse of her throat, his face buried in her black hair. "Now you belong to me," she said.

He sincerely hoped it was true. It was how he had wanted it, for as long as he could remember.

But that evening in the bathhouse Jackie sloshed across the pool, and caught up Harmakhis and gave him a hug, body to body. She pulled back and stared at Nirgal with a blank expression, her dark eyes like holes in her face. Nirgal sat frozen in the shallows, feeling his torso stiffen as if preparing for a blow. His balls were still sore from coming in her; and there she stood draped against Harmakhis, as she hadn't been in months, staring at him with a basilisk stare.

The strangest sensation swept over him—he understood that this was a moment he would remember all his life, a pivotal moment, right there in the steamy comfortable bath, under the osprey eye of the statuesque Maya, whom Jackie hated with a fine hate, who was now watching the three of them closely, suspecting something. So this was how it was. Jackie and Nirgal might belong to each other, and he certainly belonged to her— but her idea of belonging was not his. The shock of this knocked his breath out, it was a kind of collapse of the roof of his understanding of things. He looked at her, stunned, hurt, becoming angry—she hugged Harmakhis all the more—and he understood. She had collected both of them. Yes, it made sense, it was certain; and Reull and Steve and Frantz were all equally devoted to her—perhaps that was just a holdover from her rule over the little band, but perhaps not. Perhaps she had collected all of them. And clearly, now that Nirgal was a kind of foreigner to them, she was more comfortable with Harmakhis. So he was an exile in his own home, and in his own love's heart. If she had a heart!

He didn't know if any of these impressions were true, didn't know how to find out. He wasn't sure he wanted to find out. He got out of the bath and retreated into the men's room, feeling Jackie's gaze boring into his back, and Maya's too.

In the men's room he caught sight of an unfamiliar face in one of the mirrors. He stopped short and recognized it as his own face, twisted with distress.

He approached the mirror slowly, feeling the strange sensation of momentousness sweep through him again. He stared at the face in the mirror, stared and stared; it came to him that he was not the center of the universe, or its only consciousness, but a person like all the rest, seen from the outside by others, the way he saw others when he looked at them. And this strange Nirgal-in-the-mirror was an arresting black-haired brown-eyed boy, intense and compelling, a near twin to Jackie, with thick black eyebrows and a . . . a *look*. He didn't want to know any of this. But he felt the power burning at his fingertips, and recalled how people looked at him, and understood that for Jackie he might represent the same sort of dangerous power that she did for him—which would explain her consorting with Harmakhis, as an attempt to hold him off, to hold a balance, to assert her power. To show they were a matched pair—and a match. And all of a sudden the tension left his torso, and he shuddered, and then grinned, lopsidedly. They did indeed belong to each other. But he was still himself.

So when Coyote showed up and came by to ask Nirgal to join him on another trip, he agreed instantly, very thankful for the opportunity. The flash of anger on Jackie's face when she heard the news was painful to see; but another part of him exulted at his otherness, at his ability to escape her, or at least to get some distance. Match or not, he needed it.

A few evenings later he and Coyote and Peter and Michel drove away from the huge mass of the polar cap, into the broken land, black under its blanket of stars.

Nirgal looked back at the luminous white cliff with a tumultuous mix of feelings; but chief among them was relief. Back there they would burrow ever deeper under the ice, it seemed, until they lived in a dome under the South Pole—while the red world spun through the cosmos, wild among the stars. Suddenly he understood that he would never again live under the dome, never return to it except for short visits; this was not a matter of choice, but simply the way it was going to happen. His fate, or destiny. He could feel it like a redrock in his hand. Henceforth he would be homeless, unless the whole planet someday became his home, every crater and canyon known to him, every plant, every rock, every person—everything, in the green world and the white. But that (remembering the storm seen from the edge of Promethei Rupes) was a task to occupy many lives. He would have to start learning.

PART 2

The Ambassador

Asteroids with elliptical orbits that cross inside the orbit of Mars are called Amor asteroids. (If they cross inside the orbit of Earth they are called Trojans.) In 2088 the Amor asteroid known as 2034 B crossed the path of Mars some eighteen million kilometers behind the planet, and a clutch of robotic landing vehicles originating from Luna docked with it shortly thereafter. 2034 B was a rough ball about five kilometers in diameter, with a mass of about fifteen billion tons. As the rockets touched down, the asteroid became New Clarke.

Quickly the change became obvious. Some landers sank to the dusty surface of the asteroid and began drilling, excavating, stamping, sorting, conveying. A nuclear reactor power plant switched on, and fuel rods moved into position. Elsewhere ovens fired, and robot stokers prepared to shovel. On other landers payload bays opened, and robot mechanisms spidered out onto the surface and anchored themselves to the irregular planes of rock. Tunnelers bored in. Dust flew off into the space around the asteroid, and fell back down or escaped forever. Landers extended pipes and tubes into each other. The asteroid's rock was carbonaceous chrondrite, with a good percentage of water ice shot through it in veins and bubbles. Soon the linked collection of factories in the landers began to produce a variety of carbon-based materials, and some composites. Heavy water, one part in every 6,000 of the water ice in the asteroid, was separated out. Deuterium was made from the heavy water. Parts were made from the carbon composites, and other parts, brought along in another payload, were brought together with the new ones in factories. New robots appeared, made mostly of Clarke itself. And so the number of machines grew, as computers on the landers directed the creation of an entire industrial complex.

After that the process was quite simple, for many years. The principal factory on New Clarke made a cable of carbon nanotube filaments. The nanotubes were made of carbon atoms linked in chains so that the bonds holding them together were as strong as any that humans could manufacture. The filaments were only a few score meters long, but were bundled in clusters with their ends overlapping, and then the bundles were bundled, until the cable was nine meters in diameter. The factories could create the filaments and bundle them at speeds that allowed them to extrude the cable at a rate of about four hundred meters an hour, ten kilometers a day, for hour after hour, day after day, year after year.

While this thin strand of bundled carbon spun out into space, robots on another facet of the asteroid were constructing a mass driver, an engine that would use the deuterium from the indigenous water to fire crushed rock away from the asteroid at speeds of 200 kilometers a second. Around the asteroid smaller engines and conventional rockets were also being constructed and stocked with fuels, waiting for the time when they would fire, and perform the work of attitude jets. Other factories constructed long wheeled vehicles capable of running back and forth on the growing cable, and as the cable continued to appear out of the planet, small rocket jets and other machinery were attached to it.

The mass driver fired. The asteroid began to move into a new orbit.

Years passed. The asteroid's new orbit intersected the orbit of Mars such that the asteroid came within ten thousand kilometers of Mars, and the collection of rockets on the asteroid fired in a way that allowed the gravity of Mars to capture it, in an orbit at first highly elliptical. The jets continued to fire off and on, regularizing the orbit. The cable continued to extrude. More years passed.

A little over a decade after the landers had first touched down, the cable was approximately thirty thousand kilometers long. The asteroid's mass was about eight billion tons, the cable's mass was about seven billion. The asteroid was in an elliptical orbit with a periapsis of around fifty thousand kilometers. But now all the rockets and mass drivers on both New Clarke and the cable itself began to fire, some continuously but most in spurts. One of the most powerful computers ever made sat in one of the payload bays, coordinating the data from sensors and determining what rockets should fire when. The cable, at this time pointing away from Mars, began to swing around toward it, as in the pivoting of some delicate part of a timepiece. The asteroid's orbit became smaller and more regular.

More rockets landed on New Clarke for the first time since that first touch-down, and robots in them began the construction of a spaceport. The tip of the cable began to descend toward Mars. Here the calculus employed by the computer soared off into an almost metaphysical complexity, and the gravitational dance *of asteroid and cable with the planet became ever more precise, moving to a music that was in a permanent ritard, so that as the great cable grew closer to its proper position, its movements became slower and slower. If anyone had been able to see the full extent of this spectacle, it might have seemed like some spectacular physical demonstration of Zeno's paradox, in which the racer gets closer to the finish line by halving distances . . . But no one ever saw the full spectacle, for no witnesses had the senses necessary. Proportionally the cable was far thinner than a human hair—if it had been reduced to a hair's diameter, it would still have been hundreds of kilometers long—and so it was only visible for short portions of its entire length. Perhaps one might say that the computer guiding it in had the fullest sensation of it. For observers down on the surface of Mars, in the town of Sheffield, on the volcano Pavonis Mons (Peacock Mountain), the cable made its first appearance as a very small rocket, descending with a very thin leader line attached to it; something like a bright lure and a thin fishing line, being trolled by some gods in the next universe up. From this ocean-bottom perspective the cable itself followed its leader line down into the massive concrete bunker east of Sheffield with an aching slowness, until most humans simply stopped paying attention to the vertical black stroke in the upper atmosphere.*

But the day came when the bottom of the cable, firing jets to hold its position in the gusty winds, dropped down into the hole in the roof of the concrete bunker, and settled into its collar. Now the cable below the areosynchronous point was being pulled down by Mars's gravity; the part above the areosynchronous point was trying to follow New Clarke in centrifugal flight away from the planet; and the carbon filaments of the cable held the tension, and the whole apparatus rotated at the same speed as the planet, standing above Pavonis Mons in an oscillating vibration that allowed it to dodge Deimos; all of it controlled still by the computer on New Clarke, and the long battery of rockets deployed on the carbon strand.

The elevator was back. Cars were lifted up one side of the cable from Pavonis, and other cars were let down from New Clarke, providing a counterweight so that the energy needed for both operations was greatly lessened. Spaceships made their approach to the New Clarke spaceport, and when they left they were given a slingshot departure. Mars's gravity well was therefore substantially mitigated, and all its human intercourse with Earth and the rest of the solar system made less expensive. It was as if an umbilical cord had been retied.

He was in the middle of a perfectly ordinary life when they drafted him and sent him to Mars.

The summons came in the form of a fax that appeared out of his phone, in the apartment Art Randolph had rented just the month before, after he and his wife had decided on a trial separation. The fax was brief: *Dear Arthur Randolph: William Fort invites you to attend a private seminar. A plane will leave San Francisco airport at 9 A.M., February 22nd 2101.*

Art stared at the paper in amazement. William Fort was the founder of Praxis, the transnational that had acquired Art's company some years before. Fort was very old, and now his position in the transnat was said to be some kind of semiretired emeritus thing. But he still held private seminars, which were notorious although there was very little hard information about them. It was said that he invited people from all subsidiaries of the transnat; that they gathered in San Francisco, and were flown away by private jet to someplace secret. No one knew what went on there. People who attended were usually transferred afterward, and if not, they kept their mouths shut in a way that gave one pause. So it was a mystery.

Art was surprised to be invited, apprehensive but basically pleased. Before its acquisition he had been the cofounder and technical director of a small company called Dumpmines, which was in the business of digging up and processing old landfills, recovering the valuable materials that had been thrown away in a more wasteful age. It had been a surprise when Praxis had acquired them, a very pleasant surprise, as everyone in Dumpmines went from employment in a small firm to apprentice membership in one of the richest organizations in the world—paid in its shares, voting on its policy, free to use all its resources. It was like being knighted.

Art certainly had been pleased, and so had his wife, although she had been elegiac as well. She herself had been hired by Mitsubishi's synthesis management, and the big transnationals, she said, were like separate worlds. With the two of them working for different ones they were inevitably going to drift apart, even more than they already had. Neither of them needed the other anymore to obtain longevity treatments, which transnats provided much more reliably than the government. And so they were like people on different ships, she said, sailing out of San Francisco Bay in different directions. Like ships, in fact, passing in the night.

It had seemed to Art that they might have been able to commute between ships, if his wife had not been so interested in one of the other passengers on hers, a vice-chairman of Mitsubishi in charge of east Pacific development. But Art had been quickly caught up in Praxis's arbitration program, traveling frequently to take classes or arbitrate in disputes between various small Praxis subsidiaries involved in resource recovery, and when he was in San Francisco, Sharon was very seldom at home. Their ships were moving out of hailing distance, she had said, and he had become too demoralized to contest the point, and had moved out soon afterward, on her suggestion. Kicked out, one could have said.

Now he rubbed a swarthy unshaven jaw, rereading the fax for the fourth time. He was a big man, powerfully built but with a tendency to slouch—"uncouth," his wife had called him, although his secretary at Dumpmines used the term "bearlike," which he preferred. Indeed he had the somewhat clumsy and shambling appearance of a bear, also its surprising quickness and power. He had been a fullback at the University of Washington, a fullback slow of foot but decisive in direction, and very difficult to bring down. Bear Man, they had called him. Tackle him at your peril.

He had studied engineering, and afterward worked in the oil fields of Iran and Georgia, devising a number of innovations for extracting oil from extremely marginal shale. He had gotten a master's degree from Tehran University while doing this work, and then had moved to California and joined a friend who was forming a company that made deep-sea diving equipment used in offshore oil drilling, an enterprise that was moving out into ever-deeper water as more accessible supplies were exhausted. Once again Art had invented a number of improvements in both diving gear and underwater drills, but a couple of years spent in compression chambers and on the continental shelf had been enough for him, and he had sold his shares to his partner and moved on again. In quick succession he had started a cold-environments habitat construction company, worked for a solar panel firm, and built rocket gantries. Each job had been fine, but as time passed he had found that what really interested him was not the technical problems but the human ones. He became more and more involved with project management, and then got into arbitration; he liked jumping into arguments and solving them to everyone's satisfaction. It was engineering of a different kind, more engrossing and fulfilling than the mechanical stuff, and more difficult. Several of the companies he worked for in those years were part of transnationals, and he got embroiled in interface arbitration not only between his companies and others in the transnats, but also in more distant disputes requiring some kind of third-party arbitration. Social engineering, he called it, and found it fascinating.

So when starting Dumpmines he had taken the technical directorship, and had done some good work on their SuperRathjes, the giant robot vehicles that did the extraction and sorting at the landfills; but more than ever before he involved himself in labor disputes and the like. This trend in his career had accelerated after the acquisition by Praxis. And on the days when work like that went well, he always went home knowing that he should have been a judge, or a diplomat. Yes—at heart he was a diplomat.

Which made it embarrassing that he had not been able to negotiate a successful outcome to his own marriage. And no doubt the breakup was well known to Fort, or whoever had invited him to this seminar. It was even possible that they had bugged his old apartment, and heard the unhappy mess of his and Sharon's final months together, which wouldn't have been flattering to either of them. He cringed at the thought, still rubbing his rough jaw, and drifted toward the bathroom and turned on the portable water heater. The face in the mirror looked mildly stunned. Unshaven, fifty, separated, misemployed for most of his life, just beginning at his true calling—he was not the kind of person who he imagined got faxes from William Fort.

His wife or ex-wife-to-be called, and she was likewise incredulous. "It must be a mistake," she said when Art told her about it.

She had called about one of her camera lenses, now missing; she suspected that Art had taken it when he moved out. "I'll look for it," Art said. He went over to the closet to look in his two suitcases, still unpacked. He knew the lens was not in them, but he rooted loudly through them both anyway. Sharon would know if he tried to fake it. While he searched she continued to talk over the phone, her voice echoing tinnily through the empty apartment. "It just shows how weird that Fort is. You'll go to some Shangri-La and he'll be using Kleenex boxes for shoes and talking Japanese, and you'll be sorting his trash and learning to levitate and I'll never see you again. Did you find it?"

"No. It's not here." When they had separated they had divided their joint possessions: Sharon had taken their apartment, the entertainment center, the desktop array, the lectern, the cameras, the plants, the bed, and all the rest of the furniture; Art had taken the Teflon frying pan. Not one of his best arbitrations. But it meant he now had very few places to search for the lens.

Sharon could make a single sigh into a comprehensive accusation. "They'll teach you Japanese, and we'll never see you again. What could William Fort want with you?"

"Marriage counseling?" Art said.

• • •

Many of the rumors about Fort's seminars turned out to be true, which Art found amazing. At San Francisco International he got on a big powerful private jet with six other men and women, and after takeoff the jet's windows, apparently double-polarized, went black, and the door to the cockpit was closed. Two of Art's fellow passengers played at orienteering, and after the jet made several gentle banks left and right, they agreed that they were headed in some direction between southwest and north. The seven of them shared information: they were all technical managers or arbitrators from the vast network of Praxis companies. They had flown in to San Francisco from all over the world. Some seemed excited to be invited to meet the transnational's reclusive founder; others were apprehensive.

Their flight lasted six hours, and the orienteers spent the descent plotting the outermost limit of their location, a circle that encompassed Juneau, Hawaii, Mexico City, and Detroit, although it could have been larger, as Art pointed out, if they were in one of the new air-to-space jets; perhaps half the Earth or more. When the jet landed and stopped, they were led through a miniature jetway into a big van with blackened windows, and a windowless barrier between them and the driver's seat. Their doors were locked from the outside.

They were driven for half an hour. Then the van stopped and they were let out by their driver, an elderly man wearing shorts and a T-shirt advertising Bali.

They blinked in the sunlight. They were not in Bali. They were in a small asphalt parking lot surrounded by eucalyptus trees, at the bottom of a narrow coastal valley. An ocean or very big lake lay to the west about a mile, just a small wedge of it in sight. A creek drained the valley, and ran into a lagoon behind a beach. The valley's side walls were covered with dry grass on the south side, cactus on the north; the ridges above were dry brown rock. "Baja?" one of the orienteers guessed. "Ecuador? Australia?"

"San Luis Obispo?" Art said.

Their driver led them on foot down a narrow road to a small compound, composed of seven two-story wooden buildings, nestled among seacoast pines at the bottom of the valley. Two buildings by the creek were residences, and after they dropped their bags in assigned rooms in these buildings, the driver led them to a dining room in another building, where half a dozen kitchen workers, all quite elderly, fed them a simple meal of salad and stew. After that they were taken back to the residences, and left on their own.

They gathered in a central chamber around a wood-burning stove. It was warm outside, and there was no fire in the stove.

"Fort is a hundred and twelve," the orienteer named Sam said. "And the treatments haven't worked on his brain."

"They never do," said Max, the other orienteer.

They discussed Fort for a while. All of them had heard things, for William Fort was one of the great success stories in the history of medicine, their century's Pasteur: the man who beat cancer, as the tabloids inaccurately put it. The man who beat the common cold. He had founded Praxis at age twenty-four, to market several breakthrough innovations in anti-virals, and he had been a multibillionaire by the time he was twenty-seven. After that he had occupied his time by expanding Praxis into one of the world's biggest transnationals. Eighty continuous years of metastasizing, as Sam put it. While mutating personally into a kind of ultra–Howard Hughes, or so it was said, growing more and more powerful, until like a black hole he had disappeared completely inside the event horizon of his own power. "I just hope it doesn't get too weird," Max said.

The others attendants—Sally, Amy, Elizabeth, and George—were more optimistic. But all of them were apprehensive at their peculiar welcome, or lack of one, and when no one came to visit them through the rest of that evening, they retired to their rooms looking concerned.

Art slept well as always, and at dawn he woke to the low hoot of an owl. The creek burbled below his window. It was a gray dawn, the air filled with the fog that nourished the sea pines. A tocking sound came from somewhere in the compound.

He dressed and went out. Everything was soaking wet. Down on narrow flat terraces below the buildings were rows of lettuce, and rows of apple trees so pruned and tied to frameworks that they were no more than fan-shaped bushes.

Colors were seeping into things when Art came to the bottom of the little farm, over the lagoon. There a lawn lay spread like a carpet under a big old oak tree. Art walked over to the tree, feeling drawn to it. He touched its rough, fissured bark. Then he heard voices; coming up a path by the lagoon were a line of people, wearing black wetsuits and carrying surfboards, or long folded birdsuits. As they passed he recognized the faces of the previous night's kitchen crew, and also their driver. The driver waved and continued up the path. Art walked down it to the lagoon. The low sound of waves mumbled through the salty air, and birds swam in the reeds.

After a while Art went back up the trail, and in the compound's dining room he found the elderly workers back in the kitchen, flipping pancakes.

After Art and the rest of the guests had eaten, yesterday's driver led them upstairs to a large meeting room. They sat on couches arranged in a square. Big picture windows in all four walls let in a lot of the morning's gray light. The driver sat on a chair between two couches. "I'm William Fort," he said. "I'm glad you're all here."

He was, on closer inspection, a strange-looking old man; his face was lined as if by a hundred years of anxiety, but the expression it currently displayed was serene and detached. A chimp, Art thought, with a past in lab experimentation, now studying Zen. Or simply a very old surfer or hang-glider, weathered, bald, round-faced, snub-nosed. Now taking them in one by one. Sam and Max, who had ignored him as driver and cook, were looking uncomfortable, but he didn't seem to notice. "One index," he said, "for measuring how full the world is of humans and their activities, is the percent appropriation of the net product of land-based photosynthesis."

Sam and Max nodded as if this were the usual way to start a meeting. "Can I take notes?" Art asked.

"Please," Fort said. He gestured at the coffee table in the middle of the square of couches, which was covered with papers and lecterns. "I want to play some games later, so there's lecterns and workpads, whatever you like."

Most of them had brought their own lecterns, and there was a short silent scramble as they got them out and running. While they were at it Fort stood up and began walking in a circle behind their couches, making a revolution every few sentences.

"We now use about eighty percent of the net primary product of land-based photosynthesis," he said. "One hundred percent is probably impossible to reach, and our long range-carrying capacity has been estimated to be thirty percent, so we are massively overshot, as they say. We have been liquidating our natural capital as if it were disposable income, and are nearing depletion of certain capital stocks, like oil, wood, soil, metals, fresh water, fish, and animals. This makes continued economic expansion difficult."

Difficult! Art wrote. *Continued?*

"We have to continue," Fort said, with a piercing glance at Art, who unobtrusively sheltered his lectern with his arm. "Continuous expansion is a fundamental tenet of economics. Therefore one of the fundamentals of the universe itself. Because everything is economics. Physics is cosmic economics, biology is cellular economics, the humanities are social economics, psychology is mental economics, and so on."

His listeners nodded unhappily.

"So everything is expanding. But it can't happen in contradiction to the law of conservation of matter-energy. No matter how efficient your throughput is, you can't get an output larger than the input."

Art wrote on his note page, *Output larger than input—everything economics—natural capital—Massively Overshot.*

"In response to this situation, a group here in Praxis has been working on what we call full-world economics."

"Shouldn't that be overfull-world?" Art asked.

Fort didn't appear to hear him. "Now as Daly said, man-made capital and natural capital are not substitutable. This is obvious, but since most economists still say they *are* substitutable, it has to be insisted on. Put simply, you can't substitute more sawmills for fewer forests. If you're building a house you can juggle the number of power saws and carpenters, which means they're substitutable, but you can't build it with half the amount of lumber, no matter how many saws or carpenters you have. Try it and you have a house of air. And that's where we live now."

Art shook his head and looked down at his lectern page, which he had filled again. *Resources and capital nonsubstitutable—power saws/carpenters—house of air.*

"Excuse me?" Sam said. "Did you say natural capital?"

Fort jerked, turned around to look at Sam. "Yes?"

"I thought capital was by definition man-made. The produced means of production, we were taught to define it."

"Yes. But in a capitalist world, the word *capital* has taken on more and more uses. People talk about human capital, for instance, which is what labor accumulates through education and work experience. Human capital differs from the classic kind in that you can't inherit it, and it can only be rented, not bought or sold."

"Unless you count slavery," Art said.

Fort's forehead wrinkled. "This concept of *natural capital* actually resembles the traditional definition more than human capital. It can be owned and bequeathed, and divided into renewable and nonrenewable, marketed and nonmarketed."

"But if everything is capital of one sort or another," Amy said, "you can see why people would think that one kind was substitutable for another kind. If you improve your man-made capital to use less natural capital, isn't that a substitution?"

Fort shook his head. "That's efficiency. Capital is a quantity of input, and efficiency is a ratio of output to input. No matter how efficient capital is, it can't make something out of nothing."

"New energy sources . . ." Max suggested.

"But we can't make soil out of electricity. Fusion power and self-replicating machinery have given us enormous amounts of power, but we have to have basic stocks to apply that power to. And that's where we run into a limit for which there are no substitutions possible."

Fort stared at them all, still displaying that primate calm that Art had noted at the beginning. Art glanced at his lectern screen. *Natural capital—*

human capital— traditional capital— energy vs. matter—electric soil— no substitutes please— He grimaced and clicked to a new page.

Fort said, "Unfortunately, most economists are still working within the empty-world model of economics."

"The full-world model seems obvious," Sally said. "It's just common sense. Why would any economist ignore it?"

Fort shrugged, made another silent circumnavigation of the room. Art's neck was getting tired.

"We understand the world through paradigms. The change from empty-world economics to full-world economics is a major paradigm shift. Max Planck once said that a new paradigm takes over not when it convinces its opponents, but when its opponents eventually die."

"And now they aren't dying," Art said.

Fort nodded. "The treatments are keeping people around. And a lot of them have tenure."

Sally looked disgusted. "Then they'll have to learn to change their minds, won't they."

Fort stared at her. "We'll try that right now. In theory at least. I want you to invent full-world economic strategies. It's a game I play. If you plug your lecterns into the table, I can give you the starting data."

They all leaned forward and plugged into the table.

The first game Fort wanted to play involved estimating maximum sustainable human populations. "Doesn't that depend on assumptions about lifestyle?" Sam asked.

"We'll make a whole range of assumptions."

He wasn't kidding. They went from scenarios in which Earth's every acre of arable land was farmed with maximum efficiency, to scenarios involving a return to hunting and gathering; from universal conspicuous consumption, to universal subsistence diets. Their lecterns set the initial conditions and then they tapped away, looking bored or nervous or impatient or absorbed, using formulas provided by the table, or else supplying some of their own.

It occupied them until lunch, and then all afternoon. Art enjoyed games, and he and Amy always finished well ahead of the others. Their results for a maximum sustainable population ranged from a hundred million (the "immortal tiger" model, as Fort called it) to thirty billion (the "ant farm" model).

"That's a big range," Sam noted.

Fort nodded, and eyed them patiently.

"But if you look only at models with the most realistic conditions," Art said, "you usually get between three and eight billion."

"And the current population is about twelve billion," Fort said. "So, say we're overshot. Now what do we do about that? We've got companies to run, after all. Business isn't going to stop because there's too many people. Full-world economics isn't the end of economics, it's just the end of business as usual. I want Praxis to be ahead of the curve on this. So. It's low tide, and I'm going back out. You're welcome to join me. Tomorrow we'll play a game called Overfull."

With that he left the room, and they were on their own. They went back to their rooms, and then, as it was close to dinnertime, to the dining hall. Fort was not there, but several of his elderly associates from the night before were; and joining them tonight was a crowd of young men and women, all of them lean, bright-faced, healthy-looking. They looked like a track club or a swim team, and more than half were women. Sam's and Max's eyebrows shot up and down in a simple Morse code, spelling "Ah ha! Ah ha!" The young men and women ignored that and served them dinner, then returned to the kitchen. Art ate quickly, wondering if Sam and Max were correct in their suppositions. Then he took his plate into the kitchen and started to help at the dishwasher, and said to one of the young women, "What brings you here?"

"It's a kind of scholarship program," she said. Her name was Joyce. "We're all apprentices who joined Praxis last year, and we were selected to come here for classes."

"Were you by chance working on full-world economics today?"

"No, volleyball."

Art went back outside, wishing he had gotten selected to their program rather than his. He wondered if there was some big hot-tub facility, down there overlooking the ocean. It did not seem impossible; the ocean here was cool, and if everything was economics, it could be seen as an investment. Maintaining the human infrastructure, so to speak.

Back in the residence, his fellow guests were talking the day over. "I hate this kind of stuff," said Sam.

"We're stuck with it," Max said gloomily. "It's join a cult or lose your job."

The others were not so pessimistic. "Maybe he's just lonely," Amy suggested.

Sam and Max rolled their eyes and glanced toward the kitchen.

"Maybe he always wanted to be a teacher," Sally said.

"Maybe he wants to keep Praxis growing ten percent per year," George said, "full world or not."

Sam and Max nodded at this, and Elizabeth looked annoyed. "Maybe he wants to save the world!" she said.

"Right," Sam said, and Max and George snickered.

"Maybe he's got this room bugged," Art said, which cut short the conversation like a guillotine.

• • •

The days that followed were much like the first one. They sat in the conference room, and Fort circled them and talked through the mornings, sometimes coherently, sometimes not. One morning he spent three hours talking about feudalism—how it was the clearest political expression of primate dominance dynamics, how it had never really gone away, how transnational capitalism was feudalism writ large, how the aristocracy of the world had to figure out how to subsume capitalist growth within the steady-state stability of the feudal model. Another morning he talked about a caloric theory of value called eco-economics, apparently first worked out by early settlers on Mars; Sam and Max rolled their eyes at that news, while Fort droned on about Taneev and Tokareva equations, scribbling illegibly on a drawing board in the corner.

But this pattern didn't last, because a few days after their arrival a big swell came in from the south, and Fort canceled their meetings and spent all his time surfing or skimming over the waves in a birdsuit, which was a light broad-winged bodysuit, a flexible fly-by-wire hang glider that translated the flyer's muscle movements into the proper semi-rigid configurations for successful flight. Most of the young scholarship winners joined him in the air, swooping around like Icaruses, and then dropping in and planing swiftly over the cushions of air pushed up by every breaking wave, air surfing just like the pelicans that had invented the sport.

Art went out and thrashed around on a body board, enjoying the water, which was chill, but not so much as to absolutely require a wetsuit. He hung out near the break that Joyce surfed, and chatted with her between sets, and found out that the other ancient kitchen workers were good friends of Fort's, veterans of the first years of Praxis's rise to prominence. The young scholars referred to them as the Eighteen Immortals. Some of the Eighteen were based at the camp, while others dropped by for a kind of ongoing reunion, conferring about problems, advising the current Praxis leadership on policy, running seminars and classes, and playing in the waves. Those who didn't care for the water worked in the gardens.

Art inspected the gardeners closely as he hiked back up to the compound. They worked in something resembling slow motion, talking to each other all the while. Currently the main task appeared to be harvesting the tortured apple bushes.

The south swell subsided, and Fort reconvened Art's group. One day the topic was Full-World Business Opportunities, and Art began to see why he and his six fellows might have been chosen to attend: Amy and George worked in contraception, Sam and Max in industrial design, Sally and Elizabeth in agricultural technology, and he himself in resource recovery.

They all worked in full-world businesses already, and in the afternoon's games they proved fairly good at designing new ones.

Another day Fort proposed a game in which they solved the full-world problem by returning to an empty world. They were to suppose the release of a plague vector that would kill everyone in the world who had not had the gerontological treatment. What would the pros and cons of such an action be?

The group stared at their lecterns, nonplussed. Elizabeth declared that she wouldn't play a game based on such a monstrous idea.

"It is a monstrous idea," Fort agreed. "But that doesn't make it impossible. I hear things, you see. Conversations at certain levels. Among the leadership of the big transnationals, for instance, there are discussions. Arguments. You hear all kinds of ideas put out quite seriously, including some like this one. Everyone deplores them, and the subject changes. But no one claims that they are technically impossible. And some seem to think that they would solve certain problems that otherwise are unsolvable."

The group considered this thought unhappily. Art suggested that agricultural workers would be in short supply.

Fort was looking out at the ocean. "That's the fundamental problem with a collapse," he said thoughtfully. "Once you start one, it's hard to pick a point at which one can confidently say it will stop. Let's go on."

And they did, rather subdued. They played Population Reduction, and given the alternative they had just contemplated, went at it with a certain intensity. Each of them took a turn being Emperor of the World, as Fort put it, and outlined his or her plan in some detail.

When it was Art's turn, he said, "I would give everyone alive a birthright which entitled them to parent three-quarters of a child."

Everyone laughed, including Fort. But Art persevered. He explained that every pair of parents would thus have the right to bear a child and a half; after having one, they could either sell the right to the other half, or arrange to buy a half from some other couple and go on to have a second child. Prices for half children would fluctuate in classic supply/demand fashion. Social consequences would be positive; people who wanted extra children would have to sacrifice for them, and those who didn't would have a source of income to help support the one they had. When populations dropped far enough, the World Emperor might consider changing the birthright to one child per person, which would be close to a demographic steady state; but given the longevity treatment, the three-quarters limit might have to be in effect for a long time.

When Art was done outlining the proposal he looked up from the notes on his lectern. Everyone was staring at him.

"Three quarters of a child," Fort repeated with a grin, and everyone laughed again. "I like that." The laughter stopped. "It would finally establish a monetary value for a human life, on the open market. So far the work done in that area has been sloppy at best. Lifetime incomes and expenditures and the like." He sighed and shook his head. "The truth is, economists cook most of the numbers in the back room. Value isn't really an economic calculation. No, I like this. Let's see if we can estimate how much the price of a half child would be. I'm sure there would be speculation, middlemen, a whole market apparatus."

So they played the three-quarters game for the rest of the afternoon, getting right down to the commodities market and the plots for soap operas. When they finished, Fort invited them to a barbecue on the beach.

They went back to their rooms and put on windbreakers, and hiked down the valley path into the glare of the sunset. On the beach under a dune was a big bonfire, being tended by some of the young scholars. As they approached and sat on blankets around the fire, a dozen or so of the Eighteen Immortals landed out of the air, running across the sand and bringing their wings slowly down, then unzipping from their suits, and pulling wet hair out of their eyes, and talking among themselves about the wind. They helped each other out of the long wings, and stood in their bathing suits goose-pimpled and shivering: centenarian flyers with wiry arms outstretched to the fire, the women just as muscular as the men, their faces just as lined by a million years of squinting into the sun and laughing around the fire. Art watched the way Fort joked with his old friends, the easy way they toweled each other down. Secret lives of the rich and famous! They ate hot dogs and drank beer. The flyers went behind a dune and returned dressed in pants and sweatshirts, happy to stand by the fire a bit longer, combing out each other's wet hair. It was a dusky twilight, and the evening onshore breeze was salty and cold. The big mass of orange flame danced in the wind, and light and shadow flickered over Fort's simian visage. As Sam had said earlier, he didn't look a day over eighty.

Now he sat among his seven guests, who were sticking together, and stared into the coals and started talking again. The people on the other side of the fire continued in their conversations, but Fort's guests leaned closer to hear him over the wind and waves and crackling wood, looking a bit lost without their lecterns in their laps.

"You can't make people do things," Fort said. "It's a matter of changing ourselves. Then people can see, and choose. In ecology they have what they call the founder principle. An island population is started by a small number of settlers, so it has only a small fraction of the genes of the parent population. That's the first step toward speciation. Now I think we need a new species, economically speaking of course. And Praxis itself is the island. The way we structure it is a kind of engineering of the genes we came to it with. We have no obligation to abide by the rules as they stand now.

We can make a new species. Not feudal. We've got the collective ownership and decision-making, the policy of constructive action. We're working toward a corporate state similar to the civic state they've made in Bologna. That's a kind of democratic communist island, outperforming the capitalism around it, and constructing a better way to live. Do you think that kind of democracy is possible? We'll have to try playing at that one of these afternoons."

"Whatever you say," Sam remarked, which got him a sharp glance from Fort.

The following morning it was sunny and warm, and Fort decided the weather was too good to stay indoors. So they returned to the beach and set up under a big awning near the firepit, among coolers and hammocks strung between the awning poles. The ocean was a deep bright blue, the waves small but crisp, and often occupied by wetsuited surfers. Fort sat in one of the hammocks and lectured on selfishness and altruism, taking his examples from economics, sociobiology, and bioethics. He concluded that strictly speaking, there was no such thing as altruism. It was only selfishness taking the long view, acknowledging the real costs of behavior and making sure to pay them in order not to run up any long-term debts. A very sound economic practice, in fact, if properly directed and applied. As he tried to prove by means of the selfish-altruism games they then played, like Prisoner's Dilemma, or Tragedy of the Commons.

The next day they met in the surf camp again, and after a meandering talk on voluntary simplicity, they played a game Fort called Marcus Aurelius. Art enjoyed this game as he did all the others, and he played it well. But each day his lectern notes were getting shorter; for this day they read, in their entirety, *Consumption—appetite—artificial needs—real needs—real costs—straw beds! Env. Impact = population × appetite × efficiency—in tropics refrigerators not a luxury—community refrigerators—cold houses—Sir Thomas More.*

That evening the conferees ate alone, and their discussion over dinner was tired. "I suppose this place is a kind of voluntary simplicity," Art remarked.

"Would that include the young *scholars*?" Max asked.

"I don't see the Immortals doing very much with them."

"They just like to look," Sam said. "When you're that old . . ."

"I wonder how long he plans to keep us here," Max said. "We've only been here a week and it's already boring."

"I kind of like it," Elizabeth said. "It's relaxing."

Art found that he agreed with her. He was getting up early; one of the scholars marked every dawn by striking a wooden block with a big wooden mallet, in a descending interval that drew Art out of sleep every time:

tock . . . . . . tock . . . . . tock . . . . tock . . . tock . . tock, tock tock toc- toc- toc-toc-to-to-to-t-t-tttttt. After that Art went out into gray wet mornings, full of birdcalls. The sound of the waves was always there, as if invisible shells were held to his ears. When he walked the trail through the farm he always found some of the Eighteen Immortals around, chatting as they worked with hoes or pruning shears, or sat under the big oak tree looking out at the ocean. Fort was often among them. Art could hike through the hour before breakfast with the knowledge that he would spend the rest of the day in a warm room or on a warm beach, talking and playing games. Was that simple? He wasn't sure. It was definitely relaxing; he had never spent time like it.

But of course there was more to it than that. It was, as Sam and Max kept reminding them, a kind of test. They were being judged. The old man was watching them, and maybe the Eighteen Immortals as well, and the young scholars too, the "apprentices" who began to look to Art like serious powers, young hotshots who ran a lot of the day-to-day operations of the compound, and perhaps of Praxis too, even at its highest levels—in consultation with the Eighteen, or perhaps not. After listening to Fort ramble, he could see how one might be inclined to bypass him when it came to practical matters. And the conversations around the dishwasher sometimes had the tone of siblings squabbling over how to deal with incapacitated parents. . . .

Anyway, a test: one night Art went over to the kitchen to get a glass of milk before bed, and passed a small room off the dining hall, where a number of people, old and young, were watching a videotape of the morning's session with Fort. Art went back to his room, deep in thought.

The next morning in the conference room Fort circled the room in his usual way. "The new opportunities for growth are no longer in growth."

Sam and Max glanced at each other ever so briefly.

"That's what all this full-world thinking comes down to. So we've got to identify the new nongrowth growth markets, and get into them. Now recall that natural capital can be divided into marketable and nonmarketable. Nonmarketable natural capital is the substrate from which all marketable capital arises. Given its scarcity and the benefits that it provides, it would make sense according to standard supply/demand theory to set its price as infinite. I'm interested in anything that has a theoretically infinite price. It's an obvious investment. Essentially it's infrastructure investment, but at the most basic biophysical level. Infra-infrastructure, so to speak, or bioinfrastructure. And that's what I want Praxis to start doing. We obtain and rebuild whatever bioinfrastructure has been depleted by liquidation. It's long-term investment, but the yields will be fantastic."

"Isn't most bioinfrastructure publicly owned?" Art asked.

"Yes. Which means close cooperation with the governments involved. Praxis's gross annual product is much larger than most countries'. What we need to do is find countries with small GNPs and bad CFIs."

"CFI?" Art said.

"Country Future Index. It's an alternative to the GNP measurement, taking into account debt, political stability, environmental health and the like. A useful cross-check on the GNP, and it helps tag countries that could use our help. We identify those, go to them and offer them a massive capital investment, plus political advice, security, whatever they need. In return we take custody of their bioinfrastructure. We also have access to their labor. It's an obvious partnership. I think it will be the coming thing."

"How do we fit in?" Sam asked, gesturing at the group.

Fort looked at them one by one. "I'm going to give each of you a different assignment. I'll want you to keep them confidential. You'll be leaving here separately in any case, and going different places. You'll all be doing diplomatic work as a Praxis liaison, as well as specific jobs involved with bioinfrastructure investment. I'll give you the details in private. Now let's take an early lunch, and afterward I'll meet with you one at a time."

Diplomatic work! Art wrote in his lectern.

He spent the afternoon wandering around the gardens, looking at the espaliered apple bushes. Apparently he was not early in the list of personal appointments with Fort. He shrugged at that. It was a cloudy day, and the flowers in the garden were wet and vibrant. It would be tough to move back to his studio under the freeway in San Jose. He wondered what Sharon was doing, whether she ever thought of him. Sailing with her vice-chairman, no doubt.

It was nearly sunset, and he was about to go back to his room and get ready for dinner when Fort appeared on the central path. "Ah, there you are," he said. "Let's go down to the oak."

They sat by the big tree's trunk. The sun was cutting under the low clouds, and everything was turning the color of the roses. "You live in a beautiful place," Art said.

Fort didn't appear to hear him. He was looking up at the underlit clouds billowing overhead.

After a few minutes of this contemplation he said, "We want you to acquire Mars."

"Acquire Mars," Art repeated.

"Yes. In the sense that I spoke about this morning. These national-transnational partnerships are the coming thing, there's no doubt about it. The old flag-of-convenience relationships were suggestive, but they need to be taken further, so that we have more control over our investment. We did that with Sri Lanka, and we've had so much success in our deal there that the other big transnats are all imitating us, actively recruiting countries in trouble."

"But Mars isn't a country."

"No. But it is in trouble. When the first elevator crashed, its economy was shattered. Now the new elevator is in place, and things are ready to happen. I want Praxis to be ahead of the curve. Of course the other big investors are all still there too, jockeying for position, and that will only intensify now that the new elevator is up."

"Who runs the elevator?"

"A consortium led by Subarashii."

"Isn't that a problem?"

"Well, it gives them an edge. But they don't understand Mars. They think it's just a new source of metals. They don't see the possibilities."

"The possibilities for . . ."

"For development! Mars isn't just an empty world, Randolph—in economic terms, it's nearly a nonexistent world. Its bioinfrastructure has to be *constructed,* you see. I mean one could just extract the metals and move on, which is what Subarashii and the others seem to have in mind. But that's treating it like nothing more than a big asteroid. Which is stupid, because its value as a base of operations, as a planet so to speak, far surpasses the value of its metals. All its metals together total about twenty trillion dollars, but the value of a terraformed Mars is more in the neighborhood of two hundred trillion dollars. That's about one third of the current Gross World Value, and even that doesn't make proper assessment of its scarcity value, if you ask me. No, Mars is bioinfrastructure investment, just like I was talking about. Exactly the kind of thing Praxis is looking for."

"But acquisition . . ." Art said. "I mean, what are we talking about?"

"Not what. Who."

"Who?"

"The underground."

"The underground!"

Fort gave him time to think it over. Television, the tabloids, and the nets were full of tales of the survivors of 2061, living in underground shelters in the wild southern hemisphere, led by John Boone and Hiroko Ai, tunneling everywhere, in contact with aliens, and dead celebrities, and current world leaders. . . . Art stared at Fort, a bona fide current world leader, shocked by the sudden notion that these Pellucidarian fantasies might have some truth to them. "Does it really exist?"

Fort nodded. "It does. I'm not in full contact with it, you understand, and I don't know how extensive it is. But I'm sure that some of the First Hundred are still alive. You know the Taneev-Tokareva theories I talked about when you first arrived? Well, those two, and Ursula Kohl, and that whole biomedical team, they all lived in the Acheron Fin, north of Olympus Mons. During the war the facility was destroyed. But there were no bodies at the site. So about six years ago I had a Praxis team go in and rebuild the facility. When it was done we named it the Acheron Institute, and we left it empty. Everything is on-line and ready to go, but nothing is happening there, except for a small annual conference on their eco-economics. And last year, when the conference was over, one of the cleanup crew found a few pages in a fax tray. Comments on one of the papers presented. No signature, no source. But there was some work there that I'm positive was written by Taneev or Tokareva, or someone very familiar with their work. And I think it was a little hello."

A very little hello, Art thought. But Fort seemed to read his mind: "I've just gotten an even bigger hello. I don't know who it is. They're being very cautious. But they're out there."

Art swallowed. It was big news, if true. "And so you want me to . . ."

"I want you to go to Mars. We have a project there that will be your cover story, salvaging a section of the fallen elevator cable. But while you're doing that, I'll be making arrangements to get you together with this person who has contacted me. You won't have to initiate anything. They'll make the move, and take you in. But look. In the beginning, I don't want you to let them know *exactly* what you're trying to do. I want you to go to work on them. Find out who they are, and how extensive their operation is, and what they want. And how we might deal with them."

"So I'll be a kind of—"

"A kind of diplomat."

"A kind of spy, I was going to say."

Fort shrugged. "It depends on who you're with. This project has to remain a secret. I deal with a lot of the other transnat leaders, and they're scared people. Perceived threats to the current order often get attacked quite brutally. And some of them already think Praxis is a threat. So for the time being there is a hidden arm to Praxis, and this Mars investigation has to be part of that. So if you join, you join the hidden Praxis. Think you can do it?"

"I don't know."

Fort laughed. "That's why I chose you for this mission, Randolph. You seem simple."

I am simple, Art almost said, and bit his tongue. Instead he said, "Why me?"

Fort regarded him. "When we acquire a new company, we review its personnel. I read your record. I thought you might have the makings of a diplomat."

"Or a spy."

"They are often different aspects of the same job."

Art frowned. "Did you bug my apartment? My old apartment?"

"No." Fort laughed again. "We don't do that. People's records are enough."

Art recalled the late-night viewing of one of their sessions.

"That and a session down here," Fort added. "To get to know you."

Art considered it. None of the Eighteen wanted this job. Nor the scholars, perhaps. Of course it was off to Mars, and then into some invisible world no one knew anything about, maybe for good. Some people might not find it attractive. But for someone at loose ends, maybe looking for new employment, maybe with a potential for diplomacy. . . .

So all this had indeed proved to be a kind of interview process. For a job he hadn't even known existed. Mars Acquirer. Mars Acquisition Chief. Mars Mole. A Spy in the House of Ares. Ambassador to the Mars Underground. Ambassador to Mars. My oh my, he thought.

"So what do you say?"

"I'll do it," Art said.

William **F**ort **d**idn't **f**ool **a**round. The moment Art agreed to take the Mars assignment, his life speeded up like a video on fast forward. That night he was back in the sealed van, and then in the sealed jet, all alone this time, and when he staggered up the jetway it was dawn in San Francisco.

He went to the Dumpmines office, and made the round of friends and acquaintances there. Yes, he said again and again, I've taken a job on Mars. Salvaging a bit of the old elevator cable. Only temporary. The pay is good. I'll be back.

That afternoon he went home and packed. It took ten minutes. Then he stood groggily in the empty apartment. There on the stovetop was the frying pan, the only sign of his former life. He took the frying pan over to his suitcases, thinking he could fit it in and take it with him. He stopped over the cases, full and shut. He went back and sat down on the single chair, the frypan hanging from his hand.

After a while he called Sharon, hoping partly to get her answering machine, but she was home. "I'm going to Mars," he croaked. She wouldn't believe it. When she believed it she got angry. It was desertion pure and simple, he was running out on her. But you already threw me out, Art tried to say, but she had hung up. He left the frying pan on the table, lugged his suitcases down to the sidewalk. Across the street a public hospital that did the longevity treatment was surrounded by its usual crowd, people whose turn at the treatment was supposedly near, camping out in the parking lot to make sure nothing went awry. The treatments were guaranteed to all U.S. citizens by law, but the waiting lists for the public facilities were so long that it was a question whether one would survive to reach one's turn. Art shook his head at the sight, and flagged down a pedicab.

• • •

He spent his last week on Earth in a motel in Cape Canaveral. It was a lugubrious farewell, as Canaveral was restricted territory, occupied chiefly by military police, and service personnel who had extremely bad attitudes toward the "late lamented," as they called those waiting for departure. The daily extravaganza of takeoff only left everyone either apprehensive or resentful, and in all cases rather deaf. People went around in the afternoons with ears ringing, repeating, What? What? What? To counteract the problem most of the locals had earplugs; they would be dropping plates on one's restaurant table while talking to people in the kitchen, and suddenly they'd glance at the clock and take earplugs out of their pocket and stuff them in their ears, and boom, off would go another Novy Energia booster with two shuttles strapped to it, causing the whole world to quake like jelly. The late lamented would rush out into the streets with hands over their ears to get another preview of their fate, staring up stricken at the biblical pillar of smoke and the pinpoint of fire arching over the Atlantic. The locals would stand in place chewing gum, waiting for the timeout to be over. The only time they showed any interest was one morning when the tides were high and news came that a group of party-crashers had swum up to the fence surrounding the town and cut their way inside, where security had chased them to the area of the day's launch; it was said some of them had been incinerated by takeoff, and this was enough to get some of the locals out to watch, as if the pillar of smoke and fire would look somehow different.

Then one Sunday morning it was Art's turn. He woke and dressed in the ill-fitting jumper provided, feeling as if he were dreaming. He got in the van with another man looking just as stunned as he felt, and they were driven to the launching compound and identified by retina, fingerprint, voice, and visual appearance; and then, without ever really having managed to think about what it all meant, he was led into an elevator and down a short tunnel into a tiny room where there were eight chairs somewhat like dentist's chairs, all of them occupied by round-eyed people, and then he was seated and strapped in and the door was shut and there was a vibrant roar under him and he was squished, and then he weighed nothing at all. He was in orbit.

After a while the pilot unbuckled and the passengers did too, and they went to the two little windows to look out. Black space, blue world, just like the pictures, but with the startling high resolution of reality. Art stared down at West Africa and a great wave of nausea rolled through every cell of him.

• • •

He was only just getting the slightest touch of appetite back, after a timeless interval of space sickness that apparently in the real world had clocked in at three days, when one of the continuous shuttles came bombing by, after swinging around Venus and aerobraking into an Earth-Luna orbit just slow enough to allow the little ferries to catch up to it. Sometime during his space sickness Art and the other passengers had transferred into one of these ferries, and when the time was right it blasted off in pursuit of the continuous shuttle. Its acceleration was even harder than the takeoff from Canaveral, and when it ended Art was reeling, dizzy, and nauseated again. More weightlessness would have killed him; he groaned at the very thought; but happily there was a ring in the continuous shuttle that rotated at a speed that gave some rooms what they called Martian gravity. Art was given a bed in the health center occupying one of these rooms, and there he stayed. He could not walk well in the peculiar lightness of Martian g; he hopped and staggered about, and he still felt bruised internally, and dizzy. But he stayed on just the right side of nausea, which he was thankful for even though it was not a very pleasant feeling in itself.

The continuous shuttle was strange. Because of its frequent aerobraking in the atmospheres of Earth, Venus, and Mars, it had somewhat the shape of a hammerhead shark. The ring of rotating rooms was located near the rear of the ship, just ahead of the propulsion center and the ferry docks. The ring spun, and one walked with head toward the centerline of the ship, feet pointing down at the stars under the floor.

About a week into their voyage Art decided to give weightlessness one more try, as the rotating ring was without windows. He went to one of the transfer chambers for getting from the rotating ring to the nonrotating parts of the ship; the chambers were on a narrow ring that moved with the g ring, but could slow down to match the rest of the ship. The chambers looked just like freight elevator cars, with doors on both sides; when you got in one and pushed the right button, it decelerated through a few rotations to a stop, and the far door opened on the rest of the ship.

So Art tried that. As the car slowed, he began to lose weight, and his gorge began to rise in an exact correspondence. By the time the far door opened he was sweating and had somehow launched himself at the ceiling, where he hurt his wrist catching himself before hitting his head. Pain battled nausea, and the nausea was winning; it took him a couple of caroms to get to the control panel and hit the button to get him moving again, and back into the gravity ring. When the far door closed he settled gently back to the floor, and in a minute Martian gravity returned, and the door he had come in through reopened. He bounced gratefully out, suffering no more than the pain of a sprained wrist. Nausea was far more unpleasant than pain, he reflected—at least certain levels of pain. He would have to get his outside view over the TVs.

He would not be lonely. Most of the passengers and all of the crew spent the majority of their time in the gravity ring, which was therefore fairly crowded, like a full hotel in which most of the guests spent most of their time in the restaurant and bar. Art had seen and read accounts of the continuous shuttles that made them seem like flying Monte Carlos, with permanent residents made up of the rich and bored; a popular vid series had had just such a setting. Art's ship, the *Ganesh,* was not like that. It was clear that it had been hurtling around the inner solar system for a good long time now, and always at full capacity; its interiors were getting shabby, and when restricted to the ring it seemed very small, much smaller than the impression one had of these kinds of ships from watching history shows about the *Ares.* But the First Hundred had lived in about five times as much space as the *Ganesh's* g ring, and the *Ganesh* carried five hundred passengers.

Flight time, however, was only three months. So Art settled down and watched TV, concentrating on documentaries about Mars. He ate in the dining room, which was decorated to look like one of the great ocean liners of the 1920s, and he gambled a bit in the casino, which was decorated to look like one of the Las Vegas casinos of the 1970s. But mostly he slept and watched TV, the two activities melting into each other so that he dreamed very lucidly about Mars, while the documentaries took on a very surreal logic. He saw the famous videotapes of the Russell-Clayborne debate, and that night dreamed he was unsuccessfully arguing with Ann Clayborne, who, just as in the vids, looked like the farmer's wife in *American Gothic* only more gaunt and severe. Another film, taken by a flying drone, also affected him deeply; the drone had dropped off the side of one of the big Marineris cliffs, and fallen for nearly a minute before pulling out and swooping low over the jumbled rock and ice on the canyon floor. Repeatedly in the following weeks Art dreamed of making that fall himself, and woke up just before impact. It appeared that parts of his unconscious mind felt that the decision to go had been a mistake. He shrugged at this, ate his meals, and practiced his walking. He was biding his time. Mistake or not, he was committed.

Fort had given him an encryption system, and instructions to report back on a regular basis, but in transit he found there was very little to say. Dutifully he sent off a monthly report, each one the same: *We're on our way. All seems well.* There was never any reply.

And then Mars swelled up like an orange thrown at the TV screens, and soon after that they were there, crushed into their g couches by an extremely violent aerobraking, and then crushed again in their ferry's chairs; but Art came through these flattening decelerations like a veteran, and after a week in orbit, still rotating, they docked with New Clarke. New Clarke had only a very small gravity, which barely held people to the floor, and made Mars appear to be overhead. Art's space sickness returned. And he had a two-day wait before his reservation for an elevator ride.

The elevator cars proved to be like slender tall hotels, and they ran their tightly packed human cargo down toward the planet over a period of five days, with no gravity to speak of until the last couple of days, when it got stronger and stronger, until the elevator car slowed and descended gently into the receiving facility called the Socket, just west of Sheffield on Pavonis Mons, and the g came to something like the g in the *Ganesh's* g ring. But a week of space sickness had left Art completely devastated, and as the elevator car opened, and they were guided out into something very like an airport terminal, he found himself scarcely able to walk, and amazed at how much nausea decreased one's desire to live. It was four months to the day since he had gotten the fax from William Fort.

The trip from the Socket into Sheffield proper was by subway, but Art would have been too miserable to notice a view even if there had been one. Wasted and unsteady, he tiptoed bouncily down a tall hallway after someone from Praxis, and collapsed thankfully on a bed in a small room. Martian g felt blessedly solid when he was lying down, and after a while he fell asleep.

When he woke he could not remember where he was. He looked around the little room, completely disoriented, wondering where Sharon had gone and why their bedroom had gotten so small. Then it came back. He was on Mars.

He groaned, and sat up. He felt hot and yet detached from his body, and everything was pulsing slightly, though the room lights appeared to be functioning normally. There were drapes covering the wall opposite the door, and he stood and walked over, and opened them with a single pull.

"Hey!" he cried, leaping back. He woke up a second time, or so it felt.

It was like the view out an airplane window. Endless open space, a bruise-colored sky, the sun like a blob of lava; and there far below stretched a flat rocky plain—flat and round, as it lay at the bottom of an enormous circular cliff—extremely circular, remarkably circular, in fact, for a natural feature. It was difficult to estimate how distant the far side of the cliff was. Features of the cliff were perfectly clear, but structures on the opposite rim were teensy; what looked like an observatory could have fit on a pinhead.

This, he concluded, was the caldera of Pavonis Mons. They had landed at Sheffield, so really there could be no doubt about it. Therefore it was some sixty kilometers across the circle to that observatory, as Art recalled from his video documentaries, and five kilometers to the floor. And all of it completely empty, rocky, untouched, primordial—the volcanic rock as bare as if cooled the week before—nothing at all of humanity in it—no sign of terraforming. It must have looked exactly like this to John Boone, a half century before. And so . . . alien. And *big*. Art had looked into the calderas of Etna and Vesuvius, while on vacation from Tehran, and those two craters were big by Terran standards, but you could have lost a thousand of them in this, this *thing*, this *hole*. . . .

He closed the drapes and got slowly dressed, his mouth imitating the shape of the unearthly caldera.

A friendly Praxis guide named Adrienne, tall enough to be a Martian native but possessing a strong Australian accent, collected him and took him and half a dozen other new arrivals on a tour of the town. Their rooms turned out to be on the city's lowest level, though it wouldn't be lowest for long; Sheffield was in the process of burrowing downward these days, to give as many rooms as possible the view onto the caldera that had so disconcerted Art.

An elevator took them up nearly fifty stories, and let them out in the lobby of a shiny new office building. They walked out its big revolving doors and emerged on a wide grassy boulevard, and walked down it past squat buildings faced with polished stone and big windows, separated by narrow grassy side streets, and a great number of construction sites, as many buildings were still in various stages of completion. It was going to be a handsome town, the buildings mostly three and four stories tall, getting taller as they moved south, away from the caldera rim. The green streets were crowded with people, and the occasional small tram running on narrow tracks set in the grass; there was a general air of bustle and excitement, caused no doubt by the arrival of the new elevator. A boom town.

The first place Adrienne took them was across a boulevard to the caldera rim. She led the seven newcomers out into a thin curving park, to the nearly invisible tenting that encased the town. The transparent fabrics were held in place by equally transparent geodesic struts, anchored in a chest-high perimeter wall. "The tenting has to be stronger than usual up here on Pavonis," Adrienne told them, "because the atmosphere outside is still extremely thin. It'll always be thinner than the lowlands, by a factor of ten."

She led them out into a viewing blister in the tent wall and, looking down between their feet, they could see through the blister's transparent deck, straight down onto the caldera floor some five kilometers below them. People exclaimed in delicious fright, and Art bounced on the clear floor uneasily. The width of the caldera was coming into perspective for him; the north rim was just about as far away as Mount Tamalpais and the Napa hills when one descended into the San Jose airport. That was no extraordinary distance. But the depth below, the depth; over five kilometers, or about *twenty thousand feet*. "Quite a hole!" Adrienne said.

Mounted telescopes and display plaques with map drawings enabled them to spot the previous version of Sheffield, now lying on the caldera floor. Art had been wrong about the caldera's untouched primeval nature; an insignificant pile of cliff-bottom talus, with some shiny dots in it, was in fact the ruins of the original city.

Adrienne described with great gusto the destruction of the town in 2061. The falling elevator cable had, of course, crushed the suburbs east of its socket in the very first moments of the fall. But then the cable had wrapped all the way around the planet, delivering a massive second blow to the south side of town, a blow which had caused an undiscovered fault in the basalt rim to give way. About a third of the town had been on the wrong side of this fault, and had fallen the five kilometers to the caldera floor. The remaining two-thirds of the town had been knocked flat. Luckily the occupants had mostly evacuated in the four hours between the detachment of Clarke and the second coming of the cable, so loss of life had been minimized. But Sheffield had been utterly destroyed.

For many years after that, Adrienne told them, the site had lain abandoned, a wreck like so many other towns after the unrest of '61. Most of those other towns had been left in ruins, but Sheffield's location remained the ideal place for tethering a space elevator, and when Subarashii began organizing the in-space construction of a new one in the late 2080s, construction on the ground had rapidly followed. A detailed areological investigation had found no other faults in the southern rim, which had justified rebuilding right on the edge, on the same site as before. Demolition vehicles had cleared the wreckage of the old town, shoving most of it over the rim, and leaving only the easternmost section of town, around the old socket, as a kind of monument to the disaster—also as the central element of a little tourist industry, which had clearly been an important part of the town's income in the fallow years before an elevator had been reinstalled.

Adrienne's next point on the tour led them out to see this preserved bit of history. They took a tram to a gate in the east wall of the tent, and then walked through a clear tube into a smaller tent, which covered the blasted ruins, the concrete mass of the old cable facility, and the lower end of the fallen cable. They walked a roped path that had been cleared of wreckage, staring curiously at the foundations and twisted pipes. It looked like the results of saturation bombing.

They came to a halt under the butt end of the cable, and Art observed it with professional interest. The big cylinder of black carbon filaments looked nearly undamaged by the fall, although admittedly this was the part that had hit Mars with the least force. The end had jammed down into the Socket's big concrete bunker, Adrienne said, then been dragged a couple of kilometers as the cable had fallen down the eastern slope of Pavonis. That wasn't that much of a beating for material designed to withstand the pull of an asteroid swinging beyond the areosynchronous point.

And so it lay there, as if waiting to be straightened up and put back in place: cylindrical, two stories high, its black bulk encrusted by steel tracks and collars and the like. The tent only covered a hundred meters or so of it; after that it ran on uncovered, east along the wide rounded plateau of the rim, until it disappeared over the rim's outer edge, which formed their horizon—they could see nothing of the planet below. But out away from the town they could see better than ever that Pavonis Mons was huge—its rim alone was an impressive expanse, a doughnut of flat land perhaps thirty kilometers wide, from the abrupt inner edge of the caldera to the more gradual drop-off down the volcano's flanks. Nothing of the rest of Mars could be seen from their vantage point, so it seemed they stood on a high circular ring world, under a dark lavender sky.

Just to the south of them, the new Socket was like a titanic concrete bunker, the new elevator cable rising out of it like an elevator cable, standing alone as if in some version of the Indian rope trick, thin and black and straight as a plumb line dropping down from heaven—visible for only a few tall skyscrapers' worth of height, at most—and, given the wreckage they stood in, and the immensity of the volcano's bare rocky peak, as fragile-looking as if it were a single carbon nanotube filament, rather than a bundle of billions of them, and the strongest structure ever made. "This is weird," Art said, feeling hollow and unsettled.

After their tour of the ruins, Adrienne took them back to a plaza café in the middle of the new town, where they had lunch. Here they could have been in the heart of a fashionable district in any town anywhere—it could have been Houston or Tbilisi or Ottawa, in some neighborhood where a lot of noisy construction marked a fresh prosperity. When they went back to their rooms, the subway system was likewise familiar to the eye—and when they got out, the halls of the Praxis floors were those of a fine hotel. All utterly familiar—so much so that it was again a shock to walk into his room and look out the window and see the awesome sight of the caldera—the bare fact of Mars, immense and stony, seeming to exert a kind of vacuum pull on him through the window. And in fact if the windowpane were to break the pressure blowout would certainly suck him immediately into that space; an unlikely eventuality, but the image still gave him an unpleasant thrill. He closed the drapes.

And after that he kept the drapes closed, and tended to stay on the side of his room away from the window. In the mornings he dressed and left the room quickly, and attended orientation meetings run by Adrienne, which were joined by a score or so of new arrivals. After lunching with some of them, he spent his afternoons touring the town, working earnestly on his walking skills. One night he thought to send a coded report off to Fort: *On Mars, going through orientation. Sheffield is a nice town. My room has a view.* There was no reply.

Adrienne's orientation took them to a number of Praxis buildings, both in Sheffield and up the east rim, to meet people in the transnational's Martian operations. Praxis had much more of a presence on Mars than it did in America. During Art's afternoon walks he tried to gauge the relative strengths of the transnationals, just by the little plates on the sides of the buildings. All the biggest transnats were there—Armscor, Subarashii, Oroco, Mitsubishi, The 7 Swedes, Shellalco, Gentine, and so on—each occupying a complex of buildings, or even entire neighborhoods of the town. Clearly they were all there because of the new elevator, which had made Sheffield once again the most important city on the planet. They were pouring money into the town, building submartian subdivisions, and even entire tent suburbs. The sheer wealth of the transnats was obvious in all the construction—and also, Art thought, in the way people moved: there were a lot of people bouncing around the streets just as clumsily as he was, newcomer businessmen or mining engineers or the like, concentrating with furrowed brow on the act of walking. It was no great trick to pick out the tall young natives, with their catlike coordination; but they were in a distinct minority in Sheffield, and Art wondered if that was true everywhere on Mars.

As for architecture, space under the tent was at a premium, and so the completed buildings were bulky, often cubical, occupying their lots right out to the street and right up to the tent. When all the construction was finished there would only be a network of ten triangular plazas, and the wide boulevards, and the curving park along the rim, to keep the town from being a continuous mass of squat skycrapers, faced with polished stone of various shades of red. It was a city built for business.

And it looked to Art like Praxis was going to get a good share of that business. Subarashii was the general contractor for the elevator, but Praxis was supplying the software as they had for the first elevator, and also some of the cars, and part of the security system. All these allocations, he learned, had been made by a committee called the United Nations Transitional Authority, supposedly part of the UN, but controlled by the transnats; and Praxis had been as aggressive on this committee as any of the others. William Fort might have been interested in bioinfrastructure, but the ordinary kind was obviously not outside Praxis's field of operations; there were Praxis divisions building water supply systems, train pistes, canyon towns, wind-power generators, and areothermal plants. The latter two were widely regarded as marginal endeavors, as the new orbiting solar collectors and a fusion plant in Xanthe were turning out so well, not to mention the older generation of integral fast reactors. But local energy sources were the specialty of the Praxis subsidiary Power From Below, and so that was what they did, working hard in the outback.

Praxis's local salvage subsidiary, the Martian equivalent of Dumpmines, was called Ouroborous, and like Power From Below it was also fairly small. In truth, as the Ouroborous people were quick to tell Art when they met one morning, there was not a large garbage output on Mars; almost everything was recycled or put to use in creating agricultural soil, so each settlement's dump was really more of a holding facility for miscellaneous materials, awaiting their particular reuse. Ouroborous therefore got its business by finding and collecting the garbage or sewage that was somehow recalcitrant—toxic, or orphaned, or simply inconvenient—and then finding ways to turn it to use.

The Ouroborous team in Sheffield occupied one floor of Praxis's downtown skyscraper. The company had gotten its start excavating the the old town, before the ruins had been so unceremoniously shoved over the side. A man named Zafir headed the fallen cable salvage project, and he and Adrienne accompanied Art to the train station, where they got on a local train and took a short ride around to the east rim, to a line of suburb tents. One of the tents was the Ouroborous storage facility, and just outside it, among many other vehicles, was a truly gigantic mobile processing factory, called the Beast. The Beast made a SuperRathje look like a compact car— it was a building rather than a vehicle, and almost entirely robotic. Another Beast was already out processing the cable in west Tharsis, and Art was slated to go out and make an on-site inspection of it. So Zafir and a couple of technicians showed him around the inside of the training vehicle, ending up in a wide compartment on the top floor, where there were living quarters for any humans who might be visiting.

Zafir was enthusiastic about what the Beast out on west Tharsis had found. "Of course just recovering the carbon filament and the diamond gel helixes gives us a basic income stream," he said. "And we are doing well with some brecciated exotics metamorphosed in the final hemisphere of the fall. But what you'll be interested in are the buckyballs." Zafir was an expert in these little carbon geodesic spheres called buckminsterfullerenes, and he waxed enthusiastic: "Temperatures and pressures in the west Tharsis zone of the fall turned out to be similar to those used in the arc-reactor-synthesis method of making fullerenes, and so there's a hundred-kilometer stretch out there where the carbon on the bottom side of the cable consists almost entirely of buckyballs. Mostly sixties, but also some thirties, and a variety of superbuckies." And some of the superbuckies had formed with atoms of other elements trapped inside their carbon cages. These "full fullerenes" were useful in composite manufacturing, but very expensive to make in the lab because of the high amounts of energy required. So they were a nice find. "It's sorting out the various superbuckies where your ion chromatography will come in."

"So I understand," Art said. He had done work with ion chromatography during analyses in Georgia, and this was his ostensible reason for being sent into the outback. So over the next few days Zafir and some Beast technicians trained Art in dealing with the Beast, and after these sessions they had dinner together at a small restaurant in the suburb tent on the east rim. After sunset they had a great view of Sheffield, some thirty kilometers around the curve of the rim, glowing in the twilight like a lamp perched on the black abyss.

As they ate and drank, the conversation seldom turned to the matter of Art's project, and, considering it, Art decided that this was probably a deliberate courtesy on his colleagues' part. The Beast was fully self-operating, and though there were some problems to be solved in sorting out the recently discovered full fullerenes, there must have been local ion chromatographers who could have done the job. So there was no obvious reason why Praxis should have sent Art up from Earth to do it, and there had to be something more to his story. And so the group avoided the topic, saving Art the embarrassment of lies, or awkward shrugs, or an explicit appeal to confidentiality.

Art would have been uncomfortable with any of these dodges, so he appreciated their tact. But it put a certain distance in their conversations. And he seldom saw the other Praxis newcomers, outside of orientation meetings; and he didn't know anyone else in town, or elsewhere on the planet. So he was a little lonely, and the days passed in an increasing sense of uneasiness, even oppression. He kept the drapes closed on his window view, and ate in restaurants away from the rim. It began to feel a bit too much like the weeks on the *Ganesh,* which he now understood to have been a miserable time. Sometimes he had to fend off the feeling that it had been a mistake to come.

And so after their last orientation lecture, at a reception luncheon in the Praxis building, he drank more than was his custom, and took a few inhalations from a tall canister of nitrous oxide. Inhalation of recreational drugs was a local custom, fairly big among Martian construction workers, he had been told, and there were even little canisters of various gases for sale from dispensers in some public men's rooms. Certainly the nitrous added a certain extra bubbly quality to the champagne; it was a nice combination, like peanuts and beer, or ice cream and apple pie.

Afterward he walked down the streets of Sheffield bouncing erratically, feeling the nitrous champagne as a kind of antigravitational effect, which, added to the Martian baseline, made him feel altogether too light. Technically he weighed about forty kilos, but as he walked along it felt more like five. Very strange, even unpleasant. Like walking on buttered glass.

He nearly ran into a young man, slightly taller than him—a black-haired youth, as slender as a bird and as graceful, who quickly veered away from him and then steadied him with a hand to his shoulder, all in one smooth flow of movement.

The youth looked him in the eye. "Are you Arthur Randolph?"

"Yes," Art said, surprised. "I am. And who are you?"

"I'm the one who contacted William Fort," the young man said.

Art stopped abruptly, swaying to get back over his feet. The young man held him upright with a gentle pressure, his hand hot on Art's upper arm. He regarded Art with a direct look, a friendly smile. Perhaps twenty-five, Art judged, perhaps younger—a handsome youth with brown skin and thick black eyebrows, and eyes that were slightly Asian, set wide over prominent cheekbones. An intelligent look, full of curiosity and a kind of magnetic quality, hard to pin down.

Art took to him instantly, for no reason he could tell. It was just a feeling. "Call me Art," he said.

"And I am Nirgal," the youth said. "Let's go down to Overlook Park."

So Art walked with him down the grassy boulevard to the park on the rim. There they strolled the path next to the coping wall, Nirgal helping Art with his drunken turns by frankly seizing his upper arm and steering him. His grasp had an electric penetrating quality to it, and was really very warm, as if the youth had a fever, though there was no sign of it in his dark eyes.

"Why are you here?" Nirgal asked—and his voice, and the look on his face, made the question into something other than a superficial inquiry. Art checked his response, thought about it.

"To help," he said.

"So you will join us?"

Again the youth somehow made it clear that he meant something different, something fundamental.

And Art said, "Yes. Anytime you like."

Nirgal smiled, a quick delighted grin that he only partly overmastered before he said, "Good. Very good. But look, I'm doing this on my own. Do you understand? There are people who wouldn't approve. So I want to slip you in among us, as if it were an accident. That's okay with you?"

"That's fine." Art shook his head, confused. "That's how I was planning on doing it anyway."

Nirgal stopped by the observation bubble, took Art's hand and held it. His gaze, so open and unflinching, was contact of another kind. "Good. Thanks. Just keep doing what you're doing, then. Go out on your salvage project, and you'll be picked up out there. We'll meet again after that."

And he was off, walking across the park in the direction of the train station, moving with the long graceful lope that all the young natives seemed to have. Art stared after him, trying to remember everything about the encounter, trying to put his finger on what had made it so charged. Simply the look on the youth's face, he decided—not just the unselfconscious intensity one sometimes saw on the faces of the young, but more—some humorous power. Art remembered the sudden grin unleashed when Art had said (had promised) that he would join them. Art grinned himself.

When he got back to his room, he walked right to the window and opened the drapes. He went over to the table by his bed, and sat and turned on his lectern, and looked up *Nirgal*. No person listed by that name. There was a Nirgal Vallis, between Argyre Basin and Valles Marineris. One of the best examples of a water-carved channel on the planet, the entry said, long and sinuous. The word was the Babylonian name for Mars.

Art went back to the window and pressed his nose against the glass. He looked right down the throat of the thing, into the rocky heart of the monster itself. Horizontal banding of the curved walls, the broad round plain *so* far below, the sharp edge where it met the circular wall—the infinite shadings of maroon, rust, black, tan, orange, yellow, red—everywhere red, all the variations of red. . . . He drank it in, for the first time unafraid. And as he looked down this enormous coring into the planet, a new feeling leaped into him to replace the fear, and he shivered and hopped in place, in a little dance. He could handle the view. He could handle the gravity. He had met a Martian, a member of the underground, a youth with a strange charisma, and he would be seeing more of him, more of all of them. . . . He was *on Mars.*

And a few days later he was on the west slope of Pavonis Mons, driving a small rover down a narrow road that paralleled a band of disturbed volcanic rubble, with what looked like a cog railway track running right down it. He had sent a final coded message to Fort, telling him that he was taking off, and had gotten the only reply of his journey so far: *Have a nice trip.*

The first hour of his drive held what everyone had told him would be its most spectacular sight: going over the western rim of the caldera, and starting down the outer slope of the vast volcano. This occurred about sixty kilometers west of Sheffield. He drove over the southwest edge of the vast rim plateau, and started downhill, and a horizon appeared very far below, and very far away—a slightly curved hazy white bar, like the view of Earth as seen from a space plane's window—which made sense, as the peak of Pavonis was about eighty-five thousand feet above Amazonis Planitia. So it was a huge view, the most forcible reminder possible of the stupendous height of the Tharsis volcanoes. And he had a great view of Arsia Mons at that moment, in fact, the southernmost of the three volcanoes lined up on Tharsis, bulking over the horizon to his left like a neighboring world. And what looked like a black cloud, over the far horizon to the northwest, could very possibly be Olympus Mons itself!

So the first day's drive was all downhill, but Art's spirits remained high. "Toto, there is *no chance* we are in Kansas anymore. We're . . . *off* to see the *wizard*! The wonderful wizard of Mars!"

The road paralleled the fall line of the cable. The cable had hit the west side of Tharsis with a tremendous impact, not as great as during the final wrap, of course, but enough to create the interesting superbuckies Art had been sent out to investigate. The Beast he was going down to meet had already salvaged the cable in this vicinity, however, and the cable was almost entirely gone; the only thing left of it was a set of old-fashioned-looking train tracks, with a third cog rail running down the middle. The Beast had made these tracks out of carbon from the cable, and then used other parts of the cable, and magnesium from the soil, to make little self-powered cog rail mining cars, which then carried salvage cargo back up the side of Pavonis to the Ouroborous facilities in Sheffield. Very neat, Art thought as he watched a little robot car roll past him in the opposite direction, up the tracks toward the city. The little train car was black, squat, powered by a simple motor engaging the cog track, filled with a cargo that was no doubt mostly carbon nanotube filaments, and capped on top by a big rectangular block of diamond. Art had heard about this in Sheffield, and so was not surprised to see it. The diamond had been salvaged from the double helixes strengthening the cable, and the blocks were actually much less valuable than the carbon filament stored underneath them—basically a kind of fancy hatch door. But they did look nice.

On the second day of his drive, Art got off the immense cone of Pavonis, and onto the Tharsis bulge proper. Here the ground was much more littered than the volcano's side had been with loose rock, and meteor craters. And down here, everything was blanketed with a drift of snow and sand, in a mix that looked like equal shares of both. This was the firn slope of west Tharsis, an area where storms coming in from the west frequently dumped loads of snow, which never melted but instead built up year by year, packing down the snow on the bottom. So far the pack consisted only of crushed snow, called firn, but after more years of compaction the lowest layers would be ice, and the slopes glaciers.

Now the slopes were still punctuated by big rocks sticking out of the firn, and small crater rings, the craters mostly less than a kilometer across, and looking as fresh as if they had been blasted the day before, except for the sandy snow now filling them.

When he was still many kilometers away, Art caught sight of the Beast salvaging the cable. The top of it appeared over the western horizon, and over the next hour the rest of it reared into view. Out on the vast empty slope it seemed somewhat smaller than its twin up in East Sheffield, at least until he drove under its flank, when once again it became clear that it was as big as a city block. There was even a square hole in the bottom of one side which looked for all the world like the entrance to a parking garage. Art drove his rover right at this hole—the Beast was moving at three kilometers a day, so it was no trick to hit it—and once inside, he drove up a curving ramp, following a short tunnel into a lock. There he spoke by radio to the Beast's AI, and doors behind his rover slid shut, and in a minute he could simply get out of his car, and go over to an elevator door, and take an elevator up to the observation deck.

• • •

It did not take long to realize that life inside the Beast was not the essence of excitement, and after checking in with the Sheffield office, and taking a look at the ion chromatograph down in the lab, Art went back out in the rover to have a more extensive look around. This was the way things went when working the Beast, Zafir assured him; the rovers were like pilot fishes swimming around a great whale, and though the view from the observation deck was nice and high, most people ended up spending a good part of their days out driving around.

So Art did that. The fallen cable out in front of the Beast showed clearly how much harder it had been coming down here than it had back at the start of its fall. Here it was buried to perhaps a third of its diameter, and the cylinder was flattened, and marked by long cracks running along its sides, revealing its structure, which consisted of bundles of bundles of carbon nanotube filament, still one of the strongest substances known to materials science, though apparently the current elevator's cable material was stronger yet.

The Beast straddled this wreckage, about four times as tall as the cable; the charred black semicylinder disappeared into a hole at the front end of the Beast, from which came a grumbling, low, nearly subsonic vibration. And then, every day at about two in the afternoon, a door at the back of the Beast slid open over the tracks always being excreted from the back end of the Beast, and one of the diamond-capped train cars would roll out, winking in the sunlight, and glide off toward Pavonis. The trains disappeared over the high eastern horizon into the apparent "depression" now between him and Pavonis about ten minutes after emerging from their maker.

After viewing the daily departure, Art would take a drive in the pilot-fish rover, investigating craters and big isolated boulders, and, frankly, looking for Nirgal, or rather waiting for him. After a few days of this, he added the habit of suiting up and taking a walk outside for a few hours every afternoon, strolling beside the cable or the pilot fish, or hiking out into the surrounding countryside.

It was odd-looking terrain, not only because of the even distribution of millions of black rocks, but because the hard blanket of firn had been sculpted into fantastic shapes by the sandblaster winds: ridges, boles, hollows, tear-shaped tailings behind every exposed rock, etc.—sastrugi, these shapes were called. It was fun to walk around among these extravagant aerodynamic extrusions of reddish snow.

Day after day he did this. The Beast ground slowly westward. He found that the windswept bare tops of the rocks were often colored by tiny flakes that were scales of fast lichen, a kind that grew quickly, or at least quickly for lichen. Art picked up a couple of sample rocks, and took them back into the Beast, and read about the lichen curiously. These apparently were engineered cryptoendolithic lichens, meaning they lived in rock, and at this altitude they were living right at the edge of the possible—the article on them said that over ninety-eight percent of their energy was used simply to stay alive, with less than two percent going toward reproduction. And this was a big improvement over the Terran species they had been based on.

More days passed, then weeks; but what could he do? He kept on collecting lichen. One of the cryptoendoliths he found was the first species to survive on the Martian surface, the lectern said, and it had been designed by members of the fabled First Hundred. He broke apart some rocks to have a better look, and found bands of the lichen growing in the rocks' outer centimeter: first a yellow stripe right at the surface, then a blue stripe under that, then a green one. After that discovery he often stopped on his walks to kneel and put his faceplate to colored rocks sticking up out of the firn, marveling at the crusty scales and their intense pale colors—yellows, olives, khaki greens, forest greens, blacks, grays.

One afternoon he drove the pilot fish far to the north of the Beast, and got out to hike around and collect samples. When he returned, he found that the lock door in the side of the pilot fish would not open. "What the hell?" he said aloud.

It had been so long that he had forgotten that something was supposed to happen. The happening had taken the form of some kind of electronic failure, apparently. Assuming that this was the happening, and not . . . something else. He called in over the intercom, and tried every code he knew on the keypad by the lock door, but nothing had any effect. And since he couldn't get back in, he couldn't turn on the emergency systems. And his helmet's intercom had a very limited range—the horizon, in effect—which down here off Pavonis had shrunk to a Martian closeness, only a few kilometers away in all directions. The Beast was well over the horizon, and though he could probably walk to it, there would be a section of the hike where both Beast and pilot fish would be over the horizon, and himself alone in a suit, with a limited air supply. . . .

Suddenly the landscape with its dirty sastrugi took on an alien, ominous cast, dark even in the bright sunshine. "Well, hell," Art said, thinking hard. He was out here, after all, to get picked up by the underground. Nirgal had said it was going to look like an accident. Of course this was not necessarily that accident, but whether it was or it wasn't, panic was not going to help. Best to make the working assumption that it was a real problem, and go from there. He could try walking back to the Beast, or he could try getting into the pilot-fish rover.

He was still thinking things over, and typing at the keypad of the lock door like a champion speed-typist, when he was tapped hard on the shoulder. "Aaa!" he shouted, leaping around.

There were two of them, in walkers and scratched old helmets. Through their faceplates he could see them: a woman with a face like a hawk's, who looked like she would be happy to bite him; and a short thin-faced black man, with gray dreadlocks crowding the border of his faceplate, like the rope picture frames one sometimes sees in nautical restaurants.

It was the man who had tapped Art on the shoulder. Now he lifted three fingers, pointing at his wrist console. The intercom band they were using, no doubt. Art switched it on. "Hey!" he cried, feeling more relieved than he ought to, considering that this was probably Nirgal's setup, so that he had never been in danger. "Hey, I seem to be locked out of my car? Could you give me a lift?"

They stared at him.

The man's laugh was scary. "Welcome to Mars," he said.

PART 3

Long Runout

Ann Clayborne was driving down the Geneva Spur, stopping every few switchbacks to get out and take samples from the roadcuts. The Transmarineris Highway had been abandoned after '61, as it now disappeared under the dirty river of ice and boulders covering the floor of Coprates Chasma. The road was an archaeological relic, a dead end.

But Ann was studying the Geneva Spur. The Spur was the final extension of a much longer lava dike, most of which was buried in the plateau to the south. The dike was one of several—the nearby Melas Dorsa, the Felis Dorsa farther east, the Solis Dorsa farther west—all of them perpendicular to the Marineris canyons, and all mysterious in their origin. But as the southern wall of Melas Chasma had receded, by collapse and wind erosion, the hard rock of one dike had been exposed, and this was the Geneva Spur, which had provided the Swiss with a perfect ramp to get their road down the canyon wall, and was now providing Ann with a nicely exposed dike base. It was possible that it and all its companion dikes had been formed by concentric fissuring resulting from the rise of Tharsis; but they could also be much older, remnants of a basin-and-range type spread in the earliest Noachian, when the planet was still expanding from its own internal heat. Dating the basalt at the foot of the dike would help answer the question one way or the other.

So she drove a little boulder car slowly down the frost-covered road. The car's movement would be quite visible from space, but she didn't care. She had driven all over the southern hemisphere in the previous year, taking no precautions except when approaching one of Coyote's hidden refuges to resupply. Nothing had happened.

She reached the bottom of the Spur, only a short distance from the river of ice and rock that now choked the canyon floor. She got out of the car and tapped away with a geologist's hammer at the bottom of the last roadcut. She kept her back to the immense glacier, and did not think of it. She was focused on the basalt. The dike rose before her into the sun, a perfect ramp to the clifftop, some three kilometers above her and fifty kilometers to the south. On both sides of the Spur the immense southern cliff of Melas Chasma curved back in huge embayments, then out again to lesser prominences—a slight point on the distant horizon to the left, and a massive headland some sixty kilometers to the right, which Ann called Cape Solis.

Long ago Ann had predicted that greatly accelerated erosion would follow any hydration of the atmosphere, and on both sides of the Spur the cliff gave indications that she had been right. The embayment between the Geneva Spur and Cape Solis had always been a deep one, but now several fresh landslides showed that it was getting deeper fast. Even the freshest scars, however, as well as all the rest of the fluting and stratification of the cliff, were dusted with frost. The great wall had the coloration of Zion or Bryce after a snowfall—stacked reds, streaked with white.

There was a very low black ridge on the canyon floor a kilometer or two west of the Geneva Spur, paralleling it. Curious, Ann hiked out to it. On closer inspection the low ridge, no more than chest high, did indeed appear to be made of the same basalt as the Spur. She took out her hammer, and knocked off a sample.

A motion caught her eye and she jerked up to look. Cape Solis was missing its nose. A red cloud was billowing out from its foot.

Landslide! Instantly she started the timer on her wristpad, then knocked the binocular hood down over her faceplate, and fiddled with the focus until the distant headland stood clear in her field of vision. The new rock exposed by the break was blackish, and looked nearly vertical; a cooling fault in the dike, perhaps—if it too was a dike. It did look like basalt. And it looked as if the break had extended the entire height of the cliff, all four kilometers of it.

The cliff face disappeared in the rising cloud of dust, which billowed up and out as if a giant bomb had gone off. A distinct boom, almost subsonic, was followed by a faint roaring, like distant thunder. She checked her wrist; a little under four minutes. Speed of sound on Mars was 252 meters per second, so the distance of sixty kilometers was confirmed. She had seen almost the very first moment of the fall.

Deep in the embayment a smaller piece of cliff gave way as well, no doubt triggered by shock waves. But it looked like the merest rockfall compared to the collapsed headland, which had to be millions of cubic meters of rock. Fantastic to actually see one of the big landslides—most areologists and geologists had to rely on explosions, or computer simulations. A few weeks spent in Valles Marineris would solve that problem for them.

And here it came, rolling over the ground by the edge of the glacier, a low dark mass topped by a rolling cloud of dust, like time-lapse film of an approaching thunderhead, sound effects and all. It was really quite a long way out from the cape. She realized with a start that she was witnessing a long runout landslide. They were a strange phenomenon, one of the unsolved puzzles of geology. 'he great majority of landslides move horizontally less than twice the distance hey fall; but a few very large slides appear to defy the laws of friction, running 1orizontally ten times their vertical drop, and sometimes even twenty or thirty. These were called long runout slides, and no one knew why they happened. Cape Solis, now, had fallen four kilometers, and so should have run out no more than eight; but there it was, well across the floor of Melas, running downcanyon directly at Ann. If it ran only fifteen times its vertical drop, it would roll right over her, and slam into the Geneva Spur.

She adjusted the focus of her binoculars for the front edge of the slide, just visible as a dark churning mass under the tumbling dustcloud. She could feel her hand trembling against her helmet, but other than that she felt nothing. No fear, no regret—nothing, in fact, but a sense of release. All over at last, and not her fault. No one could blame her for it. She had always said that the terraforming would kill her. She laughed briefly, and then squinted, trying to get a better focus on the front edge of the slide. The earliest standard hypothesis to explain long runouts had been that the rock was riding over a layer of air trapped under the fall; but then old long runouts discovered on Mars and Luna had cast doubts on that notion, and Ann agreed with those who argued that any air trapped under the rock would quickly diffuse upward. There had to be some form of lubricant, however, and other forms proposed had included a layer of molten rock caused by the slide's friction, acoustic waves caused by the slide's noise, or merely the extremely energetic bouncing of the particles caught on the slide's bottom. But none of these were very satisfactory suggestions, and no one knew for sure. She was being approached by a phenomenological mystery.

Nothing about the mass approaching her under the dustcloud indicated one theory over another. Certainly it wasn't glowing like molten lava, and though it was loud, there was no way of judging whether it was loud enough to be riding on its own sonic boom. On it came in any case, no matter what the mechanism.

It looked as though she was going to get a chance to investigate in person, her last act a contribution to geology, lost in the moment of discovery.

She checked her wrist, and was surprised to see that twenty minutes had passed already. Long runouts were known to be fast; the Blackhawk slide in the Mojave was estimated to have traveled at 120 kilometers per hour, going down a slope of only a couple of degrees. Melas was in general a bit steeper than that. And indeed the front edge of the slide was closing fast. The noise was getting louder, like rolling thunder directly overhead. The dustcloud reared up, blocking out the afternoon sun.

Ann turned and looked out at the great Marineris glacier. She had almost been killed by it more than once, when it was an aquifer outbreak flooding down the great canyons. And Frank Chalmers had been killed by it, and was entombed somewhere in its ice, far downstream. His death had been caused by her mistake, and the remorse had never left her. It had been a moment of inattention only, but a mistake nevertheless; and some mistakes you never can make good.

And then Simon had died too, engulfed in an avalanche of his own white blood cells. Now it was her turn. The relief was so acute it was painful.

She faced the avalanche. The rock visible at the bottom was bouncing, it seemed, but not rolling over itself like a broken wave. Apparently it was indeed riding over some kind of lubricating layer. Geologists had found nearly intact meadows on top of landslides that had moved many kilometers, so this was confirmation of something known, but it certainly did look peculiar, even unreal: a low rampart advancing across the land without a rollover, like a magic trick. The ground under her feet was vibrating, and she found that her hands were clenched into fists. She thought of Simon, fighting death in his last hours, and hissed; it seemed wrong to stand there welcoming the end so happily, she knew he would not approve. As a gesture to his spirit she stepped off the low lava dike and went down onto one knee behind it. The coarse grain of its basalt was dull in the brown light. She felt the vibrations, looked up at the sky. She had done what she could, no one could fault her. Anyway it was foolish to think that way; no one would ever know what she did here, not even Simon. He was gone. And the Simon inside her would never stop harassing her, no matter what she did. So it was time to rest, and be thankful. The dustcloud rolled over the low dike, there was a wind—

Boom! She was thrown flat by the impact of the noise, picked up and dragged over the canyon floor, thrown and pummeled by rock. She was in a dark cloud, on her hands and knees, dust all around her, the roar of gnashing rock filling everything, the ground tossing underfoot like a wild thing. . . .

The jostling subsided. She was still on her hands and knees, feeling the cold rock through her gloves and kneepads. Gusts of wind slowly cleared the air. She was covered with dust, and small fragments of stone.

Shakily she stood. Her palms and knees hurt, and one kneecap was numb with cold. Her left wrist felt the stab of a sprain. She walked up to the low dike, looked over it. The landslide had stopped about thirty meters short of the dike. The ground in between was littered with rubble, but the edge of the slide proper was a black wall of pulverized basalt, sloping back at about a forty-five-degree angle, and twenty or twenty-five meters tall. If she had stayed standing on the low dike, the impact of the air would have thrown her down and killed her. "Goddamn you," she said to Simon.

The northern border of the slide had run out onto the Melas glacier, melting the ice and mixing with it in a steaming trough of boulders and mud. The dust-cloud made it hard to see much of that. Ann crossed the dike, walked up to the foot of the slide. The rocks at the bottom of it were still hot. They seemed no more fractured than the rock higher in the slide. Ann stared at the new black wall, her ears ringing. Not fair, she thought. Not fair.

She walked back to the Geneva Spur, feeling sick and dazed. The boulder car was still on the dead-end road, dusty but apparently unharmed. For the longest time she could not bear to touch it. She stared back over the long smoking mass of the slide—a black glacier, next to a white one. Finally she opened the lock door and ducked inside. There was no other choice.

Ann drove a little every day, then got out and walked over the planet, doing her work doggedly, like an automaton.

To each side of the Tharsis bulge there was a depression. On the west side was Amazonis Planitia, a low plain reaching deep into the southern highlands. On the east was the Chryse Trough, a depression that ran from the Argyre Basin through the Margaritifer Sinus and Chryse Planitia, the deepest point in the trough. The trough was an average of two kilometers lower than its surroundings, and all the chaotic terrain on Mars, and most of the ancient outbreak channels, were located in it.

Ann drove east along the southern rim of Marineris, until she was between Nirgal Vallis and the Aureum Chaos. She stopped to resupply at the refuge called Dolmen Tor, which was where Michel and Kasei had taken them at the end of their retreat down Marineris, in 2061. Seeing the little refuge again did not affect her; she scarcely remembered it. All her memories were going away, which she found comforting. She worked at it, in fact, concentrating on the moment with such intensity that even the moment itself went away, each instant a burst of light in a fog, like things breaking in her head.

Certainly the trough predated the chaos and the outbreak channels, which were no doubt located there because of the trough. The Tharsis bulge had been a tremendous source of outgassing from the hot center of the planet, all the radial and concentric fractures around it leaking volatiles out of the hot center of the planet. Water in the regolith had run downhill, into the depressions on each side of the bulge. It could be that the depressions were the direct result of the bulge, simply a matter of the lithosphere bent down on the outskirts of where it had been pushed up. Or it could be that the mantle had sunk underneath the depressions, as it had plumed under the bulge. Standard convection models would support such an idea—the upwelling of the plume had to go back down somewhere, after all, rolling at its sides and pulling the lithosphere down after it.

And then, up in the regolith, water had run downhill in its usual way, pooling in the troughs, until the aquifers burst open, and the surface over them collapsed: thus the outbreak channels, and the chaos. It was a good working model, plausible and powerful, explaining a lot of features.

So every day Ann drove and then walked, seeking confirmation of the mantle convection explanation for the Chryse trough, wandering over the surface of the planet, checking old seismographs and picking away at rocks. It was hard now to make one's way north in the trough; the aquifer outbreaks of 2061 nearly blocked the way, leaving only a narrow slot between the eastern end of the great Marineris glacier and the western side of a smaller glacier that filled the whole length of Ares Vallis. This slot was the first chance east of Noctis Labyrinthus to cross the equator without going over ice, and Noctis was six thousand kilometers away. So a piste and a road had been built in the slot, and a fairly large tent town established on the rim of Galilaei Crater. South of Galilaei the narrowest part of the slot was only forty kilometers wide, a zone of navigable plain located between the eastern arm of the Hydaspis Chaos and the western part of Aram Chaos. It was hard to drive through this zone and keep the piste and road under the horizons, and Ann drove right on the edge of Aram Chaos, looking down onto the shattered terrain.

North of Galilaei it was easier. And then she was out of the slot, and onto Chryse Planitia. This was the heart of the trough, with a gravitational potential of -0.65; the lightest place on the planet, lighter even than Hellas and Isidis.

But one day she drove onto the top of a lone hill, and saw that there was an ice sea out in the middle of Chryse. A long glacier had run down from Simud Vallis and pooled in the Chryse low point, spreading until it became an ice sea, covering the land over the horizons to north, northeast, northwest. She drove slowly around its western shore, then its northern shore. It was some two hundred kilometers across.

Near the end of one day she stopped her car on a ghost crater rim, and stared out across the expanse of broken ice. There had been so many outbreaks in '61. It was clear that there had been some good areologists working for the rebels in those days, finding aquifers and setting off explosions or reactor meltdowns precisely where the hydrostatic pressures were the greatest. Using a lot of her own findings, it seemed.

But that was the past, banished now. All that was gone. Here and now, there was only this ice sea. The old seismographs she had picked up all had records disturbed by recent temblors from the north, where there should have been very little activity. Perhaps the melting of the northern polar cap was causing the lithosphere there to rebound upward, setting off lots of small marsquakes. But the temblors recorded by the seismographs were discrete short-period shocks, like explosions rather than marsquakes.

She had studied her car's AI screen through many a long evening, mystified.

Every day she drove, then walked. She left the ice sea, and continued north onto Acidalia.

The great plains of the northern hemisphere were generally referred to as level, and they certainly were compared to the chaoses, or to the southern highlands. But still, they were not level like a playing field or a table top—not even close. There were undulations everywhere, a continuous up-and-downing of hummocks and hollows, ridges of cracking bedrock, hollows of fine drifts, great rumpled boulder fields, isolated tors and little sinkholes . . . It was unearthly. On Earth, soil would have filled the hollows, and wind and water and plant life would have worn down the bare hilltops, and then the whole thing would have been submerged or subducted or worn flat by ice sheets, or uplifted by tectonic action, everything torn away and rebuilt scores of times as the eons passed, and always flattened by weather and biota. But these ancient corrugated plains, their hollows banged out by meteor impact, had not changed for a billion years. And they were among the youngest surfaces on Mars.

It was a hard thing to drive across such lumpy terrain, and very easy to get lost when out walking, particularly if one's car looked just like all the other boulders scattered about; particularly if one was distracted. More than once Ann had to find the car by radio signal rather than visual sighting, and sometimes she walked right up to it before recognizing it—and then would wake up, or come to, hands shaking in the aftershock of some forgotten reverie.

The best driving routes were along the low ridges and dikes of exposed bedrock. If these high basalt roads had connected one to the next, it would have been easy. But they commonly were broken by transverse faults, at first no more than line cracks, which then got deeper and wider as one progressed, in sequences like loaves of sliced bread tipping open, until the faults gaped and were filled with rubble and fines, and the dike became nothing but part of a boulder field again.

She continued north, onto Vastitas Borealis. Acidalia, Borealis: the old names were so strange. She was doing her best never to think, but during the long hours in the car it was sometimes impossible not to. At those times it was less dangerous to read than it was to try staying blank. So she would read randomly in her AI's library. Often she ended up staring at areological maps, and one evening at sunset after such a session, she looked into this matter of Mars's names.

It turned out most of them came from Giovanni Schiaparelli. On his telescope maps he had named over a hundred albedo features, most of which were just as illusory as his *canali*. But when the astronomers of the

1950s had regularized a map of the albedo features everyone could agree on—features that could be photographed—many of Schiaparelli's names had been retained. It was a tribute to a certain power he had had, a power evocative if not consistent; he had been a classical scholar, and a student of biblical astronomy, and among his names there were Latin, Greek, biblical, and Homeric references, all mixed together. But he had had a good ear, somehow. One proof of his talent was the contrast between his maps and the competing Martian maps of the nineteenth century. A map by an Englishman named Proctor, for instance, had relied on the sketches of a Reverend William Dawes; and so on Proctor's Mars, which had no recognizable relations even to the standard albedo features, there was a Dawes Continent, a Dawes Ocean, a Dawes Strait, a Dawes Sea, and a Dawes Forked Bay. Also an Airy Sea, a DeLaRue Ocean, and a Beer Sea. Admittedly this last was a tribute to a German named Beer, who had drawn a Mars map even worse than Proctor's. Still, compared to them Schiaparelli had been a genius.

But not consistent. And there was something wrong in this mélange of references, something dangerous. Mercury's features were all named after great artists, Venus's were named after famous women; they would drive or fly over those landscapes one day, and feel that they lived in coherent worlds. Only on Mars did they walk about in a horrendous mishmash of the dreams of the past, causing who knew what disastrous misapprehensions of the real terrain: the Lake of the Sun, the Plain of Gold, the Red Sea, Peacock Mountain, the Lake of the Phoenix, Cimmeria, Arcadia, the Gulf of Pearls, the Gordian Knot, Styx, Hades, Utopia. . . .

On the dark dunes of Vastitas Borealis she began to run low on supplies. Her seismographs showed daily temblors to the east, and she drove toward them. On her walks outside she studied the garnet sand dunes, and their layering, which revealed the old climates like tree rings. But snow and high winds were tearing off the crests of the dunes. The westerlies could be extremely strong, enough to pick up sheets of large-grained sand and hurl them against her car. The sand would always settle in dune formations, as a simple matter of physics, but the dunes would be picking up the pace of their slow march around the world, and the record they had made of earlier ages would be destroyed.

She forced that thought from her mind, and studied the phenomenon as if there were no new artificial forces disturbing it. She focused on her work as if clenching her geologist's hammer, as if breaking apart rocks. The past was spalled away piece by piece. Leave it behind. She refused to think of it. But more than once she jerked out of sleep with the image of the long runout coming at her. And then she was awake for good, sweating and trembling, faced with the incandescent dawn, the sun blazing like a chunk of burning sulphur.

Coyote had given her a map of his caches in the north, and now she came to one buried in a cluster of house-sized boulders. She restocked, leaving a brief thank-you note. The last itinerary Coyote had given her said he was going to be dropping by this area sometime soon, but there was no sign of him, and no use waiting. She drove on.

She drove, she walked. But she couldn't help it; the memory of the landslide haunted her. What bothered her was not that she had had a brush with death, which no doubt had happened many times before, mostly in ways she had not noticed. It was simply how arbitrary it had been. It had nothing to do with value or fitness; it was pure contingency. Punctuated equilibrium, without the equilibrium. Effects did not follow from causes, and one did not get one's just desserts. She was the one who had spent too much time outdoors, after all, taking on far too much radiation; but it was Simon who had died. And she was the one who had fallen asleep at the wheel; but it was Frank who had died. It was simply a matter of chance, of accidental survival or erasure.

It was hard to believe natural selection had made any way in such a universe. There under her feet, in the troughs between the dunes, archaebacteria were growing on sand grains; but the atmosphere was gaining oxygen fast, and all the archaebacteria would die out except those that were by accident underground, away from the oxygen they themselves had respired, the oxygen that was poisonous to them. Natural selection or accident? You stood, breathing gases, while death rushed toward you— and were covered by boulders, and died, or covered by dust, and lived. And nothing you did mattered in that great either-or. Nothing you did mattered. One afternoon, reading randomly in the AI to distract herself between her return to the car and her dinner hour, she learned that the Czarist police had taken Dostoyevsky out to be executed, and only brought him back in after several hours of waiting for his turn. Ann finished reading about this incident and sat in the driver's seat of her car, feet on the dash, staring at the screen blindly. Another garish sunset poured through the window over her, the sun weirdly large and bright in the thickening atmosphere. Dostoyevsky had been changed for life, the writer declared in the easy omniscience of biography. An epileptic, prone to violence, prone to despair. He hadn't been able to integrate the experience. Perpetually angry. Fearful. Possessed.

Ann shook her head and laughed, angry at the idiot writer, who simply didn't understand. Of course you didn't *integrate the experience*. It was meaninglessness. The experience that couldn't be integrated.

• • •

The next day a tower poked over the horizon. She stopped the car, stared at it through the car's telescope. There was a lot of ground mist behind it. The temblors registering on her seismograph were very strong now, and appeared to be coming from a bit to the north. She even felt one of them herself, which, given the car's shock absorbers, meant they were strong indeed. It seemed likely there was a connection with the tower.

She got out of her car. It was almost sunset, the sky a great arch of violent colors, the sun low in the hazy west. The light would be behind her, making her very hard to see. She wound between dunes, then carefully made her way to the crest of one, and crawled the final meters of the way, and looked over the crest at the tower, now only a kilometer to the east. When she saw how close its base was she kept her chin right on the ground, among ejecta the size of her helmet.

It was some kind of mobile drilling operation, a big one. The massive base was flanked by giant caterpillar tracks, like those used to move the largest rockets around a spaceport. The drill tower rose out of this behemoth more than sixty meters, and the base and lower part of the tower clearly contained the technicians' housing and equipment and supplies.

Beyond this thing, a short distance down a gentle slope to the north, was a sea of ice. Immediately north of the drill, the crests of the great barchan dunes still stuck out of the ice—first as a bumpy beach, then as hundreds of crescent islands. But a couple of kilometers out the dune crests disappeared, and it was ice only.

The ice was pure, clean—translucent purple under the sunset sky—clearer than any ice she had ever seen on the Martian surface, and smooth, not broken like all the glaciers. It was steaming faintly, the frost steam whipping east on the wind. And out on it, looking like ants, people in walkers and helmets were ice-skating.

It came clear the moment she saw the ice. Long ago she herself had confirmed the big impact hypothesis, which accounted for the dichotomy between the hemispheres: the low smooth northern hemisphere was simply a superhuge impact basin, the result of a scarcely imaginable collision in the Noachian, between Mars and a planetesimal nearly as big as it. The rock of the impact body that had not vaporized had become part of Mars itself, and there were arguments in the literature that the irregular movements in the mantle that had caused the Tharsis bulge were late developments resulting from perturbations originating with the impact. To Ann that wasn't likely, but what was clear was that the great crash had happened, wiping out the surface of the entire northern hemisphere, and lowering it by an average of four kilometers relative to the south. An astonishing hit, but that was the Noachian. An impact of similar magnitude had in all probability caused the birth of Luna out of Earth. In fact there were some antiimpact holdouts arguing that if Mars had been hit as hard, it should have had a moon as big.

But now, as she lay flat looking at the giant drilling rig, the point was that the northern hemisphere was even lower than it first appeared, for its floor of bedrock was amazingly deep, as much as five kilometers beneath the surface of the dunes. The impact had blown that deep, and then the depression had mostly refilled, with a mixture of ejecta from the big impact, windblown sand and fines, later impact material, erosional material sliding down the slope of the Great Escarpment, and water. Yes, water, finding the lowest point as it always did; the water in the annual frost hood, and the ancient aquifer outbreaks, and the outgassing from the blistered bedrock, and the lensing from the polar cap, had all eventually migrated to this deep zone, and combined to form a truly enormous underground reservoir, an ice and liquid pool that extended in a band all the way around the planet, underlying almost everything north of 60° north latitude, except, ironically, for a bedrock island on which the polar cap itself stood.

Ann herself had discovered this underground sea many years before, and by her estimates between sixty and seventy percent of all the water on Mars was down there. It was, in fact, the Oceanus Borealis that some terraformers talked about—but buried, deeply buried, and mostly frozen, and mixed with regolith and dense fines; a permafrost ocean, with some liquid down on the deepest bedrock. All locked down there for good, or so she had thought, because no matter how much heat the terraformers applied to the planet's surface, the permafrost ocean would not thaw much faster than a meter per millennium—and even when it did melt it would remain underground, simply as a matter of gravity.

Thus the drilling rig before her. They were mining the water. Mining the liquid aquifers directly, and also melting the permafrost with explosives, probably nuclear explosives, and then collecting the melt and pumping it onto the surface. The weight of the overlying regolith would help push the water up through pipes. The weight of water on the surface would help push up more. If there were very many drilling rigs like this one, they could put a tremendous amount on the surface. Eventually they would have a shallow sea. It would refreeze and become an ice sea again for a while, but between atmospheric warming, sunlight, bacterial action, increasing winds—it would melt again, eventually. And then there would be an Oceanus Borealis. And the old Vastitas Borealis, with its world-wrapping black garnet dunes, would be sea bottom. Drowned.

•   •   •

She walked back to her car in the twilight, moving clumsily. It was difficult to operate the locks, to get her helmet off. Inside she sat before the microwave without moving for more than an hour, images flitting through her mind. Ants burning under a magnifying glass, an anthill drowned behind a mud dam. . . . She had thought that nothing could reach her anymore in this preposthumous existence she was living—but her hands trembled, and she could not face the rice and salmon cooling in the microwave. Red Mars was gone. Her stomach was a small stone in her body. In the random flux of universal contingency, nothing mattered; and yet, and yet. . . .

She drove away. She couldn't think of anything else to do. She returned south, driving up the low slopes, past Chryse and its little ice sea. It would be a bay of the larger ocean, eventually. She focused on her work, or tried. She fought to see nothing but rock, to think like a stone.

One day she drove over a plain of small black boulders. The plain was smoother than usual, the horizon its usual five kilometers away, familiar from Underhill and all the rest of the lowlands. A little world, and completely filled with small black boulders, like fossil balls from various sports, only all black, and all faceted to one extent or another. They were ventifacts.

She got out of the car to walk around and look. The rocks drew her on. She walked a long way west.

A front of low clouds rolled over the horizon, and she could feel the wind pushing at her in gusts. In the premature dark of the suddenly stormy afternoon, the boulder field took on a weird beauty; she stood in a slab of dim air, rushing between two planes of lumpy blackness.

The boulders were basalt rocks, which had been scoured by the winds on one exposed surface, until that surface had been scraped flat. Perhaps a million years for that first scraping. And then the underlying clays had been blown away, or a rare marsquake had shaken the region, and the rock had shifted to a new position, exposing a different surface. And the process had begun again. A new facet would be slowly scraped flat by the ceaseless brushing of micron-sized abrasives, until once again the rock's equilibrium changed, or another rock bumped it, or something else shifted it from its position. And then it would start again. Every boulder in that field, shifting every million years or so, and then lying still under the wind for day after day, year after year. So that there were *einkanters* with single facets, and *dreikanters* with three facets—*fierkanters, funfkanters*—all the way up to nearly perfect hexahedrons, octahedrons, dodecahedrons. Ventifacts. Ann hefted one after another of them, thinking about how many years their planed sides represented, wondering whether her mind might not reveal similar scourings, big sections worn flat by time.

It began to snow. First swirling flakes, then big soft blobs, pouring down on the wind. It was relatively warm out, and the snow was slushy, then sleety, then an ugly mix of hail and wet snow, all flailing down in a hard wind. As the storm progessed, the snow became very dirty; apparently it had been pushed up and down in the atmosphere for a long time, collecting fines and dust and smoke particulates, and crystallizing more moisture and then flying up on another updraft in the thunderhead to do it again, until what came down was nearly black. Black snow. And then it was a kind of frozen mud that was falling, filling in the holes and gaps between the ventifacts, coating their tops, then dropping off their sides, as the keening wind caused a million little avalanches. Ann staggered aimlessly, pointlessly, until she twisted an ankle and stopped, her breath racking in and out of her, a rock clutched in each cold gloved hand. She understood that the long runout was running still. And mud snow pelted down out of the black air, burying the plain.

But nothing lasts, not even stone, not even despair.

Ann got back to her car, she didn't know how or why. She drove a little every day, and without consciously intending to, came back to Coyote's cache. She stayed there for a week, walking over the dunes and mumbling her food.

Then one day: "Ann, di da do?"

She only understood the word *Ann.* Shocked at the return of her glossolalia, she put both hands to the radio speaker, and tried to talk. Nothing came out but a choking sound.

"Ann, di da do?"

It was a question.

"Ann," she said, as if vomiting.

Ten minutes later he was in her car, reaching up to give her a hug. "How long have you been here?"

"Not . . . not long."

They sat. She collected herself. It was like thinking, it was thinking out loud. Surely she still thought in words.

Coyote talked on, perhaps a bit slower than usual, eyeing her closely. She asked him about the ice-drilling rig.

"Ah. I wondered if you would run across one of those."

"How many are there?"

"Fifty."

Coyote saw her expression, and nodded briefly. He was eating voraciously, and it occurred to her that he had arrived at the cache empty. "They're putting a lot of money into these big projects. The new elevator, these water rigs, nitrogen from Titan . . . a big mirror out there between us and the sun, to put more light on us. Have you heard of that?"

She tried to collect herself. Fifty. Ah, God. . . .

It made her mad. She had been angry at the planet, for not giving her her release. For frightening her, but not backing it up with action. But this was different, a different kind of anger. And now as she sat watching Coyote eat, thinking about the inundation of Vastitas Borealis, she could feel that anger contracting inside her, like a prestellar dustcloud, contracting until it collapsed and ignited. Hot fury—it was painful to feel it. And yet it was the same old thing, anger at the terraforming. That old burnt emotion that had gone nova in the early years, now coalescing and going off again; she didn't want it, she really didn't. But dammit, the planet was melting under her feet. Disintegrating. Reduced to mush in some Terran cartel's mining venture.

Something ought to be done.

And really she had to do something, if only just to fill the hours that she had to fill before some accident had mercy on her. Something to occupy the preposthumous hours. Zombie vengeance—well, why not? Prone to violence, prone to despair. . . .

"Who's building them?" she asked.

"Mostly Consolidated. There's factories building them at Mareotis and Bradbury Point." Coyote wolfed down food for a while more, then eyed her. "You don't like it."

"No."

"Would you like to stop it?"

She didn't reply.

Coyote seemed to understand. "I don't mean stop the whole terraforming effort. But there are things that can be done. Blow up the factories."

"They'll just rebuild them."

"You never can tell. It would slow them down. It might buy enough time for something to happen on a more global scale."

"Reds, you mean."

"Yes. I think people would call them Reds."

Ann shook her head. "They don't need me."

"No. But maybe you need them, eh? And you're a hero to them, you know. You would mean more to them than just another body."

Ann's mind had gone blank again. Reds—she had never believed in them, never believed that mode of resistance would work. But now—well, even if it wouldn't work, it might be better than doing nothing. Poke them in the eye with a stick!

And if it did work. . . .

"Let me think about it."

They talked about other things. Suddenly Ann was hit by a wall of fatigue, which was strange as she had spent so much time doing nothing. But there it was. Talking was exhausting work, she wasn't used to it. And Coyote was a hard man to talk to.

"You should go to bed," he said, breaking off his monologue. "You look tired. Your hands—" He helped her up. She lay down on a bed, in her clothes. Coyote pulled a blanket over her. "You're tired. I wonder if it isn't time for another longevity treatment for you, old girl."

"I'm not going to take them anymore."

"No! Well, you surprise me. But sleep, now. Sleep."

She caravaned with Coyote back south, and in the evenings they ate together, and he told her about the Reds. It was a loose grouping, rather than any rigidly organized movement. Like the underground itself. She knew several of the founders: Ivana, and Gene and Raul from the farm team, who had ended up disagreeing with Hiroko's areophany and its insistence on viriditas; Kasei and Harmakhis and several of the Zygote ectogenes; a lot of Arkady's followers, who had come down from Phobos and then clashed with Arkady over the value of terraforming to the revolution. A good many Bogdanovists, including Steve and Marian, had become Reds in the years since 2061, as had followers of the biologist Schnelling, and some radical Japanese nisei and sansei from Sabishii, and Arabs who wanted Mars to stay Arabian forever, and escaped prisoners from Korolyov, and so on. A bunch of radicals. Not really her type, Ann thought, feeling a residual sensation that her objection to terraforming was a rational scientific thing. Or at least a defensible ethical or aesthetic position. But then the anger burned through her again in a flash, and she shook her head, disgusted at herself. Who was she to judge the ethics of the Reds? At least they had expressed their anger, they had lashed out. Probably they felt better, even if they hadn't accomplished anything. And maybe they had accomplished something, at least in years past, before the terraforming had entered this new phase of transnat gigantism.

Coyote maintained that the Reds had considerably slowed terraforming. Some of them had even kept records to try to quantify the difference they had made. There was also, he said, a growing movement among some of the Reds to acknowledge reality and admit that terraforming was going to happen, but to work up policy papers advocating various kinds of least-impact terraforming. "There are some very detailed proposals for a largely carbon dioxide atmosphere, warm but water-poor, which would support plant life, and people with facemasks, but not wrench the world into a Terran model. It's very interesting. There are also several proposals for what they call ecopoesis, or areobiospheres. Worlds in which the low altitudes are arctic, and just barely livable for us, while the higher altitudes remain above the bulk of the atmosphere, and thus in a natural state, or close to it. The calderas of the four big volcanoes would stay especially pure in such a world, or so they say."

Ann doubted most of these proposals were achievable, or would have the effects predicted. But Coyote's accounts intrigued her nevertheless. He was a strong supporter of all Red efforts, apparently, and he had been a big help to them from the start, giving them aid from the underground refuges, connecting them up with each other, and helping them to build their own refuges, which were chiefly in the mesas and fretted terrain of the Great Escarpment, where they remained close to the terraforming action, and could therefore interfere with it more easily. Yes—Coyote was a Red, or at least a sympathizer. "Really I'm nothing. An old anarchist. I suppose you could call me a Boonean, now, in that I believe in incorporating anything and everything that will help make a free Mars. Sometimes I think the argument that a human-viable surface helps the revolution is a good one. Other times not. Anyway the Reds are such a great guerrilla pool. And I take their point that we're not here to, you know, *reproduce Canada*, for God's sake! So I help. I'm good at hiding, and I like it."

Ann nodded.

"So do you want to join them? Or at least meet them?"

"I'll think about it."

Her focus on rock was shattered. Now she could not help noticing how many signs of life there were on the land. In the southern tens and twenties, ice from the outbreak glaciers was melting during summer afternoons, and the cold water was flowing downhill, cutting the land in new primitive watersheds, and turning talus slopes into what ecologists called fellfields, those rocky patches that were the first living communities after ice receded, their living component made of algae and lichens and moss. Sandy regolith, infected by the water and microbacteria flowing through it, became fellfield with shocking speed, she found, and the fragile landforms were quickly destroyed. Much of the regolith on Mars had been superarid, so arid that when water touched it there were powerful chemical reactions—lots of hydrogen peroxide release, and salt crystallizations—in essence the ground disintegrated, flowing away in sandy muds that only set downstream, in loose terraces called solifluction rims, and in frosty new proto-fellfields. Features were disappearing. The land was melting. After one long day's drive through terrain altered like this, Ann said to Coyote, "Maybe I will talk to them."

But first they returned to Zygote, or Gamete, where Coyote had some business. Ann stayed in Peter's room, as he was gone, and the room she had shared with Simon had been put to other uses. She wouldn't have stayed in it anyway. Peter's room was under Harmakhis's, a round bamboo segment containing a desk, a chair, a crescent mattress on the floor, and a window looking out at the lake. Everything was the same but different in Gamete, and despite the years she had spent visiting Zygote regularly, she felt no connection with any of it. It was hard, in fact, to remember what Zygote had been like. She didn't want to remember, she practiced forgetting assiduously; any time some image from the past came to her, she would jump up and do something that required concentration, studying rock samples or seismograph readouts, or cooking complex meals, or going out to play with the kids—until the image had faded, and the past was banished. With practice one could dodge the past almost entirely.

One evening Coyote stuck his head in the door of Peter's room. "Did you know Peter is a Red too?"

"What?"

"He is. But he works on his own, in space mostly. I think that his ride down from the elevator gave him a taste for it."

"My God," she said, disgusted. That was another random accident; by all rights Peter should have died when the elevator fell. What were the chances of a spaceship floating by and spotting him, alone in areosynchronous orbit? No, it was ridiculous. Nothing existed but contingency.

But still she was angry.

She went to sleep upset by these thoughts, and once in her uneasy slumber she had a dream in which she and Simon were walking through the most spectacular part of Candor Chasma, on that first trip they had taken together, when everything was immaculate, and nothing had changed for a billion years—the first humans to walk in that vast gorge of layered terrain and immense walls. Simon had loved it just as much as she had, and he was so silent, so absorbed in the reality of rock and sky—there was no better companion for such glorious contemplation. Then in the dream one of the giant canyon walls started to collapse, and Simon said, "Long runout," and she woke up instantly, sweating.

She dressed and left Peter's rooms and went out into the little mesocosm under the dome, with its white lake and the krummholz on the low dunes. Hiroko was such a strange genius, to conceive such a place and then convince so many others to join her in it. To conceive so many children, without the fathers' permission, without controls over the genetic manipulations. It was a form of insanity, really, divine or not.

There along the icy strand of their little lake came a group of Hiroko's brood. They couldn't be called kids anymore, the youngest were fifteen or sixteen Terran years old, the oldest—well, the oldest were out scattered over the world; Kasei was probably fifty by now, and his daughter Jackie nearly twenty-five, a graduate of the new university in Sabishii, active in demimonde politics. That group of ectogenes were back in Gamete on a visit, like Ann herself. There they were, coming along the beach. Jackie was leading the group, a tall graceful black-haired young woman, quite beautiful and imperious, the leader of her generation no doubt. Unless it might be the cheery Nirgal, or the brooding Harmakhis. But Jackie led them—Harmakhis followed her with doggy loyalty, and even Nirgal kept an eye on her. Simon had loved Nirgal, and Peter did too, and Ann could see why; he was the only one among Hiroko's gang of ectogenes who did not put her off. The rest cavorted in their self-absorption, kings and queens of their little world, but Nirgal had left Zygote soon after Simon's death, and had hardly ever come back. He had studied in Sabishii, which was what had given Jackie the idea, and now he spent most of his time in Sabishii, or out with Coyote or Peter, or visiting the cities of the north. So was he too a Red? Impossible to say. But he was interested in everything, aware of everything, running around everywhere, a kind of young male Hiroko if such a creature was possible, but less strange than Hiroko, more engaged with other people; more human. Ann had never in her life managed to have a normal conversation with Hiroko, who seemed an alien consciousness, with entirely different meanings for all the words in the language, and, despite her brilliance at ecosystem design, not really a scientist at all, but rather some kind of prophet. Nirgal on the other hand seemed intuitively to strike right to the heart of whatever was most important to the person he was talking to—and he focused on that, and asked question after question, curious, assimilative, sympathetic. As Ann watched him trailing Jackie down the strand, running here and there, she recalled how slowly and carefully he had walked at Simon's side. How he had looked so frightened that last night, when Hiroko in her peculiar way had brought him in to say good-bye. All that business had been a cruel thing to subject a boy to, but Ann hadn't objected at the time; she had been desperate, ready to try anything. Another mistake she could never repair.

She stared at the blond sand underfoot, upset, until the ectogenes had passed. It was a shame Nirgal was so hooked by Jackie, who cared so little for him. Jackie was a remarkable woman in her way, but much too much like Maya—moody and manipulative, fixated on no man, except, perhaps, for Peter—who luckily (although it had not seemed so at the time) had had an affair with Jackie's mother, and was not the least bit interested in Jackie herself. A messy business that, and Peter and Kasei were still estranged by it, and Esther had never been back. Not Peter's finest hour. And its effects on Jackie . . . Oh yes, there would be effects (there, watch out—some black blank, there in her own deep past) yes, on and on and on it went, all their sordid little lives, repeating themselves in their meaningless rounds. . . .

She tried to concentrate on the composition of the sand grains. Blond was not really a usual color for sand on Mars. A very rare granitic stuff. She wondered if Hiroko had hunted for it, or else gotten lucky.

The ectogenes were gone, down by the other side of the lake. She was alone on the beach. Simon somewhere underneath her. It was hard to keep from connecting with any of that.

A man came walking over the dunes toward her. He was short, and at first she thought it was Sax, then Coyote, but he wasn't either of these. He hesitated when he saw her, and by that motion she saw that it was indeed Sax. But a Sax greatly altered in appearance. Vlad and Ursula had been doing some cosmetic surgery on his face, enough so that he didn't look like the old Sax. He was going to move to Burroughs, and join a biotech company there, using a Swiss passport and one of Coyote's viral identities. Getting back into the terraforming effort. She looked out at the water. He came over and tried to talk to her, strangely un-Saxlike, nicer-looking now, a handsome old coot; but it was still the old Sax, and her anger filled her up so much that she could hardly think, hardly remember what they were talking about from one second to the next. "You really do look different," was all she could recall. Inanities like that. Looking at him she thought, He will never change. But there was something frightening about the stricken look on his new face, something deadly that it would evoke, if she did not stop it . . . and so she argued with him until he grimaced one last time, and went away.

She sat there for a long time, getting colder and more distraught. Finally she put her head on her knees, and fell into a kind of sleep.

She had a dream. All the First Hundred were standing around her, the living and the dead, Sax at their center with his old face, and that dangerous new look of distress. He said, "Net gain in complexity."

Vlad and Ursula said, "Net gain in health."

Hiroko said, "Net gain in beauty."

Nadia said, "Net gain in goodness."

Maya said, "Net gain in emotional intensity," and behind her John and Frank rolled their eyes.

Arkady said, "Net gain in freedom."

Michel said, "Net gain in understanding."

From the back Frank said, "Net gain in power," and John elbowed him and cried, "Net gain in happiness!"

And then they all stared at Ann. And she stood up, quivering with rage and fear, understanding that she alone among them did not believe in the possibility of the net gain of anything at all, that she was some kind of crazy reactionary; and all she could do was point a shaking finger at them and say, "*Mars. Mars. Mars.*"

That night after supper, and the evening in the big meeting room, Ann got Coyote alone and said, "When do you go out again?"

"In a few days."

"Are you still willing to introduce me to those people you talked about?"

"Yeah, sure." He looked at her with his head cocked. "It's where you belong."

She only nodded. She looked around the common room, thinking, Good-bye, good-bye. Good riddance.

A week later she was flying with Coyote in an ultralight plane. They flew north through the nights, into the equatorial region, then onward to the Great Escarpment, to the Deuteronilus Mensae north of Xanthe—wild fretted terrain, the mensae like an archipelago of stack islands, dotting a sand sea. They would become a real archipelago, Ann thought as Coyote descended between two of the stacks, if the pumping to the north continued.

Coyote landed on a short stretch of dusty sand, and taxied into a hangar cut into the side of one of the mesas. Out of the plane they were greeted by Steve and Ivana and a few others, and taken up in an elevator to a floor just under the top of the mesa. The northern end of this particular mesa came to a sharp rocky point, and high in this point a large triangular meeting room had been excavated. On entering it Ann stopped in surprise; it was jammed with people, several hundred of them at least, all seated at long tables about to start a meal, leaning over the tables to pour each other's water. The people at one table saw her, and stopped what they were doing, and the people at the next table noticed that and looked around, and saw her and likewise stopped—and so the effect rippled out through the room, until they had all gone still. Then one stood, and another, and in a ragged motion they all rose to their feet. For a moment everything was as if frozen. Then they began to applaud, their hands flailing wildly, their faces gleaming; and then they cheered.

PART 4

The Scientist As Hero

Hold it between thumb and middle finger. Feel the rounded edge, observe the smooth curves of glass. A magnifying lens: it has the simplicity, elegance, and heft of a paleolithic tool. Sit with it on a sunny day, hold it over a pile of dry twigs. Move it up and down, until you see a spot in the twigs turn bright. Remember that light? It was as if the twigs caged a little sun.

The Amor asteroid that was spun out into the elevator cable was made up mostly of carbonaceous chondrites and water. The two Amor asteroids intercepted by groups of robot landers in the year 2091 were mostly silicates and water.

The material of New Clarke was spun out into a single long strand of carbon. The material of the two silicate asteroids was transformed by their robot crews into sheets of solar sail material. Silica vapor was solidified between rollers ten kilometers long, and pulled out in sheets coated with a thin layer of aluminum, and these vast mirror sheets were unfurled by spacecraft with human crews, into circular arrays which held their shape using spin and sunlight.

From one asteroid, pushed into a Martian polar orbit and called Birch, they teased the mirror sheets out into a ring a hundred thousand kilometers in diameter. This annular mirror spun around Mars in a polar orbit, the mirror ring facing the sun, angled in so that the light reflected from it met at a point inside Mars's orbit, near its Lagrange One point.

The second silicate asteroid, called Solettaville, had been pushed near this Lagrange point. There the solar sailmakers spun the mirror sheets out into a complex web of slatted rings, all connected and set at angles, so that they looked like a lens made of circular venetian blinds, spinning around a hub that was a silver cone, with the cone's open end facing Mars. This huge delicate object, ten thousand kilometers in diameter, bright and stately as it wheeled along between Mars and the sun, was called the soletta.

Sunlight striking the soletta directly bounced through its blinds, hitting the sun side of one, then the Mars side of the next one out, and onward to Mars. Sunlight striking the annular ring in its polar orbit was reflected back and in to the inner cone of the soletta, and then was reflected again, also on to Mars. Thus light struck both sides of the soletta, and these countervailing pressures kept it moving in its position, about a hundred thousand kilometers out from Mars— closer at perihelion, farther away at aphelion. The angles of the slats were constantly adjusted by the soletta's AI, to keep its orbit and its focus.

Through the decade when these two great pinwheels were being constructed out of their asteroids, like silicate webs out of rock spiders, observers on Mars saw almost nothing of them. Occasionally someone would see an arcing white line in the sky, or random glints by day or by night, as if the brilliance of a much vaster universe were shining through loose seams in the fabric of our sphere.

Then, when the two mirrors were completed, the annular mirror's reflected light was aimed at the cone of the soletta. The soletta's circular slats were adjusted, and it moved into a slightly different orbit.

And one day people living on the Tharsis side of Mars looked up, for the sky had darkened. They looked up, and saw an eclipse of the sun such as Mars had never seen: the sun bit into, as if there were some Luna-sized moon up there to block its rays. The eclipse then proceeded as they do on Earth, the crescent of darkness biting deeper into the round blaze as the soletta floated into its position between Mars and sun, with its mirrors not yet positioned to pass the light through: the sky going a dark violet, the darkness taking over the majority of the disk, leaving only a crescent of blaze until that too disappeared, and the sun was a dark circle in the sky, edged by the whisper of a corona—then entirely gone. Total eclipse of the sun. . . .

A very faint moiré pattern of light appeared in the dark disk, unlike anything ever seen in any natural eclipse. Everyone on the daylight side of Mars gasped, squinted as they looked up. And then, as when one tugs open venetian blinds, the sun came back all at once.

Blinding light!

And now more blinding than ever, as the sun was noticeably brighter than it had been before the strange eclipse had begun. Now they walked under an augmented sun, the disk appearing about the same size as it did from Earth, the light some twenty percent greater than before—noticeably brighter, warmer on the back on the neck—the red expanse of the plains more brilliantly lit. As if *floodlights had suddenly been turned on, and all of them were now walking a great stage.*

A few months after that a third mirror, much smaller than the soletta, spun down into the highest reaches of the Martian atmosphere. It was another lens made of circular slats, and looked like a silver UFO. It caught some of the light pouring down from the soletta, and focused it still further, into points on the surface of the planet that were less than a kilometer across. And it flew like a glider over the world, holding that concentrated beam of light in focus, until little suns seemed to bloom right there on the land, and the rock itself melted, turning from solid to liquid. And then to fire.

The underground wasn't big enough for Sax Russell. He wanted to get back to work. He could have moved into the demimonde, perhaps taken a teaching position at the new university in Sabishii, which ran outside the net and covered many of his old colleagues, and provided an education for many of the children of the underground. But on reflection he decided he didn't want to teach, or remain on the periphery—he wanted to return to terraforming, to the heart of the project if possible, or as close as he could get to it. And that meant the surface world. Recently the Transitional Authority had formed a committee to coordinate all the work on terraforming, and a Subarashii-led team had gotten the old synthesis job that Sax had once held. This was unfortunate, as Sax didn't speak Japanese. But the lead in the biological part of the effort had been given to the Swiss, and was being run by a Swiss collective of biotech companies called Biotique, with main offices in Geneva and Burroughs, and close ties with the transnational Praxis.

So the first task was to insinuate himself into Biotique under a false name, and get himself assigned to Burroughs. Desmond took charge of this operation, writing a computer persona for Sax similar to the one he had given to Spencer years before, when Spencer had moved to Echus Overlook. Spencer's persona, and some extensive cosmetic surgery, had enabled him to work successfully in the materials labs in Echus Overlook, and then later in Kasei Vallis, the very heart of transnat security. So Sax had faith in Desmond's system. The new persona listed Sax's physical ID data—genome, retina, voice, and finger prints—all slightly altered, so that they still almost fit Sax himself, while escaping notice in any comparative matching searches in the nets. These data were given a new name with a full Terran background, credit rating, and immigration record, and a viral subtext to attempt to overwhelm any competing ID for the physical data, and the whole package was sent off to the Swiss passport office, which had been issuing passports to these arrivals without comment. And in the balkanized world of the transnat nets, that seemed to be doing the job. "Oh yeah, that part works no problem," Desmond said. "But you First Hundred are all movie stars. You need a new face too."

Sax was agreeable. He saw the need, and his face had never meant anything to him. And these days the face in the mirror didn't much resemble what he thought he looked like anyway. So he got Vlad to do the work on him, emphasizing the potential usefulness of his presence in Burroughs. Vlad had become one of the leading theoreticians of the resistance to the Transitional Authority, and he was quick to see Sax's point. "Most of us should just live in the demimonde," he said, "but a few people hidden in Burroughs would be a good thing. So I might as well practice my cosmetic surgery on a no-lose situation like yours."

"A no-lose situation!" Sax said. "And verbal contracts are binding. I expect to come out handsomer."

And for a wonder he did, although it was impossible to tell until the spectacular bruising went away. They capped his teeth, puffed his thin lower lip, and gave his button nose a prominent bridge, and a little bit of a bend. They thinned his cheeks and gave him more of a chin. They even cut some muscles in his eyelids so that he didn't blink so often. When the bruises went away he looked like a real movie star, as Desmond said. Like an ex-jockey, Nadia said. Or an ex–dance instructor, said Maya, who had faithfully attended Alcoholics Anonymous for many years. Sax, who had never liked the effects of alcohol, waved her off.

Desmond took photos of him and put them in the new persona, then inserted this construct successfully into the Biotique files, along with a transfer order from San Francisco to Burroughs. The persona appeared in the Swiss passport listings a week later, and Desmond chuckled when he saw it. "Look at that," he said, pointing at Sax's new name. "Stephen Lindholm, Swiss citizen! Those folks are covering for us, there's no doubt about it. I'll bet you anything they put a stopper on the persona, and checked your genome with old print records, and even with my alterations I bet they figured out who you really are."

"Are you sure?"

"No. They aren't saying, are they? But I'm pretty sure."

"Is it a good thing?"

"In theory, no. But in practice, if someone is on to you, it's nice to see them behaving as a friend. And the Swiss are good friends to have. This is the fifth time they've issued a passport to one of my personas. I even have one myself, and I doubt they were able to find out who I really am, because I was never ID'd like you folks in the First Hundred. Interesting, don't you think?"

"Indeed."

"They are interesting people. They have their own plans, and I don't know what they are, but I like the look of them. I think they've made a decision to cover for us. Maybe they just want to know where we are. We'll never know for sure, because the Swiss dearly love their secrets. But it doesn't matter why when you've got the how."

Sax winced at the sentiment, but was happy to think that he would be safe under Swiss patronage. They were his kind of people—rational, cautious, methodical.

A few days before he was going to fly with Peter north to Burroughs, he took a walk around Gamete's lake, something he had rarely done in his years there. The lake was certainly a neat bit of work. Hiroko was a fine systems designer. When she and her team had disappeared from Underhill so long ago, Sax had been quite mystified; he hadn't seen the point, and had worried that they would begin to fight the terraforming somehow. When he had managed to coax a response out of Hiroko on the net, he had been partly reassured; she seemed sympathetic to the basic goal of terraforming, and indeed her own concept of viriditas seemed just another version of the same idea. But Hiroko appeared to enjoy being cryptic, which was very unscientific of her; and during her years of hiding she had indulged herself to the point of information damage. Even in person she was none too easy to understand, and it was only after some years of co-existence that Sax had become confident that she too desired a Martian biosphere that would support humans. That was all the agreement he asked for. And he could not think of a better single ally to have in that particular project, unless it was the chairperson of this new Transitional Authority committee. And probably the chair was an ally too. There were not too many opposed, in fact.

But there on the beach sat one, as gaunt as a heron. Ann Clayborne. Sax hesitated, but she had already seen him. And so he walked on, until he stood by her side. She glanced up at him, and then stared out again at the white lake. "You really look different," she said.

"Yes." He could still feel the sore spots in his face and mouth, though the bruises had cleared up. It felt a bit like wearing a mask, and suddenly that made him uncomfortable. "Same me," he added.

"Of course." She did not look up at him. "So you're off to the over-world?"

"Yes."

"To get back to your work?"

"Yes."

She looked up at him. "What do you think science is for?"

Sax shrugged. It was their old argument, again and always, no matter what kind of beginning it had. To terraform or not to terraform, that is the question. . . . He had answered the question long ago, and so had she, and he wished they could just agree to disagree, and get on with it. But Ann was indefatigable.

"To figure things out," he said.

"But terraforming is not figuring things out."

"Terraforming isn't science. I never said it was. It's what people do with science. Applied science, or technology. What have you. The choice of what to do with what you learn from science. Whatever you call that."

"So it's a matter of values."

"I suppose so." Sax thought about it, trying to marshal his thoughts concerning this murky topic. "I suppose our . . . our disagreement is another facet of what people call the fact-value problem. Science concerns itself with facts, and with theories that turn facts into examples. Values are another kind of system, a human construct."

"Science is also a human construct."

"Yes. But the connection between the two systems isn't clear. Beginning from the same facts, we can arrive at different values."

"But science itself is full of values," Ann insisted. "We talk about theories with power and elegance, we talk about clean results, or a beautiful experiment. And the desire for knowledge is itself a kind of value, saying that knowledge is better than ignorance, or mystery. Right?"

"I suppose," Sax said, thinking it over.

"Your science is a set of values," Ann said. "The goal of your kind of science is the establishment of laws, of regularities, of exactness and certainty. You want things explained. You want to answer the whys, all the way back to the big bang. You're a reductionist. Parsimony and elegance and economy are values for you, and if you can make things simpler that's a real achievement, right?"

"But that's the scientific method itself," Sax objected. "It's not just me, it's how nature itself works. Physics. You do it yourself."

"There are human values imbedded in physics."

"I'm not so sure." He held out a hand to stop her for a second. "I'm not saying there are no values in science. But matter and energy do what they do. If you want to talk about values, better just to talk about them. They arise out of facts somehow, sure. But that's a different issue, some kind of sociobiology, or bioethics. Perhaps it would be better just to talk about values directly. The greatest good for the greatest number, something like that."

"There are ecologists who would say that's a scientific description of a healthy ecosystem. Another way of saying climax ecosystem."

"That's a value judgment, I think. Some kind of bioethics. Interesting, but. . ." Sax squinted at her curiously, decided to change tack. "Why not try for a climax ecosystem here, Ann? You can't speak of ecosystems without living things. What was here on Mars before us wasn't an ecology. It was geology only. You could even say there was a start at an ecology here, long ago, that somehow went wrong and froze out, and now we're starting it up again."

She growled at that, and he stopped. He knew she believed in some kind of intrinsic worth for the mineral reality of Mars; it was a version of what people called the land ethic, but without the land's biota. The rock ethic, one might say. Ecology without life. An intrinsic worth indeed!

He sighed. "Perhaps that's just a value speaking. Favoring living systems over nonliving systems. I suppose we can't escape values, like you say. It's strange . . . I mostly feel like I just want to figure things out. Why they work the way they do. But if you ask me why I want that—or what I would want to have happen, what I work toward. . . ." He shrugged, struggling to understand himself. "It's hard to express. Something like a net gain in information. A net gain in order." For Sax this was a good functional description of life itself, of its holding action against entropy. He held out a hand to Ann, hoping to get her to understand that, to agree at least to the paradigm of their debate, to a definition of science's ultimate goal. They were both scientists after all, it was their shared enterprise. . . .

But she only said, "So you destroy the face of an entire planet. A planet with a clear record nearly four billion years old. It's not science. It's making a theme park."

"It's using science for a particular value. One I believe in."

"As do the transnationals."

"I guess."

"It certainly helps them."

"It helps everything alive."

"Unless it kills them. The terrain is destabilized; there are landslides every day."

"True."

"And they kill. Plants, people. It's happened already."

Sax waggled a hand, and Ann jerked her head up to glare at him.

"What's this, the necessary murder? What kind of value is that?"

"No, no. They're accidents, Ann. People need to stay on bedrock, out of the slide zones, that kind of thing. For a while."

"But vast regions will turn to mud, or be drowned entirely. We're talking about half the planet."

"The water will drain downhill. Create watersheds."

"Drowned land, you mean. And a completely different planet. Oh, that's a value all right! And the people who hold the value of Mars as it is . . . We will fight you, every step of the way."

He sighed. "I wish you wouldn't. At this point a biosphere would help us more than the transnationals. The transnats can operate from the tent cities, and mine the surface robotically, while we hide and concentrate most of our efforts on concealment and survival. If we could live everywhere on the surface, it would be a lot easier for all kinds of resistance."

"All but Red resistance."

"Yes, but what's the point of that, now?"

"Mars. Just Mars. The place you've never known."

Sax looked up at the white dome over them, feeling distress like a sudden attack of arthritis. It was useless to argue with her.

But something in him made him keep trying. "Look, Ann, I'm an advocate of what people call the minimum viable model. It's a model that calls for a breathable atmosphere only up to about the two- or three-kilometer contour. Above that the air would be kept too thin for humans, and there wouldn't be much life of any kind—some high-altitude plants, and above that nothing, or nothing visible. The vertical relief on Mars is so extreme that there can be vast regions that will remain above the bulk of the atmosphere. It's a plan that makes sense to me. It expresses a comprehensible set of values."

She did not reply. It was distressing, it really was. Once, in an attempt to understand Ann, to be able to talk to her, he had done research in the philosophy of science. He had read a fair amount of material, concentrating particularly on the land ethic, and the fact-value interface. Alas, it had never proved to be of much help; in conversation with her, he had never seemed able to apply what he had learned in any useful manner. Now, looking down at her, feeling the ache in his joints, he recalled something that Kuhn had written about Priestley—that a scientist who continued to resist after his whole profession had been converted to a new paradigm might be perfectly logical and reasonable, but had *ipso facto* ceased to be a scientist. It seemed that something like this had happened to Ann, but what then was she now? A counterrevolutionary? A prophet?

She certainly looked like a prophet—harsh, gaunt, angry, unforgiving. She would never change, and she would never forgive him. And all that he would have liked to say to her, about Mars, about Gamete, about Peter—about Simon's death, which seemed to haunt Ursula more than her . . . all that was impossible. This was why he had more than once resolved to give up talking to Ann: it was so *frustrating* never to get anywhere, to be faced with the dislike of someone he had known for over sixty years. He won every argument but never got anywhere. Some people were like that; but that didn't make it any less distressing. In fact it was quite remarkable how much physiological discomfort could be generated by a merely emotional response.

Ann left with Desmond the next day. Soon after that Sax got a ride north with Peter, in one of the small stealthed planes that Peter used to fly all over Mars.

Peter's route to Burroughs led them over the Hellespontus Montes, and Sax gazed down into the big basin of Hellas curiously. They caught a glimpse of the edge of the icefield that had covered Low Point, a white mass on the dark night surface, but Low Point itself stayed over the horizon. That was too bad, as Sax was curious to see what had happened over the Low Point mohole. It had been thirteen kilometers deep when the flood had filled it, and that deep it was likely that the water had remained liquid at the bottom, and probably warm enough to rise quite a distance; it was possible that the icefield was in that region an ice-covered sea, with telltale differences at the surface.

But Peter would not change his route to get a better view. "You can look into it when you're Stephen Lindholm," he said with a grin. "You can make it part of your work for Biotique."

And so they flew on. And the next night they landed in the broken hills south of Isidis, still on the high side of the Great Escarpment. Sax then walked to a tunnel entrance, and went down into the tunnel and followed it into the back of a closet in the service basement of Libya Station, which was a little train station complex at the intersection of the Burroughs-Hellas piste and the newly rerouted Burroughs-Elysium piste. When the next train to Burroughs came in, Sax emerged from a service door and joined the crowd getting on the train. He rode into Burrough's main station, where he was met by a man from Biotique. And then he was Stephen Lindholm, newcomer to Burroughs and to Mars.

The man from Biotique, a personnel secretary, complimented him on his skillful walking, and took him to a studio apartment high in Hunt Mesa, near the center of the old town. The labs and offices of Biotique were also in Hunt, just under the mesa's plateau, with window walls looking down on the canal park. A high-rent district, as only befitted the company leading the terraforming project's bioengineering efforts.

Out the Biotique office's windows he could see most of the old city, looking about the same as he remembered it, except that the mesa walls were even more extensively lined by glass windows, colorful horizontal bands of copper or gold or metallic green or blue, as if the mesas were stratified by some truly wonderful mineral layers. Also the tents that had topped the mesas were gone, their buildings now standing free under the much larger tent that now covered all nine mesas, and everything in between and around them. Tenting technology had reached the point where they could enclose vast mesocosms, and Sax had heard that one of the transnats was going to cover Hebes Chasma, a project that Ann had once suggested as an alternative to terraforming—a suggestion that Sax himself had scoffed at. And now they were doing it. One should never underestimate the potential of materials science, that was clear.

Burroughs' old canal park, and the broad grass boulevards that climbed away from the park and between the mesas, were now strips of green, cutting through orange tile rooftops. The old double row of salt columns still stood beside the blue canal. There had been a lot of building, to be sure; but the configuration of the city was still the same. It was only

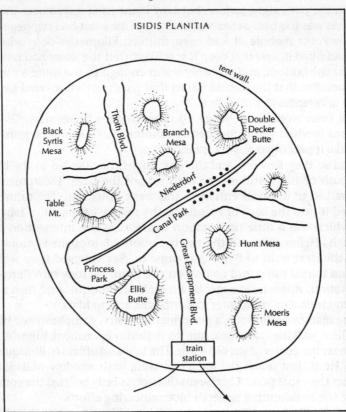

Burroughs, C. 2100 A.D.

ISIDIS PLANITIA

tent wall

Black
Syrtis
Mesa

Thoth Blvd.

Branch
Mesa

Double
Decker
Butte

Niederdorf

Table
Mt.

Canal Park

Hunt Mesa

Great Escarpment Blvd.

Princess
Park

Ellis
Butte

Moeris
Mesa

train
station

on the outskirts that one could see clearly how much things had changed, and how much larger the city really was; the city wall lay well beyond the nine mesas, so that quite a bit of surrounding land was sheltered, and much of it built upon already.

The personnel secretary gave Sax a quick tour of Biotique, making introductions to more people than he could remember. Then Sax was asked to report to his lab the next morning, and given the rest of the day to get settled in.

As Stephen Lindholm he planned to exhibit signs of intellectual energy, sociability, curiosity, and high spirits; and so he very plausibly spent that afternoon exploring Burroughs, wandering from neighborhood to neighborhood. He strolled up and down the wide swards of streetgrass, considering as he did the mysterious phenomenon of the growth of cities. It was a cultural process with no very good physical or biological analogy. He could see no obvious reason why this low end of Isidis Planitia should have become home to the largest city on Mars. None of the original reasons for siting the city here were at all adequate to explain it; so far as he knew, it had begun as an ordinary way station on the piste route from Elysium to Tharsis. Perhaps it was precisely because of its lack of strategic location that it had prospered, for it had been the only major city not damaged or destroyed in 2061, and thus perhaps it simply had had a head start on growth in the postwar years. By analogy to the punctuated equilibrium model of evolution, one might say that this particular species had accidentally survived an impact that had devastated most other species, giving it an open ecosphere to expand in.

And no doubt the bowllike shape of the region, with its archipelago of small mesas, gave it an impressive look as well. When he walked around on the wide grassy boulevards, the nine mesas appeared evenly distributed, and each mesa had a slightly different look, its rugged rock walls distinguished by characteristic knobs, buttresses, smooth walls, overhangs, cracks—and now the horizontal bands of colorful mirror windows, and the buildings and parks on the flat plateaus crowning each mesa. From any point on the streets one could always see several of the mesas, scattered like magnificent neighborhood cathedrals, and this no doubt gave a certain pleasure to the eye. And then if one took an elevator up to one of the mesa's plateau tops, all about a hundred meters higher than the city floor, then one had a view over the rooftops of several different districts, and a different perspective on the other mesas, and then, beyond those, the land surrounding the city for many kilometers, distances larger than were usual on Mars, because they were at the bottom of a bowl-shaped depression: over the flat plain of Isidis to the north, up the dark rise to Syrtis in the west, and to the south one could see the distant rise of the Great Escarpment itself, standing on the horizon like a Himalaya.

Of course whether a handsome prospect mattered to city formation was an open question, but there were historians who asserted that many ancient Greek cities were sited principally for their view, in the face of other inconveniences, so it was at least a possible factor. And in any case Burroughs was now a bustling little metropolis of some 150,000 people, the biggest city on Mars. And it was still growing. Near the end of his afternoon's sightseeing, Sax rode one of the big exterior elevators up the side of Branch Mesa, centrally located north of Canal Park, and from its plateau he could see that the northern outskirts of town were studded with construction sites all the way to the tent wall. There was even work going on around some of the distant mesas outside the tent. Clearly critical mass had been reached in some kind of group psychology—some herding instinct, which had made this place the capital, the social magnet, the heart of the action. Group dynamics were complex at best, even (he grimaced) unexplainable.

· · ·

Which was unfortunate, as always, because Biotique Burroughs was a very dynamic group indeed, and in the days that followed Sax found that determining his place in the crowd of scientists working on the project was no easy thing. He had lost the skill of finding his way in a new group, assuming he had ever had it. The formula governing the number of possible relationships in a group was $n(n-1)/2$, where n is the number of individuals in the group; so that, for the 1,000 people at Biotique Burroughs, there were 499,500 possible relationships. This seemed to Sax well beyond anyone's ability to comprehend—even the 4,950 possible relationships in a group of 100, the hypothesized "design limit" of human group size, seemed unwieldy. Certainly it had been at Underhill, when they had had a chance to test it.

So it was important to find a smaller group at Biotique, and Sax set about doing so. It certainly made sense to concentrate at first on his lab. He had joined them as a biophysicist, which was risky, but put him where he wanted to be in the company; and he hoped he could hold his own. If not, then he could claim to have come to biophysics from physics, which was true. His boss was a Japanese woman named Claire, middle-aged in appearance, a very congenial woman who was good at running their lab. On his arrival she put him to work with the team designing second- and third-generation plants for the glaciated regions of the northern hemisphere. These newly hydrated environments represented tremendous new possibilities for botanical design, as the designers no longer had to base all species on desert xerophytes. Sax had seen this coming from the very first moment he had spotted the flood roaring down Ius Chasma into Melas, in 2061. And now forty years later he could actually do something about it.

So he very happily joined in the work. First he had to bring himself up to date on what had already been put out there in the glacial regions. He read voraciously in his usual manner, and viewed videotapes, and learned that with the atmosphere still so thin and cold, all the new ice released on the surface was subliming until its exposed surfaces were fretted to a minute lacework. This meant there were billions of pockets large and small for life to grow in, directly on the ice; and so one of the first forms to have been widely distributed were varieties of snow and ice algae. These algae had been augmented with phreatophytic traits, because even when the ice started pure it became salt-encrusted by way of the ubiquitous windblown fines. The genetically engineered salt-tolerant algaes had done very well, growing in the pitted surfaces of the glaciers, and sometimes right into the ice. And because they were darker than the ice, pink or red or black or green, the ice under them had a tendency to melt, especially during summer days, when temperatures were well above freezing. So small diurnal streams had begun to run off the glaciers, and along their edges. These wet morainelike regions were similar to some Terran polar and mountain environments. Bacteria and larger plants from these Terran environments, genetically altered to help them survive the pervasive salt-iness, had first been seeded by teams from Biotique several M-years before, and for the most part these plants were prospering as the algae had.

Now the design teams were trying to build on these early successes and introduce a wider array of larger plants, and some insects bred to tol-erate the high CO_2 levels in the air. Biotique had an extensive inventory of template plants to take chromosome sequences from, and 17 M-years of field experimental records, so Sax had a lot of catching up to do. In his first weeks at the lab, and in the company arboretum on Hunt plateau, he focused on the new plant species to the exclusion of everything else, con-tent to work his way up to the bigger picture in due time.

Meanwhile, when he was not at his desk reading, or looking through the microscopes or into the various Mars jars in the labs, or up in the arboretum, there was the daily work of being Stephen Lindholm to keep him busy as well. In the lab it was not all that different from being Sax Russell. But at the end of the workdays he would often make a conscious effort and join the group that went upstairs to one of the plateau cafés, to have a drink and talk about the day's work, and then everything else.

Even there he found it surprisingly easy to "be" Lindholm, who, he discovered, asked a lot of questions, and laughed frequently; whose mouth somehow made laughter easier. Questions from the others—usually from Claire, and an English immigrant named Jessica, and a Kenyan man named Berkina—very rarely had anything to do with Lindholm's Terran past. When they did, Sax found it was easy to give a minimal response—Des-mond had given Lindholm a past in Sax's own home town of Boulder, Colorado, a sensible move—and then he could turn things around on the questioner, in a technique he had often observed Michel using. People were so happy to talk. And Sax himself had never been a particularly quiet one, like Simon. He had always pitched in his conversational ante, and if he had contributed infrequently thereafter, it was because he was only interested when the stakes reached a certain minimum level. Small talk was usually a waste of time. But it did in fact pass that time, which oth-erwise might be irritatingly blank. It also seemed to ameliorate feelings of solitude. And his new colleagues usually engaged in pretty interesting shop talk, anyway. And so he did his part, and told them about his walks around Burroughs, and asked them many questions about what he had seen, and about their past, and Biotique, and the Martian situation, and so on. It made as much sense for Lindholm as for Sax.

In these conversations his colleagues, especially Claire and Berkina, confirmed what was obvious in his walks—that Burroughs was in some sense becoming the *de facto* capital of Mars, in that the headquarters for all of the biggest transnationals were located there. The transnationals were at this point the effective rulers of Mars. They had enabled the Group of Eleven and the other wealthy industrial nations to win or at least survive the war of 2061, and now they were all intertwined in a single power structure, so that it wasn't clear who on Earth was calling the shots, the countries or the supracorporations. On Mars, however, it was obvious. UNOMA had been shattered in 2061 like one of the domed cities, and the agency that had taken its place, the United Nations Transitional Authority, was an administrative group staffed by transnat executives, its decrees enforced by transnat security forces. "The UN has nothing to do with it, really," Berkina said. "The UN is just as dead on Earth as UNOMA is here. So the name is just a cover."

Claire said, "Everyone calls it just the Transitional Authority anyway."

"They can see who is who," Berkina said. And indeed, uniformed transnational security police were to be seen frequently in Burroughs. They wore rust-colored construction jumpers, with armbands of different colors. Nothing very ominous, but there they were.

"But why?" Sax asked. "Who are they afraid of?"

"They're worried about Bogdanovists coming out of the hills," Claire said, and laughed. "It's ridiculous."

Sax raised his eyebrows, let it pass. He was curious, but it was a dangerous topic. Better just to listen when it came up on its own. Still, after that when he walked around Burroughs he watched the crowds more, checking the security police wandering around for their armband identification. Consolidated, Amexx, Oroco . . . he found it curious that they had not formed a single force. Possibly the transnationals were still rivals as well as partners, and competing security systems would naturally result. This perhaps would also explain the proliferation of identification systems, which created the gaps that made it possible for Desmond to insert his personas into one system, and have them creep elsewhere. Switzerland was obviously willing to cover for some people coming into its system from nowhere, as Sax's own experience showed; and no doubt other countries and transnationals were doing the same kind of thing.

So in the current political situation, information technology was creating not totalization but balkanization. Arkady had predicted such a development, but Sax had considered it too irrational to be a likely eventuality. Now he had to admit that it had come to pass. The computer nets could not keep track of things because they were in competition with each other; and so there were police in the streets, keeping an eye out for people like Sax.

But he was Stephen Lindholm. He had Lindholm's rooms in the Hunt Mesa, he had Lindholm's work, and his routines, and his habits, and his past. His little studio apartment looked very unlike what Sax himself would have lived in: the clothes were in the closet, there were no experiments in the refrigerator or on the bed, there were even prints on the walls, Eschers and Hundertwassers and some unsigned sketches by Spencer, an indiscretion that was certainly undetectable. He was secure in his new identity. And really, even if he was found out, he doubted the results would be all that traumatic. He might even be able to return to something like his previous power. He had always been apolitical, interested only in terraforming, and he had disappeared during the madness of '61 because it looked as if it might be fatal not to do so. No doubt several of the current transnationals would see it that way and try to hire him.

But all that was hypothetical. In reality he could settle into the life of Lindholm.

As he did, he discovered that he enjoyed his new work very much. In the old days, as head of the entire terraforming project, it had been impossible not to get bogged down in administration, or diffused across the whole range of topics, trying to do enough of everything to be able to make informed policy decisions. Naturally this had led to a lack of depth in any one discipline, with a resulting loss of understanding. Now, however, his whole attention was focused on creating new plants to add to the simple ecosystem that had been propagated in the glacial regions. For several weeks he worked on a new lichen, designed to extend the borders of the new bioregions, based on a chasmoendolith from the Wright Valleys in Antarctica. The base lichen had lived in the cracks in the Antarctic rock, and here Sax wanted it to do the same, but he was trying to replace the algal part of the lichen with a faster algae, so that the resulting new symbiote would grow more quickly than its template organism, which was notoriously slow. At the same time he was trying to introduce into the lichen's fungus some phreatophytic genes from salt-tolerant plants like tamarisk and pickleweed. These could live in salt levels three times as salty as sea water, and the mechanisms, which had to do with the permeability of cell walls, were somewhat transferable. If he managed it, then the result would be a very hardy and fast-growing new salt lichen. Very encouraging, to see the progress that had been made in this area since their first crude attempts to make an organism that would survive on the surface, back in Underhill. Of course the surface had been more difficult then. But their knowledge of genetics and their range of methods were also greatly advanced.

One problem that was proving very obdurate was adjusting the plants to the paucity of nitrogen on Mars. Most large concentrations of nitrites were being mined upon discovery and released as nitrogen into the atmosphere, a process Sax had initiated in the 2040s and thoroughly approved of, as the atmosphere was desperately in need of nitrogen. But so was the soil, and with so much of it being put into the air, the plant life was coming up short. This was a problem that no Terran plant had ever faced, at least not to this degree, so there were no obvious adaptive traits to clip into the genes of their areoflora.

The nitrogen problem was a recurrent topic of conversation in their after-work sessions at the Café Lowen, up on the mesa plateau's edge. "Nitrogen is so valuable that it's the medium of exchange among the members of the underground," Berkina told Sax, who nodded uncomfortably at this misinformation.

Their café group made its own homage to the importance of nitrogen by inhaling N_2O from little canisters, passed from person to person around the table. It was claimed, with marginal accuracy but very high spirits, that their exhalation of this gas would help the terraforming effort. When the canister came around to Sax for the first time, he regarded it dubiously. He had noticed that one could purchase the canisters in restrooms—there was an entire pharmacology inside every men's room now, wall units that dispensed canisters of nitrous oxide, omegendorph, pandorph, and other drug-laced gases. Apparently respiration was the current method of choice for drug ingestion. It was not something that interested him, but now he took the canister from Jessica, who was leaning against his shoulder. This was an area in which Stephen's and Sax's behaviors diverged, apparently. So he breathed out and then put the little facemask over his mouth and nose, feeling Stephen's slim face under the plastic.

He breathed in a cold rush of the gas, held it briefly, exhaled, and felt all the weight go out of him—that was the subjective impression. It *was* fairly humorous to see how responsive mood was to chemical manipulation, despite what it implied about the precarious balance of one's emotional equanimity, even sanity itself. Not on the face of it a pleasant realization. But at the moment, not a problem. In fact it made him grin. He looked over the rail at the rooftops of Burroughs, and noticed for the first time that the new neighborhoods to the west and north were shifting to blue tile roofs and white walls, so that they were taking on a Greek look, while the old parts of town were more Spanish. Jessica was definitely making an effort to keep their upper arms in contact. It was possible her balance was impaired by mirth.

"But it's time to get beyond the alpine zone!" Claire was saying. "I'm sick of lichen, and I'm sick of mosses and grasses. Our equatorial fellfields are becoming meadows, we've even got krummholz, and they're all getting lots of sunlight year-round, and the atmospheric pressure at the foot of the escarpment is as high as in the Himalayas."

"Top of the Himalayas," Sax pointed out, then checked himself mentally; that had been a Saxlike qualification, he could feel it. As Lindholm he said, "But there are high Himalayan forests."

"Exactly. Stephen, you've done wonders since you arrived on that lichen, why don't you and Berkina and Jessica and C.J. start working on subalpine plants. See if we can't make some little forests."

They toasted the idea with another hit of nitrous oxide, and the idea of the briny frozen borders of the aquifer outbreaks becoming meadows and forests suddenly struck them all as extremely funny. "We need moles," Sax said, trying to wipe the grin from his face. "Moles and voles are crucial in changing fellfields to meadow, I wonder if we can make some kind of CO_2-tolerant arctic moles."

His companions thought this was hilarious, but he was lost in thought for a while, and didn't notice.

"Listen, Claire, do you think we could go out and have a look at one of the glaciers? Do some of the work on-site?"

Claire stopped giggling and nodded. "Sure. In fact that reminds me. We've got a permanent experimental station out at Arena Glacier, with a good lab. And we've been contacted by a biotech group from Armscor, one with a lot of clout with the Transitional Authority. They want to be taken out to see the station and the ice. I guess they're planning to build a similar station in Marineris. We can go out with that group and show them around, and do some fieldwork, and kill two birds with one stone."

Plans to make this trip actually made it from the Lowen into the lab, and then the front office. Approval came swiftly, as was usual in Biotique. So Sax worked hard for a couple of weeks, preparing for the fieldwork, and at the end of that intensive period he packed his bag, and one morning took the subway out to West Gate. There in the Swiss garage he spotted some people from the office, gathered with several strangers. Introductions were still being made. Sax approached, and Claire saw him and drew him into the crowd, looking excited. "Here, Stephen, I want to introduce you to our guest for the trip." A woman wearing some kind of prisming fabric turned around, and Claire said, "Stephen, I'd like you to meet Phyllis Boyle. Phyllis, this is Stephen Lindholm."

"How do you do?" Phyllis said, extending a hand.

Sax took her hand and shook. "I do fine," he said.

Vlad had nicked his vocal cords to give him a different vocal print if he was ever tested, but everyone in Gamete had agreed that he sounded just the same. And now Phyllis cocked her head curiously at him, alerted by something. "I'm looking forward to the trip," he said, and glanced at Claire. "I hope I haven't held you up?"

"No no, we're still waiting for the drivers."

"Ah." Sax backed away. "Good to meet you," he said to Phyllis politely. She nodded, and with a final curious glance turned back to the people she had been talking to. Sax tried to concentrate on what Claire was saying about the drivers. Apparently driving a rover across open terrain was a specialized occupation now.

That was fairly cool, he thought. Of course coolness was a Sax trait. Probably he ought to have gushed all over her, said he knew her from the old vids and had admired her for years, etc. Although how someone could admire Phyllis he had no idea. Surely she had come out of the war fairly compromised; on the winning side, but the only one of the First Hundred to have chosen it. A quisling, did they call that? Something like that. Well, she hadn't been the only one of the First Hundred; Vasili had stayed in Burroughs throughout, and George and Edvard had been on Clarke with Phyllis when it detached from the cable and catapulted out of the plane of the ecliptic. A neat bit of work to survive that, actually. He wouldn't have thought it possible—but there she was, chattering with her host of admirers. Luckily he had heard of her survival a few years before; otherwise it would have been a shock to see her.

She still looked about sixty years old, although she had been born the same year as Sax, and so was now 115. Silver-haired, blue-eyed, her jewelry made of gold and bloodstone, her blouse made of a material that shone through all the colors of the spectrum—right now her back was a vibrant blue, but as she turned to glance over her shoulder at him, it went emerald green. He pretended not to notice the look.

Then the drivers came, and they were into the rovers and off, and for a blessing Phyllis was in one of the other cars. The rovers were big hydrazine-powered things, and they followed a concrete road north, so that Sax could not see the necessity for specialist drivers, unless it was to handle the rovers' speed; they were rolling along at about a hundred and sixty kilometers an hour, and to Sax, who was used to rover speeds about a quarter that, it felt fast and smooth. The other passengers complained at how bumpy and slow the ride was—apparently express trains now floated over the pistes at about six hundred kilometers per hour.

The Arena Glacier was some eight hundred kilometers northwest of Burroughs, spilling from the highlands of Syrtis Major north onto Utopia Planitia. It ran in one of the Arena Fossae for a distance of some three hundred fifty kilometers. Claire and Berkina and the others in the car told Sax the glacier's history, and he did his best to indicate absorbed interest; indeed it was interesting, for they were aware that Nadia had rerouted the outbreak of the Arena aquifer. Some of the people who had been with Nadia when she did it had ended up in South Fossa after the war, and the story had been told there, and had spread into the public domain.

In fact these people seemed to think they knew a lot about Nadia. "She was against the war," Claire told him confidently, "and she did everything she could to stop it and then to repair the damage, even while it was happening. People who saw her on Elysium say she never slept at all, just took stimulants to keep going. They say she saved ten thousand lives in the week she was active around South Fossa."

"What happened to her?" Sax asked.

"No one knows. She disappeared from South Fossa."

"She was headed for Low Point," Berkina said. "If she got there in time for that flood, she was probably killed."

"Ah." Sax nodded solemnly. "That was a bad time."

"Very bad," Claire said vehemently. "So destructive. It set the terraforming back decades, I'm sure."

"Although the aquifer outbreaks have been useful," Sax murmured.

"Yes, but those could have been done anyway, in a controlled manner."

"True." Sax shrugged and let the conversation go on without him. After the encounter with Phyllis it was a bit much to get into a discussion of '61.

He still couldn't quite believe she hadn't recognized him. The passenger compartment they were in had shiny magnesium panels over the windows, and there, among the faces of his new colleagues, was the little face of Stephen Lindholm. A bald old man with a slightly hooked nose, which made the eyes somewhat hawkish rather than just birdlike. Visible lips, strong jaw, a chin—no, it didn't look like him at all. No reason why she should have recognized him.

But looks weren't everything.

He tried not to think about that as they hummed north over the road. He concentrated on the view. The passenger compartment had a domed skylight, as well as windows on all four sides, so he could see a lot. They were driving up the slope of west Isidis, a section of the Great Escarpment that was like a great shaved berm. The jagged dark hills of Syrtis Major rose over the northwest horizon, sharp as the edge of a saw. The air was clearer than it had been in the old days, even though it was fifteen times thicker. But there was less dust in it, as snowstorms were knocking the fines down, and then fixing them on the surface in a crust. Of course this crust was often broken by strong winds, and the trapped fines reintroduced to the air. But these breaks were localized, and the sky-cleaning storms were slowly getting the upper hand.

And so the sky was changing color. Overhead it was a rich violet, and above the western hills it was whitish, shading up into lavender, and some color between lavender and violet that Sax didn't have a name for. The eye could distinguish differences in light frequency of only a few wavelengths, so the few names for the colors between red and blue were totally inadequate to describe the phenomena. But whatever you called them, or didn't, they were sky colors very unlike the tans and pinks of the early years. Of course a dust storm would always temporarily return the sky to that primeval ochre tone; but when the atmosphere washed out, its color would be a function of its thickness and chemical composition. Curious as to what they could expect to see in the future, Sax took his lectern from his pocket to try some calculations.

He stared at the little box, suddenly realizing that it was Sax Russell's lectern—that if checked, it would give him away. It was like carrying around a genuine passport.

He dismissed the thought, as there was nothing to be done about it now. He concentrated on the color of the sky. In clean air, sky color was caused by preferential light scattering in the air molecules themselves. Thus the thickness of the atmosphere was critical. Air pressure when they had arrived had been about 10 millibars, and now it averaged about 160. But since air pressure was created by the weight of the air, creating 160 millibars on Mars had taken about three times as much air over any given spot than would have created such a pressure on Earth. So the 160 millibars here ought to scatter light about as much as 480 millibars on Earth; meaning the sky overhead ought to have something like the dark blue color seen in photos taken in mountains about 4,000 meters high.

But the actual color filling the windows and skylight of their rover was much more reddish than that, and even on clear mornings after heavy storms, Sax had never seen it look anywhere near as blue as a Terran sky. He thought about it more. Another effect of Mars's light gravity was that the air column lofted taller than Earth's. It was possible that the smallest fines were effectively in suspension, and had been blown above the altitude of most clouds, where they escaped being scrubbed out by storms. He recalled that haze layers had been photographed that were as much as fifty kilometers high, well above the clouds. Another factor might be the composition of the atmosphere; carbon dioxide molecules were more efficient light scatterers than oxygen and nitrogen, and Mars, despite Sax's best efforts, still had much more CO_2 in its atmosphere than Earth did. The effects of that difference would be calculable. He typed up the equation for Rayleigh's law of scattering, which states that the light energy scattered per unit volume of air is inversely proportional to the fourth power of the wavelength of the illuminating radiation. Then he scribbled away on his lectern screen, altering the variables, checking handbooks, or filling in quantities by memory, or guesswork.

He concluded that if the atmosphere was thickened to one bar, then the sky would probably turn milk white. He also confirmed that in theory the present-day Martian sky ought to be a lot bluer than it was, with its scattered blue light about sixteen times the intensity of the red. This suggested that fines very high in the atmosphere were probably reddening the sky. If that was the correct explanation, one could infer that the color and opacity of the Martian sky would for many years be subject to very wide variation, depending on weather and other influences on the cleanness of the air. . . .

And so he worked on, trying to incorporate into the calculation skylight radiance intensities, Chandrasekhar's radiative transfer equation, chromaticity scales, aerosol chemical compositions, Legendre polynomials to evaluate the angular scattering intensities, Riccati-Bessel functions to evaluate the scattering cross sections, and so on—occupying the better part of the drive to Arena Glacier, concentrating hard and steadfastly ignoring the world around him and the situation in which he now found himself.

Early that afternoon they came to a small town called Bradbury, which under its Nicosia-class tent looked like something out of Illinois: treelined blacktop streets, screened-in porches fronting two-story brick houses with shingle roofs, a main street with shops and parking meters, a central park with a white gazebo under giant maples. . . .

They headed west on a smaller road, across the top of Syrtis Major. The road was made of black sand that had been cleared of rocks and sprayed with a fixative. This whole region was very dark—Syrtis Major had been the first Martian surface feature spotted through Earth telescopes, by Christiaan Huygens on November 28, 1659, and it was this dark rock that had allowed him to see it. The ground was almost black, sometimes a kind of eggplant purple; the hills and grabens and escarpments that the road

twisted through were black; the fretted mesas were black, the *thulleya* or
little ribs were black, ridge after ridge after ridge of them; the giant ejecta
erratics, on the other hand, were often rust-colored, reminding them forc-
ibly of the color from which they had temporarily escaped.

Then they drove over a black bedrock rib and the glacier lay before
them, crossing the world from left to right like a lightning bolt inlaid into
the landscape. A bedrock rib on the far side of the glacier paralleled the
one they were on, and the two ribs together looked like old lateral moraines, although really they were just parallel ridges that had channelized
the outbreak flood.

The glacier was about two kilometers across. It appeared to be no more
than five or six meters thick, but apparently it had run down a canyon, so
there were hidden depths.

Parts of its surface were like ordinary regolith, just as rocky and dusty,
with a kind of gravel surface that revealed no sign of the ice below. Other
parts looked like chaotic terrain, except clearly made of ice, with knots of
white seracs sticking up out of what looked like boulders. Some of the
seracs were broken plates, bunched like the back of a stegosaurus, translucent yellow with the setting sun behind them.

All was motionless, to every horizon—not a movement to be seen
anywhere. Of course not; Arena Glacier had been here for forty years. But
Sax could not help remembering the last time he had seen such a sight,
and he glanced involuntarily to the south, as if a new flood might burst
out at any moment.

The Biotique station was located a few kilometers upstream, on the
rim and apron of a small crater, so that it had an excellent view over the
glacier. In the last part of sunset, as some of the regulars got the station
activated, Sax went with Claire and the visitors from Armscor, including
Phyllis, up to a big observation room on the top floor of the station, to
look at the broken mass of ice in the waning moments of the day.

Even on a relatively clear afternoon like this one, the horizontal rays
of the sun turned the air a burnished dark red, and the surface of the glacier
sparked in a thousand places, the recently broken ice reflecting the light
like mirrors. The majority of these scarlet gleams lay in a rough line between them and the sun, but there were a few elsewhere on the ice, where
the reflecting surfaces stood at odd angles. Phyllis pointed out how much
larger the sun looked, now that the soletta was in position. "Isn't it wonderful? You can almost see the mirrors, can't you?"

"It looks like blood."

"It looks positively *Jurassic*."

To Sax it looked like a G-type star about one astronomical unit away.

Of course this was significant, as they were 1.5 astronomical units away. As for the talk of rubies, or dinosaur's eyes. . . .

The sun slipped over the horizon and all the points of red light disappeared at once. A great fan of crepuscular rays stretched across the sky, the pinkish beams cutting a dark purple sky. Phyllis exclaimed over the colors, which were indeed very clear and pure. She said, "I wonder what makes those magnificent rays," and automatically Sax opened his mouth to explain about the shadows of hills or clouds over the horizon, when it occurred to him that *a*, it was a rhetorical question (perhaps), and *b*, to give a technical answer would be a very Sax Russell thing to do. So he shut his mouth, and considered what Stephen Lindholm would say in such a situation. This kind of self-consciousness was new to him, and distinctly uncomfortable, but he was going to have to say things, at least some of the time, because long silences were also fairly Sax Russellish, and not at all like Lindholm as he had been playing him so far. So he tried his best.

"Just think how close those photons came to hitting Mars," he said, "and now they're going to run all the way across the universe instead."

People squinted at this odd observation. But it drew him into the group nonetheless, and so served its purpose.

After a while they went down to the dining room, to eat pasta and tomato sauce, and bread just out of the ovens. Sax stayed at the main table, and ate and talked as much as the rest, striving for the norm, doing his best to follow the elusive rules of conversation and of social discourse. These he had never understood well, and less so the more he thought about them. He knew that he had always been considered eccentric; he had heard the story of the hundred transgenic lab rats taking over his brain. —A strange moment, that, standing outside the lab door in the dark, hearing the tale being promulgated with much hilarity from one generation of postdocs to the next, experiencing the rare discomfort of seeing himself as if he were someone else, someone strikingly peculiar.

But Lindholm, now: he was a congenial fellow. He knew how to get along. Someone who could partake of a bottle of Utopian zinfandel, someone who could do his part to make a dinner party festive. Someone who understood intuitively the hidden algorithms of good fellowship, so that he would be able to operate the system without even thinking about it.

So Sax ran a forefinger up and down the bridge of his new nose, and drank the wine which did indeed suppress his parasympathetic nervous system to the point of making him less inhibited and more voluble, and he chattered away very successfully, he thought, although several times he was alarmed by the way he was drawn into conversation by Phyllis, sitting across the table from him—and by the way she looked at him—and by the way he looked back! There were protocols for this kind of thing too, but he had never understood *them* in the slightest. Now he recalled the way Jessica had leaned on him at the Lowen, and drank another half glass and smiled, and nodded, thinking uneasily about sexual attraction and its causes.

Someone asked Phyllis the inevitable question about the escape from Clarke, and as she launched into the tale she glanced frequently at Sax, seeming to assure him that she was telling the story principally to him. He attended politely, resisting a certain tendency to go cross-eyed, which might indicate his dismay.

"There was no warning of any kind," Phyllis said to the questioner. "One minute we were orbiting Mars at the top of the elevator, just sick at what was happening down on the surface, and doing our best to figure out some way to stop the unrest, and then the next minute there was a jerk like an earthquake, and we were on our way out of the solar system." She smiled and paused for the laugh that followed, and Sax saw that she had told the story many times before in just this way.

"You must have been terrified!" someone said.

"Well," Phyllis said, "it's strange how in an emergency there isn't really time for any of that. As soon as we understood what had happened, we knew that every second we stayed on Clarke diminished our chances of surviving by hundreds of kilometers. So we convened in the command center and counted heads and talked it over and took stock of what we had available. It was hectic but not panicked, if you see what I mean. Anyway, there turned out to be about the usual number of Earth-to-Mars freighters in the hangars, and the AI calculations indicated we would need the thrust of almost all of them to get ourselves back down into the plane of the ecliptic in time to intersect the Jovian system. We were on our way out as well as up, and in the general direction of Jupiter, which was a blessing. Anyway, that was when it got crazy. We had to get all the freighters outside the hangars and flying beside Clarke, and then link them together and stock them with everything they could hold of Clarke's air and fuel and so on. And we were off in that jury-rigged lifeboat only thirty hours after launching, which now that I look back on it, is almost unbelievable. Those thirty hours . . ."

She shook her head, and Sax thought he saw a real memory suddenly invade her tale, shaking her slightly. Thirty hours was a remarkably fast evacuation, and no doubt the time had flashed by in a dreamlike rush of action, in a state of mind so different from ordinary time that it might pass for transcendence.

"After that it was just a matter of cramming into a couple of crew quarters—two hundred and eighty-six of us, there were—and going out on EVAs to cut away inessential parts of the freighters. And hoping there would be enough fuel to get us on course down to Jupiter. It was more than two months before we could be positive we would intercept the Jovian system, and ten weeks before we actually did. We used Jupiter itself as a gravity handle, and swung around toward Earth, which at that time was closer than Mars. And we swung so hard around Jupiter that we needed

Earth's atmosphere and Luna's gravity to slow us down, because we were almost out of fuel at the very same time that we were the fastest humans in history, by a factor of two. Eighty thousand kilometers an hour, I think it was when we hit the stratosphere the first time. A useful speed, really, because we were running out of food and air. We got really hungry near the end. But we made it. And we saw Jupiter from about *this close,*" holding thumb and forefinger apart a couple of centimeters.

People laughed, and the gleam of triumph in Phyllis's eye had nothing to do with Jupiter. But there was a tightening at the corner of her mouth; something at the end of her tale had darkened the triumph, somehow.

"And you were the leader, right?" someone asked.

Phyllis held up a hand, to say she could not deny it though she wanted to. "It was a cooperative effort," she said. "But sometimes someone has to decide when there's an impasse, or simply a need for speed. And I had been head of Clarke before the catastrophe."

She flashed her big smile, confident that they had enjoyed the account. Sax smiled with the rest, and nodded when she looked his way. She was an attractive woman, but not, he thought, very bright. Or maybe it was just that he did not like her very much. For certainly she was very intelligent in some ways, a good biologist when she had done biology, and certain to score high on an IQ test. But there were different types of intelligence, and not all of them were subject to analytic testing. Sax had noticed this fact in his student years: that there were people who would score high on any intelligence test, and were very good at their work, but who at the same time could walk into a room of people and within an hour have many of the occupants of that room laughing at them, or even despising them. Which was not very smart. Indeed the most giddy of high school cheerleaders, say, managing to be friendly with everyone and therefore universally popular, seemed to Sax to be exercising an intelligence at least as powerful as any awkward brilliant mathematician's—the calculus of human interaction being so much more subtle and variable than any physics, somewhat like the emerging field of math called cascading recombinant chaos, only less simple. So that there were at least two kinds of intelligence, and probably many more: spatial, aesthetic, moral or ethical, interactional, analytic, synthetic, and so forth. And it was those people who were intelligent in a number of different ways who were truly exceptional, who stood out as something special.

Phyllis, however, basking in the attention of her listeners, most of them much younger than her and, at least on the surface, in awe of her historicity—Phyllis was not one of those polymaths. On the contrary, she seemed rather dim when it came to judging what people thought of her. Sax, who knew he shared the deficiency, watched her with the best Lindholm smile he could muster. But it seemed to him a fairly obviously vain performance on her part, even a bit arrogant. And arrogance was always stupid. Or else a mask for some kind of insecurity. Hard to guess what that insecurity might be, in such a successful and attractive person. And she certainly was attractive.

After supper they went back up to the observation room on the top floor, and there under a glittering bowl of stars the crowd from Biotique turned on some music. It was the kind called nuevo calypso, the current rage in Burroughs, and several members of the group brought out instruments and played along, while others moved to the middle of the room and began to dance. The music was paced at about a hundred beats a minute, Sax calculated, perfect physiological timing for stimulating the heart just a bit; the secret to most dance music, he supposed.

And then Phyllis was there by his side, grabbing for his hand and pulling him out among the dancers. Sax only just restrained himself from jerking his hand away from her, and he was sure that his response to her smiling invitation was sickly at best. He had never danced in his life, as far as he could recall. But that was Sax Russell's life. Surely Stephen Lindholm had danced a lot. So Sax began to hop gently up and down in time with the bass steel drum, wiggling his arms uncertainly at his sides, smiling at Phyllis in a desperate simulation of debonair pleasure.

Later that evening the younger Biotique crew were still dancing, and Sax took the elevator down to bring some tubs of ice milk back up from the kitchens. When he got back into the elevator Phyllis was already inside, coming back up from the dorm floor. "Here, let me help with those," she said, and took two of the four plastic bags hanging from his fingers. Then when she had them she leaned down (she was a few centimeters taller than him) and kissed him full on the mouth. He kissed back, but it was such a shock that he didn't really start to feel it until she pulled away; then the memory of her tongue between his lips was like another kiss. He tried to look less than befuddled, but by the way she laughed he knew he had failed. "I see you're not as much of a lady-killer as you look," she said, which given the situation only made him more alarmed. In point of fact, no one had ever done that to him before. He tried to rally, but the elevator slowed and the doors hissed open.

Through dessert and the rest of the party Phyllis did not approach him again. But when the timeslip began, he went to the elevators to go back to his room, and as the doors began to close Phyllis slipped through them and in, and as soon as the elevator began to drop she was kissing him again. He put his arms around her and kissed back, trying to figure out what Lindholm would do in this situation, and if there was any way out of it that wouldn't lead to trouble. When the elevator slowed Phyllis leaned back with a dreamy unfocused gaze and said, "Come walk me to my room." Reeling a bit, Sax held her upper arm like a bit of delicate lab equipment, and was led to her room, a tiny chamber like all the rest of the bedrooms. Standing in the doorway they kissed again, despite Sax's strong feeling that this was his last chance to escape, gracefully or not; but he was kissing her back pretty passionately, he noticed, and when she pulled back to murmur, "You might as well come inside," he followed without protest; indeed his penis was snagged halfway up in its blind grope toward the stars, all his chromosomes humming loudly, the silly fools, at this chance at immortality. It had been a long time since he had made love to anyone except Hiroko, and those encounters, though friendly and pleasant, were not passionate, more an extension of their bathing; whereas Phyllis, fumbling at their clothes as they fell onto her bed kissing, was clearly excited, and this excitement was transferring to Sax by a kind of immediate conduction. His erection sprang free eagerly from his pants as Phyllis got the pants down his legs, as if in illustration of the selfish gene theory, and he could only laugh and tug at the long ventral zipper of her jumpsuit. Lindholm, free of any worries, would certainly be aroused by the encounter. That was clear. And so he had to be too. And besides, although he did not especially like Phyllis, he did know her; there was that old First Hundred bond, the memories of those years together in Underhill—there was something provocative in the notion of making love to a woman he had known so long. And every one else in the First Hundred had been polygamous, it seemed, everyone but Phyllis and him. So now they were making up for it. And she was very attractive. And it was something, actually, just to be wanted.

All these rationalizations were easy in the moment itself, and indeed forgotten entirely in the rush of sexual sensation. But immediately upon completion of the act Sax began to worry again. Should he go back to his room, should he stay? Phyllis had fallen asleep with her hand on his flank, as if to assure herself that he would stay. In sleep everyone looked like a child. He surveyed the length of her body, shocked slightly once again by the various manifestations of sexual dimorphism. Breathing so calmly. Just to be wanted . . . her fingers, still tensed across his ribs. And so he stayed; but he did not sleep much.

Sax threw himself into the work on the glacier and the surrounding terrain. Phyllis went out in the field sometimes, but she was always discreet in her behavior with him; Sax doubted if Claire (or Jessica!) or anyone else realized what had happened—or realized that every few days, it was happening again. This was another complication; how would Lindholm react to Phyllis's apparent desire for secrecy? But in the end it was not an issue. Lindholm was more or less forced, as a matter of chivalry or compliance or something like that, to act as Sax would have. And so they kept their affair to themselves, much as they would have in Underhill, or on the *Ares*, or in Antarctica. Old habits die hard.

And with the distraction of the glacier, it was easy enough to keep the affair secret. The ice and the ribbed land around it were fascinating environments, and there was a lot to study and try to understand out there.

The surface of the glacier proved to be extremely broken, as the literature had suggested—mixed with regolith during the flooding, and shot through with trapped carbonation bubbles. Rocks and boulders caught on the surface had melted the ice underneath them, and then it had refrozen around them, in a daily cycle that had left them all about two-thirds submerged. All the seracs, standing above the jumbled surface of the glacier like titanic dolmens, were on close inspection found to be deeply pitted. The ice was brittle because of the extreme cold, and slow to flow downhill because of the reduced gravity; nevertheless it was moving downstream, like a river in slow motion, and because its source was emptied, the whole mass would eventually end up on Vastitas Borealis. And signs of this movement could be found in the newly broken ice seen every day—new crevasses, fallen seracs, cracked bergs. These fresh surfaces were quickly covered by crystalline ice flowers, whose saltiness only added to the speed of crystallization.

Fascinated by this environment, Sax got in the habit of going out by himself every day at dawn, following flagged trails the station crew had set out. In the first hour of the day all the ice glowed in vibrant pink and rose tones, reflecting tints of the sky. As direct sunlight struck the glacier's smashed surfaces, steam would begin to rise out of the cracks and iced-over pools, and the ice flowers glittered like gaudy jewelry. On windless mornings a small inversion layer trapped the mist some twenty meters overhead, forming a thin orange cloud. Clearly the glacier's water was diffusing fairly quickly out into the world.

As he hiked through the frigid air he spotted many different species of snow algae and lichen. The glacier-facing slopes of the two lateral ridges were especially well populated, flecked by small patches of green, gold, olive, black, rust, and many other colors—perhaps thirty or forty all told. Sax strolled over these pseudomoraines carefully, as unwilling to step on the plant life as he would be to step on any experiment in the lab. Although truthfully it looked as though most of the lichens would not notice. They were tough; bare rock and water were all they required, plus light—though not much of that appeared necessary—they grew under ice, inside ice, and even inside porous chunks of translucent rock. In something as hospitable as a crack in the moraine, they positively flourished. Every crack Sax looked in sported knobs of Iceland lichen, yellow and bronze, which under the glass revealed tiny forking stalks, fringed by spines. On flat rocks he found the crustose lichens: button lichen, stud lichen, shield lichen, *candellaria,* apple-green map lichen, and the red-orange jewel lichen that indicated a concentration of sodium nitrate in the regolith. Clumped under the ice flowers were growths of pale gray-green snow lichen, which under magnification proved to have stalks like the Iceland lichen, great masses of them looking delicate as lace. Worm lichen was dark gray, and under magnification revealed weathered antlers that appeared extremely delicate. And yet if pieces broke off, the algal cells enclosed in their fungal threads would simply keep growing, and develop into more lichen, attaching wherever they came to rest. Reproduction by fragmentation; useful indeed in such an environment.

So the lichen were prospering, and along with the species that Sax could identify, with the help of photos on his wristpad's little display screen, were many more that seemed not to correspond to any listed species. He was curious enough about these nondescripts to pluck a few samples, to take back and show to Claire and Jessica.

But lichen was only the beginning. On Earth, regions of broken rock newly exposed by retreating ice, or by the growth of young mountains, were called boulder fields, or talus. On Mars the equivalent zone was the regolith—thus effectively the greater part of the surface of the planet. Talus world. On Earth these regions were first colonized by microbacteria and lichen, which, along with chemical weathering, began to break the rock down into a thin immature soil, slowly filling the cracks between rocks.

In time there was enough organic material in this matrix to support other kinds of flora, and areas at this stage were called fellfields, *fell* being Gaelic for stone. It was an accurate name, for stone fields they were, the ground surface studded with rocks, the soil between and under them less than three centimeters thick, supporting a community of small ground-hugging plants.

And now there were fellfields on Mars. Claire and Jessica suggested to Sax that he cross the glacier, and hike downstream along the lateral moraine, and so one morning (slipping away from Phyllis) he did so, and after half an hour's hiking, stopped on a knee-high boulder. Below him, sloping into the rocky trough next to the glacier, was a wet patch of flat ground, twinkling in the late-morning light. Clearly meltwater ran over it most days—already in the utter stillness of the morning he could hear the drips of little streams under the glacier's edge, sounding like a choir of tiny wooden chimes. And on this miniature watershed, among the threads of running water, were spots of color, everywhere, leaping out at the eye— flowers. A patch of fellfield, then, with its characteristic *millefleur* effect, the gray waste peppered with dots of red, blue, yellow, pink, white. . . .

The flowers were mounted on little mossy cushions or florettes, or tucked among hairy leaves. All the plants hugged the dark ground, which would be markedly warmer than the air above it; nothing but grass blades stuck higher than a few centimeters off the soil. He tiptoed carefully from rock to rock, unwilling to step on even a single plant. He knelt on the gravel to inspect some of the little growths, the magnifying lenses on his faceplate at their highest power. Glowing vividly in the morning light were the classic fellfield organisms: moss campion, with its rings of tiny pink flowers on dark green pads; a phlox cushion; five-centimeter sprigs of blue-grass, like glass in the light, using the phlox taproot to anchor its own delicate roots . . . there was a magenta alpine primrose, with its yellow eye and its deep green leaves, which formed narrow troughs to channel water down into the rosette. Many of the leaves of these plants were hairy. There was an intensely blue forget-me-not, the petals so suffused with warming anthocyanins that they were nearly purple—the color that the Martian sky would achieve at around 230 millibars, according to Sax's calculations on the drive to Arena. It was surprising there was no name for that color, it was so distinctive. Perhaps that was cyanic blue.

The morning passed as he moved very slowly from plant to plant, using his wristpad's field guide to identify sandwort, buckwheat, pussy-paws, dwarf lupines, dwarf clovers, and his namesake, saxifrage. Rock breaker. He had never seen one in the wild before, and he spent a long time looking at the first one he found: arctic saxifrage, *Saxifraga hirculus*, tiny branches covered with long leaves, ending in small pale blue flowers.

As with the lichens, there were many plants that he couldn't identify; they exhibited features from different species, even genuses, or else they were completely nondescript, their features an odd melange of features from exotic biospheres, some looking like underwater growths, or new kinds of cacti. Engineered species, presumably, although it was surprising these weren't listed in the guide. Mutants, perhaps. Ah but there, where a wide crack had collected a deeper layer of humus and a tiny rivulet, was a clump of kobresia. Kobresia and the other sedges grew where it was wet, and their extremely absorbent turf chemically altered the soil under it quite rapidly, performing important work in the slow transition from fellfield to alpine meadow. Now that he had spotted it he could see minuscule watercourses marked by their population of sedges, running down through the rocks. Kneeling on a thinsulate pad, Sax clicked off his magnifying glasses and looked around, and as low as he was, he could suddenly see a whole series of little fellfields, scattered on the slope of the moraine like patches of Persian carpet, shredded by the passing ice.

Back at the station Sax spent a lot of time sequestered in the labs, looking at plant specimens through microscopes, running a variety of tests, and talking about the results to Berkina and Claire and Jessica.

"They're mostly polyploids?" Sax asked.

"Yes," Berkina said.

Polyploidy was fairly frequent at high altitudes on Earth, so it was not surprising. It was an odd phenomenon—a doubling or tripling or even quadrupling of the original chromosome number in a plant. Diploid plants, with ten chromosomes, would be succeeded by polyploids with twenty or thirty or even forty chromosomes. Hybridizers had used the phenomenon for years to develop fancy garden plants, because polyploids were usually larger—larger leaves, flowers, fruits, cell sizes—and they often had a wider range than their parents. That kind of adaptability made them better at occupying new areas, like the spaces in and under a glacier. There were islands in the Terran Arctic where eighty percent of the plants were polyploid. Sax supposed that it was a strategy to avoid the destructive effects of excessive mutation rates, which would explain why it occurred in high-UV areas. Intense UV irradiation would break a number of genes, but if they were replicated in the other sets of chromosomes, then there was likely to be no genotypic damage, and no impediment to reproduction.

"We find that even when we haven't started with polyploids, which we usually do, they change within a few generations."

"Have you identified the triggering mechanism that causes it?"

"No."

Another mystery. Sax stared into the microscope, vexed by this rather astonishing gap in the bizarrely rent fabric of biological science. But there was nothing to be done about it; he had looked into the matter himself in his Echus Overlook labs in the 2050s, and it had appeared that polyploidy was indeed stimulated by more UV radiation than the organism was used to, but how cells read this difference, and then actually doubled or tripled or quadrupled their chromosome count . . .

"I must say, I'm surprised at how much everything is flourishing."

Claire smiled happily. "I was afraid that after Earth you might think this was pretty barren."

"Well, no." He cleared his throat. "I guess I expected nothing. Or just algae and lichen. But those fellfields seem to be thriving. I thought it would take longer."

"It would on Earth. But you have to remember, we're not just throwing seeds out there and waiting to see what happens. Every single species has been augmented to increase hardiness and speed of growth."

"And we've been reseeding every spring," Berkina said, "and fertilizing with nitrogen-fixing bacteria."

"I thought it was denitrifying bacteria that were all the rage."

"Those are distributed specifically in thick deposits of sodium nitrate, to transpire the nitrogen into the atmosphere. But where we're gardening we need more nitrogen in the soil, so we spread nitrogen-fixers."

"It still seems to be going very fast to me. And all of this must have happened before the soletta."

"The thing is," Jessica said from her desk across the room, "there isn't any competition at this point. Conditions are harsh, but these are very hardy plants, and when we put them out there, there isn't any competition to slow them down."

"It's an empty niche," Claire said.

"And conditions here are better than most places on Mars," Berkina added. "In the south you've got the aphelion winter, and the high altitude. The stations down there report that the winterkill is just devastating. But here the perihelion winter is a lot milder, and we're only a kilometer high. It's pretty benign, really. Better than Antarctica in many ways."

"Especially in the CO_2 level," Berkina said. "I wonder if that doesn't account for some of that speed you're talking about. It's like the plants are being supercharged."

"Ah," Sax said, nodding.

So the fellfields were gardens. Aided growth rather than natural growth. He had known that, of course—it was a given everywhere on Mars—but the fellfields, so rocky and diffuse, had looked spontaneous and wild enough to momentarily confuse him. And even remembering they were gardens, he was still surprised that they were so vigorous.

"Well, and now with this soletta pouring sunlight onto the surface!" Jessica exclaimed. She shook her head, as if disapproving. "Natural insolation averaged forty-five percent of Earth's, and with the soletta it's supposed to be up to fifty-four."

"Tell me more about the soletta," Sax said carefully.

They told him in a kind of round. A group of transnationals, led by Subarashii, had built a circular slatted array of solar sail mirrors, placed between the sun and Mars and aligned to focus inward sunlight that would have just missed the planet. An annular support mirror, rotating in a polar orbit, reflected light back to the soletta to counterbalance the pressure of the sunlight, and that light was bounced back onto Mars as well. Both these mirror systems were truly huge compared to the early freighter sails Sax had enlisted to reflect light onto the surface, and the reflected light they were adding to the system was really significant. "It must have cost a fortune to build them," Sax murmured.

"Oh, it did. The big transnats are investing like you can't believe."

"And they're not done yet," Berkina said. "They're planning to fly an aerial lens just a few hundred kilometers above the surface, and this lens will focus some of the incoming light from the soletta, until it heats the surface up to fantastic temperatures, like five thousand degrees—"

"Five thousand!"

"Yes, I think that's what I heard. They plan to melt the sand and the regolith underneath, which will release all the volatiles into the atmosphere."

"But what about the surface?"

"They plan to do it in remote areas."

"In lines," Claire said. "So that they end up with ditches?"

"Canals," Sax said.

"Yes, that's right." They laughed.

"Glass-sided canals," Sax said, troubled by the thought of all those volatiles. Carbon dioxide would be prominent among them, perhaps chief among them.

But he did not want to show too much interest in the larger terraforming issues. He let it go, and soon enough the talk returned to their work. "Well," Sax said, "I guess some of the fellfields will turn into alpine meadows pretty soon."

"Oh, they're already there," Claire said.

"Really!"

"Yes, well, they're small. But hike down the western edge about three kilometers, have you done that yet? You'll see. Alpine meadows and krummholz too. It hasn't been that difficult. We planted trees without even altering them very much, because a lot of spruce and pine species turned out to have temperature tolerances much lower than they needed in their Terran habitats."

"That's peculiar."

"A holdover from the Ice Ages, I guess. But now it's coming in handy."

"Interesting," Sax said.

And he spent the rest of that day staring into the microscopes without seeing a thing, lost in thought. Life is so much spirit, Hiroko used to say. It was a very strange business, the vigor of living things, their tendency to proliferate, what Hiroko called their green surge, their viriditas. A striving toward pattern: it made him so *curious*.

• • •

When dawn arrived the next day he woke up in Phyllis's bed, with Phyllis tangled in the sheets beside him. After dinner the whole group had retired to the observation room, as was becoming habitual, and Sax had continued the conversation with Claire and Jessica and Berkina, and Jessica had been very friendly to him, as was her wont, and Phyllis had seen this, and had followed him to the bathrooms by the elevator, and pounced on him with that shocking seductive embrace of hers, and they had ended up going down to the dorm floor, and to her room. And although Sax had felt uncomfortable about disappearing without saying good-night to the others, he had made love to her passionately enough.

Now, looking at her, he remembered their precipitate departure with distaste. It did not take any more than the most simple-minded sociobiology to explain such behavior: competition for mates, a very basic animal activity. Of course Sax had never been the subject of such competition before, but there was nothing to pride oneself on in this sudden manifestation; clearly it was happening because of Vlad's cosmetic surgery, which through some chance had rearranged his face into a configuration appealing to women. Although why one arrangement of facial features should be more attractive than another was a total mystery to him. He had heard sociobiological explanations of sexual attractiveness before, and he could see that some of them might have some validity: a man would look for a mate with wide hips to be able safely to give birth to his children, with significant breasts in order to feed his children, etc.; a woman would look for a strong man to feed her children and to father strong children, etc., etc. That made a kind of sense; but none of it had anything to do with facial features. For them, sociobiological explanations got pretty tenuous: wide-set eyes for good eyesight, good teeth to aid health, a significant nose to avoid getting colds—no. It just wasn't as sensible as that. It was a matter of chance configurations, somehow appealing to the eye. An aesthetic judgment in which tiny nonfunctional features could make a great difference, which indicated that practical concerns were not a factor. A case in point was a pair of twin sisters with whom Sax had gone to high school—they had been identical twins, and had looked very much alike, and yet somehow one had been plain while the other had been beautiful. No, it was a matter of millimeters of flesh and bone and cartilage, accidentally falling into patterns that pleased or did not. So Vlad had made some alterations to his face, and now women were competing for his attentions, though he was the same person he had always been. A person Phyllis had never shown the slightest interest in before, when he had looked the way nature had made him. It was hard not to be somewhat cynical about it. To be wanted, yes; but wanted for trivialities. . . .

He got out of bed and suited up in one of the latest lightweight suits, so much more comfortable than the old stretch-fabric walkers; one had to insulate against the subfreezing temperatures, and wear a helmet and air-tank of course, but there was no longer any need to provide pressure to avoid bruising of the skin. Even 160 millibars was enough for that, and so now it was only a matter of warm clothing and boots, and the helmet. So it only took a few minutes to dress, and then he was out to the glacier again.

He crunched over the hoarfrost on the main flagged trail across the river of ice, and then wound downstream on the western bank, passing the little *millefleur* fellfields, coated with frost that was already beginning to melt in the light. He came to a place where the glacier dropped down a small escarpment, in a short crazed icefall; it also took a few degrees' turn to the left, following its bordering ribs. Suddenly a loud creak filled the air, followed by a low-frequency boom that vibrated in his stomach. The ice was moving. He stopped, listening. He heard the distant bell-sound of an under-ice stream. He hiked on, feeling lighter and happier with every step. The morning light was very clear, the steam on the ice like white smoke.

And then, in the shelter of some huge boulders, he came upon an amphitheater of fellfield, dotted with flowers like flecks of paint; and at the bottom of the field was a little alpine meadow, south-facing and shockingly green, the mats of grass and sedge all cut with ice-coated watercourses. And around the edges of the amphitheater, sheltered in cracks and under rocks, hunched a number of dwarf trees.

It was krummholz, then, which in the evolution of mountain landscapes was the next stage after alpine meadows. The dwarf trees he had spotted were actually members of ordinary species, mostly white spruce, *Picea glauca,* which in these harsh conditions miniaturized on their own, contouring into the protected spaces they sprouted in. Or had been planted in, more likely. Sax saw some lodgepole pine, *Pinus contorta,* joining the more numerous white spruce. These were the most cold-tolerant trees on Earth, and apparently the Biotique team had added salt tolerance from trees like the tamarisks. All kinds of engineering had been done to aid them, and yet still the extreme conditions stunted their growth, until trees that might have grown thirty meters high crouched in little knee-high pockets of protection, sheered off by winds and winter snowpacks as if by hedge clippers. Thus the name *krummholz,* German for "crooked wood" or perhaps "elfin wood"—the zone where trees first managed to take advantage of the soil-building work of fellfields and alpine meadows. Treelimit.

Sax wandered slowly around the amphitheater, stepping on rocks, inspecting the mosses, the sedges, the grasses, and every single individual tree. The gnarly little things were twisted as if cultivated by deranged bonsai gardeners. "Oh how nice," he said out loud more than once, inspecting a branch or a trunk, or a pattern of laminate bark, peeling away like phyllo dough. "Oh how nice. Oh for some moles. Some moles and voles, and marmots and minxes and foxes."

But the CO_2 in the atmosphere was still nearly thirty percent of the air, perhaps fifty millibars all by itself. All mammals would die very quickly in such air. This was why he had always resisted the two-stage terraforming model, which called for a massive CO_2 buildup to precede anything else. As if warming the planet were the only goal! But warming was not the goal. Animals on the surface was the goal. This was not only a good in itself, but good also for the plants, many of which needed animals. Most of these fellfield plants propagated on their own, of course, and there were some altered insects that Biotique had released, out there bumbling around in stubborn insect survivalist mode, half alive and only just managing their work of pollination. But there were many other symbiotic ecological functions that needed animals, like the soil aeration accomplished by moles and voles, or the spread of seeds by birds, and without them plants could not thrive, and some would not live at all. No, they needed to reduce the CO_2 in the air, probably right back to the ten millibars it had been when they arrived, when it had been the only air there was. Which was why the plan his colleagues had mentioned, to melt the regolith with an aerial lens, was so troubling. It would only increase their problem.

Meanwhile, this unexpected beauty. Hours passed as he inspected specimens one by one, admiring in particular the spiraling trunk and branches, the flaking bark and sprays of needles, of one little lodgepole pine—like a piece of flamboyant sculpture, really. And he was down on his knees, with his face in a sedge and his butt in the air, when Phyllis and Claire and a whole group came trooping down into the meadow, laughing at him and trampling carelessly on the living grass.

Phyllis stayed with him that afternoon, as she had one or two times before, and they walked back together, Sax trying at first to play the role of native guide, pointing out plants he had just learned the previous week. But Phyllis asked no questions about them, and did not appear even to listen when he spoke. It seemed she only wanted him to be an audience to her, a witness to her life. So he gave up on the plants and asked questions, and listened and then asked more. It was a good opportunity to learn more about the current Martian power structure, after all. Even if she exaggerated her own role in it, it was still informative. "I was amazed how fast Subarashii got the new elevator built and into position," she said.

"Subarashii?"

"They were the principal contractor."

"Who awarded the contract, UNOMA?"

"Oh no. UNOMA has been replaced by the UN Transitional Authority."

"So when you were president of the Transitional Authority, you were in effect president of Mars."

"Well, the presidency just rotates among the members, it doesn't confer much more power than any other members have. It's just for media consumption, and to run the meetings. Scut work."

"Still . . ."

"Oh, I know." She laughed. "It's a position a lot of my old colleagues wanted but never got. Chalmers, Bogdanov, Boone, Toitovna—I wonder what they would have thought if they had seen it. But they backed the wrong horse."

Sax looked away from her. "So why did Subarashii get the new elevator?"

"The steering committee of the TA voted that way. Praxis had made a bid for it, and no one likes Praxis."

"Now that the elevator is back, do you think things will change again?"

"Oh certainly! Certainly! A lot of things have been on hold since the unrest. Emigration, building, terraforming, commerce—they've all been slowed down. We've barely managed to rebuild some of the damaged towns. It's been a kind of martial law, necessary of course, given what happened."

"Of course."

"But now! All the stockpiled metals from the last forty years are ready to enter the Terran market, and that's going to stimulate the entire two-world economy unbelievably. We'll see more production out of Earth now, and more investment here, more emigration too. We're finally ready to get on with things."

"Like the soletta?"

"Exactly! That's a perfect example of what I mean. There's all kinds of plans for major investment here."

"Glass-sided canals," Sax said. It would make the moholes look trivial.

Phyllis was saying something about how bright things looked for Earth, and he shook his head to clear it of joules per square centimeter. He said, "But I thought Earth had some serious difficulties."

"Oh, Earth always has serious difficulties. We're going to have to get used to that. No, I'm very optimistic. I mean this recession has hit them hard down there, especially the little tigers and the baby tigers, and of course the less developed countries. But the influx of industrial metals from here will stimulate the economy for everyone, including the environment-control industries. And, unfortunately, it looks like the diebacks will solve a lot of their other problems for them."

Sax focused on the section of moraine they were climbing. Here solifluction, the daily melting of ground ice on a tilt, had caused the loose regolith to slide down in a series of dips and rims, and although it all looked gray and lifeless, a faint pattern like minuscule tiling revealed that it was actually covered with blue-gray flake lichen. In the dips there were clumps of what looked like gray ash, and Sax stooped to pluck a small sample. "Look," he said brusquely to Phyllis, "snow liverwort."

"It looks like dirt."

"That's a parasitic fungus that grows on it. The plant is actually green, see those little leaves? That's new growth that the fungus hasn't covered yet." Under magnification the new leaves looked like green glass.

But Phyllis didn't bother to look. "Who designed that one?" she asked, her tone of voice implying that the designer had poor taste.

"I don't know. Could be no one. Quite a few of the new species out here weren't designed."

"Can evolution be working so fast?"

"Well, you know—is polyploidy evolution?"

"No."

Phyllis moved on, not much interested in the gray little specimen. Snow liverwort. Probably very lightly engineered, or even undesigned. Test specimens, cast out here among the rest to see how they would do. And thus very interesting, in Sax's opinion.

But somewhere along the way Phyllis had lost interest. She had been a first-rate biologist once, and Sax found it hard to imagine losing the curiosity which lay at the core of science, that urge to figure things out. But they were getting old. In the course of their now unnatural lives it was likely they would all change, perhaps profoundly. Sax didn't like the idea, but there it was. Like all the rest of the new centenarians, he was having more and more trouble remembering specifics from his past, especially the middle years, things that had happened between the ages of around twenty-five to ninety. Thus the years before '61, and most of his years on Earth, were getting dim. And without fully functioning memories, they were certain to change.

So when they returned to the station he went to the lab, disturbed. Perhaps, he thought, they had gone polyploidal, not as individuals but culturally—an international array, arriving here and effectively quadrupling the meme strands, providing the adaptability to survive in this alien terrain despite all the stress-induced mutations. . . .

But no. That was analogy rather than homology. What in the humanities they would call a heroic simile, if he understood the term, or a metaphor, or some other kind of literary analogy. And analogies were mostly meaningless—a matter of phenotype rather than genotype (to use another analogy). Most of poetry and literature, really all the humanities, not to mention the social sciences, were phenotypic as far as Sax could tell. They added up to a huge compendium of meaningless analogies, which did not help to explain things, but only distorted perception of them. A kind of continuous conceptual drunkenness, one might say. Sax himself much preferred exactitude and explanatory power, and why not? If it was 200 Kelvin outside why not say so, rather than talk about witches' tits and the like, hauling the whole great baggage of the ignorant past along to obscure every encounter with sensory reality? It was absurd.

So, okay, there was no such thing as cultural polyploidy. There was just a determinate historical situation, the consequence of all that had come before—the decisions made, the results spreading out over the planet in complete disarray, evolving, or one should say developing, without a plan. Planless. In that regard there was a similarity between history and evolution, in that both of them were matters of contingency and accident, as well as patterns of development. But the differences, particularly in time scales, were so gross as to make that similarity nothing more than analogy again.

No, better to concentrate on homologies, those structural similarities that indicated actual physical relationships, that really *explained* something. This of course took one back into science. But after an encounter with Phyllis, that was just what he wanted.

So he dove back into studying plants. Many of the fellfield organisms he was finding had hairy leaves, and very thick leaf surfaces, which helped protect the plants from the harsh UV blast of Martian sunlight. These adaptations could very well be examples of homologies, in which species with the same ancestors had all kept family traits. Or they could be examples of convergence, in which species from separate phyla had come to the same forms through functional necessity. And these days they could also be simply the result of bioengineering, the breeders adding the same traits to different plants in order to provide the same advantages. Finding out which it was required identifying the plant, and then checking the records to see if it had been designed by one of the terraforming teams. There was a Biotique lab in Elysium, led by a Harry Whitebook, designing many of the most successful surface plants, especially the sedges and grasses, and a check in the Whitebook catalog often showed that his hand had been at work, in which case the similarities were often a matter of artificial convergence, Whitebook inserting traits like hairy leaves into almost every leaved plant he bred.

An interesting case of history imitating evolution. And certainly, since they wanted to create a biosphere on Mars in a short time, perhaps 10^7 times quicker than it had taken on Earth, they would have to intervene continuously in the act of evolution itself. So the Martian biosphere would not be a case of phylogeny recapitulating ontogeny, a discredited notion in any case, but of history recapitulating evolution. Or rather imitating it, to the extent possible given the Martian environment. Or even directing it. History *directing* evolution. It was a daunting thought.

Whitebook was going about the task with a lot of flair; he had bred phreatophytic lichen reefs, for instance, which built the salts they incorporated into a kind of millepore coral structure, so that the resulting plants were olive or dark green masses of semicrystalline blocks. Walking through a patch of them was like walking through a Lilliputian garden maze which had been crushed, abandoned, and half covered with sand. The individual blocks of the plant were fractured or fissured in a crackle pattern, and they were so lumpish they looked diseased, with a disease that appeared to petrify plants while they were still living, leaving them struggling to exist inside broken sheaths of malachite and jade. Strange-looking, but very successful; Sax found quite a few of these lichen reefs growing on the crest of the western moraine rib, and in the more arid regolith beyond.

He spent a few mornings studying them there, and one morning crossing the ridge he looked back over the glacier, and saw a sandy whirlwind spinning over the ice, a sparkling rust-colored little tornado that rushed downstream. Immediately afterward he was struck by a high wind, with gusts of at least a hundred kilometers an hour, and then a hundred and fifty; he ended up crouching behind a lichen reef, lifting a hand to try to estimate the wind speed. It was hard to make an accurate guess, because the thickening atmosphere had increased the force of winds, making them seem faster than they really were. All estimates based on the instincts from the Underhill days were now badly off. The gusts striking him now might have been as slow as eighty kilometers an hour. But full of sand, ticking against his faceplate and reducing visibility to a hundred meters or so. After an hour of waiting for the sandstorm to decrease he gave up and returned to the station, crossing the glacier by moving very carefully from flag to flag, careful not to lose the trail they made—important, if one wanted to stay out of dangerous crevasse zones.

Once across the ice Sax made his way back to the station quickly, pondering the little tornado that had announced the arrival of the wind. Weather was strange. Inside he called up the meteorology channel, and ran through all its information on the day's weather, and then stared at a satellite photo of their region. A cyclonic cell was bearing down on them from Tharsis. With the air thickening, the winds coming off Tharsis were powerful indeed. The bulge would forever remain an anchoring point in Martian climatology, Sax suspected. Most of the time the northern hemisphere jet stream would circle up and around its northern end, like Terra's northern jet stream did around the Rockies. But every once in a while, air masses would shove over the Tharsis crest between volcanoes, dropping their moisture on west Tharsis as they rose. Then these dehydrated air masses would roar down the eastern slope, Big Man's mistral or sirocco or foehn, with winds so fast and forceful that as the atmosphere thickened they were getting to be a problem; some tent towns on the open surface were endangered to the point where it looked like they might have to retreat into craters or canyons, or at least greatly strengthen their tenting.

As Sax considered it the whole issue of weather became so exciting that he wanted to drop his botanical studies, and go after it full-time. In the old days he would have done that, and dived into climatology for a month or a year until his curiosity was satisfied, and he had managed to think of some contribution to policy regarding any problems that were arising.

But that had been a rather undisciplined approach, as he now saw, leading to a kind of scattershot method, even to a certain dilettantism. Now, as Stephen Lindholm, working for Claire and Biotique, he had to abandon climatology with a longing glance at the satellite photos and their suggestively swirling new cloud systems, and merely tell the others about the whirlwind, and talk about weather in a recreational way in the lab or over dinner—while his main effort returned to their little ecosystem and its plants, and how to help them along. And as he was just beginning to feel he was learning the particularities of Arena, these restrictions imposed by his new identity were not a bad thing. They meant he was forced to concentrate on a single discipline in a way he hadn't since his postdoc work. And the rewards of concentration were becoming more and more evident to him. They could make him a better scientist.

The next day, for instance, with the winds merely brisk, he went back out and located the coral lichen patch he had been investigating when the sandstorm had hit. All the structure's fissures were filled with sand, which must have been true most of the time. So he brushed one of the fissures clean, and looked inside through the 20x magnifiers on his faceplate. The walls of the fissures were coated with very fine cilia, somewhat like the tiny versions of the hairs on exposed leaves of alpine cinquefoil. Clearly there was no need for protection of these already well-hidden surfaces. Perhaps they were there to release excess oxygen from the tissues of the semicrystalline outside mass. Spontaneous or planned? He read through descriptions on his wrist, and added a new one of this specimen, which because of the cilia appeared to be nondescript. He took out a little camera from his thigh pocket and took a picture, put a sample of the cilia in a bag, and put both camera and bag in his thigh pocket, and moved on.

He went down to look at the glacier, stepping onto it at one of the many junctures where its side came down and met smoothly the rising slope of the moraine rib. It was bright on the glacier at midday, as if bits of broken mirror were reflecting sunlight everywhere on it. Chunks of ice crunched underfoot. Little watersheds gathered to deep-channeled streams, which abruptly disappeared down holes in the ice. These holes, like the crevasses, were various shades of blue. The moraine ribs gleamed like gold, and seemed to bounce in the rising heat. Something in the sight reminded Sax of the soletta plan, and he whistled through his teeth.

He straightened up and stretched his lower back, feeling very alive and curious, absolutely in his element. The scientist at work. He was learning to like the ever-fresh primary effort of "natural history," its close observation of things in nature; description, categorization, taxonomy—the primal attempt to explain, or rather its first step, simply to describe. How happy the natural historians had always seemed to him in their writings, Linnaeus and his wild Latin, Lyell and his rocks, Wallace and Darwin and their great step from category to theory, from observation to paradigm. Sax could feel it, right there on Arena Glacier in the year 2101, with all these new species, this flourishing process of speciation that was half human and half Martian—a process that would need its own theories eventually, some kind of evohistory, or historico-evolution, or ecopoesis, or simply areology. Or Hiroko's viriditas, perhaps. Theories of the terraforming project—not only in what it intended, but how it was actually working.

A natural history, precisely. Very little of what was happening could be studied with experimental lab science, so natural history was going to return to its proper place among the sciences, as one among equals. Here on Mars all kinds of hierarchies were destined to fall, and that was no meaningless analogy, but simply a precise observation of what all could see.

What all could see. Would he have understood, before his time out here? Would Ann understand? Looking down the wild cracked surface of the glacier, he found himself thinking of her. Every little berg and crevasse stood out as if he still had the 20x magnification on in his faceplate, but with an infinite depth of field—every tint of ivory and pink in the pocked surfaces, every mirror gleam of meltwater, the bumpy hillocks of the far horizon—everything was, for the moment, surgically clear and focused. And it occurred to him that this vision was not a matter of accident (the lensing of tears over his cornea, for instance) but the result of a new and growing conceptual understanding of the landscape. It was a kind of cognitive vision, and he could not help but remember Ann saying angrily to him, *Mars is the place you have never seen.*

He had taken it as a figure of speech. But now he recalled Kuhn, asserting that scientists who used different paradigms existed in literally different worlds, epistemology being such an integral component of reality. Thus Aristoteleans simply did not see the Galilean pendulum, which to them was a body falling with some difficulty; and in general, scientists debating the relative merits of competing paradigms simply talked right through each other, using the same words to discuss different realities.

He had considered that too to be a figure of speech. But thinking of it now, absorbing the hallucinatory clarity of the ice, he had to admit that it certainly described what his conversations with Ann had always felt like. It had been a frustration to both of them, and when Ann had cried out that he had never seen Mars, a statement that was obviously false on some levels, she had perhaps meant only to say that he hadn't seen *her* Mars, the Mars created by her paradigm. And that was no doubt true.

Now, however, he was seeing a Mars he had never seen before. But the transformation had come by focusing for a matter of weeks on just those parts of the Martian landscape that Ann despised, the new life-forms. So he doubted that the Mars he was seeing, with its snow algae and ice lichen, and the enchanting little patches of Persian carpet fringing the glacier, was Ann's Mars. Nor was it the Mars of his colleagues in terraforming. It was a function of what he believed, and what he wanted—it was *his Mars,* evolving right before his very eyes, always in the process of becoming something new. Like a stab to the heart he felt the wish that he could seize Ann at that very moment, and pull her by the arm down the western moraine crying, See? See? See?

·   ·   ·

Instead he had Phyllis, perhaps the least philosophical person he had ever known. He avoided her when he could do it without appearing to, and passed his days on the ice, in the wind under the vast northern sky, or on the moraines, crawling around studying plants. Back in the station he talked over dinner with Claire and Berkina and the rest about what they were finding out there, and what it meant. After dinner they retired to the observation room and talked some more, dancing on some nights, especially Fridays and Saturdays. The music they played was always nuevo calypso, guitars and steel drums in fast simultaneous melodies, creating complex rhythms that Sax had great difficulty analyzing. There were often measures of 5/4 time alternating or even coexisting with 4/4, a pattern seemingly designed to throw him out of step. Luckily the current dance style was a kind of free-form movement that had little relation to the beat anyway, so when he failed in his attempts to stay in rhythm, he was pretty sure he was the only one who noticed. In fact it made a pretty good entertainment just trying to keep time, off on his own, hopping around with a little jig added to the 5/4 measures. When he returned to the tables and Jessica said to him, "You're really a good dancer, Stephen," he burst out laughing, pleased even though he knew all it revealed was Jessica's incompetence to judge dance, or her attempt to please him. Although perhaps the daily boulder-walking in the field was improving his balance and timing. Any physical action, properly studied and practiced, could no doubt be accomplished with a reasonable amount of skill, if not flair.

He and Phyllis talked or danced together only as much as they did with everyone else; and only in the secrecy of their rooms did they embrace, kiss, make love. It was the old pattern of the hidden affair, and one morning around four A.M., returning to his room from hers, a flash of fear shook him; it seemed to him suddenly that his immediate undiscussed complicity in this behavior must tag him to Phyllis as suspiciously like one of the First Hundred. Who else would fall into such a bizarre pattern so readily, as if it were the natural thing to do?

But on consideration it did not seem that Phyllis was attentive to nuances of that kind. Sax had almost given up trying to understand her thinking and her motivations, as the data were contradictory and, despite the fact that they were spending nights together on a fairly regular basis, rather sparse. She seemed interested mostly in the intertransnational maneuvering that was going on in Sheffield, and back on Earth—shifts in executive personnel and subsidiaries and stock prices that were clearly ephemeral and meaningless, but to her utterly absorbing. As Stephen he remained brightly interested in all this, and asked her questions about it to show his interest when she brought it up, but when he asked about what the daily changes meant in any larger strategic sense, she was either unable or unwilling to give him good answers. Apparently it was interesting to her more for the personal fortunes of those she knew than for the system that their careers revealed. An ex–Consolidated executive now with Subarashii had been made head of elevator operations, a Praxis executive had disappeared in the outback, Armscor was going to explode scores of hydrogen bombs in the megaregolith under the north polar cap, to stimulate growth and warming of the northern sea; and this last fact was no more interesting to her than the two previous ones.

And perhaps it made sense to pay attention to the individual careers of the people running the biggest transnationals, and the micropolitics of the jockeying for power among them. These were the current rulers of the world, after all. So Sax lay next to Phyllis, listening to her and making Stephen's comments, trying to sort out all the names, wondering if the founder of Praxis really was a senile surfer, wondering if Shellalco would be taken over by Amexx, wondering why the transnat executive teams were so fiercely competitive, given that they already ruled the world, and had everything they could conceivably want in their personal lives. Perhaps sociobiology indeed had the answer, and it was all primate dominance dynamics, a matter of increasing one's reproductive success in the corporate realm—which might not be a mere analogy, if one considered one's company as one's kin. And then again, in a world where one might live indefinitely, it could be simple self-protection. "Survival of the fittest," which Sax had always considered a useless tautology. But if social Darwinists were taking over, then maybe the concept gained importance, as a religious dogma of the ruling order. . . .

And then Phyllis would roll over onto him and kiss him, and he would enter the realm of sex, where different rules seemed to obtain. For instance, though he liked Phyllis less and less as he got to know her better, his attraction to her did not correlate to this, but fluctuated according to mysterious principles of its own, no doubt pheromone-driven and hormonally based; so that sometimes he had to steel himself to accept her touches, while other times he felt alive with a lust that seemed all the stronger because it was so unmixed with affection. Or more senseless still, a lust actually heightened by dislike. This last reaction was rare, however, and as the stay at Arena went on, and the novelty of their affair wore off, Sax more and more frequently found himself distanced from their lovemaking, and inclined to fantasize during it, and fall very deeply into Stephen Lindholm, who appeared to be thinking about caressing women Sax did not know or had scarcely heard of, like Ingrid Bergman or Marilyn Monroe.

One dawn, after a disturbing night of that sort, Sax got up to go out on the ice, and Phyllis stirred and woke, and decided to come along.

They suited up and went out into a pure purple dawn, and hiked in silence down the near moraine to the side of the glacier, ascending it by a trail of steps cut into the ice. Sax took the southernmost flagged trail across the glacier, intending to climb the west lateral moraine as far upstream as he could go in a morning.

They made their way between knee-high crenellations of ice, all holed like Swiss cheese, and stained pink with snow algae. Phyllis was charmed as always by the fantastic jumble, and commented on the more unusual seracs, comparing those they passed this morning to a giraffe, the Eiffel Tower, the surface of Europa, etc. Sax stopped often to inspect chunks of jade ice that were shot through with an ice bacteria. In one or two places the jade ice sat exposed in suncups turned pink with snow algae; the effect was strange, something like a vast field of pistachio ice cream.

So their progress was slow, and they were still on the glacier when a sequence of small tight whirlwinds popped into existence one after the next, like something out of a magic trick: brown dust devils, glittering with ice particulates, in a rough line that bore down the glacier toward them. Then the whirlwinds collapsed in some fluctuation, and with a clattery bang a gust struck them hard, whistling downslope with a surge so powerful they had to crouch into it to keep their balance. "What a gale!" Phyllis exclaimed in his ear.

"Katabatic wind," Sax said, watching a knot of seracs disappear in the dust. "Falling off Tharsis." Visibility was dropping. "We should try to get back to the station."

So they set off back along the flagged trail, moving from one emerald dot to the next. But visibility continued to decrease, until they couldn't see from one marker to the next. Phyllis said, "Here, let's get into the shelter of those icebergs."

She struck off toward the dim shape of an ice prominence, and Sax hurried after her, saying, "Be careful, a lot of seracs have crevasses at their base," and reaching forward to take her hand, when she dropped as if falling through a trap door. He caught an upflung wrist and was jerked down hard, hitting his knees painfully on the ice. Phyllis was still falling, sliding down a chute at the end of a shallow crevasse; he should have let go of her but instinctively held on, and was dragged over the edge head first. Both of them slid down into the packed snow at the bottom of the crevasse, and the snow gave under them so that they dropped again, crashing onto frosty sand after a brief but terrifying free-fall.

Sax, having landed mostly on Phyllis, sat up unhurt. Alarming sucking sounds came over the intercom from Phyllis, but it soon became clear that she had only had the wind knocked out of her. When she controlled her gasping she tested her limbs gingerly, and declared she was okay. Sax admired her toughness.

There was a rip in the fabric over his right knee, but otherwise he was fine. He took some suit tape from his thigh pocket and taped the rip; the knee still bent without pain, so he forgot about it and stood.

The hole that they had punched through the snow above them was about two meters over his outstretched hand. They were in an elongated bubble, the lower half of a crevasse that had a kind of hourglass shape. The downstream wall of their little bubble was ice, the upstream wall ice-coated rock. The rough circle of visible sky overhead was an opaque peach color, and the bluish ice wall of the crevasse gleamed with reflections of the dusty sunlight, so that the net effect was somewhat opalescent, and quite picturesque. But they were stuck.

"Our beeper signal will be cut off, and then they'll come looking," Sax said to Phyllis as she stood up beside him.

"Yes," Phyllis said. "But will they find us?"

Sax shrugged. "The beeper leaves a directional record."

"But the wind! Visibility may go right down to nothing!"

"We'll have to hope they can deal with it."

The crevasse extended to the east like a narrow low hallway. Sax ducked under a low point, and shone his headlamp down the space between ice and rock; it extended for as far as he could see, in the direction of the east side of the glacier. It seemed possible that it might reach all the way to one of the many small caves on the glacier's lateral edge, so after sharing the thought with Phyllis he set off to explore the crevasse, leaving her in position to be sure that any searchers who found the hole would also find someone at the bottom of it.

Outside the glary cone of his headlamp's beam, the ice was an intense cobalt blue, an effect caused by the same Rayleigh scattering that blued the color of the sky. There was a fair amount of light even with his headlamp off, which suggested that the ice overhead was not very thick. Probably the same approximate thickness as the height of their fall, now that he thought of it.

Phyllis's voice in his ear asked if he was all right.

"I'm fine," he said. "I think this space might have been caused by the glacier running over a transverse escarpment. So it very well might run all the way out."

But it didn't. A hundred meters farther on, the ice on the left closed in and met the ice over the rockface to the right, and that was it: dead end.

On the way back he walked more slowly, stopping to inspect cracks in the ice, and bits of rock underfoot that had perhaps been plucked from the escarpment. In one fissure the cobalt of the ice turned blue-green, and reaching into it with a gloved finger, he pulled out a long dark green mass, frozen on the surface but soft underneath. It was a long dentritic mass of blue-green algae.

"Wow," he said, and plucked a few frozen strands away, then shoved the rest back into their home crack. He had read that algae were burrowing down into the rock and ice of the planet, and bacteria were going even deeper; but actually to find some buried down here, so far from the sun, was enough to make one marvel. He turned off his headlamp again, and the luminous cobalt blue of the glacial light glowed around him, dim and rich. So dark, so cold, how did any living thing do it?

"Stephen?"

"I'm coming. Look," he said to Phyllis when he returned to her side, "it's blue-green algae, all the way down here."

He held it out for her to look at, but she only gave it the briefest glance. He sat down and got out a sample bag from his thigh pocket, and put a small strand of algae inside, then stared at it through his 20x magnifying lenses. The lenses were not powerful enough to show him all he wanted to see, but they did reveal the long strands of dentritic green, looking slimy as they thawed out. His lectern had catalogs with photos at similar magnifications, but he couldn't find the species that resembled this one in every detail. "It could be nondescript," he said. "Wouldn't that be something. It really makes you wonder if the mutation rate out here is higher than the standard rates. We should work up experiments to determine that."

Phyllis did not reply.

Sax kept his thoughts to himself as he continued to search through the catalogs. He was still at it when they heard scratchy squeals and hisses over their radio, and Phyllis began calling out over the common band. Soon they could hear voices on the intercom, and not long after that, a round helmet filled the hole overhead. "We're here!" Phyllis cried.

"Wait a second," Berkina said, "we've got a rope ladder for you."

And after an awkward swinging climb they were back on the surface of the glacier, blinking in the dusty fluctuating daylight, and crouching over to meet the gusts of wind, which were still powerful. Phyllis was laughing, explaining what had happened in her usual manner—"We were holding hands so we didn't lose each other, and boom, down we went!"— and their rescuers were describing the brute force of the strongest gusts. All seemed back to normal; but when they got inside the station, and took off their helmets, Phyllis gave him a brief searching glance, a very curious look indeed, as if he had revealed something to her out there which had made her wary—as if he had somehow reminded her of something, down in that crevasse. As if he had behaved down there in a manner which gave him away, without hope of contradiction, as her old comrade Saxifrage Russell.

Through the northern fall they worked around the glacier, and saw the days grow shorter, and the winds colder. Big intricate ice flowers grew on the glacier every night, and only melted at the edges briefly in the midafternoons, after which they hardened and served as the base for even more complex petals that appeared the next morning, the small sharp crystalline flakes bursting away in every direction from the larger fins and tines beneath. They could not help crushing entire fractal worlds with every step as they crunch-crunched over the ice, looking for the plants now covered in frost, to see how they were coping with the coming cold. Looking across the bumpy white waste, feeling the wind cut through one of the thicker insulated walkers, it seemed to Sax that a very severe winterkill was inevitable.

But looks were deceptive. Oh there would be winterkill, of course; but the plants were hardening, as the overwintering gardeners called it, acclimatizing to the onset of winter. It was a three-stage process, Sax learned, digging in the thin hard-packed snow to find the signs. First, phytochrome clocks in the leaves sensed the shorter days—and now they were getting shorter fast, with dark fronts coming through every week or so, dumping dirty white snow out of black low-bellied cumulonimbus clouds. In the second stage, growth ceased, carbohydrates translocated to the roots, and amounts of abscisic acid grew in some leaves until they fell off. Sax found lots of these leaves, yellowed or brown and still hanging from their stems, hugging the ground and providing the yet living plant with some more insulation. During this stage water was moving out of cells into intercellular ice crystals, and the cell membranes were toughening, while sugar molecules replaced water molecules in some proteins. Then in the third and coldest stage, a smooth ice formed around the cells without rupturing them, in a process called vitrification.

At this point the plants could tolerate temperatures down to 220°K, which had been approximately the average temperature of Mars before their arrival, but was now about as cold as it got. And the snow which fell in the ever more frequent storms actually served as insulation for the plants, keeping the ground that it covered warmer than the windy surface. As he dug around in the snow with numbed fingers, the subnivean environment looked to Sax to be a fascinating place, especially the adaptations to the spectrally selected blue light that was transmitted through as much as three meters of snow—another example of Rayleigh scattering. He would have liked to study this winter world in person for the entire six months of the season; he found he liked it out under the low dark waves of cloud, on the white surface of the snowy glacier, leaning into the wind and stomping through drifts. But Claire wanted him to return to Burroughs, to work with the labs there on a tundra tamarisk they were close to succeeding with in the Mars jars. And Phyllis and the rest of the crew from Armscor and the Transitional Authority were going back as well. So one day they left the station to a little crew of researcher-gardeners, and got in a caravan of cars, and drove back south together.

Sax had groaned when he heard that Phyllis and her group would be going back with them. He had hoped that mere physical separation would end the relationship with Phyllis, and get him away from that probing eye. But as they were going back together, it looked like some sort of action would have to be taken. He would have to break it off if he wanted it to end, which he did. The whole idea of getting involved with her had been a bad one to begin with; talk about the surge of the unexplainable! But the surge was over, and he was left in the company of a person who was at best irritating, and at worst dangerous. And of course it was no comfort to think that he had been acting in bad faith the entire time. No step along the way had seemed more than a little thing; but altogether it came to something rather monstrous.

So their first night back in Burroughs, when his wrist beeped and Phyllis appeared to ask him out to dinner, he agreed and ended the call, and muttered to himself uneasily. It was going to be awkward.

They went out to a patio restaurant that Phyllis knew of on Ellis Butte, west of Hunt Mesa. Because of Phyllis they were seated at a corner table, with a view over the high district between Ellis and Table Mountain, where the woods of Princess Park were ringed by new mansions. Across the park Table Mountain was so glass-walled that it looked like a giant hotel, and the more distant mesas were not much less gaudy.

Waiters and waitresses brought by a carafe of wine, and then dinner, interrupting Phyllis's chatter, which was mostly about the new construction on Tharsis. But she seemed very willing to talk with the waiters and waitresses, signing napkins for them, and asking where they were from, how long they had been on Mars, and so forth. Sax ate steadily and watched Phyllis, and Burroughs, waiting for the meal to come to an end. It seemed to go on for hours.

But finally they were done, and taking the elevator ride to the valley floor. The elevator brought back memories of their first night together, which made Sax acutely uncomfortable. Perhaps Phyllis felt the same way, for she moved to the other side of the car, and the long descent passed in silence.

And then on the streetgrass of the boulevard she pecked him on the cheek with a swift hard hug, and said, "It's been a lovely evening, Stephen, and a lovely time out at Arena as well, I'll never forget our little adventure under the glacier. But now I have to get back up to Sheffield and deal with everything that's been piling up, you know. I hope you'll come visit me if you're ever up there."

Sax struggled to control his face, trying to figure out how Stephen would feel and what he would say. Phyllis was a vain woman, and it was possible she would forget the entire affair faster if she was avoiding thought about the hurt she had caused someone by dropping him, rather than brooding over why he had seemed so relieved. So he tried to locate the minority voice inside him that was offended to be treated in such a manner. He tightened the corners of his mouth, and looked down to the side. "Ah," he said.

Phyllis laughed like a girl, and caught him up in an affectionate hug. "Come on," she admonished him. "It's been fun, hasn't it? And we'll see each other again when I visit Burroughs, or if you ever come up to Sheffield. Meanwhile, what else can we do? Don't be sad."

Sax shrugged. This made such sense that it was hard to imagine any but the most lovelorn suitor objecting, and he had never pretended to be that. They were both over a hundred, after all. "I know," he said, and gave her a nervous, rueful smile. "I'm just sorry the time has come."

"I know." She kissed him again. "Me too. But we'll meet again, and then we'll see."

He nodded, looking down again, feeling a new appreciation for the difficulties actors faced. What to do?

But with a brisk good-bye she was off. Sax said his own good-bye to a look over the shoulder, a quick wave.

He walked across Great Escarpment Boulevard, toward Hunt Mesa. So that was that. Easier than he had thought it would be, certainly. In fact, extremely convenient. But a part of him was still irritated. He looked at his reflection in the shop windows he passed on the lower floors of Hunt. A raffish old geezer; handsome? Well, whatever that meant. Handsome for some women, sometimes. Picked up by one and used as a bed partner for a few weeks, then tossed aside when it was time to move on. Presumably it had happened to many another through the years, more often to women than to men, no doubt, given the inequalities of culture and reproduction. But now, with reproduction out of the picture, and the culture in pieces. . . . She really was rather awful. But then again he had no right to complain; he had agreed to it without conditions, and had lied to her from the very start, not only about who he was, but about how he felt toward her. And now he was free of it, and all that it implied. And all that it threatened.

Feeling a kind of nitrous oxide lift, he walked up Hunt's huge atrium staircase to his floor, and down the hall to his little apartment.

Late that winter, for a couple of weeks in 2 February, the annual conference on the terraforming project took place in Burroughs. It was the tenth such conference, titled by the organizers "M-38: New Results and New Directions," and it would be attended by scientists from all over Mars, nearly three thousand of them all told. The meetings were held in the big conference center in Table Mountain, while the visiting scientists stayed in hotels all over the city.

Everyone at Biotique Burroughs went over to attend the meetings, running back to Hunt Mesa if they had experiments running that they wanted to check in on. Sax was intensely interested in every aspect of the conference, naturally enough, and on its first morning he went down early to Canal Park and grabbed a coffee and pastry, and walked up to the conference center and was nearly the first in line at the check-in table. He took his packet of program information, pinned his name tag to his coat, and wandered through the halls outside the meeting rooms, sipping his coffee, reading the program for the morning, and glancing at the poster displays set in designated parts of the halls.

Here, and for the first time in more years than he could remember, Sax felt supremely in his element. Scientific conferences were all the same, at all times and in all places, even down to the way people dressed: the men in conservative, slightly shabby professorial jackets, all tans and browns and dark rust colors; the women, perhaps thirty percent of the total population, in unusually drab and severe business dress; many people still wearing spectacles, even though it was a rare vision problem that was not correctable by surgery; most of them carrying around their program packets; everyone with their name tag on their left lapel. Inside the darkened meeting rooms Sax passed talks that were beginning, and there too all was the same as ever: speakers standing before video screens that displayed their graphs and tables and molecular structures and so on, talking in stilted cadences timed to the rhythm of their images, using a pointer to indicate the parts of overcrowded diagrams that were relevant. . . . The audiences, composed of the thirty or forty colleagues most interested in the work being described, sat in rows of chairs next to their friends, listening closely and readying questions that they would ask at the end of the presentation.

For those fond of this world, it was a very pleasant sight. Sax poked his head into several of the rooms, but none of the talks intrigued him enough to draw him in, and soon he found himself in a hall full of poster displays, so he kept on browsing.

"Solubilization of Polycyclic Aromatic Hydrocarbons in Monomeric and Micellar Surfactant Solutions." "Post-Pumping Subsidence in Southern Vastitas Borealis." "Epithelial Resistance to Third-Stage Gerontological Treatment." "Incidence of Radial Fracture Aquifers in Impact Basin Rims." "Low-voltage Electroporation of Long Vector Plasmids." "Katabatic Winds in Echus Chasma." "Base Genome for a New Cactus Genera." "Resurfacing of the Martian Highlands in the Amenthes and Tyrrhena Region." "Deposition of the Nilosyrtis Sodium Nitrate Strata." "A Method for Assessing Occupational Exposure to Chlorophenates Through Analysis of Contaminated Work Clothing."

As always, the posters were a deliciously mixed bag. They were posters rather than talks for a variety of reasons—often the work of graduate students at the university in Sabishii, or concerned with topics peripheral to the conference—but anything might be there, and it was always very interesting to browse. And at this conference there had been no strong attempt to organize the posters into hallways by subject matter, so that "Distribution of *Rhizocarpon geographicum* in the East Charitum Montes," detailing the high-altitude fortunes of a crustose lichen that could live up to four thousand years, was facing "Origins of Graupel Snow in Saline Particulates Found in Cirrus, Altostratus and Altocumulus Clouds in Cyclonic Vortexes in North Tharsis," a meteorological study of some importance.

Sax was interested in everything, but the posters that held him the longest were those that described aspects of the terraforming that he had initiated, or once had a hand in. One of these, "Estimate of the Cumulative Heat Released by the Underhill Windmills," stopped him in his tracks. He read it through twice, feeling a slight dampening of spirits as he did.

The mean temperature of the Martian surface before their arrival had been around 220°K, and one of the universally agreed-upon goals of terraforming was to raise that mean temperature to something above the freezing point of water, which was 273°K. Raising the average surface temperature of an entire planet by more than 53°K was a very intimidating challenge, requiring, Sax had figured, the application over time of no less than 3.5×10^6 joules to every square centimeter of the Martian surface. Sax in his own modeling had always aimed to reach a mean of about 274°K, figuring that with this as the average, the planet would be warm enough for much of the year to create an active hydrosphere, and thus a biosphere. Many people advocated even more warming than that, but Sax did not see the need.

In any case, all methods for adding heat to the system were judged by how much they had raised the global mean temperature; and this poster examining the effect of Sax's little windmill heaters estimated that over seven decades they had added no more than 0.05°K. And he could find nothing wrong with the various assumptions and calculations in the model outlined in the poster. Of course heating was not the only reason he had distributed the windmills; he had also wanted to provide warmth and shelter for an early engineered cryptoendolith he had wanted to test on the surface. But all those organisms had in fact died immediately upon exposure, or shortly thereafter. So on the whole the project could not be said to be one of his better efforts.

He moved on. "Application of Process-Level Chemical Data in Hydrochemical Modeling: Dao Vallis Watershed, Hellas." "Increasing CO_2 Tolerance in Bees." "Epilimnetic Scavenging of Compton Fallout Radionuclides in the Marineris Glacial Lakes." "Clearing Fines from Piste Reaction Rails." "Global Warming As a Result of Released Halocarbons."

This last one stopped him again. The poster was the work of the atmospheric chemist S. Simmon and some of his students, and reading it made Sax feel considerably better. When Sax had been made head of the terraforming project in 2042, he had immediately initiated the construction of factories to produce and release into the atmosphere a special greenhouse gas mix, composed mostly of carbon tetrafluoride, hexafluoroethane, and sulphur hexafluoride, along with some methane and nitrous oxide. The poster referred to this mix as the "Russell Cocktail," which was what his Echus Overlook team had called it in the old days. The halocarbons in the cocktail were powerful greenhouse gases, and the best thing about them was that they absorbed outgoing planetary radiation at the 8- to 12-micron wavelength, the so-called "window" where neither water vapor nor CO_2 had much absorptive ability. This window, when open, had allowed fantastic amounts of heat to escape back into space, and Sax had decided early on to attempt to close it, by releasing enough of the cocktail so that it would form ten or twenty parts per million of the atmosphere, following the classic early modeling on the subject by McKay *et al.* So from 2042 on, a major effort had been put into building automated factories, scattered all over the planet, to process the gases from local sources of carbon and sulphur and fluorite, and then release them into the atmosphere. Every year the amounts pumped out had increased, even after the twenty parts per million level had been reached, because they wanted to retain that proportion in an ever-thickening atmosphere, and also because they had to compensate for the continual high-altitude destruction of the halocarbons by UV radiation.

And as the tables in the Simmon poster made clear, the factories had continued to operate through 2061 and the decades since, keeping the levels at about twenty-six parts per million; and the poster's conclusion was that these gases had warmed the surface by around 12°K.

Sax moved on, a little smile fixed on his face. Twelve degrees! Now that was something!—over twenty percent of all the warming they needed, and all by the early and continuous deployment of a nicely designed gas cocktail. It was elegant, it truly was. There was something so comforting about simple physics. . . .

By now it was ten A.M., and a keynote talk was beginning by H. X. Borazjani, one of the best atmospheric chemists on Mars, concerning just this matter of global warming. Borazjani was apparently going to give his calculations of the contributions of all the attempts at warming that had been made up until 2100, the year before the soletta had come into operation. After estimating individual contributions, he was going to try to judge whether there were any synergistic effects taking place. This talk was therefore one of the crucial talks of the conference, as so many other people's work was going to be mentioned and evaluated in it.

It took place in one of the biggest meeting rooms, and the chamber was packed for the occasion, a couple of thousand people in there at least. Sax slipped in right at starting time, and stood at the back behind the last row of chairs.

Borazjani was a small dark-skinned white-haired man, speaking with a pointer before a large screen, which was now showing video images of the various heating methods that had been tried: black dust and lichen on the poles, the orbiting mirrors that had sailed out from Luna, the moholes, the greenhouse gas factories, the ice asteroids burning up in the atmosphere, the denitrifying bacteria, and then all the rest of the biota.

Sax had initiated every single one of these processes in the 2040s and '50s, and he watched the video even more intently than the rest of the audience. The only obvious warming strategy that he had avoided in the early years was the massive release of CO_2 into the atmosphere. Those supporting this strategy had wanted to start a runaway greenhouse effect and create a CO_2 atmosphere of up to 2 bar, arguing that this would warm the planet tremendously, and stop UV radiation, and encourage rampant plant growth. All true, no doubt; but for humans and other animals it would be poisonous, and though advocates of the plan spoke of a second phase that would scrub the CO_2 from the atmosphere and replace it with a breathable one, their methods were vague, as were their time scales, which varied from 100 to 20,000 years. And the sky milk white however long it lasted.

Sax didn't find this an elegant solution to the problem. He much preferred his single-phase model, striking directly toward the eventual goal.

It meant they had always been a bit short on heat, but Sax judged that disadvantage worth it. And he had done his best to find replacements for the heat that CO_2 would have added, as for instance the moholes. Unfortunately Borazjani's estimate of the heat released by the moholes was fairly low; altogether they had added perhaps 5°K to the mean temperature. Well, there was no getting around it, Sax thought as he tapped notes into his lectern—the only good source of heat was the sun. Thus his aggressive introduction of the orbiting mirrors, which had been growing yearly as sunsailers came out from Luna, where a very efficient production process made them from lunar aluminum. These fleets, Borazjani said, had grown large enough to have added some 5°K to the mean temperature.

The reduced albedo, an effort which had never been very vigorously pursued, had added some 2 degrees. The two hundred or so nuclear reactors scattered around the planet had added another 1.5 degrees.

Then Borazjani came to the cocktail of greenhouse gases; but instead of using the 12°K figure from Simmon's poster, he estimated it was 14°K, and cited a twenty-year-old paper by J. Watkins to support his assertion. Sax had spotted Berkina sitting in the back row near him, and now he sidled over and leaned down until his mouth was by Berkina's ear, and whispered, "Why isn't he using Simmon's work?"

Berkina grinned and whispered back, "A few years ago Simmon published a paper in which he had taken a very complex figure of the UV-halocarbon interaction from Borazjani. He modified it slightly, and that first time he attributed it to Borazjani, but after that when he used it he only cited his own earlier paper. It's made Borazjani furious, and he thinks Simmon's papers on this subject are derivative of Watkins anyway, so whenever he talks about warming he goes back to the Watkins work, and pretends Simmon's stuff doesn't exist."

"Ah," Sax said. He straightened up, smiling despite himself at Borazjani's subtle but telling little payback. And in fact Simmon was there across the room, frowning heavily.

By now Borazjani had moved on to the warming effects of the water vapor and CO_2 that had been released into the atmosphere, which he estimated together as adding another 10°K. "Some of this might be called a synergistic effect," he said, "as the desorption of CO_2 is mainly a result of other warming. But other than that I don't think we can say that synergy has been much of a factor. The sum of the warming created by all the individual methods matches pretty closely the temperatures reported by weather reports from around the planet."

The video screen displayed his final table, and Sax made a simplified copy of it into his lectern:

From Borazjani 2 February 14, 2102:

Halocarbons: 14

H_2O and CO_2: 10
Moholes: 5
Pre-Soletta Mirrors: 5
Reduced Albedo: 2
Nuclear Reactors: 1.5

Borazjani had not even included the windmill heaters, so on his lectern Sax did. Altogether it came to 37.55°K, a very respectable step, Sax thought, toward their goal of 53°+. They had only been going at it for sixty years, and already most summer days were reaching temperatures above freezing, allowing arctic and alpine plant life to flourish, as he had seen in the Arena Glacier area. And all this before the introduction of the soletta, which was raising insolation by twenty percent.

The question period had begun, and someone brought up the soletta, asking Borazjani if he thought it was necessary, given the progress being made with the other methods.

Borazjani shrugged in just the way Sax would have. "What does *necessary* mean?" he replied. "It depends how warm you want it. According to the standard model as initiated by Russell at Echus Overlook, it is important to keep CO_2 levels as low as possible. If we do this, then other warming methods are going to have to be applied to compensate for the loss of the heat that CO_2 would have contributed. The soletta might be thought of as compensating for the eventual reduction of CO_2 to breathable levels."

Sax was nodding despite himself.

Someone else rose and said, "Don't you think the standard model is inadequate, given the amount of nitrogen we now know we have?"

"Not if all the nitrogen is put into the atmosphere."

But this was an unlikely achievement, as the questioner was quick to point out. A fair percentage of the total would remain in the ground, and in fact was needed there for plants. So they were short on nitrogen, as Sax had always known. And if they kept the amount of CO_2 in the air to the lowest levels possible, that left the percentage of oxygen in the air at a dangerously high level, because of its flammability. Another person rose to state that it was possible that the lack of nitrogen could be compensated for by the release of other inert gases, chiefly argon. Sax pursed his lips; he had been introducing argon into the atmosphere since 2042, as he had seen this problem coming, and there were significant amounts of argon in the regolith. But they were not easy to free, as his engineers had found, and as other people were now pointing out. No, the balance of gases in the atmosphere was turning out to be a real problem.

A woman rose to note that a consortium of transnats coordinated by Armscor was building a continuous shuttle system to harvest nitrogen from the almost pure nitrogen atmosphere of Titan, liquefying it and flying it back to Mars and dumping it in the upper atmosphere. Sax squinted at this, and did some quick calculations on his lectern. His eyebrows shot up when he saw the result. It would take a very great number of shuttle trips to accomplish anything that way, that or else extremely large shuttles. It was remarkable that anyone had thought it worth the investment.

Now they were discussing the soletta again. It certainly had the capability of compensating for the 5 or 8°K that would be lost if they scrubbed the current amount of CO_2 from the air, and probably it would add even more heat than that; theoretically, Sax calculated on his lectern, it could add as much as 22°K. The scrubbing itself would not be easy, someone pointed out. A man standing near Sax, from a Subarashii lab, rose to announce that a demonstration talk on the soletta and the aerial lens would occur later in the conference, when some of these issues would be greatly clarified. He added before sitting down that serious flaws in the single-phase model made the creation of a two-phase model nearly mandatory.

People rolled their eyes at this, and Borazjani declared that the next meeting in the room needed to begin. No one had commented on his skillful modeling, which had sorted out so plausibly all the contributions of the various warming methods. But in a way this was a sign of respect— no one had challenged the model either, Borazjani's preeminence in this area being taken for granted. Now people stood, and some went up to talk with him; a thousand conversations broke out as the rest filed out of the room and into the halls.

Sax went to lunch with Berkina, in a café just outside the foot of Branch Mesa. Around them scientists from all over Mars ate and talked about the events of the morning. "We think it's parts per billion." "No, sulfates behave conservatively." It sounded like the people at the table next to theirs were assuming there was going to be a shift to a two-phase model. One woman said something about raising the mean temperature to 295°K, seven degrees higher than Terra's average.

Sax squinted at all these expressions of haste, of greed for heat. He saw no need to be dissatisfied with the progress that had been made so far. The ultimate goal of the project was not purely heat, after all, but a viable surface. The results so far certainly seemed to give no reason for complaint. The present atmosphere was averaging 160 millibars at the datum, and it was composed about equally of CO_2, oxygen, and nitrogen, with trace amounts of argon and other gases. This was not the mixture Sax wanted to see in the end, but it was the best they had been able to do given the inventory of volatiles they had to begin with. It represented a substantial step on the way to the final mix Sax had in mind. His recipe for this mix, following the early Fogg formulation, was as follows:

300 millibars nitrogen
160 millibars oxygen
30 millibars argon, helium, etc.
10 millibars CO_2 =

Total pressure at datum, 500 millibars

All these amounts had been fixed by physical requirements and limits of various kinds. The total pressure had to be high enough to drive oxygen into the blood, and 500 millibars was what obtained on Earth at about the 4,000-meter elevation, near the upper limit of what people could live at permanently. Given that it was near the upper limit, it would be best if such a thin atmosphere had more than the Terran percentage of oxygen in it, but it could not be too much more or else fires might be hard to extinguish. Meanwhile CO_2 had to be kept below 10 millibars, or else it would be poisonous. As for nitrogen, the more the better, in fact 780 millibars would be ideal, but the total nitrogen inventory on Mars was now estimated at less than 400 millibars, so 300 millibars was as much as one could reasonably ask to put into the air, and perhaps more. Lack of nitrogen was in fact one of the biggest problems the terraforming effort faced; they needed more than they had, both in the air and in their soil.

Sax stared down at his plate and ate in silence, thinking hard about all these factors. The morning's discussions had given him cause to wonder whether he had made the right decisions back in 2042—whether the volatile inventory could justify his attempt to go straight for a human-viable surface in a single stage. Not that there was much that could be done about it now. And all things considered, he still thought they were the right decisions; *shikata ga nai*, really, if they wanted to walk freely on the surface of Mars in their own lifetimes. Even if their lifetimes were going to be considerably extended.

But there were people who seemed more concerned with high temperatures than breathability. Apparently they were confident that they could balloon the CO_2 level, heat things tremendously, and then reduce the CO_2 without problems. Sax was dubious about that; any two-phase operation was going to be messy, so messy that Sax couldn't help wondering if they would get stuck with the 20,000-year time scales predicted in the earliest two-phase models. It made him blink to think of it. He couldn't see the need. Were people really willing to risk such a long-term problem? Could they be so impressed by the new gigantic technologies that were becoming available that they believed anything was possible?

"How was the pastrami?" Berkina asked.

"The what?"

"The pastrami. That's the kind of sandwich you just ate, Stephen."

"Oh! Fine, fine. It must have been fine."

• • •

The afternoon's sessions were mostly devoted to problems caused by the successes of the global warming campaign. As surface temperatures rose, and the underground biota began to penetrate deeper into the regolith, the permafrost down there was melting, just as hoped. But this was proving disastrous in certain permafrost-rich regions. One of these, unfortunately, was Isidis Planitia itself. A well-attended talk by an areologist from a Praxis lab in Burroughs described the situation; Isidis was one of the big old impact basins, about the size of Argyre, with its northern side completely erased, and its southern rim now part of the Great Escarpment. Underground ice had been creeping off the Escarpment and pooling in the basin for billions of years. Now the ice near the surface was melting, and in the winters freezing again. This thaw-freeze cycle was causing frost heaving on an unprecedented scale; it was pretty near the usual two-magnitude enlargement compared to similar phenomena on Earth, and karsts and pingos a hundred times the size of their Terran analogues were big holes, and big mounds. All over Isidis these giant new holes and hummocks were blistering the landscape, and after her talk and a sequence of mind-boggling slides, the areologist led a large group of interested scientists to the south end of Burroughs, past Moeris Lacus Mesa to the tent wall, where the neighborhood looked like it had been devastated by earthquake, the ground having heaved up to reveal a rising mass of ice like a bald round hill.

"This is a fine specimen of a pingo," the areologist said with a proprietary air. "The ice masses are relatively pure compared to the permafrost matrix, and they act in the matrix the same way rocks do—when the permafrost refreezes at night or in winter, it expands, and anything hard stuck in this expansion gets pushed upward toward the surface. There's a lot of pingos in Terran tundra, but none as big as this one." She led the group up the shattered concrete of what had been a flat street, and they stared out from an earthen crater rim, onto a mound of dirty white ice. "We've lanced it like a boil, and are melting it and piping it into the canals."

"Out in the country one of these coming up would be like an oasis," Sax remarked to Jessica. "It would melt in the summer, and hydrate the ground around it. We ought to develop a community of seeds and spores and rhizomes that we could scatter on any sites like this out in the country."

"True," Jessica said. "Although, to be realistic, the permafrost country is mostly going to end up under the Vastitas sea anyway."

"Hmm."

The truth was Sax had temporarily forgotten the drilling and mining in Vastitas. When they had returned to the conference center, he deliberately looked for a talk describing an aspect of that work. There was one at four: "Recent Advances in North Polar Lens Permafrost Pumping Procedures."

He watched the speaker's video show impassively. The lens of ice that extended underground from the northern polar cap was like the submerged part of an iceberg, containing some ten times as much water as the visible cap. The Vastitas permafrost contained even more. But getting that water to the surface . . . like the retrieval of nitrogen from Titan's atmosphere, it was a project so massive that Sax had never even considered it in the early years; it simply hadn't been possible then. All these big projects—the soletta, the nitrogen from Titan, the northern ocean drilling, the frequent arrival of ice asteroids—were on a scale that Sax found he was having trouble adjusting to. They were thinking big these days, the transnationals. Certainly the new abilities in design and in materials science, and the emergence of fully self-replicating factories, were what made the projects technically feasible; but the initial financial investments were still huge.

As for the technical capabilities involved, he found himself adjusting to the idea of them fairly rapidly. It was an extension of what they had done in the old days: solve some initial problems in materials, design, and homeostatic control, and one's powers grew very considerable indeed. One might say that their reach no longer exceeded their grasp. Which, given the directions their reach sometimes took, was a frightening thought.

In any case, some fifty drilling platforms were now located in the northern Sixties, boring wells and inserting permafrost melting devices at their bottoms that ranged from heated collection galleries to nuclear explosives. The new meltwater was then being pumped up and distributed over the dunes of Vastitas Borealis, where it froze again. Eventually this ice sheet would melt, partly under its own weight, and they would have an ocean in the shape of a ring around the northern Sixties and Seventies, no doubt a very good thermal sink, as all oceans were, although while it remained an ice sea the increase in albedo would probably make it a net heat loss to the global system. Yet another example of their operations cutting against each other. As was the location of Burroughs itself, relative to this new sea; the city was somewhat below the sea level most often mentioned, the datum itself. People talked of a dike, or a smaller sea, but no one knew for sure. It was all very interesting.

So Sax attended the conference every day, all day, living in the hushed rooms and halls of the conference center, chatting with colleagues, and the authors of posters, and his neighbors in audiences. More than once he had to pretend not to know old associates, and it made him nervous enough that he avoided them when he could. But people did not seem to feel that he reminded them of someone they knew, and for the most part he was able to concentrate on the science. He did that with gusto. People gave talks, asked questions, debated details of fact, discussed implications, all under the uniform fluorescent glow of the conference rooms, in the low hum of ventilators and video machines—as if they were in a world outside of time and space, in the imaginary space of pure science, surely one of the greatest achievements of the human spirit—a kind of utopian community, cozy and bright and protected. For Sax, a scientific conference *was* utopia.

The sessions at this conference, however, had a new tone, a kind of nervous edge that Sax had never witnessed before, and did not like. The questions after the presentations were more aggressive, the answers more quickly defensive. The pure play of scientific discourse which he so enjoyed (and which admittedly was never quite pure) was now more and more diluted by sheer argument, by obvious power struggles, motivated by something more than the usual egotism. It wasn't like Simmon's unconscionable lift from Borazjani, and Borazjani's exquisite riposte; it was more a matter of direct assault. As at the end of a presentation on deep moholes and the possibility of reaching the mantle, when a short bald Terran stood and said, "I don't think the basic model of the lithosphere here is valid," and then walked out of the room.

Sax witnessed this in complete disbelief. "What is his *problem*?" he whispered to Claire.

She shook her head. "He works for Subarashii on the aerial lens, and they don't like any potential competition for their regolith melting program."

"My Lord."

The question-and-answer session staggered on, shaken by this display of rudeness, but Sax slipped out of the room and stared down the hall curiously after the Subarashii scientist. What could he be thinking?

But this miscreant wasn't the only one acting strange. People were stressed, nerves were on edge. Of course the stakes were high; as the pingo below Moeris Lacus showed in a small-scale way, there were going to be some bad side effects to the procedures being studied and advocated at the conference, side effects which would cost money, time, lives. And then there were financial motivations. . . .

And now that they were entering its final days, the programming was shifting from very specific issues to more general presentations and workshops, including some presentations in the main room on the big new projects, what people were calling the "monster projects." These were going to have such major impacts that they affected almost everyone else's programs. So when they discussed them, they were arguing policy, in effect, talking about what to do next rather than about what had already happened. That always made things more of a wrangle—but never more so than now, as people began to try to plug the information from the earlier presentations into advocacy for their own causes, whatever they might be. They were entering that unfortunate zone where science began to drift into politics, where papers became grant proposals; and it was dismaying to see that degraded dark zone invade the heretofore neutral terrain of a conference.

Part of this, Sax reflected over a solitary lunch, was no doubt caused by the big-science nature of the monster projects. They were all so expensive and difficult that they had been contracted out to different transnationals. This was a plausible strategy on the face of it, an obvious efficiency move, but unfortunately it meant that the different angles of attack on the terraforming problem now had interested parties defending them as the "best" methods, twisting data in order to defend their own ideas.

Praxis, for instance, was the leader along with Switzerland in the very extensive bioengineering effort, and so its representative theoreticians defended what they called the *ecopoesis* model, which claimed that no further influx of heat or volatiles was necessary at this point, and that biological processes alone, aided by a minimum of ecological engineering, would be sufficient to terraform the planet to the levels envisioned in the early Russell model. Sax thought they were probably correct in this judgment, given the arrival of the soletta, though he deemed their time scales optimistic. And he worked for Biotique, so possibly his judgment was skewed.

The scientists from Amscor, however, were adamant that the low nitrogen inventory would cripple any ecopoetic hopes. They insisted that continued industrial intervention was necessary; and of course it was Armscor that was building the Titan nitrogen transfer shuttles. People from Consolidated, in charge of the drilling in Vastitas, emphasized the vital importance of an active hydrosphere. And people from Subarashii, in charge of the new mirrors, touted the great power of the soletta and the aerial lens to pump heat and gases into the system, allowing everything else to accelerate. It was always quite obvious why people were advocating one program over another; you could look at people's name tags and see their institutional affiliation, and predict what they were going to support or attack. To see science twisted so blatantly pained Sax a great deal, and it seemed to him that it distressed everyone there, even the ones doing it, which added to the general irritability and defensiveness. Everyone knew what was going on, and no one liked it, and yet no one would admit it.

Nowhere was this more apparent than in the last morning's panel discussion of the CO_2 question. This quickly became a defense of the soletta and the aerial lens, made very vehemently by the two Subarashii scientists on the panel. Sax sat at the back of the room and listened to their enthusiastic description of the big mirrors, feeling more and more tense and unhappy as they went on. He liked the soletta itself, which was no more than the logical extension of the mirrors he had been putting into orbit from the very beginning. But the low-flying aerial lens was clearly an *extremely* powerful instrument, and if wielded on the surface to anywhere near its full capacity, it would volatilize hundreds of millibars of gases into the atmosphere, much of it CO_2, which according to Sax's single-phase model they did not want, and which in any sensible course of action would stay bonded in the regolith. No, there were several hard questions that needed to be asked about the effects of this aerial lens, and the Subarashii people ought to be harshly censured for beginning the melting of the regolith without consulting anyone outside their UNTA rubberstamp committee about it. But Sax did not want to draw attention to himself, and so he could only sit there by Claire and Berkina with his lectern out, squirming in his seat and hoping that someone else would ask the hard questions for him.

And as they were obvious questions as well as hard, they did get asked; a scientist from Mitsubishi, which was in a perpetual hometown feud with Subarashii, stood and inquired very politely about the runaway greenhouse effect that might result from too much CO_2. Sax nodded emphatically. But the Subarashii scientists replied that this was exactly what they were hoping for, that there could not be too much heat, and that an eventual atmospheric pressure of seven or eight hundred millibars would be preferable to five hundred anyway. "But not if it's CO_2!" Sax muttered to Claire, who nodded.

H. X. Borazjani stood to say the same. He was followed by others; many in the room were still using Sax's original model as their template for action, and they insisted in many different ways on the difficulty of scrubbing any great excess of CO_2 from the air. But there were also a good many scientists, from Armscor and Consolidated as well as Subarashii, who either claimed that scrubbing CO_2 would not be difficult, or else that a CO_2-heavy atmosphere would not be so bad. An ecosystem of mostly plants, with CO_2-tolerant insects and perhaps some genetically engineered animals, would flourish in the warm thick air, and people could walk around in their shirtsleeves with nothing more cumbersome than a facemask.

This set Sax's teeth on edge, and happily he was not the only one, so he could stay in his seat while others rose to their feet to challenge this fundamental shift in the goal of terraforming. The argument quickly became heated, even rancorous.

"It's not a jungle planet we're after here!"

"You're making a hidden assumption that people can be genetically engineered to tolerate higher CO_2 levels, but it's ridiculous!"

Very soon it became clear that they were accomplishing nothing. No one was really listening, and everyone had their opinions, which were tightly aligned to their employers' interests. It was unseemly, really. A mutual distaste for the tone of the debate caused all but the immediate participants to withdraw—around Sax people were folding programs, turning off lecterns, whispering to their companions, all while people were still standing and speaking . . . bad form, no doubt about it. But it only took a moment's thought to realize that they were now arguing over policy decisions that were not going to be made at the level of working scientists anyway. No one liked that, and people actually began to get up and leave the room, right in the middle of the discussion. The overwhelmed panel moderator, an overpolite Japanese woman who was looking miserable, spoke over the rising voices, and suggested that they close the session. People trooped into the halls in little knots, some still talking heatedly to their allies, making their cases decisively now that they were only complaining to their friends.

Sax followed Claire and Jessica and the other Biotique people across the canal and into Hunt Mesa. They took the elevator up to the mesa plateau, and had lunch at Antonio's.

"They're going to flood us with CO_2," Sax said, unable to hold his tongue any longer. "I don't think they understand what a fundamental blow that will be to the standard model."

"It's a different model entirely," Jessica said. "A two-phase, heavy-industrial model."

"But it will keep people and animals in tents more or less indefinitely," Sax said.

"Maybe the transnat executives don't mind that," Jessica said.

"Maybe they like it," Berkina said.

Sax made a face.

Claire said, "It could just be that they've got this soletta and lens, and they want to use them. Like playing with toys. It's so much like the magnifying glass you use to start fires with when you're ten. But this one is so powerful. They can't stand not to use it. And then calling the burn zones canals, you know. . . ."

"That is so stupid," Sax said sharply, and when the others stared at him in some surprise, he tried to lighten his tone: "Well, it's just so silly, you know. It's such a kind of fuzzy romanticism. They won't be canals in the sense of usefully connecting one body of water with another, and even if they tried to use them, the banks would be slag."

"Glass, they're claiming," Claire said. "And it's just the idea of canals, anyway."

"But it's not a *game* we're playing here," Sax said. It was extremely hard to keep Stephen's sense of humor about it; for some reason it was really irritating to him, really distressing. Here they had started so well, sixty years of solid achievement—and now different people were hacking about with different ideas and different toys, arguing and working against each other, bringing ever more powerful and expensive methods to bear, but with ever less coordination. They were going to ruin his plan!

The afternoon's closing sessions were perfunctory, and did nothing to restore his faith in the conference as disinterested science. That evening, back in his room, he watched the environmental news on vid more closely than ever, searching for answers to questions he hadn't quite formulated. Cliffs were falling. Rocks of all sizes were being shoved out of the permafrost by the thaw-freeze cycle, the rocks arranging themselves into characteristic polygonal patterns. Rock glaciers were forming in ravines and chutes, the rocks pried free by ice and then sliding down gorges in masses that behaved much like ice glaciers. Pingos were blistering the northern lowlands, except of course where the frozen seas were pouring out of the drilling platforms, inundating the land.

It was change on a massive scale, becoming apparent everywhere now, and accelerating every year as the summers got warmer, and the submartian biota grew deeper—while everything still froze solid every winter, and froze a little bit almost every summer night. Such an intense freeze-thaw cycle would tear any landscape apart, and the Martian landscape was particularly susceptible to it, having been stalled in a cold arid stasis for millions of years. Mass wasting was causing many landslides a day, and fatalities and unexplained disappearances were not at all uncommon. Cross-country travel was dangerous. Canyons and fresh craters were no longer safe places to locate a town, or even to spend a night.

Sax stood and walked to the window of his room, looked down at the lights of the city. All of this was as Ann had predicted to him, long ago. No doubt she was noting reports of all the changes with disgust, she and all the rest of the Reds. For them every collapse was a sign that things were going wrong rather than right. In the past Sax would have shrugged them off; mass wasting exposed frozen soil to the sun, warming it and revealing potential nitrate sources and the like. Now, with the conference fresh in his mind, he was not so sure.

On the vid no one seemed to be worrying about it. There were no Reds on vid. The collapse of landforms were considered no more than an opportunity, not only for terraforming, which seemed to be considered the exclusive business of the transnats, but for mining. Sax watched a news account of a freshly revealed vein of gold ore with a sinking feeling. It was strange how many people seemed to feel the lure of prospecting. That was Mars as the twenty-second century began; with the elevator returned they were back to the old gold rush mentality, it seemed, as if it really were a manifest destiny, out on the frontier with great tools wielded left and right: cosmic engineers, mining and building. And the terraforming that had been his work, the sole focus of his life, in fact, for sixty years and more, seemed to be turning into something else. . . .

Insomnia began to plague Sax. He had never suffered the phenomenon before, and found it quite uncomfortable. He would wake, roll over, gears in his mind would catch, and everthing would start whirring. When it was clear he was not going to fall back asleep he would get up, and turn on the AI screen and watch video programs, even the news, which he had never watched before. He saw symptoms of some kind of sociological dysfunction on Earth. It did not appear, for instance, that they had even attempted to adjust their societies to the impact of the population rise caused by the gerontological treatments. That should have been elementary—birth control, quotas, sterilization, the lot—but most countries hadn't done any of that. Indeed it appeared that a permanent underclass of the untreated was developing, especially in the highly populated poor countries. Statistics were hard to come by now that the UN was moribund, but one World Court study claimed that seventy percent of the population of the developed nations had gotten the treatment, while only twenty percent had in the poor countries. If that trend held for long, Sax thought, it would lead to a kind of physicalization of class—a late emergence or retroactive unveiling of Marx's bleak vision—only more extreme than Marx, because now class distinctions would be exhibited as an actual physiological difference caused by a bimodal distribution, something almost akin to speciation. . . .

This divergence between rich and poor was obviously dangerous, but it seemed to be taken on Earth as something of a given, as if it were part of nature. Why couldn't they see the danger?

He no longer understood Earth, if he ever had. He sat there shivering through the dregs of his insomniac nights, too tired to read or to work; he could only call up one Terran news program after another, trying to understand better what was happening down there. He would have to, if he wanted to understand Mars; for the transnationals' Martian behavior was being driven by Terran ultimate causes. He *needed* to understand. But the news vids seemed beyond rational comprehension. Down there, even more dramatically than on Mars, there was no plan.

He needed a science of history, but unfortunately there was no such thing. History is Lamarckian, Arkady used to say, a notion that was ominously suggestive given the pseudospeciation caused by the unequal distribution of the gerontological treatments; but it was no real help. Psychology, sociology, anthropology, they were all suspect. The scientific method could not be applied to human beings in any way that yielded *useful* information. It was the fact-value problem stated in a different way; human reality could only be explained in terms of values. And values were very resistant to scientific analysis. Isolation of factors for study, falsifiable hypotheses, repeatable experiments—the entire apparatus as practiced in lab physics simply could not be brought to bear. Values drove history, which was whole, nonrepeatable, and contingent. It might be characterized as Lamarckian, or as a chaotic system, but even those were guesses, because what factors were they talking about, what aspects might be acquired by learning and passed on, or cycling in some nonrepetitive but patterned way?

No one could say.

He began to think again about the discipline of natural history which had so captivated him on Arena Glacier. It used scientific methods to study the natural world's history, and in many ways that history was just as problematic a methodological problem as human history, being likewise nonrepeatable and resistant to experiment. And with human consciousness out of the picture, natural history was often fairly successful, even if it was based mostly on observation and hypothesis that could be tested only by further observation. It was a real science; it had discovered, there among the contingency and disorder, some valid general principles of evolution—development, adaptation, complexification, and many more specific principles as well, confirmed by the various subdisciplines.

What he needed were similar principles influencing human history. The little reading he did in historiography was not encouraging; it was either a sad imitation of the scientific method, or art pure and simple. About every decade a new historical explanation revised all that had come before, but clearly revisionism held pleasures that had nothing to do with the actual justice of the case being made. Sociobiology and bioethics were more promising, but they tended to explain things best when working on evolutionary time scales, and he wanted something for the past hundred years, and the next hundred. Or even the past fifty and the next five.

∙   ∙   ∙

Night after night he woke, failed to fall back asleep, got up, sat at the screen and puzzled over these matters, too tired to think well. And as these night watches kept happening, he found himself returning more and more to shows about 2061. There were any number of video compilations on the events of that year, and some of them were not shy about naming it: *World War Three!* was the title of the longest series, some sixty hours' worth of video from that year, poorly edited and sequenced.

One only had to watch the series for a while to realize that the title was not entirely sensationalist. Wars had raged all over Terra in that fateful year, and the analysts reluctant to call it the Third World War seemed to think that it simply hadn't gone on long enough to qualify. Or that it hadn't been the contest of two great global alliances, but was much more confused and complex: different sources would claim it was north against south, or young against old, or UN against nations, or nations against transnationals, or transnationals against flags of convenience, or armies against police, or police against citizens—so that it began to seem every kind of conflict at once. For a matter of six or eight months the world had descended into chaos. In the course of his wanderings through "political science" Sax had stumbled across a chart by a Herman Kahn, called an "Escalation Ladder," which attempted to categorize conflicts according to their nature and severity. There were forty-four steps in Kahn's ladder, going from the first, Ostensible Crisis, up gradually through categories like Political and Diplomatic Gestures, Solemn and Formal Declarations, and Significant Mobilization, then more steeply through steps like Show of Force, Harassing Acts of Violence, Dramatic Military Confrontations, Large Conventional War, and then off into the unexplored zones of Barely Nuclear War, Exemplary Attacks Against Property, Civilian Devastation Attack, and right on up to number forty-four, Spasm or Insensate War. It was certainly an interesting attempt at taxonomy and logical sequence, and Sax could see that the categories had been abstracted from many wars of the past. And by the definitions of the table, 2061 had shot right up the ladder to number forty-four.

In that maelstrom, Mars had been no more than one spectacular war among fifty. Very few general programs about '61 devoted more than a few minutes to it, and these merely collected clips Sax had seen at the time: the frozen guards at Korolyov, the broken domes, the fall of the elevator, and then that of Phobos. Attempts at analysis of the Martian situation were shallow at best; Mars had been an exotic sideshow, with some good vid, but nothing else to distinguish it from the general morass. No. One sleepless dawn it came to him; if he wanted to understand 2061, he was going to have to piece it together himself, from the primary sources of the videotapes, from all the bouncing shots of enraged crowds torching cities, and the occasional press conferences with desperate, frustrated leaders.

Even getting these in chronological order was no easy task. And indeed this became (in his Echus style) his only interest for a few weeks, as slotting events into a chronology was the first step in piecing together what had happened—which had to precede figuring out why.

Over the weeks he began to get a sense of it. Certainly the common wisdom was correct; the emergence of the transnationals in the 2040s had set the stage, and was the ultimate cause of the war. In that decade, while Sax had been devoting every bit of his attention to terraforming Mars, a new Terran order had come into being, shaped as the thousands of multinational corporations began to coalesce into the scores of colossal transnationals. Something like planetary formation, he thought one night, planetesimals becoming planets.

It was not entirely a new order, however. The multinationals had mostly originated in the wealthy industrial nations, and so in certain senses the transnationals were expressions of these nations—extensions of their power into the rest of the world, in a way that reminded Sax of what little he knew of the imperial and colonial systems that had preceded them. Frank had said something like that: colonialism had never died, he used to declare, it just changed names and hired local cops. We're all colonies of the transnats.

This was Frank's cynicism, Sax decided (wishing that he had that hard bitter mind on hand to instruct him), because all colonies were not equal. It was true that transnats were so powerful that they had rendered national governments little more than toothless servants. And no transnat had shown any particular loyalty to any given government, or the UN. But they were children of the West—children who no longer cared for their parents, yet still supported them. For the record showed that the industrial nations had prospered under the transnats, while the developing nations had had no recourse but to fight each other for flag-of-convenience status. And thus in 2060 when the transnats had come under fire from desperate poor countries, it had been the Group of Seven and its military might that had come to their defense.

But the proximate cause? Night after night he sifted through vid of the 2040s and '50s, looking for traces of patterns. Eventually he decided that it was the longevity treatment which had pushed things over the edge. Through the 2050s the treatment had spread through the rich countries, illustrating the gross economic inequality in the world like a color stain in a microscope sample. And as the treatment spread, the situation had gotten increasingly tense, rising steadily up the steps of Kahn's ladder of crises.

The immediate cause of the explosion of '61, strangely enough, appeared to be a squabble concerning the Martian space elevator. The elevator had been operated by Praxis, but after it had started operations, in February of 2061 to be precise, it had been taken over by Subarashii, in a clearly hostile takeover. Subarashii at that time was a conglomeration of most of the Japanese corporations that had not folded into Mitsubishi, and it was a rising power, very aggressive and ambitious. Upon acquisition of the elevator—a takeover approved by UNOMA—Subarashii had immediately increased the emigration quotas, causing the situation on Mars to go critical. At the same time on Earth, Subarashii's competitors had objected to what was effectively an economic conquest of Mars, and though Praxis had confined its objections to legal action at the hapless UN, one of Subarashii's flags of convenience, Malaysia, had been attacked by Singapore, which was a base for Shellalco. By April of 2061 much of south Asia was at war. Most of the fights were long-standing conflicts, such as Cambodia versus Vietnam, or Pakistan versus India; but some were attacks on Subarashii flags, as in Burma and Bangladesh. Events in the region had shot up the escalation ladder with deadly speed as old enmities joined the new transnat conflicts, and by June wars had spread all over Terra, and then to Mars. By October fifty million people had died, and another fifty million were to die in the aftermath, as many basic services had been interrupted or destroyed, and a newly released malaria vector remained without an effective prevention or cure.

That seemed enough to qualify it as a world war to Sax, brevity notwithstanding. It had been, he concluded, a deadly synergistic combination of fights among the transnats, and revolutions by a wide array of disenfranchised groups against the transnat order. But the chaotic violence had convinced the transnats to resolve their disputes, or at least table them, and all the revolutions had failed, especially after the militaries of the Group of Seven intervened to rescue the transnats from dismemberment in their flags of convenience. All the giant military-industrial nations had ended up on the same side, which had helped to make it a very short world war compared to the first two. Short, but terrible—about as many people had died in 2061 as in the first two world wars together.

Mars had been a minor campaign in this Third World War, a campaign in which certain of the transnats had overreacted to a flamboyant but disorganized revolt. When it was over, Mars had been seized firmly in the grip of the major transnationals, with the blessing of the Group of Seven and the transnats' other clients. And Terra had staggered on, a hundred million people fewer.

But nothing else had changed. None of its problems had been addressed. So it all might happen again. It was perfectly possible. One might even say that it was likely.

Sax continued to sleep poorly. And though he spent his days in the ordinary routines of work and habit, it seemed that he saw things differently than he had before the conference. Another proof, he supposed glumly, of the notion of vision as a paradigm construct. But now it was so obvious the transnationals were everywhere. In terms of authority, there was hardly anything else. Burroughs was a transnat town, and from what

Phyllis had said, Sheffield was too. There were none of the national scientific teams that had proliferated in the years before the treaty conference; and with the First Hundred dead or in hiding, the whole tradition of Mars as a research station was extinct. What science there was was devoted to the terraforming project, and he had seen what kind of science that was becoming. No, the research was applied only, these days.

And there were very few other signs of the old nation-states, now that he looked. The news gave the impression that they were mostly bankrupt, even the Group of Seven; and the transnats were holding the debts, if anybody was. Some reports made Sax think that in a sense the transnats were even taking on smaller countries as a kind of capital asset, in a new business/government arrangement that went far beyond the old flag-of-convenience contracts.

An example of this new arrangement in a slightly different form was Mars itself, which seemed effectively in the possession of the big transnats. And now that the elevator was back, the export of metals and the import of people and goods had vastly accelerated. Terran stock markets were ballooning hysterically to mark the action, with no end in sight, despite the fact that Mars could only provide Terra with certain metals in certain quantities. So the stock market rise was probably some kind of bubble phenomenon, and if it burst it might very well be enough to bring everything down again. Or perhaps not; economics was a bizarre field, and there were senses in which the whole stock market was simply too unreal to have impacts beyond itself. But who knew till it happened? Sax, wandering the streets of Burroughs looking at the stock market displays in the office windows, certainly didn't claim to. People were not rational systems.

This profound truth was reinforced when Desmond showed up one evening at his door. The famous Coyote himself, the stowaway, Big Man's little bro, standing there small and slight in a brightly colored construction worker's jumper, diagonal slashes of aquamarine and royal blue leading the eye down to lime-green walker boots. Many construction workers in Burroughs (and there were a lot of them) wore the new light and flexible walker boots all the time as a kind of fashion statement, and all were brightly colored, but very few achieved the stunning quality of Desmond's fluorescent greens.

He grinned his cracked grin as Sax stared at them. "Yes, so beautiful aren't they? And very distracting."

Which was just as well, as his dreadlocks were stuffed into a voluminous red, yellow, and green beret, an unusual sight anywhere on Mars. "Come on, let's go out for a drink."

He led Sax down to a cheap canalside bar, built into the side of a massive emptied pingo. The construction crowd here was tightly packed around long tables, and sounded mostly Australian. At the canalside itself a particularly rowdy group were throwing ice shotputs the size of cannon-balls out into the canal, and very occasionally thumping one down on the grass of the far bank, which caused cheers and often a round of nitrous oxide for the house. Strollers on the far bank were giving that part of the canalside a wide berth.

Desmond got them four shots of tequila and one nitrous inhaler. "Pretty soon we'll have agave cactus growing on the surface, eh?"

"I think you could do it now."

They sat at the end of one table, with their elbows bumping and Desmond talking into Sax's ear as they drank. He had a whole wish list of things he wanted Sax to steal from Biotique. Seed stocks, spores, rhizomes, certain growth media, certain hard-to-synthesize chemicals. . . . "Hiroko says to tell you she really needs all of it, but especially the seeds."

"Can't she breed those herself? I don't like taking things."

"Life is a dangerous game," Desmond said, toasting the thought with a big whiff of nitrous, followed by a shot of tequila. "Ahhhhhhhhh," he said.

"It's not the danger," Sax said. "I just don't like doing it. I work with those people."

Desmond shrugged and did not answer. It occurred to Sax that these scruples might strike Desmond, who had spent most of the twenty-first century living by theft, as a bit overfine.

"You won't be taking it from those people," Desmond said at last. "You'll be taking it from the transnat that owns Biotique."

"But that's a Swiss collective, and Praxis," Sax said. "And Praxis doesn't look so bad. It's a very loose egalitarian system, it reminds me of Hiroko's, actually."

"Except that they're part of a global system that has a fairly small oligarchy running the world. You have to remember the context."

"Oh believe me, I do," Sax, said, remembering his sleepless nights. "But you have to make distinctions as well."

"Yes, yes. And one distinction is that Hiroko needs these materials and cannot make them, given the necessity to hide from the police hired by your wonderful transnational."

Sax blinked disgruntledly.

"Besides, theft of materials is one of the few resistance actions left to us these days. Hiroko has agreed with Maya that obvious sabotage is simply an announcement of the underground's existence, and an invitation for reprisal and a shutdown of the demimonde. Better simply to disappear for a while, she says, and make them think that we never existed in any great numbers."

"It's a good idea," Sax said. "But I'm surprised you're doing what Hiroko says."

"Very funny," Desmond said with a grimace. "Anyway, I think it's a good idea too."

"You do?"

"No. But she talked me into it. It may be for the best. Anyway there's still a lot of materials to be obtained."

"Won't theft itself tip off the police that we're still out there?"

"No way. It's so widespread that what we do can't be noticed against the background levels. There's a whole lot of inside jobs."

"Like me."

"Yes, but you're not doing it for money, are you."

"I still don't like it."

Desmond laughed, revealing his stone eyetooth, and the odd asymmetricality of his jaw and his whole lower face. "It's hostage syndrome. You work with them and you get to know them, and have a sympathy for them. You have to remember what they're doing here. Come on, finish that cactus and I'll show you some things you haven't seen, right here in Burroughs."

There was a commotion, as an ice shot had hit the other bank and rolled up the grass and bowled over an old man. People were cheering and lifting the woman who had made the throw onto their shoulders, but the group with the old man was charging down to the nearest bridge. "This place is getting too noisy," Desmond said. "Come on, drink that and let's go."

Sax knocked back the liquor while Desmond popped the last of the inhaler. Then they left quickly to avoid the developing brouhaha, walking up the canalside path. A half hour's walk took them past the rows of Bareiss columns and up into Princess Park, where they turned right and walked up the steep wide grassy incline of Thoth Boulevard. Beyond Table Mountain they turned left down a narrower swath of streetgrass, and came to the westernmost part of the tent wall , extending in a big arc around Black Syrtis Mesa. "Look, they're getting back to the old coffin quarters for workers again," Desmond pointed out. "That's Subarashii's standard housing now, but see how these units are set into the mesa. Black Syrtis contained a plutonium processing plant in the early days of Burroughs, when it was well out of town. But now Subarashii has built workers' quarters right next to it, and their jobs are to oversee the processing and the removal of the waste, north to Nili Fossae, where some integral fast reactors will use it. The cleanup operation used to be almost completely robotic, but the robots are hard to keep on-line. They've found it's cheaper to use people for a lot of the jobs."

"But the radiation," Sax said, blinking.

"Yes," Desmond said with his savage grin. "They take on forty rem a year."

"You're kidding!"

"I am not kidding. They tell the workers this, and give them hardship pay, and after three years they get a bonus, which is the treatment."

"Is it withheld from them otherwise?"

"It's expensive, Sax. And there are waiting lists. This is a way to skip up the list, and cover the costs."

"But forty rems! There's no way to be sure the treatment will repair the damage that could do!"

"We know that," Desmond said with a scowl. There was no need to refer to Simon. "But they don't."

"And Subarashii is doing this just to cut costs?"

"That's important in such a large capital investment, Sax. All kinds of cost-cutting measures are showing up. The sewage systems in Black Syrtis are all the same system, for instance—the med clinic and the coffins and the plants in the mesa."

"You're kidding."

"I am not kidding. My jokes are funnier than that."

Sax waved him off.

"Look," Desmond said, "there are no regulatory agencies anymore. No building codes or whatever. That is what the transnational success in sixty-one really means—they make their own rules now. And you know what their one rule is."

"But this is simply stupid."

"Well, you know, this particular division of Subarashii is run by Georgians, and they're in the grip of a big Stalin revival there. It's a patriotic gesture to run their country as stupidly as possible. That means business too. And of course the top managers of Subarashii are still Japanese, and they believe Japan became great by being tough. They say they won in sixty-one what they lost in World War Two. They're the most brutal transnat up here, but all the rest are imitating them to compete successfully. Praxis is an anomaly in that sense, you must remember that."

"So we reward them by stealing from them."

"You're the one who went to work for Biotique. Maybe you should change jobs."

"No."

"Do you think you can get these materials from one of Subarashii's firms?"

"No."

"But you could from Biotique."

"Probably. Security is pretty tight."

"But you could do it."

"Probably." Sax thought about it. "I want something in return."

"Yes?"

"Will you fly me out to have a look at this soletta burn zone?"

"Certainly! I would like to see it again myself."

·   ·   ·

So the next afternoon they left Burroughs and trained south up the Great Escarpment, getting off at Libya Station, some seventy kilometers from Burroughs. There they slipped into the basement and their closet door, down their tunnel and out into the rocky countryside. Down in a shallow graben they found one of Desmond's cars, and when night came they drove east along the Escarpment to a small Red hideout in the rim of Du Martheray Crater, next to a stretch of flat bedrock the Reds used as an airstrip. Desmond did not identify Sax to their hosts. They were led into a little cliffside hangar, where they got into one of Spencer's old stealth planes and taxied out to the bedrock, then took off in an undulant acceleration down the runway. Once in the air they flew east slowly through the night.

They flew in silence for a while. Sax saw lights on the dark surface of the planet only three times: once a station in Escalante Crater, once the tiny moving line of lights of a round-the-world train, and the last an unidentified blink in the rough land behind the Great Escarpment. "Who do you think that is?" Sax asked.

"No idea."

After a few minutes more Sax said, "I ran into Phyllis."

"Really! Did she recognize you?"

"No."

Desmond laughed. "That's Phyllis for you."

"A lot of old acquaintances haven't recognized me."

"Yeah, but Phyllis . . . Is she still president of the Transitional Authority?"

"No. She didn't seem to think it was a powerful post, anyway."

Desmond laughed again. "A silly woman. But she did get that group on Clarke back to civilization, I'll give her that. I thought they were goners, myself."

"Do you know much about that?"

"I talked with two of the people who were on it, yeah. One night in Burroughs at the Pingo Bar, in fact. You couldn't get them to shut up about it."

"Did anything happen near the end of their flight?"

"The end? Well, yeah—someone died. I guess some woman got a hand crushed when they were evacuating Clarke, and Phyllis was the closest thing they had to a doctor, so Phyllis took care of her through the whole trip, and thought she was going to make it, but I guess they ran out of something, the two telling me the story weren't too clear on it, and she took a turn for the worse. Phyllis called a prayer meeting for her and prayed for her, but she died anyway, a couple of days before they came into the Terran system."

"Ah," Sax said. Then: "Phyllis doesn't seem all that . . . religious anymore."

Desmond snorted. "She was never religious, if you ask me. Hers was the religion of business. You visit real Christians like the folks down in Christianopolis, or Bingen, and you don't find them talking profits at breakfast, and lording it over you with that horrible unctuous *righteousness* they have. Righteousness, good Lord—it is a most unpleasant quality in a person. You know it has to be a house built on sand, eh? But the demimonde Christians are not like that. They're gnostics, Quakers, Baptists, Baha'i Rastafarians, whatever—the most agreeable people in the underground if you ask me, and I've traded with everybody. So helpful. And no airs about being best friends with Jesus. They're tight with Hiroko, and the Sufis as well. Some kind of mystic networking going on down there." He cackled. "But Phyllis, now, and all those business fundamentalists—using religion to cover extortion, I hate that. Actually I never heard Phyllis speak in a religious manner after we landed. "

"Did you have much opportunity to hear Phyllis speak after we landed?"

Another laugh. "More than you might think! I saw more than you did in those years, Mister Lab Man! I had my little hidey-holes *everywhere*."

Sax made a skeptical noise, and Desmond shouted a laugh and slapped him on the shoulder. "Who else could tell you that you and Hiroko were an item in the Underhill years, eh?"

"Hmm."

"Oh yes, I saw a lot. Of course you could make that particular observation about practically any man in Underhill and be right. That vixen was keeping us all as a *harem*."

"Polyandry?"

"Two-timing, goddammit! Or twenty-timing."

"Hmm."

Desmond laughed at him.

Just after dawn they caught sight of a white column of smoke, obscuring the stars over a whole quadrant of the sky. For a while this dense cloud was the only anomaly they could see in the landscape. Then, as they flew on and the terminator of the planet rolled under them, a broad swath of bright ground appeared on the eastern horizon ahead—an orange strip, or trough, running roughly northeast to southwest across the land, obscured by smoke that poured out of one section of it. The trough under the smoke was white and turbulent, as if a small volcanic eruption were confined to that one spot. Above it stood a beam of light—a beam of illuminated smoke, rather, so tight and solid that it was like a physical pillar, extending straight up and becoming less distinct as the cloud smoke thinned, and disappearing where the smoke reached its maximum height of around ten thousand meters.

At first there was no sign of the origin of this beam in the sky—the aerial lens was some four hundred kilometers overhead, after all. Then Sax thought he saw something like the ghost of a cloud, soaring very far above. Maybe that was it, maybe it wasn't. Desmond wasn't sure.

At the foot of the pillar of light, however, there was no question of visibility—the pillar of light had a kind of biblical presence, and the melted rock under it was truly incandescent, a very brilliant white. That was what 5000°K looked like, exposed to the open air. "We have to be careful," Desmond said. "We fly into that beam and it would be like a moth in a flame."

"I'm sure the smoke is very turbulent as well."

"Yes. I plan to stay windward of it."

Down where the pillar of lit smoke met the orange channel, new smoke was spewing out in violent billows, weirdly lit from underneath. To the north of the white spot, where the rock had had a chance to cool, the melted channel reminded Sax of film of the eruptions of the Hawaiian volcanoes. Bright yellow-orange waves surged north in the channel of fluid rock, occasionally meeting resistances and splashing up onto the dark banks of the molten channel. The channel was about two kilometers wide, and ran over the horizon in both directions; they could see perhaps two hundred kilometers of it. South of the pillar of light, the channel bed was almost covered with cooling black rock, webbed by dark orange cracks. The straightness of the channel, and the pillar of light itself, were the only obvious signs that it was not some kind of natural lava channel; but these signs were more than enough. Besides, there hadn't been any volcanic activity on the surface of Mars for many thousands of years.

Desmond closed on the sight, then banked their plane sharply and headed north. "The beam from the aerial lens is moving south, so up the line we should be able to fly closer."

For many kilometers the channel of melted rock ran northeast without changing. Then as they got farther away from the current burn zone, the orange of the lava darkened and began to cake over from the sides with a black surface, broken by more orange cracks. Beyond that the channel surface was black, as were the banks on each side of it; a straight swath of pure black, running over the rust-colored highlands of Hesperia.

Desmond banked and turned south again, and flew closer to the channel. He was a rough pilot, shoving the light plane around ruthlessly. When the orange cracks reappeared, a thermal updraft bucked the plane hard, and he slid to the west a little. The light of the molten rock itself illuminated the banks of the channel, which appeared to be smoking lines of hills, very black. "I thought they were supposed to be glass," Sax said.

"Obsidian. Actually I've seen some different colors. Swirls of various minerals in the glass."

"How far does this burn extend?"

"They're cutting from Cerberus to Hellas, running just west of Tyr-rhena and Hadriaca volcanoes."

Sax whistled.

"They say it will be a canal between the Hellas Sea and the northern ocean."

"Yes, yes. But they're volatilizing carbonates much too fast."

"Thickens the atmosphere, right?"

"Yes, but with CO_2! They're wrecking the plan! We won't be able to breathe the atmosphere for years! We'll be stuck in the cities."

"Maybe they think they'll be able to scrub the CO_2 out when things are warmed up." Desmond glanced at him. "Have you seen enough?"

"More than enough."

Desmond laughed his unsettling laugh, and banked the plane sharply. They began to chase the terminator to the west, flying low over the long shadows of the dawn terrain.

"Think about it, Sax. For a while people are forced to stay in the cities, which is convenient if you want to keep control of things. You burn cuts with this flying magnifying glass, and fairly quickly you have your one-bar atmosphere, and your warm wet planet. Then you have some method for scrubbing the air of carbon dioxide—they must have something in mind, industrial or biological or both. Something they can sell, no doubt. And presto, you have another Earth, and very quickly. It might be expensive—"

"It's definitely expensive! All these big projects must be setting the transnationals back by huge amounts, and they're doing it even though we're a good step on the way to two-seventy-three K. I don't get it."

"Maybe they feel two-seventy-three is too modest. An average of freezing is a bit chilly, after all. Kind of a Sax Russell vision of terraforming, you might call that. Practical, but . . ." He cackled. "Or maybe they're feeling rushed. Earth is in a mess, Sax."

"I know that," Sax said sharply. "I've been studying it."

"Good for you! No, really. So you know that the people who haven't got the treatment are getting desperate—they're getting older, and their chances of ever getting it seem to be getting worse. And the people who have gotten the treatment, especially the ones at the top, are looking around trying to figure out what to do. Sixty-one taught them what can happen if things get out of control. So they're buying up countries like bad mangoes at the end of market day. But it doesn't seem to be helping. And here right next door they see a fresh empty planet, not quite ready for occupation, but close. Full of potential. It could be a new world. Beyond the reach of the untreated billions."

Sax thought it over. "A kind of bolt-hole, you mean. To escape to if there's trouble."

"Exactly. I think there are people in these transnationals who want Mars terraformed just as quickly as possible, by any means necessary."

"Ah," Sax said. And was silent all the way back.

Desmond accompanied him back into Burroughs, and as they walked from South Station to Hunt Mesa, they could see across the treetops of Canal Park, through the slot between Branch Mesa and Table Mountain to Black Syrtis. "Are they really doing things as stupid as that all over Mars?" Sax said.

Desmond nodded. "I will bring you a list next time."

"Do that." Sax shook his head as he pondered it. "It doesn't make sense. It doesn't take into account the long run."

"They are short-run thinkers."

"But they're going to live a long time! Presumably they'll still be in charge when these policies collapse on them!"

"They may not see it that way. They change jobs a lot up at the top. They try to establish a reputation by building a company very quickly, then get hired upward somewhere else, then try to do it again. It's musical chairs up there."

"It won't matter what chair they're in, it's the whole room that's going to come down! They aren't paying attention to the laws of physics!"

"Of course not! Haven't you noticed that before, Sax?"

". . . I guess not."

Of course he had seen that human affairs were irrational and unexplainable. This no one could miss. But he realized now that he had been making the assumption that the people who involved themselves in governance were making a good-faith effort to run things in a rational manner, with a view to the long-term well-being of humanity and its biophysical support system. Desmond laughed at him as he tried to express this, and irritably he exclaimed, "But why else take on such compromised work, if not to that end?"

"Power," Desmond said. "Power and gain."

"Ah."

Sax had always been so uninterested in those things that it was hard for him to understand why anyone else would be. What was personal gain but the freedom to do what you wanted to do? And what was power but the freedom to do what you wanted to do? And once you had that freedom, any more wealth or power actually began to restrict one's options, and reduce one's freedom. One became a servant of one's wealth or power, constrained to spend all one's time protecting it. So that properly seen, the freedom of a scientist with a lab at his command was the highest freedom possible. Any more wealth and power only interfered with that.

Desmond was shaking his head as Sax described this philosophy. "Some people like to tell others what to do. They like that more than freedom. Hierarchy, you know. And their place in the hierarchy. As long as it's high enough. Everyone bound into their places. It's safer than freedom. And a lot of people are cowards."

Sax shook his head. "I think it's simply an inability to understand the concept of diminishing returns. As if there can never be too much of a good thing. It's very unrealistic. I mean, there is no process in nature that is a constant irrespective of quantity!"

"Speed of light."

"Bah. Irrelevant. Physical reality is clearly not a factor in these calculations."

"Well put."

Sax shook his head, frustrated. "Religion again. Or ideology. What was it Frank used to say? An imaginary relationship to a real situation?"

"There was a man who loved power."

"True."

"But he was very imaginative."

They stopped at Sax's apartment and changed clothes, then went up to the top of the mesa, to get breakfast at Antonio's. Sax was still thinking about their discussion. "The problem is that people with a hypertrophied regard for wealth and power achieve positions that give them these gifts in excess, and then they find that they're as much slaves to them as masters. And then they become dissatisfied and bitter."

"Like Frank, you mean."

"Yes. So the powerful almost always seem to have a dysfunctional aspect to them. Everything from cynicism to full-blown destructiveness. They're not happy."

"But they are powerful."

"Yes. And thus our problem. Human affairs"—Sax paused to eat one of the rolls just brought to their table; he was famished—"you know, they ought to be run according to principles of systems ecology."

Desmond laughed out loud, hastily grabbing up a napkin to clean off his chin. He laughed so hard that people at other tables looked over at them, worrying Sax somewhat. "What a concept!" he cried, and started to laugh again. "Ah ha ha! Oh, my Saxifrage! Scientific management, eh?"

"Well, why not?" Sax said mulishly. "I mean, the principles governing the behavior of the dominant species in a stable ecosystem are fairly straightforward, as I recall. I'll bet a council of ecologists could construct a program that would result in a stable benign society!"

"If only you ran the world!" Desmond cried, and started laughing again. He put his face right down on the table and howled.

"Not just me."

"No, I am joking." He composed himself. "You know Vlad and Marina have been working on their eco-economics for years now. They have even had me using it in the trade between the underground colonies."

"I didn't know that," Sax said, surprised.

Desmond shook his head. "You have to pay more attention, Sax. In the south we have lived by eco-economics for years now."

"I'll have to look into that."

"Yes." Desmond grinned widely, on the verge of cracking up yet again. "You have a lot to learn."

Their orders arrived, with a carafe of orange juice, and Desmond poured their glasses full. He clinked his glass against Sax's, offered a toast: "Welcome to the revolution!"

Desmond left for the south, having extracted a promise that Sax would pilfer what he could from Biotique for Hiroko. "I've got to go meet Nirgal." He gave Sax a hug and was gone.

A month or so passed, during which Sax thought about all he had learned from Desmond and the videos, sifting through it slowly, getting more and more disturbed as he did. His sleep was still broken nearly every night by hours of wakefulness.

Then one morning after one of these restless, fruitless bouts of insomnia, Sax got a call on his wristpad. It was Phyllis, in town for meetings, and she wanted to get together for dinner.

Sax agreed, with his surprise and Stephen's enthusiasm. He met her that evening, at Antonio's. They kissed in the European style, and were led to one of the corner tables, overlooking the city. There they ate a meal that Sax scarcely noticed, talking inconsequentially about the latest events in Sheffield and Biotique.

After cheesecake they lingered over brandies. Sax was in no hurry to leave, as he was not sure what Phyllis had in mind for afterward. She had given no clear sign, and she seemed in no hurry either.

Now she leaned back in her chair, and regarded him cheerfully. "It really is you, isn't it."

Sax tilted his head to indicate his incomprehension.

Phyllis laughed. "It's hard to believe, really. You were never like this in the old days, Sax Russell. I wouldn't have guessed in a hundred years that you would be such a lover."

Sax squinted uncomfortably and looked around. "I would hope that says more about you than me," he said with Stephen's insouciance. The nearby tables were all empty, and the waiters were leaving them alone. The restaurant would close in a half hour or so.

Phyllis laughed again, but her eyes had a hard look to them, and suddenly Sax saw that she was angry. Embarrassed, no doubt, at being fooled by a man she had known for some eighty years. And angry that he had decided to fool her. And why not? It showed a very fundamental lack of trust, after all, especially from someone who was sleeping with you. The bad faith of his behavior at Arena was coming back to him with a vengeance, making him quite queasy. But what to do about it?

He recalled that moment in the elevator when she had kissed him, when he had been similarly nonplussed. Taken aback first by her nonrecognition, and now by her recognition. It had a certain symmetry. And both times he had gone along with it.

"Don't you have anything more to say?" Phyllis demanded.

He spread his hands. "What makes you think this?"

Again she laughed angrily, then regarded him with lips tight. "It's so easy to see it now," she said. "They just gave you a nose and a chin, I suppose. But the eyes are the same, and the head shape. It's funny what you remember and what you forget."

"That's true."

Actually it was not a matter of forgetting, but of being unable to recollect. Sax suspected the memories were still there, in storage.

"I can't really remember your old face," Phyllis said. "To me you were always in a lab with your nose pressing a screen. You might as well have worn a white lab coat, that's the way I see you in my memories. A kind of giant lab rat." Now her eyes were glittering. "But somewhere along the line you managed to learn to imitate human behavior pretty well, didn't you? Well enough to fool an old friend who liked the way you looked."

"We are not old friends."

"No," she snapped. "I guess we're not. You and your old friends tried to kill me. And they did kill thousands of other people, and destroyed most of this planet. And obviously they're still out there, or else you wouldn't be here, would you. In fact they must be pretty widespread, because when I ran a DNA check on your sperm, the official TA records had you as Stephen Lindholm. That put me off the trail for a while. But there was something about you that made me wonder. When we fell in that crevasse. That did it—it reminded me of something that happened when we were in Antarctica. You and Tatiana Durova and I were up on Nussbaum Riegel when Tatiana tripped and sprained her ankle, and it got windy and late and they had to helicopter us back down to the base, and while we were waiting, you found some kind of rock lichen . . ."

Sax shook his head, truly surprised. "I don't remember that." And he didn't. The year of training and evaluation in Antarctica's dry valleys had been intense, but now the entire year was a dim blur to him, and that incident would not come back at all; it was hard to believe it had happened. He couldn't even remember what poor Tatiana Durova had looked like.

Absorbed in his thoughts, and in a concerted push for his memories of that year, he missed a bit of what Phyllis was saying, but then he caught " . . . checked again with one of my old copies of my AI's memory, and there you were."

"Your AI's memory units may be degrading," he said absently. "They're finding that the circuitry tends to get scrambled by cosmic radiation if it isn't reinforced from time to time."

She ignored that weak sally. "The point is, people who can change Transitional Authority records like that are still worth watching out for. I'm afraid I can't just let this pass. Even if I wanted to."

"What do you mean?"

"I'm not sure. It depends what you do. You could just tell me where you were hiding, and who with, and what's going on. You just showed up at Biotique a year ago, after all. Where were you before that?"

"On Earth."

Her smile had a bad twist to it. "If that's the course you take, I'll be forced to ask for help from some of my associates. There are security people in Kasei Vallis who will be able to refresh your memory."

"Come on."

"I don't mean that metaphorically. They won't beat the information out of you or anything like that. It's more a matter of extraction. They put you under, stimulate the hippocampus and the amygdala, and ask questions. People simply answer."

Sax considered this. The mechanisms of memory were still very poorly understood, but no doubt something crude could be applied to the areas they knew were involved. Fast MRI, point-specific ultrasound, who knew what. It would surely be dangerous, however. . . .

"Well?" Phyllis said.

He stared at her smile, so angry and triumphant. A sneer. Random thoughts flickered through his mind, images without words: Desmond, Hiroko, the kids in Zygote shouting Why, Sax, why? He had to hold his face steady to keep it from revealing his dislike for her, suddenly pouring through him in a wave. Perhaps this sort of distaste was what people called hatred.

After a time he cleared his throat. "I suppose I'd rather just tell you."

She nodded firmly, as if this was the decision she would have made herself. She looked around: the whole restaurant was empty now, the waiters sitting at one table, nursing glasses of grappa. "Come on," she said, "let's go to my offices."

Sax nodded and rose stiffly. His right leg had gone asleep. He limped after her. They said good-night to the mobilizing waiters and left.

They got into the elevator, and Phyllis punched the button for the subway level. The door closed and they dropped. In an elevator again; Sax took a deep breath, then jerked his head down as if to look at something unusual on the control panel. Phyllis followed his gaze and with a jerky motion he slugged her on the side of the jaw. She crashed into the side of the elevator and collapsed in a heap, dazed and breathing in gasps. The two biggest knuckles of his right hand hurt horribly. He hit the button for the floor two above the subway, which had a long passageway through Hunt Mesa, lined with shops that would be closed at this hour. He grabbed Phyllis by the armpits and hauled her up; she was taller than him, loose and heavy, and when the elevator door opened, he prepared himself to shout for help. But no one stood outside the door, and he pulled one of her arms over his neck and dragged her over to one of the little carts that sat by the elevator for the convenience of people who wanted to cross the mesa quickly, or with a load. He dumped her onto the backseat and she groaned, sounding as if she was coming to. He sat down ahead of her in the driver's seat and stomped the accelerator pedal to the floor, and the little vehicle hummed down the hallway. He found he was breathing hard, and sweating.

He passed a pair of rest rooms, and stopped the cart. Phyllis rolled helplessly off the seat and onto the floor, moaning louder than ever. Soon she would regain consciousness, if she hadn't already. He got out and ran over to see if the men's room was unlocked. It was, so he ran to the cart and pulled Phyllis up by the shoulders, up and over his back. He staggered under her weight until he reached the men's room door, then flopped her down; her head cracked against the concrete floor, and her moaning stopped. He opened the door and pulled her through it, then closed and locked it.

He sat on the bathroom floor beside her, gasping. She was still breathing, and her pulse was shallow but steady. She seemed okay, but knocked out even more definitively than when he had hit her. Her skin was pale and damp, and her mouth hung open. He felt sorry for her, until he remembered her threat to give him to security technicians, to tear his secrets out of him. Their methods were advanced, but still it was torture. And if they had succeeded they would know about the refuges in the south, and all the rest. Once they had a general idea of what he knew, they could coax the specifics out of him; it wouldn't be possible to resist their combinations of drugs and behavior modification.

And even now Phyllis knew too much. The fact that he had such a good false ID implied a whole infrastructure that up until now had been hidden. Once they knew of its existence, they could probably ferret it out. Hiroko, Desmond, Spencer who was deep in the system in Kasei Vallis, all exposed . . . Nirgal and Jackie, Peter, Ann . . . all of them. Because he had not been clever enough to avoid a stupid awful woman like Phyllis.

He looked around the men's room. It was the size of two toilet stalls, one stall with a toilet, the other with a sink, a mirror, and the usual wall of dispensers: sterility pills, recreational gases. He stared at these, catching his breath and thinking things over. As plans tumbled in his mind he whispered instructions to the AI in his wristpad. Desmond had given him some very destructive viral programs, and he plugged his wristpad into Phyllis's, and waited for the transfers to take place. With luck he could crash her entire system: personal security measures were nothing against Desmond's military-based viruses, or so Desmond claimed.

But there was still Phyllis. The recreational gases in the wall dispenser were mostly nitrous oxide, in individual inhalers containing about two or three cubic meters of gas. The room was, he judged, about thirty-five or forty cubic meters. The ventilation grill was next to the ceiling, and could be blocked with a strip of the towel, on its roll by the sink.

He stuck money cards in the dispenser and bought all the recreational gases in it: twenty little pocket-sized bottles, with nose-and-mouth masks. And nitrous oxide would be slightly heavier than Burroughs air.

He took the little scissors out of the key compartment on his wristpad, and cut a sheet out of the continuous roll of towel. He climbed onto the toilet tank and covered the ventilation grill, stuffing the sheet into the slits. There were still gaps, but they were small. He climbed back down and went over to the door. There was a gap at the bottom of the door, almost a centimeter tall. He cut some more strips from the towel. Phyllis was snoring. He went to the door, opened it, kicked the gas bottles out and stepped out after them. He took one last look at Phyllis, prone on the floor, and then closed the door. He stuffed the towel strips under the door, leaving only a small opening at one corner. Then, after glancing up and down the hall, he sat down and took a bottle and shaped the flexible mask to the hole he had left, and shot the contents of the bottle into the men's room. He did that twenty times, stuffing the empty bottles in his pockets until they were full, and then making a little satchel for the remainder out of the last strip of towel. He got up and clanked over to the cart and sat down in the driver's seat. He stepped on the accelerator and the cart jerked forward, in a movement the opposite of the sudden stop that had thrown Phyllis off the back-seat and onto the floor. That would have hurt.

He stopped the cart. He got out and ran back to the men's room, clinking and clanking. He jerked open the door, walked in holding his breath, and grabbed Phyllis's ankles and hauled her out into the air. She was still breathing, and had a little smile on her face. Sax resisted the impulse to kick her, and ran back to the cart.

He drove to the other side of Hunt Mesa at full speed, and then took the elevator there down to the subway level. He got on the next subway train, and waited out the trip across town to South Station. He observed that his hands were trembling, and the two big knuckles on his right hand were swollen and turning blue. They hurt a good deal.

At the station he bought a ticket south, but when he gave the ticket and his ID to the ticket-taker at the track entrance, the man's eyes went round and he and his associates actually pulled their pistols to make the arrest, calling out nervously for help from people in another room. Apparently Phyllis had come to faster than his calculations had led him to expect.

PART 5

Homeless

Biogenesis is in the first place psychogenesis. This truth was never more manifest than on Mars, where noosphere preceded biosphere—the layer of thought first enwrapping the silent planet from afar, inhabiting it with stories and plans and dreams, until the moment when John stepped out and said Here we are—from which point of ignition the green force spread like wildfire, until the whole planet was pulsing with viriditas. It was as if the planet itself had felt something missing, and at the tap of mind against rock, noosphere against lithosphere, the absent biosphere had sprung into the gap with the startling suddenness of a magician's paper flower.

Or so it seemed to Michel Duval, who was passionately devoted to every sign of life in the rust waste; who had seized Hiroko's areophany with the fervor of a drowning man thrown a buoy. It had given him a new way of seeing. To practice this sight he had taken on Ann's habit of walking outside in the hour before sunset, and in the long-shadowed landscapes he found every patch of grass a piercing delight. In each little tangle of sedge and lichen he saw a miniature Provence.

This was his task, as he now conceived it: the hard work of reconciling the centrifugal antinomy of Provence and Mars. He felt that in this project he was part of a long tradition, for recently in his studies he had noticed that the history of French thought was dominated by attempts to resolve extreme antinomies. For Descartes it had been mind and body, for Sartre, Freudianism and Marxism, for Teilhard de Chardin, Christianity and evolution—the list could be extended, and it seemed to him that the particular quality of French philosophy, its heroic tension and its tendency to be a long march of magnificent failures, came from this repeated attempt to yoke together impossible opposites. Perhaps they were all, including his, attacks on the same problem, the struggle to knit together spirit and matter. And perhaps this was why French thought had so often welcomed complex rhetorical apparatuses such as the semantic rectangle, structures which might bind these centrifugal oppositions in nets strong enough to hold them.

So now it was Michel's work patiently to knit green spirit and rust matter, to discover the Provence in Mars. Crustose lichen, for instance, made parts of the red plain look as if they were being plated with apple jade. And now, in the lucid indigo evenings (the old pink skies had made grass look brown), the sky's color allowed every blade of grass to radiate such pure greens that the little meadow lawns seem to vibrate. The intense pressure of color on the retina . . . such delight.

And it was awesome as well, to see how fast this primitive biosphere had taken root, and flowered, and spread. There was an inherent surge toward life, a green electric snap between the poles of rock and mind. An incredible power, which here had reached in and touched the genetic chains, inserted sequences, created new hybrids, helped them to spread, changed their environments to help them grow. The natural enthusiasm of life for life was everywhere clear, how it struggled and so often prevailed; but now there were guiding hands as well, a noosphere bathing all from the start. The green force, bolting into the landscape with every touch of their fingertips.

So that human beings were miraculous indeed—conscious creators, walking this new world like fresh young gods, wielding immense alchemical powers. So that anyone Michel met on Mars he regarded curiously, wondering as he looked at their often innocuous exteriors what kind of new Paracelsus or Isaac of Holland stood before him, and whether they would turn lead to gold, or cause rocks to blossom.

The American rescued by Coyote and Maya was no more or less remarkable on first acquaintance than any other person Michel had met on Mars; more inquisitive perhaps, more ingenuous it seemed; a bulky shambling man with a swarthy face and a quizzical expression. But Michel was used to looking past that kind of surface to the transformative spirit within, and quickly he concluded that they had a mysterious man on their hands.

His name was Art Randolph, he said, and he had been salvaging useful materials from the fallen elevator. "Carbon?" Maya had asked. But he had missed or ignored her sarcastic tone and replied, "Yes, but also—" and he had rattled off a whole list of exotic brecciated minerals. Maya had only glared at him, but he had not appeared to notice. He only had questions. Who were they? What they doing out there? Where were they taking him? What kind of cars were these? Were they really invisible from space? How did they get rid of their thermal signals? Why did they need to be invisible from space? Could they be part of the legendary lost colony? Were they part of the Mars underground? Who were they, anyway?

No one was quick to answer these questions, and it was Michel who finally said to him, "We are Martians. We live out here on our own."

"The underground. Incredible. I would have said you guys were a myth, to tell you the truth. This is great."

Maya only rolled her eyes, and when their guest asked to be dropped off at Echus Overlook, she laughed nastily and said, "Get serious."

"What do you mean?"

Michel explained to him that as they could not release him without revealing their presence, they might not be able to release him at all.

"Oh, I wouldn't tell anyone."

Maya laughed again.

Michel said, "It's a matter that is too important for us to trust a stranger. And you might not be able to keep it a secret. You would have to explain how you had gotten so far from your vehicle."

"You could take me back to it."

"We don't like to spend time around things like that. We wouldn't have come close to it if we hadn't noticed you were in trouble."

"Well, I appreciate it, but I must say this isn't much of a rescue."

"Better than the alternative," Maya told him sharply.

"Very true. And I do appreciate it, really. But I promise I won't tell anyone. And you know it isn't as if people don't know you're out here. TV back home has shows about you all the time."

Even Maya was silenced by that. They drove on. Maya got on their intercom and had a brief bursted exchange in Russian with Coyote, who was traveling in the rover ahead of them, with Kasei, Nirgal, and Harma-khis. Coyote was adamant; as they had saved the man's life, they could certainly rearrange it for a time to keep themselves out of danger. Michel reported the gist of the exchange to their prisoner.

Randolph frowned briefly, then shrugged. Michel had never seen a faster adjustment to the rerouting of a life; the man's sangfroid was impressive. Michel regarded him attentively, while also keeping one eye on the front camera screen. Randolph was already asking questions again, about the rover's controls. He only made one more reference to his situation, after looking at the radio and intercom controls. "I hope you'll let me send some kind of message to my company, so they'll know I'm safe. I worked for Dumpmines, a part of Praxis. You and Praxis have a lot in common, really. They can be very secretive too. You ought to contact them just for your own sake, I swear. You must have some coded bands that you use, right?"

No response from Maya or Michel. And later, when Randolph had gone into the rover's little toilet chamber, Maya hissed, "He's obviously a spy. He was out there deliberately so we would pick him up."

That was Maya. Michel did not try to argue with her, but only shrugged. "We're certainly treating him like one."

And then he was back out among them, and asking more questions. Where did they live? What was it like hiding all the time? Michel began to be amused at what seemed more and more like a performance, or even a test; Randolph appeared perfectly open, ingenuous, friendly, his swarthy face almost that of a moon-calf simpleton—and yet his eyes watched them very carefully, and with every unanswered question he looked more interested and more pleased, as if their answers were coming to him by telepathy. Every human was a great power, every human on Mars an alchemist; and though Michel had given up psychiatry a long time ago, he could still recognize the touch of a master at work. He almost laughed at the growing urge he felt in himself, to confess everything to this hulking quizzical man, still clumsy in the Martian g.

Then their radio beeped, and a compressed message lasting no more than two seconds buzzed over the speakers. "See," Randolph said help-fully, "you could get a message out to Praxis just like that."

But when the AI finished running the message through the decryption sequence, there was no more joking. Sax had been arrested in Burroughs.

At dawn they drew up with Coyote's car, and spent the day conferring about what to do. They sat in a cramped circle in the living compartment, their faces all lined and etched with worry—all except their prisoner, who sat between Nirgal and Maya. Nirgal had shaken hands with him and nod-ded as if they were old friends, although neither had said a word. But the language of friendship was not in words.

The news about Sax had come from Spencer, by way of Nadia. Spencer was working in Kasei Vallis, which was a kind of new Korolyov, a security town, very sophisticated and at the same time very low-profile. Sax had been taken to one of the compounds there, and Spencer had found out about it and made the call out to Nadia.

"We have to get him out," Maya said, "and fast. They've only had him a couple days."

"*The* Sax Russell?" Randolph was saying. "Wow. I can't believe it. Who are you all, anyway? Hey, are you Maya Toitovna?"

Maya cursed him in livid Russian. Coyote ignored them all; he hadn't said anything since the message had arrived, and was busy at his AI screen, looking at what appeared to be weather satellite photos.

"You might as well let me go," Randolph said into the silence. "I couldn't tell them anything they won't get out of Russell."

"He won't tell them anything!" Kasei said hotly.

Randolph waggled a hand. "Scare him, maybe hurt him a little, put him under, plug him in, dope him up and zap his brain in the right places—they'll get answers to whatever they ask. They've got it down to a science, as I understand it." He was staring at Kasei. "You look familiar too. Never mind! Anyway, if they can't tweak it out, they can usually do it more crudely."

"How do you know all this?" Maya demanded.

"Common knowledge," Randolph said. "So maybe it's all wrong, but . . ."

"I want to go get him," Coyote said.

"But they'll know we're out here," Kasei said.

"They know that anyway. What they don't know is where we are."

"Besides," Michel said, "it's our Sax."

Coyote said, "Hiroko won't object."

"If she does, tell her to fuck off!" Maya exclaimed. "Tell her *shikata ga nai*!"

"It would be my pleasure," Coyote said.

• • •

The western and northern slopes of the Tharsis bulge were unpopulated relative to the eastern drop to Noctis Labyrinthus; there were a few areothermal stations and aquifer wells, but much of the region was covered in a year-round blanket of snow and firn and young glaciers. Winds out of the south collided with the strong northwest winds coming around Olympus Mons, and the blizzards could be fierce. The protoglacial zone extended up from the six- or seven-kilometer contour nearly to the base of the great volcanoes; it was not a good place to build, nor was it a good place for stealth cars to hide. They drove hard over the sastrugi and along ropy lava mounds that served as roads, north past the bulk of Tharsis Tholus, a volcano that was about the size of Mauna Loa, though under the rise of Ascraeus it looked like a cinder cone. The next night they made it off the snow and northeast across Echus Chasma, and hid for the day under the stupendous eastern wall of Echus, just a few kilometers north of Sax's old headquarters at the top of the cliff.

The east wall of Echus Chasma was the Great Escarpment at its absolute greatest—a cliff three kilometers tall, running in a straight line north and south for a thousand kilometers. The areologists were still arguing over its origin, as no ordinary force of landscape formation seemed adequate to have created it. It was simply a break in the fabric of things, separating the floor of Echus Chasma from the high plateau of Lunae Planum. Michel had visited Yosemite Valley in his youth, and he still recalled those towering granite cliffs; but this wall standing before them was as long as the whole state of California, and three kilometers high, for most of that length: a vertical world, its massive planes of redrock staring out blankly to the west, glowing in each empty sunset like the side of a continent.

At its northern end this incredible cliff finally became less tall, and less steep, and just above 20° North it was cut by a deep broad channel, which ran east through Lunae plateau, down onto the Chryse basin. This big canyon was Kasei Vallis, one of the clearest manifestations of ancient flooding anywhere on Mars. A single glance at a satellite photo and it was obvious that a very large flood had run down Echus Chasma once upon a time, until it reached a break in its great eastern wall, perhaps a graben. The water had turned right down this valley and smashed through it with fantastic force, eroding the entrance until it was a smooth curve, slopping over the outside bank of the turn and ripping at joints in the rock until they were a complex gridwork of narrow canyons. A central ridge in the main valley had been shaped into a long lemniscate or tear-shaped island, the shape as hydrodynamic as a fishback. The inner bank of the fossil watercourse was incised by two canyons that had been mostly untouched by water, ordinary fossae that showed what the main channel had probably looked like before the flood. Two late meteor strikes on the highest part of the inner bank had completed the shaping of the terrain, leaving fresh steep craters.

From the ground, driving slowly onto the rise of the outer bank, it was a rounded elbow of a valley, with the lemniscate ridge, and the round ramparts of the craters on the rise of the inner bank, the most prominent features. It was an attractive landscape, reminiscent of the Burroughs region in its spatial majesty, the great sweep of the main channel just begging to be filled with running water, which no doubt would be a shallow braided stream, coursing over pebbles and cutting new beds and islands every week. . . .

But now it was the site for the transnationals' security compound. The two craters on the inner bank had been tented, as had big sections of the gridwork terrain on the outer bank, and part of the main channel on both sides of the lemniscate island; but none of this work was ever shown on the video, or mentioned in the news. It was not even on the maps.

Spencer had been there since the beginning of construction, however, and his infrequent reports out had told them what the new town was for. These days almost all the people found guilty of crimes on Mars were sent out to the asteroid belt, to work off their sentences in mining ships. But there were people in the Transitional Authority who wanted a jail on Mars itself, and Kasei Vallis was it.

Outside the valley entrance they hid their boulder cars in a knot of boulders, and Coyote studied weather reports. Maya fumed at the delay, but Coyote shrugged her off. "This isn't going to be easy," he told her sternly, "and it isn't possible at all except in certain circumstances. We need to wait for some reinforcements to arrive, and we need to wait on the weather. This is something Spencer and Sax himself helped me to set up, and it is very clever, but the initial conditions have to be right."

He returned to his screens, ignoring them all, talking to himself or to the screens alchemist, his dark thin face flickering in their light. Alchemist indeed, Michel thought, muttering as if over alembic or crucible, working his transmutations on the planet . . . a great power. And now focused on the weather. Apparently he had discovered some prevailing patterns in the jet stream, tied to certain anchoring points in the landscape. "It's a question of the vertical scale," he said brusquely to Maya, who with all her questions was beginning to sound like Art Randolph. "This planet has a thirty-k span top to bottom. Thirty thousand meters! So there are strong winds."

"Like the mistral," Michel offered.

"Yes. Katabatic winds. And one of the strongest of them drops off the Great Escarpment here."

The prevailing winds in the region, however, were westerlies. When these hit the Echus cliff, towering updrafts resulted, and flyers living in Echus Overlook took advantage of them for sport, flying all day in gliders or birdsuits. But fairly frequently cyclonic systems came by, bringing winds from the east, and when that happened cold air ran over the snow-covered Lunae plateau, scouring snow and becoming denser and colder, until the entire drainage area was funneled out through notches in the great cliff's edge, and the winds then fell like an avalanche.

Coyote had studied these katabatic winds for some time, and his calculations had led him to believe that when conditions were right—sharp temperature contrasts, a developed storm track east to west across the plateau—then very slight interventions in certain places would cause the downdrafts to turn into vertical typhoons, smashing down into Echus Chasma and blasting north and south with immense power. When Spencer had identified for them the nature and purpose of the new settlement in Kasei Vallis, Coyote had immediately decided to try to create the means to effect these interventions.

"Those idiots built their prison in a wind tunnel," he muttered at one point, in answer to Maya's inquisition. "So we built a fan. Or rather a switch to turn the fan on. We dug in some silver nitrate dispensers at the top of the cliff. Big monster jet hoses. Then some lasers to burn the air just over the flow zone. That creates an unfavorable pressure gradient, damming up the normal outflow so that it's stronger when it finally breaks through. And explosives installed all down the cliff face, to push dust into the wind and make it heavier. See, wind heats up as it falls, and that would slow it down some if it weren't so full of snow and dust. I climbed down that cliff five times to set it all up, you should have seen it. Set some fans as well. Of course the power of the whole apparatus is negligible compared to the total wind force, but sensitive dependence is the whole key to weather, you see, and our computer modeling located the spots to push the initial conditions the way we want. Or so we hope."

"You haven't tried it?" Maya asked.

Coyote stared at her. "We tried it in the computer. It works fine. If we get initial conditions of hundred-and-fifty kilometer cyclonic winds over Lunae, you'll see."

"They must know about these katabatic winds in Kasei," Randolph pointed out.

"They do. But what they calculated as once-a-millennium winds, we think we can create any time the initial conditions are there on top."

"Guerrilla climatology," Randolph said, eyes bugged out. "What do you call that, climatage? Attack meteorology?"

Coyote pretended to ignore him, although Michel saw a brief grin through the dreadlocks.

But his system would only work with the proper initial conditions. There was nothing to do but sit and wait, and hope they developed.

During these long hours it seemed to Michel that Coyote was trying to project himself through his screen, out into the sky. "Come on," the wiry little man urged under his breath, nose against glass. "Push, push, push. Come over that hill, you bastard wind. Tuck and turn, spiral tight. Come on!"

He wandered the darkened car when the rest of them were trying to sleep, muttering, "Look, yes, look," and pointing at features of satellite photos that none of the rest of them could see. He sat brooding over scrolling meteorological data, chewing on bread and cursing, whistling like a wind. Michel lay on his narrow cot, head propped on his hand, watching in fascination as the wild man prowled through the dimness of the car, a small, shadowy, secretive, shamanesque figure. And the bearish lump of their prisoner, one eye agleam, was likewise awake to witness this nocturnal scene, rubbing his scruffy jaw with an audible rasping, glancing at Michel as the whispering continued. "Come on, damn you, come on. Shooooooooooo . . . Blow like an October hurricane . . ."

Finally, at sunset on their second day of waiting, Coyote stood and stretched like a cat. "The winds have come."

During the long wait some Reds had driven from Mareotis to aid in the rescue, and Coyote had worked out a plan of attack with them, based on information Spencer had sent out. They were going to split up, and come on the town from several angles. Michel and Maya were to drive one car onto the cracked terrain of the outer bank, where they could hide at the foot of a small mesa within sight of the outer-bank tents. One of these tents contained a medical clinic where Sax was being taken some of the time, a fairly low-security place according to Spencer, at least compared to the holding compound on the inner bank, where Sax was being kept between sessions in the clinic. His schedule was staggered, and Spencer could not be sure which location he would be in at any given time. So when the wind hit, Michel and Maya were going to enter the outer-bank tent and meet Spencer, who would be there ready to guide them to the clinic. The bigger car, with Coyote, Kasei, Nirgal, and Art Randolph, was going to converge, with some of the Reds from Mareotis, on the inner bank. Other Red cars would be doing their best to make the raid look like a full-scale attack from all directions, particularly the east. "We will make the rescue," Coyote said, frowning at his screens. "The wind will make the attack."

So the next morning Maya and Michel sat in their car, waiting for the winds to arrive. They had a view down the slope of the outer bank to the big lemniscate ridge. Through the day they could see into the green bubble worlds under the tents on the outer bank and the ridge—little terrariums, overlooking the red sandy sweep of the valley, connected by clear transit tubes and one or two arching bridge tubes. It looked like Burroughs some forty years before, patches of a city growing to fill a big desert arroyo.

Michel and Maya slept; ate; sat; watched. Maya paced the car. She had been getting more nervous every day, and now she padded about like a caged tigress that has smelled the blood of a meal. Static electricity jumped off her fingertips as she caressed Michel's neck, making her touch painful. It was impossible to calm her down; Michel stood behind her when she sat in the pilot's chair, massaging her neck and shoulders as she had his, but it was like trying to knead blocks of wood, and he could feel his arms getting tense from the contact.

Their talk was disconnected and desultory, wandering in random jumps of free association. In the afternoon they found themselves talking for an hour about the days in Underhill—about Sax, and Hiroko, and even Frank and John.

"Do you remember when one of the vaulted chambers collapsed?"

"No," she said irritably. "I don't. Do you remember the time Ann and Sax had that big argument about the terraforming?"

"No," Michel said with a sigh, "I can't say I do."

They could go back and forth like that for a long time, until it seemed they had lived in completely different Underhills. When they both remembered an event, it was cause for cheer. All the First Hundred's memories were growing spotty, Michel had noticed, and it seemed to him that most of them recalled their childhoods on Earth better than they did their first years on Mars. Oh, they remembered their own biggest events, and the general shape of the story; but the little incidents that somehow stuck in mind were different for everyone. Memory retention and recollection were getting to be big clinical and theoretical problems in psychology, exacerbated by the unprecedented longevities now being achieved. Michel had read some of the literature on it from time to time, and though he had long ago given up the clinical practice of therapy, he still asked questions of his old comrades in a kind of informal experiment, as he did now with Maya: Do you remember this, do you remember that? No, no, no. What *do* you remember?

The way Nadia bossed us around, Maya said, which made him smile. The way the bamboo floors felt underfoot. And do you remember the time she screamed at the alchemists? Why no! he said. On and on it went, until it seemed that the private Underhills they inhabited were separate universes, Riemannian spaces that intersected each other only at the plane at infinity, each of them meanwhile wandering in the long reach of his or her own idiocosmos.

"I hardly remember any of it," Maya said at last, darkly. "I can still barely stand to think of John. And Frank too. I try *not* to. And then something will trigger something, and I'll be lost to everything else while I remember it. Those kinds of memories are as intense as if what you remember only happened an hour before! Or as if it were happening again." She shuddered under his hands. "I hate them. Do you know what I mean?"

"Of course. *Mémoire involuntaire.* But I remember also that the very same thing happened to me when we were living in Underhill. So it isn't just getting old."

"No. It's life. What we can't forget. Still, I can hardly look at Kasei . . ."

"I know. Those children are strange. Hiroko is strange."

"She is. But were you happy, then? After you left with her?"

"Yes." Michel thought back on it, working hard to recall. Recollection was certainly the weak link in the chain. . . . "I was, certainly. It was a matter of admitting things I had tried to suppress in Underhill. That we are animals. That we are sexual creatures." He kneaded her shoulders harder than ever, and she rolled them under his hands.

"I didn't need reminding of that," she said with a short laugh. "And did Hiroko give that back to you?"

"Yes. But not just Hiroko. Evgenia, Rya—all of them, really. Not directly, you know. Well, sometimes directly. But just in admitting that we had bodies, that we were bodies. Working together, seeing and touching each other. I needed that. I was really having trouble. And they managed to connect it to Mars as well. You never seemed to have trouble with that part either, but I did, I really did. I was sick. Hiroko saved me. For her it was a sensuous matter to make our home and food out of Mars. A kind of making love to it, or impregnating it, or midwifing it—in any case, a sensuous act. It was this that saved me."

"This and their bodies, Hiroko's and Evgenia's and Rya's." She looked over her shoulder at him with a wicked grin, and he laughed. "That you remember well enough, I bet."

"Well enough."

It was midday, but to the south, up the long throat of Echus Chasma, the sky was darkening. "Maybe the wind is coming at last," Michel said.

Clouds topped the Great Escarpment, a tall mass of highly turbulent cumulonimbus clouds, their black bottoms flickering with lightning, striking the top of the cliff. The air in the chasm was hazy, and the tents of Kasei Vallis were defined sharply under this haze, little blisters of clear air standing over the buildings and curiously still trees, like glass paperweights dropped on the windy desert. It was only just past noon. They would have to wait until dark even if the winds did come. Maya stood and paced again, radiating energy, muttering to herself in Russian, ducking down to take looks out of their low windows. Gusts were picking up and striking the car, whistling and keening over the broken rock at the foot of the little mesa behind them.

Maya's impatience made Michel nervous. It really was like being trapped with a wild beast. He slumped down in one of the drivers' seats, looking up at the clouds rolling off the Escarpment. Martian gravity allowed thunderheads to tower tremendous heights into the sky, and these immense white anvil-topped masses, along with the stupendous cliff face under them, made the world seem surrealistically big. They were ants in such a landscape, they were the little red people themselves.

Certainly they would make the rescue attempt that night; they had had to wait too long as it was. On one of her restless turns Maya stopped behind him again, and took the muscles between his shoulders and neck and squeezed them. The squeezes sent great shocks of sensation down his back and flanks, and then along the insides of his thighs. He flexed in her clutches, and turned in the rotating seat so that he could put his arms around her waist, and his ear against her sternum. She continued to work his shoulders, and he felt his pulse pumping in him, and his breath grow short. She leaned over and kissed the top of his head. They worked their way against each other until they were tightly wrapped together, Maya kneading his shoulders all the while. For a long time they stayed like that.

Then they moved back into the living compartment of the car, and made love. Tight with apprehension as they both were, they fell into it with intensity. No doubt the talk of Underhill had started this; Michel recalled vividly his illicit lusts for Maya in those years, and buried his face in her silvery hair, and tried his best to merge with her, to climb right into her. Such a big feline animal she was, pushing back in an equally wild attempt to take him in, which effort carried him completely away. It was good to be by themselves, to be free to disappear into surprised ravishment, nothing but a series of moans and yelps and electric rushes of sensation.

Afterward he lay on her, still inside her, and she held his face and stared at him. "In Underhill I loved you," he said.

"In Underhill," she said slowly, "I loved you too. Truly. I never did anything about it because I would have felt foolish, what with John and Frank. But I loved you. That was why I was so angry at you when you left. You were my only friend. You were the only one I could talk with honestly. You were the only one who really listened to me."

Michel shook his head, remembering. "I didn't do a very good job of that."

"Maybe not. But you cared about me, didn't you? It wasn't just your job?"

"Oh no! I loved you, yes. It is never just a job with you, Maya. Not for anyone or anything."

"Flatterer," she said, pushing him. "You always did that. You tried to put the best interpretation on all the horrible things I did." She laughed shortly.

"Yes. But they weren't so horrible."

"They were." She pursed her mouth. "But then you disappeared!" She slapped his face lightly. "You left me!"

"I left, anyway. I had to."

Her mouth tightened unhappily, and she looked past him, into the deep chasm of all their years. Sliding back down the sine curve of her moods, into something darker and deeper. Michel watched it happen with a sweet resignation. He had been happy for a very long time; and just in that expression on her face, he could see that he would, if he stayed with this, be trading his happiness—at least that particular happiness—for her. His "optimism by policy" was going to become more of an effort, and he would now have another antinomy to reconcile in his life, as centrifugal as Provence and Mars—which was simply Maya and Maya.

They lay side by side, each in his or her own thoughts, looking outside and feeling the rover bounce on its shock absorbers. The wind was still rising, the dust now pouring down Echus Chasma and then Kasei Vallis, in a ghostly mimicry of the great outflow that had first carved the channel. Michel pushed up to check the screens. "Up to two hundred kilometers per hour." Maya grunted. Winds had been far faster in the old days, but with the atmosphere so much thicker, these slower speeds were deceptive; present-day gales were much more forceful than the old insubstantial screamers.

Clearly they would go in tonight, it was only a matter of getting Coyote's bursted signal. So they lay back down together and waited, tense and relaxed at the same time, giving each other thorough massages to pass the time and relieve the tension, Michel marveling throughout at the catlike grace of Maya's long muscular body, ancient by the dates, but in most respects the same as ever. As beautiful as ever.

Then finally sunset stained the hazy air, and the monumental clouds to the east, clouds which now covered the cliff face. They got up and sponged down, and ate a meal, and dressed and sat in the drivers' seats, getting nervous again as the quartz sun disappeared and the stormy twilight fell away.

In the dark the wind was sheer noise, and an irregular trembling of the rover on its stiff shock absorbers. Gusts buffeted the car so hard that it was sometimes held down against the full crush of the shocks for seconds at a time, the car struggling to rise on the springs and failing, like an animal fighting to free itself from the bottom of a stream. Then the gust would let off and the car would jerk up wildly. "Are we going to be able to walk in this?" Maya asked.

"Hmm." Michel had been out in some hard blows before, but in the dark one couldn't be sure if this was worse than those or not. It certainly seemed like it, and the rover anemometer was now registering gusts of 230 kilometers per hour, but in the lee of their little mesa it was unclear whether these represented true maximums or not.

He checked the fines gauge, and was not surprised to find it was now a full-blown dust storm as well. "Let's drive down closer," Maya said. "It will get us there quicker, and make it easier to relocate the car as well."

"Good idea."

They sat in the drivers' seats and took off. Out of the shelter of the mesa, the wind was ferocious. At one point the bouncing grew so severe it felt as if they might be flipped over, and if they had been side-on to the wind, they might have been; as it was, with the wind behind them, they rolled on at fifteen kilometers per hour when they should have been going ten, and the motor hummed unhappily as it braked the car from going even faster. "This is too much wind, isn't it?" Maya asked.

" I don't think Coyote has much control over it."

"Guerrilla climatology," Maya said with a snort. "That man is a spy, I'm sure of it."

"I don't think so."

The cameras showed nothing but a starless black rush. The car's AI was guiding them by dead reckoning, and on the screen's map they were shown within two kilometers from the outer bank's southernmost tent. "We'd better walk from here," Michel said.

"How will we find the car again?"

"We'll have to get out the Ariadne thread."

They suited up and got in the lock. When the outer door slid open the air sucked out instantly, pulling them hard. The wind keened across the doorway.

They stepped out of the lock and were slammed by great blows to the back. One knocked Michel to his hands and knees, and he could just see through the dust to Maya, in the same position beside him. He reached back into the lock and took the thread reel in one hand, Maya's hand in the other. He clipped the reel to his forearm.

By careful experiment they found they could stand if they stayed crouched forward, helmets at waist level and hands up and ready to catch themselves if they were knocked down. They stumbled ahead slowly, crashing down when strong gusts made it impossible to stand. The ground under them was just barely visible, and a knee striking a rock was all too possible. Coyote's wind had indeed come down too strong. But there was nothing to be done about it. And clearly the inhabitants of the Kasei tents were not going to be out wandering around.

A gust knocked them down again, and Michel let the wind pour over him. It was hard to keep from being rolled. His wristpad was connected to Maya's by a phone cord, and he said, "Maya, are you all right?"

"Yes. And you?"

"I'm okay."

Though there seemed to be a small tear in his glove, over the ball of his thumb. He bunched his fist, felt the cold seeping up his wrist. Well, it wouldn't be instant frostbite the way it used to be, nor pressure bruising. He took a suit patch from his wristpad compartment, stuck it on. "I think we'd better stay down like this."

"We can't crawl two kilometers!"

"We can if we have to."

"But I don't think we do. Just stay low, and be ready to go down."

"Okay."

They stood again, bent double, and shuffled cautiously forward. Black dust flew past them with amazing rapidity. Michel's navigation display lit his faceplate, down in front of his mouth: the first bubble tent was still a kilometer away, and to his astonishment the green numbers of the clock showed 11:15:16—they had been out an hour. The howl of the wind made it hard to hear Maya, even with his intercom right against his ear. Over on the inner bank Coyote and the others, and the Red groups as well, were presumably making their raid on the living quarters—but there was no way of telling. They had to take it on faith that the shocking wind had not halted that part of the action, or slowed it down too much.

It was hard work to shuffle forward doubled over, connected by the telephone cord. On and on it went, until Michel's thighs burned and his lower back hurt. Finally his navigation display indicated they were very close to the southernmost tent. They could see nothing of it. The wind became stronger than ever, and they crawled the final few hundred meters, over painfully hard bedrock. The clock numerals froze at 12:00:00. Sometime soon thereafter they banged into the concrete coping of the tent's foundation. "Swiss timing," Michel whispered. Spencer was expecting them in the timeslip, and they had thought they would have to wait at the wall until it came. He reached up and put a hand gently on the tent's outermost layer. It was very taut, pulsing in time with the onslaught of air. "Ready?"

"Yes," Maya said, her voice tight.

Michel took a small air gun from his thigh pocket. He could feel Maya doing the same. The guns were used with a variety of attachments, for everything from driving nails to giving inoculations; now they hoped to use them to break the tough and elastic fabrics of the tent.

They disconnected the phone cord between them, and put their two guns against the taut vibrating invisible wall. With a tap of the elbows they shot together.

Nothing happened. Maya plugged the phone cord back into her wrist. "Maybe we'll have to slash it."

"Maybe. Let's put the two guns together, and try again. This material is strong, but still, with the wind . . ."

They disconnected, got set, tried it again—their arms were jerked over the coping, and they slammed into the concrete wall. A loud boom was followed by a lesser one, then a cascading roar, and a series of explosions. All four layers of the tent were peeling away, between two of the buttresses and maybe all across the south side, which would surely explode the whole thing. Dust was flying among the dimly lit buildings ahead of them. Windows were going dark as buildings lost lights; some appeared to be losing their windows to the sudden depressurization, although this was nowhere near as severe as it once would have been.

"You okay?" Michel said over the intercom. He could hear Maya's breath sucking through her teeth. "Hurt my arm," she said. Over the roar of the wind they could hear the high ringing of alarms. "Let's find Spencer," she said harshly. She pushed up and was blown violently over the coping, and Michel quickly followed, falling hard inside and rolling into her. "Come on," she said. They stumbled into the prison city of Mars.

Inside the tent it was chaos. Dust made the air into a kind of black gel, pouring through the street in a fantastically fast torrent, shrieking so that Michel and Maya could just barely hear each other, even when they reconnected their phone line. Decompression had blown out some windows and even a wall, so that the streets were littered with shards of glass and chunks of concrete. They moved side by side, kicking ahead cautiously with every step, hands often touching to confirm positions. "Try your IR heads-up display," Maya recommended.

Michel turned his on. The infrared display was nightmarish, the blown buildings glowing like green fires.

They came to the large central building that Spencer had said would contain Sax, and found it too was bright green all along one wall. Hopefully there were bulkheads protecting the underground clinic where Spencer had said Sax was being taken; if not their rescue attempt might already have killed their friend. All too possible, Michel judged; the surface floors of the building were wrecked.

And getting down onto the lower floors was going to be a problem. There was presumably a stairwell that functioned as an emergency lock, but it wasn't going to be easy to locate it. Michel switched to the common band, and eavesdropped on a frantic discussion of trouble across the valley; the tent over the smaller of the two craters on the inner bank had blown away, and there were calls for help. Over the phone Maya said, "Let's hide and see if someone comes out."

They lay down behind a wall and waited, protected somewhat from the wind. Then before them a door banged open, and suited figures rushed down the street and disappeared. When they were gone Maya and Michel went to the door, and entered.

It was a hallway, still depressurized; but its lights were on, and a panel in one wall was lit up with red lights. It was an emergency lock, and quickly they closed the outer door and got the little space repressurized. They stood before the inner door, looking at each other through dusty faceplates. Michel wiped his clear with a glove and shrugged. Back in the rover they had discussed this moment, the crux of the operation; but there hadn't been all that much they could foresee or plan, and now the moment was here, and the blood was flying in Michel's veins as if impelled by the wind outside.

They disconnected the phone cord between them, took taser pistols that Coyote had given them from their thigh pockets. Michel hit the door pad, and it opened with a hiss. They were met by three men in suits but without helmets, looking scared. Michel and Maya shot them and they went down, twitching. Thunderbolts from the fingertips indeed.

They dragged the three men into a side room, and shut them in. Michel wondered if they had shot them too many times; cardiac arrhythmias were common when that happened. His body seemed to have expanded until it was constricted by his walker, and he was very hot, and breathing hard, and ferociously jumpy. Maya apparently felt the same, and she led the way down a hall, almost running. The hallway suddenly went dark. Maya turned on her headlamp, and they followed its dusty cone of light to the third door on the right, where Spencer had said Sax would be. It was locked.

Maya took a small explosive charge from her thigh pocket and placed it over the handle and lock, and they went back down the hall several meters. When she blew the charge the door slammed outward, propelled by air bursting out from inside. They ran in and found two men struggling to latch helmets onto their suits; when they saw Michel and Maya one reached for a waist holster while the other went for a desk console, but hampered by the necessity of getting their helmets secured, they accomplished neither of these tasks before the two intruders shot them. The men went down.

Maya went back and closed the door they had come through. They walked down another hall, the final one. They came to the door of another room, and Michel pointed. Maya held out her pistol in both hands, nodded her readiness. Michel kicked the door in and Maya rushed through with Michel close after her. There was a figure in suit and helmet standing by what looked like a surgical gurney, working over the head of a recumbent body. Maya shot the standing figure several times and it crashed down as if struck by fists, then rolled over the floor, contorted by muscular spasms.

They rushed to the man on the gurney. It was Sax, although Michel recognized him by his body rather than his face, which was a deathmask apparition, with two blackened eyes, and a mashed nose between them. He appeared unconscious at best. They worked to detach him from body restraints. There were electrodes stuck to several places on his shaved head, and Michel winced as Maya simply tore them all away. Michel pulled a thin emergency suit from his thigh pocket, and set about pulling it up over Sax's inert legs and torso, manhandling him in his haste; but Sax didn't even groan. Maya came back and took an emergency fabric headpiece and small tank out of Michel's backpack, and they hooked them to Sax's suit, and turned the suit on.

Maya's hand was clutching Michel's wrist so hard that he feared the bones would crack. She plugged her phone line back into his wrist. "Is he alive?"

"I think so. Let's get him out of here, we can find out later."

"Look what they've done to his face, those fascist murderers."

The person on the floor, a woman, was stirring, and Maya stalked over and kicked her hard in the gut. She leaned over and looked in the faceplate, cursed in a surprised voice. "It's Phyllis."

Michel pulled Sax out of the room and down the hall. Maya caught up with them. Someone appeared before them and Maya aimed her gun, but Michel knocked her hand aside—it was Spencer Jackson, he recognized him by the eyes. Spencer spoke, but with their helmets on they couldn't hear him. He saw that, and shouted: "Thank God you came! They were done with him—they were going to kill him!"

Maya said something in Russian and ran back to the room and threw something inside, then ran back toward them. An explosion shot smoke and debris out of the room, peppering the wall opposite the door.

"No!" Spencer cried. "That was Phyllis!"

"*I know*," Maya shouted viciously; but Spencer couldn't hear her.

"Come on," Michel insisted, picking up Sax in his arms. He gestured at Spencer to get helmeted. "Let's go while we can." No one seemed to hear him, but Spencer got on a helmet, and then helped Michel carry Sax along the hall and up the stairs to the ground floor.

Outside it was louder than ever, and just as black. Objects were rolling along the ground, even flying through the air. Michel took a shot to the faceplate that knocked him down.

After that he was two steps behind everything that happened. Maya plugged a phone jack into Spencer's wristpad and hissed orders at both of them, her voice hard and precise. They hauled Sax bodily to the tent wall and over it, and crawled back and forth until they found the iron spool anchoring their Ariadne thread.

It was immediately clear that they could not walk into the wind. They had to crawl on hands and knees, the middle person with Sax draped over his or her back, the other two supporting on each side. They crawled on, following the thread; without it they wouldn't have had a hope of relocating the rover. With it they could crawl on, straight toward their goal, their hands and knees going numb with the cold. Michel stared down at a black flow of dust and sand under his faceplate. At some point he realized that the faceplate was badly scarred.

They stopped to rest when shifting Sax to the next carrier. When his turn was done Michel knelt, panting and resting his faceplate right on the ground, so that the dust flew over him. He could taste red grit on his tongue, bitter and salty and sulphuric—the taste of Martian fear, of Martian death—or just of his own blood; he couldn't say. It was too loud to think, his neck hurt, there was a ringing in his ears, and red worms in his eyes, the little red people finally coming out of his peripheral vision to dance right in front of him. He felt he was on the verge of blacking out. Once he thought he was going to vomit, which was dangerous in a helmet, and his whole body clenched in the effort to hold it down, a sweaty gross pain in every muscle, every cell of him. After a long struggle the urge passed.

They crawled on. An hour of violent and wordless exertion passed, and then another. Michel's knees were losing their numbness to sharp stabbing pains, going raw. Sometimes they just lay on the ground, waiting for a particularly maniacal gust to pass. It was striking how even at hurricane speeds the wind came in individual buffets; the wind was not a steady pressure, but a series of shocking blows. They had to lie prone for so long waiting out these hammerstrokes that there was time to get bored, to have one's mind wander, to doze. It seemed they might be caught out by dawn.

But then he saw the shattered numerals of his faceplate clock—it was actually only 3:30 A.M. They crawled on.

And then the thread lifted, and they nosed right into the lock door of the rover, where the Ariadne thread was tied. They cut it free and blindly hauled Sax into the lock, then climbed in wearily after him. They got the outer door closed, and pumped the chamber. The floor of the lock was deep in sand, and fines swirled away from the pump ventilator, staining the overbright air. Blinking, Michel stared into the small faceplate of Sax's emergency headpiece; it was like looking into a diving mask, and he saw no sign of life.

When the inner door opened, they stripped off helmets and boots and suits, and limped into the rover and closed the door quickly on the dust. Michel's face was wet, and when he wiped it he discovered it was blood, bright red in the overlit compartment. He had had a bloody nose. Though the lights were bright it was dim in his peripheral vision, and the room was strangely still and silent. Maya had a bad cut across one thigh, and the skin around it was white with frostnip. Spencer seemed exhausted, unhurt but obviously very shaken. He pulled off Sax's headpiece, gabbling at them as he did. "You can't just yank people out of those probes, you're very likely to damage them! You should have waited until I got there, you didn't know what you were doing!"

"We didn't know whether you would come," Maya said. "You were late."

"Not by much! You didn't have to panic like that!"

"We didn't panic!"

"Then why did you just tear him out of there? And why did you kill Phyllis?"

"She was a torturer, a murderer!"

Spencer shook his head violently. "She was just as much a prisoner as Sax."

"She was not!"

"You don't know. You killed her just because of how it looked! You're no better than they are."

"Fuck that! They're the ones torturing us! You didn't stop them and so we had to!"

Cursing in Russian, Maya stalked to one of the drivers' seats and started the rover. "Send the message to Coyote," she snapped at Michel.

Michel struggled to recall how to operate the radio. His hand tapped out the release for the bursted message that they had Sax. Then he went back to Sax, who was lying on the couch breathing shallowly. In shock. Patches of his scalp had been shaved. He too had had a bloody nose. Spencer gently wiped it, shaking his head. "They use MRI, and focused ultrasound," he said dully. "Taking him out like that could have . . ." He shook his head.

Sax's pulse was weak and irregular. Michel went to work getting the suit off him, watching his own hands move like floating starfish; they were disconnected from his own volition, it was as if he were trying to work a damaged teleoperator. I've been stunned, he thought. I'm concussed. He felt nauseated. Spencer and Maya were shouting at each other angrily, really getting furious, and he couldn't follow why.

"She was a bitch!"

"If people were killed for being bitches you never would have made it off the *Ares*!"

"Stop it," he said to them weakly. "Both of you." He did not quite comprehend what they were saying, but it was clearly a fight, and he knew he had to mediate. Maya was incandescent with rage and pain, crying and shouting. Spencer was shouting back, his whole body trembling. Sax was still comatose. I'm going to have to start doing psychotherapy again, Michel thought, and giggled. He navigated his way to a driver's seat and tried to comprehend the driver's controls, which pulsed blurrily under the flying black dust outside the windshield. "Drive," he said desperately to Maya. She was in the seat next to him weeping furiously, both hands clenching the steering wheel. Michel put a hand to her shoulder and she knocked it aside; it flew away as if on a string rather than the end of his arm, and he almost fell out of his chair. "Talk later," he said. "What's done is done. Now we have to get home."

"We have no home," Maya snarled.

PART 6

Tariqat

—————————

Big Man came from a big planet. He was just as much a visitor to Mars as Paul Bunyan only passing by when he spotted it and stopped to look around, and he was still there when Paul Bunyan dropped in, and that's why they had the fight. Big Man won that fight, as you know. But after Paul Bunyan and his big blue ox Babe were dead, there was no one else around to talk to, and Mars for Big Man was like trying to live on a basketball. So he wandered around for a while tearing things apart, trying to make them fit, and then he gave up and left.

After that, all the bacteria inside Paul Bunyan and his ox Babe left their bodies, and circulated in the warm water lying on the bedrock, deep underground. They ate methane and hydrogen sulfide, and withstood the weight of billions of tons of rock, as if they were living on some neutron planet. Their chromosomes began to break, mutation after mutation, and at the reproduction rate of ten generations per day, it didn't take long for good old survival of the fittest to make its natural selections. And billions of years passed. And before long there was an entire submartian evolutionary history, moving up through the cracks in the regolith and the spaces between sand grains, right up into the cold desert sunshine. All kinds of creatures, the whole spread—but everything was tiny. That's all there was room for underground, see, and by the time they hit the surface certain patterns were set. And there wasn't much to encourage growth up there anyway. So a whole chasmoendolithic biosphere developed, in which everything was small. Their whales were the size of first-day tadpoles, their sequoias were like antler lichen, and so on down the line. It was as if the two-magnitude ratio, *which always has things on Mars a hundred times bigger than their counterparts on Earth, had finally gone the other way, and piled it on.*

And so their evolution produced the little red people. They're like us—or they look kind of like us when we see them. But that's because we only ever see them out of the corner of our eyes. If you get a clear look at one you will see that it looks like a very tiny standing salamander, dark red, although the skin apparently does have some chameleon abilities, and they are usually the same color as the rocks they are standing among. If you see one really clearly you'll notice that its skin resembles plate lichen mixed with sand grains, and its eyes are rubies. It's fascinating, but don't get too excited because the truth is you're not ever going to see one of them that clearly. It's just too hard. When they hold still we flat can't see them. We would never see them at all, except that some of them when they get in a mood are so confident that they can freeze and disappear that they will jump around when they're in your peripheral vision, just to blow your mind. So you see that, but then they stop moving when you turn your eye to look, and you never can spot them again.

They live everywhere, including all our rooms. Usually there's a few in every pile of dust in the corners. And how many can say their rooms don't have some dust in their corners? I thought not. It makes a good abrasive when you get around to swiping down, doesn't it. Yes, on those days the little red people all have to run like hell. Disasters for them. They figure we're crazy huge idiots that every once in a while have fits and go on a rampage.

Yes, it is true that the first human to see the little red people was John Boone. What else would you expect? He saw them within hours of his landing. Later he learned to see them even when they were still, and then he began talking to the ones he spotted in his rooms, until they finally cracked and talked back. John and them taught each other their languages, and you can still hear the little red people use all kinds of John Booneisms in their English. Eventually a whole crowd of them traveled with Boone wherever he went. They liked it, and John wasn't a very neat person, so they had their spots. Yes, there were several hundred of them in Nicosia the night he was killed. That's what actually got those Arabs who died later that night—a whole gang of the little ones went after them. Gruesome.

Anyway, they were John Boone's friends, and they were just as sad as the rest of us when he was killed. There's no human since who has learned their language, or gotten to know them anywhere near as close. Yes, John was also the first to tell stories about them. A lot of what we know about them comes from him, because of that special relationship. Yes, it is said that excessive use of omegendorph causes faint red crawling dots in the abuser's peripheral vision. But why do you ask?

Anyway, since John's death the little red people have been living with us and laying low, watching us with their ruby eyes and trying to find out what we're like, and why we do what we do. And how they can deal with us, and get what they want—which is people they can talk to and be friends with, who won't sweep them out every few months or wreck the planet either. So they're watching us. Whole caravan cities are carrying the little red people around with us. And they're getting ready to talk to us again. They're figuring out who they should talk to. They're asking themselves, which of these giant idiots knows about Ka?

That's their name for Mars, yes. They call it Ka. The Arabs love that fact because the Arabic for Mars is Qahira, and the Japanese like it too because their name for it is Kasei. But actually a whole lot of Earth names for Mars have the sound ka in them somewhere—and some little red dialects have it as m'kah, which adds a sound that's in a lot of other Terran names for it too. It's possible that the little red people had a space program in earlier times, and came to Earth and were our fairies, elves and little people generally, and at that time told some humans where they came from, and gave us the name. On the other hand it may be that the planet itself suggests the sound in some hypnotic way that affects all conscious observers, whether standing right on it or seeing it as a red star in the sky. I don't know, maybe it's the color that does it. Ka.

And so the ka watch us and they ask, who knows Ka? Who spends time with Ka, and learns Ka, and likes to touch Ka, and walks around on Ka, and lets Ka seep into them, and leaves the dust in their rooms alone? Those are the humans we're going to talk to. Pretty soon we're going to introduce ourselves, they say, to just as many of you as we can find who seem like Ka. And when we do, you'd better be ready. We're going to have a plan. It'll be time to drop everything and walk right out on the streets into a new world. It'll be time to free Ka.

They drove south in silence, the car bobbing under the wind's on-slaughts. Hour followed hour, and there was no word from Michel and Maya; they had arranged for bursted radio signals that sounded very similar to the static caused by lightning, one for success and one for failure. But the radio only hissed, barely audible over the roaring wind. Nirgal got more and more frightened the longer they waited; it seemed that some kind of disaster had overtaken their companions on the outer bank, and given how extreme their own night had been—the desperate crawling through the howling blackness, the hurtling debris, the wild firing by some of the people inside the broken tents—the possibilities were grim. The whole plan now looked crazy, and Nirgal wondered at Coyote's judgment, Coyote who was studying his AI screen muttering to himself and rocking over his hurt shins . . . of course the others had agreed to the plan, as had Nirgal, and Maya and Spencer had helped to formulate it, along with the Mareotis Reds. And no one had expected the katabatic hurricane to become this severe. But Coyote had been the leader, no doubt about it. And now he was looking as distraught as Nirgal had ever seen him, angry, worried, frightened.

Then the radio crackled just as if a pair of lightning bolts had struck nearby, and the decryption of the message followed immediately. *Success.* Success. They had found Sax on the outer bank, and got him out.

The mood in the car went from gloom to elation as if launched from a slingshot. They shouted incoherently, they laughed, they embraced each other; Nirgal and Kasei wiped tears of joy and relief from their eyes, and Art, who had stayed in the car during the raid, and then taken it on himself to drive around picking them up out of the black wind, gave them slaps on the back that knocked them all over the compartment, shouting, "Good job! Good job!"

Coyote, dosed thoroughly with painkillers, laughed his crazed laugh. Nirgal felt physically light, as if the gravity in his chest had lessened. Such extremes of exertion, fear, anxiety—now joy—giddily he understood that these were the moments that etched themselves on one's mind forever, when one was struck by the shocking reality of reality, so seldom felt, now igniting in him like a fuse. And he could see the same stark glory lighting all his companions' faces, wild animals glowing with spirit.

The Reds took off north for their refuge in Mareotis. Coyote drove south hard, to the rendezvous with Maya and Michel. They met in a dim chocolate dawn, far up Echus Chasma. The group from the inner-bank car hurried over into Michel and Maya's car, ready to renew the celebration. Nirgal tumbled through the lock and shook hands with Spencer, a short round-faced drawn-looking man, whose hands were trembling. Nevertheless he inspected Nirgal closely. "Good to meet you," he said. "I've heard about you."

"It went really well," Coyote was saying, to a chorus of shouted protest from Kasei and Art and Nirgal. In fact they had barely escaped with their lives, crawling around on the inner bank trying to survive the typhoon and the panicked police inside the tent, trying to find the car while Art tried to find them. . . .

Maya's glare cut short their merriment. In fact with the initial joy of the rendezvous over, it was becoming clear that things were not right in her car. Sax had been saved, but a bit too late. He had been tortured, Maya told them curtly. It was not clear how much damage had been done to him, as he was unconscious.

Nirgal went to the back of the compartment to see him. He lay on the couch senselessly, his smashed face a shocking sight. Michel came back and sat down, woozy from a blow to the head. And Maya and Spencer appeared to be having some kind of disagreement, they weren't explaining but they did not look at each other, or speak to each other. Maya was clearly in a foul mood, Nirgal recognized the look from childhood, although this one was worse, her face hard and her mouth set in a down-turned sickle.

"I killed Phyllis," she told Coyote.

There was silence. Nirgal's hands went cold. Suddenly, looking around at the others, he saw that they all felt awkward. It was the sole woman among them who was the killer, and for a second there was something strange in that which they all felt, including Maya—who drew herself up, scornful of their cowardice. None of this was rational or even conscious in them, Nirgal saw as he read their faces, but rather something primal, instinctive, biological. And so Maya only stared them down the more, contemptuous of their horror, glaring at them with an eagle's alien hostility.

Coyote stepped to her side and went on his toes to peck her on the cheek with a kiss, meeting her glare foursquare. "You did good," he said, putting a hand to her arm. "You saved Sax."

Maya shrugged him off and said, "We blew up the machine they had Sax hooked into. I don't know if we managed to wreck any records. Probably not. And they know they had him, and that someone took him back. So there's no reason to celebrate. They'll come after us now with everything they've got."

"I don't think they're that well organized," Art offered.

"You shut up," Maya told him.

"Well, okay, but look, now that they know about you, you won't have to hide so much, right?"

"Back in business," Coyote muttered.

They drove south together through that day, as the dust torn up by the katabatic storm was enough to hide them from satellite cameras. Tension remained high; Maya was in a black fury, and could not be spoken to. Michel handled her like an unexploded bomb, trying always to get her focused on the practical matters of the moment, so that she might forget their terrible night out. But with Sax lying on a couch in the living compartment of their car, unconscious and looking like a racoon with all his bruises, this was no easy thing to forget. Nirgal sat beside Sax for hours on end, a hand placed flat on his ribs, or the top of his head. Other than that there was nothing to be done. Even without the black eyes he wouldn't have looked much like the Sax Russell whom Nirgal had known as a child. It was a visceral shock to see the signs of physical abuse on him, proof positive that they had deadly enemies in the world. This was something Nirgal had been wondering about in recent years, so that the sight of Sax was an ugly, sickening thing—not just that they had enemies, but that there were people who would do this kind of thing, had always been doing it all through history, just as the unbelievable accounts had it. They were real after all. And Sax only one of millions of victims.

As Sax slept, his head rolled from side to side. "I'm going to give him a shot of pandorph," Michel said. "Him and then me."

"There's something wrong with his lungs," Nirgal said.

"Is there?" Michel put his ear to Sax's chest, listened for a time, hissed. "Some fluid in there, you're right."

"What were they doing to him?" Nirgal asked Spencer.

"They were talking to him while they had him under. You know, they have located several memory centers in the hippocampus very precisely, and with drugs and a very minute ultrasound stimulation, and fast MRI to track what they're doing . . . well, people just answer whatever questions they are asked, often at great length. They were doing that to Sax when the wind hit and they lost power. The emergency generator kicked in right away, but—" He gestured at Sax. "Then, or when we took him out of the apparatus . . ."

This was why Maya had killed Phyllis Boyle, then. The end of the collaborator. Murder among the First Hundred. . . .

Well, Kasei muttered under his breath in the other car, it wouldn't be the first time. There were people who suspected Maya of arranging the assassination of John Boone, and Nirgal had heard of people who suspected that Frank Chalmers's disappearance might also have been her doing. The Black Widow, they called her. Nirgal had discounted these stories as malicious gossip, spread by people who obviously hated Maya, like Jackie. But certainly Maya now looked poisonously dangerous, sitting in her car glaring at the radio, as if considering breaking their silence to send word to the south: white-haired, hawk-nosed, mouth like a wound . . . it made Nirgal nervous just to get in the same car with her, though he fought against the sensation. She was one of his most important teachers after all, he had spent hours and hours absorbing her impatient instruction in math and history and Russian, learning her more than any of the subject material; and he knew very well that she did not want to be a murderer, that under her moods both bold and bleak (both manic and depressive) there writhed a lonely soul, proud and hungry. So that in yet another way this affair had become a disaster, despite their ostensible success.

Maya was adamant that they should all get down immediately into the southern polar region, to tell the underground what had happened.

"It is not so easy," Coyote said. "They know we were in Kasei Vallis, and since they had time to get Sax to talk, they probably know we'll be trying to get back south. They can look at a map as well as we can, and see that the equator is basically blocked, from west Tharsis all the way to the east of the chaoses."

"There's the gap between Pavonis and Noctis," Maya said.

"Yes, but there's several pistes and pipelines crossing that, and two wraps of the elevator. I've got tunnels built under all those, but if they're looking they might find some of them, or see our cars."

"So what are you saying?"

"I think we have to go around, north of Tharsis and Olympus Mons, and then down Amazonis, and cross the equator there."

Maya shook her head. "We need to get south fast, to let them know they've been found out."

Coyote thought about it. "We can split up," he said. "I've got a little ultralight plane stashed in a hideout near the foot of Echus Overlook. Kasei can lead you and Michel to it, and fly you back south. We'll follow by way of Amazonis."

"What about Sax?"

"We'll take him straight to Tharsis Tholus, there's a Bogdanovist med clinic there. That's only two nights away."

Maya talked it over with Michel and Kasei, never even glancing at Spencer. Michel and Kasei were agreeable, and finally she nodded. "All right. We're off south. Come down as quickly as you can."

They drove by night and slept by day, in their old pattern, and in two nights made their way across Echus Chasma to Tharsis Tholus, a volcanic cone on the northern edge of the Tharsis bulge.

There a Nicosia-class tent town called Tharsis Tholus was located on the black flank of its namesake. The town was part of the demimonde: most of its citizens were living ordinary lives in the surface net, but many of them were Bogdanovists, who helped support Bogdanovist refuges in the area, as well as Red sanctuaries in Mareotis and on the Great Escarpment; and they helped other people in the town who had left the net, or been off it since birth. The biggest med clinic in town was Bogdanovist, and served many of the underground.

So they drove right up to the tent, and plugged into its garage, and got out. And soon a little ambulance car came and rushed Sax to the clinic, near the center of town. The rest of them walked down the grassy main street after him, feeling the roominess after all those days in the cars. Art goggled at their open behavior, and Nirgal briefly explained the demimonde to him as they walked to a café with some safe rooms upstairs, across from the clinic.

At the clinic itself they were already at work on Sax. A few hours after their arrival, Nirgal was allowed to clean up and change into sterile clothes, and then to go in to sit with him.

They had him on a ventilator, which was circulating a liquid through his lungs. One could see it in the clear tubes and the mask covering his face, looking like clouded water. It was an awful thing to see, as if they were drowning him. But the liquid was a perfluorocarbon-based mixture, and it transferred to Sax three times as much oxygen as air would have, and flushed out the gunk that had been accumulating in his lungs, and reinflated collapsed airways, and was spiked with a variety of drugs and medicines. The med tech working on Sax explained all this to Nirgal as she worked. "He had a bit of edema, so it's kind of a paradoxical treatment, but it works."

And so Nirgal sat, his hand on Sax's arm, watching the fluid inside the mask that was taped to Sax's lower face, swirling in and out of him. "It's like he's back in an ectogene tank," Nirgal said.

"Or," the med tech said, looking at him curiously, "in the womb."

"Yes. Being reborn. He doesn't even look the same."

"Keep that hand on him," the tech advised, and went away. Nirgal sat and tried to feel how Sax was doing, tried to feel that vitality struggling in its own processes, swimming back up into the world. Sax's temperature fluctuated in alarming little swoops and dives. Other medical people came in and held instruments against Sax's head and face, talking among themselves in low voices. "Some damage. Anterior, left side. We'll see."

The same tech came in a few nights later when Nirgal was there, and said, "Hold his head, Nirgal. Left side, around the ear. Just above it, yeah. Hold it there and . . . yeah, like that. Now do what you do."

"What?"

"You know. Send heat into him." And she left hastily, as if embarrassed to have made such a suggestion, or frightened.

Nirgal sat and collected himself. He located the fire within, and tried running some of it into his hand, and across into Sax. Heat, heat, a tentative jolt of whiteness, sent into the injured green . . . then feeling again, trying to read the heat of Sax's head.

Days passed, and Nirgal spent most of them at the clinic. One night he was coming back from the kitchens when the young tech came running down the hall to him, grabbing him by the arm and saying, "Come on, come on," and the next thing he knew he was down in the room, holding Sax's head, his breath short and all his muscles like wires. There were three doctors in there and some more techs. One doctor put out an arm toward Nirgal, and the young tech stepped in between them.

He felt something inside Sax stir, as if going away, or coming back—some passage. He poured into Sax every bit of viriditas he could muster, suddenly terrified, stricken with memories of the clinic in Zygote, of sitting with Simon. That look on Simon's face, the night he died. The perfluorocarbon liquid swirled in and out of Sax, a quick shallow tide. Nirgal watched it, thinking about Simon. His hand lost its heat, and he couldn't bring it back. Sax would know who it was with hands so warm. If it mattered. But as it was all he could do . . . he exerted himself, pushed as if the world were freezing, as if he could pull back not only Sax but also Simon, if he pushed hard enough. "Why, Sax?" he said softly into the ear by his hand. "But why? Why, Sax? But why? Why, Sax? But why? Why, Sax? But why?"

The perfluorocarbon swirled. The overlit room hummed. The doctors worked at the machines and over Sax's body, glancing at each other, at Nirgal. The word *why* became nothing but a sound, a kind of prayer. An hour passed and then more hours, slow and anxious, until they fell into a kind of timeless state, and Nirgal couldn't have said whether it was day or night. Payment for our bodies, he thought. We pay.

One evening, about a week after their arrival, they pumped Sax's lungs clear, and took the ventilator off. Sax gasped loudly, then breathed. He was an air-breather again, a mammal. They had repaired his nose, although it was now a different shape, almost as flat as it had been before his cosmetic surgery. His bruises were still spectacular.

About an hour after they took the ventilator off, he regained consciousness. He blinked and blinked. He looked around the room, then looked very closely at Nirgal, clutching his hand hard. But he did not speak. And soon he was asleep.

Nirgal went out into the green streets of the small town, dominated by the cone of Tharsis Tholus, rising in black and rust majesty to the north, like a squat Fuji. He ran in his rhythmic way, around and around the tent wall as he burned off some of his excess energy. Sax and his great unexplainable. . . .

They were staying in rooms over a café across the street, and there he found Coyote hobbling restlessly from window to window, muttering and singing wordless calypso tunes. "What's wrong?" Nirgal said.

Coyote waggled both hands. "Now that Sax is stabilized, we should get out of here. You and Spencer can tend to Sax in the car, while we drive west around Olympus."

"Okay," Nirgal said. "When they say Sax is ready."

Coyote stared at him. "They say you saved him. That you brought him back from the dead."

Nirgal shook his head, frightened at the very thought. "He never died."

"I figured. But that's what they're saying." Coyote regarded him thoughtfully. "You'll have to be careful."

They drove by night, contouring around the slope of north Tharsis, Sax propped on the couch in the compartment behind the drivers. Within hours of their departure Coyote said, "I want to hit one of the mining camps run by Subarashii in Ceraunius." He looked at Sax. "It's okay with you?"

Sax nodded. His raccoon bruises were now green and purple.

"Why can't you talk?" Art asked him.

Sax shrugged, croaked once or twice.

They rolled on.

From the bottom of the northern side of the Tharsis bulge there extends an array of parallel canyons called the Ceraunius Fossae. There are as many as forty of these fractures, depending on how you count them, as some of the indentations are canyons, while others are only isolated ridges, or deep cracks, or simply corrugations in the plain—all running north and south, and all cutting into a metallogenic province of great richness, a basalt mass rifted with all kinds of ore intrusions from below. So there were a lot of mining settlements and mobile rigs in these canyons, and now, as he contemplated them on his maps, Coyote rubbed his hands together. "Your capture set me free, Sax. Since they know we're out here anyway, there's no reason we shouldn't put some of them out of business, and grab some uranium while we're at it."

So he stopped one night at the southern end of Tractus Catena, the longest and deepest of the canyons. Its beginning was a strange sight—the relatively smooth plain was disrupted by what looked like a ramp that cut into the ground, a ramp about three kilometers wide, and eventually about three hundred meters deep, running right over the horizon to the north in a perfectly straight line.

They slept through the morning, and then spent the afternoon sitting in the living compartment nervously, looking at satellite photos and listening to Coyote's instructions.

"Is there a chance we'll kill these miners?" Art asked, pulling at his big whiskery jaw.

Coyote shrugged. "It might happen."

Sax shook his head back and forth vehemently.

"Not so rough with your head," Nirgal said to him.

"I agree with Sax," Art said quickly. "I mean, even setting aside moral considerations, which I don't, it's still stupid just as a practical matter. It's stupid because it makes the assumption that your enemies are weaker than you, and will do what you want if you murder a few of them. But people aren't like that. I mean, think about how it will fall out. You go down that canyon and kill a bunch of people doing their jobs, and later other people come along and find the bodies. They'll hate you forever. Even if you do take over Mars someday they'll still hate you, and do anything they can to screw things up. And that's all you will have accomplished, because they'll replace those miners quick as that."

Art glanced at Sax, who was sitting up on the couch, watching him closely. "On the other hand, say you go down there and do something that causes those miners to run into their emergency shelter, and then you lock them in the shelter and wreck their machines. They call for help, they hang out there, and in a day or two somebody comes to rescue them. They're mad but also they're thinking we could be dead, those Reds wrecked our stuff and were gone in a flash, we never even saw them. They could have killed us but they didn't. And the people who rescued them will be thinking the same. And then later on, when you've taken over Mars or when you're trying to, they remember and they all dive off into hostage syndrome and start rooting for you. Or working with you."

Sax was nodding. Spencer was looking at Nirgal. And then they all were, all but Coyote, who was looking down at the palms of his hands, as if reading them. And then he looked up, and he too was looking at Nirgal.

For Nirgal it was simple, and he regarded Coyote with some concern. "Art's right. Hiroko will never forgive us if we start killing people for no reason."

Coyote's face twisted, as if in disgust for their softness. "We just killed a bunch of people in Kasei Vallis," he said.

"But that was different!" Nirgal said.

"How so?"

Nirgal hesitated, unsure, and Art said quickly, "Those were a bunch of police torturers who had your buddy and were microwaving his brain. They got what was coming to them. But these guys down this canyon are just digging up rocks."

Sax nodded. He was staring at them all with the utmost intensity, and it seemed certain that he understood everything, and was deeply engaged in it; but mute as he was, it was hard to be sure.

Coyote stared hard at Art. "Is this a Praxis mine?"

"I don't know. I don't care, either."

"Hmm. Well—" Coyote looked at Sax; then at Spencer; then at Nirgal, who could feel his cheeks burning. "All right then. We'll try it your way."

And so at the end of the day Nirgal climbed out of the rover with Coyote and Art. The sky above was dark and starry, the western quadrant still purple, casting a florid light in which everything was quite visible but at the same time unfamiliar. Coyote led the way, and Art and Nirgal followed him closely. Through his faceplate Nirgal could see that Art's eyes were pressing glass.

The floor of Tractus Catena was broken at one point by a transverse fault system called Tractus Traction, and the trellis fracturing in this zone had formed a system of crevasses impenetrable to vehicles. The Tractus miners reached their camp from the canyon wall above it, descending in elevators. But Coyote said it was possible to walk through Tractus Traction, following a path of connecting crevasses he had marked for himself. Many of his resistance actions involved crossing "impassable" terrain like this, making possible some of his more legendary impossible visitations, and sending him through badlands no one else had ever even approached. And with Nirgal to run some of the raids, they had performed some truly miraculous-seeming ventures—just by getting out and traveling by foot.

So they jogged down the canyon floor, in the steady Martian lope that Nirgal had perfected, and had tried with partial success to teach to Coyote. Art was not graceful—his stride was too short, and he stumbled frequently—but he kept up. Nirgal began to feel the loose joy of running, the boulder ballet of it, the rapid crossing of long stretches of land under his own power. Also the rhythmic breathing, the bounce of his air tank on his back, the trancelike state that he had learned over the years, with help from the issei Nanao, who had been taught *lung-gom* on Earth by a Tibetan adept. Nanao claimed that some of the old *lung-gom-pas* had had to carry weights to keep from flying away, and on Mars it seemed entirely possible. The way he could fly over rocks was exhilarating, a kind of rapture.

He had to restrain himself. Neither Coyote nor Art knew *lung-gom*, and they couldn't keep up, though they were both pretty good, Coyote for his age, Art for his recent arrival on Mars. Coyote knew the land, and ran in short mincing dance steps, efficient and clean. Art bombed over the landscape like a badly programmed robot, staggering often as he hit wrong in the starlight, but keeping up a pretty good head of steam nevertheless. Nirgal ranged in front of them like a dog. Twice Art went down in a cloud of dust and Nirgal ran over to check on him, but both times Art got up jogging, and in their intercom silence he only waved to Nirgal and ran on.

After half an hour's run down the canyon, which was so straight that it seemed cut by design, cracks appeared on the ground, and quickly deepened and connected up with one another, until progress over the canyon floor proper would have been impossible, as it was now the plateau tops of a collection of islands. The deep slots separating these islands were in places only two or three meters wide, but thirty or forty meters deep.

Walking through these generally flat-floored alleys was a strange business, but Coyote led the way through the maze without delaying at any of the many forks, following a path only he knew, turning left and right a score of times. One slot was so narrow they could touch both walls at once, and they had to scrape through a turn.

When they came out the northern side of the crevasse maze, emerging from a draw in the riven steep escarpment which was the end of the plateau islands, a small tent stood before them against the western canyon wall. Its arc of fabric glowed like the bulb of a dusty lamp. Within the tent were mobile trailers, rovers, drills, earthmovers, and other mining equipment. It was a uranium mine, called Pitchblende Alley, because this lower section of the canyon was floored with a pegmatite extremely rich in uraninite. It was a very productive mine, and Coyote had heard that the processed uranium stockpiled at it during the years between elevators had not yet been shipped out.

Now Coyote ran over the canyon floor toward the tent, and Nirgal and Art followed. There was no one visible inside the tent; the only illumination was provided by a few night lights, and the lit windows of a big trailer set near the center of things.

Coyote walked right up to the tent's nearest lock gate, and the other two followed him. He plugged his wristpad jack into the keyhole by the lock gate, and began to tap on his wristpad. The outer lock door opened. No alarms seemed to go off; no figures appeared out of the door of the trailer. They got in the lock, closed the outer door, waited for the lock to suck and pump, then opened the inner door. Coyote ran toward the settlement's little physical plant, beside the trailer; Nirgal went for the living quarters, hopping up the steps to the trailer's door. He held one of Coyote's "locking bars" under the door handle, turned the dial that released the fixative, and pushed the bar against the door and wall of the trailer. The trailer was made of a magnesium-based alloy, and the polymer fixative would make what was in effect a ceramic bond between the locking bar and the trailer, so that the door would be stuck. He ran around the trailer and did the same to the other door, then dashed back toward the gate, feeling his blood fly through him as if it were pure adrenaline. It was so much like a prank that he had to consciously remember the explosive charges that Coyote and Art were distributing through the settlement, in warehouses, against the tent fabric, and in the parking lot for the mining behemoths. Nirgal joined them in running from vehicle to vehicle, climbing the stairs on their sides, opening doors manually or electronically, tossing small boxes Coyote had provided into the cabs or cabins.

But there were also hundreds of tons of processed uranium that Coyote wanted to haul away. This was impossible, fortunately. They did run over to a warehouse, however, where they filled a number of the mine's own robot trucks with loads, and programmed them with instructions to head off into the canyonlands to the north, burying loads in regions where the apatite concentrations might be high enough to disguise the boxed uranium's radioactivity, and make the loads hard to relocate. Spencer had doubted this strategy would work, but Coyote said it beat leaving the uranium at the mine, and all of them were happy to help in any plan that would keep him from putting tons of uranium in the storage hold of their boulder car, radproof containers or not.

When that was done they ran back to the gate, and got back outside, and ran hard. Halfway to the escarpment they heard a series of pops and booms from the tent, and Nirgal glanced over his shoulder, but saw nothing different—the tent was still mostly dark, the trailer windows lit.

He turned and ran on, feeling as if he were flying, and was astonished to see Art racing over the canyon floor ahead of him, every stride a huge wild leap, bounding like some cheetah-bear all the way to the escarpment, where he had to wait for Coyote to catch up, and lead them back through the crevasse maze. Once out of it he took off again, so fast that Nirgal decided to try to catch him, just to feel how fast it was. He got into the rhythm of the sprint, pressing harder and harder, and as he passed Art he saw that his own springbok strides were almost twice as long as Art's even in sprint mode, where both their legs were pumping as fast as possible.

They got to the boulder car long before Coyote, and waited for him in the lock, catching their breath, grinning through their faceplates at each other. A few minutes later Coyote was there and in with them, and Spencer had the rover moving, with the timeslip just past, and six more hours of night to drive in.

Inside they laughed hard at Art's mad run, but he only grinned and waved them off. "I wasn't scared, it's this Martian gravity I tell you, I was just running the way I usually would but my legs were leaping along like a tiger! Amazing."

They rested through the day, and after dark they were off again. They passed the mouth of a long canyon that ran from Ceraunius to Jovis Tholus; it was an oddity in that it was neither straight nor sinuous, and was called Crooked Canyon. When the sun rose they were hidden on the apron of Crater Qr, just north of Jovis Tholus. Jovis Tholus was a bigger volcano than Tharsis Tholus, bigger in fact than any volcano on Earth, but it was located on the high saddle between Ascraeus Mons and Olympus Mons, and both were visible on skysills to east and west, bulking like vast plateau continents, and making Jovis seem compact, friendly, comprehensible—a hill you could walk up if you wanted to.

That day Sax sat and stared silently at his screen, tapping at it tentatively and getting a random assortment of texts, maps, diagrams, pictures, equations. He tilted his head at each, with no sign of recognition. Nirgal sat down beside him. "Sax, can you hear what I'm saying?"

Sax looked at him.

"Can you understand my words? Nod if you understand."

Sax tilted his head to the side. Nirgal sighed, held by that inquisitive look. Sax nodded, hesitantly.

That night Coyote drove west again, toward Olympus, and near dawn he directed the rover right up to a wall of pocked and riven black basalt. This was the edge of a tableland cut by innumerable narrow twisting ravines, like Tractus Traction only on a much larger scale, creating a badlands like an immense expansion of the Traction's maze. The tableland was a fan of broken ancient lava, the remnant of one of the earliest flows from Olympus Mons, capping softer tuff and ash from even earlier eruptions. Where the wind-cut ravines had worn deep enough, their bottoms broke through into the layer of softer tuff, so that some ravines were narrow slots with tunnels at their bottoms, rounded by eons of wind. "Like upsidedown keyholes," Coyote said, though Nirgal had never seen a keyhole remotely like these shapes.

Coyote drove the rover right into one of the black-and-gray tunnel ravines. Several kilometers up the tunnel he stopped the car, beside a wall of tenting that cut off a kind of embolism in the tunnel, a widened outer curve.

This was the first hidden sanctuary that Art had ever seen, and he looked suitably startled. The tent was perhaps twenty meters tall, containing a section of the curve a hundred meters long; Art exclaimed over the size of it until Nirgal had to laugh. "Someone else is already here using it," Coyote said, "so be quiet for a second."

Art nodded quickly, and leaned over Coyote's shoulder to hear what he was saying over the intercom. Parked before the tent lock was another car, just as lumpish and rocky as their own. "Ah," said Coyote, pushing Art back. "It's Vijjika. They'll have oranges, and maybe some kava. We'll have a party this morning for sure."

They rolled up to the tent lock, and a coupler tube reached out and clamped around their exterior door. When all the lock doors were opened they made their way into the tent, bending and shuffling to carry Sax through the tube with them.

They were met inside by eight tall, dark-skinned people, five women and three men—a loud group, happy to have company. Coyote introduced them all, although Nirgal knew Vijjika from the university in Sabishii, and gave her a big hug. She was pleased to see him again, and led them all back to the smooth curve of the cliff wall, into a clearing between trailers, under a skylight provided by a vertical crack in the old lava. Under this shaft of diffuse daylight, and the even more diffuse light from the deep ravine outside the tent, the visitors sat on broad flat pillows around low tables, while several of their hosts went to work at a clutch of round-bellied samovars. Coyote was talking with acquaintances, catching up on the news. Sax looked around, blinking, and Spencer, beside him, did not look much less confused; he had been living in the surface world since '61, and his knowledge of the sanctuaries must have been almost entirely secondhand. Forty years of a double life; it was no wonder he looked stunned.

Coyote went to the samovars, and began handing out tiny cups from a freestanding cabinet. Nirgal sat next to Vijjika, an arm around her waist, soaking in her warmth and buzzing with the long contact of her leg against his. Art sat down on her other side, his broad face thrust into the conversation like a dog's. Vijjika introduced herself to him, and shook his hand; he clasped her long delicate fingers in his big paw as if he wanted to kiss them. "These are Bogdanovists," Nirgal explained to Art, laughing at his expression and handing him one of the little ceramic cups from Coyote. "Their parents were prisoners in Korolyov before the war."

"Ah," Art said. "We're a long way from there, right?"

Vijjika said, "Yes, well, our parents took the Transmarineris Highway north, just before it was flooded, and eventually they came here. Here, take that tray from Coyote and go pass out cups, and introduce yourself to everyone."

So Art made the rounds, and Nirgal caught up on news with Vijjika. "You won't believe what we've found in one of these tuff tunnels," she told him. "We've become most fantastically rich." Everyone had their cup, so they all paused for a moment and took their first sips together, then after some whoops and a general smacking of the lips they went back to their conversations. Art returned to Nirgal's side.

"Here, have some yourself," Nirgal told him. "Everyone needs to join the toast, that's the way they do it."

Art took a sip from his cup, looking dubious at the liquid, which was blacker than coffee, and foul-smelling. He shuddered. "It's like coffee with licorice mixed into it. Poisoned licorice."

Vijjika laughed. "It's kavajava," she said, "a mixture of kava and coffee. Very strong, and it tastes like hell. And hard to come by. But don't give up on it. If you can get a cup down you'll find it's worth it."

"If you say so." Manfully he downed another swallow, shuddering again. "Horrible!"

"Yes. But we like it. Some people just extract the kavain from the kava, but I don't think that's right. Rituals should have some unpleasantness, or you don't appreciate them properly."

"Hmm," Art said. Nirgal and Vijjika watched him. "I'm in a refuge of the Martian underground," he said after a while. "Getting high on some weird awful drug, in the company of some of the most famous lost members of the First Hundred. As well as young natives never known to Earth."

"It's working," Vijjika observed.

Coyote was talking to a woman, who, though sitting in the lotus position on one of the pillows, was just below his eye level as he stood before her. "Sure I'd like to have romaine lettuce seeds," the woman said. "But you have to take fair for something so valuable."

"They're not that valuable," Coyote said in his plausible style. "You're already giving us more nitrogen than we can burn."

"Sure, but you have to get nitrogen before you can give it."

"I know that."

"Get before you give, and give before you burn. And here we've found this enormous vein of sodium nitrate, it's pure *caliche blanco,* and these badlands are stuffed with it. It looks like there's a band of it between the tuff and the lava, about three meters thick and extending, well, we don't even know how far yet. It's a huge amount of nitrogen, and we've got to get rid of it."

"Fine, fine," Coyote said, "but that's no reason to start potlatching on us."

"We're not potlatching. You're going to burn eighty percent of what we give you—"

"Seventy."

"Oh yeah, seventy, and then we'll have these seeds, and we'll finally be able to eat decent salads with our meals."

"If you can get them to grow. Lettuce is delicate."

"We'll have all the fertilizer we need."

Coyote laughed. "I guess so. But it's still out of whack. Tell you what, we'll give you the coordinates for one of those trucks of uranium we sent off into Ceraunius."

"Talk about potlatching!"

"No no, because there's no guarantee that you'll be able to recover the stuff. But you'll know where it is, and if you do recover it, then you can just burn another picobar of nitrogen, and we'll be even. How about that?"

"It still seems like too much to me."

"You're going to be feeling like that all the time with this *caliche blanco* you've found. There's really that much of it?"

"Tons of it. Millions of tons of it. These badlands are layered through and through with it."

"All right, maybe we can get some hydrogen peroxide from you too. We're going to need the fuel for the trip south."

Art leaned toward them as if pulled by a magnet. "What's *caliche blanco?*"

"It's nearly pure sodium nitrate," the woman said. She described the areology of the region. Rhyolitic tuff—the light-colored rock surrounding them—had been overlaid by the dark andesite lava that roofed the tableland. Erosion had carved the tuff wherever cracks in the andesite exposed it, forming the tunnel-bottomed ravines, and also revealing great seams of *caliche*, trapped between the two layers. "The *caliche* is loose rock and dust, cemented together with salts and the sodium nitrates."

"Microorganisms *must* have laid that layer down," a man beyond the woman said, but she instantly disagreed:

"It could have been areothermal, or lightning attracted by the quartz in the tuff."

They argued in the way people do when they are repeating a debate for the thousandth time. Art interrupted to ask again about the *caliche blanco*. The woman explained that *blanco* was a very pure *caliche*, up to eighty percent pure sodium nitrate, and thus, on this nitrogen-poor world, extremely valuable. A block of it sat on the table, and she passed it over to Art and went back to arguing with her friend, while Coyote bartered on with another man, talking about teeter-totters and pots, kilograms and calories, equivalence and overburden, cubic meters per second and pico-bars, haggling expertly and getting a lot of laughs from the people listening.

At one point the woman interrupted Coyote with a cry: "Look, we can't just take an unknown pot of uranium that we can't be sure we'll get or not! That's either gross potlatching or else ripping us off, depending on whether we can find the truck or not! What kind of a deal is that, I mean it's a lousy deal either way!"

Coyote wagged his head mischievously. "I had to bring it in, or else otherwise you were going to bury me in *caliche blanco*, weren't you. We're out here on the road, we've got some seeds but not much else—certainly not millions of tons of new *caliche* deposits! And we actually need the hydrogen peroxide and the pasta too, it's not just a luxury like lettuce seeds. Tell you what, if you find the truck you can burn its equivalent, and you'll still have given us fair. If you don't find it, then you'll owe us one, I admit it, but in that case you can burn a gift, and then we'll have given you fair!"

"It'll take us a week's work and a bunch of fuel to recover the truck."

"All right, we'll take another ten picobars, and burn six of it."

"Done." The woman shook her head, baffled. "You're a hard bastard."

Coyote nodded and got up to go refill their cups.

Art swung his head around and stared at Nirgal, his mouth hanging open. "Explain to me what just went on there."

"Well," said Nirgal, feeling the benevolence of the kava flowing through him, "they were trading. We need food and fuel, so we were at a disadvantage, but Coyote did pretty well."

Art hefted the white block. "But what's this get nitrogen, and give nitrogen, and *burn* nitrogen? What, do you torch your money when you get it?"

"Well, some of it, yeah."

"So both of them were trying to lose?"

"To lose?"

"To come out short in the deal?"

"Short?"

"To give more than they got?"

"Well, sure. Of course."

"Oh, of course!" Art rolled his eyes. "But you . . . you can't give *too* much more than you get, did I understand that?"

"Right. That would be potlatching."

Nirgal watched his new friend mull this over.

"But if you always give more than you get, how do you get anything to give, if you see what I mean?"

Nirgal shrugged, glanced at Vijjika, hugged her waist suggestively. "You have to find it, I guess. Or make it."

"Ah."

"It's the gift economy," Vijjika told him.

"The gift economy?"

"It's part of how we run things out here. There's a money economy for the old buy-and-pay system, using units of hydrogen peroxide as the money. But most people try to do as much as they can by the nitrogen standard, which is the gift economy. The Sufis started that, and the people in Nirgal's home."

"And Coyote," Nirgal added. Although, as he glanced over at his father, he could see that Art might find it hard to envision Coyote as any sort of economic theorist. At the moment Coyote was tapping madly at a keyboard beside another man, and when he lost the game they were playing he shoved the man off his pillow, explaining to everyone that his hand had slipped. "I'll arm wrestle you double or nothing," he said, and he and the man plonked their elbows on the table and tensed their forearms, and went at it.

"Arm wrestling!" Art said. "Now that's something I can understand."

Coyote lost in seconds, and Art sat down to challenge the winner. He won in seconds, and it quickly became obvious that no one could resist him; the Bogdanovists even clustered across from him, and got three and then four hands clasping his hand and wrist, but he smacked every combination of them down onto the table. "Okay I win," he said at last, and flopped back on his pillow. "How much do I owe you?"

To avoid the aureoles of shattered terrain clustered north of Olympus Mons, they had to circle far to the north. They drove by night, and slept by day.

Art and Nirgal spent many hours of these nights driving the car and talking. Art asked questions by the hundred, and Nirgal asked just as many back, as fascinated by Earth as Art was by Mars. They were a matched pair, each very interested in the other, which as always made a fertile ground for friendship.

Nirgal had been frightened by the idea of contacting Terrans on his own, when it first occurred to him in his student years. It was clearly a dangerous notion, which had come to him one night in Sabishii and never let go. He had spent many hours over many months thinking about the idea, and doing research to figure out who he should contact, if he decided to act on the thought. The more he learned, the stronger grew his sense that it was a good idea, that having an alliance with a Terran power was critical to their hopes. And yet he was sure that all the members of the First Hundred he knew would not want to risk contact. If he did it, he would have to do it on his own. The risk, the stakes. . . .

He tried Praxis because of what he had read about it. It was a shot in the dark, as most critical acts are. An instinctive act: the trip to Burroughs, the walk into the Praxis offices in Hunt Mesa, the repeated requests for a line to William Fort.

He got the line, although that in itself meant nothing. But later, in the first moment he had approached Art on the street in Sheffield, he knew that he had done well. That Praxis had done well. There had been, just in the look of the big man, some quality that Nirgal had found instantly reassuring—some openness, an easy, friendly ability. To use his childhood vocabulary, a balance of the two worlds. A man he trusted.

One sign of a good action is that in retrospect it appears inevitable. Now, as the long rolling nights of their journey passed in the light of the IR imagers, the two men spoke to each other as if they too saw each other in the infrared. Their dialogue went on and on and on, and they got to know each other—to become friends. Nirgal's impulsive reach to Earth was going to work out, he could see it right there in front of him hour after hour, just in the look on Art's face, the curiosity, the *interest*.

They talked about everything, in the way people will. Their pasts, their opinions, their hopes. Nirgal spent most of his time trying to explain Zygote, and Sabishii. "I spent some years in Sabishii. The issei there run an open university. There's no records kept. You just attend the classes you want, and deal with your teacher and no one else. A lot of Sabishii operates off the record. It's the capital of the demimonde, like Tharsis Tholus only much bigger. A *great* city. I met a lot of people there, from all over Mars."

The romance of Sabishii poured through his mind, memories flooding speech in all their profusion of incident, of feeling—all the individual emotions of that time, contradictory and incompatible though they were, experienced again simultaneously, in a dense polyphonic chord.

"That must have been quite an experience," Art remarked, "after growing up in a place like Zygote."

"Oh it was. It was wonderful."

"Tell me about it."

Nirgal crouched forward in his chair, shivering a bit, and tried to convey some of what it had been like.

At first it had been so strange. The issei had done incredible things; while the First Hundred had squabbled, fought, fissioned all over the planet, started a war, and were now dead or in hiding, the first group of Japanese settlers, the 240 who had founded Sabishii just seven years after the First Hundred had arrived, had stayed right next to their landing site, and built a city. They had absorbed all the changes that had followed, including the location of a mohole right next to their town; they had simply taken over the dig, and used the tailings for construction materials. When the thickening atmsophere made it possible they had gardened the surrounding terrain, which was rocky and high, not at all easy land, until they lived in the midst of a diffuse dwarfish forest, a bonsai krummholz, with alpine basins in the highlands above it. In the catastrophes of 2061 they had never moved, and, considered neutral, had been left alone by the transnats. In that solitude they had taken the excavated rock from their mohole and built it into long snaking mounds, all shot through with tunnels and rooms, ready to hide people from the south.

Thus they had invented the demimonde, the most sophisticated and complex society on Mars, full of people who passed each other on the street like strangers but met at night in rooms, to talk, and make music, and make love. And even the people not part of the underworld were interesting, because the issei had started a university, the University of Mars, where many of the students, perhaps a third of the total, were young and Martian-born. And whether these young natives were surface-world or underground in origin, they recognized each other without the slightest difficulty, as people *at home* in a million subtle ways, in ways no Terran-born ever could be. And so they talked, and made music, and made love, and naturally quite a few of the surface natives were thus initiated into knowledge of the underground, until it began to seem as if all the natives knew all, and were natural allies.

The professors included many of the Sabishiian issei and nisei, as well as distinguished visitors from all over Mars, and even from Terra. The students came from everywhere as well. There in the large handsome town they lived and studied and played, in streets and gardens and open pavilions, by ponds and in cafés, and on broad streetgrass boulevards, in a kind of Martian Kyoto.

Nirgal had first seen the city on a brief visit with Coyote. He had found it too big, too crowded, too many strangers. But months later, tired of wandering the south with Coyote, so solitary for so much of the time, he had recalled the place as if it were the only destination possible. Sabishii!

He had gone there and moved into a room under a roof, smaller than his bamboo room in Zygote, barely bigger than his bed. He joined classes, runs, calypso bands, café groups. He learned just how much his lectern held. He found out just how incredibly provincial and ignorant he was. Coyote gave him blocks of hydrogen peroxide, which he sold to the issei for what money he needed. Every day was an adventure, almost entirely unscheduled, just a tumble of encounters from hour to hour, on and on until he dropped, often wherever he was. During the days he studied areology and ecological engineering, giving these disciplines he had begun to learn in Zygote a mathematical underpinning, and finding in the tutorials with Etsu, and in the work itself, that he had inherited some of his mother's gift for seeing clearly the interplay of all the components of a system. The days were devoted to this extraordinarily fascinating work. So many human lives, given over to the gaining of this body of knowledge! So varied, the powers this knowledge gave them in the world!

Then at night he might crash on the floor at a friend's, after talking to a 140-year-old Bedouin about the Transcaucasus War, and the next night be playing bass steel drum or marimbas till dawn with twenty other kavajavaed Latin Americans and Polynesians, the next after that be in bed with one of the dusky beauties from the band, women as cheerful as Jackie at her best, and much less complicated. The following night he might go with friends to a performance of Shakespeare's *King John*, and observe the great X that the play's structure made, with John's fortunes starting high and ending low, and the bastard's starting low and ending high—and sit shaking as he watched the critical scene at the crossing of the X, in which John orders the death of young Arthur. And afterward walk with his friends all through the night city, talking about the play and what it said about the fortunes of certain of the issei, or about the various forces on Mars, or the Mars-Earth situation itself. And then the night after that, after some of them had spent the day out fell running, exploring high basins in his quest to see as much of the land as he could, they might stay out to sleep in a little survival tent, camping in one of the high cirques east of the city, heating a meal in the dusk as stars popped out everywhere in the purple sky, and the alpine flowers faded away into the basin of rock that held them all, as if in the palm of a giant hand.

Day after day of this ceaseless interaction with strangers taught him at least as much as he learned in the classes. Not that Zygote had left him completely ignorant; its inhabitants had included such a great variety of human behavior as to have left few surprises for Nirgal on that score. In fact, as he began to understand, he had been raised in something like an asylum of eccentrics, people bent hard by those first overpressured years on Mars.

But there still were some surprises, nevertheless. The natives from the northern cities, for instance—and not only them, but almost everyone not from Zygote—were much less physical with each other than Nirgal was used to being. They did not touch or hug or caress each other as much, or shove or strike—nor did they bathe together, although some learned to in Sabishii's public baths. So Nirgal was always surprising people by his touch. He said odd things; he liked to run all day; whatever the reasons, as the months passed and he got involved in endlessly connected groups, bands, cells, and gangs, he was aware that he stuck out somehow, that he was the focal point of some groups—that a party was following him from café to café, from day to day. That there was such a thing as "Nirgal's crowd." Quickly he learned to deflect this attention if he didn't want it. But sometimes he found he did.

Often it was when Jackie was there.

"Jackie again!" Art observed. It was not the first time she had come up, or the tenth.

Nirgal nodded, feeling his pulse jump.

Jackie too had moved to Sabishii, soon after Nirgal. She had taken rooms nearby, and attended some of the same classes. And in the fluctuating group of their peers, they sometimes showed off to each other—especially in the very common situation in which one or the other of them was involved in seducing someone or in being seduced.

But they soon learned that they could not indulge themselves in that, if they did not want to drive away other partners. Which neither did. So they left each other alone, except if one actively disliked the other's choice of partner. So that in a way they were judging each other's partners, and acquiescing to each other's influence. And all this without a word, with this rare behavior the only visible sign of their power over each other. They were both fooling around with a lot of other people, making new relationships, friendships, having affairs. Sometimes they didn't see each other for weeks. And yet at some deeper level (Nirgal shook his head unhappily as he tried to express this to Art) they "belonged to each other."

If one of them ever needed to confirm that bond, the other responded to the seduction in a blaze of excitement, and off they went. That had only happened three times in the three years they were in Sabishii, and yet Nirgal knew by those meetings that the two of them were linked—by their shared childhood and all that had happened in it, certainly, but also by something more. Everything they did together was different than when they did it with other people, more intense.

With the rest of his acquaintances, there was nothing so fraught with significance, or danger. He had friends—a score, a hundred, five hundred. He always said yes. He asked questions and listened, and rarely slept. He went to the meetings of fifty different political organizations, and agreed with them all, and spent many a night talking, deciding the fate of Mars, and then of the human race. Some people he hit it off with better than others. He might talk to a native from the north and feel an immediate empathy, starting a friendship that would endure forever. Much of the time it happened that way. But then once in a while he would be utterly surprised by some action totally foreign to his understanding, and be reminded yet again what a cloistered, even claustrophobic upbringing he had had in Zygote—leaving him as innocent, in some ways, as a fairy brought up under an abalone shell.

"No, it's not Zygote that made me," he said to Art, looking behind them to make sure that Coyote was really sleeping. "You can't choose your childhood, it's just what happens to you. But after that you choose. I chose Sabishii. And that's really what made me."

"Maybe," Art said, rubbing his jaw. "But childhood isn't just those years. It's also the opinions you form about them afterward. That's why our childhoods are so long."

One dawn the deep plum color of the sky illuminated the spectacular fin ridge of Acheron to the north, looming like a Manhattan of solid rock, as yet uncut into individual skyscrapers. The canyonland underneath the fin was particolored, giving the fractured land a painted look. "That's a lot of lichen," Coyote said. Sax climbed into the seat beside him and leaned almost nose to windshield, showing as much animation as he had since the rescue.

Under the very top of the Acheron fin, there was a line of mirror windows like a diamond necklace, and on top of the ridge itself, a long tuft of green, under the ephemeral glint of tenting. Coyote exclaimed, "It looks like it's been reoccupied!"

Sax nodded.

Spencer, looking over their shoulders, said, "I wonder who's in there."

"No one is," Art said. They stared at him, and he went on: "I heard about it in my orientation in Sheffield. It's a Praxis project. They rebuilt it, and got everything ready. And now they're just waiting."

"Waiting for what?"

"For Sax Russell, basically. For Taneev, Kohl, Tokareva, Russell . . ." He looked at Sax, shrugging almost apologetically.

Sax croaked something wordlike.

"Hey!" Coyote said.

Sax cleared his throat hard, tried again. His mouth pursed to a little O, and a horrible noise started deep in his throat: "W-w-w-w-w-" He looked over at Nirgal, gestured as if Nirgal would know.

"Why?" Nirgal said.

Sax nodded.

Nirgal felt his cheeks burn as an electric flush of acute relief ran through his skin, and he leaped up and gave the little man a hard hug. "You do understand!"

"Well," Art was saying, "they did it as a kind of gesture. It was Fort's idea, the guy who founded Praxis. 'Maybe they'll come back,' he supposedly said to the Praxis people in Sheffield. I don't know if he thought out the practicalities or not."

"This Fort is strange," Coyote said, and Sax nodded again.

"True," Art said. "But I wish you could meet him. He reminds me of the stories you tell about Hiroko."

"Does he know we're out here?" Spencer asked.

Nirgal's pulse leapt, but Art showed no sign of discomfort. "I don't know. He suspects. He wants you to be out here."

"Where does he live?" Nirgal asked.

"I don't know." Art described his visit to Fort. "So I don't know exactly where he is. Somewhere on the Pacific. But if I could get word to him . . ."

No one responded.

"Well, maybe later," Art said.

Sax was looking out the rover's low windshield at the distant rock fin, at the tiny line of lit windows marking the labs behind them, empty and silent. Coyote reached out and squeezed his neck. "You want it back, don't you."

Sax croaked something.

On the empty plain of Amazonis there were few settlements of any kind. This was the back country, and they rolled rapidly south through it, night after night, and slept in the darkened cabin of the car through the days. Their biggest problem was finding adequate hiding places. On flat open plains the boulder car stood out like a glacial erratic, and Amazonis was almost nothing but flat open plain. They usually tucked into the apron of ejecta around one of the few craters they passed. After the dawn meals Sax sometimes exercised his voice, croaking incomprehensible words, trying to communicate with them and failing. This upset Nirgal even more than it seemed to bother Sax himself, who, though clearly frustrated, did not seem pained. But then he had not tried to talk to Simon in those last weeks. . . .

Coyote and Spencer were pleased with even this much progress, and they spent hours asking Sax questions, and running him through tests they got out of the AI lectern, trying to figure out just what the problem was. "Aphasia, obviously," Spencer said. "I'm afraid his interrogation caused a stroke. And some strokes cause what they call nonfluent aphasia."

"There's such a thing as *fluent* aphasia?" Coyote said.

"Apparently. Nonfluent is where the subject can't read or write, and has difficulty speaking or finding the right words, and is very aware of the problem."

Sax nodded, as if to confirm the description.

"In fluent aphasia the subjects talk at great length, but are unaware that what they're saying makes no sense."

Art said, "I know a lot of people with that problem."

Spencer ignored him. "We've got to get Sax down to Vlad and Ursula and Michel."

"That's what we're doing." Coyote gave Sax a squeeze on the arm before retiring to his mat.

On the fifth night after leaving the Bogdanovists, they approached the equator, and the double barrier of the fallen elevator cable. Coyote had passed the barrier in this region before, using a glacier formed by one of the aquifer outbursts of 2061, in Mangala Vallis. During the unrest water and ice had poured down the old arroyo for a hundred and fifty kilometers, and the glacier left behind when the flood froze had buried both passes of the fallen cable, at 152° longitude. Coyote had located a route over an unusually smooth stretch of this glacier, which had taken him across the two passes of the cable.

Unfortunately, when they approached Mangala Glacier—a long tumbled mass of gravel-covered brown ice, filling the bottom of a narrow valley—they found that it had changed since Coyote had last been there. "Where's that rampway?" he kept demanding. "It was right here."

Sax croaked, then made kneading motions with his hands, staring all the while through the windshield at the glacier.

Nirgal had a difficult time comprehending the glacier's surface; it was a kind of visual static, all patches of dirty white and gray and black and tan, tumbled together until it was hard to distinguish size, shape, or distance. "Maybe it isn't the same place," he suggested.

"I can tell," Coyote said.

"Are you sure?"

"I left markers. See, there's one there. That trail duck on the lateral moraine. But beyond it should be a rampway up onto smooth ice, and it's nothing but a wall of icebergs. Shit. I've been using this trail for ten years."

"You're lucky you had it that long," Spencer said. "They're slower than Terran glaciers, but they still flow downhill."

Coyote only grunted. Sax croaked, then tapped at the inner lock door. He wanted to go outside.

"Might as well," Coyote muttered, looking at a map on the screen. "We'll have to spend the day here anyway."

So in the predawn light Sax wandered the rubble plowed up by the glacier's passage: a little upright creature with a light shining out of his helmet, like some deep-sea fish poking about for food. Something in the sight made Nirgal's throat tighten, and he suited up and went outside to keep the old man company.

He wandered through the lovely chill gray morning, stepping from rock to rock, following Sax in his winding course through the moraine. Illuminated one by one in the cone of Sax's headlamp were eldritch little worlds, the dunes and boulders interspersed with spiky low plants, filling cracks and hollows under rocks. Everything was gray, but the grays of the plants were shaded olive or khaki or brown, with occasional light spots, which were flowers—no doubt colorful in the sun, but now light luminous grays, glowing among thick furry leaves. Over his intercom Nirgal could hear Sax clearing his throat, and the little figure pointed at a rock. Nirgal crouched to inspect it. In cracks on the rock were growths like dried mushrooms, with black dots all over their shriveled cups, and sprinkled with what looked like a layer of salt. Sax croaked as Nirgal touched one, but he could not say what he wanted. "R-r-r . . ."

They stared at each other. "It's okay," Nirgal said, stricken again by the memory of Simon.

They moved to another patch of foliage. The areas that supported plants appeared like little outdoor rooms, separated by zones of dry rock and sand. Sax spent about fifteen minutes in each frosty fellfield, stumbling around awkwardly. There were a lot of different kinds of plants, and only after they had visited several glens did Nirgal begin to see some that appeared again and again. None of them resembled the plants he had grown up with in Zygote, nor were they like anything in the arboretums of Sabishii. Only the first-generation plants, the lichens, mosses, and grasses, looked at all familiar, like the ground cover in the high basins above Sabishii.

Sax didn't try to speak again, but his headlamp was like a pointed finger, and Nirgal often trained his headlamp on the same area, doubling the illumination. The sky turned rosy, and it began to feel like they were in the planet's shadow, with sunlight just overhead.

Then Sax said, "Dr—!" and aimed his headlamp at a steep slope of gravel, over which a network of woody branches grew, like a mesh put there to hold the rubble in place. "Dr—!"

"Dryad," Nirgal said, recognizing it.

Sax nodded emphatically. The rocks under their feet were covered with light green patches of lichen, and he pointed at a patch, and said, "Ap-ple. Red. Map. Moss."

"Hey," Nirgal said. "You said that really well."

The sun rose, throwing their shadows over the gravel slope. Suddenly the dryad's little flowers were picked out by the light, the ivory petals cupping gold stamens. "Dry-ad," Sax croaked. Their headlamp beams were now invisible, and the flowers blazed with daylight color. Nirgal heard a sound over the intercom and looked into Sax's helmet, and saw that the old man was crying, the tears streaming down his cheeks.

Nirgal pored over maps and photos of the region. "I have an idea," he said to Coyote. And that night they drove to Nicholson Crater, four hundred kilometers to the west. The falling cable had to have landed across this large crater, at least on its first pass, and it seemed to Nirgal that there might be some kind of break or gap near the rim.

Sure enough, when they rolled up the low flat-topped hill that was the crater's north apron, they came to the eroded rim and saw the weird vision of a black line, crossing the middle of the crater some forty kilometers away, looking like an artifact of some long-forgotten race of giants. "Big Man's . . ." Coyote began.

"Hair strand," Spencer suggested.

"Or black dental floss," Art said.

The inner wall of the crater was much steeper than the outer apron, but there were a number of rim passes to choose from, and they drove without trouble down the stabilized slope of an ancient landslide, then crossed the crater floor, following the curve of the western inner wall. As they approached the cable, they saw that it emerged from a depression it had crushed in the rim, and drooped gracefully to the crater floor, like the suspension cable of a buried bridge.

They drove slowly under it. Where it left the rim, it was nearly seventy meters off the crater floor, and it didn't touch down until it was over a kilometer out. They pointed the boulder car's cameras up, and watched the view on the screen curiously; but the black cylinder was featureless against the stars, and they could only speculate about what the burn of the descent had done to the carbon.

"That's nifty," Coyote remarked as they drove up a smooth slope of eolian deposit, over another rim pass and out of the crater. "Now let's hope there's a way over the next pass."

From the southern flank of Nicholson they could see south for many kilometers, and midway to the horizon was the black line of the cable's second time around. This section had impacted many times harder than the first pass, and two swaths of ejecta paralleled the cable like henge mounds. It appeared that the cable just barely stuck out of the trench it had smashed into the plain.

As they got closer to it, weaving between ejecta boulders, they could see that the cable was a shattered mass of black rubble, a mound of carbon three to five meters higher than the plain, and steep on its sides, so that it did not look like it would be possible to drive over it in the boulder car.

Off to the east, however, was a dip in the mound of wreckage, and when they drove down the line to investigate, they found that a meteor impact subsequent to the cable's fall had landed on the wreckage itself, smashing the cable and the ejecta swaths on both sides, and creating a new low crater that was all flecked and studded with black cable fragments, and occasional chunks of the diamond matrix that had spiraled inside the cable. It was a disordered mess of a crater, with no well-defined rim to block their way; and it looked like it would be possible to find a route through.

"Incredible," said Coyote.

Sax shook his head vigorously. "Dei—Dei—"

"Phobos," Nirgal said, and Sax nodded.

"Do you think so?" Spencer exclaimed.

Sax shrugged, but Spencer and Coyote discussed the possibility enthusiastically. The crater appeared oval, a so-called bathtub crater, which would support the idea of a low-angle impact. And while a random meteor hitting the cable in the forty years since its fall would be quite a coincidence, the fragments of Phobos had fallen entirely in the equatorial zone, and so a piece of it hitting the cable was much less surprising. "Although still very useful," Coyote noted after he had negotiated their way over the little crater, and gotten the car south of the ejecta zone.

They parked next to one of the last big chunks of ejecta, and suited up and went back to have a look at the site.

There were brecciated chunks of rock everywhere, so that it was not obvious which were pieces of the meteor and which ejecta excavated by the cable's fall. But Spencer was pretty good at rock ID, and he collected several samples that he said were exotic carbonaceous chondrite, very likely to be pieces of the impact rock. It would take a chemical analysis to be sure, but back in the car he looked at them under magnification, and declared himself confident that these were pieces of Phobos. "Arkady showed me a piece just like it, the first time he came down." They passed around a heavy burned-looking black chunk. "Impact brecciation has metamorphosed it," Spencer said, inspecting the stone when it came back to him. "I suppose it has to be called phobosite."

"Not the rarest rock on Mars, either," Coyote said.

To the southeast of Nicholson Crater, the two big parallel canyons of the Medusae Fossae ran for over three hundred kilometers, into the heart of the southern highlands. Coyote decided to drive up East Medusa, the bigger of the two fractures. "I like to go through canyons when I can, see if the walls have any overhangs or caves. That's how I've found most of my cache sites."

"What if you run into a transverse scarp that crosses the whole canyon?" Nirgal asked.

"I backtrack. I've done an inhuman lot of backtracking, no doubt about that."

So they drove up the canyon, which proved mostly flat-floored, for the rest of the night. The following night, as they continued south, the floor of the canyon began to rise, in steps that they were always able to negotiate. Then they reached a new and higher level of flat floor, and Nirgal, who was driving, braked the car. "There's buildings up there!"

They all crowded around to look through the windshield. On the horizon, under the eastern wall of the canyon, a cluster of small white stone buildings stood silently.

After a half hour's examination with the car's various imagers and scopes, Coyote shrugged. "No obvious electricity or warmth. Doesn't look like anyone's home. Let's go have a look."

So they drove toward the structures, and stopped beside a massive chunk of the cliff wall, which had rolled well out on the floor. From this distance they could see that the buildings were freestanding, with no tent around them; they appeared to be solid blocks of whitish rock, like the *caliche blanco* in the badlands north of Olympus. Small white figures stood motionlessly between these buildings, on white plazas ringed by white trees. It was all made of stone.

"A statue," Spencer said. "A town of stone!"

"Mud," Sax croaked, then pounded the dashboard angrily, giving it four sharp slams that startled them all. "Muh!—du!—sa!"

Spencer and Art and Coyote laughed. They clapped Sax on the shoulders as if they were trying to pile-drive him into the floor. Then they all suited up again, and went out to have a closer look.

The white walls of the buildings glowed eerily in the starlight, like giant soap carvings. There were some twenty buildings, and many trees, and a couple of hundred people—and also a few score lions, mixed freely among the people. All carved from white stone, which Spencer identified as alabaster. The central plaza seemed to have been petrified during an active morning; there was a crowded farmers' market, and a group clustered around two men playing chess, with waist-high pieces on a large board. The black chess pieces and the black squares of the chessboard stood out dramatically in their surroundings—onyx, in an alabaster world.

Another group of statues watched a juggler, who looked up at invisible balls. Several of the lions were watching this exhibition closely, as if ready to bat something out of the air if the juggler came too close. All the faces of the statues, human or feline, were rounded and almost featureless, but every one of them somehow expressed an attitude.

"Look at the circular arrangement of the buildings," Spencer said over the intercom. "It's Bogdanovist architecture, or something like."

"No Bogdanovist ever mentioned this to me," Coyote said. "I don't think any of them have ever been in this region. I don't know anyone who has. This is pretty remote." He looked around, a grin showing through his faceplate. "Someone spent a bit of time at this!"

"It's strange what people will do," Spencer said.

Nirgal wandered around the edges of the construct, ignoring the talk on the intercom, looking into one blurred face after another, looking into white stone doorways and white stone windows, his blood stirring. It was as if the sculptor had made the place in order to speak to him, to strike him with his own vision. The white world of his childhood, thrusting right out into the green—or, out here, into the red. . . .

And there was something in the peace of the place. Not just the stillness, but the marvelous relaxation in all the figures, the flowing calm of their stances. Mars could be this way. No more hiding, no more strife, the children racing around the market, the lions walking among them like cats. . . .

After an extended tour of the alabaster town, they returned to the car and drove on. About fifteen minutes later Nirgal spotted another statue, a white bas-relief face only, emerging from the cliff face opposite the town. "The Medusa herself," Spencer said, pausing in his nightly drink. The basilisk glare of the Gorgon was directed back at the town, and the stone snakes of her hair twisted away from her head and back into the cliffside, as if the rock had only just seized her by a serpentine ponytail, preventing her from emerging completely from the planet.

"Beautiful," Coyote said. "Remember that face—if that's not a self-portrait of the sculptor, I'm much mistaken." He drove on without stopping, and Nirgal stared at the stone face curiously. It seemed to be Asian, although perhaps that was only the effect of having the snake hair pulled back. He tried to memorize the features, feeling it was someone he already knew.

They came out of the Medusa's canyon before dawn, and stopped to hide through the day, and chart their next move. Beyond Burton Crater, which lay before them, the Memnonia Fossae cut the land east to west for hundreds of kilometers, blocking their way south. They had to go west, toward Williams and Ejriksson craters, then south again toward Columbus Crater, and after that weave through a narrow gap in the Sirenum Fossae farther south—and so on. Doing a continuous dance around craters, cracks, escarpments, and hollows. The southern highlands were extremely rough compared to the smooth long vistas of the north—Art commented on the difference, and Coyote said irritably, "It's a planet, man. There's all kind of land."

Every day they woke to an alarm set for an hour before sunset, and spent the last light of day eating a spare breakfast, and watching the garish alpenglow colors spread with the shadows over the rugged landscape. Then every night they drove, without ever being able to use the autopilot, navigating the broken terrain kilometer by kilometer. Nirgal and Art took the graveyard shift together on most nights, and continued their long conversations. Then as the stars faded, and dawn's pure violet light stained the eastern sky, they found places where the boulder car would be inconspicuous—in this latitude the work of a moment, almost just a matter of stopping, as Art said—and ate a leisurely supper, watching the sharp blast of sunrise and its sudden creation of great fields of shadow. A couple of hours later, after a planning session, and occasional trips out, they would darken the windshield, and sleep through the day.

At the end of another long night's conversation about their respective childhoods, Nirgal said, "I suppose it wasn't until Sabishii that I realized that Zygote was . . ."

"Unusual?" Coyote said from his sleeping mat behind them. "Unique? Bizarre? Hirokolike?"

Nirgal was not surprised to discover that Coyote was awake; the old man slept poorly, and often muttered a dreamy commentary to Nirgal and Art's narrative, which they generally ignored, as he was mostly asleep. But now Nirgal said, "Zygote reflects Hiroko, I think. She's very inward."

"Ha," Coyote said. "She didn't use to be."

"When was that?" Art pounced, swiveling in his chair to include Coyote in their little circle of talk.

"Oh, back before the beginning," Coyote said. "In prehistoric times, back on Earth."

"Is that when you met her?"

Coyote grunted affirmatively.

This was where he always stopped, when he was talking to Nirgal. But now with Art there, with just the three of them awake in all the world, in a little circle lit by the infrared imager, Coyote's thin crooked face had a different expression than its usual mulish dismissal, and Art leaned over him and said firmly, "So just how did you get to Mars, anyway?"

"Oh God," Coyote said, and rolled onto his side, propping his head up on one hand. "It's hard to remember something that long ago. It's almost like an epic poem I memorized once, and can barely recite anymore."

He glanced up at them, then closed his eyes, as if recalling the opening lines. The two younger men stared down at him, waiting.

"It was all due to Hiroko, of course. She and I were friends. We met young, when we were students at Cambridge. We were both cold in England, so we warmed each other. This was before she met Iwao, and long before she became the great mother goddess of the world. And back then we shared a lot of things. We were outsiders at Cambridge, and we were good at the work. And so we lived together for a couple of years there. Very much like what Nirgal has been saying about Sabishii. Even what he said about Jackie. Although Hiroko . . ."

He closed his eyes, as if trying to see it in his mind.

"You stayed together?" Art asked.

"No. She went back to Japan, and I went with her for a while, but I had to go back to Tobago when my father died. So things changed. But she and I stayed in touch, and met at scientific conferences, and when we met we fought, or promised to love each other forever. Or both. We didn't know what we wanted. Or how we could get it, if we admitted what we wanted. And then the selection of the First Hundred began. But I was in jail in Trinidad, for objecting to the flag-of-convenience laws. And even if I had been free, I wouldn't have had a chance of being selected anyway. I'm not even sure I wanted to go. But Hiroko either remembered our promises, or thought I would be useful to her, I have never decided which. So she contacted me, and told me that if I wanted she would hide me in the farm on the *Ares,* and then in the colony on Mars. She has always been a bold thinker, I give her that."

"Didn't it strike you as a crazy plan?" Art asked, his eyes round.

"Yes it did!" Coyote laughed. "But all the good plans are crazy, aren't they. And at that time my prospects were dim. And if I hadn't gone for it, I would never have seen Hiroko again." He looked at Nirgal, smiled crookedly. "So I agreed to try it. I was still in prison, but Hiroko had some unusual friends in Japan, and one night I found myself being led out of my cell by a trio of masked men, and every guard in the jail sedated. We took a helicopter to a tanker ship, and I sailed on that to Japan. The Japanese were building the space station that the Russians and Americans were using for the construction of the *Ares,* and I was flown up in one of the new Earth-to-space planes, and slipped into the *Ares* just as construction was ending. They popped me in with some of the farm equipment Hiroko had ordered, and after that it was up to me. I lived by my wits from that moment on, all the way to this very moment! Which meant I was pretty hungry at times, until the *Ares* began its flight. After that, Hiroko took care of me. I slept in a storage compartment behind the pigs, and stayed out of sight. It was easier than you might think, because the *Ares* was big. And when Hiroko got confident in the farm crew, she introduced me to them, and it was easier yet. Where it got hard was on the ground, in those first weeks after we landed. I went down in a lander filled with only the farm crew, and they helped me get settled in a closet in one of the trailers. Hiroko got the greenhouses built fast mostly to get me out of that closet, or so she would tell me."

"You lived in a closet?"

"For a couple of months. It was worse than jail. But after that I lived in the greenhouse, and started work on stockpiling the materials we needed to take off on our own. Iwao had hidden the contents of a couple of freight boxes, right from the start. And after we built a rover out of spare parts I spent most of my time away from Underhill, exploring the chaotic terrain and finding a good place for our hidden shelter, and moving stuff out there. I was out on the surface more than anyone, even Ann. By the time the farm team moved out there to it, I was used to spending a lot of time on my own. Just me and Big Man, out wandering the planet. I tell you, it was like heaven. No, not heaven—it was Mars, pure Mars. I guess I lost my mind in a way. But I loved it so . . . I can't really talk about it."

"You must have taken a lot of radiation."

Coyote laughed. "Oh yes! Between those journeys and the solar storm on the *Ares*, I took on more rems than anyone in the First Hundred, except maybe for John. Maybe that's what did it. Anyway"— he shrugged, looked up at Art and Nirgal—"here I am. The stowaway."

"Amazing," Art said.

Nirgal nodded; he had never gotten his father to reveal even a tenth as much information about his past, and now he looked from Art to Coyote and back again, wondering how Art had done it. And done it to him as well—for Nirgal had tried to tell not only what had happened to him, but what it had meant, which was much more difficult. Apparently this was a talent Art had, though it was very hard to pin down what it consisted of; just the look on his face, somehow, that cross-eyed intensity of interest, those bald bold questions, trampling on the niceties and going right to the heart of things—assuming that every person wanted to talk, to shape the meaning of their life. Even secretive weird old hermits like Coyote.

"Well, it was not that hard," Coyote was saying now. "Concealment is never as hard as people think, you must understand that. It's action while hiding that is the hard part."

At that thought he frowned, then pointed a finger at Nirgal. "This is why we will have to come out eventually, and fight in the open. This is why I got you to go to Sabishii."

"What? You told me I shouldn't go! You said it would ruin me!"

"That was how I got you to go."

They kept up this nocturnal, conversational life for the better part of a week, and at the end of it they approached a small settled region surrounding the mohole that had been dug in the midst of craters Hipparchus, Eudoxus, Ptolemaeus, and Li Fan. There were some uranium mines on the aprons of these craters, but Coyote did not suggest any sabotage attempts, and they drove hard past the Ptolemaic mohole, getting away from the region as quickly as possible. Soon they came to the Thaumasia Fossae, the fifth or sixth big fracture system they had encountered on their trip. Art found this curious, but Spencer explained to him that the Tharsis bulge was surrounded by fracture systems caused by its uplift, and as they were in effect circumnavigating the bulge, they kept running into them. Thaumasia was one of the biggest of these systems, and the location of the large town of Senzeni Na, which had been founded next to another of the 40° latitude moholes, one of the first moholes to be dug, and still one of the deepest. At this point they had been traveling for over two weeks, and they needed to restock at one of Coyote's caches.

They drove south of Senzeni Na, and near dawn were weaving between rocky ancient hillocks. But when they came to the bottom end of a landslide coming off a low broken scarp, Coyote started cursing. The ground was marked by rover tracks, and a scattering of crushed gas cylinders, food boxes and fuel containers.

They stared at the sight. "Your cache?" Art asked, which provoked another outburst of swearing.

"Who were they?" Art asked. "Police?"

No one answered immediately. Sax went to one of the drivers' seats to check supply gauges. Coyote continued cursing furiously, plopping meanwhile into the other driver's seat. Finally he said to Art, "It wasn't police. Not unless they've started using Vishniac rovers. No. These thieves were from the underground, damn them. Probably an outfit I know based in Argyre. I can't think of anyone else who would do it. But this crowd knows where some of my old caches were, and they've been mad at me ever since I sabotaged a mining settlement in the Charitums, because it closed down after that, and they lost their main source of supplies."

"You folks should try to stay on the same side," Art said.

"Fuck off," Coyote advised him.

Coyote started up the boulder car and drove away. "It's the same old story," he said bitterly. "The resistance begins fighting itself, because that's the only thing it can beat. Happens every time. You can't get any movement larger than five people without including at least one fucking idiot."

He went on in that vein for quite some time. Finally Sax tapped at one of the gauges, and Coyote said roughly, "I know!"

It was full daylight, and he stopped the car in a cleft between two of the ancient hillocks, and they blacked the windows, and lay in the dark on their narrow mattresses.

"So how many underground groups are there?" Art asked.

"No one knows," Coyote said.

"You're kidding."

Nirgal answered before Coyote started in again. "There's about forty in the southern hemisphere. And some long-standing disagreements among them are getting nasty. There are some tough groups out there. Radical Reds, Schnelling splinter groups, different kinds of fundamentalists . . . it's causing trouble."

"But aren't you all working for the same thing?"

"I don't know." Nirgal recalled all-night arguments in Sabishii, sometimes quite violent, among students who were basically friends. "Maybe not."

"But haven't you talked it over?"

"Not in any formal way, no."

Art looked surprised. "You should do that," he said.

"Do what?" Nirgal asked.

"You should convene some kind of meeting of all the underground groups, and see if you can't agree about what you're all trying to do. How to settle disputes, and like that."

Aside from a skeptical snort from Coyote, there was no response to this. After a long time Nirgal said, "My impression is that some of these groups are wary of Gamete, because of the First Hundred in it. No one wants to give up any autonomy to what's already perceived as the most powerful sanctuary."

"But they could work on that at a meeting," Art said. "That's part of what it would be for. Among other things. You all need to work together, especially if the transnat police get more active after what they found out from Sax."

Sax nodded at this. The rest of them considered it in silence. Somewhere in the consideration Art started to snore, but Nirgal was awake for hours, thinking about it.

They approached Senzeni Na in some need. Their food supplies were adequate if they rationed them, and the car's water and gases were recycling so efficiently that there was little loss there. But they were simply short of fuel to run the car. "We need around fifty kilos of hydrogen peroxide," Coyote said.

He drove up to the rim of Thaumasia's biggest canyon; and there in the far wall was Senzeni Na, behind great sheets of glass, the arcades all full of tall trees. The canyon floor in front of it was covered with walktubes, small tents, the great factory apparatus of the mohole, the mohole itself, which was a giant black hole at the south end of the complex, and the tailings mound, which ran up the canyon far to the north. This was reputed to be the deepest mohole on Mars, so deep that the rock was getting a bit plastic at the bottom, "squishing in," as Coyote put it—eighteen kilometers deep, with the lithosphere in the area about twenty-five.

The mohole operation was almost completely automated, and the majority of the town's population never went near it. And many of the robot trucks hauling rock out of the hole used hydrogen peroxide for fuel, so the warehouses down on the canyon floor next to the mohole would have what they needed. And security down there dated from before the unrest, and had been designed in part by John Boone himself, so it was woefully inadequate to withstand Coyote's methods, particularly since he had all of John's old programs in his AI.

The canyon was exceptionally long, however, and Coyote's best way down to the canyon floor from the rim was a climbing trail, some ten kilometers downcanyon from the mohole. "That's fine," Nirgal said. "I'll get it on foot."

"Fifty kilos?" Coyote said.

"I'll go with him," said Art. "I may not be able to do mystic levitation, but I can run."

Coyote thought it over, nodded. "I'll lead you down the cliff."

So he did that, and in the timeslip Nirgal and Art took off with empty backpacks draped over their air tanks, running along easily over the smooth canyon floor, north to Senzeni Na. It seemed to Nirgal that it was going to be a simple operation. They came up on the mohole complex without a problem, the starlight now augmented by the diffuse light of the town shining out of the glass, and reflecting off the far wall. Coyote's program got them through a garage lock and into the warehouse area as quickly as if they had every right to be there, with no sign that they had tripped any alarms. But then when they were in the warehouse itself, stuffing small hydrogen peroxide containers in their backpacks, all the lights in the place went on at once, and emergency doors slid shut.

Art ran immediately to the wall away from the door, and set a charge and moved aside. The charge exploded with a loud bang, blowing a sizable hole in the thin warehouse wall, and then the two of them were outside and skulking between gigantic draglines to the perimeter wall. Suited figures came racing out of the walktube lock from the town, and the two intruders had to dive behind one of the draglines, a structure so big that they could stand in the crack between individual tractor treads. Nirgal felt his heart pounding against the metal. The suited figures went into the warehouse, and Art ran out and set another charge; the flash of light from this one blinded Nirgal, and he ducked through the gap in the fence and ran for it without seeing a thing, without feeling the thirty kilograms of fuel packets bouncing on his back and crushing the air tanks into his spine. Art was ahead of him again, badly out of control in the Martian g but nonetheless bounding along with those great surging strides. Nirgal almost laughed as he worked to catch up with him, hitting his rhythm and then, as he drew abreast of him, trying to show him by example how to use his arms properly, in a sort of swimming motion, rather than the rapid pumping that was throwing Art off balance so often. Despite the dark and their speed it seemed to Nirgal that Art's arms began to slow down.

And they ran. Nirgal took the lead, and tried to pick the cleanest route over the canyon floor, the one least littered with rocks. The starlight seemed more than sufficient to illuminate their way. Art kept pounding up to his right, pressing him to hurry. It almost became a kind of race, and Nirgal ran much faster than he would have on his own, or in any normal circumstances. So much of it was rhythm, and breath, and the dispersal of heat from the torso out into the skin and then the walker. It was surprising to see how well Art could keep up with him, without the advantage of any of the disciplines. He was a powerful animal.

They almost ran right by Coyote, who leaped out from behind a rock and scared them enough to knock them down like ninepins. Then they clambered up the rocky trail he had marked on the cliff wall, and were on the rim, under the full dome of the stars again, the bright lights of Senzeni Na like a spaceship that had dived into the opposite cliff.

Back in the boulder car Art gasped for air, still out of breath from the run down the canyon. "You're going to have to—teach me that *lung-gom,*" he said to Nirgal. "My Lord you run fast."

"Well, you too. I don't know how you do it."

"Fear." He shook his head, sucked at the air. "This kind of thing is dangerous," he complained to Coyote.

"It wasn't my idea," Coyote snapped. "If those bastards hadn't stolen my supplies, we wouldn't have had to do it."

"Yeah, but you do stuff kind of like this all the time, right? And it's dangerous. I mean, you need to be doing something other than sabotage in the outback. Something systemic."

It turned out that fifty kilos was the absolute minimum they needed to get home, so they limped south with all noncritical systems shut off, so that the interior of the car was dark, and fairly cold. It was cold outside as well; through the lengthening nights of the early southern winter they began to encounter frost on the ground, and snowdrifts. Salt crystals on top of the drifts served as the seed points for ice flakes, which grew into thickets of ice flowers. They navigated between these white crystalline fields, dimly glowing in the starlight, until the fields merged into one great white blanket of snow, frost, rime, and ice flowers. Slowly they drove over it, until one night the hydrogen peroxide ran out. "We could have got more," Art said.

"Shut up," Coyote replied.

They ran on battery power, which would not last long. In the dark of the unlit car, the light cast by the white world outside was ghostly. None of them talked, except to discuss the essentials of driving. Coyote was confident that the distance the batteries would take them would be enough to see them home, but they were cutting it awfully fine, and if anything failed, if one of the ice-clogged wheels jammed in its well—they would have to try walking, Nirgal thought. Running. But Spencer and Sax wouldn't be able to run far.

On the sixth night after the raid on Senzeni Na, however, around the end of the timeslip, the frosty ground ahead became a pure white line, which thickened on the horizon, and then came clear of it: the white cliffs of the southern polar ice cap. "It looks like a wedding cake," Art said, grinning.

They were almost out of battery power, to the point that the car was slowing down. But Gamete was just a few kilometers clockwise around the polar cap. And so just after dawn, Coyote guided the halting car into the outlying garage in Nadia's crater rim complex. They walked the last stretch, crunching over new frost in the raw long-shadowed morning light, under the great white overhang of dry ice.

Gamete gave Nirgal the same feeling it always did, that he was trying to fit into old clothes that were much too small. But this time Art was there with him, and so the visit had the interest of showing a new friend an old home. Every day Nirgal took him around, explaining features of the place and introducing him to people. As he watched the range of expressions plainly exposed on Art's face, from surprise to amazement to disbelief, the whole enterprise of Gamete began to strike Nirgal as truly odd. The white ice dome; its winds, mists, birds; the lake; the village, always freezing, weirdly shadowless, its white-and-blue buildings dominated by the crescent of bamboo treehouses . . . it was a strange place. And Art found all of the issei equally amazing; he shook their hands, saying, "I've seen you on the vids, very pleased to meet you." After introductions to Vlad and Ursula, Marina and Iwao, he muttered to Nirgal, "It's like a wax museum."

Nirgal took him down to meet Hiroko, and she was her usual benign, distant self, treating Art with about the same reserved friendliness she gave to Nirgal. Mother goddess of the world. . . . They were in her labs, and feeling obscurely annoyed by her, Nirgal took Art by the ectogene tanks, and explained what they were. Art's eyes went perfectly round when he was surprised, and now they were like big white-and-blue marbles. "They look like refrigerators," he said, and stared closely at Nirgal. "Was it lonesome?"

Nirgal shrugged, looked down at the small clear windows, like portholes. Once he had floated in there, dreaming and kicking. . . . It was hard to imagine the past, hard to believe in it. For billions of years he had not existed, and then one day, inside this little black box . . . a sudden appearance, green in the white, white in the green.

"It's so cold here," Art remarked when they went back outside. He was wearing a big borrowed fiberfill coat, with the hood over his head.

"We have to keep a water ice layer coating the dry ice, so the air stays good. So it's always a little under freezing, but not much. I like it myself. It strikes me as the best temperature of all."

"Childhood."

"Yeah."

They visited Sax every day, and he would croak "Hello" or "Goodbye" in greeting, and try his best to talk. Michel was spending several hours a day working with him. "It's definitely aphasia," he told them. "Vlad and Ursula did a scan, and the damage is in the left anterior speech center. Nonfluent aphasia, sometimes called Broca's aphasia. He has trouble finding the word, and sometimes he thinks he's got it, but what comes out will be synonyms, or antonyms, or taboo words. You should hear the way he can say *Bad results*. It's frustrating for him, but improvement from this particular injury is often good. Slow, however. Essentially, other parts of the brain have to learn to take over the functions of the damaged part. So—we work on it. It's nice when it goes well. And it could be worse, obviously."

Sax, who had been staring at them through this, nodded quizzically. He said, "I want to teach. To *speech*."

Of all the people in Gamete to whom Nirgal introduced Art, the one Art hit it off with best was Nadia. They were drawn to each other instantly, to Nirgal's surprise. But it pleased him to see it, and he watched his old teacher fondly as she made her own kind of confession in response to Art's question barrage, her face looking very ancient except for her startling light brown eyes, with the green flecks around the pupil—eyes that radiated friendly interest and intelligence, and amusement at Art's interrogation.

The three of them ended up spending hours together in Nirgal's room talking, looking down at the village, or out the other window to the lake. Art walked around the little cylinder from window to door to window, fingering the cuts in the glossy green wood. "Do you call it wood?" he asked, looking at the bamboo. Nadia laughed. "I call it wood," she said. "It's Hiroko's idea to live in these things. And a good one; good insulation, incredible strength, no carpentry but door and window installation . . ."

"I guess you wish you had these bamboo in Underhill, eh?"

"The spaces we had were too small. Maybe in the arcades. Anyway this species wasn't developed until recently."

She turned the interrogation on him, and asked him scores of questions about Earth. What did they use for housing materials now? Were they going to use fusion power commercially? Was the UN irrevocably damaged by the war of '61? Were they trying to build a space elevator for Earth? How much of the population had gotten the aging treatments? Which of the big transnationals were the most powerful? Were they fighting among themselves for preeminence?

Art answered these questions as fully as he could, and though he shook his head at the inadequacy of his answers, Nirgal for one learned a lot from them, and Nadia seemed to feel the same. And they both found themselves laughing fairly often.

When Art asked Nadia questions in turn, her answers were friendly, but varied greatly in length. Talking about her current projects she went on in detail, happy to describe the scores of construction sites she was working on in the southern hemisphere. But when he asked her questions about the early years in Underhill, in that bold direct way of his, she usually just shrugged, even if he asked about building details. "I don't really remember it very well," she would say.

"Oh come on."

"No, I'm telling the truth. It's a problem, actually. How old are you?"

"Fifty. Or fifty-one, I guess. I've lost track of the date."

"Well, I am one hundred and twenty. Don't look so shocked! With the treatments it's not so old—you'll see! I just had the treatment again two years ago, and I'm not exactly like a teenager, but I feel pretty good. Very good in fact. But I think memory may be the weak link. It may be the brain just won't hold that much. Or maybe I just don't try. But I'm not the only one having the problem. Maya is even worse than me. And everyone my age complains about it. Vlad and Ursula are getting concerned. I'm surprised they didn't think of this back when they developed the treatments."

"Maybe they did and then forgot."

Her laugh seemed to take her by surprise.

Later at dinner, after talking about her construction projects again, Art said to her, "You really ought to try to convene a meeting of all these underground groups."

Maya was at their table, and she looked at Art as suspiciously as she had in Echus Chasma. "It isn't possible," she declared. She looked much better than she had when they had parted, Nirgal thought—rested, tall, rangy, graceful, glamorous. She seemed to have shrugged off the guilt of murder as if it were a coat she didn't like.

"Why not?" Art asked her. "You'd be a lot better off if you could live on the surface."

"This is obvious. And we could move into the demimonde, if it were just that simple. But there is a large police force on the surface and in orbit, and the last time they saw us they were trying to kill us as quickly as possible. And the way they treated Sax does not give me any confidence that things have changed."

"I'm not saying they have. But I think there are things you could do to oppose them more effectively. Getting together, for instance, and making a plan. Making contact with surface organizations that would help you. That kind of thing."

"We have such contacts," Maya said coldly. But Nadia was nodding. And Nirgal's mind was racing with images of his years in Sabishii. A meeting of the underground. . . .

"The Sabishiians would come for sure," he said. "They're already doing stuff like this all the time. That's what the demimonde is, in effect."

Art said, "You should think about contacting Praxis as well. My ex-boss William Fort would be very interested in such a meeting. And the whole membership of Praxis is involved in innovations you would like."

"Your *ex*-boss?" Maya said.

"Sure," Art said with an easy smile. "I'm my own boss now."

"You could say you are our prisoner," Maya pointed out sharply.

"When you're the prisoner of anarchists it's the same thing, right?"

Nadia and Nirgal laughed, but Maya scowled and turned away.

Nadia said, "I think a meeting would be a good idea. We've let Coyote run the network for too long."

"I heard that!" Coyote called from the next table.

"Don't you like the idea?" Nadia asked him.

Coyote shrugged. "We have to do something, no doubt of that. They know we're down here now."

This caused a thoughtful silence.

"I'm going north next week," Nadia said to Art. "You can come with me if you like—Nirgal, you too if you want. I'm going to drop in on a lot of sanctuaries, and we can talk to them about a meeting."

"Sure," Art said, looking pleased. And Nirgal's mind was still racing as he thought of the possibilities. Being in Gamete again brought dormant parts of his mind back alive, and he saw clearly the two worlds in one, the white and the green, split into different dimensions, folded through each other—like the underground and the surface world, joined clumsily in the demimonde. A world out of focus. . . .

So the next week Art and Nirgal joined Nadia, and drove north. Because of Sax's arrest Nadia did not want to risk staying in any of the open towns along their way, and she did not even seem to trust the other hidden sanctuaries; she was one of the most conservative of the old ones in terms of secrecy. Over the years of hiding she, like Coyote, had built a whole system of small shelters of her own, and now they drove from one to the next, spending the short days sleeping and waiting in relative comfort. They could not drive during the winter days because the fog hood had been lessening in thickness and area for several years now, and this year was often no more than a light mist, or patchy low clouds, swirling over the rough lumpy land. Once they were descending a rough drop in a foggy morning, after a 10 A.M. dawn, and Nadia was explaining that Ann had identified it as the remnant of an earlier Chasma Australe—"She says there are literally scores of fossil Chasma Australes down here, cut at different angles during earlier points in the cycle of precession"—and the fog swept away, and they could suddenly see for many kilometers, all the way to the shaggy ice walls at the mouth of the present Chasma Australe, gleaming in the distance. They were exposed—then the clouds closed over them again, very swiftly, enveloping them in murky flowing white, as if they were traveling in a snowstorm in which the snowflakes were so fine that they defied gravity, and blew about in suspension forever.

Nadia hated that kind of exposure, no matter how brief, and so she continued to hide through the days. They looked out the little windows of her shelters onto swirling clouds, which sometimes caught the light in sparkling arrays, so bright it hurt to look at them. Sunbeams cut through gaps between clouds, striking the long ridges and scarps of the blindingly white land. Once they even experienced a full whiteout, when all shadows disappeared, and everything else: a pure white world, in which it was impossible to make out even the horizon.

On other days icebows threw curves of pale pastel color against the intense whites, and once when the sun broke through, low over the land, it was surrounded by a ring of light as bright as it was. The landscape blazed white under this display, not uniformly but in patches, all shifting rapidly in the ceaseless winds. Art laughed to see it, and he never stopped exclaiming over the ice flowers, now as large as shrubs, and studded with spikes and lacy fans, and growing into each other at their edges, so that in many areas the ground itself completely disappeared, and they drove across a crackling surface of shard blooms, crushing hundreds of them under their wheels. The long dark nights were almost a comfort after days like that.

Days passed, one like the next. Nirgal found it very comfortable to travel with Art and Nadia; they were both even-tempered, calm, funny; Art was 51 and Nadia 120, and Nirgal only 12, which was around 25 Terran years; but despite the discrepancies in age they interacted as equals. Nirgal could test his ideas on them freely, and they never laughed or scoffed, even when they saw problems and pointed them out. And in fact their ideas meshed fairly well, for the most part. They were, in Martian political terms, moderate green assimilationists—Booneans, Nadia called it. And they had similar temperaments, which was something that Nirgal had never felt before about anyone, not for the rest of his family in Gamete or his friends in Sabishii.

As they talked, night after night, they dropped in briefly on some of the big sanctuaries of the south, introducing Art to the people there, and broaching the idea of a meeting or congress. They took him to Bogdanov Vishniac, and amazed him with the giant complex built deep into the mohole, so much bigger than any other sanctuary. Art's pop-eyed face was as eloquent as a speech, and brought back to Nirgal most acutely the feeling he had had as a child when he first visited it with Coyote.

The Bogdanovists were clearly interested in a meeting, but Mikhail Yangel, one of the only one of Arkady's associates to survive '61, asked Art what the long-range purpose of such a meeting would be.

"To retake the surface."

"I see!" Mikhail's eyes were wide. "Well, I'm sure you would have our support for that! People have been afraid to even bring that subject up."

"Very good," Nadia told Art as they drove on north. "If the Bogdanovists support a meeting, then it will probably happen. Most of the hidden sanctuaries are either Bogdanovist or else heavily influenced by them."

From Vishniac they visited the sanctuaries around Holmes Crater, known as the "industrial heartland" of the underground. These colonies were also mostly Bogdanovist, with any number of small social variations among them, influenced by early Martian social philosophers such as the prisoner Schnelling, or Hiroko, or Marina, or John Boone. The Francophone utopians in Prometheus, on the other hand, had structured their settlement on ideas taken from sources ranging from Rousseau and Fourier to Foucault and Nemy, subtleties Nirgal had not been aware of when he had first visited. Currently they were being strongly influenced by the Polynesians who had recently arrived on Mars, and their big warm chambers sported palm trees and shallow pools, so that Art said it seemed more like Tahiti than Paris.

In Prometheus they were joined by Jackie Boone herself, who had been left there by friends traveling through. She wanted to go directly on to Gamete, but she was willing to travel with Nadia rather than wait longer, and Nadia was willing to take her. So when they took off again, they had Jackie with them.

The easy camaraderie of the first part of their journey disappeared. Jackie and Nirgal had parted in Sabishii with their relationship in its usual unsettled undefined state, and Nirgal was displeased to have the growth of his new friendships interrupted. Art was obviously agog at her physical presence—she was actually taller than he was, and heavier than Nirgal, and Art watched her in a way he thought surreptitious, but which the others were all aware of, including Jackie of course. It made Nadia roll her eyes, and she and Jackie quarreled over little things like sisters. Once after they did, and Jackie and Nadia were elsewhere in one of Nadia's shelters, Art whispered to Nirgal, "She's just like Maya! Doesn't she remind you? The voice, the mannerisms—"

Nirgal laughed. "Tell her that and she'll kill you."

"Ah," Art said. He regarded Nirgal with a sidelong glance. "So you two are still . . . ?"

Nirgal shrugged. In a way it was interesting; he had told Art enough about his relationship with Jackie that the older man knew there was something fundamental between the two. Now Jackie was almost certain to come on to Art, to add him to her minions as she routinely did with men she liked or thought important. At this point she had not figured out how important Art was, but when she did she would act in her usual way, and then what would Art do?

So their voyage was no longer the same, Jackie imparting her usual spin to things. She argued with Nirgal and Nadia; she casually rubbed up to Art, charming him at the same time she judged him, just as an automatic part of acquaintanceship. She would pull off her shirt to sponge down in Nadia's shelters, or put a hand to his arm when asking questions about Terra—then at other times ignore him completely, veering off into worlds of her own. It was like living with a big cat in the rover, a panther that might purr in your lap or bat you across the compartment, but either way stalk about in a perfect nervous grace.

Ah, but that was Jackie. And there was her laugh, ringing through the car at things Art or Nadia said; and her beauty; and her intense enthusiasm for discussing the Martian situation, so that when she discovered what they were doing on this trip, she immediately fell into it. Life was heightened with her around, no doubt about it. And Art, though he goggled at her when she bathed, had what Nirgal suspected was a sly edge to his smile as he enjoyed her mesmerizing attentions; and once Nirgal caught him giving a look to Nadia that was positively amused. So though he liked her well enough, and liked looking at her, he did not seem hopelessly smitten. This was possibly a matter of his friendship with Nirgal; Nirgal couldn't be sure, but he liked the idea, which had not been a common one in either Zygote or Sabishii.

For her part, Jackie seemed inclined to dismiss Art as a factor in the organizing of a general meeting, as if she would take it over herself. But then they visited a small neomarxist sanctuary in the Mountains of Mitchel (which were no more mountainous than the rest of the southern highlands, the name being an artifact of the telescope era) and these neomarxists proved to be in communication with the city of Bologna in Italy, and with the Indian province of Kerala—and with Praxis offices in both these places. So they had a lot to talk about with Art, and they obviously enjoyed it, and at the end of the visit one of them said to him, "It's wonderful what you're doing, you're just like John Boone."

Jackie jerked her head around to stare at Art, who was sheepishly shaking his head. "No he's not," she said automatically.

But after that she treated him more seriously. Nirgal could only laugh. Any mention of the name John Boone was like a magic spell to Jackie.

When she and Nadia discussed John's theories, he could understand a little why she felt that way; much of what Boone had wanted for Mars made excellent sense, and it seemed to him that Sabishii in particular was a kind of Boonean space. For Jackie, however, it went beyond a rational response—it had to do with Kasei and Esther, and Hiroko, even Peter—with some complex of feelings that touched her on a level that nothing else did.

They continued north, into lands even more violently disarranged than those they had left behind. This was volcanic country, where the harsh sublimity of the southern highland was augmented by the ancient craggy peaks of Australis Tholus and Amphitrites Patera. The two volcanoes bracketed a region of lava flows, where the blackish rock of the land was frozen in weird lumps, waves, and rivers. Once these flows had poured over the surface in streams of white-hot fluid, and even now, hard and black and shattered by the ages, and covered with dust and ice flowers, the liquid origins were completely evident.

The most prominent of these lava remnants were long low ridges, like dragon tails now fossilized to solid black rock. These ridges snaked across the land for many kilometers, often disappearing over the horizon in both directions, forcing the travelers to make long detours. These dorsa were ancient lava channels; the rock they were made of had proved harder than the countryside they had originally flowed over, and in the eons since, the countryside had been worn away, leaving the black mounds lying on the surface somewhat like the fallen elevator cable only very much larger.

One of the dorsa, in the Dorsa Brevia region, had recently been turned into a hidden sanctuary. So Nadia drove their rover on a tortuous path through outlying lava ridges, and then into a capacious garage in the side of the largest black mound they had seen. They got out of their car, and were greeted by a small group of friendly strangers, several of whom Jackie had met before. There was no indication in the garage that the chamber beyond it was going to be any different from any other they had visited, and so when they walked into a big cylindrical lock and out the other door, it was a great shock to find before them an open space that clearly occupied the whole interior of the ridge. The ridge was hollow; the empty space inside it was roughly cylindrical, a tube perhaps two hundred meters floor to ceiling, three hundred meters wall to wall, and extending for as far as they could see in both directions. Art's mouth was like a cross-section model of the tunnel: "Wow!" he kept exclaiming. "Wow, look at this! Wow!"

Quite a few dorsa were hollow, their hosts told them. Lava tunnels. There were many of them on Terra, but the usual two-magnitude scale jump obtained, and this tube was in fact a hundred times bigger than the biggest Terran tube. When the lava streams had flowed, a young woman named Ariadne explained to Art, they had cooled and hardened at their edges, and then on their surfaces—after which hot lava had continued to run through the sleeve, until the flows had stopped, and the remaining lava had emptied out onto some lake of fire, leaving behind cylindrical caves that were sometimes fifty kilometers long.

The floor of this particular tunnel was approximately flat, and now it was covered by rooftops and grassy parks, ponds, and hundreds of young trees, planted in groves of mixed bamboo and pine. Long cracks in the roof of the tunnel had served as the basis for filtered skylights, made of layered materials which gave off the same visual and thermal signals as the rest of the ridge, but let into the tunnel long curtains of sunny brown air, so that even the dimmest sections of the tunnel were only as dim as a cloudy day.

Dorsa Brevia's tunnel was forty kilometers long, Ariadne informed them as they walked down a staircase, although there were places where the roof had caved in, or plugs of lava almost filled the cavity. "We haven't closed off the whole thing, of course. It's more than we need, and more than we could keep warm and pumped anyway. But we've closed off about twelve kilometers now, in kilometer-long segments, with tent-fabric bulkheads between them."

"Wow," Art said again. Nirgal felt just as impressed, and Nadia was clearly delighted. Even Vishniac was nothing compared to this.

Jackie was already near the bottom of the long staircase that led from the garage lock to a park below them. As they followed her Art said, "Every colony you've taken me to I've figured has to be the biggest one, and I'm always wrong. Why don't you just tell me now if the next one is going to be like all of Hellas Basin or something."

Nadia laughed. "This is the biggest one I know of. Bigger!"

"So why do you all stay in Gamete, when it's so cold and small and dim? Couldn't the people from all the sanctuaries fit into this space?"

"We don't want to all be in one place," she replied. "As for this one, it wasn't even here a few years ago."

Down on the floor of the tunnel they appeared to be in a forest, under a black stone sky rent by long jagged bright cracks. The four travelers followed a group of their hosts to a complex of buildings with thin wooden walls and steep roofs upturned at the corners. In one of these they were introduced to a group of elderly women and men in colorful baggy clothing, and invited to share a meal.

As they ate they learned more about the sanctuary, mostly from Ariadne, who sat beside them. It had been built and occupied by the descendants of people who had come to Mars and joined the disappeared in the 2050s, leaving the cities and occupying small refuges in this region, aided in their efforts by the Sabishiians. They had been heavily influenced by Hiroko's areophany, and their society was described by some as a matriarchy. They had studied some ancient matriarchal cultures, and based some of their customs on the ancient Minoan civilization and the Hopi of North America. Thus they worshipped a goddess who represented life on Mars, something like a personification of Hiroko's viriditas, or a deification of Hiroko herself. And in daily life the women owned the households, and would pass them on to their youngest daughters: ultimogeniture, Ariadne called it, a custom of the Hopi. And as with the Hopi, men moved into their wives' houses on marriage.

"Do the men like it?" Art asked curiously.

Ariadne laughed at his expression. "There's nothing like happy women for making happy men, that's what we say." And she gave Art a look that seemed to pull him right over the bench toward her.

"Makes sense to me," Art said.

"We all share the work—extending the tunnel segments, farming, raising the children, whatever needs doing. Everybody tries to get good at more than just their specialty, which is a custom that comes from the First Hundred, I think, and the Sabishiians."

Art nodded. "And how many of you are there?"

"About four thousand now."

Art whistled his surprise.

That afternoon they were taken down the tunnel through several kilometers of transformed segments, many of them forested, and all containing a large stream that ran down the floor of the tunnel, widening in some segments to form big ponds. When Ariadne brought them back up to the first chamber, called Zakros, almost a thousand people showed up for an open-air meal in the largest park. Nirgal and Art wandered around talking to people, enjoying a plain meal of bread and salad and broiled fish. The people there appeared receptive to the idea of a congress of the underground. They had tried something like it years before, but had not gotten many takers at the time—had lists of the sanctuaries in their region—and one of the older women said, with authority, that they would be happy to host it, as they had a space large enough to handle a great number of guests.

"Oh, that would be marvelous," Art said, glancing at Ariadne.

Later Nadia agreed. "It will help a lot," she said. "A lot of people will be resistant to the idea of a meeting, because they suspect the First Hundred of trying to take charge of the underground. But if it's held here, and the Bogdanovists are behind it . . ."

When Jackie came over and heard of the offer, she gave Art a hug. "Oh, it's going to happen! And it's just what John Boone would have done. It's like the meeting he called on Olympus Mons."

They left Dorsa Brevia and headed north again, on the east side of the Hellas Basin. During the nights of this drive Jackie often brought out John Boone's AI, Pauline, which she had studied and cataloged. She played back selections from his thoughts about an independent state, which were disorganized and rambling, the reflections of a man with more enthusiasm (and omegendorph) than analytic ability; but sometimes he would get on a roll, and ad-lib in the manner of the famous speeches, and that could be fascinating. He had had a knack for free association which made his ideas sound like logical progression even when they weren't.

"See how often he talks about the Swiss," Jackie said. She sounded like John, Nirgal noticed suddenly. She had been working with Pauline extensively for a long time, and her manner had been affected by it. John's voice, Maya's manner; in such ways they carried the past with them. "We have to make sure some Swiss are at the congress."

"We've got Jurgen and the group at Overhangs," Nadia said.

"But they're not really so Swiss, are they?"

"You'll have to ask them," Nadia said. "But if you mean Swiss officials, there are a lot of them in Burroughs, and they've been helping us there, without ever even talking to us about it. About fifty of us have Swiss passports now. They're a big part of the demimonde."

"As is Praxis," Art put in.

"Yes yes. Anyway, we'll talk to the group at Overhangs. They'll have contacts with the surface Swiss, I'm sure."

Northeast of the volcano Hadriaca Patera, they visited a town that had been founded by Sufis. The original structure was built into the side of a canyon cliff, in a kind of high-tech Mesa Verde—a thin line of buildings, inserted into the break point where the cliff's imposing overhang began to slope back out and down to the canyon floor. Steep staircases in walktubes ran down the lower slope to a small concrete garage, and around the garage had sprung up a number of blister tents and greenhouses. These tents were occupied by people who wished to study with the Sufis. Some came from the sanctuaries, some from the cities of the north; many were natives, but quite a few were newcomers from Earth. Together they hoped to roof the entire canyon, using materials developed for the new cable to support an immense spread of tent fabric. Nadia was immediately drawn into discussions of the construction problems such a project would encounter, which she happily told them would be various and severe. Ironically, the thickening atmosphere made all dome projects more difficult, because the domes could not be floated by the air pressures underneath them to the extent they once had been; and though the tensile and load-bearing strengths of the new carbon configurations were more than they would need, anchoring points that would hold such weights as they had in mind would be almost impossible to find. But the local engineers were confident that lighter tent fabrics and new anchoring techniques might serve, and the walls of the canyon, they said, were solid. They were in the very upper reach of Reull Vallis, and ancient sapping had cut back into very hard material. Good anchoring points should be everywhere.

No attempt was being made to hide any of this activity from satellite observation. The Sufis' circular mesa dwelling in Margaritifer, and their main settlement in the south, Rumi, were similarly unconcealed. Yet they had never been harassed in any way by anybody, or even contacted by the Transitional Authority. This made one of their leaders, a small black man named Dhu el-Nun, think the fears of the underground were exaggerated. Nadia politely disagreed, and when Nirgal pressed her on the point, curious about it, she looked at him steadily. "They hunt the First Hundred."

He thought it over, watching the Sufis lead the way up the walktube staircases to their cliff dwelling. They had arrived well before dawn, and Dhu had invited everyone up to the cliff for a brunch to welcome the visitors. So they followed the Sufis up to the dwelling, and sat at a great long table, in a long room with its outer wall a continuous great window, overlooking the canyon. The Sufis dressed in white, while the people from the tents in the canyon wore ordinary jumpers, most of them rust-colored. People poured each other's water, and talked as they ate. "You are on your *tariqat*," Dhu el-Nun said to Nirgal. This was one's spiritual path, he explained, one's road to reality. Nirgal nodded, struck by the aptness of the description—it was just how his life had always felt to him. "You must feel lucky," Dhu said. "You must pay attention."

After a meal of bread and strawberries and yogurt, and then mud-thick coffee, the tables and chairs were cleared, and the Sufis danced a *sema* or whirling dance, spinning and chanting to the music of a harpist and several drummers, and the chanting of the canyon dwellers. As the dancers passed their guests, they placed their palms very briefly to the guests' cheeks, their touches as light as the brush of a wing. Nirgal glanced at Art, expecting him to be as goggle-eyed as he usually was at the various phenomena of Martian life, but in fact he was smiling in a knowing way, and tapping his forefinger and thumb together in time to the beat, and chanting with the rest. And at the end of the dance he stepped out and recited something in a foreign language, which caused the Sufis to smile and, when he was done, to applaud loudly.

"Some of my professors in Tehran were Sufis," he explained to Nirgal and Nadia and Jackie. "They were a big part of what people call the Persian Renaissance."

"And what did you recite?" Nirgal asked.

"It's a Farsi poem by Jalaluddin Rumi, the master of the whirling dervishes. I never learned the English version very well—

'I died from a mineral and plant became,
   Died from the plant, took a sentient frame;
   Died from the beast, donned a human dress—
   When by my dying did I ever grow less . . .'

"Ah, I can't remember the rest. But some of those Sufis were very good engineers."

"They'd better be here too," Nadia said, glancing at the people she had been talking to about doming the canyon.

In any case the Sufis here proved to be very enthusiastic about the idea of an underground congress. As they pointed out, theirs was a syncretic religion, which had taken some of its elements not only from the various types and nationalities of Islam, but also from the older religions of Asia that Islam had encountered, and also newer ones such as Baha'i. Something similarly flexible was going to be needed here, they said. Meanwhile, their concept of the gift had already been influential throughout the underground, and some of their theoreticians were working with Vlad and Marina on the specifics of eco-economics. So as the morning passed and they waited for the late winter sunrise, standing at the great window and looking across the dark canyon to the east, they were quick to make very practical suggestions about the meeting. "You should go talk to the Bedouin and the other Arabs as quickly as possible," Dhu told them. "They won't like being late in the list of those consulted."

Then the eastern sky lightened, very slowly, from dark plum to lavender. The opposite cliff was lower than the one they were on, and they could see over the dark plateau to the east for a few kilometers, to a low range of hills that formed the horizon. The Sufis pointed out the cleft in the hills where the sun would rise, and some began to chant again. "There is a group of Sufis in Elysium," Dhu told them, "who are exploring backwards to our roots in Mithraism and Zoroastrianism. Some say there are Mithraists on Mars now, worshipping the sun, Ahura Mazda. They consider the soletta to be religious art, like a stained glass window in a cathedral."

When the sky was an intense clear pink the Sufis gathered around their four guests and gently pushed them into a pattern against the windows: Nirgal next to Jackie, Nadia and Art behind them. "Today you are our stained glass," Dhu said quietly. Hands lifted Nirgal's forearm until his hand was touching Jackie's, and he took it. They exchanged a quick glance and then stared forward to the hills on the horizon. Art and Nadia were likewise holding hands, and their outside hands were placed on Nirgal's and Jackie's shoulders. The chanting around them got louder, the chorus of voices intoning words in Farsi, the long and liquid vowels stretching out for minutes on end. And then the sun cracked the horizon and the fountain of light exploded over the land, pouring in the wide window and over them so that they had to squint, and their eyes watered. Between the soletta and the thickening atmosphere the sun was visibly larger than it had been in the past, bronze and oblate and shimmering up through the horizontal slicing of distant inversion layers. Jackie squeezed Nirgal's hand hard, and on an impulse he looked behind them; there on the white wall all their shadows made a kind of linked tapestry, black on white, and in the intensity of the light, the white nearest their shadows was the brightest white of all, tinged just barely by the colors of the rainbow glory, embracing them all.

They took the Sufis' advice when they left, and headed for the Lyell mohole, one of the four 70° south latitude moholes. In this region the Bedouin from western Egypt had located a number of caravanserai, and Nadia was acquainted with one of their leaders. So they decided to try and find him.

As they drove Nirgal thought hard about the Sufis, and what their influential presence said about the underground and the demimonde. People had left the surface world for many different reasons, and that was important to remember. All of them had thrown everything away, and risked their lives, but they had done so intent on very different goals. Some hoped to establish radically new cultures, as in Zygote, or Dorsa Brevia, or in the Bogdanovist sanctuaries. Others, like the Sufis, wanted to hold on to ancient cultures they felt were under assault in the Terran global order. Now all these parts of the resistance were scattered in the southern highlands, mixed but still separate. There was no obvious reason why they should all want to become one single thing. Many of them had been trying specifically to get away from dominant powers—transnationals, the West, America, capitalism—all the totalizing systems of power. A central system was just what they had gone to great lengths to get away from. That did not bode well for Art's plan, and when Nirgal expressed this worry, Nadia agreed. "You are American, this is trouble for us." Which made Art go cross-eyed. But then Nadia added, "Well, America also stands for the melting pot. The idea of the melting pot. It was the place where people could come from anywhere and be a part of it. Such was the theory. There are lessons there for us."

Jackie said, "What Boone finally concluded was that it wasn't possible to invent a Martian culture from scratch. He said it should be a mix of the best of everyone that came here. That's the difference between Booneans and Bogdanovists."

"Yes," Nadia said, frowning, "but I think they were both wrong. I don't think we can invent it from scratch, and I don't think there will be a mix. At least not for a very long time. In the meantime, it will be a matter of a lot of different cultures coexisting, I think. But whether such a thing is possible . . ." She shrugged.

The problems they were going to face in any congress were made flesh during their visit to the Bedouin caravanserai. These Bedouin were mining the region of the far south between Dana Crater, Lyell Crater, the Sisyphi Cavi, and Dorsa Argentea. They were traveling about in mobile mining rigs, in the style honed on the Great Escarpment, now traditional—harvesting surface deposits, and then moving on. The caravanserai was just a small tent, left in place like an oasis, for people to use in emergencies, or when they wanted to stretch out a little.

Nobody could have made more of a contrast with the ethereal Sufis than the Bedouin; these reserved unsentimental Arabs dressed in modern jumpers, and seemed to be mostly male. When the travelers arrived there was a mining caravan about to leave, and when they heard what the travelers wanted to discuss, they frowned and left anyway. "More Booneism. We don't want anything to do with it."

The travelers ate a meal with a group of men in the largest rover left in the caravanserai, with women appearing from a tube from the car next door to serve the dishes. Jackie glowered at this, with a dark expression that was straight off Maya's face. When one of the younger Arab men sitting beside her tried to strike up a conversation, he found it hard going indeed. Nirgal suppressed a smile at this, and attended to Nadia and an old Bedu named Zeyk, the leader of this group, and the one Nadia had known from before. "Ah, the Sufis," he said genially. "No one bothers them because they are clearly harmless. Like birds."

Later in the meal Jackie warmed to the young Arab, of course, as he was a strikingly handsome man, with long dark eyelashes framing liquid brown eyes, an aquiline nose, full red lips, a sharp jaw, and an easy confident manner that appeared unintimidated by Jackie's own beauty, which was similar in some ways to his own. His name was Antar, and he came from an important Bedu family. Art, sitting across the low table from them, looked shocked at this developing friendship, but after their years in Sabishii Nirgal had seen it coming even before Jackie had, and in a strange way it was almost a pleasure to watch her at work. Quite a sight, in fact— she the proud daughter of the greatest matriarchy since Atlantis, Antar the proud heir of the most extreme patriarchy on Mars, a young man with a grace and ease of manner so pure it was as if he were king of the world.

After the meal the two of them disappeared. Nirgal settled back with scarcely a twinge, and talked with Nadia and Art and Zeyk, and Zeyk's wife, Nazik, who came out to join them. Zeyk and Nazik were Mars old-timers, who had met John Boone, and been friends of Frank Chalmers. Contrary to the Sufis' prediction, they were very friendly to the idea of a congress, and they agreed that Dorsa Brevia would be a good place to hold it.

"What we need is equality without conformity," Zeyk said at one point, squinting seriously as he chose his words. This was close enough to what Nadia had been saying on the drive there that it caught Nirgal's attention even more than it otherwise would have. "This is not an easy thing to establish, but clearly we have to try, to avoid fighting. I'll spread the word through the Arab community. Or at least the Bedu. I must say, there are Arabs in the north who are very much involved with the transnationals, with Amexx especially. All the African Arab countries are falling into Amexx, one after the next. A very odd pairing. But money . . ." He rubbed his fingers together. "You know. Anyway, we will contact our friends. And the Sufis will help us. They are becoming the mullahs down here, and the mullahs don't like it, but I do."

Other developments worried him. "Armscor has taken on the Black Sea Group, and that's a very bad combination—old Afrikaaner leadership, and security from all the member states, most of them police states— Ukraine, Georgia, Moldova, Azerbaijan, Armenia, Bulgaria, Turkey, Romania." He ticked them off on his fingers, wrinkling his nose. "Think about those histories for a while! And they have been building bases on the Great Escarpment, a band around Mars, in effect. And they're in tight with the Transitional Authority." He shook his head. "They will crush us if they can."

Nadia nodded her agreement, and Art, looking surprised at this assessment, pumped Zeyk with a hundred questions. "But you don't hide," he noted at one point.

"We have sanctuaries if we need them," Zeyk said. "And we are ready to fight."

"Do you think it will come to that?" Art asked.

"I am sure of it."

Much later, after several more tiny cups of mudlike coffee, Zeyk and Nazik and Nadia talked to each other about Frank Chalmers, all three of them smiling peculiar fond smiles. Nirgal and Art listened, but it was hard to get a sense of that man, dead long before Nirgal had been born. In fact it was a shocking reminder of just how old the issei were, that they had known such a figure from the videotapes. Finally Art blurted out, "But what was he *like?*"

The three old ones thought it over.

Slowly Zeyk said, "He was an angry man. He listened to Arabs, though, and respected us. He lived with us for a time and learned our language, and truthfully there are few Americans who have ever done that. And so we loved him. But he was no very easy man to know. And he was angry. I don't know why. Something in his years on Earth, I suppose. He never spoke of them. In fact he never spoke about himself at all. But there was a gyroscope in him, spinning like a pulsar. And he had black moods. Very black. We sent him out in scouting rovers, to see if he could help himself. It didn't always work. He would rip us from time to time, even though he was our guest." Zeyk smiled, remembering. "Once he called us all slaveowners, right to our faces over coffee."

"Slaveowners?"

Zeyk waved a hand. "He was angry."

"He saved us, there at the end," Nadia told Zeyk, stirring from deep in her own thoughts. "In sixty-one." She told them of a long drive down Valles Marineris, accomplished at the very same time that the Compton Aquifer outbreak was flooding the great canyon; and how when they were almost clear of it, the flood had caught Frank and swept him away. "He was out getting the car off a rock, and if he hadn't acted so quickly, the whole car would have gone."

"Ah," said Zeyk. "A happy death."

"I don't think he thought so."

The issei all laughed, briefly, then reached together for their empty cups, and made a small toast to their late friend. "I miss him," Nadia said as she put her cup down. "I never thought I would say that."

She went silent, and watching her Nirgal felt the night cosseting them, hiding them. He had never heard her speak of Frank Chalmers. A lot of her friends had died in the revolt. And her partner too, Bogdanov, whom so many people still followed.

"Angry to the last," Zeyk said. "For Frank, a happy death."

From Lyell they continued counterclockwise around the South Pole, stopping at sanctuaries or tent towns, and exchanging news and goods. Christianopolis was the largest tent town in the region, center of trade for all the smaller settlements south of Argyre. The sanctuaries in the area were mostly occupied by Reds. Nadia asked all the Reds they met to convey news of the congress to Ann Clayborne. "We're supposed to have a phone link, but she's not answering me." A lot of the Reds clearly thought a meeting was a bad idea, or at least a waste of time. South of Schmidt Crater they stopped at a settlement of Bologna communists who lived in a hollowed-out hill, lost in one of the wildest zones of the southern highlands, a region very hard to travel in because of the many wandering scarps and dikes, which rovers could not negotiate. The Bolognese gave them a map marking some tunnels and elevators they had installed in the area, to allow passage through dikes, and up or down scarps. "If we didn't have them our trips would be nothing but detours."

Located next to one of their hidden dike tunnels was a small colony of Polynesians, living in a short lava tunnel, which they had floored with water and three islands. The dike was piled high with ice and snow on its southern flank, but the Polynesians, most of whom were from the island of Vanuatu, kept the interior of their refuge at homey temperatures, and Nirgal found the air so hot and humid that it was hard to breathe, even when just sitting on a sand beach, between a black lake and a line of tilting palm trees. Clearly, he thought as he looked around, the Polynesians could be counted among those trying to build a culture incorporating some aspects of their archaic ancestors. They also proved to be scholars of primitive government everywhere in Earth's history, and they were excited at the idea of sharing what they had learned in these studies at the congress, so it was no problem getting them to agree to come.

To celebrate the idea of the congress they had gathered for a feast on the beach. Art, seated between Jackie and a Polynesian beauty named Tanna, beamed blissfully as he sipped from a half coconut shell filled with kava. Nirgal lay stretched out on the sand before them, listening as Jackie and Tanna talked animatedly about the indigenous movement, as Tanna called it. This was not any simple back-to-the-past nostalgia, she said, but rather an attempt to invent new cultures, which incorporated aspects of early civilizations into high-tech Martian forms. "The underground itself is a kind of Polynesia," Tanna said. "Little islands in a great stone ocean, some on the maps, some not. And someday it will be a real ocean, and we'll be out on the islands, flourishing under the sky."

"I'll drink to that," Art said, and did. Clearly one part of the archaic Polynesian culture that Art hoped they were incorporating was their renowned sexual friendliness. But Jackie was mischievously complicating things by leaning on Art's arm, either to tease him or to compete with Tanna. Art was looking happy but concerned; he had drunk his cup of the noxious kava fairly quickly, and between that and the women, appeared lost in a blissful confusion. Nirgal nearly laughed out loud. It seemed possible that some of the other young women at the feast might also be interested in sharing the archaic wisdom, judging by their glances his way.

On the other hand Jackie might leave off teasing Art. It did not matter; it was going to be a long night, and New Vanuatu's little tunnel ocean was kept as warm as the old Zygote baths. Nadia was already out there, swimming in the shallows with some men a quarter her age. Nirgal stood and pulled off his clothes, walked out into the water.

It was getting to be late enough in the winter that even at 80° latitude the sun rose for an hour or two around noon, and during these brief intervals the shifting fogs glowed in tones pastel or metallic—on some days violet and rose and pink, on others copper and bronze and gold. And in all cases the delicate shades of color were captured and reflected by the frost on the ground, so that it looked sometimes as if they traversed a world made entirely of jewels, of amethysts, rubies, sapphires.

On other days the wind would roar, throwing a weight of frost that coated the rover, and gave the world a flowing, underwater look. In the brief hours of sunlight they worked at clearing the rover's wheels, the sun in the fog like a patch of yellow lichen. Once, after one of these windstorms had cleared, the fog hood was gone as well, and the land to every horizon was a spectacular complexity of ice flowers. And over the northern horizon of this rumpled diamond field stood a tall dark cloud, pouring up into the sky from some source that appeared to be not far over the horizon.

They stopped and dug out one of Nadia's little shelters. Nirgal stared out at the dark cloud and looked at the map. "I think it might be the Rayleigh mohole," he said. "Coyote started up the robot excavators in that one, during that first trip I took with him. I wonder if something's come of it."

"I've got a little scout rover stashed in the garage here," Nadia said. "You can take that over and have a look if you want. I'd go too but I need to get back to Gamete. I'm supposed to meet Ann there day after tomorrow. Apparently she's heard about the congress, and wants to ask me some questions."

Art expressed an interest in meeting Ann Clayborne; he had been impressed by a video about her he had seen on the flight to Mars. "It would be like meeting Jeremiah."

Jackie said to Nirgal, "I'll come with you."

So they agreed to meet in Gamete, and Art and Nadia headed there directly in the big rover, while Nirgal took off with Jackie in Nadia's scout car. The tall cloud still stood over the icescape ahead of them, a dense pillar of dark gray lobes, torn flat in the stratosphere, in different directions at different times. As they got closer, it seemed more and more certain that the cloud was pouring up out of the silent planet. And then as they rolled to the edge of one low scarp, they saw that the land in the distance was clear of ice, the ground as rocky as it would be in high summer, but blacker, a nearly pure black rock that was smoking from long orange fissures in its bulbous, pillowy surface. And just beyond the horizon, which here was six or seven kilometers off, the dark cloud was roiling up, like a mohole thermal cloud gone nova, the hot gaseous smoke exploding outward and then tumbling up hastily.

Jackie drove their car to the top of the highest hill in the region. From there they could see all the way to the source of the cloud, and it was just as Nirgal had guessed the moment he had seen it: the Rayleigh mohole was now a low hill, black except for its pattern of angry orange cracks. The cloud poured out of a hole in this hill, the smoke dark and dense and roiling. A tongue of rough black rock stretched downhill to the south, in their direction and then off to their right.

As they sat in the car, silently watching, a big part of the low black hill covering the mohole tipped over and broke apart, and liquid orange rock ran quickly between the black chunks, sparking and splashing yellow. The intense yellow quickly turned orange, and then darkened further.

After that nothing moved but the column of smoke. Over the ventilator and engine hums they could hear a rumbling basso continuo, punctuated by booms that were timed to sudden explosions of smoke from the vent. The car trembled slightly on its shock absorbers.

They stayed on the hill watching, Nirgal rapt, Jackie excited and talkative, commenting at length, then going silent as chunks of lava broke away from the hill, releasing more spills of melted rock. When they looked through the car's IR viewer the hill was a brilliant emerald with blazing white cracks in it, and the tongue of lava licking the plain was bright green. It took about an hour for orange rock to turn black in visible light, but through the IR the emerald went dark green in about ten minutes. Green pouring up into the world, with the white bursting through it.

They ate a meal, and as they cleaned their plates Jackie moved Nirgal around the cramped kitchen with her hands, friendly in the way she had been in New Vanuatu, her eyes bright, a small smile on her lips. Nirgal knew these signs, and he caressed her as she passed in the small space behind the drivers' seats, happy at the renewed intimacy, so rare and so precious. "I'll bet it's warm outside," he said.

And her head snapped around as she looked at him, her eyes wide.

Without another word they dressed and got into the lock, and held gloved hands as they waited for it to suck and open. When it did they stepped out of the car, and walked across the dry rust rubble, holding hands and squeezing hard, winding around bumps and hollows and chest-high boulders toward the new lava. Each carried a thinsulate pad in his other outside hand. They could have talked but they didn't. The air pushed at them from time to time, and even through the layers of his walker Nirgal could feel that it was warm. The ground trembled slightly underfoot, and the rumble was distinct, vibrating in his stomach; it was punctuated every few seconds by a dull boom, or a sharper cracking noise. No doubt it was dangerous to be out here. There was a small rounded hill, very like the one their car was parked on, overlooking the tongue of hot lava from a somewhat closer distance, and without consultation they headed for it, climbing its final slope with big steps, always holding hands, gripping hard.

From the top of the little hill they could see far over the new black flow and its shifting network of fiery orange cracks. The noise was considerable. It seemed clear that any new lava would run off the other side of the black mass, the downhill side. They were on a high point in the bank of a stream, with an obvious watercourse running left to right as they looked down on it. Of course a sudden great flood might overwhelm them, but it seemed unlikely, and in any case they were in no more danger here than they had been in the car.

All such calculations disappeared as Jackie pulled her hand free of his and began to take off her glove. Nirgal did the same, rolling the stretching fabric up until the wrist was exposed and his thumb free. The glove popped off his fingertips. It was about 278 degrees, he reckoned, brisk but not particularly cold. And then a wave of warm air buffeted him, followed by a wave of hot air, perhaps 315°K, which quickly passed and was followed by the jostling cool air his hand had been exposed to first. As he peeled off his other glove it became clear that the temperature was all over the place, each knock of the wind distinctly different. Jackie had already unzipped her jacket from her helmet, and down the front, and now as Nirgal watched she pulled it off, baring her upper body. The air struck her and goose-pimples ran over her skin like cat's paws over water. She leaned over to get off her boots, and her air tank lay in the hollow of her spine, her ribs standing out under her skin. Nirgal stepped over and pulled her pants down over her bottom. She reached back and pulled him to her and wrestled him to the ground, and they went down together in a tangle, twisting fast to get onto the thinsulate pads; the ground was very chill. They got their clothes off, and she lay back with her air tank above her right shoulder. He lay on her; in the chill air her body was amazingly warm, radiating heat like the lava, buffets of heat pushing him from below and from the side, the wind airy and cooked, her body pink and muscular, wrapping him hard with arms and legs, startlingly tangible in the sunlight. They bonked faceplates. Their helmets were pumping out air hard, to compensate for the leaks around shoulders, backs, chests, collarbones. For a time they looked each other in the eye, separated by the double layer of glass, which seemed the only thing keeping them from fusing into one being. The sensation was so powerful it felt dangerous—they bonked and bonked, expressing the desire to fuse, but knowing they were safe. Jackie's eyes had a strange vibrant border between iris and pupil. The little black round windows were deeper than any mohole, a drop to the center of the universe. He had to look away, he had to! He lifted off her to look at her long body, which, stunning as it was, was still less stunning than the depths of her eyes. Wide rangy shoulders, oval navel, the so-feminine length of her thighs—he closed his eyes, he had to. The ground trembled under them, moving with Jackie so that it felt as if he were plunging into the planet itself, a wild muscular female body—he could lie perfectly still, they both lay perfectly still, and still the world vibrated them, in a gentle but intense seismic ravishment. This living rock. As his nerves and skin began to thrum and sing he turned his head to look out at the flowing magma and then everything was coming together.

They left the Rayleigh volcano, and rolled back down into the fog hood's darkness. On the second night after leaving Rayleigh they approached Gamete. In the dark gray of an especially thick noon twilight they came up and under the great overhang of ice, and suddenly Jackie leaned forward with a cry and slapped off the autopilot, then kicked down the brake.

Nirgal had been dozing, and he caught himself on his steering wheel, staring out to see what the trouble was.

The cliff where the garage had been was shattered—a great ice fall spilled away from the cliff, covering where the garage had been. The ice at the top of the break was heavily starred, as by explosion. "Oh," Jackie cried, "they've blown it up! They've killed them all!"

Nirgal felt as if he had been punched in the stomach; he was amazed to find what a physical blow fear could wield. In his mind he was numb, and seemed to feel nothing—no anguish, no despair, nothing. He reached out and squeezed Jackie's shoulder—she was shaking—and peered anxiously through the thick blowing mist.

"There's the bolt-hole," he said. "They wouldn't have been caught unawares." The tunnel led through an arm of the polar cap to Chasma Australe, where there was a shelter in the ice wall.

"But—" Jackie said, and swallowed. "But if they didn't get any warning!"

"Let's get around to the shelter in Australe," Nirgal said, taking over the controls.

He bounced them over the ice flowers at the car's top speed, concentrating on the terrain and trying not to think. He did not want to get to the other shelter—get there and find it empty, taking away his last hope, the only way he had of staving off this disaster. He wanted never to arrive, to keep driving clockwise around the polar cap forever, no matter the torque of apprehension that was causing Jackie to hiss as she breathed, and to moan from time to time. In Nirgal it was only a numbness, an inability to think. I don't feel a thing, he thought wonderingly. But unbidden images of Hiroko kept flashing before him as if projected on the windshield, or standing ghostlike out in the driving mists. There was a chance that the assault had come from space, or by missile from the north, in which case there might not have been any warning. Wiping the green world out of the universe, and leaving only the white world of death. The colors drained from everything, as in this gray-fog winter world.

He pursed his lips and concentrated on the icescape, driving with a ruthless touch he had not known he had. The hours passed and he did his best not to think of Hiroko or Nadia or Art or Sax or Maya or Harmakhis or any of the rest: his family, neighborhood, town, and nation, all under that one small dome. He bent over his twisted stomach and focused on the world of driving, on each little bump and hollow to be dodged in the vain attempt to make it a less rattled ride.

They had to go clockwise for three hundred kilometers, and then most of the way up the length of Chasma Australe, which in late winter narrowed and became so choked with ice blocks that there was only a single route through, marked by weak little directional transponders. There he was forced to slow down, but under the dark mist they could drive at all hours, and they did so until they reached the low wall that marked the refuge. It was just fourteen hours after their departure from the gate of Gamete—an accomplishment, over such jagged frosty terrain—but Nirgal didn't even note it. If the refuge was empty—

If it was empty . . . The numbness in him was eroding fast as they approached the low wall at the head of the chasm; there was no sign of anyone or anything there, and his fear was breaking through the numbness like orange magma out of the cracks in black lava, it gushed out and billowed through him, became an unbearable ripping tension in every cell of him. . . .

Then a light flickered from low on the wall, and Jackie cried "Ah!" as if stuck with a pin. Nirgal accelerated and the car bounded toward the ice wall, he almost crashed the car right into it; he slammed on the brakes and the big wire wheels of the car skidded very briefly, then ground to a halt. Jackie popped on her helmet and dashed into the lock, and Nirgal followed, and after an agonizing suck and pump they dropped out of the lock onto the ground, and hurried to the lock door in a shallow recess in the ice. The door opened and four suited figures leaped out holding guns; Jackie cried out over the common band, and in a second the four were hugging them; so far so good, although it was conceivable that they were just comforting them, and Nirgal was still in an agony of suspense, when he saw Nadia's face behind one of the faceplates. She gave him the thumbs-up sign, and he realized that he had been holding his breath for what seemed like the last fifteen hours entire, though no doubt it was only since he had jumped out of the car. Jackie was crying with relief and Nirgal felt that he wanted to cry too, but the sudden disintegration of the numbness and then the fear had left him merely shattered, exhausted, beyond tears.

Nadia led him into the refuge lock by hand, as if she understood this, and when the lock was closed and pumping up Nirgal began to understand the voices on the common band: "I was so scared, I thought you were dead." "We got out the escape tunnel, we saw them coming—"

Inside the shelter they took off their helmets and went through a hundred rounds of embracing. Art slapped him on the back, his eyes popping out like eggs: "So glad to *see* you two!" He pulled Jackie into a rough hug, then held her out at arm's length and looked at her wet snotty red-eyed girlish face with approval and admiration, as if just this moment accepting that she was human too, and not some feline goddess.

As they staggered down the narrow tunnel to the refuge's rooms, Nadia told them the story, scowling as she recalled it. "We saw them coming and got way up the back tunnel, and then brought down both domes, and all the tunnels. So we may have killed a good number of them, but I don't know—I don't know how many they sent in, or how far they got. Coyote's out shadowing them to see if he can tell. Anyway, it's done."

At the end of the tunnel was a crowded refuge of several little chambers, roughly walled, floored and ceilinged by insulation panels, set right against cavities in the ice. Every room radiated from a larger central chamber that served as kitchen and dining hall. Jackie hugged everyone in there but Maya, ending with Nirgal. They held each other hard, and Nirgal felt her trembling, and realized he was trembling as well, in a kind of synchronic vibration. The silent, desperate, fearful drive would strengthen the bond as much as their lovemaking by the volcano, or more—it was hard to tell—he was too tired to be able to read the powerful vague emotions sloshing through him. He disengaged from Jackie and sat, feeling suddenly exhausted to tears. Hiroko sat beside him, and he listened to her as she told him what had happened in more detail. The attack had started with the sudden appearance of several space planes, dropping onto the flat outside the hangar in a group. So they had had very little warning inside, and the people at the hangar had reacted in confusion, telephoning in to warn the others, but failing to activate Coyote's defense system, which apparently they had simply forgotten. Coyote was disgusted about this, Hiroko said, and Nirgal could well believe it. "You have to stop paratrooper attacks at the very moment of landing, he said." Instead the people at the hangar had retreated into the dome. After some confusion they had gotten everyone up into the escape tunnel, and once they were past the blast point Hiroko had ordered them to use the Swiss defense and bring down the dome, and Kasei and Harmakhis had obeyed her, and so the whole dome had been blown down, killing whatever part of the attack force was inside, burying them in million of tons of dry ice. Radiation readings seemed to indicate that the Rickover had not suffered a meltdown, although it certainly had been crushed along with everything else. Coyote had disappeared down a side tunnel with Peter, out a bolt-hole of his own, and

Hiroko didn't know exactly where they had gone. "But I think those space planes may be in trouble."

So Gamete was gone, and the shell of Zygote too. In some future age the polar cap would sublime away and reveal their flattened remnants, Nirgal thought absently; but for now it was buried, utterly unreachable.

And here they were. They had gotten out with only some AIs, and the walkers on their backs. And now they were at war with the Transitional Authority (presumably), with some part of the force that had assaulted them still out there.

"Who were they?" Nirgal asked.

Hiroko shook her head. "We don't know. Transitional Authority, Coyote said. But there are a lot of different units in UNTA security, and we need to find out if this is the full Transitional Authority's new policy, or if some unit has gone on a rampage."

"What will we do?" Art asked.

At first no one answered.

Finally Hiroko said, "We'll have to ask for shelter. I think Dorsa Brevia has the most room."

"What about the congress?" Art asked, reminded of it by the mention of Dorsa Brevia.

"I think we need it now more than ever," Hiroko said.

Maya was frowning. "It could be dangerous to congregate," she pointed out. "You've told a lot of people about this."

"We had to," Hiroko said. "That's the point of it." She looked around at them all, and even Maya did not dare contradict her. "Now we have to take the risk."

PART 7

What Is to Be Done?

The few big buildings in Sabishii were faced with polished stone, picked for colors that were unusual on Mars: alabaster, jade, malachite, yellow jasper, turquoise, onyx, lapis lazuli. The smaller buildings were wooden. After traveling by night and hiding by day, the visitors found it a pleasure to walk in the sunlight between low wooden buildings, under plane trees and fire maples, through stone gardens and across wide boulevards of streetgrass, past canals lined by cypress, which occasionally widened into lily-covered ponds, crossed by high arching bridges. They were almost on the equator here, and winter meant nothing; even at aphelion hibiscus and rhododendron were flowering, and pine trees and many varieties of bamboo shot high into the warm breezy air.

The ancient Japanese greeted their visitors as old and valued friends. The Sabishii issei dressed in copper jumpsuits, went barefoot, and wore long ponytails, and many earrings and necklaces. One of them, bald, with a wispy white beard and a deeply wrinkled face, took the visitors on a walk, to stretch their legs after their long drives. His name was Kenji, and he had been the first Japanese to step on Mars, though no one remembered that anymore.

At the city wall they looked out at enormous boulders balancing on nearby hilltops, carved into one fantastic shape after another.

"Have you ever been to the Medusae Fossae?"

Kenji only smiled and shook his head. The kami stones on the hills were honeycombed with rooms and storage spaces, he told them, and along with the mohole mound maze they now could house a very great number of people, as many as twenty thousand, for as long as a year. The visitors nodded. It seemed possible it might become necessary.

Kenji took them back to the oldest part of town, where the visitors had been given rooms in the original compound. The rooms were smaller and more spare than most of the town's student apartments, and had a patina of age and use that made them more like nests than rooms. The issei still slept in some of them.

As the visitors walked through these rooms, they did not look at each other. The contrast between their history and those of the Sabishiians was too stark. They stared at the furniture, disturbed, distracted, withdrawn. And after that evening's meal, after a lot of sake had gone down the hatches, one said, "If only we had done something like this."

Nanao began to play a bamboo flute.

"It was easier for us," Kenji said. "We were all Japanese together. We had a model."

"It doesn't seem much like the Japan I remember."

"No. But that isn't the true Japan."

They took their cups and a few bottles, and climbed up stairs to a pavilion on top of a wooden tower next to their compound. Up there they could see the trees and rooftops of the city, and the jagged array of boulders standing on the black skysill. It was the last hour of twilight, and except for a wedge of lavender in the west the sky was a rich midnight blue, liberally flecked with stars. A string of paper lanterns hung in a grove of fire maples below.

"We are the true Japanese. What you see in Tokyo today is transnational. There is another Japan. We can never go back to that, of course. It was a feudal culture in any case, and had features we cannot accept. But what we do here has its roots in that culture. We are trying to find a new way, a way which rediscovers the old one, or reinvents it, for this new place."

"Kasei Nippon."

"Yes, but not just for Mars! For Japan also. As a model for them, you see? An example of what they can become."

And so they drank rice wine under the stars. Nanao played his flute, and down in the park under the paper lanterns someone laughed. The visitors sat leaning against each other, drinking and thinking. They talked for a while about all the sanctuaries, how different they were and yet how much they had in common. They got drunk.

"This congress is a good idea."

The visitors nodded, in various degrees of assent.

"It's just what we need. I mean, we have been getting together to celebrate John's festival for how many years now? And it's been good. Very pleasant. Very *important. We have needed it, for our own sakes. But now things are changing fast. We can't pretend to be a cabal. We have to deal with the rest of them."*

They talked specifics for a while: attendants at the congress, security measures, problem issues.

"Who attacked the egg—the egg?"

"A security team from Burroughs. Subarashii and Armscor have organized what they call a sabotage investigation unit, and they've gotten the Transitional Authority to bless the operation. They'll be coming south again, no doubt of that. We have almost waited too long."

"They got the institution—the information—from me?"

A snort. "You should resist thinking you are so important."

"It doesn't matter anyway. It's the return of the elevator driving all this."

"And they are building one for Earth as well. And so . . . "

"We had better act."

Then as the stone sake bottles kept going around, and emptying, they gave up on such seriousness, and talked about the past year, things they had seen in the outback, gossip about mutual acquaintances, new jokes heard. Nanao got out a packet of balloons, and they filled them and tossed them out into the city's night breeze, and watched them float down onto the trees and the old habitats. They passed around a canister of nitrous oxide, took breaths and laughed. The stars made a thick net overhead. One told stories of space, of the asteroid belt. They tried to nick exposed bits of wood with their pocket knives and failed. "This congress will be what we call nema-washi. Preparing the ground."

Two stood, arms around each other, and swayed until they had caught their balance, then held out their little cups in a toast.

"Next year on Olympus."

"Next year on Olympus," the others repeated, and drank.

It was Ls 180, M-year 40, when they began to arrive at Dorsa Brevia, in small cars and planes from all over the south. A group of Reds and caravan Arabs checked people's credentials in the wasteland approaches, and more Reds and Bogdanovists were stationed in bunkers located all around the dorsa, armed, in case there was any trouble. The Sabishiian intelligence experts, however, thought that the conference was unknown in Burroughs or Hellas or Sheffield, and when they explained why they thought so, people tended to relax, for clearly they had penetrated far into the halls of UNTA, and indeed throughout the whole structure of transnational power on Mars. That was another advantage to the demimonde; they could work in both directions.

When Nadia arrived, with Art and Nirgal, they were led to their guest quarters in Zakros, the southernmost segment of the tunnel. Nadia dropped her pack in a little wooden room, and wandered the big park, and then through the segments farther north, finding old friends and meeting strangers, feeling in a mood of good hope. It was encouraging to see all these people milling about the green parks and pavilions, representing so many different groups. She looked around at the crowd thronging the canalside park, perhaps three hundred people in view at that moment, and laughed.

The Swiss from Overhangs arrived on the day before the conference was supposed to begin; people said they had been camped outside in their rovers, waiting for the date specified. They brought with them a whole set of procedures and protocols for the meeting, and as Nadia and Art listened to a Swiss woman describing their plans, Art elbowed Nadia and whispered, "We've created a monster."

"No no," Nadia whispered back, happy as she looked over the big central park in the third-from-the-south segment of the tunnel, called Lato. The skylight overhead was a long bronze crack in the dark roof, and morning light filled the giant cylindrical chamber with the kind of photon rain she had been craving all winter, brown light everywhere, the bamboo and pine and cypress rising over the tile rooftops and blazing like green water. "We need a structure, or it would be a free-for-all. The Swiss are form without content, if you see what I mean."

Art nodded. He was very quick, sometimes even hard to understand, because he jumped five or six steps at a time and assumed she had followed him. "Just get them to drink kava with the anarchists," he muttered, and got up to walk around the edges of the meeting.

And in fact that night, on her way with Maya through Gournia to a canalside row of open-air kitchens, Nadia passed by Art and saw that he was doing just that, dragging Mikhail and some of the other Bogdanovist hard-liners over to a table of Swiss, where Jurgen and Max and Sibilla and Priska were chatting happily with a group standing around them, switching languages as if they were translation AIs, but in every language exhibiting the same buoyant guttural Swiss accent. "Art is an optimist," Nadia said to Maya as they walked on.

"Art is an idiot," Maya replied.

By now there were about five hundred visitors in the long sanctuary, representing about fifty groups. The congress was to begin the following morning, so on this night the partying was loud, from Zakros to Falasarna, the timeslip filled with wild shouting and singing, Arab ululations harmonizing with yodels, the strains of "Waltzing Matilda" forming a descant to "The Marseillaise."

Nadia got up early the next morning. She found Art already out at the pavilion in the Zakros park, rearranging chairs into a circular formation, in classic Bogdanovist style. Nadia felt a prick of pain and regret, as if Arkady's ghost had walked through her; he would have loved this meeting, it was just what he had often called for. She went to help Art. "You're up early."

"I woke up and couldn't fall back asleep." He needed a shave. "I'm nervous!"

She laughed. "This is going to take weeks, Art, you know that."

"Yes, but starts are important."

By ten all the seats were filled, and behind the chairs the pavilion was crowded with standing observers. Nadia stood at the back of the Zygote wedge of the circle, watching curiously. There appeared to be slightly more men than women in attendance, and slightly more natives than emigrants. Most people wore standard one-piece jumpers—the Reds' were rust-colored—but a significant number were dressed in a colorful array of ceremonial styles: robes, dresses, pantaloons, suits, embroidered shirts, bare chests, a lot of necklaces and earrings and other jewelry. All the Bogdanovists wore jewelry containing pieces of phobosite, the black chunks shining where they had been cut flat and polished.

The Swiss stood in the center, somber in gray bankers' suits, Sibilla and Priska in dark green dresses. Sibilla called the meeting to order, and she and the rest of the Swiss alternated as they explained in excruciating detail the program they had worked out, pausing to answer questions, and asking for comments at every change of speaker. As they did this a group of Sufis in pure white shirts and pantaloons worked their way around the outer perimeter of the circle, passing out jugs of water and bamboo cups, moving with their customary dancelike grace. When everyone had cups, the delegates at the front of each group poured water for the party on their left, and then they all drank. Out in the crowd of spectators the Vanuatuans were at a table filling tiny cups of kava or coffee or tea, and Art was passing these out to those who wanted them. Nadia smiled at the sight of him, shambling through the crowds like a Sufi in slow motion, sipping from the cups of kava he was distributing.

The Swiss's program was to begin with a series of workshops on specific topics and problems, working in open rooms scattered through Zakros, Gournia, Lato, and Malia. All of the workshops were to be recorded. Conclusions, recommendations, and questions from the workshops were to serve as the basis for a subsequent day's discussion at one of the two general ongoing meetings. One of these would focus roughly on the problems of achieving independence, the other on what came after—the means and ends meetings, as Art noted when he stopped briefly at Nadia's side.

When the Swiss were done describing the program, they were ready to start; it had not occurred to them to have any ceremonial opening. Werner, speaking last, reminded people that the first workshops would begin in an hour, and that was that. They were done.

But before the crowd dispersed, Hiroko stood at the back of the Zygote crowd, and walked slowly into the center of the circle. She wore a bamboo-green jumper, and no jewelry—a tall slight figure, white-haired, unprepossessing—and yet every eye there was locked onto her. And when she lifted her hands, everyone seated got to their feet. In the silence that followed, Nadia's breath caught in her throat. We should stop now, she thought. No meetings—this is it right here, our presence together, our shared reverence for this single person.

"We are children of Earth," Hiroko said, loud enough for all to hear. "And yet here we stand, in a lava tunnel on the planet Mars. We should not forget how strange a fate that is. Life anywhere is an enigma and a precious miracle, but here we see even better its sacred power. Let's remember that now, and make our work our worship."

She spread her hands wide, and her closest associates walked humming into the center of the circle. Others followed suit, until the space around the Swiss was full of a milling horde of friends, acquaintances, strangers.

The workshops were held in gazebos scattered through the parks, or in three-walled rooms in the public buildings that edged these parks. The Swiss had assigned small groups to run the workshops, and the rest of the conferees attended whichever meetings interested them the most, so that some involved five people, others fifty.

Nadia spent the first day wandering from workshop to workshop, up and down the four southernmost segments of the tunnel. She found that quite a few people were doing the same, none more so than Art, who appeared to be trying to observe all the workshops, so that he caught only a sentence or two at each site.

She dropped in on a workshop discussing the events of 2061. She was interested, although not surprised, to find in attendance Maya, Ann, Sax, Spencer, and even Coyote, as well as Jackie Boone and Nirgal, and many others. The room was packed. First things first, she supposed, and there were so many nagging questions about '61: What had happened? What had gone wrong, and why?

Ten minutes' listening, however, and her heart sank. People were upset, their recriminations heartfelt and bitter. Nadia's stomach knotted in a way it hadn't in years, as memories of the failed revolt flooded into her.

She looked around the room, trying to concentrate on the faces, to distract herself from the ghosts within. Sax was watching birdlike as he sat next to Spencer; he nodded as Spencer asserted that 2061 taught them that they needed a complete assessment of all the military forces in the Martian system. "This is a *necessary precondition* for any successful action," Spencer said.

But this bit of common sense was shouted down by someone who seemed to consider it an excuse to avoid action—a Marsfirster, apparently, who advocated immediate mass ecotage, and armed assault on the cities.

Quite vividly Nadia recalled an argument with Arkady about this very matter, and suddenly she couldn't stand it. She walked down to the center of the room.

After a while everyone went silent, stilled by the sight of her. "I'm tired of this matter being discussed in purely military terms," she said. "The whole model of revolution has to be rethought. This is what Arkady failed to do in sixty-one, and this is why sixty-one was such a bloody mess. Listen to me, now—there can be no such thing as a successful armed revolution on Mars. The life-support systems are too vulnerable."

Sax croaked, "But if the surface is vivable—is *viable*—then the support systems not so—so . . . "

Nadia shook her head. "The surface is not viable, and won't be for many years. And even when it is, revolution has to be rethought. Look, even when revolutions have been successful, they have caused so much destruction and hatred that there is always some kind of horrible backlash. It's inherent in the method. If you choose violence, then you create enemies who will resist you forever. And ruthless men become your revolutionary leaders, so when the war is over they're in power, and likely to be as bad as what they replaced."

"Not in—*American*," Sax said, cross-eyed with the effort to force the right words out in a timely manner.

"I don't know about that. But mostly it's been true. Violence breeds hatred, and eventually there is a backlash. It's unavoidable."

"Yes," said Nirgal with his usual intent look, not all that different from Sax's grimace. "But if people are attacking the sanctuaries and destroying them, then we don't have much choice."

Nadia said, "The question is, who's sending those forces out? And who are the people actually in these forces? I doubt that those individuals bear us any ill will. At this point they might just as easily be on our side as against us. It's their commanders and owners we should focus on."

"De-cap-i-ta-tion," Sax said.

"I don't like the sound of that. You need a different term."

"Mandatory retirement?" Maya suggested acidly. People laughed, and Nadia glared at her old friend.

"Forced disemployment," Art said loudly from the back, where he had just appeared.

"You mean a coup," Maya said. "Not to fight the entire population on the surface, but just the leadership and their bodyguards."

"And maybe their armies," Nirgal insisted. "We have no sign that they are disaffected, or even apathetic."

"No. But would they fight without orders from their leaders?"

"Some might. It's their job, after all."

"Yes, but they have no great stake beyond that," Nadia said, thinking it out as she spoke. "Without nationalism or ethnicity, or some other kind of home feeling involved, I don't think these people will fight to the death. They know they're being ordered around to protect the powerful. Some more egalitarian system makes an appearance, and they might feel a conflict of loyalties."

"Retirement benefits," Maya mocked, and people laughed again.

But from the back Art said, "Why not put it in those terms? If you don't want revolution conceptualized as war, you need something else to replace it, so why not economics? Call it a change in practice. This is what the people in Praxis are doing when they talk about human capital, or bioinfrastructure—modeling everything in economic terms. It's ludicrous in a way, but it does speak to those for whom economics is the most important paradigm. That certainly includes the transnationals."

"So," Nirgal said with a grin, "we disemploy the local leadership, and give their police a raise while job-retraining them."

"Yeah, like that."

Sax was shaking his head. "Can't reach them," he said. "Need force."

"Something has to be changed to avoid another sixty-one!" Nadia insisted. "It has to be rethought. Maybe there are historical models, but not the ones you've been mentioning. Something more like the velvet revolutions that ended the Soviet era, for instance."

"But those involved unhappy populations," Coyote said from the back, "and took place in a system that was falling apart. The same conditions don't obtain here. People are pretty well off. They feel lucky to be here."

"But Earth—in trouble," Sax pointed out. "Falling apart."

"Hmm," Coyote said, and he sat down by Sax to talk about it. Talking with Sax was still frustrating, but as a result of all his work with Michel, it could be done. It made Nadia happy to see Coyote conferring with him.

The discussion went on around them. People argued theories of revolution, and when they tried to talk about '61 itself, they were hampered by old grievances, and a basic lack of understanding of what had happened in those nightmare months. At one point this became especially clear, as Mikhail and some ex-Korolyov inmates began arguing about who had murdered the guards.

Sax stood and waved his AI over his head.

"Need facts—*first*," he croaked. "Then the dialysis—the *analysis*."

"Good idea," Art said instantly. "If this group can put together a brief history of the war to give to the congress at large, that would be really useful. We can save the discussion of revolutionary methodology for the general meetings, okay?"

Sax nodded and sat down. Quite a few people left the meeting, and the rest calmed down, and gathered around Sax and Spencer. Now they were mostly veterans of the war, Nadia noticed, but there also were Jackie and Nirgal and some other natives. Nadia had seen some of the work Sax had done in Burroughs on the question of '61, and she was hopeful that with eyewitness accounts from other veterans, they could come to some basic understanding of the war and its ultimate causes—nearly half a century after it was over, but as Art said when she mentioned this to him, that was not atypical. He walked with a hand on her shoulder, looking unconcerned by what he had seen that morning, in his first full exposure to the fractious nature of the underground. "They don't agree about much," he admitted. "But it always starts that way."

• • •

Late on the second afternoon Nadia dropped in on the workshop devoted to the terraforming question. This was probably the most divisive issue facing them, Nadia judged, and attendance at the workshop reflected it; the room on the border of Lato's park was packed, and before the meeting began the moderator moved it out into the park, on the grass overlooking the canal.

The Reds in attendance insisted that terraforming itself was an obstruction to their hopes. If the Martian surface became human-viable, they argued, then it would represent an entire Earth's worth of land, and given the acute population and environmental problems on Earth, and the space elevator currently being constructed there to match the one already on Mars, the gravity wells could be surmounted and mass emigration would certainly follow, and with it the disappearance of any possibility of Martian independence.

People in favor of terraforming, called greens, or just green, as they were not a party as such—argued that with a human-viable surface it would be possible to live anywhere, and at that point the underground would be on the surface, and infinitely less vulnerable to control or attack, and thus in a much better position to take over.

These two views were argued in every possible combination and variation. And Ann Clayborne and Sax Russell were both there, in the center of the meeting, making points more and more frequently—until the others in attendance stopped speaking, silenced by the authority of those two ancient antagonists. Watching them go at it yet again.

Nadia observed this slow-developing collision unhappily, anxious for her two friends. And she wasn't the only one who found the sight unsettling. Most of the people there had seen the famous videotape of Ann and Sax's argument in Underhill, and certainly their story was well known, one of the great myths of the First Hundred—a myth from a time when things had been simpler, and distinct personalities could stand for clearcut issues. Now nothing was simple anymore, and as the old enemies faced off again in the middle of this new hodgepodge group, there was an odd electricity in the air, a mix of nostalgia and tension and collective déjà vu, and a wish (perhaps just in herself, Nadia thought bitterly) that the two of them could somehow effect a reconciliation, for their own sakes and for all of them.

But there they were, standing in the center of the crowd. Ann had already lost this argument in the world itself, and her manner seemed to reflect this; she was subdued, disinterested, almost uninterested; the fiery Ann of the famous tapes was nowhere to be seen. "When the surface is viable," she said—*when*, Nadia noted, not *if*—"they'll be here by the billions. As long as we have to live in shelters, logistics will keep the population in the millions. And that's the size it needs to be if you want a successful revolution." She shrugged. "You could do it today if you wanted. Our shelters are hidden, and theirs aren't. Break theirs open, they have no one to shoot back at—they die, you take over. Terraforming just takes away that leverage."

"I won't be a part of that," Nadia said promptly, unable to help herself. "You know what it was like in the cities in sixty-one."

Hiroko was there, sitting at the back observing, and now she spoke out for the first time. "A nation founded in genocide is not what we want."

Ann shrugged. "You want a bloodless revolution, but it's not possible."

"It is," Hiroko said. "A silk revolution. An aerogel revolution. An integral part of the areophany. That is what I want."

"Okay," Ann said. No one could argue with Hiroko, it was impossible. "But even so, it would be easier if you didn't have a viable surface. This coup you're talking about—I mean, think about it. If you take over the power plants in the major cities and say, 'We're in control now,' then the population is likely to agree, out of necessity. If there are billions of people here, however, on a viable surface, and you disemploy some people and declare yourself in control, then they're likely to say, 'In control of what?' and ignore you."

"This," Sax said slowly. "This suggests—take over—while surface non-vivable. Then continue process—as independent."

"They'll want you," Ann said. "When they see the surface open up, they'll come get you."

"Not if they collapse," Sax said.

"The transnationals are in firm control," Ann said. "Don't think they're not."

Sax was watching Ann most intently, and instead of dismissing her points, as he had in the debates of old, he seemed on the contrary hyperfocused on them, observing her every move, blinking as he considered her words, and then replying with even more hesitation than his speech problems would explain. With his altered face it sometimes seemed to Nadia that someone else was arguing with her this time, not Sax but some brother of his, a dance instructor or ex-boxer with a broken nose and a speech impediment, struggling patiently to choose the right words, and often failing.

And yet the effect was the same. "Terraforming—irreversible," he croaked. "Would be tactically hard—*technically* hard—to start—to *stop*. Effort equal to one—made. And might not—. And—environment can be a— a weapon in our case—in our *cause*. At any stage."

"How so?" several people asked, but Sax did not elaborate. He was concentrating on Ann, who was looking back at him with a curious expression, as if exasperated.

"If we're on course to viability," she said to him, "then Mars represents an incredible prize to the transnationals. Maybe even their salvation, if things go really wrong down there. They can come here and take over and have their own new world, and let Earth go to hell. That being the case, we're out of luck. You saw what happened in sixty-one. They have giant militaries at their disposal, and that's how they'll keep their power here."

She shrugged. Sax blinked as he considered this; he even nodded. Looking at them, Nadia felt her heart wrench; they were so dispassionate it was almost as if they didn't care, or as if the parts of them that cared just barely outweighed the parts that didn't, and tipped the balance to speech. Ann like a weatherbeaten sodbuster from the early daguerreotypes, Sax incongruously charming—they both appeared to be in their early seventies, so that seeing them, and feeling her own nervous pulse, it was hard for Nadia to believe that they were over 120 now, inhumanly ancient, and so . . . changed, somehow—worn down, overexperienced, jaded, used up—or at the very least, long past getting too passionate about any mere exchange of words. They knew now how little importance words had in the world. And so they fell silent, still looking into each other's eyes, locked in a dialectic nearly drained of anger.

But others more than compensated for their thoughtfulness, and the younger hotheads went at it hammer and tongs. The younger Reds regarded terraforming as nothing more than part of the imperial process; Ann was a moderate compared to them, they raged even at Hiroko in their fury—"*Don't* call it areoforming," one of them shouted at her, and Hiroko stared nonplussed at this tall young woman, a blond Valkyrie made nearly rabid by the use of the word—"it's *terraforming* you mean and *terraforming* you're doing. Calling it areoforming is a sickening lie."

"We terraform the planet," Jackie said to the woman, "but the planet areoforms us."

"And that's a lie too!"

Ann stared grimly at Jackie. "Your grandfather said that to me," she said, "a long time ago. As you may know. But I'm still waiting to see what *areoforming* is supposed to mean."

"It's happened to everyone born here," Jackie said confidently.

"How so? You were born on Mars—how are you any different?"

Jackie glowered. "Like the rest of the natives, Mars is all I know, and all I care about. I was brought up in a culture made of strands from many different Terran predecessors, mixed to a new Martian thing."

Ann shrugged. "I don't see how you're so different. You remind me of Maya."

"To hell with you!"

"As Maya would say. And that's your areoforming. We're human and human we remain, no matter what John Boone said. He said a lot of things, but none of them ever came true."

"Not yet," Jackie said. "But the process is slowed when it's in the hands of people who haven't had a new thought for fifty years." A lot of the younger ones laughed at this. "And who are in the habit of introducing gratuitous personal insults into a political argument."

And she stood there watching Ann, looking calm and relaxed, except for the flash in her eye, which reminded Nadia again of what a power Jackie was. Almost all the natives there were behind her, no doubt about it.

"If we have not changed here," Hiroko said to Ann, "how do you explain your Reds? How do you explain the areophany?"

Ann shrugged. "They are the exceptions."

Hiroko shook her head. "There is a spirit of place in us. Landscape has profound effects on the human psyche. You are a student of landscapes, and a Red. You must acknowledge this to be true."

"True for some," Ann replied, "but not for all. Most people obviously don't feel that spirit of place. One city is much like another—in fact they're interchangeable in all the important ways. So people come to a city on Mars, and what's the difference? There isn't any. So they think no more of destroying the land outside the city than they did back on Earth."

"These people can be taught to think differently."

"No, I don't think they can. You've caught them too late. At best you can order them to act differently. But that's not being areoformed by the planet, that's indoctrination, reeducation camps, what have you. Fascist areophany."

"Persuasion," Hiroko countered. "Advocacy, argument by example, argument by argument. It need not be coercive."

"The aerogel revolution," Ann said sarcastically. "But aerogel has very little effect on missiles."

Several people spoke at once, and for a moment the thread of discourse was lost; the discussion immediately fissioned into a hundred smaller debates, as many there had something to say which they had been holding back. It was obvious they could go on like this for hour after hour, day after day.

Ann and Sax sat back down. Nadia made her way out of the crowd, shaking her head. On the edge of the meeting she ran into Art, who shook his head soberly. "Unbelievable," he said.

"Believe it."

The days of the congress unfolded much as the first few had, with workshops good or bad leading to dinner, and then long evenings of talk or partying. Nadia noticed that while the old emigrants were likely to go back to work after dinner, the young natives tended to regard the conferences as daytime work only, with the nights given over to celebration, often around the big warm pond in Phaistos. Once again this was only a matter of tendencies, with many exceptions either way, but she found it interesting.

She herself spent most of her evenings on the Zakros dining patios, making notes on the day's meetings, talking to people, thinking things over. Nirgal often worked with her, and Art too, when he was not getting people who had been arguing during the day to drink kava together, and then go up to party in Phaistos.

In the second week she got in the habit of taking an evening walk up the tube, often all the way to Falasarna, after which she would walk back and join Nirgal and Art for their final postmortem on the day, which they convened on a patio set on a little lava knob in Lato. The two men had become good friends during their long trek home from Kasei Vallis, and under the pressure of the congress they were becoming like brothers, talking over everything, comparing impressions, testing theories, laying out plans for Nadia's judgment, and deciding to take on the task of writing some kind of congress document. She was part of it—the elder sister perhaps, or maybe just the babushka—and once when they shut down and staggered off to bed Art spoke of "the triumvirate." With her as Pompey, no doubt. But she did her best to sway them with her analyses of the larger picture.

There were many different kinds of disagreements among the groups there, she told them, but some were basic. There were those for and against terraforming. There were those for and against revolutionary violence.

There were those who had gone underground to hold on to cultures under assault, and those who had disappeared in order to create radical new social orders. And it seemed more and more evident to Nadia that there were also significant differences between those who had immigrated from Earth, and those who had been born on Mars.

There were all kinds of disagreements, then, and no obvious alignments to be found among them. One night Michel Duval joined the three of them for a drink, and as Nadia described to him the problem he got out his AI, and began to make diagrams based on what he called the "semantic rectangle." Using this schema they made a hundred different sketches of the various dichotomies, trying to find a mapping that would help them to understand what alignments and oppositions might exist among them. They made some interesting patterns, but it could not be said that any blinding insights jumped off the screen at them—although one particularly messy semantic rectangle seemed suggestive, at least to Michel: violence and nonviolence, terraforming and antiterraforming formed the initial four corners, and in the secondary combination around this first rectangle he had located Bogdanovists, Reds, Hiroko's areophany, and the Muslims and other cultural conservatives. But what this *combinatoire* indicated in terms of action was not clear.

Nadia began to attend the daily meetings devoted to general questions concerning a possible Martian government. These were just as disorganized as the discussions of revolutionary methods, but less emotional, and often more substantive. They took place every day in a small amphitheater which the Minoans had cut into the side of the tunnel in Malia. From this rising arc of benches the participants looked out over bamboo and pine trees and terra-cotta rooftops all the way up and down the tunnel, from Zakros to Falasarna.

The talks were attended by a somewhat different crowd than the revolutionary debates. A report would come in from the smaller workshops for discussion, and then most of the people who had attended that workshop would join the larger meeting, to see what comments were made on the report. The Swiss had set up workshops for all aspects of politics, economics, and culture generally, and so the general discussions were very wide-ranging indeed.

Vlad and Marina sent over frequent reports from their workshop on finances, each report sharpening and expanding their evolving concept of eco-economics. "It's very interesting," Nadia reported to Nirgal and Art in their nightly gathering on the knob patio. "A lot of people are critiquing Vlad and Marina's original system, including the Swiss and the Bolognese, and they're basically coming around to the conclusion that the gift system that we first used in the underground is not sufficient by itself, because it's too hard to keep balanced. There are problems of scarcity and hoarding, and when you start to set standards it's like compelling gifts from people, which is a contradiction. This is what Coyote always said, and why he set up his barter network. So they're working toward a more rationalized system, in which basic necessities are distributed in a regulated hydrogen peroxide economy, where things are priced by calculations of their caloric value. Then when you get past the necessities, the gift economy comes into play, using a nitrogen standard. So there are two planes, the need and the gift, or what the Sufis in the workshop call the animal and the human, expressed by the different standards."

"The green and the white," Nirgal said to himself.

"And are the Sufis pleased with this dual system?" Art asked.

Nadia nodded. "Today after Marina described the relationship of the two planes, Dhu el-Nun said to her, 'The Mevlana could not have put it any better.' "

"A good sign," Art said cheerfully.

Other workshops were less specific, and therefore less fruitful. One, working on a prospective bill of rights, was surprisingly ill-natured; but Nadia quickly saw that this topic tapped into a huge well of cultural concerns. Many obviously considered the topic an opportunity for one culture to dominate the rest. "I've said it ever since Boone," Zeyk exclaimed. "An attempt to impose one set of values on all of us is nothing but Ataturkism. Everyone must be allowed their own way."

"But this can only be true up to a point," said Ariadne. "What if one group here asserts its right to own slaves?"

Zeyk shrugged. "This would be beyond the pale."

"So you agree there should be some basic bill of human rights?"

"This is obvious," Zeyk replied coldly.

Mikhail spoke for the Bogdanovists: "All social hierarchy is a kind of slavery," he said. "Everyone should be completely equal under the law."

"Hierarchy is a natural fact," Zeyk said. "It cannot be avoided."

"Spoken like an Arab man," Ariadne said. "But we are not natural here, we are Martian. And where hierarchy leads to oppression, it must be abolished."

"The hierarchy of the right-minded," Zeyk said.

"Or the primacy of equality and freedom."

"Enforced if necessary."

"Yes!"

"Enforced freedom, then." Zeyk waved a hand, disgusted.

Art rolled a drink cart onto the stage. "Maybe we should focus on some actual rights," he suggested. "Maybe look at the various declarations of human rights from Earth, and see if they can be adapted to suit us here."

Nadia moved on to check out some of the other meetings. Land use, property law, criminal law, inheritance . . . the Swiss had broken down the matter of government into an amazing number of subcategories. The anarchists were irritated, Mikhail chief among them: "Do we *really* have to go through all this?" he asked again and again. "None of this should obtain, none of it!"

Nadia would have expected Coyote to be among those arguing with him, but in fact he said, "We have to argue all of it! Even if you want no state, or a minimal state, then you still have to argue it point by point. Especially since most minimalists want to keep exactly the economic and police system that keeps them privileged. That's libertarians for you—anarchists who want police protection from their slaves. No! If you want to make the minimum-state case, you have to argue it from the ground up."

"But," Mikhail said, "I mean, *inheritance law*?"

"Sure, why not? This is critical stuff! I say there should be no inheritance at all, except for a few personal objects passed on, perhaps. But all the rest should go back to Mars. It's part of the gift, right?"

"All the rest?" Vlad inquired with interest. "But what would that consist of, exactly? No one will own any of the land, water, air, the infrastructure, the gene stock, the information pool—what's left to pass on?"

Coyote shrugged. "Your house? Your savings account? I mean, won't we have money? And won't people stockpile surpluses of it if they can?"

"You have to come to the finance sessions," Marina said to Coyote. "We are hoping to base money on units of hydrogen peroxide, and price things by energy values."

"But money will still exist, right?"

"Yes, but we are considering reverse interest on savings accounts, for instance, so that if you don't put what you've earned back into use, it will be released to the atmosphere as nitrogen. You'd be surprised how hard it is to keep a positive personal balance in this system."

"But if you did it?"

"Well, then I agree with you—on death it should pass back to Mars, be used for some public purpose."

Sax haltingly objected that this contradicted the bioethical theory that human beings, like all animals, were powerfully motivated to provide for their own offspring. This urge could be observed throughout nature and in all human cultures, explaining much behavior both self-interested and altruistic. "Try to change the baby logical—the *biological*—basis of culture—by decree . . . Asking for trouble."

"Maybe there should be a minimal inheritance allowed," Coyote said. "Enough to satisfy that animal instinct, but not enough to perpetuate a wealthy elite."

Marina and Vlad clearly found this intriguing, and they began to tap new formulas into their AIs. But Mikhail, sitting by Nadia and flipping through his program for the day, was still frustrated. "Is this *really* part of a constitutional process?" he said, looking at the list. "Zoning codes, energy production, *waste disposal,* transport systems—pest management, property law, grievance systems, criminal law—arbitration—*health codes?"*

Nadia sighed. "I guess so. Remember how Arkady worked so hard on architecture."

"School schedules? I mean I've heard of micropolitics, but this is ridiculous!"

"Nanopolitics," Art said.

"No, picopolitics! Femtopolitics!"

Nadia got up to help Art push the drink cart to the workshops in the village below the amphitheater. Art was still running from one meeting to the next, wheeling in food and drink, then catching a few minutes of the talk before moving on. There were eight to ten meetings per day, and Art was still dropping in on all of them. In the evenings, while more and more of the delegates spent their time partying, or going for walks up and down the tunnel, Art continued to meet with Nirgal, and they watched tapes at a moderate fast forward so that everyone spoke like a bird, only slowing them down to take notes, or talk over some point or other. Getting up in the middle of the night to go to the bathroom, Nadia would pass the dim lounge where the two of them worked on their write-ups, and see the two of them asleep in their chairs, their slack open-mouthed faces flickering under the light of the Keystone Kops debate on the screen.

But in the mornings Art was up with the Swiss, getting things started. Nadia tried to keep pace with him for a few days, but found that the breakfast workshops were chancy. Sometimes people sat around tables sipping coffee and eating fruit and muffins, staring at each other like zombies: Who are you? their bleary gazes said. What am I doing here? Where are we? Why aren't I asleep in my bed?

But it could be just the opposite: some mornings people came in showered and refreshed, alert with coffee or kavajava, full of new ideas and ready to work hard, to make progress. If the others there were of like mind, things could really fly. One of the sessions on property went like that, and for an hour it seemed as though they had solved all the problems of reconciling self and society, private opportunity and the common good, selfishness and altruism. . . . At the end of the session, however, their notes looked just about as vague and contradictory as those taken at any of the more fractious meetings. "It's the tape of the whole session that will have to represent it," Art said, after trying to write down a summary.

The majority of the meetings, however, were not as successful. In fact most of them were merely protracted arguments. One morning Nadia came in on Antar, the young Arab whom Jackie had spent time with during their tour, saying to Vlad, "You will only repeat the socialist catastrophe!"

Vlad shrugged. "Don't be too hasty to judge that period. The socialist countries were under assault from capitalism without and corruption within, and no system could survive that. We must not throw the baby socialism out with the Stalinist bathwater, or we lose many concepts of obvious fairness that we need. Earth is in the grip of the system that defeated socialism, and it is clearly an irrational and destructive hierarchy. So how can we deal with it without being crushed? We have to look everywhere for answers to this, including the systems that the current order defeated."

Art was pulling a food cart to the next room, and Nadia left with him.

"Man, I wish Fort was here," Art muttered. "He should be, I really think he should."

In the next meeting they were arguing about the limits to tolerance, the things that simply wouldn't be allowed no matter what religious meaning anyone gave them, and someone shouted, "Tell that to the Muslims!"

Jurgen came out of the room, looking disgusted. He took a roll from the cart and walked with them, talking through his food: "Liberal democracy says that cultural tolerance is essential, but you don't have to get very far away from liberal democracy for liberal democrats to get very intolerant."

"How do the Swiss solve that?" Art asked.

Jurgen shrugged. "I don't think we do."

"*Man*, I wish Fort were here!" Art said. "I tried to reach him a while back and tell him about this, I even used the Swiss government lines, but I never got any reply."

The congress went on for almost a month. Sleep deprivation, and perhaps an overreliance on kava, made Art and Nirgal increasingly haggard and groggy, until Nadia started coming by at night and putting them to bed, pushing them onto couches and promising to write summaries of the tapes they had not reviewed. They would sleep right there in the room, muttering as they rolled over on the narrow foam-and-bamboo couches. One night Art sat up suddenly from his couch: "I'm losing the content of things," he said to Nadia seriously, still half dreaming. "I'm just seeing forms now."

"Becoming Swiss, eh? Go back to sleep."

He flopped back down. "It was crazy to think you folks could do anything together," he murmured.

"Go back to sleep."

Probably it was crazy, she thought as he snuffed and snored. She stood up, went to the door. She felt the mental whirr in her head that told her she was not going to be able to sleep, and walked outside, into the park.

The air was still warm, the black skylights stuffed with stars. The length of the tunnel suddenly reminded her of one of the full rooms on the *Ares,* here vastly enlarged, but with the same aesthetics employed: dimly lit pavilions, the dark furry clumps of little forests. . . . A world-building game. But now there was a real world at stake. At first the attendants of the congress had been almost giddy with the enormous potential of it, and some, like Jackie and other natives, were young and irrepressible enough to feel that way still. But for a lot of the older representatives, the intractable problems were beginning to reveal themselves, like knobby bones under shrinking flesh. The remnant of the First Hundred, the old Japanese from Sabishii—they sat around these days, watching, thinking hard, with attitudes ranging from Maya's cynicism to Marina's anxious irritation.

And then there was the Coyote, down below her in the park, strolling tipsily out of the woods with a young woman holding him by the waist. "Ah, love," he shouted down the long tunnel, throwing his arms wide, "could thou and I with fate conspire—to grasp this sorry scheme of things entire—would we not shatter it to bits, and then—remold it nearer to the heart's desire!"

Indeed, Nadia thought, smiling, and went back to her room.

There were some reasons for hope. For one thing Hiroko persevered, attending meetings all day long, adding her thoughts and giving people the sense that they had chosen the most important meeting going on at that moment. And Ann worked—though she seemed critical of everything, Nadia thought, blacker than ever—and Spencer, and Sax, and Maya and Michel, and Vlad and Ursula and Marina. Indeed the First Hundred seemed to Nadia more united in this effort than in anything they had done since setting up Underhill—as if this were their last chance to get things right, to recover from the damage done. To make something for their dead friends' sake.

And they weren't the only ones to work. As the meetings went on people got a sense of who wanted the congress to achieve something tangible, and these people got in the habit of attending the same meetings, working hard on finding compromises and getting results onto screens, in the form of recommendations and the like. They had to tolerate visits by those who were more interested in grandstanding than results, but they kept hammering away.

Nadia focused on these signs of progress, and worked to keep Nirgal and Art informed, also fed and rested. People dropped by their suite: "We were told to bring this over to the big three." Many of the serious workers were interesting; one of the women from Dorsa Brevia, named Charlotte, was a constitutional scholar of some note, and she was building a kind of framework for them, a Swisslike thing in which topics to be dealt with were ordered without being filled in. "Cheer up," she told the three of them one morning, when they were sitting around looking glum. "A clash of doctrines is an *opportunity*. The American constitutional congress was one of the most successful ever, and they went into it with several very strong antagonisms. The shape of the government they made reflects the distrust these groups had for each other. Small states came in afraid they were going to be overwhelmed by large states, and so there's a Senate where all states are equals, and a House where the larger states have their greater numbers represented. The structure is a response to a specific problem, see? Same with the three-way checks and balances. It's an institutionalized distrust of authority. The Swiss constitution has a lot of that too. And we can do it here."

So out they went, ready to work, two sharp young men and one blunt old woman. It was strange, Nadia thought, to see who emerged as leaders in situations like these. It wasn't necessarily the most brilliant or well-informed, as Marina or Coyote would serve to show, though both qualities helped, and those two people were important. But the leaders were the ones people would listen to. The magnetic ones. And in a crowd of such powerful intellects and personalities, such magnetism was very rare, very elusive. Very powerful. . . .

She attended a meeting devoted to a discussion of Mars-Earth relations in the postindependence period. Coyote was in there, exclaiming, "Let them go to hell! It's their own doing! Let them pull together if they can, and if they do, we can visit and be neighbors. But without that, if we try to help them it will only destroy us."

Many of the Reds and Marsfirsters in there nodded emphatically, Kasei prominent among them. Kasei had been coming into his own recently, as a leader of the Marsfirst group, a separatist wing of the Reds, whose members wanted nothing to do with Earth, who were willing to back sabotage, ecotage, terrorism, armed revolt—any means necessary to get what they wanted. One of the least tractable groups there, in fact, and Nadia found it sad to see Kasei seizing their cause, and even leading it.

Now Maya stood to reply to Coyote. "Nice theory," she said, "but it's impossible. It's like Ann's redness. We're going to have to deal with Earth, so we might as well figure out how, and not just hide from it."

"As long as they're in chaos, we're in danger," Nadia said. "We have to do what we can to help. To exert influence in the direction we want them to go."

Someone else said, "The two planets are one system."

"What do you mean by that?" Coyote demanded. "They're different worlds, they could certainly be two systems!"

"Information exchange."

Maya said, "We exist for Earth as a model or experiment. A thought experiment for humanity to learn from."

"A real experiment," Nadia said. "This is no longer a game, we can't afford to take attractively pure theoretical positions." She was looking at Kasei and Harmakhis and their comrades as she said this; but it made no impact, she could see.

More meetings, more talk, a quick meal, and another meeting with the Sabishii issei, to discuss the demimonde as a springboard for their efforts. Then it was off to the nightly conference with Art and Nirgal; but the men were beat, and she sent them to bed. "We'll talk over breakfast."

She too was tired, but very far from sleepy. So she took her night walk, north from Zakros through the tunnel. She had recently discovered a high trail running along the west wall of the tunnel, cut into the basalt where the curve of the cylinder made the wall about a forty-five-degree slope. From this trail she could look out over the treetops, down into the parks. And where the trail veered out onto a little spur in Knossos, she could see up and down the length of the tunnel all the way to both horizons, the entire lengthy narrow world dimly lit, by streetlights surrounded by irregular green globes of leaves, and by the few windows with lights still on inside, and by a string of paper lanterns hung in the pines of Gournia's park. It was such an elegant piece of construction, it hurt her slightly to think of the long years spent in Zygote, under ice, in frigid air and artificial light. If only they had known about these lava tunnels. . . .

The next segment, Phaistos, had its floor nearly filled by a long shallow pond, where the canal that coursed slowly down from Zakros widened. Underwater lights at one end of the pond turned its water into a strange sparkling dark crystal, and she could see a group of people splashing about in it, their bodies gleaming in the lit water, disappearing into the dark. Amphibious creatures, salamanders. . . . Once, very long ago on Earth, there had been water animals that had crawled up gasping onto the shore. They must have had some pretty serious policy debates, Nadia thought sleepily, down in that ocean. To emerge or not to emerge, how to emerge, when to emerge. . . . Sound of distant laughter, the stars packing the jagged skylights. . . .

She turned and walked down a staircase to the tunnel floor, then back to Zakros, on the paths and streetgrass, following the canal, thinking in scattered darting images. Back at their suite she lay on her bed and fell asleep instantly, dreaming at dawn of dolphins swimming through the air.

But in the midst of that dream she was awakened roughly by Maya, who said in Russian, "There's some Terrans here. Americans."

"Terrans," Nadia repeated. And was afraid.

She dressed and went out to see. It was true; Art was standing with a small group of Terrans, men and women her own size, and apparently about her own age, unsteady on their feet as they craned their necks, looking at the great cylindrical chamber in amazement. Art was trying to introduce them and explain them at the same time, which was giving even his motor-mouth some difficulty. "I invited them, yes, well, I didn't know—hi, Nadia—this is my old boss, William Fort."

"Speak of the devil," Nadia said, and shook the man's hand. He had a strong grip; a bald snub-nosed man, tanned and wrinkled, with a pleasant vague expression.

"—They just arrived, the Bogdanovists brought them in. I invited Mr. Fort some while ago, but never heard back from him and didn't know he was going to come I'm quite surprised and pleased of course."

"*You* invited him?" Maya said.

"Yes you see he's very interested in helping us that's the thing."

Maya was glaring, not at Art but at Nadia. "I told you he was a spy," she said in Russian.

"Yes you did," Nadia said, then spoke to Fort in English. "Welcome to Mars."

"I'm happy to be here," Fort said. And it looked like he meant it; he was grinning goofily, as if too pleased to keep a straight face. His companions did not seem as sure; there were about a dozen of them, both young and old, and some were smiling, but many looked disoriented and cautious.

After an awkward few minutes Nadia took Fort and his little group of associates over to the Zakros guest quarters, and when Ariadne arrived, they assigned the visitors rooms. What else could they do? The news had already gone the length of Dorsa Brevia and back, and as people came down to Zakros their faces expressed displeasure as much as curiosity—but there the visitors were, after all, leaders of one of the biggest transnationals, and apparently alone, and without tracking devices on them, or so the Sabishiians had declared. One had to do something with them.

Nadia got the Swiss to call a general meeting at the lunch hour, and then she invited the new guests to freshen up in their rooms and afterward speak at the meeting. The Terrans accepted the invitation gratefully, the uncertain ones among them looking reassured. Fort himself seemed to be already composing a speech in his mind.

Back outside the Zakros guest quarters, Art was facing a whole crowd of upset people. "What makes you think you can make decisions like that for us?" Maya demanded, speaking for many of them. "You, who don't even belong! You, a kind of spy among us! Making friends with us, and then betraying us behind our backs!"

Art spread his hands, red-faced with embarrassment, shifting his shoulders as if dodging abuse, or sliding through it to make an appeal to the people behind Maya, the ones who might just be curious. "We need help," he said. "We can't accomplish what we want all by ourselves. Praxis is different, they're more like us than them, I'm telling you."

"It is not your right to tell us!" Maya said. "You are our prisoner!"

Art squinted, waggled his hands. "You can't be a prisoner and a spy at the same time, can you?"

"You can be every kind of treacherous thing at once!" Maya exclaimed.

Jackie walked up to Art and looked down on him, her face stern and intent. "You know this Praxis group may have to become permanent Martians now, whether they want to be or not. Just like you."

Art nodded. "I told them that might happen. Obviously they didn't care. They want to help, I'm telling you. They represent the only transnational that's doing things differently, that has goals similar to ours. They've come here by themselves to see if they can help. They're *interested*. Why should you be so upset by that? It's an *opportunity*."

"Let's see what Fort says," Nadia said.

The Swiss had convened the special meeting in the Malia amphitheater, and as the crowd of delegates gathered, Nadia helped guide the newcomers through the segment gates to the site. They were still obviously awestruck at the size of Dorsa Brevia's tunnel. Art was scurrying around them with his eyes bugged out, wiping sweat from his brow with his sleeve, intensely nervous. It made Nadia laugh. Somehow Fort's arrival had put her in a good mood; she did not see how they could lose from it.

So she sat down in the front row with the Praxis group, and watched as Art led Fort onto the stage and introduced him. Fort nodded and spoke a sentence, then tilted his head and looked up at the back row of the amphitheater, realizing that he was unamplified. He took a breath and started again, and his usually quiet voice floated out with the assurance of a veteran actor, carrying nicely to everyone there.

"I'd like to thank the people of Subarashii for bringing me south to this conference."

Art cringed as he returned to his seat, and turned and cupped a hand by his mouth: "That's Sabishii," he said in an undertone to Fort.

"What's that?"

"Sabishii. You said Subarashii, which is the transnational. The settlement you went through to get here is called Sabishii. Sabishii means 'lonely.' Subarashii means 'wonderful.' "

"Wonderful," Fort said, staring curiously at Art. Then he shrugged and was off and running, an old Terran with a quiet but penetrating voice, and a somewhat wandering style. He described Praxis, how it had begun and how it operated now. When he explained the relationship of Praxis to the other transnationals, Nadia thought there were similarities to the relationship on Mars between the underground and the surface worlds, no doubt cleverly highlighted by Fort's description. And it seemed to her from the silence behind her that Fort was doing pretty well at capturing the crowd's interest. But then he said something about ecocapitalism, and regarding Earth as a full world while Mars was still an empty one; and three or four Reds popped to their feet.

"What do you mean by that?" one of them called out. Nadia saw Art's hands clench in his lap, and soon she could see why; Fort's answer was long and strange, describing what he called ecocapitalism, in which nature was referred to as the bioinfrastructure, while people were referred to as human capital. Looking back Nadia saw many people frowning; Vlad and Marina had their heads together, and Marina was tapping away at her wrist. Suddenly Art popped to his feet, and interrupted to ask Fort what Praxis was doing now, and what he thought Praxis's role might be on Mars.

Fort stared at Art as if he didn't recognize him. "We've been working with the World Court. The UN never recovered from 2061, and is now widely regarded as an artifact of World War Two, just as the League of Nations was an artifact of World War One. So we've lost our best arbitrator of international disputes, and meanwhile conflicts have been ongoing, and some are serious. More and more of these conflicts have been brought before the World Court by one party or another, and Praxis has started a Friends of the Court organization, which tries to give it aid in every way possible. We abide by its rulings, give it money, people, try to work out arbitration techniques, and so on. We've been part of a new technique, where if two international bodies of any kind have a disagreement and decide to submit to arbitration, they enter into a yearlong program with the World Court, and its arbitrators try to find a course of action that satisfies both sides. At the end of the year the World Court rules on any outstanding problems, and if it works, a treaty is signed, and we try to support the treaties any way we can. India has been interested, and went through the program with Sikhs in the Punjab, and it's working so far. Other cases have proved more difficult, but it's been instructive. The concept of semiautonomy is receiving a lot of attention. At Praxis we believe nations were never truly sovereign, but were always semiautonomous in relation to the rest of the world. Metanationals are semiautonomous, individuals are semiautonomous, culture is semiautonomous in relation to the economy, values are semiautonomous in relation to prices . . . there's a new branch of math that is trying to describe semiautonomy in formal logical terms."

Vlad and Marina and Coyote were trying to listen to Fort and confer among themselves and write down notes all at once. Nadia stood and waved at Fort.

"Do the other transnationals support the World Court as well?" she asked.

"No. The metanationals avoid the World Court, and use the UN as a rubber stamp. I'm afraid they still believe in the myth of sovereignty."

"But this sounds like a system that only works when both sides agree to it."

"Yes. All I can tell you is that Praxis is very interested, and we're trying to build bridges between the World Court and all powers on Earth."

"Why?" Nadia asked.

Fort raised his hands, in a gesture just like one of Art's. "Capitalism only works if there is growth. But growth is no longer growth, you see. We need to grow inward, to recomplicate."

Jackie stood. "But you could grow on Mars in classic capitalist style, right?"

"I suppose, yes."

"So maybe that's all you want from us, right? A new market? This empty world you spoke of earlier?"

"Well, in Praxis we've been coming to think that the market is only a very small part of a community. And we're interested in all of it."

"So what do you want from us?" someone yelled from the back.

Fort smiled. "I want to watch."

The meeting ended soon after that, and the afternoon's regular sessions took place. Of course in all of them the arrival of the Praxis group dominated at least part of the discussion. Unfortunately for Art, it became evident as they sat around that night reviewing the tapes that Fort and his team affected the congress as a separator rather than a bonding agent. Many could not accept a Terran transnational as a valid member of the congress, and that was that. Coyote came by and said to Art, "Don't tell me about how different Praxis is. That's the oldest dodge in the book. If only the rich would behave decently, then the system would be okay. That's crap. The system overdetermines everything, and it's the system that has to change."

"Fort's talking about changing it," Art objected. But here Fort was his own worst enemy, with his habit of using classic economic terms to describe his new ideas. The only ones interested in that approach were Vlad and Marina. For the Bogdanovists, and Reds, and Marsfirsters—for most of the natives, and many of the immigrants—it represented Terran business as usual, and they wanted no part of it. No dealing with a transnat, Kasei exclaimed on one tape to applause, no dealing with Terra however they phrased it! Fort was beyond the pale! The only question for this crowd was whether he and his group were going to be allowed to leave or not; some felt that they, like Art, were now prisoners of the underground.

Jackie, however, stood up in that same meeting, to take the Boonean position that everything ought to be put to use in the cause. She was contemptuous of those rejecting Fort on principle. "Since you're going to take visitors hostage," she said sharply to her father, "why not put them to use? Why not talk to them?"

So in effect they had a new split to add to all their others: isolationists and two-worlders.

In the next few days Fort handled the controversy surrounding him by ignoring it, to the extent that it seemed to Nadia that he might not even be aware of it. The Swiss asked him to run a workshop on the current Terran situation, and this was packed, with Fort and his companions answering questions at length in every session. In these sessions Fort seemed content to accept whatever they told him about Mars, and regarding it he advocated nothing. He stuck to Terra, and he only described. "The transnationals have collapsed down into the couple dozen largest of them," he said in response to one question, "all of which have entered into development contracts with more than one national government. We call those the metanationals. The biggest are Subarashii, Mitsubishi, Consolidated, Amexx, Armscor, Mahjari, and Praxis. The next ten or fifteen are also quite big, and after that you're back down to transnat size, but these are being quickly incorporated into the metanats. The big metanats are now the major world powers, insofar as they control the IMF, the World Bank, the Group of Eleven, and all their client countries."

Sax asked him to define a metanational in more detail.

"About a decade ago we at Praxis were asked by Sri Lanka to come into their country and take over the economy and work on arbitration between the Tamils and the Singhalese. We did that and the results were good, but during the time of the arrangement it was clear that our relationship with a national government was a new kind of thing. It got noticed in certain circles. Then some years ago Amexx got into a disagreement with the Group of Eleven, and pulled all of its assets out of the Eleven and relocated them in the Philippines. The mismatch between Amexx and the Philippines, estimated in gross yearly product to be on the order of a hundred to one, resulted in a situation where Amexx in effect took that country over. That was the first real metanational, though it wasn't clear that it was a new thing until their arrangement was imitated by Subarashii, when they shifted many of their operations into Brazil. It became clear that this was something new, not like the old flag-of-convenience relationship. A metanational takes over the foreign debt and the internal economy of its client countries, kind of like the UN did in Cambodia, or Praxis in Sri Lanka, but much more comprehensively. In these arrangements the client government becomes the enforcement agency of the metanational's economic policies. In general they enforce what are called austerity measures, but all government employees are paid much more than they were before, including the army and police and intelligence operations. So at that point, the country is bought. And every metanational has the resources to buy several countries. Amexx has that kind of relationship with the Philippines, the North African countries, Portugal, Venezuela, and five or six smaller countries."

"Has Praxis done this as well?" Marina asked.

Fort shook his head. "In a way yes, but we've tried to give the relationships a different nature. We've dealt with countries large enough to make the partnership more balanced. We've had dealings with India, China, and Indonesia. These were all countries that were shortchanged on Mars by the treaty of 2057, and so they encouraged us to come here and make inquiries like this one. We've also initiated dealings with some other countries that are still independent. But we haven't moved into these countries exclusively, and we haven't tried to dictate their economic policies. We've tried to stick to our version of the transnational format, but on the scale of the metanationals. We hope to function for the countries we deal with as alternatives to metanationalism. A resource, to go along with the World Court, Switzerland, and some other bodies outside the emerging metanational order."

"Praxis is *different*," Art declared.

"But the system is the system," Coyote insisted from the back of the room.

Fort shrugged. "We make the system, I think."

Coyote only shook his head.

Sax said, "We have to steal it—to *deal* with it."

And he started asking Fort questions. "Which is the boggest—the *biggest*?" They were halting, ragged, croaking questions—but Fort ignored his difficulties, and answered in great detail, so that most of three consecutive Praxis workshops consisted of an interrogation of Fort by Sax, in which everyone learned a great deal about the other metanationals, their leaders, their internal structures, their client countries, their attitudes toward each other, and their history, particularly the roles taken by their predecessor organizations in the chaos surrounding 2061. "Why respond—why crack the eggs—no, I mean the *domes*?"

Fort was weak on historical detail, and sighed unhappily at the failures of his personal memory of that period; but his account of the current Terran situation was fuller than any they had gotten before, and it helped clarify questions about metanational activity on Mars that all of them had wondered about. The metanets used the Transitional Authority as a way to mediate their own disagreements. They disagreed over territories. They left the demimonde alone because they felt its underground aspects were negligible and easily monitored. And so on. Nadia could have kissed Sax— she did kiss him—and she kissed Spencer and Michel too for their support of Sax during these sessions, because although Sax doggedly pushed through his speech difficulties, he was often red-faced with frustration, and often hit tables with his fist. Near the end he said to Fort, "What does Praxis want from men—" *Bam!* "—from Mars, then?"

Fort said, "We feel that what happens here will have effects back home. At this point we've identified an emerging coalition of progressive elements on Earth, the biggest of which are China, Praxis, and Switzerland. After that there are scores of smaller elements, but they are less powerful. Which way India goes in this situation could be critical. Most of the metanats seem to regard it as a development sink, meaning that no matter how much they pour into it, nothing there will change. We don't agree with that. And we think Mars is critical as well, in a different way, as an emergent power. So we wanted to find the progressive elements here too, you see, and show you what we're doing. And see what you think of it."

"Interesting," Sax said.

And so it was. But many people remained adamantly opposed to dealing with a Terran metanational. And meanwhile all the other arguments about all the other issues continued unabated, often becoming more polarized the longer they talked about them.

That night at their patio meeting Nadia shook her head, marveling at the capacity people had for ignoring what they had in common, and fighting bitterly over whatever small differences existed between them. She said to Art and Nirgal, "Maybe the world is simply too complex for any one plan to work. Maybe we shouldn't be trying for a global plan, but just something to suit us. And then hope Mars can get along using several different systems."

Art said, "I don't think that will work either."

"But what will?"

He shrugged. "Don't know yet." And he and Nirgal went off to review tapes, pursuing what suddenly seemed to Nadia an ever-receding mirage.

Nadia went to bed. If it were a construction project, she thought as she lay falling asleep, she would tear it down and start over again.

The hypnogogic image of a falling building jerked her awake. After a while, sighing, she gave up on sleep, and went out for another night walk. Art and Nirgal were asleep in the tape room, their faces squashed on the tabletop, flickering under the fast-forward light from the screen. Outside the air whooshed north through the gates into Gournia, and she followed it, taking the high trail. Clicking bamboo leaves, stars in the skylights overhead . . . then the faint sounds of laughter, pealing down the tunnel from Phaistos pond.

The pond's underwater lights were on, and a crowd was bathing again. But now on the far side of the tunnel, about as high on the curved wall as she was on her side, there was a lit platform with perhaps eight people jammed onto it. One of them was getting onto a board of some kind, crouching down; then he dropped away from the platform, crouching down and holding the front of the board, which clearly had very little friction—a naked man with wet hair whipping behind him, flying down the curving black side of the tunnel, accelerating until he shot up a lip of rock and flew out over the pond, cartwheeling, crashing into the water with a great splash, shooting back up with a whoop, to cheers all around.

Nadia walked down to have a look. Someone else was running the board back up a staircase to the platform, and the man who had ridden it down was standing in the shallows, pulling his hair back. Nadia didn't recognize him until she was at the edge of the pond and he sloshed into the liquid light from below. It was William Fort.

Nadia shed her clothes and walked out into the water, which was very warm, body temperature or a bit higher. With a shout another figure came shooting down the incline, like a surfer on an immense rock wave. "The drop looks severe," Fort was saying to one of his companions, "but with the gravity so light you can just handle it."

The woman riding the board was projected out over the water; she arched back in a perfect swan dive until making a final tuck and splash into the pond, and was cheered loudly on emergence. Another woman had retrieved the board and was climbing out of the pond, near the foot of the stairs cut into the slope.

Fort greeted Nadia with a nod, standing waist-deep in the water, his body wiry under ancient wrinkled skin. On his face was the same look of vague pleasure it had worn in the workshops. "Want to try it?" he asked her.

"Maybe later," she said, looking around at the people in the water, trying to sort out who was there and what parties at the congress they represented. When she realized what she was doing she snorted in disgust, at herself and at the pervasiveness of politics—how it could infect everything if you let it.

But still, she noted that the people in the water were mostly young natives, from Zygote, Sabishii, New Vanuatu, Dorsa Brevia, Vishniac mohole, Christianopolis. Hardly any of them were active speaking delegates, and their power was something Nadia couldn't gauge. Probably it didn't signify all that much that they were gathering together here at night, naked in warm water, partying—most of them came from places where public baths were the norm, so they were used to splashing with someone they might fight elsewhere.

Another rider came screaming down the slope, then flying out into the depths of the pond. People swam to her like sharks to blood. Nadia ducked under the water, which tasted slightly salty; opening her eyes she saw crystal bubbles exploding everywhere, then swimming bodies twisting like dolphins over the smooth dark surface of the pond bottom. An unearthly sight. . . .

She came back up, squeezed her hair dry. Fort stood among the youngsters like a decrepit Neptune, surveying them with his curious impassive relaxation. Perhaps, Nadia thought, these natives were in fact the new Martian culture that John Boone had talked about, springing up among them without their actually noticing. Generational transmission of information always contained a lot of error; that was how evolution happened. And even though people had gone underground on Mars for very different reasons, still, they all seemed to be converging here, in a kind of life that had certain paleolithic aspects to it, harking back perhaps to some ur-culture behind all their differences, or forward to some new synthesis—it did not matter which—it could be both at once. So that there was a possible bond there.

Or so Fort's mild expression of pleasure seemed to say to Nadia, somehow, as Jackie Boone in all her Valkyrie glory came shooting down the tunnel wall, and flew out over them as if shot from a circus cannon.

The program devised by the Swiss came to its end. The organizers quickly called for a three-day rest, to be followed by a general meeting.

Art and Nirgal spent these days in their little conference room, going over videotapes twenty hours a days, talking endlessly and typing at their AIs in a kind of hammering desperation. Nadia kept them going, and broke ties when they disagreed, and wrote the sections they deemed too hard. Often when she walked in one of them would be asleep in his chair, the other staring transfixed by his screen. "Look," he would croak, "what do you think of this?" Nadia would read the screen and make comments while putting food under their noses, which often woke the sleeping one. "Looks promising. Let's get back to work."

And so on the morning of the general meeting Art and Nirgal and Nadia walked out onto the stage of the amphitheater together, and Art took his AI with him to the proscenium. He stood looking out at the assembled crowd, as if stunned by the sight of it, and after a long pause said, "We actually agree on many things."

This got a laugh. But Art held his AI overhead like the stone tablets, then read aloud from the screen: "Work points for a Martian government!"

He peered over the screen at the crowd, and they subsided into an attentive silence.

"One. Martian society will be composed of many different cultures. It is better to think of it as a world rather than a nation. Freedom of religion and cultural practice must be guaranteed. No one culture or group of cultures should be able to dominate the rest.

"Two. Within this framework of diversity, it still must be guaranteed that all individuals on Mars have certain inalienable rights, including the material basics of existence, health care, education, and legal equality.

"Three. The land, air, and water of Mars are in the common stewardship of the human family, and cannot be owned by any individual or group.

"Four. The fruits of an individual's labor belong to the individual, and cannot be appropriated by another individual or group. At the same time, human labor on Mars is part of a communal enterprise, given to the common good. The Martian economic system must reflect both these facts, balancing self-interest with the interests of society at large.

"Five. The metanational order ruling Earth is currently incapable of incorporating the previous two principles, and cannot be applied here. In its place we must enact an economics based on ecologic science. The goal of Martian economics is not 'sustainable development' but a sustainable prosperity for its entire biosphere.

"Six. The Martian landscape itself has certain 'rights of place' which must be honored. The goal of our environmental alterations should therefore be minimalist and ecopoetic, reflecting the values of the areophany. It is suggested that the goal of environmental alterations be to make only that portion of Mars lower than the four-kilometer contour human-viable. Higher elevations, constituting some thirty percent of the planet, would then remain in something resembling their primeval conditions, existing as natural wilderness zones.

"Seven. The habitation of Mars is a unique historical process, as it is the first inhabitation of another planet by humanity. As such it should be undertaken in a spirit of reverence for this planet and for the scarcity of life in the universe. What we do here will set precedents for further human habitation of the solar system, and will suggest models for the human relationship to Earth's environment as well. Thus Mars occupies a special place in history, and this should be remembered when we make the necessary decisions concerning life here."

Art let his AI fall to his side, and stared out at the crowd. They looked down at him in silence. "Well," he said, and cleared his throat. He gestured at Nirgal, who came up and stood beside him.

Nirgal said, "That's all that we could pick out from the workshops that it seemed to us everyone here might agree to. There's lots more that we feel would be accepted by a majority of the groups here, but not by all. We've made lists of those partial consensus points as well, and we'll post them all for your inspection. We feel very strongly that if we can come away from here with even a very general kind of document, then we will have accomplished something significant. The tendency in a congress like this is to become more and more aware of our differences, and I think this tendency is exaggerated in our situation, because at this point a Martian government remains a kind of theoretical exercise. But when it becomes a practical problem—when we have to act—then we'll be looking for common ground, and a document like this will help us find it.

"We have a lot of specific notes for each of the main points of the document. We've talked with Jurgen and Priska about them, and they suggest setting up a week of meetings with a day devoted to each of the seven main points, so that everyone can make comments and revisions. Then at the end we can see if we have anything left."

There was a weak laugh. A lot of people were nodding.

"What about gaining independence in the first place?" Coyote called from the back.

Art said, "We couldn't figure out any similar points of agreement to write down. Maybe there can also be a workshop that tries to do that."

"*Maybe* there should!" Coyote exclaimed. "Anyone can agree things should be fair, and the world just. The way to get there is *always* the real problem."

"Well, yes and no," Art said. "What we've got here is more than a wish that things be fair. As for the methods, maybe if we go at it again with these goals in mind, things will suggest themselves. That is to say, what will get us to these goals most surely? What kind of means do these ends imply?"

He looked around at the crowd, and shrugged. "Look, we've tried to compile a composite of what you've all been saying here in your different ways, so if there is a lack of specific suggestions for means of achieving independence, it's perhaps because you've all gotten stuck at the level of general philosophies of action, where many of you disagree. The only thing I can think to suggest is that you try to identify the various forces on the planet, and rate how resistant to independence they might be, and tailor your actions to match the resistance. Nadia talked about reconceptualizing the whole methodology of revolution, and some have suggested economic models, the idea of a leveraged buyout or something, but when I was thinking about this notion of a tailored response, it reminded me of integrated pest management, you know—the system in agriculture where a variety of methods of varying severity are used to deal with the pests you have."

People laughed at this, but Art didn't seem to notice; he looked taken aback by the lack of approval of the general document. Disappointed. And Nirgal looked angry.

Nadia turned and said loudly, "How about a round of applause for our friends here, for managing to synthesize anything at all out of this!"

People clapped. A few cheered. For a moment it sounded quite enthusiastic. But quickly it ended, and they filed out of the amphitheater, talking among themselves, arguing again already.

So the debates continued, now structured around Art and Nirgal's document. Reviewing the tapes, Nadia saw that there was a fair amount of agreement over the substance of all the points except for number six, concerning the level of terraforming. Most of the Reds would not accept the low-elevation viability concept, pointing out that most of the planet lay under the four-kilometer contour, and that the higher elevations would be significantly contaminated if the lower elevations were viable. They spoke of dismantling the industrial terraforming processes that were now under way, of returning to the very slowest biological methods called for in the radical ecopoesis model. Some advocated the growth of a thin CO_2 atmospshere, supporting plants but not animals, as being a situation more natural to Mars's volatile inventory and its past history. Other advocated leaving the surface as close to how they had found it as possible, and keeping a very small population in tented valleys. These people decried the rapid destruction of the surface by the industrial terraforming in outraged tones, condemning particularly the inundation of Vastitas Borealis, and the outright melting of the landscape by use of the soletta and the aerial lens.

But as the seven days passed, it became more and more obvious that this point of the draft declaration was the only one being really debated, while the others were for the most part being subjected to fine-tuning only. A lot of people were pleasantly surprised to find even this much assent to the draft statement, and more than once Nirgal said irritably, "Why be surprised? We didn't make those points up, we just wrote down what people were saying."

And people would nod at this, interested, and go back to the meetings, and work on the points again. And it began to seem to Nadia that agreement was popping up everywhere, called out of chaos by Art and Nirgal's assertion that it existed. Several of the sessions that week ended in a kind of kavajava high of political consensus, the various aspects of a state finally hammered into a shape to which many of the parties could agree.

But the argument over methods only got more vehement. Back and forth it would go, Nadia against Coyote, Kasei, the Reds, the Marsfirsters, and many of the Bogdanovists. "You can't get to what we want by murder!" "They won't give this planet up! Political power begins at the end of a gun!"

One night after one of these donnybrooks, a big gathering of them floated in the shallows of the Phaistos pond, trying to relax. Sax sat on an underwater bench and shook his head. "Classic problem of punishment—no—of *violence*," he said. "Radical, liberal. Who never managed to agree again. Before."

Art plunged his head in the water, and pulled it out spluttering. Weary, frustrated, he said, "What about integrated pest management? What about that mandatory retirement idea?"

"Forced disemployment," Nadia corrected.

"Decapitation," Maya said.

"Whatever!" Art said, splashing them. "Velvet revolution. Silk revolution."

"Aerogel," Sax said. "Light, strong. Invisible."

"It's worth a try!" Art said.

Ann shook her head. "It will never work."

"It's better than another sixty-one," Nadia said.

Sax said, "Better if we agree on a play. On a *plan*."

"But we can't," Maya said.

"The front is broad," Art insisted. "Let's go out there and do what we're comfortable with."

Sax and Nadia and Maya all shook their heads at once; seeing it, Ann unexpectedly laughed out loud. And then they were all sitting in the pond together, giggling at they knew not what.

The final general meeting took place in the late afternoon, in the Zakros park where it had all begun. It had a strangely confused air, Nadia felt, with most people only grudgingly satisfied with the Dorsia Brevia Declaration, now several times longer than Art and Nirgal's original draft. Each point was read aloud by Priska, and each was cheered in a consensual vote of approval; but different groups cheered more loudly for some points than for others, and when the reading was done, the general applause was brief and perfunctory. No one could be happy with that, and Art and Nirgal looked exhausted.

The applause ended, and for a moment everyone just sat there. No one knew what to do next; the lack of agreement on the matter of methods seem to extend right into that very moment. What next? What now? Did they just go home? Did they have a home? The moment stretched out, uncomfortable, even vaguely painful (how they needed John!), so that Nadia was relieved when someone shouted something—an exclamation that seemed to break a malign spell. She looked around as people pointed.

There on a staircase, high on the black tunnel wall, stood a green woman. She was unclothed, green-skinned, glowing in a shaft of afternoon sun that shot down from a skylight—gray-haired, barefoot, without jewelry—completely naked, except for a coat of green paint. And what was common at night in the pond was, in this vivid daylight, dangerous and provocative—a shock to the senses, a challenge to their notion of what a political congress was, or could be.

It was Hiroko. She began to step down the staircase, in a steady measured pace. Ariadne and Charlotte and several other Minoan women stood at the bottom of the stairs waiting for her, along with Hiroko's closest followers from the hidden colony—Iwao, Rya, Evgenia, Michel, all the rest of that little band. As Hiroko descended they started to sing. When she reached them, they draped her with strings of bright red flowers. A fertility rite, Nadia thought, reaching directly into some paleolithic part of their minds, and intermingling there with Hiroko's areophany.

When Hiroko left the foot of the stairs she had a little train of followers, singing the names of Mars, "Al-Qahira, Ares, Auqakuh, Bahram," and so on, a great mélange of archaic syllables, into which some of them were interjecting "Ka . . . ka . . . ka . . . "

She led them down the path, through trees, out again onto the grass, into the meeting in the park. She walked right through the middle of the crowd, with a solemn, distant expression on her green face. Many stood as she passed. Jackie Boone came out of the crowd and joined the group of followers, and her green grandmother took her by the hand. The two of them led the way through the crowd, the old matriarch tall, proud, thoroughly ancient, gnarled like a tree, and as green as a tree's leaves; Jackie taller still, young and graceful as a dancer, her black hair flowing halfway down her back. A rustle went through the crowd, a sigh; and as the two and the group following them walked down to the central path by the canal, people stood and followed, the Sufis among them dancing a braid around their circumference. *"Ana el-Haqq, ana Al-Qahira, ana el-Haqq, ana Al-Qahira . . . "* And so a thousand people walked down the canal path after the two women and their train, the Sufis singing, others chanting pieces of Hiroko's areophany, the rest content to follow.

Nadia walked along holding hands with Nirgal and Art, feeling happy.

They were animals, after all, no matter where they chose to live. She felt something like worship, an emotion very rare in her experience—worship for the divinity of life, which took such beautiful forms.

At the pond Jackie took off her rust jumper, and she and Hiroko stood in ankle-deep water, facing each other and holding their clasped hands as far overhead as they could reach. The other Minoan women joined this bridge. Old and young, green and pink. . . .

The hidden colonists passed under the bridge first, among them Maya herself, hand in hand with Michel. And then all kinds of people were filing under the mother bridge, in what felt like the millionth repetition of a million-year-old ritual, something everyone had coded in their genes and had practiced all their life. The Sufis danced under the clasped hands still wearing their white billowing clothes, and this gave a model to others, who stayed clothed but surged right out into the water, ducking under the naked women, Zeyk and Nazik leading the way, chanting, *"Ana Al-Qahira, ana el-Haqq, ana Al-Qahira, ana el-Haqq,"* looking like Hindus in the Ganges, or Baptists in the Jordan. So that in the end many shed their clothes, but all walked into the water. And they stared around at this instinctive and yet highly conscious rebirth, many drumming on the water surface, making rhythmic slapping splashes to accompany the singing and chanting. . . . Nadia saw again and again how beautiful humans were. Nakedness was dangerous to the social order, she thought, because it revealed too much reality. They stood before each other with all their imperfections and their sexual characteristics and their intimations of mortality—but most of all with their astonishing beauty, which in the ruddy light of the tunnel sunset could scarcely be believed, could scarcely be comprehended or answered. Skin at sunset had a lot of red in it—but not enough for some of the Reds, apparently, who were sponging one of their women down with a red dye they had located, to make a counter figure to Hiroko, apparently. Political bathing! Nadia groaned. Actually all the colors were coming off in the pond, turning the water brown.

Maya swam through the shallows and knocked Nadia deeper into the pond with an impetuous hug. "Hiroko is a genius," she said in Russian. "She may be a mad genius, but a genius she is."

"Mother goddess of the world," Nadia said, and switched to English as she plowed through the warm water to a little knot of the First Hundred and the Sabishii issei. There were Ann and Sax standing side by side, Ann tall and thin, Sax short and round, looking just as they had in the old days in the baths of Underhill, debating something or other, Sax talking with his face all screwed up in concentration. Nadia laughed at the sight, splashing them.

Fort swam to her side. "Should have run the whole conference like this," he observed. "Ooh, he's going to crash." And indeed a board rider coming down the curved wall slipped off his plummeting board, and slid ignominiously into the pond. "Look, I need to get back home to be able to help. Also a great-great-great-granddaughter is getting married in four months."

"Can you get back that fast?" Spencer asked.

"Yes, my ship is fast." A Praxis space division built rockets that used a modified Dyson propulsion to accelerate and then decelerate continuously through the flight, which took a very direct line between the planets.

"Executive style," Spencer said.

"They're open for use by anyone in Praxis, if they're in a hurry. You might want to visit Earth yourself, see what conditions are like firsthand."

No one took him up on that, though it raised some eyebrows. But there was no more talk of detaining him, either.

People drifted like jellyfish in a slow whirlpool, calmed at last by the warmth, by the water and wine and kava being passed around in bamboo cups, by the accomplishment of finishing what they had come to do. It was not perfect, people said—definitely not perfect—but it was something, especially the remarkable nature of point four, or three—quite a declaration, in fact—a beginning, a real beginning—seriously flawed—especially point six—definitely not perfect—but likely to be remembered. "Well, but this here is religion," someone sitting in the shallows was saying, "and I like all the pretty bodies, but mixing state and religion is a dangerous business . . . "

Nadia and Maya walked out into deeper water, arm in arm, talking with everyone they knew. A group of the youngsters from Zygote saw them, Rachel and Tiu and Frantz and Steve and the rest, and they cried, "Hey, the two witches!" and came over to squish them together with hugs and kisses. Kinetic reality, Nadia thought, somatic reality, haptic reality— the power of the touch, ah, my . . . her ghost finger was throbbing, which hadn't happened in ages.

They walked on, trailing the Zygote ectogenes, and came on Art, who was standing with Nirgal and a few other men, all drawn as by magnet to where Jackie still stood by the half-green Hiroko, her wet hair slicked over her bare shoulders, her head thrown back laughing, the sunset glaring off her and giving her a kind of hyperreal, heraldic power. Art was looking happy indeed, and when Nadia hugged him, he put an arm over her shoulder and left it there. Her good friend, a very solid somatic reality.

"It was well done," Maya told him. "It was like John Boone would have done it."

"It was not," Jackie said automatically.

"I knew him," Maya said, giving her a sharp look, "and you didn't. And I say it was like John would have done it."

They stood staring at each other, the ancient white-haired beauty and the young black-haired beauty—and it seemed to Nadia there was something primal in the sight, primal, primeval, primate . . . *these* are the two witches, she wanted to say to Jackie's sibs behind her. But then again they no doubt knew that. "No one is like John was," she said, trying to break the spell. She squeezed Art's waist. "But it was well done."

Kasei came splashing up; he had been standing by silently, and Nadia wondered at him a little, the man with the famous father, famous mother, famous daughter.... And slowly becoming a power himself, among the Reds and the radical Marsfirsters, out there on the edge in a splinter movement, as the congress had proved. No, it was hard to tell what Kasei thought of his life. He gave Jackie a glance that was too complex to read—pride, jealousy, some sort of rebuke—and said, "We could use John Boone now." His father—the first man on Mars—her cheery John, who used to love to swim the butterfly in Underhill, in afternoons that had felt like this ceremony, except that it had been their everyday reality, for a year or so there in the beginning. . . .

"And Arkady," Nadia said, still trying to defuse things. "And Frank."

"We can do without Frank Chalmers," Kasei said bitterly.

"Why do you say that?" Maya exclaimed. "We would be lucky to have him here now! He would know how to handle Fort, and Praxis, and the Swiss and you Reds and the greens, all of it. Frank, Arkady, John—we could use all three of them now." Her mouth was hard and downturned. She glared at Jackie and Kasei as if daring them to speak; then her lip curled, and she looked away.

Nadia said, "This is why we must avoid another sixty-one."

"We will," Art said, and gave her another squeeze.

Nadia shook her head sadly. The peak always passed so fast. "It's not our choice," she told him. "It's not something that is entirely in our hands. So we will see."

"It will be different this time," Kasei insisted.

"We will see."

PART 8

Social
Engineering

Where were you born?
Denver.
Where did you grow up?
Rock. Boulder.
What were you like as a child?
I don't know.
Give me your impressions.
I wanted to know why.
You were curious?
Very curious.
Did you play with science kits?
All of them.
And your friends?
I don't remember.
Try for anything.
I don't think I had many friends.
Were you ambidextrous as a child?
I don't remember.
Think about your science experiments. Did you use both hands when you did them?
I believe it was often necessary.
You wrote with your right hand?
I do now. I—I did then as well. Yes. As a child.

And did you do anything with your left hand? Brush your teeth, comb your hair, eat, point at things, throw balls?

I did all those things with my right hand. Would it matter if I hadn't?

Well, you see, in cases of aphasia, the strong right-handers all conform pretty well to a certain profile. Activities are located, or it is better to say coordinated, at certain places in the brain. When we determine precisely the problems the aphasic is experiencing, we can tell pretty well where the lesions in the brain are located. And vice versa. But with left-handers and ambidextrous people there is no such pattern. One might say that every left-handed and ambidextrous brain is organized differently.

You know most of Hiroko's ectogene children are left-handed.

Yes, I know. I've spoken with her about it, but she claims she doesn't know why. She says it may be a result of being born on Mars.

Do you find this plausible?

Well, handedness is still poorly understood in any case, and the effects of the lighter gravity . . . we'll be sorting those out for centuries, won't we.

I suppose so.

You don't like the idea of that, do you?

I would rather get answers.

What if all your questions were answered? Would you be happy then?

I find it hard to imagine such a—state. A fairly small percentage of my questions have answers.

But that's rather wonderful, don't you agree?

No. It wouldn't be scientific to agree.

You conceive of science as nothing more than answers to questions?

As a system for generating answers.

And what is the purpose of that?

. . . To know.

And what will you do with your knowledge?

. . . Find out more.

But why?

I don't know. It's the way I am.

Shouldn't some of your questions be directed that way—to finding out why you are the way you are?

I don't think you can get good answers to questions about—human nature. Better to think of it as a black box. You can't apply the scientific method. Not well enough to be sure of your answers.

In psychology we believe we have scientifically identified a certain pathology in which a person needs to know everything because he is afraid of not knowing. It's a pathology of monocausotaxophilia, as Pöppel called it, the love of single causes that explain everything. This can become fear of a lack of causes. Because the lack might be dangerous. The knowledge-seeking becomes primarily defensive, in that it is a way of denying fear when one really is afraid. At its worst it isn't even knowledge-seeking, because when the answers arrive they cease to be of interest, as they are no longer dangerous. So that reality itself doesn't matter to such a person.

Everyone tries to avoid danger. But motivations are always multiple. And different from action to action. Time to time. Any patterns are a matter of—observer's speculation.

Psychology is a science in which the observer becomes intimately involved with the subject of observation.

That's one of the reasons I don't think it's a science.

It is certainly a science. One of its tenets is, if you want to know more, care more. Every astronomer loves the stars. Otherwise why study them so?

Because they are mysteries.

What do you care about?

I care about truth.

The truth is not a very good lover.

It isn't love I'm looking for.

Are you sure?

No surer than anyone else who thinks about—motivations.

You agree we have motivations?

Yes. But science cannot explain them.

So they are part of your great unexplainable.

Yes.

And so you focus your attention on other things.

Yes.

But the motivations are still there.

Oh yes.

What did you read when you were young?

All kinds of things.

What were some of your favorite books?

Sherlock Holmes. Other detective stories. The Thinking Machine. Dr. Thorndyke.

Did your parents punish you if you got upset?

I don't think so. They didn't like me making a fuss. But I think they were just ordinary in that respect.

Did you ever see them get upset?

I don't remember.

Did you ever see them shout, or cry?

I never heard them shout. Sometimes my mom cried, I think.

Did you know why?

No.

Did you wonder why?

I don't remember. Would it matter if I had?

What do you mean?

I mean, if I had had one kind of past. I could still have turned into any kind of person. Depending on my reaction to the—events. And if I had had another kind of past. The same variations would have followed. So that your line of questioning is useless. In that it has no explanatory rigor. It's an imitation of the scientific method.

I consider your conception of science to be as parsimonious and reductive as your scientific activities. Essentially you are saying we should not study the human mind in a scientific manner because it is too complex to make the study easy. That's not very bold of you. The universe outside us is complex too, but you don't advise avoiding that. Why so with the universe inside?

You can't isolate factors, you can't repeat conditions, you can't set up experiments with controls, you can't make falsifiable hypotheses. The whole apparatus of science is unavailable to you.

Think about the first scientists for a while.

The Greeks?

Before that. Prehistory was not just a formless timeless round of the seasons, you know. We tend to think of those people as if they resembled our own unconscious minds, but they were not like that. For a hundred thousand years at least we have been as intellectual as we are now. Probably more like half a million years. And every age has its great scientists, and they all had to work in the context of their times, like we do. For the early ones, there were hardly explanations for anything—nature was as whole and complex and mysterious as our own minds are to us now, but what could they do? They had to begin somewhere, eh? This is what you must remember. And it took thousands of years to learn the plants, the animals, the use of fire, rocks, axes, bows and arrows, shelter, clothing. Then pottery, crops, metallurgy. All so slowly, with such effort. And all passed along by word of mouth, from one scientist to the next. And all the while there were no doubt people saying, it's too complex to be sure of anything. Why should we try at all? Galileo said, "The ancients had good reason to think the first scientists among the gods, seeing that common minds have so little curiosity. The small hints that began the great inventions were part of not a trivial but a superhuman spirit." Superhuman! Or merely the best parts of ourselves, the bold minds of each generation. The scientists. And over the millennia we have pieced together a model of the world, a paradigm that is quite precise and powerful, yes?

But haven't we tried just as hard all these years—with little success—to understand ourselves?

Say we have. Maybe it takes longer. But look, we have made quite a bit of progress there too. And not just recently. By observation alone the Greeks discovered the four temperaments, and only recently have we learned enough about the brain to say what the neurological basis of this phenomenon is.

You believe in the four temperaments?

Oh yes. They are confirmable by experiment, if you will. As are so many, many things about the human mind. Perhaps it is not physics, perhaps it will never be physics. It could be that we are simply more complex and unpredictable than the universe.

That hardly seems likely. We are made of atoms after all.

But animated! Driven by the green force, alive with spirit, the great unexplainable!

Chemical reactions . . .

But why life? It's more than reactions. There is a drive toward complexification that is directly opposed to the physical law of entropy. Why should that be?

I don't know.

Why do you dislike it so when you can't say why?

I don't know.

This mystery of life is a holy thing. It is our freedom. We have shot out of physical reality, we exist now in a kind of godlike freedom, and the mystery is integral to it.

No. We are still physical reality. Atoms in their rounds. Determined on most scales, random on some others.

Ah well. We disagree. But either way, the scientist's job is to explore everything. No matter the difficulties! To stay open, to accept ambiguity. To attempt to fuse with the object of knowledge. To admit that there are values shot through the whole enterprise. To love it. To work toward discovering the values by which we should live. To work to enact those values in the world. To explore—and more than that—to create!

I'll have to think about that.

Observation is never enough. Besides it wasn't their experiment anyway. Desmond came to Dorsa Brevia, and Sax went to find him. "Is Peter still flying?"

"Why yes. He spends a fair amount of time in space, if that's what you mean."

"Yes. Can you get me in touch with him?"

"Sure I can." Quizzical expression on Desmond's cracked face. "Your speech is getting better and better, Sax. What have they been doing to you?"

"Gerontological treatments. Also growth hormone, L-dopa, serotonin, other chemicals. Stuff out of starfish."

"Grew you a new brain, did they?"

"Yes. Parts anyway. Synergic synaptic stimulus. Also a lot of talking with Michel."

"Uh-oh!"

"It's still me."

Desmond's laugh was an animal noise. "I can see that. Listen, I'll be off again in a couple days, and I'll take you to Peter's airport."

"Thanks."

Grew a new brain. Not an accurate way of putting it. The lesion had been sustained in the posterior third of the inferior frontal convolution. Tissues dead as a result of interruption of focused ultrasound memory-speech stimulation during interrogation. A stroke. Broca's aphasia. Difficulty with motor apparatus of speech, little melody, difficulty in initiating utterances, reduction to telegramese, mostly nouns and simplest forms of verbs. A battery of tests determined that most other cognitive functions were unimpaired. He wasn't so sure; he had understood people speaking to him, his thinking had been much the same as far as he could tell, and he had had no trouble with the spatial and other nonlinguistic tests. But when he tried to talk, sudden betrayal—in the mouth and in the mind. Things lost their names.

Strangely enough, without names they were still things. He could see them and think about them in terms of shapes, or numbers. Formula of description. Various combinations of conic sections and the six surfaces of revolution symmetrical around an axis, the plane, the sphere, the cylinder, the catenoid, the unduloid, and the nodoid; shapes without the names, but the shapes alone were like names. Spatializing language.

But it turned out that remembering without words was hard. A method had to be borrowed, the palace-of-memory method, spatial to begin with. A space in the mind was established to resemble the inside of the Echus Overlook labs, which he recalled well enough to walk around in in his mind, names or no. And in each place an object. Or another place. On one counter, all the Acheron labs. On top of the refrigerator, Boulder, Colorado. And so he remembered all the shapes he thought by their location in the mental lab.

And then sometimes the name would come. But when he knew the name and tried to say it, it was very possible that the wrong one would come out of his mouth. He had always had a tendency this way. After sessions of his best thinking, when everything had been quite clear to him, it had sometimes been difficult to translate his thoughts onto the plane of language, which did not match well the kind of thinking he had been doing. So that talking had been work. But nothing like this, this halting, erratic, treacherous groping, which usually either failed or betrayed. Frustrating in the extreme. Painful. Although preferable to Wernicke's aphasia, certainly, in which one babbled volubly, unaware that one was making no sense at all. Just as he had had a premorbid tendency to lose the words for things, there were people who tended towards Wernicke's without the excuse of brain damage. As Art had noted. Sax preferred his own problem.

Ursula and Vlad had come to him. "Aphasia is different for every person," Ursula said. "There are patterns, and clusters of symptoms that usually go with certain lesion patterns in right-handed adults. But in extraordinary minds there are a lot of exceptions. Already we see that your cognitive functions have remained very high for someone with your degree of language difficulties. Probably a lot of your thought in math and physics did not take place using language."

"That's right."

"And if it was geometrical thinking rather than analytical, it probably took place in the right hemisphere of the brain rather than the left. And your right hemisphere was spared."

Sax nodded, not trusting himself to speak.

"So, prospects for recovery vary widely. There is almost always improvement. Children in particular are very adaptable. When they have head injuries even a circumscribed lesion may cause serious problems, but there is almost always recovery. A whole hemisphere of the brain can be removed from a child if a problem makes it necessary, and all the functions be relearned by the remaining half. This is because of the incredible growth in the child's brain. For adults it is different. Specialization has occurred, so that circumscribed lesions cause a specific limited damage. But once a skill has been destroyed in a mature brain, you don't often see significant improvement."

"The treat. The treatment."

"Exactly. But you see, the brain is precisely one of the places where the gerontological treatment has the most trouble penetrating. We've been working on that, however. We've designed a stimulus package to be used in concert with the treatment, when faced with cases of brain damage. It may become a regular part of the treatment, if the trials continue to have good results. We haven't done this in too many human trials yet, you see. The injection increases brain plasticity by stimulating axon and dendritic spine growth, and the sensitivity of Hebb synapses. The corpus callosum is particularly affected, and the hemisphere opposite to the lesioned side. Learning can build whole new neural networks there."

"Do it," Sax said.

Destruction is creation. Become as a little child. Language as space, a kind of mathematical notation, geometric locations in the lab of memory. Reading. Maps. Codes, substitutions, the secret names of things. The glorious inrush of a word. The joy of chatter. Every color's wavelength, by number. That sand is orange, tan, blond, yellow, sienna, umber, burnt umber, ochre. That sky is cerulean, cobalt, lavender, mauve, violet, Prussian, indigo, egglant, midnight. Just to look at color charts with words, the rich intensity of colors, the sounds of the words—he wanted more. A name for every wavelength of the visible spectrum, why not? Why be so stingy? The .59-micron wavelength is so much more blue than .6, and .61 is so much more red. . . . They needed more words for purples, the way Eskimos needed more words for snow. People always used that example, and Eskimos did have about twenty words for snow; but scientists had over three hundred words for snow, and who ever gave scientists credit for paying attention to their world? No two snowflakes alike. Thisness. Buh, buh. Bean, bear, bun, burr, bent, bomb. Buh. That place where my arm bends is my elbow! Mars looks like a pumpkin! The air is cold. And poisoned by carbon dioxide.

There were parts of his inner speech which were composed entirely of old clichés, coming no doubt from what Michel called "overlearned" activities in his past, which had so permeated his mind that they had survived the damage. Clean design, good data, parts per billion, bad results. Then cutting through these comfortable formulations, as if from a separate language entirely, were the new perceptions, and the new phrases groping to express them. Synaptic synergies. Actual speech from either realm was still welcome. The exhilaration of normality. How he had taken it for granted. Michel came by to talk every day, helping him to build this new brain. Michel harbored some very alarming beliefs for a man of science. The four elements, the four temperaments, alchemical formulations of all kinds, philosophical positions parading as science. . . . "Didn't you once ask me if I could change lead to gold?"

"I don't think so."

"Why do you spend so much time talking to me, Michel?"

"I like talking to you, Sax. You say something new every day."

"I like this throwing things with my left hand."

"I can see that. It's possible you may end up a left-hander. Or ambidextrous, because your left brain is so powerful, I can't imagine it will lag much, no matter the lesion."

"Mars looks like an iron-cored ball of old planetesimals."

Desmond flew him to the Red sanctuary in Wallace Crater, where Peter often stayed. And Peter was there, Peter son of Mars, tall fast and strong, graceful, friendly although impersonal, distant, absorbed in his own work and his own life. Simonlike. Sax told him what he wanted to do, and why. He still stumbled in his speech occasionally. But it was so much better than it had been before that he hardly minded when he did. Forge on! Like talking in a foreign language. All languages were foreign languages to him now. Except his idiolect of shapes. But it was no aggravation—on the contrary, such a relief to do even so well. To have the fog clearing away from the names, have the mind-mouth connections restored. Even if in a new and chancy way. A chance to learn. Sometimes he liked the new way. One's reality might indeed depend on one's scientific paradigm, but it mostly definitely depended on one's brain structure. Change that and your paradigms might as well follow. You can't fight progress. Nor progressive differentiation. "Do you understand?"

"Oh, I understand," Peter said, grinning widely. "I think it's a very good idea. Very important. It will take me a few days to get the plane ready."

Ann arrived at the shelter, looking tired and old. She greeted Sax curtly, her old antipathy as strong as ever. Sax did not know what to say to her. Was this a new problem?

He decided to wait until Peter had talked to her, and see if that made any difference. He waited. Nowadays if he didn't talk no one bothered him. Advantages everywhere.

She came back from a talk with Peter, to eat a meal with the other Reds in their little commons, and yes she stared at him curiously. Looking over the heads of the others at him as if inspecting a new cliff on the Martian landscape. Intent and objective. Evaluative. A status change in a dynamic system is a data point that speaks to a theory. Supporting or troubling. What are you? Why are you doing this?

He met her stare calmly, tried to field it, to turn it around. Yes I am still Sax. I have changed. Who are you? Why haven't you changed? Why do you still look at me like that? I have experienced an injury. The premorbid individual is not there anymore, not quite. I have been given an experimental treatment, I feel fine, I am not the man you knew. And why haven't you changed?

If enough data points trouble the theory, the theory may be wrong. If the theory is basic, the paradigm may have to change.

She sat down to eat. It was doubtful she had read his mind in that much detail. But a great pleasure nevertheless, to be able to meet her eye!

He got in the little cockpit with Peter and just after the timeslip they bounced down the bedrock runway, accelerating hard and tilting up at the black sky, the big streamlined space plane vibrating under them. Sax lay back, crushed into his seat, and waited for the plane to curve over that asymptotic hill at the top of its course, slowing as it rose less steeply, until it was in a gentle rise through the high stratosphere, making the transition from plane to rocket as the atmosphere thinned to its last attenuated level, a hundred kilometers high, where the gases of the Russell cocktail were annihilated daily by incoming UV rays. The plane's skin was glowing with heat. Through the filtered glass of the cockpit it was the color of the sun at sunset. No doubt it was affecting their night vision. Below the planet was all dark, except for very faint patches of starlit glaciers in Hellas Basin. They were rising still. A widening gyre. Stars packed the blackness of what looked like an enormous black hemisphere, standing on an enormous black plane. Night sky, night Mars. They rose and rose again. The incandescent rocket was translucent yellow, hallucinatorily bright and sleek. The latest thing from Vishniac, designed in part by Spencer, and made of an intermetallic compound, chiefly gamma titanium aluminum, rendered superplastic for the manufacture of heat-resistant engine parts as well as the exterior skin, which dimmed a bit as they rose higher and it cooled.

He could imagine the beautiful latticework of the gamma titanium aluminum, patterned in a tapestry of nodoids and catenoids like hooks and eyes, vibrating madly with the heat. They were building such things these days. Ground-to-space planes. Walk out into your backyard and fly to Mars in an aluminum can.

Sax described what he wanted to do next after this. Peter laughed. "Do you think Vishniac can do it?"

"Oh yeah."

"There are some design problems."

"I know, I know. But they'll solve them. I mean you don't have to be a rocket scientist to be a rocket scientist."

"That's very true."

Peter sang to pass the hours. Sax joined in when he knew the words— as in "Sixteen Tons," a satisfying song. Peter told the story of how he had escaped from the falling elevator. What it had been like to float in an EVA suit, alone for two days. "Somehow it gave me a taste for it, that's all. I know that sounds strange."

"I understand." The shapes out here were so big and pure. The color of things.

"What was it like to learn to talk again?"

"I have to concentrate to do it. I have to think hard. Things surprise me all the time. Things I used to know and forgot. Things I never knew. Things I learned just before the injury. That period is usually occluded forever. But it was so important. When I was working around the glacier. I have to talk to your mom about that. It isn't like she thinks. You know, the land. The new plants out there. The yellow butterfly sun. It doesn't have to be . . . "

"You should talk to her."

"She doesn't like me."

"Talk to her when we get back."

The altimeter indicated 250 kilometers above the surface. The plane plowed up toward Cassiopeia. Every star had a distinct color, different from any other. Or there were at least fifty of them. Below them, on the eastern edge of the black disk, the terminator appeared, zebra-banded sandy ochre and shadowy black. The thin crescent of sunlit Mars gave him the sudden clear perception of the disk as a great spheroid. A ball spinning through the galaxy of stars. The great huge continent-mountain of Elysium bulked over the horizon, its shape perfectly delineated by the horizontal shadows. They were looking down the length of its long saddleback, Hecates Tholus almost hidden behind the cone of Elysium Mons, Albor Tholus off to the side.

"There it is," Peter said, and pointed up through the clear cockpit. Above them, to the east, the eastern edge of the aerial lens was silver in the morning light, the rest of it still in the planet's shadow.

"Are we close enough yet?" Sax asked.

"Almost."

Sax looked down again at the thickening crescent of the morning. There on the dark rough highlands of Hesperia, a cloud of smoke was billowing up from the dark surface just beyond the terminator, into the morning light. Even at their height they were in that cloud still, in the part that was no longer visible. The lens itself was surfing on that invisible thermal, using its lift and the pressure of sunlight to hold its position over the burn zone.

Now the entire lens was in the sunlight, looking like an enormous silver parachute with nothing underneath it. Its silver was also violet, sky-colored. The cup was a section of a sphere, a thousand kilometers across, its center some fifty kilometers above its rim. Spinning like a Frisbee. There was a hole at the peak, where the sunlight poured straight through. Everywhere else the circular mirror strips that made up the cup were reflecting the light from the sun and the soletta, inward and down onto a moving point on the surface below, bringing to bear so much light that it was igniting basalt. The lens mirrors heated up to almost 900°K, and the liquefied rock down there was reaching 5,000°K. Degassing volatiles.

Into Sax's mind, as he considered the great object flying over them, came the image of a magnifying glass, held over dry weeds and an aspen branch. Smoke, flame, fire. The concentrated rays of the sun. Photon assault. "Aren't we close enough yet? It looks like it's right over us."

"No, we're well out from under the edge. It wouldn't do to get under that thing, although I suppose the focus wouldn't be right to fry us. Anyway it's moving over the burn zone at almost a thousand kilometers an hour."

"Like jets when I was young."

"Uh." Green lights blinked on one of his consoles. "Okay, here we go."

He pulled back on the stick and the plane stood on its tail, rising straight at the lens, which was still another hundred kilometers higher than they were, and well to the west of them. Peter pushed a button on the console. The whole plane jerked as a bank of fletched missiles appeared from under the plane's stubby wings, lofting with them and then igniting like magnesium flares and shooting up and away, toward the lens. Pinpricks of yellow fire against that huge silvery UFO, eventually disappearing from sight. Sax waited, lips pursed, and tried to stop his blinking.

The front edge of the lens began to unravel. It was a flimsy thing, nothing but a great spinning cup of solar sail bands, and it came apart with startling rapidity, its front edge rolling under it until it was tumbling forward and down, trailing long looping streamers which looked like the tangled tails of several broken kites, all falling together. A billion and a half kilograms of solar sail material, in fact, all unraveling as it fluttered down in its long trajectory, looking slow because it was so big, though probably the great mass of material was still moving at well above terminal velocity. A good portion of it would burn up before it hit the surface. Silica rain.

Peter turned and followed it in its descent, keeping well to the east of it. And so they could still see it below them, there in the violet morning sky, as the main mass of it heated to an incandescent glare and caught fire, like a great yellow comet with a hairy tangled silver tail, dropping down to the tawny planet. All fall down.

"Good shot," Sax said.

Back in Wallace Crater they were welcomed as heroes. Peter deflected all congratulations: "It was Sax's idea, the flight itself was no big deal, just another reconnaissance except for the firing, I don't know why we didn't think of it before."

"They'll just drop another one into position," Ann said from the edge of the crowd, staring at Sax with a very curious expression.

"But they're so vulnerable," Peter said.

"Surface-to-space missiles," Sax said, feeling nervous. "Can you invent—can you *inventory* all orbiting objects?"

"We already have," Peter said. "Some of them we don't have ID'd, but most are obvious."

"I'd like to see the list."

"I'd like to talk to you," Ann told him darkly.

And the rest quickly left the room, wagging their eyebrows at each other like a bunch of Art Randolphs.

Sax sat down in a bamboo chair. It was a little room, without a window. It could have been one of the barrel vaults in Underhill, back in the beginning. The shape was right. The textures. Brick was such a stable staple. Ann pulled a chair over and sat across from him, leaning forward to stare in his face. She looked older. The vaunted Red leader, vaunted, gaunted, haunted. He smiled. "Are you about due for a gerontological treatment?" his mouth said, surprising them both.

Ann brushed the question off as an impertinence. "Why did you want to bring down the lens?" she said, her gaze boring into him.

"I didn't like it."

"I know *that*," she said. "But why?"

"It wasn't necessary. Things are warming up fast enough. There's no reason to go faster. We don't even need much more heat. And it was releasing very large amounts of carbon dioxide. That will be hard to scrub. And it was very nicely stuck—it's hard to get CO_2 out of carbonates. As long as one doesn't melt the rock, it stays." He shook his head. "It was stupid. They were just doing it because they could. Canals. I don't believe in canals."

"So it just wasn't the right kind of terraforming for you."

"That's right." He met her stare calmly. "I believe in the terraforming outlined in Dorsa Brevia. You signed off too. As I recall."

She shook her head.

"No? But the Reds signed?"

She nodded.

"Well . . . it makes sense to me. I said this to you before. Human-viable to a certain elevation. Above that, air too thin and cold. Go slow. Ecopoesis. I don't like any of the big new heavy-industry methods. Maybe some nitrogen from Titan. But not any of the rest."

"What about the oceans?"

"I don't know. See what happens without pumping?"

"What about the soletta?"

"I don't know. The extra insolation means less warming needed from industrial gassing. Or other methods. But—we could have done without it. I thought the dawn mirrors were enough."

"But it's not in your hands anymore."

"No."

They sat in silence for a while. Ann appeared to be thinking. Sax watched her weathered face, wondering when she had last had the treatment. Ursula recommended repeating it every forty years, at a minimum.

"I was wrong," his mouth said. As she stared at him, he tried to follow the thought. It was a matter of shapes, geometries, mathematical elegance. Cascading recombinant chaos. Beauty is the creation of a strange attractor. "We should have waited before we started. A few decades of study of the primal state. It would have told us how to proceed. I didn't think things would change so fast. My original idea was something more like ecopoesis."

She pursed her lips. "But now it's too late."

"Yes. I'm sorry." He turned a palm up, inspected it. All the lines there were the same as always. "You ought to get the treatment."

"I'm not taking the treatment anymore."

"Oh Ann. Don't say that. Does Peter know? We need you. I mean—we need you."

She got up and left the room.

His next project was more complex. Although Peter was confident, the Vishniac people were dubious. Sax explained as best he could. Peter helped. Their objections turned to practicalities. Too large? Enlist more Bogdanovists. Impossible to stealth? Interrupt the surveillance network. Science is creation, he told them. This isn't science, Peter replied. It's engineering. Mikhail agreed, but liked that part of it. Ecotage, a branch of ecological engineering. But very difficult to arrange. Enlist the Swiss, Sax told them. Or at least let them know. They don't like surveillance anyway. Tell Praxis.

Things began to shape up. But it was a long time before he and Peter took off in a space plane again. This time they rocketed out of the stratosphere entirely, and then far above it. Twenty thousand kilometers above it, until they were closing on Deimos. And then making a rendezvous with it.

The gravity of the little moon was so slight that it was more a docking than a touchdown. Jackie Boone, who had helped on the project, mostly to be close to Peter (the shape was clear), guided the plane in. As they approached, Sax had an excellent view through the cockpit window. Deimos's black surface looked to be covered by a thick coat of dusty regolith—all the craters were nearly buried in it, their rims soft round dimples in the blanket of dust. The little oblong moon was not regular, but was rather composed of several rounded facets. A triaxial ellipsoid, almost. An old robot lander sat near the middle of Voltaire Crater, its landing pads buried, its coppery articulated struts and boxes dimmed by a fine dark dust.

They had chosen their own landing site on one of the ridges between facets, where lighter bare rock protruded from the blanket of dust. The ridges were old spallation scars, marking where early impacts had knapped pieces of the moonlet away. Jackie brought them down gently toward a ridge to the west of Swift and Voltaire craters. Deimos was tidally fixed, as Phobos had been, which was convenient for their project. The sub-Mars point served as 0° for both longitude and latitude, a most sensible plan. Their touchdown ridge was near the equator, at 90° longitude. About a ten-kilometer walk from the sub-Mars point.

As they approached the ridge, the rim of Voltaire disappeared under the black curved horizon. Dust blew away from the ridge as the plane's rockets shot exhaust over it. There was only a few centimeters of dust covering the bedrock. Carbonaceous chondrite, five billion years old. They docked with a hard thump, bounced away, slowly drifted down again. He could feel the pull toward the floor of the plane, but it was very slight. Probably he didn't weigh more than a couple of kilograms, if that.

Other rockets began to land on the ridge to either side of them, kicking clouds of dust into the vacuum, where they drifted slowly down. All the planes bounced on impact, then came down gently through their dust-clouds. Within half an hour there were eight planes lined up on the ridge, running along it to the tight horizons in both directions. Together they made a weird sight, the intermetallic compounds of their rounded surfaces gleaming like chitin under the surgical glare of unfiltered sunlight, the clarity of the vacuum making all their edges overfocused. Dreamlike.

Each plane carried a component of the system. Robot drillers and tunnelers and stamps. Water-collection galleries, there to melt the veins of ice in Deimos. A processing plant to separate out heavy water, about one part in 6,000 of the ordinary water. Another plant to process deuterium from the heavy water. A small tokamak, to be powered by a deuterium-deuterium fusion reaction. Lastly guidance jets, though most of these were in planes that had landed on the other sides of the moon.

The Bogdanovist technicians who had come up with the equipment were doing most of the installation. Sax got suited up in one of the bulky pressure suits on board, and went out the lock and onto the surface, thinking to look and see if the plane carrying the guidance jet for the Swift-Voltaire region had landed.

The big heated boots were weighted, and he was glad of it; escape velocity was no more than twenty-five kilometers an hour, meaning that with a running start one could jump right off the moon. It was quite difficult to keep his balance. Millions of tiny motions carried one along. Every step kicked up a healthy cloud of black dust, which slowly fell to the ground. There were rocks scattered on top of the dust, usually in little pockets they had made on landing. Ejecta which had no doubt circled the moonlet many times after ejection, before dropping in again. He picked up one rock like a black baseball. Throw it at the right speed, turn around, wait for it to go around the world, catch it chest high. Out at first. A new sport.

The horizon was only a few hundred meters away, and it changed markedly with every step—crater rims, spallation ridges, and boulders popping up over the dusty edge as he trudged toward it. People back on the ridge, between the planes, already stood at a different upright than he did, and were tilted away from him. Like the Little Prince. The clarity was starting. His footprints made a deep trail through the dust. The dustclouds hanging over the footprints got lower the farther back they were, until they settled, four or five steps back.

Peter came out of the lock and walked in his direction, and Jackie followed. Peter was the only man Sax had ever seen Jackie really attracted to, in that intense helpless manner of the orbiting object, the lovelorn, yearning for orbital decay. Peter was also the only man Sax had ever seen who did not respond to Jackie's amorous attentions in any way. The perversity of the heart. As in his attraction to Phyllis, a woman he had not liked. Or as in his desire for the approval of Ann, a woman who had not liked him. A woman with crazy views. But perhaps there was a rationality to it. If someone moons over you, you have to wonder at their judgment. Something like that.

Now Jackie trailed Peter like a dog, and though their faceplates were a copper color, Sax could tell just by her movements that she was talking to him, cajoling him somehow. Sax turned to the common band and came in on their conversation.

"—why they're named Swift and Voltaire," Jackie said.

"Both of them predicted the existence of the Martian moons," Peter said, "in books they wrote a century before the moons were seen. In *Gulliver's Travels* Swift even gives their distances from the planet and their orbit times, and he wasn't that far off."

"You're kidding!"

"No."

"How in the world did he do that?"

"I don't know. Blind luck, I guess."

Sax cleared his throat. "Sequence."

"What?" they said.

"Venus had no moon, Earth one, Jupiter four. Mars should have had two. Since they couldn't see them, they were probably small. And close. Therefore fast."

Peter laughed. "Swift must have been a smart man."

"Or his source. But it was still blind luck. The sequence being a coincidence."

They stopped on another spallation ridge, from which they could see the rim of Swift Crater, as a nearly buried ridge on the next horizon. A small gray rocket plane stood on the black dust like a miracle. Above them Mars filled most of the sky, a vast orange world. Night was falling across the eastern crescent. Isidis was directly above them, and though he could not make out Burroughs, the plains to the north of it were patched with great white splotches. Glaciers meeting up to become ice lakes, and the beginnings of an ice sea. Oceanus Borealis. A corrugated layer of clouds lay pasted right against the land, reminding him suddenly of what Earth had looked like from the *Ares*. That was a cold front, coming down Syrtis Major. The pattern of white clouds was just what it would have been on Terra. Cyclical waves of condensation particles.

He left the ridge, walked back toward the planes. The tall stiff boots were the only things that kept him upright, and his ankles hurt. Like walking on the sea bottom, only with no resistances. Universe ocean. He reached down and dug in the dust; no bedrock for ten centimeters, then twenty; it could have been five or ten meters deep, or even more. The dustclouds he had kicked up dropped back to the surface in about fifteen seconds. The dust was so fine that in any kind of atmosphere they might have stayed in suspension indefinitely. But in the vacuum they fell like anything else. Ejecta. There simply wasn't much to pull them back. One might be able to kick dust into space. He crossed a low ridge and abruptly could see over the sloping plain of the next facet. It was so obvious that the moonlet was shaped like some paleolithic hand tool, with facets knapped off by ancient strikes. Triaxial ellipsoid. Curious that it had such a circular orbit, one of the most circular in all the solar system. Not what you would expect of a captured asteroid, nor of ejecta flung up from Mars in one of the big impacts. Leaving what? Very old capture. With other bodies in other orbits, to regularize it. Knapp, knapp. Spall. Spallation. Language was so beautiful. Rocks striking rocks, in the ocean of space. Knocking bits off and flying away. Until they all either fell into the planet or skittered off. All but two. Two out of billions. Moon bomb. Gun stand. Rotating just faster than Mars above, so that any point on the Martian surface had it in the sky for sixty hours at a time. Convenient. The known was more dangerous than the unknown. No matter what Michel said. Clomp, clomp, on the virgin rock, of a virgin moon, with a virgin mind. The Little Prince. The planes rising over the horizon looked absurd, like insects from a dream, chitinous, articulated, colorful, tiny in the starry black, on the dust-blanketed rock. He climbed back into the lock.

It was months later, and he was alone in Echus Chasma, when the robots on Deimos finished their construction, and the starter deuterium ignited the drive engine. One thousand tons of crushed rock were thrown out by the engine every second, at a speed of 200 kilometers per second. All flying out tangent to the orbit and in the orbit plane. In four months, when about a half percent of the moon's mass had been ejected, the engine would cut off. Deimos would then be 614,287 kilometers away from Mars, according to Sax's calculations, and on its way completely out of Mars's influence, to become a free asteroid again.

Now it flew in his night sky, an irregular gray potato, less luminous than Venus or Terra, except that there was a new comet blazing out of its side. Quite a sight. News all over both worlds. Scandalous! Controversial even in the resistance, where people argued pro and con. All that squabbling. Hiroko was going to get tired of it and light out for the territory, he could feel the shape of it. Yes, no, what, where. Who did it? Why?

Ann came on the wrist to ask the same questions, looking furious.

"It was a perfect weapons platform," Sax said. "If they made it into a military base, like they did Phobos. We would have been helpless under it."

"So you did this on the off chance it might get turned into a military base?"

"If Arkady and his crew hadn't fixed Phobos on the off chance, we couldn't have dealt with it. We would have been killed. Anyway, the Swiss heard it was going to happen."

Ann was shaking her head, staring at him as if he were mad. A crazed saboteur. Rather a case of the pot calling the kettle black, in his opinion. Resolutely he met the look. When she cut the connection he shrugged and called the Bogdanovists. "The Reds have a catalog of—all the objects in orbit around Mars. Then we need surface-to-space delivery systems. Spencer will help. Equatorial silos. Inactive moholes. Do you understand?"

They said they did. You didn't have to be a rocket scientist. And so if it ever came to it again, they would not be pounded from space.

Sometime later, he could not be sure how long, Peter appeared on the little screen of the boulder car Sax had borrowed from Desmond. "Sax, I'm in contact with some friends who work on the elevator, and with Deimos accelerating, the cable oscillations to dodge it have been thrown off in their timing. It looks like the next pass in its orbit might collide with the elevator, but my friends can't get the cable's navigation AI to respond to them. Apparently it's really hardened to outside input, to prevent sabotage you know, and the idea of Deimos changing speed is something they can't get it to accept. Do you have any suggestions?"

"Let it see for itself."

"What?"

"Feed the data on Deimos into it. It must get that anyway. And it's programmed to avoid it. Direct its attention to the data. Explain what happened. Trust it."

"Trust it?"

"Well, talk to it."

"We're trying, Sax. But the antisabotage programming is real strong."

"It's running the oscillations to avoid Deimos. As long as that's in its list of goals, you should be okay. Just give it the data."

"Okay. We'll try."

It was night, and Sax went outside. Wandering in the darkness, under the immense cliff of the Great Escarpment, in the region just north of where Kasei Vallis broke through the wall. *Sei* meant star in Japanese, *ka* fire. Fire star. It was the same in Chinese, in which *huo* was the syllable the Japanese pronounced as *ka*, and *hsing*, *sei*. A Chinese word to start with, *Huo Hsing*: fire star, burning in the sky. They said Ka was what the little red men called it. We live on fire. Sax was distributing seeds in the ground, the hard little nuts pushed just under the surface of the sand flooring the chasm. Johnny Fireseed. There in the southern sky Deimos burned, slowly losing way through the stars, rolling westward at its own slow pace. Now pushed by the pinpoint comet burst on its eastern edge. The elevator rising over Tharsis was invisible, the new Clarke perhaps one of the dimmer stars in the southwest sky, it was impossible to say. He kicked a rock by accident, bent down and planted another seed. After the seeds were all out, there were starter packets of a new lichen to distribute. A chasmoendolithic strain, very hardy, very fast to propagate, very quick to pump out oxygen. Very high surface-to-volume ratio. Very dry.

A bip on the wrist. He switched the voice into his helmet intercom as he continued to take the little nuts out of his thigh pocket and shove them into the sand, careful to avoid damaging the roots of any of the sedges or other ground cover that dotted the ground like furry black rocks.

It was Peter, sounding excited. "Sax, Deimos is coming up on them now, and the AI seems to have acknowledged that it's not in its usual spot in its orbit. It's been mulling it over, they say. The attitude jets all through their sector have started a bit early, so we're hopeful that the system is responding."

"Can't you calculate the oscillation?"

"Yes, but the AI is proving recalcitrant. It's a stubborn bastard, the security programs are pretty watertight. We can just figure out enough from independent calculations to see that it's going to be a pretty close pass."

Sax straightened up and tapped out calculations of his own on his wristpad. Orbital period of Deimos had started at approximately 109,077 seconds. The drive engine had been on for some, he wasn't sure, say a million seconds, speeding the moonlet by a significant amount already, but also expanding the radius of its orbit. . . . He tapped away in the great silence. Usually when Deimos passed by the elevator cable, the cable was at the full extension of its oscillation in that sector, some fifty kilometers or more away, far enough away that the gravitational perturbation was so small it did not have to be factored into the adjustments of the cable jets. This time the acceleration and movement outward of Deimos would throw the timing off; the cable would be moving back in toward Deimos's orbital plane too soon. So it was a matter of slowing the Clarke oscillation, and adjusting for that all up and down the cable. Complicated stuff, and no wonder the AI was not able to display what it was doing in much detail. It was likely to be busy linking up to other AIs to gain the calculating capacity necessary to perform the operation. The shapes of the situation—Mars, the cable, Clarke, Deimos—were beautiful to contemplate.

"Okay, here it comes at them," Peter said.

"Are your friends at the elevation of the orbit?" Sax asked, surprised.

"They're a couple hundred kilometers below it, but their elevator car is on its way up. They've linked me up to their cameras, and hey, here it comes . . . Yes! Oh! Ka wow, Sax, it must have missed the cable by about three kilometers! It just flashed right by their camera!"

"A miss is as good as a mile."

"What's that?"

"At least in a vacuum it is." But now it was more than just a passing rock. "What about the tail of ejecta from the drive engine?"

"I'll ask. . . . They ended up crossing in front of Deimos, they say."

"Good." Sax clicked off. Good foresight on the AI's part. A few more passes and Deimos would be above Clarke, and the cable would no longer have to dodge it. Meanwhile, as long as the navigational AI believed in the danger, as obviously it did now, they would be okay.

Sax was of two minds about this. Desmond had said he would be happy to see the cable come down again. But there were few who seemed to agree with him. Sax had decided against taking unilateral action on the matter, since he was not sure what he felt about that tie to Earth. Best to limit unilateral action to things he was sure about. And so he bent over and planted another seed.

PART 9

The Spur of the Moment

Inhabiting new country is always a challenge. As soon as the tenting of Nirgal Vallis was done, Séparation de L'Atmosphère set up some of their largest mesocosm aerators, and soon the tent was filled with 500 millibars of a nitrogen-oxygen-argon mix that had been pulled and filtered out of the ambient air, now at 240 millibars. And the settlers started moving in, from Cairo and Senzeni Na, and everywhere else on the two worlds.

First people lived in mobile trailers, next to small portable greenhouses, and while they worked on the soils of the canyon with bacteria and plows, they used the greenhouses to grow their starter crops, and the trees and bamboo they would use to build their houses, and the desert plants they would spread outside the farms. The smectite clays on the canyon floor were a very good base for a soil, though they had to add biota, nitrogen, potassium—there was plenty of phosphorus, and more salts than they wanted, as usual.

So they spent their days augmenting the soil, and growing greenhouse crops, and planting hardy salt-desert plants. They traded all up and down the valley, and little market hamlets sprang up almost the day people moved in, as well as trails between homesteads, and a trunk road running down the middle of the valley, next to the stream. Nirgal Vallis had no aquifer at its head, and so a pipeline from Marineris pumped enough water to the head to start a small stream running. Its waters were collected at the Uzboi Gate and piped back up to the top of the tent again.

The homesteads were about half a hectare each, and almost everyone was trying to grow the bulk of their food on that space. Most divided their land up into six miniature fields, rotating crops and pasturage each season. Everyone had

*their own theories of cropping and soil augmentation. Most people grew a small
cash crop, nuts or fruits or lumber trees. Many kept chickens, some kept sheep,
goats, pigs, cows. The cows were almost all miniatures, no bigger than pigs.*

They tried to keep the farms down on the canyon floor by the stream, leaving
the higher rougher ground under the canyon walls to wild land. They introduced
an American Southwest community of desert animals, so that lizards and turtles
and jackrabbits began to live nearby, and coyotes, bobcats, and hawks to make
depredations among their chickens and sheep. They had an infestation of alli-
gator lizards, then one of toads. Populations slowly settled into their sizes, but
there were frequent sharp fluctuations. The plants began to spread on their own.
The land began to look as if its life belonged there. The redrock walls stood
unchanged, sheer and craggy over the new riverine world.

Saturday morning was market day, and people drove down to the market
hamlets in full pickups. One morning in the early winter of '42 they gathered in
Playa Blanco under dark cloudy skies, to sell late vegetables, and dairy products,
and eggs. "You know how you can tell which eggs have live chicks in them—you
take them all, and put them in a tub of water, and wait until it's all gone completely still. Then the eggs that tremble just a little bit are the ones with live
chicks in them. You can put those back under the hens, and eat the rest."

"A cubic meter of hydrogen peroxide is like twelve hundred kilowatt-hours!
And besides it weighs a ton and a half. No way you'll need that much."

"We're trying to get it into the parts per billion range, but no luck yet."

"Centro de Educación y Tecnología in Chile, they've really done some great
work on rotation, you won't believe it. Come over and see."

"Storm coming."

"We keep bees too."

"Maja is Nepali, Bahram is Farsi, Mawrth is Welsh. Yeah, it does sound
like a lisp, but I'm probably not pronouncing it right. Welsh spelling is bizarre.
They probably pronounce it Moth, or Mort, or Mars."

Then word spread through the marketplace, leaping from group to group like
a fire. "Nirgal is here! Nirgal is here! He's going to talk at the pavilion—"

And there he was, walking fast at the head of a growing crowd, greeting old
friends and shaking hands with people who approached him. Everyone in the
hamlet followed him, jamming into the pavilion and volleyball court at the western end of the market. Wild howls rang out over the crowd buzz.

Nirgal stood on a bench and began to speak. He talked about their valley,
and the other new tented land on Mars, and what it meant. But as he was getting
to the larger situation of the two worlds, the storm overhead broke big-time.

Lightning began to stab all the lightning rods, and in quick succession they saw rain, snow, sleet, and then mud.

The tenting over the valley was pitched as steep as a church roof, and dust and fines were repelled by the static charge of its piezoelectric outer layer; rain ran right off it, and snow slid down and piled up against the bottom of the sides, forming drifts that were blown away by huge robotic snowplows with long angled blower extensions, which rolled up and down the foundation road during snowstorms. Mud, however, was a problem. Mixed with the snow it formed cold, concrete-hard packs on the tenting just above the foundation, and this dense pack could get heavy enough to cause tent failure—it had happened once before in the north.

So when this storm turned ugly, and the light in the canyon was like the color of a branch, Nirgal said, "We'd better get up there," and they all piled into the trucks and drove to the nearest elevator that ran up inside the canyon wall to the rim. Up on top the people who knew how took over the snowplows and drove them by hand, with the great blowers now spraying steam over the drifts to wash them off the tenting. Everyone else teamed up and took hand-pulled steam carts out, and worked on moving the piles of sludge brought down by the snowplows away from the foundation. This was what Nirgal helped with, running around with a steam hose like he was playing some strenuous new sport. No one could keep up his pace, but quickly they were all thigh-deep in cold swirling mud, with winds over 150, and solid low black clouds spitting more mud down on them all the time. The winds surged to 180 kilometers an hour, but no one minded; it helped clear the tent of the mud. They made sweep after sweep, moving east with the wind, pushing rivers of mud over the drop into uncovered Uzboi Vallis.

When the storm ended, the tenting was fairly clear, but the land on both sides of Nirgal Vallis was deep in frozen mud, and the crews were soaked. They piled back into elevators and dropped to the canyon floor, exhausted and cold, and when they got out at the bottom they looked at each other, entirely black figures except for their faceplates. Nirgal pulled off his helmet and there he was, laughing hard, irrepressible, and when he scooped mud off his helmet and threw it at them, the fight was on. Most found it prudent to keep their helmets on, and it was a strange sight there on the dark floor of that canyon, blind muddy figures throwing clumps of mud at each other and running out into the stream, slipping around as they wrestled and dove.

Maya Katarina Toitovna woke in a foul mood, disturbed by a dream that she deliberately forgot as she rolled out of bed. Like flushing the toilet after that first trip to the bathroom. Dreams were dangerous. She dressed with her back to the little mirror over the sink, then went downstairs to the dining common. All of Sabishii had been built in its signature Martian/ Japanese style, and her neighborhood had the look of a Zen garden, all pine and moss scattered among polished pink boulders. It was beautiful in a spare way that Maya found unpleasant, a kind of rebuke to her wrinkles. She ignored it as best she could, and concentrated on breakfast. The dead boredom of the daily necessities. At another table Vlad and Ursula and Marina were eating with a group of the Sabishii issei. The Sabishiians had all shaved their heads, and in their work jumpers looked like Zen monks. One of them turned on a tiny screen over their table and a Terran news show began, a metanational production from Moscow that had the same relationship to reality that *Pravda* had once had. Some things never changed. This was the English-language version, the speaker's English better than her own, even after all these years. "Now the latest on this fifth day of August, 2114."

Maya stiffened in her chair. In Sabishii it was Ls 246, very near perihelion—the fourth day of 2 November—the days short, the nights warmish for this M-year 44. Maya had had no idea what the Terran date was, and hadn't for years. But back there it was her birthday. Her—she had to calculate . . . her 130th birthday.

Feeling sick, she scowled and threw her half-eaten bagel on her plate, stared at it. Thoughts burst in her head like birds scattering out of a tree; she couldn't track them; it was like being blank. What did it mean, this horrible unnatural age? Why had they turned on the screen at just that moment?

She left the half-moon of bread, which had taken on an ominous look, and walked outside into the autumn morning light. Down the lovely main boulevard of Sabishii's old quarter, green with streetgrass, red with broad-topped fire maples—there was one maple blocking the low sun, and flaring scarlet. Across the plaza outside their dorm she saw Yeli Zudov, playing skittlebowl with a young child, perhaps Mary Dunkel's great-great-granddaughter. There were a lot of the First Hundred in Sabishii now, it was working well as their demimonde, all of them tucked into the local economy and the old quarter, with false identities and Swiss passports—everything amazingly solid, enabling them to live surface lives. And all without the need for the kind of cosmetic surgery that had so altered Sax, because age had done that surgery for them: they were unrecognizable just as they were. She could walk the streets of Sabishii and people would see only one ancient crone among many others. If Transitional Authority officials stopped her they would identify one Ludmilla Novosibirskaya. But the truth was, they would not stop her.

She walked through the city, trying to get away from herself. From the north end of the tent she could see outside the town to the great mound of rock that had been brought up out of Sabishii mohole. It formed a long sinuous hill, running uphill to the horizon, across the high krummholz basins of Tyrrhena. They had designed the mound so that from above it formed the image of a dragon, clutching the egglike tents of the town in its talons. A shadowed cleft crossing the mound marked where a talon left the scaled flesh of the creature. The morning sun shone like the dragon's silver eye, staring back over its shoulder at them.

Her wristpad beeped, and irritably she took the call. It was Marina. "Saxifrage is here," she said. "We're going to meet out in the western stone garden in an hour."

"I'll be there," Maya said, and cut the connection.

What a day it was turning out to be. She wandered west along the city perimeter, abstracted and depressed. One hundred thirty years old. There were Abkhasians down in Georgia, on the Black Sea, who were reputed to have lived to such ages without the treatment. Presumably they were still doing without—the gerontological treatments had been only partially distributed on Earth, following the isobars of money and power, and the Abkhasians had always been poor. Happy but poor. She tried to remember what it had been like in Georgia, in the region where the Caucasus met the Black Sea. Sukhumi, the town was called. She felt she had visited it in her youth, her father had been Georgian. But she could call no image to mind, not a scrap. In fact she could scarcely remember anything of any part of Earth—Moscow, Baikonur, the view from *Novy Mir*—none of it. Her mother's face across the kitchen table, laughing blackly as she ironed or cooked. Maya knew that had happened because she rehearsed the words of the memory from time to time, when she was feeling sad. But the actual images. . . . Her mother had died only ten years before the treatment became available, or she might be alive yet. She would be 150, not at all unreasonable; the current age record was around 170, and rising all the time, with no sign that it would ever stop. Nothing but accidents and rare diseases and the occasional medical mistake were killing the treated these days. Those and murder. And suicide.

She came to the western rock gardens without having seen any of the neat narrow streets of Sabishii's old quarter. That was how the old ended up not remembering recent events—by not seeing them in the first place. Memory lost before it ever came to be, because one was focusing so intently on the past.

Vlad and Ursula and Marina and Sax were seated on a park bench across from Sabishii's original habitats, which were still in use, at least by geese and ducks. The pond and bridge, and banks of riprap and bamboo, were straight out of an old woodblock or silk painting: a cliché. Beyond the tent wall the great thermal cloud of the mohole billowed whitely, thicker than ever as the hole got deeper, and the atmosphere more humid.

She sat down on the bench across from her old companions, stared at them grimly. Mottled wrinkled codgers and crones. They looked almost like strangers, people she had never met. Ah, but there were Marina's sultry hooded eyes, and Vlad's little smile—not surprising on the face of a man who had lived with two women, apparently in harmony and certainly in a completely isolated intimacy, for eighty years. Although it was said that Marina and Ursula were a lesbian couple, and Vlad only a sort of companion or pet. But no one could say for sure. Ursula too looked content, as always. Everybody's favorite aunt. Yes—with concentration, one could see them. Only Sax looked utterly different, a dapper man with a broken nose that he still had not had straightened. It stood in the middle of his newly handsome face like an accusation against her, as if she had done it to him and not Phyllis. He did not meet her eye, but only stared mildly at the ducks clacking around his feet, as if studying them. The scientist at work. Except he was a mad scientist now, wreaking havoc with all their plans, completely beyond rational discourse.

Maya pursed her lips and looked at Vlad.

"Subarashii and Amexx are increasing the number of Transitional Authority troops," he said. "We got a message from Hiroko. They've bulked up the unit that attacked Zygote into a kind of expeditionary force, and it's now moving south, between Argyre and Hellas. They don't seem to know where most of the hidden sanctuaries are, but they're checking hot spots one by one, and they entered Christianopolis, and took it over as a base of operations. There's about five hundred of them, heavily armed and protected from orbit. Hiroko says she's only just barely keeping Coyote and Kasei and Harmakhis from leading the Marsfirst guerrillas in an attack on them. If they find many more sanctuaries the radicals are bound to call for an attack."

Meaning the wild youngsters of Zygote, Maya thought bitterly. They had brought them up poorly, the ectogenes and that whole sansei generation—almost forty now, and itching for a fight. And Peter and Kasei and the rest of the nisei generation were nearing seventy, and in the ordinary course of things should have long since become the leaders of their world; and yet here they were always in the shadow of their undying parents, and how did that make them feel? How might they act on those feelings? Perhaps some of them were figuring that another revolution would be just the thing to give them their chance. Perhaps the only thing. Revolution was the empire of the young, after all.

The old ones sat around watching the ducks in silence. A somber, dispirited group. "What happened to the Christians?" Maya asked.

"Some went to Hiranyagarbha. The rest stayed."

If the Transitional Authority forces took over the southern highlands, then the underground might have infiltrated the cities, but to what purpose? Scattered so thinly they couldn't budge the two-world order, based as it was on Earth. Suddenly Maya had the ugly feeling that the whole independence project was no more than a dream, a compensatory fantasy for the decrepit survivors of a losing cause.

"You know why this step-up in security has happened," she said, glaring at Sax. "Those big sabotages were what did it."

Sax showed no sign of hearing her.

Vlad said, "It's too bad we couldn't have fixed on some sort of plan of action at Dorsa Brevia."

"Dorsa Brevia," Maya said scornfully.

"It was a good idea," Marina said.

"Maybe it was. But without a plan of action, agreed on by all, the constitutional stuff was just—" Maya waved a hand. "Building sandcastles. A game."

"The notion was that each group would do what it thought best," Vlad said.

"That was the notion in sixty-one," Maya pointed out. "And now, if Coyote and the radicals start a guerrilla war and it touches things off, then we're right back in sixty-one all over again."

"What do you think we should do?" Ursula asked her curiously.

"We should take over ourselves! *We* make the plan, *we* decide what to do. We disseminate it through the underground. If we don't take responsibility for this, then whatever happens will be our fault."

"That's what Arkady tried to do," Vlad pointed out.

"At least Arkady tried! We should build on what was good in his work!" She laughed shortly. "I never thought I would hear myself say that. But we should work with the Bogdanovists, and then everyone else who will join. We have to take charge! We are the First Hundred, we are the only ones with the authority to pull it off. The Sabishiians will help us, and the Bogdanovists will come along."

"We need Praxis too," Vlad said. "Praxis, and the Swiss. It has to be a coup rather than a general war."

"Praxis wants to help," Marina said. "But what about the radicals?"

"We have to coerce them," Maya said. "Cut off their supplies, take away their members—"

"That way leads to civil war," Ursula objected.

"Well, they must be stopped! If they start a revolt too soon and the metanationals come down on us before we're ready, then we're doomed. All these uncoordinated strikes at them ought to stop. They accomplish nothing, they only increase the levels of security and make things more difficult for us. Things like knocking Deimos out of its orbit only make them more aware of our presence, without doing anything else."

Sax, still observing the ducks, spoke in his odd lilting way: "There are a hundred and fourteen Earth-to-Mars transit ships. Forty-seven objects in Mars obit—Mars *orbit*. The new Clarke is a fully defended space station. Deimos was available to become the same. A military base. A weapons platform."

"It was an empty moon," Maya said. "As for the vehicles in orbit, we will have to deal with those at the appropriate time."

Again Sax did not appear to notice she had spoken. He stared at the damned ducks, blinking mildly, glancing from time to time at Marina.

Marina said, "It has to be a matter of decapitation, like Nadia and Nirgal and Art said in Dorsa Brevia."

"We'll see if we can find the neck," Vlad said drily.

Maya, getting angrier and angrier at Sax, said, "We should each take one of the major cities, and organize people there into a unified resistance. I want to return to Hellas."

"Nadia and Art are in South Fossa," Marina said. "But we'll need all the First Hundred to join us, for this to work."

"The first thirty-nine," Sax said.

"We need Hiroko," Vlad said, "and we need Hiroko to talk some sense into Coyote."

"No one can do that," Marina said. "But we do need Hiroko. I'll go to Dorsa Brevia and talk to her, and we'll try to hold the south in check."

"Sax?" Vlad said.

Sax jerked out of his reverie, blinked at Vlad. Still not a glance for Maya, even though they were discussing her plan. "Integrated pest management," he said. "You grow tougher plants among the weeds. And then the tougher plants push them out. I'll take Burroughs."

Furious at Sax's snubbing of her, Maya got up and walked around the little pond. She stopped on the opposite bank, gripped the railing by the path in both hands. She glared at the group across the water, sitting on their benches like retired pensioners chatting about food and the weather and ducks and the last chess match. Damn Sax, damn him! Would he hold Phyllis against her forever, that vile woman—

Suddenly she heard their voices, tiny but clear. There was a curving ceramic wall behind the path, running almost all the way around the pond, and she was almost precisely across the pond from them; apparently the wall functioned as a sort of whispering gallery, she could hear them in perfect miniature, the airy voices a fraction of a second behind their mouths' little movements.

"Too bad Arkady didn't survive," Vlad said. "The Bogdanovists would come around a lot easier."

"Yes," said Ursula. "Him and John. And Frank."

"Frank," Marina said scornfully. "If he hadn't killed John none of this would have happened."

Maya blinked. The railing was holding her up.

"What?" she shouted, without thinking. Across the pond the little figures jerked and looked at her. She detached herself from the railing one hand at a time, and half ran around the pond, stumbling twice.

"What do you mean?" she shouted at Marina as she neared them, the words bursting from her without volition.

Vlad and Ursula met her a few steps from the benches. Marina remained seated, looking away sullenly. Vlad had his hands out and Maya tore right through them to get at Marina. "What do you mean saying such foul things?" she shouted, her voice painful in her own throat. "Why? Why? It was Arabs who killed John, everyone knows that!"

Marina grimaced and shook her head, looking down.

"Well?" Maya cried.

"It was a manner of speaking," Vlad said from behind. "Frank did a lot to undermine John in those years, you know that's true. Some say he inflamed the Moslem Brotherhood against John, that's all."

"Pah!" Maya said. "We have all argued with each other, it means nothing!"

Then she noticed that Sax was looking right at her—finally, now that she was furious—staring at her with a peculiar expression, cold and impossible to read—a glare of accusation, of revenge, of what? She had shouted in Russian and the others had replied in kind, and she didn't think Sax spoke it. Perhaps he was just curious about what had upset them so. But the antipathy in that steady stare—as if he were confirming what Marina had said—hammering it into her like a nail!

Maya turned and fled.

She found herself in front of the door to her room with no memory of crossing Sabishii, and threw herself inside as if into her mother's arms; but in the beautiful spare wooden chamber she drew up short of the bed, shocked by the memory of some other room that had turned from womb to trap on her, in some other moment of shock and fear . . . no answers, no distraction, no escape. . . . Over the little sink she caught sight of her face as if in a framed portrait—haggard, ancient, eyes bright red around the rims, like the eyes of a lizard. A nauseating image. That was it—the time she had caught sight of the stowaway on the *Ares*, the face seen through an algae jar. Coyote: a shock which had proved not hallucination, but reality.

And so it might be with this news of Frank and John.

She tried to remember. She tried with all her might to remember Frank Chalmers, to really remember him. She had spoken with him that night in Nicosia, in an encounter unremarkable for its awkwardness and tension, Frank as always acting aggrieved and rejected. . . . They had been together at the very moment John was being knocked unconscious, and dragged into the farm and left to die. Frank couldn't have. . . .

But of course there were surrogates. You could always pay people to act for you. Not that the Arabs would have been interested in money per se. But pride, honor—paid in honor, or in some political *quid pro quo,* the kind of currency Frank had been so expert at printing. . . .

But she could remember so little of those years, so little of the *specifics.* When she put her mind to it, and forced herself to *remember,* to recollect, it was frightening how little came up. Fragments; moments; potsherds of an entire civilization. Once she had been so angry she had knocked a coffee cup off a table, the broken handle bare like a half-eaten bagel on a table. But where had that been, and when, and with whom? She couldn't be sure! "Aahh," she cried involuntarily, and the haggard antediluvian face in the mirror suddenly disgusted her with its pathetic reptile pain. So *ugly.* And once upon a time she had been a beauty, she had been proud of that, she had used it like a scalpel. Now . . . her hair had gone from pure white to a dull gray in recent years, changed somehow in the last treatment. And now it was thinning, for God's sake, and only in some places while not in others. Disgusting. And once a beauty, once upon a time. That hawkish regal face—and now—As if the Baroness Blixen, also a rare beauty in her youth, had crumbled into the syphilitic witch Isak Dinesen and then lived on for centuries after that, like a vampire or a zombie—a ravaged living lizard of a corpse, 130 years old, happy birthday to you, happy birthday to you. . . .

She strode to the sink and yanked on the side of the mirror, revealing a crowded medicine cabinet. Nail scissors on the top shelf. Somewhere on Mars they made nail scissors, of magnesium no doubt. She took them down and pulled a hank of hair out from her head till it hurt, and cut it off right against her scalp. The blades were dull, but if she pulled hard enough they worked. She had to be careful not to cut her scalp, some tiny remnant of her vanity would not allow that. So it was a long, tedious, painstaking and pain-giving job. But a comfort, somehow, to be so distracted, so methodical, so destructive.

The initial cut was ragged enough to require a great deal of trimming, which took a long time. An hour. But she could not make the hairs come to the same length, and finally she got out the razor from the shower, and finished by shaving, patting with toilet paper the cuts that bled copiously, ignoring the old scars revealed, the awful bumps and hollows of the bare skull, so close under the skin. It was hard to do it all without ever looking at the monstrous face hanging from the front of the skull.

When she was done she stared ruthlessly at the freak in the mirror—androgynous, withered, insane. The eagle become vulture: skin head, wattled neck, beady eyes, hook nose, and the lipless downturned little mouth. Staring at this hideous face, there were long, long moments when she could not remember a single thing about Maya Toitovna. She stood frozen in the present, a stranger to everything.

A knock at the door made her jump, and released her. She hesitated, suddenly ashamed, even frightened. Another part of her croaked, "Come in."

The door opened. It was Michel. He saw her and stopped in the doorway. "Well?" she said, staring at him and feeling naked.

He swallowed, cocked his head. "Beautiful as ever." With a crooked grin.

She had to laugh. She sat on her bed and began to weep. She sniffed and sniffed. "Sometimes," she said, wiping her eyes, "sometimes I wish I could stop being Toitovna. I get so tired of it, of everything that I've done."

Michel sat beside her. "We're locked in our selves to the end. This is the price one pays for thought. But which would you rather be—convict, or idiot?"

Maya shook her head. "I was down in the park with Vlad and Ursula and Marina and Sax who hates me, and looking at them all, and we have to do something, we really do, but looking at them and remembering everything—trying to remember—we suddenly all seemed such damaged people."

"A lot has happened," Michel said, and put his hand on hers.

"Do you have trouble remembering?" Maya shivered, and clasped his hand like a life raft. "Sometimes I get so scared, that I'll forget everything." She sniffed a laugh. "I guess that means I'd rather be a convict than an idiot, to answer your question. If you forget, you're free of the past, but nothing means anything. So there's no escape"—she started to cry again—"remember or forget, it hurts just as bad."

"Memory problems are pretty common at our age," Michel said gently. "Especially events in the middle distance, so to speak. There are exercises that help."

"It's not a muscle."

"I know. But the power of recollection seems to strengthen with use.

And the act of remembering apparently strengthens the memories them-selves. It makes sense when you think about it. Synapses physically rein-forced or replaced, that sort of thing."

"But then, if you can't face what you remember—oh Michel—" She took in a big unsteady breath. "They said—Marina said that Frank had murdered John. She said it to the others when she thought I couldn't hear, said it as if it was something they all knew!" She clutched him by the shoulder, squeezed as if she could rip the truth out of him with her claws. "Tell me the truth, Michel! Is it true? Is that what you all think happened?"

Michel shook his head. "No one knows what happened."

"I was there! I was in Nicosia that night and they weren't! I was with Frank when it happened! He had no idea, I swear!"

Michel squinted, uncertain, and she said, "Don't *look* like that!"

"I'm not, Maya, I'm not. I don't mean anything by it. I have to tell you everything I've heard, and I'm trying to remember myself. There have been rumors—all kinds of rumors!—about what happened that night. It's true, some say Frank was—involved. Or connected to the Saudis who killed John. That he met with the one who died later the next day, and so on."

Maya began to weep harder. She bent over her clenched stomach and put her face on Michel's shoulder, her ribs heaving. "I can't stand it. If I don't know what happened . . . how can I remember? How can I even think of them?"

Michel held her, soothed her with his embrace. He squeezed the mus-cles of her back, over and over. "Ah, Maya."

After a long time she sat up, went to the sink and washed her face in cold water, avoiding the mirror's gaze. She returned to the bed and sat, utterly despondent, a seeping blackness in every muscle.

Michel took her hand again. "I wonder if it might not help to know. Or at least, to know as much as you can. To investigate, you know. To read about John and Frank. There are books now, of course. And to ask the other people who were in Nicosia, particularly the Arabs who saw Selim el-Hayil before he died. That kind of thing. It would give you a kind of control, you see. It wouldn't be remembering exactly, but it wouldn't be forgetting either. Those aren't the only two alternatives, strange as it may seem. We have to assume our past, you see? We have to make it a part of what we are now, by an act of the imagination. It's a creative thing, an active thing. It's not a simple process. But I know you, and you are always better when you are active, when you have a little control."

"I don't know if I can," she said. "I can't stand not to know, but I'm afraid to know. I don't want to know. Especially if it's true."

"See how you feel about it," Michel suggested. "Try it and see. Given that both alternatives are painful, it might be you prefer action to the alternative."

"Well." She sniffed, took a single glance across the room. From the room on the other side of the mirror, an ax murderer stared out at her.

"My *God* I am *so ugly*," she said, revulsion making her nauseated to the verge of vomiting.

Michel stood, went to the mirror. "There is a thing called body dysmorphic disorder," he said. "It's related to obsessive-compulsive disorders, and to depression. I've noticed signs of it in you for a long time now."

"It's my birthday."

"Ah. Well, it's a treatable problem."

"Birthdays?"

"Body dysmorphic disorder."

"I won't take drugs."

He put a towel over the mirror, turned to look at her. "What do you mean? It may be a simple lack of serotonin. A biochemical insufficiency. A disease. Nothing to be ashamed of in that. We all take drugs. Clomipramine is very helpful for this problem."

"I'll think about it."

"And no mirrors."

"I'm not a child!" she snarled. "I know what I look like!" She leaped up and tore the towel off the mirror. Insane reptile vulture, pterodactylic, ferocious—it was impressive, in a way.

Michel shrugged. He had a little smile on his face, which she wanted to punch, or kiss. He liked lizards.

She shook her head to clear it. "Well. Take action, you say." She thought about it. "I certainly prefer action to the alternative, in the current situation we're in." She told him about the news from the south, and her proposal to the others. "They make me so angry. They're just waiting for disaster to strike again. All but Sax, and he is a loose cannon with all his sabotages, consulting with no one but these fools he has—we have to do something *coordinated!*"

"Good," he said emphatically. "I agree. We need this."

She regarded him. "Will you come to Hellas Basin with me?"

And he smiled, a spontaneous grin of pure pleasure. Of delight that she had asked! It pierced her heart to see it.

"Yes," he said. "I have some business to finish here, but I can do that quickly. Just a few weeks." And he smiled again. He loved her, she saw; not just as a friend or therapist, but as a lover too. And yet with a certain kind of distance, a Michel distance, some kind of therapist thing. So that she could still breathe. Be loved and still breathe. Still have a friend.

"So you can still stand to be with me, even though I look like this."

"Oh Maya." He laughed. "Yes, you are still beautiful, if you want to know. Which you still do, thank God." He gave her a hug, pulled back and inspected her. "It is a trifle austere. But it will do."

She pushed him away. "And no one will recognize me."

"No one who doesn't know you." He stood. "Come on, are you hungry?"

"Yes. Let me change clothes."

He sat on the bed and watched her as she did, soaking her up, the old goat. Her body was still a human body, amazingly enough, demonstrably female even at this ridiculous posthumous age. She could walk over and squash a breast into his face and he would suckle it like a child. Instead she dressed, feeling her spirits scrape off the bottom and begin their rise; the best moment in the whole sine wave, like the winter solstice for the paleolithics, the moment of relief when you know the sun will come back again, someday. "This is good," Michel said. "We need you to lead again, Maya. You have the authority, you see. The natural authority. And it's good to spread the work around, and for you to concentrate on Hellas. A very good plan. But you know—it will take more than anger."

She pulled a sweater over her head (her scalp felt funny, bare and raw), then looked at him, surprised. He raised a finger admonishingly. "Your anger will help, but it can't be everything. Frank was nothing but anger, remember? And you see where it got him. You have to fight not only against what you hate, but for what you love, you see? And so you have to find what it is you love. You have to remember it, or create it."

"Yes yes," she said, suddenly irritated. "I love *you*, but shut up now." She lifted her chin imperiously. "Let's go eat."

The train from Sabishii out to the Burroughs-Hellas piste was only four cars long, a little locomotive and three passenger cars, none more than half full. Maya walked through them to the last seats of the final car; people glanced at her, but only briefly. No one seemed perturbed by her lack of hair. There were a lot of vulture women on Mars after all, even some on this very train, also wearing work jumpers of cobalt or rust or light green, also old and UV-weathered: a kind of cliché, the ancient Mars veterans, here from the beginning, seen it all, ready to bore you to tears with tales of dust storms and stuck lock doors.

Well, it was just as well. It would not have done to have people nudging each other and exclaiming There's Toitovna! Still she could not help sitting down feeling ugly and forgotten. Which was stupid. She needed to be forgotten. And ugliness helped that; the world wants to forget the ugly.

She plumped into her seat and stared forward. Apparently Sabishii had been visited by a contingent of Terran Japanese tourists, all of them clustered in facing seats at the front of the car, chattering and looking around with their vid spectacles, no doubt recording every minute of their life movies, recordings that no one would ever watch.

The train slid gently forward and they were off. Sabishii was still a small tent town in the hills, but the hummocky land between the town and the main piste was studded with carved peak boulders, and small shelters cut into the cliffs. All north-facing slopes were caked with the snow of the autumn's first storms, and the sun bounced in blinding flashes off slick mirrors of ice as they floated by frozen ponds. The low dark shrubs were all based on ancestors from Hokkaido, and the vegetation gave the land a spiky black-green texture; it was a collection of bonsai gardens, each of them an island separated by a harsh sea of broken rock.

The Japanese tourists naturally found this landscape enchanting. Although possibly they were from Burroughs, new emigrants down to visit the Japanese first landing site, as if making a trip from Tokyo to Kyoto. Or perhaps they were natives, and had never seen Japan. She would be able to tell when she saw them walk; but it didn't matter.

The piste ran just north of Jarry-Desloges Crater, which from outside appeared to be a big round mesa. The apron was a broad fan of snowy debris, dotted with ground-hugging trees and a piebald array of dark greens and bright lichen and alpine flowers and heather, each species with its signature color, and the whole field starred by the scattering of erratic boulders that had fallen back from the sky when the crater was formed. The effect was of a field of redrock, being drowned from below by a rainbow tide.

Maya stared out at the vivid hillside, feeling mildly stunned. Snow, lichen, heather, pine: she knew that things had changed in the world while she had hidden under the polar cap—that before it had been different, and she had lived in a rock world and had experienced all the intense events of those years, had had her heart smashed to stishovite under their impact. But it was so hard to connect with any of that. Either to remember it, or to feel anything about what she could remember. She sat back in her seat and closed her eyes, and tried to relax, to let whatever would come to her come.

. . . It was not so much a specific memory of a specific event, but rather a kind of composite: Frank Chalmers, angrily denouncing or deriding or fulminating. Michel was right: Frank had been an angry man. And yet that was not all he had been. She more than anyone knew that, perhaps, had seen him at peace, or if not at peace—perhaps she had never seen that— at least happy. Or something like. Scared of her, solicitous of her, in love with her—she had seen all that. And shouting at her furiously for some small treachery, or for nothing at all; she had certainly seen that too. Because he had loved her.

But what had he been *like*, really? Or rather, why had he been that way? Was there ever any explaining why they were themselves? There was so little she knew about him before they had met: a whole life back there in America, an incarnation that she had not seen. The bulky dark man she had met in Antarctica—even that person was almost lost to her, overlaid by everything that had happened on the *Ares,* and on Mars. But before that nothing, or next to nothing. He had headed NASA, got the Mars program off the ground, no doubt with the same corrosive style he had exhibited in later years. He had been married briefly, or so she seemed to recall. What had that been like? Poor woman. Maya smiled. But then she heard Marina's tiny voice again, saying, "If Frank hadn't killed John," and she shuddered. She stared at the lectern in her lap. The Japanese passengers at the front of the car were singing a song, a drinking song apparently, as they had a flask out and were passing it around. Jarry-Desloges was behind them now, and they were gliding along the northern rim of the Iapygia Sink, an oval depression that they could see a fair way across before the horizon cut it off. The depression was saturated with craters, and now inside each ring was a slightly separate ecology; it was like looking down into a bombed florist's shop, the baskets scattered everywhere and mostly broken, but here a basket of yellow tapestry, there of pink palimpsest, of whitish or bluish or green Persian carpets. . . .

She tapped on her lectern, and typed out *Chalmers*.

It was an immense bibliography: articles, interviews, books, videos, a whole library of his communiqués to Earth, another library of commentaries, diplomatic, historical, biographical, psychological, psychobiographical—histories, comedies, and tragedies, in every medium, including, apparently, an opera. Meaning some villainous coloratura was down there on Earth, singing her thoughts.

She clicked off the lectern, appalled. After a few minutes of deep breathing she clicked it back on, and called up the file. She couldn't bear to look at any video or still images; she went for the shortest biographical articles in print, from popular magazines, and called one up at random and began to read.

He was born in Savannah, Georgia, in 1976, and grew up in Jacksonville, Florida. His mother and father divorced when he was seven, and after that he lived mostly with his father, in apartments near Jacksonville Beach, an area of cheap stucco beach property built in the 1940s, behind an aging boardwalk of shrimp shacks and hamburger joints. Sometimes he lived with an aunt and uncle near the downtown, which was dominated by big skyscrapers built by insurance companies. His mother moved to Iowa when he was eight. His father joined Alcoholics Anonymous three separate times. He was his high school's class president, and the captain of its football team, on which he played center, and of its baseball team, on which he played catcher. He led a project to clear the choking hyacinths from the St. Johns River. "His entry in his senior yearbook is so long you just know something had to be wrong!" He was accepted by Harvard and given a scholarship, then after one year transferred to MIT, where he earned degrees in engineering and astronomy. For four years he lived alone, in a room above a garage in Cambridge, and very little information about him survived; few people seemed to have known him. "He went through Boston like a ghost."

After college he took a National Service Corps job in Fort Walton Beach, Florida, and here was where he burst onto the national scene. He ran one of the most successful civilian works programs associated with the NSC, building housing for Caribbean immigrants coming through Pensacola. Here thousands of people knew him, at least in his work life. "They all agree he was an inspirational leader, dedicated to the immigrants, working nonstop to help their integration into American society." It was in these years that he married Priscilla Jones, the beautiful daughter of a prominent Pensacola family. People spoke of a political career. "He was on top of the world!"

Then in 2004 the NSC was terminated, and in 2005 he joined the astronaut program in Huntsville, Alabama. His marriage broke up that same year. In 2007 he became an astronaut, and moved quickly into a "flying administration" post. One of his longest space flights was six weeks on the American space station, alone with fellow rising star John Boone. He became head of NASA in 2015, while Boone became captain of the space station. Chalmers and Boone together rode the "Mars Apollo" project through the American government, and after Boone made the first landing in 2020, they both joined the First Hundred, and went to Mars in 2027.

Maya stared at the clear black letters of the Roman alphabet. The pop articles with their one-liners and exclamation points had their suggestive moments, no doubt about it. A motherless boy with a father who drank; a hardworking idealistic youth, riding high and then losing a job and a marriage in the same year; that 2005 would be worth looking into in more detail. After that, he seemed pretty clearly in it for himself. That was what being an astronaut generally meant, in NASA or Glavkosmos; always trying to get more space time, doing administration to get the power to get out more often. . . . By that time in his life, the brief descriptions chimed with the Frank she had known. No, it was the youth, the childhood; it was hard to see that, hard to imagine it as Frank.

She called up the index again, and ran down the list of biographical materials. There was an article called "Broken Promises: Frank Chalmers and the National Service Corps." Maya tapped out the calling code for it and the text appeared. She scrolled down until she saw his name.

> Like many people with basic structural problems in their lives, Chalmers coped in his Pensacola years by filling the days with ceaseless activity. If he had no time to rest, then he had no time to think. This had been a successful strategy for him all the way back to high school, when in addition to all his school activities, he had worked twenty hours a week in a literacy program. And in Boston his academic load made him what one classmate called an "invisible man." We know less about this period of his life than any other. There are reports that he lived out of his car through his first Boston winter, using the bathrooms of a gym on campus. Only when he had secured the transfer to MIT do we have an address for him—

Maya hit fast forward, *click click.*

The Florida panhandle was one of the poorest areas of the nation at the beginning of the twenty-first century, with Caribbean immigration, the closure of the local military bases, and Hurricane Dale combining to cause great misery. "You felt like you were working in Africa," one National Service Corps worker said. In his three years there we get our fullest view of Chalmers as a social creature, as he secured grants to expand a jobs program that made an immense impact on the entire coast, helping thousands who had moved into makeshift shelters after Dale. Training programs taught people to build their homes, meanwhile learning skills that could be put to use elsewhere. The programs were immensely popular among the recipients, but there was opposition to them from the local development industry. Chalmers was therefore controversial, and in the first years of the new century he appears often in the local media, enthusiastically defending the program and advocating it as part of a mass surge of grassroots social action. In a guest editorial for the *Fort Walton Beach Journal* he wrote, "The obvious solution is to turn all our energies on the problem and work on it as a systemic thing. We need to build schools to teach our children to read, and send them off to become doctors to heal us, and lawyers to work the powers that be, so we get our fair share. We need to build our own homes and our own farms, and feed ourselves."

The results in Pensacola and Fort Walton Beach got the local NSC larger grants from Washington, and matching grants from participating corporations. At the high point, in 2004, the Pensacola Coast NSC employed 20,000 people, and was one of the main factors responsible for what was called the "Gulf Renaissance." Chalmers's marriage to Priscilla Jones, daughter of one of the old money families from Panama City, seemed to symbolize this new synthesis of poverty and privilege in Florida, and the two were a prominent couple in the society of the Gulf Coast for about two years.

The election of 2004 ended this period. The abrupt cancellation of the NSC was one of the new administration's first acts. Chalmers spent two months in Washington testifying before House and Senate subcommittees, trying to aid the passage of a bill reinstating the program. The bill passed, but the two Democratic Florida senators and the congressman from the Pensacola district did not support it, and Congress was unable to override the executive veto. The NSC "threatened market forces," the new administration said, and so it came to an end. The indictment and conviction of 19 congressmen (including Pensacola's representative) for lobbying irregularities originating in the building industry came eight years later, and by that time the NSC was a dead issue, its veterans scattered.

For Frank Chalmers it was a watershed. He retreated into a privacy from which in many respects he never emerged. The marriage did not survive the move to Huntsville, and Priscilla soon remarried a friend of the family she had known before Chalmers's arrival in the area. In Washington, Chalmers led an austere life in which NASA appeared to be his exclusive interest; he was famous for his 18-hour days, and the enormous impact they had on NASA's fortunes. These successes made Chalmers nationally famous, but no one at NASA or elsewhere in Washington claimed to know him well. The obsessive overscheduling served again as a mask, behind which the idealistic social worker of the Gulf Coast disappeared for good.

A disturbance at the front of the car caused Maya to look up. The Japanese were standing, pulling down luggage, and it was clear now that they were Burroughs natives; most of them were about two meters tall, gangly kids with toothy laughs and uniformly brilliant black hair. Gravity, diet, whatever it was, people born on Mars grew tall. This group of Japanese reminded Maya of the ectogenes in Zygote, those strange kids who had grown like weeds. . . . Now scattered over the planet, that whole little world gone, like all the others before it.

Maya grimaced, and on an impulse fast-forwarded her lectern to the article's illustrations. There she found a photo of Frank at age twenty-three, in the beginning of his work with the NSC: a dark-haired kid with a sharp confident smile, looking at the world as if he were ready to tell it something it didn't know. So young! So young and so knowing. At first glance Maya thought it was the innocence of youth to look so knowing, but in fact the face did not look innocent. His had not been an innocent childhood. But he was a fighter, and he had found his method, and was prevailing. A power that couldn't be beaten, or so the smile seemed to say.

But kick the world, break your foot. As they said in Kamchatka.

The train slowed and glided to a smooth stop. They were in Fournier Station, where the Sabishii branch met the main Burroughs-to-Hellas piste.

The Burroughs Japanese filed out of the car, and Maya clicked off her lectern and followed. The station was only a small tent, south of Fournier Crater; its interior was simple, a T-shaped dome. Scores of people wandered the three levels of the interior, in groups or singly, most of them in plain work jumpers, but many in business suits or metanational uniforms, or in casual clothes, which these days consisted of loose pantaloons, blouses, and moccasins.

Maya found the sight of so many people a bit alarming, and she moved awkwardly past the kiosk lines and the crowded cafés fronting the pistes. No one met the eye of such a bald withered androgyne. Feeling the artificial breeze on her scalp, she took her place at the front of the line to get on the next train south, turning over in her mind the photo from the book. Had they ever really been that young?

At one o'clock the train floated in from the north. Security guards came out of a room by the cafés, and under their bored eye she put her wrist to a portable checker, and boarded. A new procedure, and simple; but as she found a seat her heart was racing. Clearly the Sabishiians, with the help of the Swiss, had beaten the Transitional Authority's new security system. But still she had reason to be afraid—she was Maya Toitovna, one of the most famous women in history, one of the most wanted criminals on Mars, with the passengers in their seats looking up at her as she passed down the aisle, naked under a blue cotton jumper.

Naked but invisible, by reason of unsightliness. And the truth was that at least half the occupants of the car looked as old as her, Mars vets who looked seventy and could have been twice that, wrinkled, gray-haired, balding, irradiated and bespectacled, scattered among all the tall fresh young natives like autumn leaves among evergreens. And there among them, what looked like Spencer Jackson. As she flung her bag onto the overhead rack, she looked at the seat three ahead; the man's bald pate told her little, but she was pretty sure it was him. Bad luck. On general principle the First Hundred (the First Thirty-nine) tried never to travel together. But there was always the chance that chance itself would screw them up.

She sat in the window seat, wondering what Spencer was doing. Last she had heard, he and Sax had formed a technological team in Vishniac mohole, doing weapons research that they weren't telling anyone else about, or so Vlad had said. So he was part of Sax's crazy outlaw ecotage team, at least to some extent. It didn't seem like him, and she wondered if he had been the moderating influence one recently noticed in Sax's activities. Was Hellas his destination, or was he returning to the southern sanctuaries? Well—she wouldn't find out until Hellas at best, as the protocol was to ignore each other until they were in private.

So she ignored Spencer, if it was him, and she ignored the passengers still filing into the car. The seat next to her remained empty. Across from her were two fiftyish men in suits, emigrants by the look of them, apparently traveling with the two just like them who were seated in front of her. As the train pulled out of the station tent they discussed some game they had all played together: "He hit it a mile! He was lucky to ever find it again!" Golf, apparently. Americans, or something like. Metanational executives, off to oversee something in Hellas, they didn't mention what. Maya took out her lectern and headphones and put the headphones on. She called up *Novy Pravda* and watched the tiny images from Moscow. It was hard to concentrate on the voices, and it made her drowsy. The train flew south. The reporter was deploring the growing conflict between Armscor and Subarashii over the terms of the Siberian development plan. This was a case of crocodile tears, as the Russian government had been hoping for years to play the two giants off against each other and create an auction situation for the Siberian oil fields, rather than be met by a united metanat front dictating all terms. It was surprising in fact that the two metanats had broken ranks like this. Maya did not expect that it would last; it was in the metanats' interest to hold together, to make sure it was always a matter of parceling out the available resources and never fighting for them. If they squabbled, the fragile balance of power might collapse on them, a possibility of which they were surely aware.

She put her head back drowsily and looked out the window at the passing land. Now they were gliding down into the Iapygia Sink, and had a long view to the southwest. It looked like the Siberian taiga/tundra border, as depicted on the news program she had just been watching—a great frost-fractured jumble of a slope, all caked with snow and ice, the bare rock coated with lichen and amorphous mounds of olive and khaki mosses, the coral cacti and dwarf trees filling every low hollow. Pingoes dotting one flat low valley looked like a rash of acne, smeared with a dirty ointment. Maya dozed for a while.

The image of Frank at twenty-three jerked her awake. She thought drowsily about what she had read, trying to piece it together. The father; what had made him join Alcoholics Anonymous three times, and quit it twice (or three times)? It had a bad sound. And after that, as if in response to it, the kind of workaholic habits that were just like the Frank she had known, even if the work seemed un-Frankishly idealistic. Social justice was not something that the Frank she had known had believed in. He had been a political pessimist, engaged in a constant rearguard action to keep the worse from coming to the worst. A career of damage control—and, if some were to be believed, personal aggrandizement. No doubt true. Although Maya felt he had always craved power in order to effect more damage control. But no one could tease the strands of those two motives apart; they were tangled like the moss and the rock out there in the Sink. Power was a many-faceted thing.

If only Frank hadn't killed John. . . . She stared at the lectern, turned it on, tapped in John's name. The bibliography was endless. She checked: 5,146 entries. And it was a selected list. Frank had had several hundred at most. She switched to index mode, and looked up "Death of."

Scores of entries, hundreds! Cold and yet sweating, Maya ran swiftly down the list. The Bern connection, the Moslem Brotherhood, MarsFirst, UNOMA, Frank, her, Helmut Bronski, Sax, Samantha; by title alone she could see that all theories of agency in his death would be advocated. Of course. Conspiracy theory was tremendously popular, always and forever. People wanted such catastrophes to mean something more than mere individual madness, and so the hunt was on.

Disgust at the crackpot inclusiveness of the list almost caused her to shut the file. But then again, perhaps she was just afraid? She opened one of the many biographies, and there on the screen was a photo of John. A ghost of her old pain passed through her, leaving a kind of bleached, emotionless desolation. She clicked to the final chapter.

The Nicosia riot was an early manifestation of the tensions informing Martian society which would later explode in 2061. There were already a great number of Arab technicians living in minimal housing arrangements, in close proximity to ethnic groups with whom they had historical grievances, also to administration personnel whose better housing and travel and walker privileges were obvious. A volatile mix of several groups descended on Nicosia for its dedicatory celebration, and for several days the town was extremely crowded.

click click

The violence has never been satisfactorily explained. Jensen's theory, that the intra-Arab conflict, stimulated by the Lebanese war of liberation from Syria, sparked the Nicosia riot, is insufficient; there were also documented attacks on the Swiss, as well as a high level of random violence, all impossible to explain in terms of the Arab conflict alone.

The official depositions of the people in Nicosia that night still leave the ignition of the conflict a mystery. A number of reports suggest the presence of an *agent provocateur,* never identified

click click

At midnight, when the timeslip began, Saxifrage Russell was at a café midtown, Samantha Hoyle was on a tour of the city wall, and Frank Chalmers and Maya Toitovna had met in the western park where the speeches had been given a few hours before. Fighting had already broken out in the medina. John Boone went down the central boulevard to investigate the disturbance, as did Sax Russell from another direction. At approximately ten minutes into the timeslip, Boone was set upon by a group of between three and six young men, sometimes identified as "Arab." Boone was knocked down and whisked into the medina before any witnesses could react, and an impromptu search turned up no sign of him. It was not until 12:27 A.M. that he was located by a larger search party in the town's farm, and taken from there to the nearest hospital, on Boulevard of the Cypresses. Russell, Chalmers, and Toitovna helped to carry him—

Again a disturbance in the car drew Maya out of the text. Her skin was clammy, and she was shivering slightly. Some memories never really went away, no matter how you suppressed them: despite herself Maya remembered perfectly the glass on the street, a figure on its back on the grass, the puzzled look on Frank's face, the so different puzzlement on John's.

But those were officials, there at the front of the car, standing in the aisle and moving slowly down it. Checking IDs, travel documentation; and there were another two stationed at the back of the car.

Maya tapped off her lectern. She watched the three policemen move down the car, feeling her pulse knocking hard through her body. This was new; she had never seen it before, and it seemed the others on board hadn't either. The car was hushed; everyone watched. Anyone in the car could have had irregular ID, and that fact made for a kind of solidarity in their silence; all eyes focused on the police; no one looked around to see who might be blanching.

The three policemen were oblivious to this observation, and almost seemed oblivious to the very people they interviewed. They joked among themselves as they discussed the restaurants of Odessa, and they moved from row to row rapidly, like conductors, gesturing for people to put their wrists up to the little reader, then cursorily checking the results, comparing for only a few seconds people's faces to the photos called up by their IDs.

They came to Spencer, and Maya's heart rate picked up. Spencer (if it was Spencer) merely held up a steady hand to the reader, apparently looking straight at the seat back in front of him. Suddenly something about his hand was deeply familiar—there under the veins and the liver spots was Spencer Jackson, no doubt of it. She knew it by the bones. He was answering a question now, in a low voice. The policeman with the voice-and-eye reader held it to Spencer's face briefly, and then they all waited. Finally they got a quick line on the reader, and moved on. Two away from Maya. Even the exuberant businessmen were subdued, eyeing each other with sardonic grimaces and raised eyebrows, as if it were ludicrous to have such measures imported into the cars themselves. No one liked this; it was a mistake to do it. Maya took heart from that, and looked out the window. They were ascending the southern side of the Sink, the train gliding up the gentle grade of the piste over low hills, each higher than the next, the train always moving at the same speed, as if moving by magic carpet, over the even-more-magic carpet of the millefleur landscape.

They stood over her. The one closest wore a belt over his rust uniform jumper, with several instruments hanging from the belt, including a stun gun. "ID wrist please." He wore an ID tag, with photo and dosimeter, and a label that said "United Nations Transitional Authority." A thin-faced young emigrant of about twenty-five, though it was easier to guess that from the photo than the face itself, which looked tired. The man turned and said to the woman officer behind him, "I like the veal parmesan they do there."

The reader was warm on her wrist. The woman officer was observing her closely. Maya ignored the look and stared at her wrist, wishing she had a weapon. Then she was looking into the camera eye of the voice-and-eye reader. "What is your destination?" the young man asked.

"Odessa."

A moment's suspended silence.

Then a high beep. "Enjoy your stay." And they were off.

Maya tried to regulate her breathing, to slow it down. The wrist readers took pulses, and if you were over 110 or so they notified the applicator; it was a basic lie detector in that sense. Apparently she had stayed under the line. But her voice, her retinas; those had never been changed. The Swiss passport identity must be powerful indeed, overriding the earlier IDs when they were consulted, at least in this security system. Had the Swiss done that, or the Sabishiians, or Coyote, or Sax, or some force she didn't know? Had she actually been successfully identified and let go, to be tracked so that she would lead them to more of the fugitive Hundred? It seemed as likely as the idea of overmastering the big data banks—as likely or more.

But for the moment, she was left alone. The police were gone. Maya's finger knocked on the lectern, and without thinking about it she called back what she had been reading. Michel was right; she felt tough and hard, diving back into this stuff. Theories to explain the death of John Boone. John had been killed, and now she was being checked by police while traveling over Mars in an ordinary train. It was hard not to feel that there was some sort of cause and effect there, that if John had lived, it wouldn't be this way.

All the principal figures in Nicosia that night have been accused of being behind the assassination: Russell and Hoyle on the basis of sharp disagreements in MarsFirst policy; Toitovna on the basis of a lovers' quarrel; and the various ethnic or national groups in town on the basis of political quarrels either real or imaginary. But certainly the most suspicion over the years has fallen on the figure of Frank Chalmers. Though he was observed to be with Toitovna at the time of the attack (which in some theories gets Toitovna called an accessory or coconspirator), his relationship with the Egyptians and Saudis in Nicosia that night, and his long-standing conflict with Boone, make it inevitable that he is often identified as the ultimate cause of Boone's murder. Few if any deny that Selim el-Hayil was the leader of the three Arabs who eventually confessed before their suicide/murders. But this only adds to suspicion of Chalmers, as he was a known acquaintance of el-Hayil's. Samizdat and one-read documents are reputed to tell the story that "the stowaway" was in Nicosia, and spotted Chalmers and el-Hayil in conversation that night. As "the stowaway" is a myth mechanism by which people convey the anonymous perceptions of the common Martian, it is quite possible that such a tale expresses the observations of people who did not want to be identified as witnesses.

Maya clicked to the end.

El-Hayil was in the late stages of a fatal paroxysm when he broke into the hotel occupied by the Egyptians and confessed to the murder of Boone, asserting that he had been the leader, but had been aided by Rashid Abou and Buland Besseisso of the Ahad wing of the Moslem

Brotherhood. The bodies of Abou and Besseisso were found later that afternoon in a room in the medina, poisoned by coagulants that appeared to be self-administered or given to each other. The actual murderers of Boone were dead. Why they acted, and with whom they may have acted, will never be known. Not the first time such a situation has existed, and not the last; for we hide as much as we seek.

Scrolling through footnotes, Maya was struck again by what a Topic this was, debated by historians and scholars and conspiracy nuts of every persuasion. With a shudder of revulsion she tapped the lectern off, and faced the double window and shut her eyes hard, trying to restore the Frank she had known, and the Boone. For years she had scarcely ever thought of John, the pain was so great; and in a different way she hadn't wanted to think of Frank either. Now she wanted them back. The pain had become the ghost of pain, and she needed to have them back, for her own life's sake. She needed to know.

The "mythical" stowaway.... She ground her teeth, feeling the weightless hallucinatory fear of that first sight of him, his brown face distorted and big-eyed through the glass . . . did he know anything? Had he really been in Nicosia? Desmond Hawkins, the stowaway, the Coyote—he was a strange man. Maya had never been able to talk to him well. Hard to say if she would be able now that she needed to, but she doubted it.

What is it? she had asked Frank when they heard the shouting.

A hard shrug, a look away. Something done on the spur of the moment. Where had she heard that before? He had looked away as he said it, as if he could not bear her gaze. As if he had somehow said too much.

The mountain ranges ringing the Hellas Basin were widest in the western crescent called the Hellespontus Montes, the range on Mars most reminiscent of Terran mountains. To the north, where the piste from Sabishii and Burroughs crossed into the basin, the range was narrower and lower, not so much a matter of mountainous terrain as of an uneven drop to the basin floor, the land seemingly shoved to the north in low concentric waves. The piste threaded its way down this hilly slope, and often it had to switchback down long ramps cut into the sides of the rock waves, each new one lower than the last. The train slowed greatly for the turns, and for many minutes at a time Maya could look out her window either straight at the bare basalt of the wave they were descending, or out over a big expanse of northwest Hellas, still three thousand meters below them: a wide flat plain, ochre and olive and khaki in the foreground, then, out on the horizon, a dirty jumble of white, winking like a broken mirror. That was the glacier over Low Point, still mostly frozen, but thawing more each year, with melt ponds on its surface, and deeper pods of water far below—

pods which teemed with life, and occasionally broke onto the surface of the ice, or even the adjacent land—for this lobe of ice was growing fast. They were pumping water out of aquifers below the surrounding mountains onto the basin floor. The deep depression in the northwest part of the basin, where Low Point and the mohole had been, was the center of this new sea, which was over a thousand kilometers long, and at its widest, over Low Point, three hundred kilometers across. And situated in the lowest point on Mars. A situation rich with promise, as Maya had been maintaining from the very moment they had landed.

The town Odessa had been established well up the north slope of the basin, at the −1-kilometer elevation, where they planned to stabilize the final level of the sea. Thus it was a harbor town waiting for water, and with that in mind the southern edge of the town was a long boardwalk or corniche, a wide grassy esplanade that ran inside the tent, which was secured in the edge of a tall seawall that now stood above bare land. The view of the seawall as the train approached gave one the impression that it was a half-town, with a southern part that had split off and disappeared.

Then the train was coasting into the town's train station, and the view was cut off. The train stopped and Maya pulled down her bag and walked out, following Spencer. They did not look at each other, but once out of the station they went with a loose group of people to a tram stop, and got on the same little blue tram, which ran behind the corniche park bordering the seawall. Near the west end of town they both got off at the same stop.

There, behind and above an open-air market shaded by plane trees, was a three-story apartment complex inside a walled courtyard, with young cypresses lining the side walls. Each floor of the building stepped back from the one below, so that there were balconies for the two higher levels, sporting potted trees and flower boxes hung on their railings. As she climbed the stairs up to the gate of the courtyard, Maya found the architecture of the building somewhat reminiscent of Nadia's buried arcades; but up here in the late afternoon sun behind the market, its walls whitewashed and its shutters blue, it had the look of the Mediterranean or the Black Sea—not all that unlike some fashionable seaside apartment blocks in Terra's Odessa. At the gate she turned to look back over the plane trees of the market; the sun was setting over the Hellespontus Mountains to the west, and out on the distant ice, blinks of sunlight gleamed as yellow as butter.

She followed Spencer through the garden and into the building, checked in with the concierge right after he did, got her key, and went to the apartment that had been assigned to her. The whole building belonged to Praxis, and some apartments functioned as safe houses, including hers, and no doubt Spencer's. They got in the elevator together and went to the third floor, not speaking. Maya's apartment was four doors down from Spencer's. She went inside. Two spacious rooms, one with a kitchen nook;

a bathroom, an empty balcony. The view from the kitchen window over-looked the balcony, and the distant ice.

She put her bag on the bed and went back out, down to the market to buy dinner. She bought from vendors with carts and umbrellas, and sat on a bench placed on the grass bordering the corniche, eating souvlakia and drinking from a little bottle of retsina, watching the evening crowd make their leisurely promenade up and down the corniche. The closest edge of the ice sea looked to be about forty kilometers away, and now all but the easternmost part of the ice was in the shadow of the Hellespontus, a dusky blue shading in the east to alpenglow pink.

Spencer sat down beside her on the bench. "Nice view," he remarked.

She nodded and continued eating. She offered him the bottle of ret-sina, and he said, "No thank you," holding up a half-eaten tamale. She nodded and swallowed.

"What are you working on?" she asked when she was done.

"Parts for Sax. Bioceramics, among other things."

"For Biotique?"

"For a sister company. She Makes Seashells."

"What?"

"It's the name of the company. Another Praxis division."

"Speaking of Praxis . . . " She glanced at him.

"Yes. Sax wants these parts pretty bad."

"For weapons?"

"Yes."

She shook her head. "Can you keep him on a leash for a while?"

"I can try."

They watched the sunlight drain out of the sky, flowing westward like a liquid. Behind them lights flicked on in the trees over the market, and the air began to chill. Maya felt grateful that there was an old friend sitting beside her, in comfortable silence. Spencer's behavior toward her made a telling contrast to Sax; in his friendliness was his apology for his recrimi-nations in the car after Kasei Vallis, and his forgiveness for what she had done to Phyllis. She appreciated it. And in any case he was one of the primal family, and it was nice to have that during yet another move. A new start, a new city, a new life—how many was it now?

"Did you know Frank very well?" she said.

"Not really. Not like you and John knew him."

"Do you think . . . do you think he could have been involved in John's murder?"

Spencer continued to look out at the blue ice on the black horizon. Finally he took the retsina bottle from the bench beside her, drank. He looked at her. "Does it matter anymore?"

She had spent many of the early years working in the Hellas Basin, convinced as she had been that its low elevation was going to make it an obvious site for settlement. Now the land just above the −1-kilometer contour was being settled in places all around the basin, places she had been among the first to explore. She had her old notes on them in her AI, and now, as Ludmilla Novosibirskaya, she got to put them to use.

Her job was in the administration of the hydrological company that was flooding the basin. The team was part of a conglomerate of organizations developing the basin, among them the Black Sea Economic Group's oil companies, the Russian company that had tried to resuscitate the Caspian and Aral seas, and her company, Deep Waters, which was Praxis-owned. Maya's job involved coordinating the many hydrological operations in the region, so again she got to see the heart of the Hellas project, just as in the old days when she had been the driving force behind the entire thing. This was satisfying in various ways, some of them strange—for instance her town Low Point (a mistaken siting, she had to admit) was out there getting drowned deeper every day. That was fine: drown the past, drown the past, drown the past. . . .

So she had her work, and her apartment, which she filled with used furniture and hanging kitchen implements and potted plants. And Odessa proved to be a pleasant town. It was built principally of yellow stone and brown tile, and placed on a part of the slope of the basin rim that curved inward more than usual, so that every part of town looked down on the center of the dry waterfront, and every part had a great view over the basin to the south. The lower districts were devoted to shops and business and parks, the higher ones to residential neighborhoods and garden strips. The town lay just above 30° latitude in the south, and so she had gone from autumn to spring, with the big hot sun shining down the stepped streets of the upper town, and melting away the winter's snow from the ice mass's edge, and the peaks of the Hellespontus Mountains on their western horizon. A handsome little town.

And about a month after her arrival, Michel came down from Sabishii, and took over the apartment right next door to hers. At her suggestion he installed a connecting door between their two living rooms, and after that they wandered between the two apartments as if in one, living their lives in a conjugal domesticity which Maya had never experienced before, a normality that she found very restful. She did not love Michel passionately, but he was a good friend, a good lover, and a good therapist, and having him around was like having an anchor inside her, keeping her from flying away into exhilarations of hydrology or revolutionary fervor, also from sinking too deep into terrible abysses of political despair or personal repugnance. Cycling up and down the sine wave of her moods was a helpless oscillation that she hated, and anything Michel did in the way of amplitude modulation she appreciated. They kept no mirrors in the apartments, which along with clomipramine helped to dampen the cycle. But the bottoms of pots, and the windows at night, gave her the bad news if she cared to have it. As often enough she did.

With Spencer down the hall, the building had just the slightest feeling of Underhill to it, reinforced occasionally by visitors from out of town, using their apartment in its capacity as safe house. When others of the First Hundred came through, they would go out and walk the waterless waterfront, looking at the ice horizon and exchanging the news like old folks anywhere. Marsfirst, led by Kasei and Harmakhis, was becoming more and more radical. Peter was working on the elevator, drawn like a moth back to its moon. Sax had stopped his mad ecotage campaign for the time being, thank God, and was concentrating on his industrial effort in Vishniac mohole, building surface-to-space missiles and the like. Maya shook her head at this news. It was not military might that would do it for them; on that issue she sided with Nadia and Nirgal and Art. They would need something else, something she could not yet visualize. And this gap in her thinking was one of the things that would start her downward in the sine wave of her moods, one of the things that made her mad.

Her work coordinating the various aspects of the flooding project began to get interesting. She trammed or walked down to the offices in the center of town, and there worked hard to process all the reports sent in by the many dowsing crews and drilling operations—all full of glowing estimates of the amounts of water they might put into the basin, and all accompanied by requests for more equipment and personnel, until altogether they added up to much more than Deep Waters could supply. Judging the competing claims was difficult from the office, and her technical staff usually just rolled their eyes and shrugged. "It's like judging a liars' contest," one said.

And then also reports were coming in from all around the basin of the new settlements under construction, and by no means all of the people building these settlements came from the Black Sea Group, or the metanats involved with them. A lot of them were simply unidentified—one of her dowsing crews would note the presence of a tent town which had no official existence, and leave it at that. And the two big canyon projects, in Dao Vallis and the Harmakhis-Reull system, were clearly populated by many more people than could be accounted for in the official documentation—people who must therefore be living under assumed identities, like her, or else living out of the net entirely. Which was very interesting indeed.

A circumHellas piste had just been completed the year before, a difficult piece of engineering as the rim of the basin was riven by cracks and ridges, and cratered by a heavy dose of ejecta reentry. But now the piste was in place, and Maya decided to satisfy her curiosity by taking a trip out to inspect all the Deep Waters projects in person, and look into some of the new settlements.

To accompany her on this trip she requested the company of one of their areologists, a young woman named Diana, whose reports had been coming in from the east basin. Her reports were terse and unremarkable, but Maya had learned from Michel that she was the child of Esther's son, Paul. Esther had had Paul very soon after leaving Zygote, and as far as Maya knew, she had never told anyone who Paul's father was. So it could have been Esther's husband Kasei, in which case Diana was Jackie's niece, and John and Hiroko's great-granddaughter—or else it could have been Peter, as many supposed, in which case she was Jackie's half-niece, and Ann and Simon's great-granddaughter. Either way Maya found it intriguing, and in any case the young woman was one of the yonsei, a fourth-generation Martian, and as such interesting to Maya no matter what her ancestry.

Interesting also in her own right, as it turned out when Maya met her in the Odessa offices a few days before their trip. With her great size (over two meters tall, and yet very rounded and muscular) and her fluid grace, and her high-cheekboned Asiatic features, she seemed a member of a new race, there to keep Maya company in this new corner of the world.

It turned out that Diana was completely obsessed with the Hellas Basin and its hidden water, and she talked about it for hours, at such length and in such detail that Maya became convinced that the mystery of parentage was solved—such a marsmaniac must be related to Ann Clayborne, and so it followed that Paul had been fathered by Peter. Maya sat in the train seat beside the big young woman, watching her or looking out the window at the steep northern slope of the basin, asking questions, observing as Diana shifted her knees against the seat back in front of her. They did not make train seats big enough for the natives.

One thing that fascinated Diana was that the Hellas Basin had proved to be ringed by much more underground water than had been predicted by the areological models. This discovery, made in the field over the last decade, had inspired the current Hellas project, turning the hypothetical sea from a nice idea into a tangible possibility. It had also forced the areologists to reconsider their theoretical models of early Martian history, and caused people to start looking around the rims of the other big impact basins on the planet; reconnaissance expeditions were under way in the Charitum and Nereidum Montes encircling Argyre, and in the hills ringing south Isidis.

Around Hellas itself they were near to completing the inventory, and they had found perhaps thirty million cubic meters all told, though some dowsers argued they were by no means finished. "Is there a way to know when they're finished?" Maya asked Diana, thinking about all the requests for resources flooding her office.

Diana shrugged. "After a while you've just looked everywhere."

"What about the basin floor itself? Might the flooding be destroying our ability to get to some aquifers out there?"

"No." Almost no water, she told Maya, was located under the basin floor itself. The floor had been desiccated by the original impact, and now it consisted of about a kilometer's depth of eolian sediment, underlain by a hard cake of brecciated rock, formed during the brief but stupendous pressures of the impact. These same pressures had also caused deep fracturing all around the rim of the basin, and it was this fracturing that had allowed unusually large amounts of outgassing from the interior of the planet. Volatiles from below had seeped up and cooled, and the water portion of the volatiles had pooled in liquid aquifers, and in many zones of highly saturated permafrost.

"Quite an impact," Maya observed.

"It was big all right." As a general rule, Diana said, impactors were about one-tenth the size of the crater or basin they made (like historical figures, Maya thought); so the impacting planetesimal in this case had been a body about two hundred kilometers in diameter, coming down on ancient cratered highland terrain. Signature traces of it indicated it had probably been an ordinary asteroid, carbonaceous chondrite for the most part, with lots of water and some nickel-iron in it. It had had a speed on arrival of about 72,000 kilometers per hour, and had hit at a slightly eastward angle, which explained the huge devastated region east of Hellas, as well as the high, relatively well-organized concentric ridges of the Hellespontus Montes to the west.

Then Diana described another rule of thumb which caused Maya to free-associate analogies to human history: the bigger an impactor, the less of it survived the impact. Thus almost every bit of this one had vaporized in the cataclysmic strike—though there was a small gravitational bolide under Gledhill Crater, which some areologists claimed was almost certainly the buried remainder of the planetesimal, perhaps one ten-thousandth of the original or less, which they claimed would supply all the iron and nickel that they would ever need if they cared to go digging for it.

"Is that feasible?" Maya asked.

"Not really. Cheaper just to mine the asteroids."

Which they were doing, Maya thought darkly. That was what a prison sentence meant now, under the latest UNTA regime—years in the asteroid belt, operating the very strictly circumscribed mining ships and robots. Efficient, the Transitional Authority said. Prisons that were both remote and profitable.

But Diana was still thinking about the basin's awesome birth. The impact had occurred about three and a half billion years before the present, when the planet's lithosphere had been thinner, and its interior hotter. Energies released by the impact were hard to imagine: the total energy created by humanity through all history was as nothing to it. And so the resulting volcanic activity had been considerable. Surrounding Hellas were a number of ancient volcanoes, which just post-dated the impact, including Australis Tholus to the southwest, Amphitrites Patera to the south, and Hadriaca Patera and Tyrrhena Patera to the northeast. All of these volcanic regions had been found to have liquid water aquifers near them.

Two of these aquifers had burst onto the surface in ancient times, leaving on the eastern slope of the basin two characteristic sinuous water-carved valleys: Dao Vallis, originating on the corrugated slopes of Hadriaca Patera; and farther south, a linked pair of valleys known as the Harmakhis-Reull system, which extended for a full thousand kilometers. The aquifers at the heads of these valleys had refilled over the eons since their outbreaks, and now big construction crews had tented Dao and were working on Harmakhis-Reull, and were letting the water from the aquifers run down the long enclosed canyons, to outlets on the basin floor. Maya was extremely interested in these big new additions to the habitable surface, and Diana, who knew them well, was going to take her to visit some friends in Dao.

Their train glided along the northern rim of Hellas for all the first day, with the ice in view on the basin floor almost continually. They passed a little hillside town called Sebastopol, its stone walls Florentine yellow in the afternoon, and after that came to Hell's Gate, the town at the bottom end of Dao Vallis. They walked out of the Hell's Gate train station late in the afternoon, and looked down into a big new tent town, located under an enormous suspension bridge. The bridge supported the train piste, spanning Dao Vallis just up from the canyon's mouth, so that its towers were over ten kilometers apart. From the canyon rim by the bridge, where the train station was, they could see down the widening mouth of the canyon onto the basin floor, stretching out under a lattice of kinky sun-stained clouds. In the other direction there was a view well up into the steep narrow world of the canyon proper. As they walked down a staired and switchbacked street into the town, the new tenting over the canyon was visible only as a certain red haze to the color of the evening sky, the result of a dusting of fines on the tenting materials. "We'll go upstream tomorrow by way of the rim road," Diana said, "and get an overview. Then come back down on the canyon floor, so you can see what it's like down there."

They descended the street, which had 700 numbered steps. In Hell's Gate's downtown they walked around and had dinner, and then climbed back up to the Deep Waters office, which was on the valley wall just under the bridge. They stayed in rooms there, and next morning they went to a garage by the train station, and borrowed a small company rover.

Diana took the wheel and drove them northeast, paralleling the canyon rim on a road that ran next to the massive concrete foundation for the canyon's tenting. Even though the fabrics were diaphanous to the point of vanishing, the sheer size of the roof made it a heavy weight to anchor. The concrete bulk of the foundation blocked their view down into the canyon itself, and so when they came to the first overlook, Maya had not seen into it since Hell's Gate. Diana drove into a little parking lot up on the broad foundation itself, and they parked and put on helmets and got out of the car, and walked up a wooden staircase that seemed to ascend freestanding into the sky, although a closer look revealed first the clear aerogel beam supporting the staircase, and then the layers of tenting, stretching away from their beam to others that could not be seen. At the top of the stairs was a small railed viewing platform, with a prospect that gave a view of the canyon for many kilometers both upstream and downstream.

And there was indeed a stream; the floor of Dao Vallis had a river in it. The canyon floor was dotted with green, or to be more precise, a collection of greens. Maya identified tamarisk, cottonwood, aspen, cypress, sycamore, scrub oak, snow bamboo, sage—and then, on the steep talus and boulder slopes footing the canyon walls, many varieties of shrubs and low creepers, and of course sedge, and moss, and lichen. And running through this exquisite arboretum, a river.

It was not a blue stream with white rapids. The water in the slower stretches was opaque, and the color of rust. In the rapids and waterfalls it foamed bright shades of pink. Classic Martian tones, caused, Diana said, by the fines that were suspended in the water like glacial silt—also by the reflected color of the sky, which was today a kind of hazy mauve, going lavender around the veiled sun, as yellow as the iris of a tiger's eye.

But no matter the color of the water—it was a running river, in an obviously riverine valley, placid in some places, agitated in others, with gravel fords, sandbars, braided sections, crumbling lemniscate islands, there a big deep lazy oxbow, frequent rapids, and far upstream, a couple of small falls. Under the tallest waterfall they could see the pink foam turn almost white, and patches of white were then carried downstream, to catch on boulders and snags sticking out from the bank.

"Dao River," Diana said. "Also called the Ruby River by the people who live down there."

"How many are there?"

"A few thousand. Most live pretty close to Hell's Gate. Upstream there are family homesteads and the like. And of course then the aquifer station at the head of the canyon, where a few hundred of them work."

"It's one of the biggest aquifers?"

"Yes. About three million cubic meters of water. So we're pumping it out at a flow rate—well, you see it there. About a hundred thousand cubic meters a year."

"So in thirty years, no more river?"

"Right. Although they could pump some water back upstream in a pipe, and let it out again. Or who knows, if the atmosphere gets humid enough, the slopes of Hadriaca might collect a snowpack big enough to serve as a watershed. Then the river would fluctuate with the seasons, but that's what rivers do, don't they."

Maya stared down at the scene, which looked so much like something from her youth, some river . . . the upper Rioni, in Georgia? The Colorado, seen once on a visit to America? She couldn't recall. So fuzzy, all that life. "It's beautiful. And so . . . " She shook her head; the sight had a quality she could not recall ever seeing before, as if it were out of time, a prophetic glimpse into a distant future.

"Here, let's go up the road a bit farther and see Hadriaca."

Maya nodded, and they returned to the car. Once or twice as they continued uphill, the road rose far enough above the foundation to give them another view down onto the canyon floor, and Maya saw that the little river continued to cut through rocks and vegetation. But Diana did not pause, and Maya saw no sign of settlements.

At the upper end of the tented canyon there was a big concrete block of a physical plant, housing the gas exchange mechanisms, and the pumping station. A forest of windmills stood on the rising slope to the north of this station, the big props all facing west and slowly spinning. Above that array rose the broad low cone of Hadriaca Patera, a volcano whose sides were unusually furrowed by a dense crisscrossing network of lava channels, the later ones cutting over the earlier ones. Now the winter's snowpack had filled the channels, but not the exposed black rock between them, which had been blown clear by the strong winds accompanying the snowstorms. The result was an enormous black cone sticking into the bruised sky, festooned with hundreds of tangled white ribbons.

"Very handsome," Maya said. "Can they see it from the canyon floor?"

"No. But a lot of them at this end work up on the rim anyway, at the well or the power station. So they see it every day."

"These settlers—who are they?"

"Let's go meet them and see," Diana said. Maya nodded, enjoying Diana's style, which still reminded her a bit of Ann. The sansei and yonsei were all strange to Maya, but Diana much less than most—a bit private perhaps, but compared to her more exotic contemporaries, and the Zygote kids, welcomely ordinary.

While Maya observed Diana, thinking this, Diana drove their rover into the canyon, down a steep road laid over a giant ancient talus slope near the head of Dao. This was where the original aquifer outburst had occurred, but there was very little chaotic terrain—just titanic talus slopes, permanently settled at the angle of repose.

The canyon floor itself was basically flat and unbroken. Soon they were driving down it, on a regolith track sprayed with a fixative. The track ran by the stream where it could. After about an hour's driving they passed a green meadow, tucked into the lazy curve of a fat oxbow. In the center of this meadow, in a knot of piñon pine and aspen, huddled a gathering of low shingled roofs, with faint smoke rising from a solitary chimney.

Maya stared at the settlement (corral and pasture, truck garden, barn, bee boxes), marveling at its beauty, and its archaic wholeness, its seeming detachment from the great redrock desert plateau above the canyon—detachment from everything really, from history, from Time itself. A mesocosm. What did they think in those little buildings of Mars and Earth, and all their troubles? Why should they care?

Diana stopped the car, and a few people came out and crossed the meadow to see who they were. Pressure under the tent was 500 millibars, which helped to support the weight of the tenting, as the atmosphere at large was averaging about 250 millibars now. So Maya popped the lock of the car, and got out without her helmet on, feeling undressed and uncomfortable.

These settlers were all young natives. Most of them had come down in the last few years from Burroughs and Elysium. Some Terrans lived in the valley too, they said—not many, but there was a Praxis program that brought up groups from smaller countries, and here in the valley they had recently welcomed some Swiss, and Greeks, and Navajo. And there was a Russian settlement down near Hell's Gate. So they heard some different languages in the valley, but English was the lingua franca, and the first tongue of almost all of the natives. They had accents to their English that Maya had not heard before, and made odd mistakes in grammar, at least to her ear; almost every verb after the first one was in present tense, for instance. "We went downstream and see some Swiss are working on the river. Stabilizing the banks in some places, with plants or rocks. They say in a few years the streambed is flushed enough for the water to clear."

Maya said, "It will still be the color of the cliffs, and the sky."

"Yeah, of course. But clear water looks better than silty water, somehow."

"How do you know?" Maya enquired.

They squinted and frowned, thinking about it. "Just from the way it looks in your hand, eh?"

Maya smiled. "It's wonderful you have so much room. Unbelievable what big spaces they can roof these days, isn't it?"

They shrugged, as if they hadn't thought of it that way. One said, "We look forward to the day when we take the tenting off, actually. We miss the rain, and the wind."

"How do you know?"

But they knew.

She and Diana drove on, passing very small villages. Isolated farms. A pasture of sheep. Vineyards. Orchards. Cultivated fields. Big packed greenhouses, gleaming like labs. Once a coyote ran across the track ahead of their car. Then on a high little lawn under a talus slope Diana spotted a brown bear, and later some Dall sheep. In the little villages people were trading food and tools in open marketplaces, and talking over the day's events. They did not monitor the news from Earth, and seemed to Maya astonishingly ignorant of it. All but a little community of Russians, who spoke a mongrel Russian which nevertheless brought tears to Maya's eyes, and who told her that things on Earth were falling apart. As usual. They were happy to be in the canyon.

In one of the small villages there was an outdoor market in full swing, and there in the middle of the crowd was Nirgal, chomping an apple and nodding vigorously as someone spoke to him. He saw Maya and Diana get out of the car and rushed over and hugged her, lifting her off the ground. "Maya, what are you doing here?"

"On a tour from Odessa. This is Diana, Paul's daughter. What are you doing here?"

"Oh, visiting the valley. They've got some soil problems I'm trying to help with."

"Tell me about it."

Nirgal was an ecological engineer, and seemed to have inherited some of Hiroko's talent. The valley mesocosm was relatively new, they were still planting seedlings all up and down it, and though the soil had been prepped, nitrogen and potassium deficiencies were causing many plants not to thrive. As they walked around the marketplace Nirgal discussed this, and pointed out local crops and imported goods, describing the economics of the valley. "So they're not self-sufficient?" Maya asked.

"No no. Not even close. But they do grow a lot of their own food, and then trade other crops, or give them away."

He was working on eco-economics as well, it seemed. And he already had a lot of friends here; people kept coming up to hug him, and as he had his arm over Maya's shoulders, she got pulled into these embraces and then introduced to one young native after another, all of them looking delighted to see Nirgal again. He remembered all their names, asked how they were doing, kept up the questions as they continued to circulate through the market, past tables of bread and vegetables, and bags of barley and fertilizer, and baskets of berries and plums, until there was a whole little crowd of them like a mobile party, which finally settled around long pine tables outside a tavern. Nirgal kept Maya at his side throughout the rest of the afternoon, and she watched all the young faces, relaxed and happy, observing how much Nirgal was like John—how people warmed to him, and then were warm to each other—every occasion like a festival, touched by his grace. They poured each other's drinks, they fed Maya a big meal "all local, all local," they talked with each other in their quick Martian English, detailing gossip and explaining their dreams. Oh, he was a special boy all right, as fey as Hiroko and yet utterly normal, at one and the same time. Diana for instance was simply latched to his other side, and a lot of the other young women there looked like they wished they were in her place, or Maya's. Perhaps had been in the past. Well, there were some advantages to being an ancient babushka. She could mother him shamelessly and he only grinned, and nothing they could do. Yes, there was something charismatic about him: lean jaw, mobile humorous mouth, wide-set, brown, slightly Asiatic eyes, thick eyebrows, unruly black hair, long graceful body, though he was not as tall as muot of them. Nothing exceptional. It was mostly his manner, friendly and curious and prone to hilarity.

"What about politics?" she asked him late that night, as they walked together from the village down to the stream. "What do you say to them?"

"I use the Dorsa Brevia document. My notion is that we should enact it immediately, in our daily lives. Most of the people in this valley have left the official network, you see, and are living in the alternative economy."

"I noticed. That's one of the things that got me up here."

"Yeah, well, you see what's happening. The sansei and yonsei like it. They think of it as a homegrown system."

"The question is, what does UNTA think of it."

"But what can they do? I don't think they care, from what I can see." He was constantly traveling, and had been now for years, and had seen a lot of Mars—much more than Maya had, she realized. "We're hard to see, and we don't appear to be challenging them. So they don't bother with us. They're not even aware how widespread we are."

Maya shook her head dubiously. They stood on the bank of the stream, which in this spot was noisily gurgling over shallows, the night-purple surface scarcely reflecting the starlight. "It's so silty," Nirgal said.

"What do you call yourselves?" she asked.

"What do you mean?"

"It's a kind of political party, Nirgal, or a social movement. You must call it something."

"Oh. Well, some say we're Booneans, or a kind of Marsfirst wing. I don't think that's right. I don't name it, myself. Maybe Ka. Or Free Mars. We say that, as a kind of greeting. Verb, noun, whatever. Free Mars."

"Hmm," Maya said, feeling the chill humid wind on her cheek, Nirgal's arm around her waist. An alternative economy, functioning without the rule of law, was intriguing but dangerous; it could turn into a black economy run by gangsters, and there was very little that any idealistic village could do about it. So that as a solution to the Transitional Authority it was somewhat illusory, she judged.

But when she expressed these reservations to Nirgal, he agreed. "I don't think of this as the final step. But I think it helps. It's what we can do now. And then, when the time comes . . . "

Maya nodded in the darkness. It was another Creche Crescent, she thought suddenly. They walked back up to the village together, where the party was still going on. There five young women at least began jockeying to be the last one at Nirgal's side when the party ended, and with a laugh only slightly edged (if she were young they would not have had a *chance*) Maya left them to it and went to bed.

After two days' driving downstream from the market village, still forty kilometers from Hell's Gate, they came around a bend in the canyon and could see down the length of it, to the towers of the piste's suspension bridge. Like something out of a different world, Maya thought, with a different technology entirely. The towers were six hundred meters high, and ten kilometers apart—a truly immense bridge, dwarfing the town of Hell's Gate itself, which did not roll over the horizon for another hour, and then came visible from the rim downward, its buildings spilling down the steep canyon walls like some dramatic seafront village in Spain or Portugal—but all in the shadow of the enormous bridge. Enormous, yes—and yet there were bridges twice as big as it in Chryse, and with the continual improvements in materials, there was no end in sight. The new elevator cable's carbon nanotube filament had a tensile strength that was overkill even for the elevator's needs, and using it you could build just about any surface bridge you could possibly imagine; people spoke of bridging Marineris, and there were jokes about running cable car lines between the prince volcanoes on Tharsis, to save people the fifteen-kilometer vertical drops between the three peaks.

Back in Hell's Gate Maya and Diana returned the car to the garage, and had a big dinner in a restaurant about halfway up the wall of the valley, under the bridge. After that Diana had friends she wanted to see, so Maya excused herself and went to the Deep Waters offices, and her room. But outside the glass doors of her room, above its little balcony, the great span of the bridge arched through the stars, and remembering Dao Canyon and its people, and black Hadriaca ribboned white with its snow-filled channels, she had great difficulty getting to sleep. She went out and sat curled in a blanket, on a chair on her balcony, for a good part of the night, watching the underside of the giant bridge and thinking about Nirgal and the young natives, and what they meant.

The next morning they were supposed to take the next circumHellas train, but Maya asked Diana to drive her out onto the basin floor instead, to see in person what happened to the water running down the Dao River. Diana was happy to oblige.

At the lower end of the town, the stream poured into a narrow reservoir, dammed by a thick concrete dam and pump, located right at the tent wall. Outside the tent, water was carried off across the basin in a fat insulated pipeline, set on three-meter pylons. The pipeline ran down the broad gentle eastern slope of the basin, and they followed it in another company rover, until the crumbled cliffs of Hell's Gate disappeared over the low dunes of the horizon behind them. An hour later the towers of the bridge were still visible, poking up over the skyline.

A few kilometers farther on, the pipeline ran out over a reddish plain of cracked ice—a kind of glacier, except that it fanned out right to left over the plain for as far as they could see. It was the current shore of their new sea, in fact, or at least one lobe of it, frozen in its place. The pipeline ran out over the ice, then descended into it, disappearing a couple of kilometers from shore.

A small, nearly submerged crater ring stuck out into the ice like a curving double peninsula, and Diana followed tracks onto one peninsula and drove until they were as far out in the ice as they could get. The visible world before them was completely covered with ice; behind them lay the rising slope of sand. "This lobe extends out a long way now," Diana said. "Look there—" She pointed at a silver twinkling on the western horizon.

Maya took a pair of binoculars from the dash. On the horizon she could make out what appeared to be the northern edge of the lobe of ice, where it gave way again to rising sand dunes. As she watched, a mass of ice at this border toppled, looking like a Greenland glacier caving into the sea, except that when it hit the sand it shattered into hundreds of white pieces. Then there was a spill of water, running as dark as the Ruby River out over the sand. Dust dashed up and away from this stream, and blew south on the wind. The edges of the new flow began to whiten, but Maya saw that it was nothing like the frightening speed with which the flood in Marineris had frozen in '61. It stayed liquid, with hardly any frost steam, for minute after minute, right out there in the open air! Oh the world was warmer, all right, and the atmosphere thicker; up to 260 millibars sometimes down here in the basin, and the temperature outside at the moment was 271°K. A very pleasant day! She surveyed the surface of the ice lobe through the binoculars, and saw that it was liberally dotted by the bright white sheens of meltwater ponds that had refrozen clean and flat.

"Things are changing," Maya said, although not to Diana; and Diana did not reply.

Eventually the flood of new dark water whitened all over its surface, and stopped moving. "It's coming out somewhere else now," Diana said. "It works like sedimentation in a river delta. The main channel for this lobe is actually well to the south of here."

"I'm glad I saw this. Let's get back."

They drove back to Hell's Gate, and that night had supper together again, on the same restaurant terrace under the great bridge. Maya asked Diana a great number of questions about Paul and Esther and Kasei and Nirgal and Rachel and Emily and Reull and the rest of Hiroko's brood, and their children and their children's children. What were they doing now? What were they going to do? Did Nirgal have lots of followers?

"Oh yes, of course. You saw how it is. He travels all the time, and there's a whole network of natives in the northern cities who take care of him. Friends, and friends of friends, and so on."

"And you think these people will support a . . . "

"Another revolution?"

"I was going to say independence movement."

"Whatever you call it, they'll support it. They'll support Nirgal. Earth looks like a nightmare to them, a nightmare trying to drag us down into it. They don't want that."

"They?" Maya said, smiling.

"Oh me too." Diana smiled back. "Us."

As they continued clockwise around Hellas, Maya had cause to remember that conversation. A consortium from Elysium, without any metanat or UNTA connections that Maya could discover, had just finished roofing over the Harmakhis-Reull valleys, using the same method that had been used to roof Dao. Now there were hundreds of people in those two linked canyons, outfitting the aerators and working up soils, and seeding and planting the nascent biosphere of the canyons' mesocosm. Their on-site greenhouses and manufacturing plants were producing much of what they needed for this work, and metals and gases were being mined out of the badlands of Hesperia to the east, and brought into the town at the mouth of Harmakhis Vallis called Sukhumi. These people had the starter programs and the seeds, and they did not appear to put much stock in the Transitional Authority; they had not asked permission from it to engage in their project, and they actively disliked the official crews from the Black Sea Group, who were usually Terran metanat representatives.

They were hungry for manpower, however, and were happy to get more technicians or generalists from Deep Waters, and any equipment they could cadge from its headquarters. Practically every group Maya met in the Harmakhis-Reull region made a pitch for aid, and most of them were young natives, who seemed to think they had just as much chance at the equipment as anyone else, even though they were not affiliated with Deep Waters or any other company.

And everywhere south of Harmakhis-Reull, in the ragged ejecta hills behind the rim of the basin, there were dowsing crews, out looking for aquifers. As in the roofed canyons, most of these crews had been born on Mars, and a lot of them had been born on Mars since '61. And they were different, profoundly different, sharing interests and enthusiasms perfectly incommunicable to any other generation, as if genetic drift or disruptive selection had produced a bimodal distribution, so that members of the old *Homo sapiens* were now coinhabiting the planet with a new *Homo ares*, creatures tall and slender and graceful and utterly at home, chattering to each other in a profound self-absorption as they did the work that would make Hellas Basin into a sea.

And this gigantic project was perfectly natural work to them. At one stop on the piste Maya and Diana got out and drove with some friends of Diana's out onto one of the ridges of the Zea Dorsa, which ran out onto the southeast quarter of the basin floor. Now most of these dorsa were peninsulas running out under another ice lobe, and Maya looked down at the crevasse-riven glaciers to each side and tried to imagine a time when the surface of the sea would in fact lie hundreds of meters overhead, so that these craggy old basalt ridges would be nothing but blips on some ship's sonar, home to starfish and shrimp and krill and extensive varieties of engineered bacteria. That time was not far off, amazing though it was to realize it. But Diana and her friends, these in particular of Greek ancestry, or was it Turkish—these young Martian dowsers were not awed by this imminent future, nor by their project's vastness. It was their work, their life—to them it *was* human scale, there was nothing unnatural about it. On Mars, simply enough, human work consisted of pharaonic projects like this one. Creating oceans. Building bridges that made the Golden Gate look like a toy. They weren't even watching this ridge, which would only be visible for a while longer—they were talking about other things, mutual friends in Sukhumi, that sort of thing.

"This is a stupendous act!" Maya told them sharply. "This is magnitudes bigger than anything people have been able to do before! This sea is going to be the size of the Caribbean! There's never been any project anything like this on Earth—*no* project! Not even close!"

A pleasant oval-faced woman with beautiful skin laughed. "I don't give a damn about Earth," she said.

The new piste curved around the southern rim, crossing transversely some steep ridges and ravines which were called the Axius Valles. These corrugations ran from the rim's rough hills down into the basin, forcing the piste viaduct to alternate between great arching bridges and deep cuts, or tunnels. The train they had boarded after the Zea Dorsa was a short private one belonging to the Odessa office, so Maya got it to stop at most of the small stations along this stretch, and she got out to meet and talk with the dowsing and construction crews. At one stop they were all Earthborn emigrants, and to Maya much more comprehensible than the blithe natives—normal-sized people, staggering around amazed and enthusiastic, or dismayed and complaining, in any case aware of how strange their enterprise was. They took Maya down a tunnel in a ridge, and it turned out that the ridge was a lava tunnel running down from Amphitrites Patera, its cylindrical cavity much the same size as Dorsa Brevia's, but tilted at a sharp angle. The engineers were pumping the Amphitrites aquifer's water into it, and using it as their pipeline to the basin floor. So now, as the grinning Earthborn hydrologists showed her as she stepped into an observation gallery cut into the side of the lava tube, black water was racing down the bottom of the huge tunnel, barely covering its bottom even at 200 cubic meters a second, the roar of its splashing echoing in the empty cylinder of basalt. "Isn't it great?" the emigrants demanded, and Maya nodded, happy to be with people whose reactions she could understand. "Just like a damn big storm drain, isn't it?"

But back at the train, the young natives nodded at Maya's exclamations—lava tube pipeline, of course—very big, yes, it would be wouldn't it—saved her some pipe for the less fortunate operations, yes? And then they went back to discussing some feature out on the basin floor that Maya could not see.

As the train continued they rounded the southwest arc of the basin, and the piste led them north. They rode over four or five more big pipelines, snaking out of high canyons in the Hellespontus Montes to their left, canyons between bare serrated ridges of rock, like something out of Nevada or Afghanistan, the peaks whitened with snow. Out the windows to the right, down on the basin floor, there were more spreading patches of dirty broken ice, often marked by the flat white patches of newer spills. They were building on the hilltops by the piste, little tent towns like places out of the Tuscan Renaissance. "These foothills will be a popular place to live," Maya said to Diana. "They'll be between the mountains and the sea, and some of these canyon mouths should end up as little harbors."

Diana nodded. "Nice sailing."

As they came around the last curve of their circumnavigation, the piste had to cross the Niesten Glacier, the frozen remainder of the massive outburst that had drowned Low Point in '61. There was no easy way to make this crossing, as the glacier was thirty-five kilometers wide at its narrowest point, and no one had yet marshaled the time and equipment to build a suspension bridge over it. Instead several support pylons had been rammed through the ice and secured in the rock below. These pylons had prows like icebreakers on their upstream side, and on their downstream side there was attached a kind of pontoon bridge, which rode over the passing ice of the glacier using cushioned smart pads that expanded or contracted to compensate for drops and rises in the ice.

The train slowed for the crossing of this pontoon, and as they glided over it Maya looked upstream. She could see where the glacier fell out of the gap between two fanglike peaks, very near Niesten Crater. Never-identified rebels had broken open the Niesten aquifer with a thermonuclear explosion, and released one of the five or six largest outbursts of '61, almost as big as the one that had harrowed the Marineris canyons. The ice under them was still a bit radioactive. But now it lay under the bridge frozen and still, the aftermath of that terrible flood nothing more than an astonishingly broken field of ice blocks. Beside her Diana said something about climbers who liked to ascend the icefalls on the glacier for the fun of it. Maya shuddered with disgust. People were so crazy. She thought of Frank, carried away by the Marineris flood, and cursed out loud.

"You don't approve?" Diana asked.

She cursed again.

An insulated pipeline ran down the midline of the ice, under the pontoon and down toward Low Point. They were still draining the bottom of the broken aquifer. Maya had overseen the building of Low Point, she had lived there for years and years, with an engineer whose name she could not now recall—and now they were pumping up what was left at the bottom of Niesten aquifer, to add to the water over that drowned city. The great outburst of '61 was now reduced to a slender pipeline's worth of water, channelized and regulated.

Maya felt the turbulent maelstrom of emotions inside her, stirred by all she had seen on her circumnavigation, by all that had happened and

all that was going to happen . . . ah, the floods within her, the flash floods
in her mind! If only she could accomplish the same yoking of her spirit
that they had with this aquifer—drain it, control it, make it sane. But the
hydrostatic pressures were so intense, the outbreaks when they came so
fierce. No pipeline could hold it.

"Things are changing," she told Michel and Spencer. "I don't think we understand things anymore."

She settled back into her life in Odessa, happy to be back but also disturbed, inquisitive, seeing everything anew. On the wall above her desk at the office she kept a drawing by Spencer, of an alchemist flinging a big volume into a turbulent sea. At the bottom he had written, "I'll drown my book."

She left the apartment every morning early, and walked down the corniche to the Deep Waters offices near the dry waterfront, next to another Praxis firm called Séparation de L'Atmosphère. There she worked through the days directing the synthesis team, coordinating the field units, and concentrating now on the small mobile operations that were moving around the basin floor, doing last-minute mineral mining and rearrangement of the ice. Occasionally she worked on the design of these little roving hamlets, enjoying the return to ergonomics, her oldest skill aside from cosmonautics itself. Working one day on changing room cabinets, she looked down at her sketches and felt a wash of déjà vu, and wondered if she had done exactly this bit of work before, sometime in the lost past. She wondered also why it was that skills were so robust in the memory, while knowledge was so fragile. She could not for the life of her recall the education that had given her this ergonomic expertise, but she had it nevertheless, despite the many decades that had passed since she had last put it to use.

But the mind was strange. Some days the sense of déjà vu returned as palpably as an itch, such that every single event of that day felt like something that had happened before. It was a sensation that became more and more uncomfortable the longer it persisted, she found, until the world became an acute frightful prison, and she nothing more than a creature of fate, a clockwork mechanism unable to do anything that she had not done before in some forgotten past. Once, when it lasted almost a week, she was almost paralyzed by it; she had never had the meaning of life assaulted so viciously, never. Michel was quite concerned about it, and assured her it was probably the mental manifestation of a physical problem; this Maya believed, sort of, but as nothing he prescribed helped to ease the feeling, it was of little practical help. She could only endure, and hope for the sensation to pass.

When it did pass, she did her best to forget the experience. And then when it recurred, she would say to Michel "Oh my God, I'm feeling it again," and he would say "Hasn't this happened before?" and they would laugh, and she would do her best to make do. She would dive into the particulars of her current work, planning for the dowsing teams, giving them their assignments based on the areographers' reports from the rim, and the results of other dowsing teams coming back in. It was interesting, even exciting work, a sort of gigantic treasure hunt, which necessitated a continuing education in areography, in the secret habits of submartian water. This absorption helped with the déjà vu quite a bit, and after a while it became just another of the odd sensations with which her mind afflicted her, worse than the exhilarations but better than the depressions, or the occasional moments when rather than feeling that something had happened before, she was struck by the sense that nothing like this had ever happened ever, even though she might be doing something like stepping onto a tram. *Jamais vu*, Michel called it, looking concerned. Quite dangerous, apparently. But nothing to be done about it. Sometimes it was less than helpful, living with someone trained in psychological problems. One could easily become nothing more than a spectacular case study. They would need several pseudonyms to describe her.

In any case, on the days she was lucky and feeling well she worked completely abstracted, and quit somewhere between four and seven, tired and satisfied. She walked home in the characteristic light of the late day in Odessa: the whole town in the shadow of the Hellespontus, the sky therefore intense with light and color, the clouds brilliantly lit as they sailed east over the ice, and everything below burnished with reflected light, in that infinite array of colors between blue and red, different every day, every hour. She strolled lazily under the leaves of the trees in the park, and through the locked gate into the Praxis building, then up to the apartment to eat supper with Michel, who usually had finished a long day of doing therapy with homesick newcomers from Earth, or old-timers with a variety of complaints like Maya's déjà vu or Spencer's dissociation—memory loss, anomie, phantom smells and the like—odd gerontological problems, which had seldom cropped up in shorter-lived people, giving ominous warnings that the treatments might not be penetrating the brain quite as fully as they needed them to.

Very few nisei or sansei or yonsei ever came to visit him, however, which surprised him. "No doubt it is a good sign for the long-term prospects of Martian habitation," he said one evening as he came up from a quiet day in his office on the bottom floor.

Maya shrugged. "They could be crazy and not know it. It looked like it might be that way to me, when I went around the basin."

Michel eyed her. "Do you mean crazy or just different?"

"I don't know. They just seem unaware of what they're doing."

"Every generation is its own secret society. And these are what you might call areurges. It is their nature to operate the planet. You have to give them that."

Usually by the time Maya got home the apartment would already be fragrant with the smells of Michel's attempts at Provençal cooking, and there would be an open bottle of red wine on the table. Through most of the year they ate out on the balcony, and when he was in town and feeling up to it Spencer joined them, as would their frequent visitors. As they ate they talked over the day's work, and the events around the world, and back on Earth.

And so she lived the ordinary days of an ordinary life, *la vie quotidienne*, and Michel would share it with his sly smile, a bald man with an elegant Gallic face, ironic and good-humored, and ever so objective. The evening light would concentrate itself into the band of sky over the black jagged peaks of the Hellespontus, brilliant pinks and silvers and violets shading up into dark indigos and bruised blacks, and their voices would soften in that last part of the twilight Michel called *entre chien et loup*. And then they would pick up the plates, and go back inside, and clean up the kitchen— everything habitual, everything known, deep in that déjà vu that one determines oneself, that makes one happy.

And then, on some evenings, Spencer would have arranged for her to attend a meeting, usually in one of the communes in the upper town. These were loosely affiliated with Marsfirst, but the people who came to the meetings did not seem much like the radical Marsfirsters whom Kasei had led at the Dorsa Brevia congress—they were more like Nirgal's friends in Dao, younger, less dogmatic, more self-absorbed, happier. It disturbed Maya to meet them even though she wanted to, and she spent the day before a meeting in a state of restless anticipation. Then after dinner a small band of Spencer's friends would join them at the Praxis building, and accompany her as they made their way through town, taking trams and then walking, usually up into the upper reaches of Odessa, where the more crowded apartments were located.

Here entire buildings were becoming alternative strongholds, in which the occupants paid their rent and held some downtown jobs, but otherwise disconnected themselves from the official economy; they farmed in greenhouses and on terraces and roofs, and did programming and construction and small instrument and agritool manufacture, for selling and trading and giving among themselves. Their meetings took place in communal living rooms, or out in the little parks and gardens of the upper town, under the trees. Sometimes groups of Reds from out of town joined them.

Maya started by asking people to introduce themselves, and she learned more then: that most of them were in their twenties or thirties or forties, born in Burroughs, or on Elysium or Tharsis, or in camps on Acidalia or the Great Escarpment. There was also a regular small percentage of old Mars vets, and some new emigrants, often from Russia, which pleased Maya. They were agronomists, ecological engineers, construction workers, technicians, technocrats, city operators, service personnel. Much of this work was being done more and more within their developing alternative economy. Their communal buildings had begun as warrens of one-room apartments, with the bathrooms down the hall. They walked or trammed to their downtown jobs, past the fortress mansions behind the corniche, occupied by the visiting metanat executives. (Everyone in Praxis lived in apartments like theirs, which they had noted with approval.) They had all gotten the treatment, and took that to be normality—they were shocked to hear the way it was being used as an instrument of control back on Earth, but then added that to their list of Terran evils. They were in excellent health, and knew very little about sickness, or crowded health clinics. It was a folk cure among them to go out in a walker and let in a single breath of the ambient air. This was said to kill any ailment you could have. They were big and strong. They had a look in their eye that one night Maya recognized: it was the look on the youthful Frank's face, in that photo she had seen in her lectern—that idealism, that edge of anger, that knowledge that things were not right, that confidence that they could set them right. The young, she thought. Revolution's natural constituency.

And there they were, in their small rooms, meeting to argue the issues at hand, looking tired but happy. These were parties as much as anything else, part of their social life. It was important to understand that. And Maya would go to the middle of the room and sit on a tabletop, if possible, and say, "I am Toitovna. I was here since the beginning."

She would talk about that—about what it had been like in Underhill—working to remember until she became as urgent in her manner as History herself, trying to explain why things on Mars were the way they were. "Look," she told them, "you can never go back." Physiological changes had closed Earth to them forever, emigrants and native-born alike, but especially the natives. They were Martian now, no matter what. They needed to be an independent state, sovereign perhaps, semiautonomous at least. Semiautonomy might be enough, given the realities of the two worlds; semiautonomy would justify calling it a free Mars. But in the current state of things they were no more than property, and had no real power over their own lives. Decisions were made for them a hundred million kilometers away. Their home was being chopped up into metal bits and shipped away. It was a waste, it benefited no one except a small metanational elite who were running the two worlds like feudal fiefdoms. No, they needed to be free—and not so that they could cast loose from Earth's terrible situation, not at all—rather, to be able to exert some real influence over what was happening down there. Otherwise they were only going to be helpless witnesses to catastrophe. And then sucked down into the maelstrom after the first sets of victims. That was intolerable. They had to act.

The communal groups were very receptive to this message, as were the more traditional Marsfirst groups, and the urban Bogdanovists, and even some of the Reds. To all of them, in every meeting, Maya stressed the importance of coordinating their actions. "Revolution is no place for anarchy! If we tried to fill Hellas each on our own we might easily wreck each other's work, and maybe even overfill the minus one contour, and wreck everything we've been working for. It's the same with this. We need to work together. We didn't in sixty-one, and that's why it was such a fiasco. It was interference rather than synergy, you understand? That was stupid. This time we have to work together."

Tell that to the Reds, the Bogdanovists would say. And Maya would impale them with a look and say, "I'm talking to *you* right now. You don't want to hear how I talk to *them*." Which might make them laugh, relaxing as they imagined her castigating someone else. That awareness of her as the Black Widow—the evil witch who might curse them, the Medea who might kill them—this was not an unimportant part of her hold on them, and so she let the knives show from time to time. She asked them hard questions, and although usually they were hopelessly naïve, sometimes their answers were really impressive, especially when they were talking about Mars itself. Some of them were collecting tremendous amounts of information: inventories of metanat armories, airport systems, communication center layouts, lists and location programs for satellites and spacecraft, networks, databases. Sometimes, listening to them, it seemed like the whole thing might be possible. They were young, of course, and astonishingly ignorant in many ways, so that it was easy to feel superior to them; but then there was their animal vitality, their health and energy. And they were adults, after all, so that other times watching them Maya understood that the vaunted experience of age was perhaps only a matter of wounds and scarring—that young minds to old minds might be as young bodies to old bodies: stronger, more vital, less twisted by damage.

So she would keep that in mind even as she lectured them as sternly as she had the kids in Zygote, and after her lessons she took pains to mingle among them and just talk, share some food, listen to their stories. After an hour of that, Spencer would announce that she had to leave. The implication throughout was that she was visiting from another city—although, as she had seen some of their faces on the streets of Odessa, they certainly must have seen her as well, and knew at least that she spent a lot of time in the town. But afterward Spencer and his friends would take her through an elaborate routine, to make sure they were not followed. And most of the group would fade away into the staircased alleys of the upper town before they reached the western quarter, and the Praxis apartment building. Then they would slip in through the gate, and the door would shut with a clang, reminding her that the sunny double apartment she shared with Michel was a safe house.

One night after a very sharp meeting with a group of young engineers and areologists, as she was telling Michel about it, she tapped away at her lectern, and found the photo of the young Frank in that article, and printed out a copy of it. The article had taken the photo out of a newspaper of the time, and it was black and white, and quite grainy. She taped the photo to the side of the cabinet over the kitchen sink, feeling odd and turbulent.

Michel looked up from his AI and peered at it, and nodded approvingly. "It's amazing how much you can read from people's faces."

"Frank didn't think so."

"He was just afraid of the ability."

"Hmm," Maya said. She couldn't remember. She recalled instead the looks on the faces of the people at that night's meeting. It was true, they had revealed everything—they had been like masks expressing exactly the sentences their owners had spoken. The metanats are out of control. They're screwing things up. They're selfish, they only care about themselves. Metanationalism is a new kind of nationalism, but without any home feeling. It's money patriotism, a kind of disease. People are suffering, not so much here, but on Earth. And if it doesn't change it will happen here too. They will infect us.

All said with the look from the photo, that knowing confident righteous blaze. It could change to cynicism, no doubt about it; Frank was the proof of that. It was possible to break that fervor, or lose it, in cynicism which could be so contagious. They would have to act before that happened; not too soon, but not too late. Timing would be everything. But if they timed it right. . . .

One day at the office, news came in from the Hellespontus. They had discovered a new aquifer, very deep compared to the others, very far away from the basin, and very big. Diana speculated that earlier glacial ages had run west off the Hellespontus range, and come to rest out there, underground—some twelve million cubic meters, more than any other aquifer, raising the amount of located water from 80 percent to 120 percent of the amount need to fill the basin to the −1-kilometer contour.

It was amazing news, and the whole headquarters group gathered in Maya's office to discuss it and plot it onto the big maps, the areographers already charting pipeline routes over the mountains, and debating the relative merits of different kinds of pipeline. The Low Point sea, called "the pond" in the office, already supported a robust biotic community based on the Antarctic krill food chain, and there was a spreading melt zone at its bottom, heated by the mohole and the accumulating weight of the many tons of ice pressing down from above. Increased air pressure and ever-warming temperatures meant that there would be more and more surface melting as well; bergs would be slipping and crashing together and breaking up, exposing more surfaces, and warming things with friction and sunlight, until they reached a kind of pack ice, and then brash ice. At that point newly pumped-in water, properly aimed to reinforce the Coriolis forces, would start a counterclockwise current.

On and on they talked about it, getting further and further ahead of the game, until when they went out to celebrate with a big lunch, it was almost a shock to see the corniche standing over the rocky plain of the empty basin floor. But today they would not be deterred by the present. They all had a lot of vodka with lunch, so much so that they gave themselves the rest of the afternoon off.

And so when Maya went back to the apartment, she was in no shape to deal with the sight of Kasei, Jackie, Antar, Art, Harmakhis, Rachel, Emily, Frantz, and several of their friends, all there in her living room. They were passing through on a trip to Sabishii, where they planned to meet with some Dorsa Brevia friends, and enter Burroughs and spend a few months working there. They were perfunctory in their congratulations on the discovery of the new aquifer, all but Art; they weren't really interested. This and the sudden crowding of her apartment made Maya cross, and it did not help that she was still affected by the vodka, or that Jackie was so effervescent, with her hands all over both proud Antar (the unbeaten knight of the pre-Islamic epic, as he had once explained to her) and dour Harmakhis—both of whom stretched under her touch without appearing to mind when she was on the other one, or playing with Frantz. Maya ignored it. Who knew what perversion the ectogenes were capable of, brought up like a litter of cats as they were. And now they were rovers, gypsies, radicals, revolutionaries, whatever—like Nirgal, except not, as he had a profession, and a plan, while this crowd—well, she forced herself to suspend judgment. But she had her doubts.

She talked to Kasei, who was usually much more serious than the younger ectogenes—a gray-haired mature man, who somewhat resembled John in feature but not in expression, his stone eyetooth exposed like a fang as he darkly eyed his daughter's behavior. Unfortunately this time through he was full of plans for ridding the world of the Kasei Vallis security compound. Obviously he felt that the relocation of Korolyov to his namesake valley had been a kind of personal affront, and the damage done to the complex by their raid to rescue Sax had not been enough to assuage him—indeed, it seemed only to have given him a taste for more. A brooding man, Kasei, with a temper—perhaps that had come from John—though really he was not much like either John or Hiroko, which Maya found endearing. But his plan to destroy Kasei Vallis was a mistake. Apparently he and Coyote had worked up a decryption program that had broken all the lock codes for the Kasei Vallis compound, and now he planned to storm the sentries, shut the occupants of the city into rovers on a locked course for Sheffield, and then blow up all the structures in the valley.

It might work or it might not, but either way it was a declaration of war, a very serious break in the rough strategy that had held ever since Spencer had managed to stop Sax from knocking things out of the sky. The strategy consisted of simply disappearing from the face of Mars—no reprisals, no sabotage, nobody home in whatever sanctuaries they happened to stumble on. . . . Even Ann seemed to be paying at least some attention to this plan. Maya reminded Kasei of this while praising his idea highly, and encouraging him to use it when the proper time came.

"But we won't necessarily be able to break the codes then," Kasei complained. "It's a one-time opportunity. And it's not as if they don't know we're out here, after what Sax and Peter did to the aerial lens, and Deimos. They probably think we're even bigger than we are!"

"But they don't know. And we want to keep that sense of mystery, that invisibility. Invisible is invincible, as Hiroko says. But remember how much they increased their security presence after Sax went on his rampage? And if they lose Kasei Vallis, they might bring up a huge replacement force. And that only makes it harder to take over in the end."

Stubbornly Kasei shook his head. Jackie interrupted from across the room and said cheerily, "Don't worry, Maya, we know what we're doing."

"Something you can be proud of! The question is, do any of the rest of us? Or are you princess of Mars now?"

"Nadia is the princess of Mars," Jackie said, and went to the kitchen nook. Maya scowled at her back, and noticed Art watching her curiously. He did not flinch when she stared at him, and she went to her room to change clothes. Michel was in there cleaning up, making room for people to sleep on the floor. It was going to be an irritating evening.

The next morning when she got up early to go to the bathroom, feeling hung over, Art was already up. Over the sleeping bodies on the floor he whispered, "Want to go out and get breakfast?"

Maya nodded. When she was dressed they walked down the stairs and out, through the park and along the corniche, which was lurid in the horizontal beams of dawn sunlight. They stopped in a café that had just washed down its section of sidewalk. On the dawn-stained white wall of the building, a sentence had been painted with the help of a stencil, so that it was neat and small, and brilliantly red:

YOU CAN NEVER GO BACK

"My God," Maya exclaimed.

"What?"

She pointed at the graffito.

"Oh, yeah," Art said. "You see that painted all over Sheffield and Burroughs these days. Pithy, eh?"

"Ka wow."

They sat in the chill air by a small round table, and ate pastries and drank Turkish coffee. The ice on the horizon blinked like diamonds, revealing some movement under the ice. "What a fantastic sight," Art said.

Maya looked at the bulky Terran closely, pleased at his response. He was an optimist like Michel, but more canny about it, more natural; with Michel it was policy, with Art, temperament. She had always considered him to be a spy, from the first moment they had rescued him from his too-convenient breakdown out in their path: a spy for William Fort, for Praxis, perhaps for the Transitional Authority, perhaps for others as well. But now he had been among them for so long—a close friend of Nirgal, of Jackie, of Nadia as well . . . and they were in fact working with Praxis now, depending on it for supplies, and protection, and information about Earth. So she was no longer so sure—not only whether Art was a spy, but what, in this case, a spy was.

"You've got to stop them from making this assault on Kasei Vallis," she said.

"I don't think they're waiting on my permission."

"You know what I mean. You can talk them out of it."

Art looked surprised. "If I could talk people out of things that well, we'd be free already."

"You know what I mean."

"Well," Art said. "I suppose they're afraid they won't be able to break the code again. But Coyote seems pretty confident he has the protocol. And it was Sax helped him work it out."

"Tell them that."

"For what it's worth. They listen to you more than me."

"Right."

"We could have a contest—who does Jackie listen to least?"

Maya laughed out loud. "Everyone would win."

Art grinned. "You should slip your recommendations into Pauline. Get it to imitate Boone's voice."

Maya laughed again. "Good idea!"

They talked about the Hellas project, and she described the import of the new discovery west of Hellespontus. Art had been in contact with Fort, and he described the intricacies of the latest World Court decision, of which Maya had not heard. Praxis had brought a suit against Consolidated for arranging to tether their Terran space elevator in Colombia, which was so close to the site in Ecuador that Praxis had planned to use that both sites would be endangered. The court had decided in favor of Praxis, but had been ignored by Consolidated, who had gone ahead and built a base in their new client country, and were already prepared to maneuver their elevator cable down onto it. The other metanats were happy to see the World Court defied, and they were backing Consolidated in every way possible, which was creating trouble for Praxis.

Maya said, "But these metanationals are squabbling all the time, yes?"

"That's right."

"The thing to do would be to start a big fight between some of them."

Art's eyebrows shot up. "A dangerous plan!"

"For who?"

"For Earth."

"I don't give a damn about Earth," Maya said, tasting the words on her tongue.

"Join the crowd," Art said ruefully, and she laughed again.

Happily. Jackie's troop soon left for Sabishii. Maya decided to travel out to the site of the newly discovered aquifer. She took a train counterclockwise around the basin, over Niesten Glacier and south down the great western slope, past the hill town of Montepulciano to a tiny station called Yaonisplatz. From there she drove a little car along a road that followed a mountain valley through the violent ridges of the Hellespontus.

The road was no more than a rough cut in the regolith, secured by a fixative, marked by transponders, and obstructed in shadowed places by drifts of dirty hard summer snow. It ran through strange country. From space the Hellespontus had a certain visual and areomorphological coherence, as the ejecta had been thrown back from the basin in concentric rings. But on the surface these rough rings were almost impossible to make out, and what was left was random pilings of rock, stone dropped from the sky chaotically. And the fantastic pressures engendered by the impact had resulted in all manner of bizarre metamorphoses, the most common being giant shattercones, which were conical boulders fractured on every scale by the impact, so that some had faults you could drive into, while others were simply conical rocks on the ground, with microscopic flaws that covered every centimeter of their surfaces, like old china.

Maya drove through this fractured landscape feeling somewhat spooked by the frequent *kami* stones: shattercones that had landed on their points and stood balanced; others that had had the softer material underneath them eroded away, until they became immense dolmens; giant rows of fangs; tall capped lingam columns, such as the one known as Big Man's Hardon; crazily stacked strata piles, the most prominent of them called Dishes In the Sink; great walls of columnar basalt, patterned in hexagons; other walls as smooth and gleaming as immense chunks of jasper.

The outermost concentric ring of ejecta was the one that most resembled a conventional mountain range, appearing on this afternoon like something out of the Hindu Kush, bare and huge under galloping clouds. The road crossed this range by means of a high pass between two lumpy peaks. In the windy pass Maya stopped her car and looked back, and saw nothing but ragged mountains, a whole world of them—peaks and ridges all piebald with clouds' shadows and snow, and here and there the occasional crater ring to give things a truly unearthly look.

Ahead the land dropped to the crater-pocked Noachis Planum, and down there was a camp of mining rovers, drawn up in a circle like a wagon train. Maya drove hard down the rough road to this camp, reaching it in the late afternoon. There she was welcomed by a small contingent of old Bedouin friends, plus Nadia, who was visiting to consult on the drilling rig for the newly discovered aquifer. They all were impressed with this one. "It extends past Proctor Crater, and probably out to Kaiser," Nadia said. "And it looks like it goes way far south, so far it might be coextensive with the Australis Tholus aquifer. Did you ever establish a northern boundary for that one?"

"I think so," Maya said, and started tapping at her wristpad to find out. They talked about water through an early dinner, only occasionally pausing to exchange other news. After dinner they sat in Zeyk and Nazik's rover, and relaxed eating sherbet that Zeyk passed around, while staring into the coals of a little brazier fire on which Zeyk had earlier cooked shish kebab. The talk turned inevitably to the current situation, and Maya said again what she had said to Art—that they should foment trouble between the metanationals back on Earth, if they could.

"That means world war," Nadia said sharply. "And if the pattern holds, it would be the worst one yet." She shook her head. "There has to be a better way."

"It will not take our meddling for it to start," Zeyk said. "They're on the spiral down into it now."

"Do you think so?" Nadia said. "Well, if it happens . . . then we'll have our chance for a coup here, I guess."

Zeyk shook his head. "This is their escape hatch. It will take a lot of coercion to make the powerful give up a place like this."

"There are different kinds of coercion," Nadia said. "On a planet where the surface is still deadly, we should be able to find some kinds that don't involve shooting people. There should be a whole new technology for waging war. I've talked with Sax about this, and he agrees."

Maya snorted, and Zeyk grinned. "His new ways resemble the old ones, as far as I can tell! Bringing down that aerial lens—we loved that! As for firing Deimos out of orbit, well. But I can see his point, to an extent. When the cruise missiles come out . . . "

"We have to make sure it doesn't come to that." Nadia had the mulish expression she got when her ideas were set in concrete, and Maya regarded her with surprise. Nadia, revolutionary strategist—Maya wouldn't have believed it possible. Well, she no doubt thought of it as protecting her construction projects. Or a construction project itself, in a different medium.

"You should come talk to the communes in Odessa," Maya suggested to her. "They're followers of Nirgal, basically."

Nadia agreed, and leaned forward with a miniature poker to tap one of the coals back into the center of the brazier. They watched the fire burn; a rare sight on Mars, but Zeyk liked fires enough to take the trouble. Films of gray ash fluttered over the Martian orange of hot coals. Zeyk and Nazik talked in low voices, describing the Arab situation on the planet, which was complex as usual. The radicals among them were almost all out in caravans, prospecting for metals and water and areothermal sites, looking innocuous and never doing a thing to reveal that they were not part of the metanat order. But they were out there, waiting, ready to act.

Nadia got up to go to bed, and when she had gone, Maya said hesitantly, "Tell me about Chalmers."

Zeyk stared at her, calm and impassive. "What do you want to know?"

"I want to know how he was involved with Boone's murder."

Zeyk squinted uncomfortably. "That was a very complicated night in Nicosia," he complained. "The talk about it among Arabs is endless. It gets tiresome."

"So what do they say?"

Zeyk glanced at Nazik, who said. "The problem is they all say different things. No one knows what really happened."

"But you were there. You saw some of it. Tell me first what you saw."

At this Zeyk eyed her closely, then nodded. "Very well." He took a breath, composed himself. Solemnly, as if giving witness, he said, "We were gathered at the Hajr el-kra Meshab, after the speeches you gave. People were angry at Boone because of a rumor that he had stopped a plan to build a mosque on Phobos, and his speech hadn't helped. We never liked that new Martian society he talked about. So we were there grumbling when Frank came by. I must say, it was an encouraging sight to see him at that moment. It seemed to us that he was the only one with a chance to counter Boone. So we looked to him, and he encouraged us to—he slighted Boone in subtle ways, made jokes that made us angrier at Boone while making Frank seem the only bastion against him. I was actually annoyed with Frank for stirring up the young ones even more. Selim el-Hayil and several of his friends from the Ahad wing were there, and they were in a state—not just at Boone, but also at the Fetah wing. You see the Ahad and Fetah were split over a variety of issues—pan-Arab versus nationalist, relations to West, attitude to the Sufis . . . it was a fundamental division in that younger generation of the Brotherhood."

"Sunni-Shiite?" Maya asked.

"No. More conservative and liberal, with the liberals thought to be secular, and the conservatives religious, either Sunni or Shiite. And el-Hayil was a leader of the conservative Ahad. And he had been in the caravan

Frank had traveled with that year. They had talked often, and Frank had asked him a lot of questions, really bored into him, in that way he had, until he felt that he understood you, or understood your party."

Maya nodded, recognizing the description.

"So Frank knew him, and that night el-Hayil almost spoke at one point, and decided not to when Frank gave him a look. I saw this. Then Frank left, and el-Hayil left almost immediately after."

Zeyk paused to sip coffee and think it over.

"That was the last I saw of either of them for the next couple of hours. It began to get ugly well before Boone was killed. Someone was cutting slogans on the windows of the medina, and the Ahad thought it was the Fetah, and some Ahad attacked a group of Fetah. After that they were fighting throughout the city, and fighting some American construction crews as well. Something happened. There were other fights going on as well. It was as if everyone had suddenly gone crazy."

Maya nodded. "I remember that much."

"So, well, we heard that Boone had disappeared, and we were down at the Syrian Gate checking the lock codes to see if he had gone out that way, and we found someone had gone out and hadn't come back in, so we were on our way out when we heard the news about him. We couldn't believe it. We went down to the medina and everyone was gathered there, and they all told us it was true. I got into the hospital after about a half hour of moving through the crowd. I saw him. You were there."

"I don't remember."

"Well, you were, but Frank had already left. So I saw him, and went back out and told the others it was true. Even the Ahad were shocked, I am sure of that—Nasir, Ageyl, Abdullah. . . . "

"Yes," Nazik said.

"But el-Hayil and Rashid Abou, and Buland Besseisso, were not there with us. And we were back at the residence facing Hajr el-kra Meshab when there was a very hard knocking at the door, and when we opened it el-Hayil fell into the room. He was already very sick, sweating and trying to vomit, and his skin all flushed and blotchy. His throat had swollen and he could barely talk. We helped him into the bathroom and saw he was choking on vomit. We called Yussuf in, and were trying to get Selim out to the clinic in our caravan when he stopped us. 'They have killed me,' he said. We asked him what he meant, and he said, 'Chalmers.' "

"He said that?" Maya demanded.

"I said, 'Who did this?' and he said, 'Chalmers.' "

As if from a great distance Maya heard Nazik say, "But there was more."

Zeyk nodded. "I said, 'What do you mean?' and he said, 'Chalmers has killed me. Chalmers and Boone.' He was choking it out word by word. He said, 'We planned to kill Boone.' Nazik and I groaned to hear this, and Selim seized me by the arm." Zeyk reached out with both hands and clutched an invisible arm. " *'He was going to kick us off Mars.'* He said this in such a way—I will never forget it. He truly believed it. That Boone was somehow going to kick us off Mars!" He shook his head, still incredulous.

"What happened then?"

"He—" Zeyk opened his hands. "He had a seizure. He held his throat first, then all his muscles—" He clenched his fists again. "He seized up and stopped breathing. We tried to get him breathing, but he never did. I didn't know—tracheotomy? Artificial respiration? Antihistamines?" He shrugged. "He died in my arms."

There was a long silence as Maya watched Zeyk remembering. It had been half a century since that night in Nicosia, and Zeyk had been old at the time.

"I'm surprised how well you remember," she said. "My own memory, even of nights like that . . . "

"I remember everything," Zeyk said gloomily.

"He has the opposite problem to everyone else," Nazik said, watching her husband. "He remembers too much. He does not sleep well."

"Hmph." Maya considered it. "What about the other two?"

Zeyk's mouth pursed. "I can't say for sure. Nazik and I spent the rest of that night dealing with Selim. There was an argument about what to do with his body. Whether to take it out to the caravan and then hide what had happened, or to get the authorities in immediately."

Or to go to the authorities with a lone dead assassin, Maya thought, watching Zeyk's guarded expression. Perhaps that had been argued as well. He was not telling the story in the same way. "I don't know what really happened to them. I never found out. There were a lot of Ahad and Fetah in town that night, and Yussuf heard what Selim had said. So it could have been their enemies, their friends, themselves. They died later that night, in a room in the medina. Coagulants."

Zeyk shrugged.

Another silence. Zeyk sighed, refilled his cup. Nazik and Maya refused.

"But you see," Zeyk said, "that is just the start. That's what we saw, what we could tell you for sure. After that, whew!" He made a face. "Arguments, speculation—conspiracy theories of all kind. The usual thing, right? No one is ever simply assassinated anymore. Ever since your Kennedys, it is always a matter of how many stories you can invent to explain the same body of facts. That is the great pleasure of conspiracy theory—not explanation, but narrative. It is like Scheherazade."

"You don't believe in any of them?" Maya asked, feeling suddenly hopeless.

"No. I have no reason to. The Ahad and Fetah were in conflict, I know that. Frank and Selim were connected somehow. How that affected Nicosia—whether it did—" He blew out a breath. "I don't know, and I don't see how one could know. The past . . . Allah forgive me, the past seems a sort of demon, here to torture my nights."

"I'm sorry." Maya stood. The brilliant little chamber suddenly seemed cramped and florid. Catching a glimpse of the evening stars in a window, she said, "I'm going to go for a walk."

Zeyk and Nazik nodded, and Nazik helped her get her helmet on. "Don't be long," she said.

The sky was matted with the usual spectacular array of stars, with a band of mauve on the western horizon. The Hellespontus reared to the east, late alpenglow turning its peaks a dark pink that sawed at the indigo above it, both colors so pure that the transition line seemed to vibrate.

Maya walked slowly toward an outcropping perhaps a kilometer away. There was something growing in the cracks underfoot, lichen or piggyback moss, its greens all black. She stepped on rocks where she could. Plants had it hard enough on Mars without being stepped on as well. All living things. The chill of the twilight seeped into her, until she could feel the X of the heating filaments in her pants against her knees as she walked. She stumbled and blinked to clear her vision. The sky was full of blurry stars. Somewhere north, in the Aureum Chaos, the body of Frank Chalmers lay in a wash of ice and sediments, his walker for a coffin. Killed while saving the rest of them from being swept away. Though he would have scorned such a description with all his heart. An accident of timing, he would insist, nothing more. The result of having more energy than anyone else, energy fueled by his anger—at her, at John, at UNOMA and all the powers of Earth. At his wife. At his father. At his mother, and himself. At everything. The angry man; the angriest man who had ever lived. And her lover. And the murderer of her other lover, the great love of her life, John Boone, who might have saved them all. Who would have been her partner forever.

And she had set them on each other.

Now the sky was starry black, with no more than a dark purple band left on the western skyline. Her tears were gone, along with her feelings; nothing left but the black world and a slash of purple bitterness, like a wound bleeding into the night.

Some things you must forget. *Shikata ga nai.*
    Back in Odessa Maya did the only thing she could with what she had learned, and forgot it, throwing herself into the work of the Hellas project, spending long hours at the office poring over reports, and assigning crews to the various drilling and construction sites. With the discovery of the Western Aquifer the dowsing expeditions lost their urgency, and more emphasis was placed on tapping and pumping the aquifers already found, and constructing the infrastructure of the rim settlements. So drillers followed dowsers, and pipeline crews went out after the drillers, and tent teams were out all around the piste, and up the Reull canyon above Harmakhis, helping the Sufis deal with a badly fretted canyon wall. New emigrants were arriving at a spaceport built between Dao and Harmakhis, and moving into upper Dao, and helping to transform Harmakhis-Reull, and also settling the other new tent towns around the rim. It was a massive exercise in logistics, and in almost every respect it conformed to Maya's old dream of development for Hellas. But now that it was actually happening, she felt extremely jangly and odd; she was no longer sure what she wanted for Hellas, or for Mars, or herself. Often she felt at the mercy of her mood swings, and in the months after the visit to Zeyk and Nazik (though she did not make this correlation) they were especially violent, an irregular oscillation from elation to despair, with the equinox time in the middle wrecked by the knowledge that she was either on her way up or down.
    She was often hard on Michel in these months, often annoyed by his composure, by the way he seemed so at peace with himself, humming along through his life as if his years with Hiroko had answered all his questions. "It's your fault," she told him, pushing to get a reaction. "When I needed you, you were gone. You weren't doing your job."

Michel would ignore that, would soothe and soothe until it made her angry. He was not her therapist now but her lover, and if you couldn't make your lover angry, then what kind of lover was he? She saw the awful bind that one was put in when one's lover was also one's therapist—how that objective eye and soothing voice could become the distancing device of a professional manner. A man doing his job—it was intolerable to be judged by such an eye, as if he were somehow above it all, and did not have any problems himself, any emotions that he could not control. That had to be disproved. And so (forgetting to forget): "I killed them both! I snared them and played them against each other, to increase my own power. I did it on purpose and you were *no help at all*! It was your fault too!"

He muttered something, beginning to get worried, as he could see what was coming, like one of the frequent storms that blew over the Hellespontus into the basin, and she laughed and slapped him hard in the face, punching him as he retreated, shouting "Come on, you coward, stand up for yourself!" until he ran out onto the balcony and held the door shut with the heel of his foot, staring over the trees of the park and cursing out loud in French while she battered the door. Once she even broke one of the panes and showered glass over his back, and he yanked the door open, still cursing in French as he shoved by her and out the door, out of the building.

But usually he just waited until she collapsed and started to cry, and then he came back in and spoke in English, which marked the return of his composure. And with only a slightly disgusted air he would return to the intolerable therapy again. "Look," he would say, "we were all under great pressure then, whether we could tell it or not. It was an extremely artificial situation, and dangerous as well—if we had failed in any number of different ways, we all could have died. We had to succeed. Some of us dealt with the pressure better than others. I did not do so well, and neither did you. But here we are now. And the pressures are still there, some different, some the same. But we are doing better at dealing with them, if you ask me. *Most* of the time."

And then he would leave and go out to a café on the corniche, and nurse a cassis for an hour or two, drawing sketches of faces in his lectern, mordant caricatures that he erased at the moment of completion. She knew this because some nights she would go out and find him, and sit by him in silence with her glass of vodka, apologizing with the set of her shoulders. How to tell him that it helped her to fight now and then, that it started her on the upward curve again—tell him without causing that sardonic little shrug of his, melancholy and oppressed? Besides, he knew. He knew and he forgave. "You loved them both," he would say, "but in different ways. And there were things you didn't like about them as well. Besides, whatever you did, you can't take responsibility for their actions. They chose to do what they did, and you were only one factor."

It helped her to hear that. And it helped her to fight. It would be all right; she would feel better, for a few weeks or days at least. The past was so shot full of holes anyway, a ragged collection of images—eventually she would forget for real, surely. Although the memories that held the firmest seemed to stick because of a glue made of pain, and remorse. So it might take a while to forget them, even though they were so corrosive, so painful, so useless. Useless! Useless. Better to focus on the present.

Thinking that one afternoon, in the apartment by herself, she stared for a long time at the photo of the young Frank by the sink—thinking that she would take it down, and throw it away. A murderer. Focus on the present. But she too was a murderer. And also the one who had driven him to murder. If one ever drove anyone to anything. In any case he was her companion in that, somehow. So after a long time thinking about it, she decided to leave the photo up.

Over the months, however, and the long rhythms of the timeslipped days and the six-month seasons, the photo became little more than part of the decor, like the rack of tongs and wooden paddles, or the hanging row of copper-bottomed pots and pans, or the little sailing-ship salt and pepper shakers. Part of the stage set for this act of the play, as she sometimes thought of it, which however permanent it seemed would be struck at some point—would disappear utterly, as all the previous sets had disappeared, while she passed through to the next reincarnation. Or not.

So the weeks passed and then the months, twenty-four per year. The first of the month would fall on a Monday for so many months in a row that it would seem fixed forever; then a third of a Martian year would have passed, and a new season finally have made its appearance, and a twenty-seven-day month would pass and suddenly the first would be on a Sunday, and after a while that too would begin to seem the eternal norm, for month after month. And this went on and on; the long Martian years made their slow wheel. Out around Hellas, they seemed to have discovered most of the significant aquifers, and the effort shifted entirely to mining and piping. The Swiss had recently developed what they called a walking pipeline, made specifically for the work in Hellas, and up on Vastitas Borealis. These contraptions rolled over the landscape, distributing the groundwater evenly over the land, so that they could cover the basin floor without creating mountains of ice directly outside the ends of fixed pipelines, as they had tended to before.

Maya went out with Diana to look at one of these pipes in action. Seen from a dirigible floating overhead, they looked remarkably like a garden hose lying on the ground, snaking back and forth under the high pressure of the spurting water.

Down on the ground it was more impressive, even bizarre; the pipeline was huge, and it rolled majestically over layers of smooth ice already deposited, held a couple of meters over the ice on squat pylons that ended in big pontoon skis. The pipeline moved at several kilometers an hour, pushed by the pressure of the water spewing out of its nozzle, which pointed at various angles set by computer. When the pipeline had skiied out to the end of its arc, motors would turn the nozzle, and the pipeline slow down, stop, and reverse direction.

The water shot out of the nozzle in a thick white stream, arcing out and splashing onto the surface in a spray of red dust and white frost steam. Then the water flowed over the ground, in great muddy lobate spills, slowing down, pooling, settling flat, then whitening, and shifting slowly to ice. This was not pure ice, however; nutrients and several strains of ice bacteria had been added to the water from big bioreservoirs located back at the beachline, and so the new ice had a milky pink cast, and melted quicker than pure ice. Extensive melt ponds, actually shallow lakes many square kilometers in area, were a daily event in the summer, and on sunny spring and fall days. The hydrologists also reported big melt pods under the surface. And as worldwide temperatures continued to rise, and the ice deposits in the basin got thicker, the bottom layers were apparently melting under the pressure. So great plates of ice over these melt zones would slip down even the slightest of slopes, piling up in great broken heaps over all the lowest points on the basin floor, in areas that were fantastic wastelands of pressure ridges, seracs, melt pools that froze every night, and blocks of ice like fallen skyscrapers. These great unstable ice piles shifted and broke as they melted in the day's heat, with explosive booms like thunder, heard in Odessa and every other rim town. Then the piles froze again every night, booming and cracking, until many places on the basin floor were an inconceivably shattered chaos.

No travel was possible across such surfaces, and the only way to observe the process over the majority of the basin was from the air. One week in the fall of M-48, Maya decided to join Diana and Rachel and some others taking a trip out to the little settlement on the rise in the center of the basin. This was already called Minus One Island, although it was not yet quite an island, as the Zea Dorsa were not yet covered. But the last of the Zea Dorsa was going to be inundated in a matter of days, and Diana, along with several other hydrologists at the office, thought it would be a good idea to go out and see the historic occasion.

Just before they were scheduled to leave, Sax showed up at their apartment, by himself. He was on his way from Sabishii down to Vishniac, and had dropped in to see Michel. Maya was glad to think that she would be off soon, and so not be around during his stay, which would surely be brief. She still found it unpleasant to be around him, and it was clear that the feeling was mutual; he continued to avoid her eye, and did his talking with Michel and Spencer. Never one word for her! Of course he and Michel had spent hundreds of hours talking during Sax's rehabilitation, but still, it made her furious.

Thus when he heard about her impending trip to Minus One, and asked if he could come along, she was very unpleasantly surprised. But Michel gave her a beseeching glance, quick as a lightning bolt, and Spencer quickly asked if he could come along too, no doubt to keep her from pushing Sax out of the dirigible. And so she agreed, very grumpily.

Thus when they took off a couple of mornings later they had "Stephen Lindholm" and "George Jackson" along with them, two old men whom Maya did not bother to explain to the others, seeing that Diana and Rachel and Frantz all knew who they were. The youngsters were all a bit more subdued as they climbed the steps into the dirigible's long gondola, which made Maya purse her lips irritably. It was not going to be the same trip it would have been without Sax.

The flight from Odessa out to Minus One Island took about twenty-four hours. The dirigible was smaller than the old arrowhead-shaped behemoths of the early years; this one was a cigar-shaped craft called the *Three Diamonds,* and the gondola that formed the bag's keel was long and capacious. Though its ultralight props were powerful enough to drive it at some speed, and directly into fairly strong winds, it still felt to Maya like a barely controlled drift, the hum of the motors scarcely audible under the whoosh of the west wind. She went to one window and looked down, her back to Sax.

The view out the windows was a marvel from the very moment of the first ascent, for Odessa was a handsome banked leaf-and-tile vision in its tent on the north slope. And after a couple of hours of plowing through the air to the southeast, the basin's ice plain covered the entire visible surface of the world, as if they flew over an Arctic Ocean, or an ice world.

They sailed at an altitude of some thousand meters, at about fifty kilometers an hour. Through the afternoon of the first day the shattered icescape beneath them was everywhere a dirty white, liberally dotted with sky-purple melt pools, occasionally blazing silver as they mirrored the sun. For a while they could see a pattern of spiral polynyas to the west, the long black streaks of open water marking the location of the drowned mohole at Low Point.

At sunset the ice became a jumble of opaque pinks and oranges and ivories, streaked by long black shadows. Then they flew through the night, under the stars, over a luminous crackled whiteness. Maya slept uneasily on one of the long benches under the windows, and woke before dawn, which was another wonder of coloration, the purples of the sky appearing much darker than the pink ice below, an inversion that made everything look surreal.

Around midmorning of that day they caught sight of land again; over the horizon floated an oval of sienna hills rising out of the ice, about a hundred kilometers long and fifty wide. This rise was Hellas's equivalent of the central knob found on the floor of medium-sized craters, and it was high enough to remain well above the planned water level, giving the future sea a fairly substantial central island.

At this stage the Minus One settlement, on the northwest point of the high ground, was no more than an array of runways, rocket pads, dirigible masts, and an untidy collection of small buildings—a few under a small station tent, the rest standing isolate and bare, like concrete blocks dumped from the sky. No one lived there but a small technical and scientific staff, although visiting areologists dropped in from time to time.

The *Three Diamonds* swung around and latched on to one of the poles, and was hauled down to the ground. The passengers left the gondola by a jetway, and were given a short tour of the airport and residential habitat by the stationmaster.

After a forgettable dinner in the dining hall of the habitat, they suited up and took a walk outside, wandering through the scattered utilitarian buildings, downhill to what one of the locals said would eventually be the shoreline. They found when they got there that no ice was yet visible from this elevation; it was a low sandy rubble-strewn plain, all the way out to the nearby horizon, some seven kilometers away.

Maya strolled aimlessly behind Diana and Frantz, who seemed to be commencing a romance. Beside them walked another native couple who were based at the station, both even younger than Diana, arm in arm, very affectionate. They were both well over two meters tall, but not lithe and willowy like most of the young natives—this couple had worked out with weights, bulking up until they had the proportions of Terran weight lifters, despite their great height. They were huge people, and yet still very light on their feet, doing a kind of boulder ballet over the scattered rocks of this empty shore. Maya watched them, marveling again at the new species. Behind her Sax and Spencer were coming along, and she even said something about it over the old First Hundred band. But Spencer only said something about phenotype and genotype, and Sax ignored the remark, and took off down the slope of the plain.

Spencer went with him, and Maya followed them, moving slowly over all the other new species: there were grass tufts dotting the sand between the rocks of the rubble, also low flowering plants, weeds, cacti, shrubs, even some very small gnarled trees, tucked into the sides of rocks. Sax wandered around stepping gingerly, crouching down to inspect plants, standing back up with an unfocused look, as if the blood had left his head while he was crouching. Or perhaps this was the look of Sax surprised, something Maya could not recall seeing before. She stopped to stare around her; it was in fact surprising to discover such profligate life, out here where no one had cultivated anything. Or perhaps the scientists stationed at the airport had done it. And the basin was low, and warm, and humid. . . . The young Martians upslope danced over it all, gracefully avoiding the plants without taking any notice of them.

Sax stopped in front of Spencer and tilted his helmet back so that he was staring up into Spencer's faceplate. "These plants will all be drowned," he said querulously, almost as if asking a question.

"That's right," Spencer said.

Sax briefly glanced toward Maya. His gloved fingers were clenching in agitation. What, was he accusing her of murdering plants now too?

Spencer said, "But the organic matter will help sustain later aquatic life, isn't that right?"

Sax merely looked around. As he looked past her, Maya could see he was squinting, as if in distress. Then he took off again across the intricate tapestry of plants and rocks.

Spencer met Maya's gaze and lifted his gloved hands, as if to apologize for the way Sax was ignoring her. Maya turned and walked back upslope.

Eventually the whole group walked up a spiraling ridge, above the −1 contour to a knoll just north of the station, where they were high enough to get a view of the ice on the western horizon. The airport lay below them, reminding Maya of Underhill or the Antarctic stations—unplanned, unstructured, with no sense at all of the island town that was sure to come. The youngsters as they stepped gracefully over the rocks speculated about what that town would look like—a seaside resort, they were sure, every hectare built up or gardened, with boat harbors in every little indentation of the shoreline, and palm trees, beaches, pavilions. . . . Maya closed her eyes and tried to imagine what the young ones were describing—opened them again, to see rock and sand and scrubby little plants. Nothing had come to her mind. Whatever the future brought would be a surprise to her—she could form no image of it, it was a kind of *jamais vu*, pressing at the present. A sudden premonition of death washed over her, and she struggled to shrug it off. No one could imagine the future. A blank there in her mind meant nothing; it was normal. It was only the presence of Sax that was disturbing her, reminding her of things she could not afford to think of. No, it was a blessing that the future was blank. The freedom from déjà vu. An extraordinary blessing.

Sax trailed behind, looking off at the basin below them.

The next day they climbed back in the *Three Diamonds* and took to the air again and floated southeast, until the captain dropped an anchor line just to the west of the Zea Dorsa. It had been quite a while since Maya had driven out onto them with Diana and her friends, and now the ridges were no more than skinny rock peninsulas, extending out into the shattered ice toward Minus One, and diving under the ice one after the next—all except for the largest one, which was still an unbroken ridge, dividing two rough ice masses, the western ice mass clearly about two hundred meters lower than the eastern one. This, Diana said, was the final line of land connecting Minus One and the basin rim. When this isthmus was overwhelmed, the central rise would be an actual island.

The ice mass on the eastern side of the remaining dorsum was at one point very near to the ridgeline. The dirigible captain let out more anchor line and they floated east on the prevailing wind until they were directly over the ridge, where they could see clearly that only meters of rock remained to be overcome. And off to the east was a walking pipeline, a blue hose sliding slowly back and forth on its ski pylons as its nozzle shot water onto the surface. Under the drone of the props, they could hear occasional creaks and moans from below, a muffled boom, a high crack like a gunshot. There was liquid water below the ice, Diana explained, and the weight of new water on top was causing some sections of ice to scrape over barely submerged dorsa. The captain pointed to the south, and Maya saw a line of icebergs fly into the air as if propelled by explosives, arcing in various directions and falling back onto the ice, breaking into thousands of pieces. "Maybe we'd better back off a little," the captain said. "It would be better for my reputation if we did not get shot out of the sky by an iceberg."

The walking pipeline's nozzle was pointing their way. And then, with a faint seismic roar, the last complete ridge was overwhelmed. A rush of dark water ran up the rock, and then poured down the western side of the ridge in a waterfall some hundred meters wide. It fell the two hundred meters of its descent in a slow lazy sheet. In the context of the great ice world stretching to the horizon in every direction, it was no more than a trickle—but it kept pouring steadily, the water on the eastern mass now channelized by ice on its sides, the falls booming like thunder, the water on the western side fanning out in a hundred streams through the broken ice—and the hair on Maya's neck lifted in fear. Probably a memory of the Marineris flood, she decided, but couldn't say for sure.

Slowly the volume of the waterfall decreased, and in less than an hour it had all slowed and then frozen, at least on the surface; though a sunny fall day, it was eighteen degrees below freezing down there, and a line of ragged cumulonimbus clouds was approaching from the west, indicating a cold front. So the waterfall eventually stilled. But left behind was a fresh icefall, coating the rock ridge with a thousand smooth white tubes. So now the ridge had become two promontories which did not quite meet, like all the other ridges of the Zea Dorsa, all diving into the ice like sets of matching ribs: matching peninsulas. The Hellas Sea was continuous now, and Minus One truly an island.

•   •   •

After that, the circumHellas train trips and the various overflights felt different to Maya, as she perceived the interlaced network of glaciers and ice chaoses in the basin to be the new sea itself, rising and filling and sloshing around. And in fact the liquid sea under the surface ice near Low Point was growing much faster in the springs and summers than it was shrinking in the autumns and winters. And strong winds kicked up waves in the polynyas, which in the summers broke the ice between them, creating regions of brash ice, a floating pack of ice chunks which growled so loudly as they rode the steep little swells that conversation in dirigibles overhead was difficult.

And in the year M-49, the flow rates from all the tapped aquifers reached their maximums, combining to pump 2,500 cubic meters a day into the sea, an amount that would fill the basin to the −1-kilometer contour in about six M-years. To Maya this did not seem long at all, especially as they could see the progress, right there on Odessa's horizon. In winters the black storms that poured over the mountains would blanket the whole basin floor with startling white snow; in the springs the snow would melt, but the new edge of the ice sea would be closer than it had been the previous autumn.

It was much the same in the northern hemisphere, as news reports and her infrequent trips to Burroughs made clear. The great northern dunes of Vastitas Borealis were being rapidly inundated, as the truly enormous aquifers under Vastitas and the north polar region were being pumped onto the surface by drilling platforms that rose on the ice as the ice accumulated under them. In the northern summers, great rivers were pouring off the melting northern polar cap, cutting channels through the laminate sands and running down to join the ice. And a few months after Minus One had been islanded, news reports showed video of an uncovered stretch of ground in Vastitas, disappearing under a dark flood from west and east and north. This apparently created the last link between the lobes of ice; so now there was a world-wrapping sea in the north. Of course it was patchy still, and covered only about half of the land between the sixtieth and seventieth latitudes, but as satellite photos showed, there were already great bays of ice extending south into the deep depressions of Chryse and Isidis.

Submerging the rest of Vastitas would take about twenty more M-years, as the amount of water necessary to fill Vastitas Borealis was much greater than that needed to fill Hellas. But the pumping operation up there was bigger as well, so things were proceeding apace, and all the acts of Red sabotage combined could do no more than put a dent in this progress. In fact progress was accelerating despite increasing acts of sabotage and ecotage, because some of the new mining methods being put into use were quite radical, and very effective. The news programs showed video of the latest method, which set off big underground thermonuclear explosions, very deep under Vastitas. This melted the permafrost over large areas, providing the pumps with more water. On the surface these explosions were manifested as sudden icequakes, which reduced the surface ice overhead to a bubbling slurry, the liquid water soon freezing on the surface, but tending to stay liquid underneath. Similar explosions under the northern polar cap were causing floods nearly as vast as the great outbursts of '61. And all that water was pouring downhill into Vastitas.

Down at the office in Odessa, they followed all of this with professional interest. A recent assessment of the amount of underground water in the north had encouraged the Vastitas engineers to shoot for a final sea level very near the datum itself, the 0-kilometer contour that had been set back in the days of sky areology. Diana and other hydrologists in Deep Waters thought that subsidence of the land in Vastitas, as a result of the mining of aquifers and permafrost, would cause them to end up with a sea level somewhat lower than the datum. But up there they seemed confident they had factored that in, and would reach the mark.

Fooling around with various sea levels on an office AI map made it clear what shape the coming ocean was likely to have. In many places the Great Escarpment would form its southern shoreline. Sometimes that would mean a gentle slope; in the fretted terrain, archipelagos; in certain regions, dramatic seaside cliffs. Broached craters would provide good harbors. The Elysium massif would become an island continent, and the remains of the northern polar cap would as well—the land under the cap was the only part of the north well above the 0-kilometer contour.

No matter which exact sea level they chose to display on the maps, a big southern arm of the ocean was going to cover Isidis Planitia, which was lower than most of Vastitas. And aquifers in the highlands around Isidis were being pumped down into it as well. So a big bay was going to fill the old plain, and because of that, construction crews were building a long dike in an arc around Burroughs. The city was located fairly close to the Great Escarpment, but its elevation was just below the datum. It was therefore going to become a port city every bit as much as Odessa, a port city on a world-wrapping ocean.

The dike they were building around Burroughs was two hundred meters high and three hundred meters wide. Maya found the concept of a dike to protect the city disturbing, though it was clear from the aerial shots taken of it that it was another pharaonic monument, tall and massive. It ran in a horseshoe shape, with both its ends up on the slope of the Great Escarpment, and it was so big that there were plans to build on it, to make it into a fashionable Lido district, containing small boat harbors on its water side. But Maya remembered once standing on a dike in Holland, with the land on one side of her lower than the North Sea on the other side of her; it had been a very disorienting sensation, more unbalancing than weightlessness. And, on a more rational level, as news programs from Earth now showed, all dikes there were currently stressed by a very slight rise in sea level, caused by global warming initiated two centuries before. As little as a meter's rise endangered many of the low-lying areas of Earth, and Mars's northern ocean was supposed to rise in the coming decade by a full kilometer. Who could say whether they would be able to fine-tune its ultimate level so accurately as to make a dike sufficient? Maya's work in Odessa made her worry about such control, though of course they were trying for it themselves in Hellas, and thought that they probably had it. They had better, as Odessa's location gave them little margin for error. But the hydrologists also talked about using the "canal" that had been burned by the aerial lens before its destruction, as a runoff into the northern ocean, if such a runoff became necessary. Fine for them, but the northern ocean would have no such recourse.

"Oh," Diana said, "they could always pump any excess up into Argyre Basin."

On Earth, riots, arson, and sabotage were becoming daily weapons of the people who had not gotten the treatment—the mortals, as they were called. Springing up around all the great cities were walled towns, fortress suburbs where those who had gotten the treatment could live their entire lives inside, using telelinks, teleoperation, portable generators, even green-house food, even air filtration systems: like tent towns on Mars, in fact.

One evening, tired of Michel and Spencer, Maya went out to eat by herself. Often she was feeling an urge to get off alone. She walked down to a corner café on the sidewalk facing the corniche, and sat at one of its outdoor tables, under trees strung with lights, and ordered antipasto and spaghetti, and ate abstractedly while she drank a small carafe of chianti, and listened to a small band of musicians play. The leader played a kind of accordion with nothing but buttons on it, called a bandoneon, and his companions played violin, guitar, piano, and an upright bass. A bunch of wizened old men, guys her age, rollicking their way with a tight nimble attack through gaily melancholy tunes—gypsy songs, tangos, odd scraps they seemed to be improvising together. . . . When her meal ended she sat for a long time, listening to them, nursing a last glass of wine and then a coffee, watching the other diners, the leaves overhead, the distant ice-scape beyond the corniche, the clouds tumbling in over the Hellespontus. Trying to think as little as possible. For a while it worked, and she made a blissful escape into some older Odessa, some Europe of the mind, as sweet and sad as the duets of violin and accordion. But then the people at the next table began to debate what percentage of Earth's population had re-ceived the treatment—one argued ten percent, another forty—a sign of the information war, or simply the level of chaos that obtained there. Then as she turned away from them, she noticed a headline on the newspaper screen placed over the bar, and read the sentences scrolling right to left after it: the World Court had suspended operations in order to move from the Hague to Bern, and Consolidated had seized the opportunity of the break to attempt a hostile takeover of Praxis holdings in Kashmir, which in effect meant starting a large coup or small war against the government of Kashmir, from Consolidated's base in Pakistan. Which would of course draw India into it. And India had been dealing with Praxis lately as well. India versus Pakistan, Praxis versus Consolidated—most of the world's population, untreated and desperate. . . .

That night when Maya went home, Michel said that this assault marked a new level of respect for the World Court, in that Consolidated had timed its move to the court's recess; but given the devastation in Kashmir, and the reversal for Praxis, Maya was in no mood to listen to him. Michel was so stubbornly optimistic that it made him stupid sometimes, or at least painful to be around. One had to admit it; they lived in a darkening situation. The cycle of madness on Earth was coming around again, caught in its inexorable sine wave, a sine wave more awful even than Maya's, and soon they would be back in the midst of one of those paroxysms, out of control, struggling to avoid obliteration. She could feel it. They were falling back in.

She began eating in the corner café regularly, to hear the band, and be alone. She sat with her back to the bar, but it was impossible not to think about things. Earth: their curse, their original sin. She tried to understand, she tried to see it as Frank would have seen it, tried to hear his voice analyzing it. The Group of Eleven (the old G-7 plus Korea, Azania, Mexico, and Russia) were still in titular command of much of Terra's power, in the form of their militaries and their capital. The only real competitors to these old dinosaurs were the big metanationals, which had coalesced like Athenas out of the transnats. The big metanats—and there was only room in the two-world economy for about a dozen of them, by definition—were of course interested in taking over countries in the Group of Eleven, as they had so many smaller countries; the metanats that succeeded in this effort would probably win the dominance game among themselves. And so some of them were trying to divide and conquer the G-11, doing their best to pit the Eleven against each other, or to bribe some to break ranks. All the while competing among themselves, so that while some had allied themselves with G-11 countries, in an attempt to subsume them, others had concentrated on poor countries, or the baby tigers, to build up their strength. So there was a kind of complex balance of power, the strongest old nations against the biggest new metanationals, with the Islamic League, India, China, and the smaller metanats existing as independent loci of power, forces that could not be predicted. Thus the balance of power, like any moment of temporary equipoise, was fragile—necessarily so, as half the population of the Earth lived in India and China, a fact

Maya could never quite believe or comprehend—history was so *strange*—and there was no knowing what side of the balance this half of humanity might come down on.

And of course all this begged the question of why there was so much conflict to begin with. Why, Frank? she thought as she sat listening to the cutting melancholy tangos. What is the motivation of these metanational rulers? But she could see his cynical grin, the one from the years when she had known him. Empires have long half-lives, as he had remarked to her once. And the idea of empire has the longest half-life of all. So that there were people around still trying to be Genghis Khan, to rule the world no matter the cost—executives in the metanats, leaders in the Group of Eleven, generals in the armies. . . .

Or, suggested her mental Frank, calmly, brutally—Earth had a carrying capacity. People had overshot it. Many of them would therefore die. Everyone knew this. The fight for resources was correspondingly fierce. The fighters, perfectly rational. But desperate.

The musicians played on, their tart nostalgia made even more poignant as the months passed, and the long winter came on, and they played through the snowy dusks with the whole world darkening, *entre chien et loup*. Something so small and brave in that bandoneon wheeze, in those little tunes pattering on in the face of it all: normal life, clung to so stubbornly, in a patch of light under bare-branched trees.

So familiar, this apprehension. This was how it had felt in the years before '61. Even though she could not remember any of the individual incidents and crises that had constituted the prewar period last time around, she could still remember the feel of it as fully as if stimulated by a familiar scent; how nothing seemed to matter, how even the best days were pale and chill under the black clouds that lay massed to the west. How the pleasures of town life took on an antic, desperate edge, everyone with their backs to the bar, so to speak, doing their best to counteract a feeling of diminution, of helplessness. Oh yes, this was déjà vu all right.

So when they traveled around Hellas and met with Free Mars groups, Maya was thankful to see the people who came, who made the effort to believe that their actions could make a difference, even in the face of the great vortex swirling below them. Maya learned from them that everywhere he went, Nirgal was apparently insisting to the other natives that the situation on Earth was critical to their own fortunes, no matter how distant it seemed. And this was having an effect; now the people who came to the meetings were full of the news of Consolidated and Amexx and Subarashii, and of the recent new incursions into the southern highlands by the UNTA police, incursions which had forced the abandonment of Overhangs, and many hidden sanctuaries. The south was being emptied, all the hidden ones flooding into Hiranyagarbha or Sabishii, or Odessa and the east Hellas canyons.

Some of the young natives Maya met seemed to think that the UNTA appropriation of the south was basically a good thing, as it began the countdown to action. She was quick to denounce such thinking. "It's not them who should have control of the timetable," she told them. "*We* have to control the timing of this, we have to wait for our moment. And then all act together. If you don't see that—"

Then you're *fools*!

But Frank had always lashed out at his audiences. These people needed something more—or, to be precise, they deserved something more. Something positive, something to draw them as well as to drive them. Frank had said this too, but he had seldom acted on it. They needed to be seduced, like the nightly dancers on the corniche. Probably these people were out on their own waterfronts on all the other nights of the week. And politics needed to co-opt some of that erotic energy, or else it was only a matter of *ressentiment* and damage control.

So she seduced them. She did it even when she was worried or frightened, or in a bad mood. She stood among them thinking about sex with the tall lithe young men, and then she sat down in their midst, and asked them questions. She caught their gazes one by one, all of them so tall that when she sat on tables she was eye to eye with them as they sat in chairs, and she engaged them in conversation as intimate and pleasurable as she could make it. What did they want from life, from Mars? Often she laughed out loud at their responses, caught unawares by their innocence or their wit. They had themselves already dreamed Marses more radical than any she could believe in, Marses that were truly independent, egalitarian, just and joyous. And in some ways they had already enacted these dreams: many of them now had made their little warrens into extensive communal apartments, and they worked in their alternative economy that had less and less connection with the Transitional Authority or the metanats—an economy governed by Marina's eco-economics and Hiroko's areophany, by the Sufis and by Nirgal, by his roving gypsy government of the young. They felt they were going to live forever; they felt they lived in a world of sensuous beauty; their confinement in tents was normality, but a stage only, a confinement in warm womb mesocosms, which would be inevitably followed by their emergence onto a free living surface—by their birth, yes! They were embryo areurges, to use Michel's term, young gods operating their world, people who knew they were meant to be free, and were confident they would get there, and soon. Bad news would come from Earth and attendance at the meetings would rise—and in these meetings the air was not one of fear but of determination, of the look on Frank's face in the photo over her sink. A struggle between ex-allies Armscor and Subarishii over Nigeria resulted in the use of biological weapons (both sides disclaimed responsibility) so that the people, animals, and plants of Lagos and the surrounding area were devastated by grotesque diseases; and in the meetings that month, the young Martians spoke angrily, their eyes flashing, of the lack of any rule of law on Earth—the lack of any authority that could be trusted. The metanational global order was too *dangerous* to be allowed to rule Mars!

Maya let them talk for an hour before she said anything but "I know." And she did know! It almost made her weep to look at them, to see how shocked they were by injustice and cruelty. Then she went over the points of the Dorsa Brevia Declaration one by one, describing how each had been argued out, what it meant, and what its implementation in the real world would feel like in their lives. They knew more about this than she did, and these parts of the discussion got them more fired up than any complaints about Earth—less anxious, and more enthusiastic. And in trying to envision a future based on the declaration she often got them laughing: ludicrous scenarios of collective harmony, everyone at peace and happy—they knew the squabbling cramped reality of their shared apartments, and so it really was funny. The light in the eyes of laughing young Martians—even she, who never laughed, felt a small smile rearranging the unseen map of wrinkles that was her face.

And so she would end the meeting, feeling that it was work well done. What use was utopia without joy, after all? What was the point of all their striving if it did not include the laughter of the young? This was what Frank had never understood, at least not in his latter years. And so she would abandon Spencer's security procedures, and lead the people in the meetings out of their rooms and down to the dry waterfronts, or into parks or cafés, to have a walk or a drink or a late meal, feeling that she had found one of the keys to revolution, a key that Frank had never known existed, but only suspected when looking at John.

"Of course," Michel said when she returned to Odessa, and tried to tell him about it. "But Frank was not a believer in revolution anyway. He was a diplomat, a cynic, a counterrevolutionary. Joy was not in his nature. It was all damage control to him."

But Michel was often contrary with her these days. He had learned to explode rather than soothe if she showed signs she needed a fight, and she appreciated that so much that she found she didn't need to fight nearly so often. "Come on," she objected at this characterization of Frank, and shoved Michel onto their bed and ravished him, just for the fun of it, just to drag him into the realm of joy and make him admit it. She knew perfectly well that he felt it was his duty to pull her always back toward the midline of her mood oscillations, and she could see his point, no one more so, and appreciated the anchoring he tried to provide; but sometimes, soaring up at the top of the curve, she saw no reason not to enjoy it a little, those brief moments of no-g flight, something like a spiritual *status orgasmus.* . . . And so she would pull him up by the cock to that level, and make him smile for an hour or two. Then it was possible for them to walk together downstairs and out the gate, and down through the park, over to her café in a mood of relaxation and peace, there to sit with their backs to the bar, and listen to the flamenco guitarist or the old tango band, playing its *piazzollas.* Talking casually about the work around the basin. Or not talking at all.

One evening in the late summer of M-year 49, they walked down with Spencer to the café and sat through the long twilight, watching dark copper clouds that sat glowing over the distant ice, under the purple sky. The prevailing westerlies drove air masses up over the Hellespontus, so that dramatic fronts of cloud over the ice were part of their daily life, but some clouds were special—metallic lobed solid objects, like mineral statues which could never just waft away on a wind. Spitting lightning from their black bottoms onto the ice below.

And then as they watched these particular statues, there was a low rumble, and the ground trembled slightly underfoot, and the silverware chattered across the table. They grabbed their glasses and stood, along with everyone else in the café—and in the shocked silence Maya saw they were all automatically looking to the south, out toward the ice. People were pouring out of the park onto the corniche, and then standing against the tent wall in silence, looking outward. There in the fading indigo of sunset, under the copper clouds, it was just possible to see movement, a winking black and white at the edge of the white-and-black mass. Moving toward them across the plain. "Water," someone at the next table said.

Everyone moved as if in a tractor beam, glasses in hand, all other thoughts gone as they came to the tent coping at the edge of the waterfront and stood together against the chest-high wall, squinting into the shadows on the plain: black on black, with a salting of white spots, tumbling this way and that. For a second Maya recalled again the Marineris flood, and she shuddered, forced the memory back down like chyme in her esophagus, choking slightly on the acidity, doing her best to kill that part of her mind. It was the Hellas Sea coming toward her—her sea, her idea, now inundating the slope of the basin. A million plants were dying, as Sax had taught her to remember. The Low Point melt pod had been getting bigger and bigger, connecting up to other pods of liquid water, melting the rotten ice between and around them, warmed by the long summer and the bacteria and the surges of steam from explosions set in the surrounding ice. One of the northern ice walls must have broken, and now the flood was blackening the plain south of Odessa. The nearest edge was no more than fifteen kilometers away. Now most of what they could see of the basin was a salt-and-pepper jumble, the predominant pepper in the foreground shifting even as they watched to more and more salt—the land lightening at the same time that the sky was darkening, which as always gave things an unnatural aspect. Frost steam swirled up from the water, glowing with what looked to be reflected light from Odessa itself.

Perhaps half an hour passed, with everyone on the corniche standing still and watching, in a general silence that only began to end when the flood was frozen, and the twilight ended. Then there was a sudden return of human voices, and electric music from a café two down. A peal of laughter. Maya went to the bar and ordered champagne for the table, feeling her high spirits sizzle. For once her mood was in tune with events, and she was ready to celebrate the bizarre sight of their own powers unleashed, lying out there on the landscape for their inspection. She offered a toast to the café at large:

"To the Hellas Sea, and all the sailors who will sail it, dodging icebergs and storms to reach the far shore!"

Everyone cheered, and people all up and down the corniche picked it up and cheered as well, a wild moment. The gypsy band struck up a tango version of a sea chantey, and Maya felt the small smile shifting the stiff skin of her cheeks for the entire rest of that evening. Even a long discussion of the possibility of another surge washing up and over Odessa's seawall could not take that smile off her face. Down at the office they had calculated the possibilities very finely indeed, and any slopover, as they called it, was unlikely or even impossible. Odessa would be all right.

But news kept flooding in from afar, threatening to overwhelm them in its own way. On Earth the wars in Nigeria and Azania had caused bitter worldwide economic conflict between Armscor and Subarashii. Christian, Muslim, and Hindu fundamentalists were all making a vice of necessity and declaring the longevity treatment the work of Satan; great numbers of the untreated were joining these movements, taking over local governments and making direct, human-wave assaults on the metanational operations within their reach. Meanwhile all the big metanationals were trying to resuscitate the UN, and put it forth as an alternative to the World Court; and many of the biggest metanat clients, and now the Group of Eleven, were going along with it. Michel considered this a victory, as it again showed fear of the World Court. And any strengthening of an international body like the UN, he said, was better than none. But now there were two competing arbitration systems erected, one controlled by the metanats, which made it easier to avoid the one they didn't like.

And on Mars things were little better. The UNTA police were roving in the south, unhindered except by occasional unexplained explosions among their robot vehicles, and Prometheus was the latest hidden sanctuary to have been discovered and shut down. Of all the big sanctuaries only Vishniac remained hidden, and they had gone dormant in an effort to stay that way. The south polar region was no longer part of the underground.

In this context it was no surprise to see how frightened the people who came to the meetings sometimes were. It took courage to join an underground that was visibly shrinking, like Minus One Island. People were driven to it by anger, Maya supposed, and indignation and hope. But they were frightened as well. There was no assurance that this move would do any good.

And it would be so easy to plant a spy among these newcomers. Maya found it hard to trust them, sometimes. Could all of them be what they claimed to be? It was impossible to be sure of that, impossible. One night at a meeting with a lot of newcomers there was a young man in the front with a look she didn't like, and after the meeting, which was uninspired, she had gone with Spencer's friends right back to the apartment, and told Michel about it. "Don't worry," he said.

"What do you mean, *don't worry*."

He shrugged. "The members keep track of each other. They try to make sure they're all known to each other. And Spencer's team is armed."

"You never told me that."

"I thought you knew."

"Come on. Don't treat me as if I was stupid."

"I don't, Maya. Anyway, it's all we can do, unless we hide entirely."

"I'm not proposing to do that! What do you think I am, a coward?"

A sour expression crossed his face, and he said something in French. Then he took a deep breath and shouted at her in French, one of his curses. But she could see that this was a deliberate decision on his part—that he had decided the fights were good for her, and cathartic for him, so that they could be pursued, when inevitable, as a kind of therapeutic method— and this of course was intolerable. An act, a manipulation of her—without another thought she took a step into the kitchen area and picked up a copper pot and heaved it at him, and he was so surprised that he barely managed to knock it away.

"Putaine!" he roared. *"Pourquoi ce ça? Pourquoi?"*

"I won't be patronized," she told him, satisfied that he was genuinely angry now, but still blazing herself. "You damned head-shrinker, if you weren't so bad at your job the whole First Hundred wouldn't have gone crazy and this world wouldn't be so fucked up. It's all your fault." And she slammed out the door and went down to the café to brood over the awfulness of having a shrink as a partner, also over her own ugly behavior, so quick to leap out of her control and attack him. He did not come down and join her that time, though she sat around till closing.

And then, just after she had gotten home and lain down on the couch and fallen asleep, there was a knock at the door, rapid and light in a way immediately frightening, and Michel ran to it and looked through the peephole. He saw who it was and let her in. It was Marina.

Marina sat down heavily on the couch beside Maya, and with shaking hands holding theirs, said, "They took over Sabishii. Security troops. Hiroko and her whole inner circle were there visiting, as well as all the southerners who had come up since the raids. And Coyote too. All of them were there, and Nanao, and Etsu, and all the issei . . . "

"Didn't they resist?" Maya said.

"They tried. There were a bunch of people killed at the train station. That slowed them down, and I think some people might have gotten into the mohole mound maze. But they had surrounded the whole area, and they came in through the tent walls. It was just like Cairo in sixty-one, I swear."

Suddenly she started to cry, and Maya and Michel sat down on each side of her, and she put her face in her hands and sobbed. This was so out of character for the usually severe Marina that the reality of her news hit home.

She sat up and wiped her eyes and nose. Michel got her a tissue. Calmly she went on: "I'm afraid a lot of them may be killed. I was out with Vlad and Ursula in one of those outlying hermitage boulders, and we stayed there for three days, and then walked to one of the hidden garages and got out in boulder cars. Vlad went to Burroughs, Ursula to Elysium. We're trying to tell as many of the First Hundred as we can. Especially Sax and Nadia."

Maya got up and put on her clothes, then went down the hall and knocked on Spencer's door. She returned to the kitchen and put on water for tea, refusing to look at the photo of Frank, who watched her saying *I told you so. This is the way it happens.* She took teacups back into the living room, and saw that her own hands were shaking so much that hot liquid was spilling down over her fingers. Michel's face was pale and sweaty, and he wasn't hearing anything Marina was saying. Of course—if Hiroko's group had been there, then his entire family was gone, either captured or killed. She handed out the teacups, and as Spencer came in and had the story told to him, she got a robe and draped it over Michel's shoulders, excoriating herself for the miserable timing of her assault on him. She sat by him, squeezing his thigh, trying to tell him by touch that she was there, that she was his family too, and that all her games were over, to the best of her ability—no more treating him as pet or punching bag. . . . That she loved him. But his thigh was like warm ceramic, and he obviously didn't notice her hand, was scarcely even aware she was there. And it came to her that it was precisely in the moments of greatest need when people could do the least for each other.

She got up and got Spencer some tea, avoiding looking at the photo or the pale image of her face in the dark kitchen window, the pinched bleak vulture eye that she could never meet. You can never look back.

For the moment there was nothing to do but sit there, and get through the night. Try to absorb the news, to withstand it. So they sat, they talked, they listened to Marina tell her story in greater and greater detail. They made calls out on the Praxis lines, trying to find out more. They sat, slumped and silent, caged in their own reflections, their solitary universes. The minutes passed like hours, the hours like years: it was the hellish twisted spacetime of the all-night vigil, that most ancient of human rituals, where people fought without success to wrench meaning into each random catastrophe.

Dawn when it finally came was overcast, the tent spattered with raindrops. A few painfully slow hours later, Spencer began the process of contacting all the groups in Odessa. Over the course of that day and the next they spread the news, which had been suppressed on Mangalavid and the other infonets. But it was clear to all that something had happened, because of the sudden absence of Sabishii from the ordinary discourse, even in matters of common business. Rumors flew everywhere, gaining momentum in the absence of hard news, rumors of everything from Sabishii's independence to its razing. But in the tense meetings of the following week Maya and Spencer told everyone what Marina had said, and then they spent the subsequent hours discussing what should be done. Maya did her best to convince people that they should not be pushed into acting before they were ready, but it was hard going; they were furious, and frightened, and there were a lot of incidents in town and around Hellas that week, all over Mars in fact—demonstrations, minor sabotage, assaults on security positions and personnel, AI breakdowns, work slowdowns. "We've got to show them they can't get away with this!" Jackie said over the net, seeming everywhere at once. Even Art agreed with her: "I think civil protests by as much of the general population as we can muster might slow them down. Make those bastards think twice about doing anything like this again."

Nevertheless, the situation stabilized after a while. Sabishii returned to the net and to train schedules, and life there resumed, although it was not the same as before, as a big police force stayed in occupation, monitoring the gates and the station, and trying to discover all the cavities of the mound maze. During this time Maya had a number of long talks with Nadia, who was working in South Fossa, and with Nirgal and Art, and even with Ann, who called in from one of her refuges in the Aureum Chaos. They all agreed that no matter what had happened in Sabishii, they needed to hold back for the moment from any attempt at a general insurrection. Sax even called in to Spencer, to say he "needed time." Which Maya found comforting, as it supported her gut feeling that the time was not right. That they were being provoked in the hopes they would try a revolt prematurely. Ann and Kasei and Jackie and the other radicals—Harmakhis, Antar, even Zeyk—were unhappy at the wait, and pessimistic about what it meant. "You don't understand," Maya told them. "There's a whole new world growing out there, and the longer we wait, the stronger it gets. Just hold on."

Then about a month after the closing of Sabishii, they got a brief message on their wrists from Coyote—a short clip of his lopsided face, looking unusually serious, telling them that he had gotten away through the maze of secret tunnels in the mohole mound, and was now back in the south, in one of his own hideouts. "What about Hiroko?" Michel said instantly. "What about Hiroko and the rest of them?"

But Coyote was already gone.

"I don't think they got Hiroko either," Michel said instantly, walking around the room without noticing he was moving. "Not Hiroko or any of them! If they had been captured, I'm sure the Transitional Authority would have announced it. I'll bet Hiroko has taken the group underground again. They haven't been pleased with things since Dorsa Brevia, they're just not good at compromise, that's why they took off in the first place. Everything that has happened since has only confirmed their opinion that they can't trust us to build the kind of world they want. So they've used this chance and disappeared again. Maybe the crackdown on Sabishii forced them to do it without warning us."

"Maybe so," Maya said, careful to sound like she believed it. It sounded like denial on Michel's part, but if it helped him, who cared? And Hiroko was capable of anything. But Maya had to make her response plausibly Mayalike, or he would see she was only reassuring him: "But where would they go?"

"Back into the chaos, I would guess. A lot of the old shelters are still there."

"But what about you?"

"They'll let me know."

He thought it over, looked at her. "Or maybe they figure that you're my family now."

So he had felt her hand, in that first horrible hour. But he gave her such a sad crooked smile that she winced, and caught him up and tried to crush him with a hug, really crack a rib, to show him how much she loved him and how little she liked such a wan look. "They're right about that," she said harshly. "But they ought to contact you anyway."

"They will. I'm sure they will."

Maya had no idea what to think of this theory of Michel's. Coyote had in fact escaped through the mound maze, and he was likely to have helped as many of his friends as he could. And Hiroko would probably be first on that list. She would certainly grill Coyote about it next time she saw him; but then he had never told her anything before. In any case, Hiroko and her inner circle were gone. Dead, captured, or in hiding, no matter which it was a cruel blow to the cause, Hiroko being the moral center for so much of the resistance.

But she had been so strange. A part of Maya, mostly subconscious and unacknowledged, was not entirely unhappy to have Hiroko off the scene, however it had happened. Maya had never been able to communicate with Hiroko, to understand her, and though she had loved her, it had made her nervous to have such a great random force wandering about, complicating things. And it had been irritating also to have another great power among the women, a power that she had had absolutely no influence over. Of course it was horrible if the whole of her group had been captured, or worse, killed. But if they had decided to disappear again, that would not be a bad thing at all. It would simplify things at a time when they desperately needed simplification, giving Maya more potential control over the events to come.

So she hoped with all her heart that Michel's theory was true, and nodded at him, and pretended to agree in a reserved realistic way with his analysis. And then went off to the next meeting, to calm down yet another commune of angry natives. Weeks passed, then months; it seemed they had survived the crisis. But things were still degenerating on Earth, and Sabishii, their university town, the jewel of the demimonde, was functioning under a kind of martial law; and Hiroko was gone, Hiroko who was their heart. Even Maya, initially pleased in some sense to be rid of her, felt more and more oppressed by her absence. The concept of Free Mars had been part of the areophany, after all—and to be reduced to mere politics, to the survival of the fittest. . . .

The spirit seemed gone from things. And as the winter passed, and the news from Earth told of escalating conflicts, Maya noticed that people seemed more and more desperate for distraction. The partying got louder and wilder; the corniche was a nightly celebration, and on special nights, like Fassnacht or New Year's, it was jammed with everyone in town, all dancing and drinking and singing with a kind of ferocious gaiety, under the little red mottoes painted on every other wall. YOU CAN NEVER GO BACK. FREE MARS. But how? How?

New Year's that winter was especially wild; it was M-year 50, and people were celebrating the big anniversary in style. Maya walked with Michel up and down the corniche, and from behind her domino she watched curiously as the undulating dance lines passed them by, she stared at all the long young dancing bodies, the figures masked but naked to the waist for the most part, as if out of an ancient Hindu illustration, breasts and pecs bobbing gracefully to nuevo calypso steel-drum ponking. . . . Oh, it was strange! And these young aliens were ignorant, but how beautiful! How beautiful! And this town she had helped to build, standing over its dry waterfront. . . . She felt herself taking off inside, past the equinox and into the glorious rush to euphoria, and maybe it was only an accident of her biochemistry, probably so given the grim situation of the two worlds, *entre chien et loup,* but nevertheless it existed, and she felt it in her body. And so she pulled Michel into a dance line, and danced and danced until she was slippery with sweat. It felt great.

For a while they sat together in her café—quite a little reunion of the First Thirty-nine, as it turned out: she and Michel and Spencer, and Vlad and Ursula and Marina, and Yeli Zudov and Mary Dunkel, who had slipped out of Sabishii a month after the shutdown, and Mikhail Yangel, up from Dorsa Brevia, and Nadia, down from South Fossa. Ten of them. "A decimation," Mikhail noted. They ordered bottle after bottle of vodka, as if they could drown the memory of the other ninety, including their poor farm crew, who at best had just disappeared on them again, and at worst had been murdered. The Russians among them, strangely in the majority that night, began to offer up all the old toasts from home. Let's pig up! Let's get healthier! Let's pour behind the cellar! Let's get glassed! Let's get fucked! Let's fill the eyes with it! Let's lick it out! Let's wet the back of the throat! Let's buy for three! Let's suck it, pour it, knock it, grab it, beat it, flog it, swing it—and so on and so on, until Michel and Mary and Spencer were looking amazed and appalled. It's like Eskimos and snow, Mikhail told them.

And then they went back out to dance, the ten of them forming a line of their own, weaving dangerously through the crowds of youngsters. Fifty long Martian years, and still they survived, still they danced! It was a miracle!

But as always in the all-too-predictable fluctuation of Maya's moods, there came that stall at the top, that sudden downturn—tonight, begun as she noticed the drugged eyes behind the other masks, saw how everyone was on their way out, doing their best to escape into their own private world, where they didn't have to connect with anyone except that night's lover. And they were no different. "Let's go home," she said to Michel, who was still bouncing along before her in time to the bands, enjoying the sight of all the lean Martian youngsters. "I can't stand this."

But he wanted to stay, and so did the others, and in the end she went home by herself, through the gate and the garden and up the stairs to their apartment. The noise of the celebration was loud behind her.

And there on the cabinet over the sink the young Frank smiled at her distress. Of course it goes this way, the youth's intent look said. I know this story too—I learned it the hard way. Anniversaries, marriages, happy moments—they blow away. They're gone. They never meant a thing. The smile tight, fierce, determined; and the eyes . . . it was like looking in the windows of an empty house. She knocked a coffee cup off the counter and it broke on the floor; the handle spun there and she cried out loud, sank to the floor and wrapped her arms around her knees and wept.

Then in the new year came news of heightened security measures in Odessa itself. It seemed that UNTA had learned the lesson of Sabishii, and was going to clamp down on the other cities more subtly: new passports, security checks at every gate and garage, restricted access to the trains. It was rumored they were hunting the First Hundred in particular, accusing them of attempting to overthrow the Transitional Authority.

Nevertheless Maya wanted to keep going to the Free Mars meetings, and Spencer kept agreeing to take her. "As long as we can," she said. And so one night they walked together up the long stone staircases of the upper town. Michel was with them for the first time since the assault on Sabishii, and it seemed to Maya that he was recovering fairly well from the blow of the news, from that awful night after Marina's knock on the door.

But they were joined at this meeting by Jackie Boone and the rest of her crowd, Antar and the zygotes, who had arrived in Odessa on the circumHellas train, on the run from the UNTA troops in the south, and rabidly angry at the assault on Sabishii, more militant than ever. The disappearance of Hiroko and her inner group had sent the ectogenes over the edge; Hiroko was mother to many of them, after all, and they all seemed in agreement that it was time to come out from cover and start a full-scale rebellion. Not a minute to lose, Jackie told the meeting, if they wanted to rescue the Sabishiians and the hidden colonists.

"I don't think they got Hiroko's people," Michel said. "I think they went underground with Coyote."

"You wish," Jackie told him, and Maya felt her upper lip curl.

Michel said, "They would have signaled us if they were truly in trouble."

Jackie shook her head. "They wouldn't go into hiding again, now that things are going critical." Harmakhis and Rachel nodded. "And besides, what about the Sabishiians, and the lockup of Sheffield? And it's going to happen here too. No, the Transitional Authority is taking over everywhere. We have to act now!"

"The Sabishiians have sued the Transitional Authority," Michel said, "and they're all still in Sabishii, walking around."

Jackie just look disgusted, as if Michel were a fool, a weak overoptimistic frightened fool. Maya's pulse jumped, and she could feel her teeth pressing together.

"We can't act now," she said sharply. "We're not ready."

Jackie glared at her. "We'll never be ready according to you! We'll wait until they've got a lock on the whole planet, and then we won't be able to do anything even if we wanted to. Which is just how you'd like it, I'm sure."

Maya shot out of her chair. "There is no *they* anymore. There are four or five metanationals fighting over Mars, just like they're fighting over Earth. If we stand up in the middle of it we'll just get cut down in the crossfire. We need to pick our moment, and that has to be when they've hurt each other, and we have a real chance to succeed. Otherwise we get the moment imposed on us, and it's just like sixty-one, it's just flailing about and chaos and people getting killed!"

"Sixty-one," Jackie cried, "it's always sixty-one with you—the perfect excuse for doing nothing! Sabishii and Sheffield are shut down and Burroughs is close, and Hiranyag and Odessa will be next, and the elevator is bringing down police every day and they've got hundreds of people killed or imprisoned, like my grandmother who is the real leader of us all, and all you talk about is sixty-one! Sixty-one has made you a coward!"

Maya lunged out and slapped her hard on the side of the head, and Jackie leaped on her and Maya fell back into a table's edge and the breath whooshed out of her. She was being punched but managed to catch one of Jackie's wrists, and she bit into the straining forearm as hard as she could, really trying to sever things. Then they were jerked apart and held onto, the room bedlam, everyone shouting including Jackie, who shouted "Bitch! Bitch! Bitch! *Murderer!*" and Maya heard words grating out of her own throat as well, "Stupid little slut, stupid little slut," between gasps for air. Her ribs and teeth hurt. People were holding hands over her mouth and Jackie's too, people were hissing "Sssh, sssh, quiet, they'll hear us, they'll report us, the police will come!"

Finally Michel took his hand from Maya's mouth and she hissed "Stupid little slut" one last time, then sat back in a chair and looked at them all with a glare that caught and stilled at least half of them. Jackie was released and she started to curse in a low voice and Maya snapped, *"Shut up!"* so viciously that Michel stepped between them again. "Towing all your boys around by the cock and thinking you're a leader," Maya snarled in a whisper, "and all without a single thought in your empty head—"

"I won't listen to this!" Jackie cried, and everyone said *"Ssssh!"* and she was off, out into the hall. That was a mistake, a retreat, and Maya stood back up and used the time to castigate the rest of them in a tearing whisper for their stupidity—and then, when she had controlled her temper a little, to argue the case for biding their time, the excoriating edge of her anger just under the surface of a rational plea for patience and intention and control, an argument that was essentially unanswerable. All through this peroration everyone in the room was of course staring at her as if she were some bloodied gladiator, the Black Widow indeed, and as her teeth still hurt from sinking them into Jackie's arm she could scarcely pretend to be the perfect model of intelligent debate; she felt like her mouth must be puffed up, it throbbed so, and she fought a rising sense of humiliation and carried on, cold and passionate and overbearing. The meeting ended in a sullen and mostly unspoken agreement to delay any mass insurrection and continue lying low, and the next thing she knew she was slumped on a tram seat between Michel and Spencer, trying not to cry. They would have to put up Jackie and the rest of her group while they were in Odessa— theirs was the safe house, after all. So it was a situation she wasn't going to be able to escape. And meanwhile there were police officers standing in front of the town's physical plant and offices, checking wrists before they let people inside. If she didn't go to work again they very well might try to track her down to ask why, and if she went to work and got checked, it wasn't certain that her wrist ID and Swiss passport would pass her. There were rumors that the post-'61 balkanization of information was beginning to collapse back into some larger integrated systems, which had recovered some prewar data; thus the requirement of new passports. And if she ran into one of those systems, that would be that. Shipped off to the asteroids or to Kasei Vallis, to be tortured and have her mind wrecked like Sax. "Maybe it is time," she said to Michel and Spencer. "If they lock up all the cities and the pistes, what other choice do we have?"

They didn't answer. They didn't know what to do any more than she did. Suddenly the whole independence project again seemed a fantasy, a dream that was just as impossible now as it had been when Arkady had espoused it, Arkady who had been so cheerful and so wrong. They would never be free of Earth, never. They were helpless before it.

"I want to talk to Sax first," Spencer said.

"And Coyote," Michel said. "I want to ask him more about what happened in Sabishii."

"And Nadia," Maya said, and her throat tightened; Nadia would have been ashamed of her if she had seen her at that meeting, and that hurt. She needed Nadia, the only person on Mars whose judgment she still trusted.

"There's something odd going on with the atmosphere," Spencer complained to Michel as they changed trams. "I really want to hear what Sax has to say about it. Oxygen levels are rising faster than I would have expected, especially on north Tharsis. It's like some really successful bacteria has been distributed without any suicide genes in it. Sax has basically reassembled his old Echus Overlook team, everyone still alive, and they've been working at Acheron and Da Vinci on projects they're not telling us about. It's like those damn windmill heaters. So I want to talk to him. We have to get together on this, or else—"

"Or else sixty-one!" Maya insisted.

"I know, I know. You're right about that, Maya, I mean I agree. I hope enough of the rest of us do."

"We're going to have to do more than hope."

Which meant she was going to have to get out there and do it herself. Go fully underground, move from city to city, from safe house to safe house as Nirgal had been doing for years, without a job or a home, meeting with as many of the revolutionary cells as she could, trying to hold them on board. Or at least keep them from popping off too soon. Working on the Hellas Sea project wasn't going to be possible anymore.

So this life was over. She got off the tram and glanced briefly through the park down the corniche, then turned and walked up to their gate and through the garden, up the stairwell, down the familiar hall, feeling heavy and old and very, very tired. She stuck the right key into the lock without thinking about it, and walked into the apartment and looked at her things, at Michel's stacks of books, the Kandinsky print over the couch, Spencer's sketches, the battered coffee table, the battered dining table and chairs, the kitchen nook with everything in its place, including the little face on the cabinet by the sink. How many lifetimes ago had she known that face? All these pieces of furniture would go their ways. She stood in the middle of the room, drained and desolate, grieving for these years that had slipped by almost without noticing; almost a decade of productive work, of real life, now blowing away in this latest gale of history, a paroxysm that she was going to have to try to direct or at least ride out, trying her best to nudge it in ways that would allow them to survive. Damn the world, damn its intrusiveness, its mindless charge, its inexorable roll through the present, wrecking lives as it went. . . . She had liked this apartment and this town and this life, with Michel and Spencer and Diana and all her colleagues at work, all her habits and her music and her small daily pleasures.

She looked glumly at Michel, who stood behind her in the doorway, staring around as if trying to commit the place to memory. A Gallic shrug: "Nostalgia in advance," he said, trying to smile. He felt it too—he understood—it wasn't just her mood, this time, but reality itself.

She made an effort and smiled back, walked over and held his hand. Downstairs there was a clatter as the Zygote gang came up the stairs. They could stay in Spencer's apartment, the bastards. "If it works out," she said, "we'll come back someday."

They walked down to the station in the fresh morning light, past all the cafés, still chairs-on-tables wet. At the station they risked their old IDs and got tickets without trouble, and took a counterclockwise train down to Montepulciano, and got into rented walkers and helmets, and walked out of the tent and down the hill and off the map of the surface world, into one of the steep ravines of the foothills. There Coyote was waiting for them in a boulder car, and he drove them through the heart of the Hellespontus, up a forking network of valleys, over pass after pass in this mountain range that was just as chaotic as rock falling from the sky implied, a nightmare maze of a wilderness—until they were down the western slope, past Rabe Crater and onto the crater-ringed hills of the Noachis highlands. And so they were off the net again, wandering as Maya never had before.

Coyote helped a lot in the early part of this period. He was not the same, Maya thought—subdued by the takeover of Sabishii, even worried. He wouldn't answer their questions about Hiroko and the hidden colonists; he said "I don't know" so often that she began to believe him, especially when his face finally twisted up into a recognizably human expression of distress, the famous invulnerable insouciance finally shattered. "I truly don't know whether they got out or not. I was already out in the mound maze when the takeover started, and I got out in a car as fast as I could, thinking I could help the most from outside. But no one else came out from that exit. But I was on the north side, and they could have gotten out to the south. They were staying in the mound maze too, and Hiroko has emergency shelters just like I do. But I just don't know."

"Then let's go see if we can find out," she said.

So he drove them north, at one point going under the Sheffield-Burroughs piste, using a long tunnel just bigger than his car; they spent the night in this black slot, restocking from recessed closets and sleeping the uneasy sleep of spelunkers. Near Sabishii they descended into another hidden tunnel, and drove for several kilometers until they came into a small cave of a garage; it was part of the Sabishiians' mound maze, and the squared stone caves behind it were like Neolithic passage tombs, now lit with strip lighting and warmed from vents. They were greeted down there by Nanao Nakayama, one of the issei, who seemed just as cheerful as ever. Sabishii had been returned to them, more or less, and though there were UNTA police in town and especially at the gates and the train station, the police were still unaware of the full extent of the mound complexes, and so not able to completely stop Sabishii's efforts to help the underground. Sabishii was no longer an open demimonde, as he put it, but they were still working.

And yet he, too, did not know what had happened to Hiroko. "We didn't see the police take any of them away," he said. "But we didn't find Hiroko and her group down here either, after things had calmed down. We don't know where they went." He tugged at his turquoise earring, obviously mystified. "I think they are probably off on their own. Hiroko was always careful to have a bolt-hole everywhere she went, that is what Iwao told me once when we drank a lot of sake down at the duck pond. And it seems to me that disappearance is a habit of Hiroko's, but not of the Transitional Authority. So we can infer that she chose to do this. But come on—you must want a bath and some food, and then if you could talk to some of the sansei and yonsei who have gone into hiding with us, that would be good for them."

So they stayed in the maze for a week or two, and Maya met with several groups of the newly disappeared. She spent most of her time encouraging them, assuring them that they would be able to reemerge onto the surface, even into Sabishii itself, quite soon; security was hardening, but the nets were simply too permeable, and the alternative economy too large, to allow for total control. Switzerland would give them new passports, Praxis would give them jobs, and they would be back in business. The important thing was to coordinate their efforts, and to resist the temptation to lash out too early.

Nanao told her after one such meeting that Nadia was making similar appeals in South Fossa, and that Sax's team was begging them for more time; so there was some agreement on the policy, at least among the old-timers. And Nirgal was working closely with Nadia, supporting the policy as well. So it was the more radical groups that they would have to work hardest to rein in, and here Coyote had the most influence. He wanted to visit some of the Red refuges in person, and Maya and Michel went with him, to catch a ride up to Burroughs.

The region between Sabishii and Burroughs was saturated with crater impacts, so that they wound through the nights between flat-topped circular hills, stopping every dawn at small rim shelters crowded with Reds who were none too hospitable to Maya and Michel. But they listened to Coyote very attentively, and traded news with him about scores of places Maya had never heard of. On the third night of this they came down the steep slope of the Great Escarpment, through an archipelago of mesa islands, and abruptly onto the smooth plain of Isidis. They could see down the slope of the basin for a long way, all the way out to where a mound like the Sabishiians' mohole mound ran across the land, in a great curve from Du Martheray Crater on the Great Escarpment, northwest toward Syrtis. This was the new dike, Coyote told them, built by a robot collection pulled from the Elysium mohole. The dike was truly massive, and looked like one of the basalt dorsa of the south, except that its velvety texture revealed it to be excavated regolith rather than hard volcanic rock.

Maya stared at the long ridge. The cascading recombinant consequences of their actions were, she thought, out of their control. They could try to build bulwarks to contain them—but would the bulwarks hold?

Then they were back in Burroughs, in through the Southeast Gate on their Swiss IDs, and secured in a safe house run by Bogdanovists from Vishniac, now working for Praxis. The safe house was an airy light-filled apartment about halfway up the northern wall of Hunt Mesa, with a view out over the central valley to Branch Mesa and Double Decker Butte. The apartment above it was a dance studio, and many of the hours of the day they lived to a faint *thump, thump, thump-thump, thump-thump.* Just over the horizon to the north an irregular cloud of dust and steam marked where the robots were working still on the dike; every morning Maya looked out at it, thinking over the news reports on Mangalavid and in the long messages from Praxis. Then it was into the day's work, which was entirely underground, and often confined to meetings in the apartment, or to work there on video messages. So it was not at all like life in Odessa, and it was hard to develop any habits, which made her feel jangly and dark.

But she could still walk the streets of the great city, one anonymous citizen among thousands of others—strolling by the canal, or sitting in restaurants around Princess Park, or on one of the less trendy mesa tops. And everywhere she went, she saw the neat red print of their stenciled graffiti: FREE MARS. Or GET READY. Or, as if she were hallucinating a warning made to her by her own soul: YOU CAN NEVER GO BACK. These messages were ignored by the populace as far as she could tell, never discussed, and often removed by cleaning crews; but they kept popping up in their neat red, usually in English but sometimes in Russian, the old alphabet like a long-lost friend, like some subliminal flash out of their collective unconscious, if they had one; and somehow the messages never lost their little electric shock. It was strange what powerful effects could be created with such simple means. People might come to do almost anything, if they talked about it long enough.

Her meetings with small cells of the various resistance organizations went well, although it became clearer to her that there were profound divisions of all kinds among them, particularly the dislike that the Reds and Marsfirsters had for the Bogdanovists and Free Mars groups, whom the Reds considered green, and thus one more manifestation of the enemy. That could be trouble. But Maya did what she could, and everyone at least listened to her, so that she felt she made some progress. And slowly she warmed to Burroughs, and her hidden life there. Michel arranged a routine for her with the Swiss and Praxis, and with the Bogdanovists now tucked away in the city—a secure routine, which allowed her to meet groups fairly frequently without ever compromising the integrity of the safe houses they had established. And every meeting seemed to help a little. The only intransigent problem was that so many groups seemed to want to revolt immediately—Red or green, they tended to follow the radical lead of Ann's Reds in the outback, and the young hotheads surrounding Jackie, and there were more and more incidents of sabotage in the cities, which caused a corresponding increase in police surveillance, until it seemed very possible that things could break wide open. Maya began to see herself as a kind of brake, and she often lost sleep worrying about how little people wanted to hear that message. On the other hand she was also the one who had to keep the old Bogdanovists and other veterans aware of the power of the native movement, cheering them up when they got depressed. Ann in the outback with the Reds, grimly wrecking stations: "It's not going to happen like that," Maya told her over and over, though there was no sign that Ann was getting the message.

Still, there were encouraging signs. Nadia was in South Fossa, building a strong movement there which seemed under her influence, and closely aligned with Nirgal and his crowd. Vlad and Ursula and Marina had re-occupied their old labs at Acheron, under the aegis of the Praxis bio-engineering company nominally in charge. They were in constant communication with Sax, who was in a refuge in Da Vinci Crater with his old terraforming team, being supported by the Dorsa Brevia Minoans. The inhabitation of that great lava tube had extended north much farther than it had been during the time of the congress, and most of the new segments apparently were devoted to shelter for the refugees from the wrecked or abandoned sanctuaries farther south, and a whole string of manufactories. Maya watched videos of people driving about in little cars from segment to tented segment, working under the clear brown light pouring down from the filtered skylights, engaged in what could only be called military production; they were building stealth fliers, stealth cars, surface-to-space missiles, reinforced block shelters (some of which were already installed in the lava tube itself, in case it was ever broached)—also air-to-ground missiles, antivehicle weapons, handguns, and, the Minoans told Maya, a variety of ecological weapons Sax was designing himself.

This kind of work, and the destruction of the southern sanctuaries, had created what looked from a distance like a sort of war fever in Dorsa Brevia, and Maya was worried by that too. Sax, at the heart of it, was a stubborn secretive brilliant brain-damaged loose cannon, a bona fide mad scientist. He had still never spoken to her directly; and his strikes against the aerial lens and Deimos, while very effective, had in her opinion caused UNTA's intensification of the assault on the south. She kept sending down messages advising restraint and patience, until Ariadne replied irritably, "Maya, we know. We're working with Sax here, we've got an idea of what we're up to, and what you're saying is either obvious or wrong. Talk to the Reds if you want to help, but we don't need it."

Maya cursed the video and talked to Spencer about it. Spencer said, "Sax thinks if we're going to pull this off we might need some weapons, if only in reserve. It seems sensible to me."

"What happened to the idea of a decapitation?"

"Maybe he thinks he's building the guillotine. Look, talk to Nirgal and Art about that. Or even Jackie."

"Right. Look, I want to talk to *Sax*. He's *got* to talk to me sometime, goddammit. Get him to talk to me, will you?"

Spencer agreed to try, and one morning he arranged a call over his private line to Sax. It was Art who answered the call, but he promised to try to get Sax to come to the line. "He's busy these days, Maya. I like to see it. People are calling him General Sax."

"God forbid."

"That's all right. They talk about General Nadia too, and General Maya."

"That's not what they call me." The Black Widow, more like, or the Bitch. The Killer. She knew.

And Art's squint told her she was right. "Well," he said, "whatever. With Sax it's kind of a joke. People talk about the revenge of the lab rats, that kind of thing."

"I don't like it." The idea of another revolution seemed to be gaining a life of its own now, a momentum independent of any real logic; it was just something they were doing, were always going to have done. Out of her control, and out of anyone else's control. Even their collective efforts, scattered and hidden as they were, seemed not to be coordinated or conceived with any clear idea of what they were going to try to do, or why. It was just happening.

She tried to express some of this to Art, and he nodded. "That's history, I guess. It's messy. You just have to ride the tiger and hold on. You've got a lot of different people in this movement, and they all have their own ideas. But look, I think we're doing better than last time. I'm working on some initiatives back on Earth, negotiating with Switzerland and some people at the World Court and so on. And Praxis is keeping us really well informed about what's going on among the metanationals on Earth, which means we won't just get swept into something we don't understand."

"True," Maya admitted. The news and analysis packages sent up from Praxis were more thorough by far than any commercial news shows, and as the metanationals continued to drift into what was being called the metanatricide, they on Mars, in their sanctuaries and safe houses, were able to follow it blow by blow. Subarashii taking over Mitsubishi, and then its old foe Armscor, and then falling out with Amexx, which was working hard on breaking the United States out of the Group of Eleven; they saw it all from the inside. Nothing could have been less like the situation in the 2050s. And that was a comfort, if a very small one.

And then there was Sax on the screen behind Art, and looking at her. He saw who it was, and said, "Maya!"

She swallowed hard. Was she forgiven, then, for Phyllis? Did he understand why she had done it? His new face gave her no clues—it was as impassive as his old one had been, and harder to read because so unfamiliar still.

She collected herself, asked him what his plans were.

He said, "No plan. We're still making preparations. We need to wait for a *trigger*. A trigger event. Very important. There are a couple of possibilities I'm keeping an eye against. But nothing yet."

"Fine," she said. "But listen, Sax." And then she told him everything she had been worrying about—the strength of the Transitional Authority troops, bolstered as they were by the big centrist metanats; the constant edging toward violence in the more radical wings of the underground; the feeling that they were falling into the same old pattern. And as she spoke he blinked in his old fashion, so that she knew it was really him listening under that new face—finally listening to her again, so that she went on longer than she had intended to, pouring out everything, her distrust of Jackie, her fear at being in Burroughs, everything. It was like talking to a confessor, or pleading—begging their pure rational scientist not to let things go crazy again. Not to go crazy again himself. She heard herself babbling, and realized how frightened she was.

And he blinked in what seemed a kind of neuter, ratlike sympathy. But in the end he shrugged and said little. This was General Sax now, remote, taciturn, speaking to her from the strange world inside his new mind.

"Give me twelve months," he said to her. "I need twelve more months."

"Okay, Sax." She felt reassured, somehow. "I'll do my best."

"Thanks, Maya."

And he was gone. She sat there staring at the little AI screen, feeling drained, teary, relieved. Absolved, for the hour.

So she returned to the work with a will, meeting groups almost every week, and making occasional off-the-net trips to Elysium and Tharsis, to talk to cells in the high cities. Coyote took charge of her travel, flying her across the planet in night voyages that reminded her of '61. Michel took charge of her security, protecting her with the help of a team of natives, including several of the Zygote ectogenes, who moved her from safe house to safe house in every city they visited. And she talked and talked and talked. It was not just a matter of getting them to wait, but also coordinating them, forcing them to agree they were on the same side. Sometimes it seemed that she was having an effect, she could see it on the faces of the people who came to listen. Other times her whole effort was devoted to applying the brakes (worn, burning) to radical elements. There were a lot of these now, and more every day: Ann and the Reds, Kasei's Marsfirsters, the Bogdanovists under Mikhail, Jackie's "Booneans," the Arab radicals led by Antar, who was one of Jackie's many boyfriends—Coyote, Harmakhis, Rachel. . . . It was like trying to stop an avalanche that she herself was caught up in, grasping at clumps even as she rolled down with them. In such a situation the disappearance of Hiroko began to loom as more and more of a disaster.

The attacks of déjà vu returned, stronger than ever. She had lived in Burroughs before, in a time like this—perhaps that was all it was. But the feeling was so disturbing when it struck, this profound unshakable conviction that everything had happened before in exactly this way, as ineluctably as if eternal recurrence were really true. . . . So that she would wake up and go to the bathroom, and certainly all that had happened before in just that way, including all the stiffness and small aches and pains; and then she would walk out to meet with Nirgal and some of his friends, and recognize that it was a genuine attack and not just a coincidence. Everything had happened just like this before, it was all clockwork. Strokes of fate. Okay, she would think, ignore it. That's reality, then. We are creatures of fate. At least you don't know what will happen next.

She talked endlessly with Nirgal, trying to understand him, and get him to understand her. She learned from him, she imitated him in meetings now—his bright friendly quiet confidence, which so obviously drew people to him. They both were famous, they both were talked about on the news, they both were on UNTA's wanted list. They both had to stay off the streets now. So they had a bond, and she learned all she could from him, and she thought he learned from her as well. She had an influence, anyway. It was a good relationship, her best link to the young. He made her happy. He gave her hope.

But to have it all happen in the remorseless grip of an overmastering fate! The seen-again, the always-already: nothing but brain chemistry, Michel said. There was simply a neural delay or repetition, which was giving her the sensation that the present was a kind of past as well. As maybe it was. So she accepted his diagnosis, and took whatever drugs he prescribed, without complaint and without hope. Every morning and evening she opened the pocket in the container strip he prepared for her every week, and took whatever pills were in it, without asking questions. She did not lash out at him; she no longer felt the urge. Perhaps the night of the vigil in Odessa had cured her. Perhaps he had finally mixed the right cocktail of drugs. She hoped so. She went out with Nirgal to meetings, returned to the apartment under the dance studio, exhausted. And yet very often insomniac. Her health got bad, she was sick often, digestive troubles, sciatica, chest pains. . . . Ursula recommended another course of the gerontological treatment. Always helps, she said. And with the latest genomic mismatch scanning techniques, faster than ever. She would only have to take a week off, at most. But Maya didn't feel like she had a week to take off. Later, she told Ursula. When this is all over.

Some nights when she couldn't sleep, she read about Frank. She had taken the photo from the Odessa apartment with her, and now it was stuck to the wall by her bed in the Hunt Mesa safe house. She still felt the pressure of that electrifying gaze, and so sometimes in the sleepless hours she read about him, and tried to learn more about his diplomatic efforts. She hoped to find things he had been good at to imitate, and also to identify what he had done that she thought had been wrong.

One night in the apartment, after a tense visit to Sabishii and the community still hidden in its mound maze, she fell asleep over her lectern, which had been displaying a book about Frank. Then a dream about him woke her. Restlessly she went out to the living room of the apartment and got a drink of water, and went back and began to read the book again.

This one focused on the years between the treaty conference of 2057 and the outbreak of the unrest in 2061. These were the years when Maya had been closest to him, but she remembered them poorly, as if by flashes of lightning—moments of electric intensity, separated by long stretches of pure darkness. And the account in this particular book sparked no feelings of recognition in her at all, despite that fact that she was mentioned fairly frequently in the text. A kind of historical *jamais vu*.

Coyote was sleeping on the couch, and he groaned in some dream of his own, and woke and looked around to find the source of the light. He padded behind her on the way to the bathroom, looked over her shoulder.

"Ah," he said meaningfully. "They say a lot about him." And he went down the hall.

When he came back Maya said, "I suppose you know better."

"I know some things about Frank that they don't, that's for sure."

Maya stared at him. "Don't tell me. You were in Nicosia too." Then she remembered reading that, somewhere.

"I was, now you mention it."

He sat down heavily on his couch, stared at the floor. "I saw Frank that night, throwing bricks through windows. He started that riot single-handed."

He looked up, met her stare. "He was speaking to Selim el-Hayil in the apex park, about a half hour before John was attacked. You figure it out for yourself."

Maya clenched her teeth and stared at the lectern, ignoring him.

He stretched out on the couch and began to snore.

It was old news, really. And as Zeyk had made clear, no one would ever untangle that knot, no matter what they had seen or thought they remembered seeing. No one could be sure of anything that far in the past, not even of their own memories, which shifted subtly at every rehearsal. The only memories one could trust were those unbidden eruptions from the depths, the *mémoires involuntaires,* which were so vivid they had to be true—but often concerned unimportant events. No. Coyote's was just one more unreliable account among all the rest.

When the words of the text on the screen started registering again, she read on.

> Chalmers's efforts to stop the outbreak of violence in 2061 were unsuccessful because in the end he was simply ignorant of the full extent of the problem. Like most of the rest of the First Hundred, he could never quite imagine the actual population of Mars in the 2050s, which was well over a million; and while he thought that the resistance was led and coordinated by Arkady Bogdanov, because he knew him, he was unaware of the influence of Oskar Schnelling in Korolyov, or of the widespread red movements such as Free Elysium, or the unnamed disappeareds who left the established settlements by the hundreds. Through ignorance and a failure of the imagination, he addressed only a small fraction of the problem.

Maya pulled back, stretched, looked over at Coyote. Was that really true? She tried to think back into those years, to remember. Frank had been aware, hadn't he? "Playing with needles when the roots are sick." Hadn't Frank said that to her, sometime in that period?

She couldn't remember. *Playing with needles when the roots are sick.* The statement hung there, separated from anything else, from any context that could give it meaning. But she had the very strong impression that Frank had been aware that there was a huge unseen pool of resentment and resistance out there; no one had been more aware of it, in fact! How could this writer have missed that! For that matter how could any historian, sitting in a chair and sifting through the records, ever know what they had known, ever capture the way it had felt at the time, the fractured kaleidoscopic nature of the daily crisis? Each moment of the storm they had struggled. . . .

She tried to remember Frank's face, and there came to her an image of him, hunched over miserably at a café table, a white coffee cup handle spinning under his feet; and she had broken the coffee cup; but why? She couldn't remember. She clicked forward through the book on the screen, flying through months with every paragraph, the dry analysis utterly divorced from anything like what she could recall. Then a sentence caught her eye, and she read on as if a hand were at her throat, forcing her to:

> Ever after their first liaison in Antarctica, Toitovna had a hold over Chalmers that he never broke, no matter how much it damaged his own plans. Thus when he returned from Elysium in the final month before the Unrest broke out, Toitovna met him in Burroughs, and they stayed together for a week, during which it was clear to others they were fighting; Chalmers wanted to stay in Burroughs, where the conflict was at a crisis; Toitovna wanted him to return to Sheffield. One night he showed up in one of the cafés by the canal so angry and distraught that the waiters were afraid, and when Toitovna appeared, they expected him to explode. But he only sat there as she reminded him of every connection they had ever had, every debt owed, all their past together, such as it was; and finally he bowed to her wishes, and returned to Sheffield, where he was unable to control the growing violence in Elysium and Burroughs. And so the revolution came.

Maya stared at the screen. It was wrong, wrong, wrong, all wrong— nothing like that had happened! A liaison in Antarctica? No, never!

But she had once confronted him at some restaurant . . . no doubt it was possible they had been observed . . . so hard to say. But this book was stupid—stuffed with unwarranted speculation—not history at all. Or maybe all the histories would be like that, if one had really been there and so could judge them properly. All lies. She tried to call it back—she clenched her teeth, and stiffened, and her fingers curled as if she could dig out thoughts with them. But it was like clawing at rock. And now when she tried to remember that particular confrontation in a café, no visual image at all came into her mind; the phrases from the book overlaid them, *She reminded him of every connection they had ever had* no! No! A figure hunched at a table, there it was, the image itself—and it finally looked up at her—

But it was the youthful face from her kitchen wall in Odessa.

She groaned; she began to cry; she chewed at her clenched fists and wept.

"You okay?" Coyote said blearily from the couch.

"No."

"Find something?"

"No."

Frank was being erased by books. And by time. The years had passed, and for her, even for her, Frank Chalmers was becoming nothing but one tiny historical figure among many others, standing out there like a person seen through the wrong end of the telescope. A name in a book. Someone to read about, along with Bismarck, Talleyrand, Machiavelli. And her Frank . . . gone.

She spent a few hours of most days going over the Praxis reports with Art, trying to find patterns and comprehend them. They were getting such great amounts of data through Praxis that they had the reverse of the problem they had had in the pre-'61 crisis—not too little information, but too much. Every day the screws tightened in a multitude of crises, and Maya often ended up near despair. Several countries attending the UN, all of them Consolidated or Subarashii clients, requested that the World Court be abolished, as its functions were redundant. Most of the metanats immediately declared their support for this idea, and as the World Court had long ago begun as an agency of the UN, there were those who claimed the action would be legal and have some historical reason for being—but the first result was to disrupt some of the arbitrations in process, leading to fighting in Ukraine and Greece. "Who's responsible?" Maya exclaimed to Art. "Is there anyone *doing* this stuff?"

"Of course. Some metanats have presidents, and they all have executive boards, and they get together and talk things over, and decide what orders to give. It's like Fort and the eighteen immortals in Praxis, although Praxis is more democratic than most. And then the metanat boards appoint the executive committee for the Transitional Authority, and the Authority makes some local decisions, and I could give you their names, but I don't think they're as powerful as the folks back home."

"Never mind." Of course people were responsible. But no one was in control. It was the same on both sides, no doubt. Certainly it was true in the resistance. Sabotage, against the Vastitas ocean platforms particularly, was now pandemic, and she knew whose idea that was. She talked with Nadia about getting in touch with Ann, but Nadia just shook her head. "Not a chance. I haven't been able to talk to Ann since Dorsa Brevia. She's one of the most radical Reds there is."

"As always."

"Well, I don't think she used to be. But it doesn't matter now."

Maya shook her head and went back to work. She spent more and more time working with Nirgal, taking his instruction and advising him in turn. More than ever he was her best contact among the young, and the most powerful, and a moderate to boot; he wanted to wait for a trigger and then organize a concerted action just like she did, and this of course was one of the reasons she gravitated to him. But it was also just a matter of his character, his warmth and high spirits, his regard for her. He couldn't have been more different than Jackie, although Maya knew the two of them had a very close complex relationship, going right back into their childhoods. But they appeared to be estranged these days, which she was not at all unhappy to see, and very much at odds politically. Jackie, like Nirgal, was a charismatic leader, and recruiting big new crowds into her "Boonean" wing of Marsfirst, which advocated immediate action, and thus aligned her much more with Harmakhis than Nirgal, politically in any case. Maya did everything she could to back Nirgal in this split among the natives: in every meeting she argued for policies and actions that were green, moderate, nonviolent, and coordinated from a center. But she could see that the majority of the newly politicized natives in the cities were attracted to Jackie and Marsfirst, which was generally Red, radical, violent, and anarchic—or so she saw it. And the increasing strikes, demonstrations, street fights, sabotage, and ecotage tended to support her analysis.

And it wasn't just most of the new native recruits going to Jackie, but also great numbers of disaffected emigrants, the most recent arrivals. This tendency baffled her, and she complained about it to Art one day after they had gone through the Praxis report.

"Well," he said diplomatically, "it's good to have as many emigrants on our side as possible."

Of course when he wasn't on-line to Earth he was spending much of his time shuttling around between resistance groups trying to get them to agree, so this was his party line. "But why are they joining *her?*" Maya demanded.

"Well . . . " Art said, waggling a hand, "you know, these emigrants arrive, and some of them hear about the demonstrations, or they see one, and they ask around and hear stories, and some hear that if they go out and join in a demonstration then the natives will really like them for it, you know? Some of the young native women maybe, who they hear can be friendly, right? *Very* friendly. So they go out there thinking that maybe if they help out, one of these big girls will take them home at the end of the day."

"Come on," Maya said.

"Well, you know," Art said. "It does happen to some of them."

"And so of course our Jackie gets all the new recruits."

"Well, I'm not sure it isn't a factor for Nirgal as well. And I don't know that people are making that much of a party distinction between them. That's a fine point, something you're more aware of than them."

"Hmm."

She remembered Michel, telling her it was important to argue for what she loved, as well as against what she hated. And she loved Nirgal, it was true. He was a wonderful young man, the finest native of them all. Certainly it was not right to scorn those kinds of motivations, that erotic energy taking people into the streets. . . . Still, if only people would be more *sensible*. Jackie was doing her damnedest to lead them into yet another spastic unplanned revolt, and the results of that could be *disastrous.*

"It's part of why people follow you too, Maya."

"What?"

"You heard me."

"Come on. Don't be a fool."

Although it was nice to think so. Perhaps she could extend the struggle for control to that level too. Although she would be at a disadvantage. Create a party of the old. Well, in effect that's what they were already. That had been her whole idea, back in Sabishii—that the issei would take over the resistance, and guide it on the right course. And a good number of them had devoted many years of their life to doing just that. But in fact it hadn't worked. They were outnumbered. And the new majority was a new species, with new minds of their own. The issei could only ride the tiger. Do the best they could. She sighed.

"Tired?"

"Exhausted. This work is going to kill me."

"Get some rest."

"Sometimes when I talk to these people I feel like such a cautious, conservative coward of a naysayer. Always don't do this, don't do that. I get so sick of it. I wonder sometimes if Jackie isn't right."

"Are you kidding?" Art said, eyes wide. "You're the one holding this show together, Maya. You and Nadia and Nirgal. And me. But you're the one with the, the aura." The reputation as a murderer, he meant. "You're just tired. Get some rest. It's almost the timeslip."

Michel woke her up some other night: on the other side of the planet Armscor security units supposedly integrated into Subarashii had taken control of the elevator from regular Subarashii police, and in the hour of uncertainty a group of Marsfirsters had tried to seize the new Socket outside Sheffield. The attempt had failed, and most of the assault group had been killed, and Subarashii had ended up back in control of Sheffield and Clarke and everything in between, and most of Tharsis as well. Now it was late afternoon there, and a huge crowd had appeared on the streets of Sheffield to demonstrate against the violence, or the takeover, it was impossible to say; it had no purpose; groggily Maya watched with Michel as police units in walkers and helmets cut the demonstrating groups into segments, and drove them off with tear gas and rubber batons. "Fools!" Maya cried. "Why are they doing this! They'll bring down the whole Terran military on our heads!"

"It looks like they're dispersing," Michel said as he stared into the little screen. "Who knows, Maya. Images like this may galvanize people. They win this battle, but they lose support everywhere."

Maya splayed out over a couch in front of the screen, not yet awake enough to think. "Maybe," she said. "But it's going to be harder than ever to hold people back as long as Sax wants."

Michel waved this off, face to the screen. "How long can he expect you to manage that?"

"I don't know."

They watched as the Mangalavid reporters described the riots as terrorist-sponsored violence. Maya groaned. Spencer was at another AI screen, talking to Nanao in Sabishii. "Oxygen is rising so fast, there has to be something out there without suicide genes. Carbon dioxide levels? Yeah, dropping fast as well. . . . A bunch of really good carbon-fixing bacteria out there, proliferating like a weed. I've asked Sax about it and he just blinks. . . . Yeah, he's as out of control as Ann. And she's out there sabotaging every project she can get her hands on."

When Spencer got off, Maya said to him, "Just how long is Sax going to want us to hold out?"

Spencer shrugged. "Until we get something he thinks is a trigger, I guess. Or a coherent strategy. But if we can't stop the Reds and the Marsfirsters, it won't matter what Sax wants."

So the weeks crept by. A campaign of regular street demonstrations began in Sheffield and South Fossa. Maya thought this would only bring more security down on them, but Art argued in their favor. "We've got to let the Transitional Authority know how widespread the resistance is, so that when the moment comes, they don't try to crush us out of ignorance, see what I mean? At this point we need them to feel disliked and outnumbered. Hell, mass numbers of people in the streets are about the only thing that scare governments, if you ask me."

And whether Maya agreed or not, there was nothing she could do about it; every day passed and she could only work as hard as possible, traveling and meeting group after group, while inside her body her muscles were turning to wire with the tension, and she could barely sleep at night, nothing more than an exhausted hour or two near dawn.

• • • •

One morning in the northern spring of M-52, year 2127, she woke feeling more refreshed than usual. Michel was still sleeping, and she dressed and went out alone, and walked across the great central promenade to the cafés by the canal. This was the wonderful thing about Burroughs; despite tightened security at the gates and stations, one could still walk around freely inside the city at some hours, and among the throngs there was very little danger of being picked out. So she sat and drank coffee and ate pastries and looked at the low gray clouds rolling overhead, down the slope of Syrtis and toward the dike to the east. Air circulation under the tent was high, to give some kinetic match to the visuals overhead. That was strange, that; how used she had gotten to the sky visuals not matching the feel of the wind under the tents. The long slender arched tube of the bridge from Ellis Butte to Hunt Mesa was filled with the colorful ant-figures of people, hurrying about their morning's work. Living normal lives; abruptly she got up and paid her bill, and went for a long walk herself. She strolled along the rows of white Bareiss columns, up through Princess Park to the new tents, around the pingo hills where the currently fashionable apartments were located. Here in the high western district one could look back down and see the whole spread of the city, the trees and rooftops split by the promenade and its canals, the mesas huge and widely spaced, resembling vast cathedrals. Their sheer rock sides were cracked and furrowed, horizontal lines of twinkling windows the only clue that they were hollowed out inside, each of them a city of its own, a little world, living together on the red sand plain, under the immense invisible tent, connected by soaring footbridges that glinted like the visible sheen of soap bubbles. Ah, Burroughs!

So she walked back with the clouds, through narrow streets walled by apartment blocks and gardens, to Hunt Mesa and their home under the dance studio. Michel and Spencer were out, and for a long time she just stood in the window and looked at the clouds racing over the city, trying to do Michel's job for him, to lasso her moods and pull them back to some kind of stable center. From the ceiling came little uncoordinated *thump thump thumps*. Another class beginning. Then the thumps were in the hall before the door, and there was a hard knock. She went to answer it, heart pounding like the ceiling.

It was Jackie and Antar, and Art and Nirgal, and Rachel and Frantz and the rest of the Zygote ectogenes, pouring in and talking at the speed of sound, so that she couldn't quite understand them. She greeted them as cordially as she could, given Jackie's presence among them, and then collected herself and removed all hatred from her eyes, and talked with all of them, even Jackie, about their plans. They had come to Burroughs to help organize a demonstration down in the canal park. Word had been sent out through the cells, and they were hoping that a lot of the unaligned citizenry would join them as well. "I hope it doesn't precipitate any crackdowns," Maya said.

Jackie smiled at her, in triumph of course. "Remember, you can never go back," she said.

Maya rolled her eyes and went to put water on the stove, trying to quell her bitterness. They would meet with all the cell leaders in the city, and Jackie would take over the meeting, and exhort them to immediate rebellion, no sense or strategy involved. And there was nothing Maya could do about it—the time for beating the shit out of her had passed, unfortunately.

So she went around taking off people's coats and giving them bananas and kicking their feet off the couch cushions, feeling like a dinosaur among the mammals, a dinosaur in a new climate, among quick hot creatures who disdained her gallumphing around, who dodged her slow blows and ran end runs behind her dragging tail.

Art came slouching out to help her with the teacups, scruffy and relaxed as always. She asked him what he'd heard from Fort, and he gave her the daily report from Earth. Subarashii and Consolidated were under attack by fundamentalist armies, in what looked like a fundamentalist alliance, although that was an illusion as the Christian and Muslim fundamentalists hated each other, and despised the fundamentalist Hindus. The big metanats had used the new UN to give warning that they would protect their interests with appropriate force. Praxis and Amexx and Switzerland had urged use of the World Court, and India had done so, but no one else. Michel said, "At least they're still afraid of the World Court." But to Maya it looked like the metanatricide was shifting to a war between the well-to-do and the "mortals," which could be much more explosive—total war, rather than decapitations.

She and Art talked the situation over as they served the people in the apartment tea. Spy or not, Art knew Terra, and had an incisive political judgment, which she found helpful. He was like a mellow Frank. Was that right? Somehow she was reminded of Frank, and though she couldn't pin down why, she was obscurely pleased. No one else could have seen any resemblance in this lumbering sly man, it was her perception and hers alone.

Then more people began to crowd into the apartment, cell leaders and visitors from out of town. Maya sat at the back and listened as Jackie spoke to them. Everyone in the resistance, Maya thought as she listened to her, was in it for themselves. The way Jackie used her grandfather as a symbol, waving him like a flag to rally her troops, was sickening. It wasn't John who had gotten her her followers, but her white scoop blouse, the slut. No wonder Nirgal was estranged from her.

Now she exhorted them with her usual incendiary message, enthusiastically advocating immediate rebellion, no matter what the agreed-upon strategy was. And to these so-called Booneans, Maya was nothing more than an old paramour of the great man, or perhaps the reason he had been killed: a fossil odalisque, a historical embarrassment, an object of men's desire, like Helen of Troy called back by Faustus, insubstantial and weird. Ach, it was maddening! But she kept a calm face, and got up and walked in and out of the kitchen with her head averted, doing what paramours did, keeping people comfortable and fed. Nothing more to be done, at this point.

She stood in the kitchen, staring out the window at the rooftops below. She had lost whatever influence she had ever had on the resistance. The whole thing was going to come unraveled before Sax or any of the rest of them who counted were ready. Jackie was ranting on cheerily in the living room, organizing a demonstration that might get ten thousand people into the park, maybe fifty, who could say? And if security responded with tear gas and rubber bullets and truncheons, people would get hurt, some killed; killed for no strategic purpose, people who might have lived a thousand years. And still Jackie went on, bright and enthusiastic, burning like a flame. Overhead the sun gleamed through a break in the clouds, bright silver, ominously large. Art came into the kitchen and sat at the table, switching on his AI and sticking his face into it. "Got a note from home Praxis on the wrist." He read the screen, nose practically touching it.

"Are you nearsighted?" Maya said irritably.

"I don't think so . . . oh man. Ka boom. Is Spencer out there? Get Spencer in here."

Maya went to the doorway and signaled Spencer, who came in. Jackie ignored the disturbance and went on talking. Spencer sat down at the kitchen table beside Art, who was now sitting back, round-eyed and round-mouthed. Spencer read for five seconds and sat back in his chair, looked over at Maya with a strange expression. "This is it!" he said.

"What?"

"The trigger."

Maya went to him, and stood reading over his shoulder.

She held on to him, feeling a bizarre sensation of weightlessness. No more staving off the avalanche. She had done her job, she had just barely done it. At the very moment of failure, fate had turned.

Nirgal came into the kitchen to ask what was going on, attracted by something in their low voices. Art told him and his eyes lit, he couldn't conceal his excitement. He turned to Maya and said, "It's true?"

She could have kissed him for that. Instead she nodded, not trusting herself to speak, and went to the doorway to the living room. Jackie was still in the midst of her exhortation, and it gave Maya the greatest of pleasure to interrupt her. "The demonstration's off."

"What do you mean?" Jackie said, startled and annoyed. "Why?"

"Because we're having a revolution instead."

PART 10

Phase Change

Phase Change

They were pelican surfing when apprentices jumping up and down on the beach alerted them that something was wrong. They flew back in to the beach and stuck their landings on the wet sand, and got the news. An hour later they were up to the airport, and soon after that taking off in a little Skunkworks space plane called the Gollum. *They headed south, and when they reached 50,000 feet they were somewhere over Panama, and the pilot tilted it up and kicked in the rockets, and they were pressed back in their big g chairs for a few minutes. The three passengers were in cockpit seats behind the pilot and copilot, and out their windows they could see the exterior skin of the plane, which looked like pewter, begin to glow, and then quickly turn a vivid glowing yellow with a touch of bronze to it, brighter and brighter until it looked as if they were Shadrach, Meshach and Abednego, sitting together in the fiery furnace and coming to no harm.*

When the skin lost some of its glow, and the pilot leveled them off, they were about eighty miles above the Earth, and looking down on the Amazon, and the beautiful spinal curve of the Andes. As they flew south one of the passengers, a geologist, told the other two more about the situation.

"The West Antarctic ice sheet was resting on bedrock that is below sea level. It's continental land, though, not ocean bottom, and under West Antarctica it's a kind of basin and range zone, very geothermally active."

"West Antarctica?" Fort asked, squinting.

"That's the smaller half, with the peninsula sticking up toward South America, and the Ross ice shelf. The west ice sheet is between the mountains of the peninsula and the Transantarctic Mountains, in the middle of the continent.

Here, look, I brought a globe." He pulled from his pocket an inflatable globe, a child's toy, and blew it up and passed it around the cockpit.

"So, the western ice sheet, there, was resting on bedrock below sea level. But the land down there is warm, and there are some under-ice volcanoes down there, and so the ice on the bottom gets melted a bit. This water mixes with sediments from the volcanoes, and forms a substance called till. It has a consistency kind of like toothpaste. Where the ice is riding over this till it moves faster than usual, so within the west ice sheet there were ice streams, like fast glaciers with their banks made of slower ice. Ice Stream B ran two meters a day, for instance, while the ice around it moved two meters a year. And B was fifty kilometers across, and a kilometer deep. So that was one hell of a river, running off with about half a dozen other ice streams into the Ross ice shelf." He indicated these invisible streams with a fingertip.

"Now, where the ice streams and the ice sheet in general came off the bedrock, and started floating in the Ross Sea—that was called the grounding line."

"Ah," said one of Fort's friends. "Global warming?"

The geologist shook his head. "Our global warming has had very little effect on all this. It's raised temperatures and sea levels a little bit, but if that was all that was happening it wouldn't make much difference here. The problem is we're still in the interglacial warming that began at the end of the last Ice Age, and that warming sends what we call a thermal pulse down through the polar ice sheets. That pulse has been moving down for eight thousand years. And the grounding line of the west ice sheet has been moving inland for eight thousand years. And now one of the under-ice volcanoes down there is erupting. A major eruption. About three months old now. The grounding line had already started to retreat at an accelerated rate some years ago, and it was very close to the volcano that's erupted. It looks like the eruption has brought the grounding line right to the volcano, and now ocean water is running between the ice sheet and the bedrock, right into an active eruption. And so the ice sheet is breaking up. Lifting up, sliding out into the Ross Sea, and being carried away by currents."

His listeners stared at the little inflatable globe. By this time they were over Patagonia. The geologist answered their questions, pointing out features on the globe as he did. This kind of thing had happened before, he told them, and more than once. West Antarctica had been ocean, dry land, or ice sheet, many times in the millions of years since tectonic movement had deposited that continent in that position. And there appeared to be several unstable points in the long-term temperature changes—"instability triggers," he called them, causing massive

changes in a matter of years. "This climatological stuff is practically instanta-neous as far as geologists are concerned. Like, there's good evidence in the Green-land ice sheet that one time we went from glacial to interglacial in three years."
The geologist shook his head.

"And these ice sheet breakups?" Fort asked.

"Well, we think they might go typically in a couple hundred years, which is still very fast, mind you. A trigger event. But this time the volcano cruption makes it much worse. Hey look, there's the Banana Belt."

He pointed down, and across Drake Strait they saw a narrow icy mountain-ous peninsula, pointing in the same direction as the coccyx of Tierra del Fuego.

The pilot banked to the right, then more gently to the left, beginning a wide lazy turn. Below them as they stared down was the familiar image of Antarctica as seen in satellite photos, but everything was now brilliantly colored and artic-ulated: the cobalt blue of the ocean, the daisy chain of cyclonic cloud systems spinning away to the north, the textured sheen of the sun on the water, the great gleaming mass of the ice, and the flotillas of tiny icebergs, so white in the blue.

But the familiar Q shape of the continent was now strangely mottled in the area behind the comma of the Antarctic peninsula, with gaping blue-black cracks in the white. And the Ross Sea was even more fractured, by long ocean-blue fjords, and a radial pattern of turquoise-blue cracks; and offshore from the Ross Sea, floating up toward the South Pacific, were some tabular icebergs that were like pieces of the continent itself, sailing away. The biggest one looked to be about the same size as New Zealand's South Island, or even bigger.

After they had pointed out the biggest tabular bergs to each other, and the various features of the broken and reduced western ice sheet (the geologist indi-cated where he thought the volcano under the ice was, but it looked no different from the rest of the sheet), they simply sat in their seats and watched.

"That's the Ronne ice shelf, there," the geologist said after a while, "and the Weddell Sea. Yeah, there's some slippage down into it too.... Up there's where McMurdo used to be, on the far side of the Ross ice shelf. Ice was pushed across the bay and ran up over the settlement."

The pilot started a second lap around the continent.

Fort said, "Now say again what effect this will have?"

"Well, theoretical models have world sea levels rising about six meters."

"Six meters!"

"Well, it will take a few years for the full rise, but it's definitely started. This catastrophic break will raise sea levels about two or three meters, in a matter

of weeks. What's left of the sheet will be afloat in a matter of months, or a few years at most, and that will add another three meters."

"How could it raise the whole ocean that much?"

"It's a lot of ice."

"It can't be that much ice!"

"Yes it can. That's most of the fresh water in the world, right down there under us. Just be thankful the East Antarctic ice sheet is nice and stable. If it were to slide off, sea levels would rise sixty meters."

"Six meters is plenty," Fort said.

They finished another lap. The pilot said, "We should be getting back."

"That's it for every beach in the world," Fort said, pulling his face back from the window. Then: "I guess we'd better go get our stuff."

When the second Martian revolution began, Nadia was in the upper canyon of Shalbatana Vallis, north of Marineris. In a sense one could say that she started it.

She had left South Fossa temporarily to oversee the Shalbatana closure, which was similar to those over Nirgal Vallis and the east Hellas valleys: a long tent roof over a temperate ecology, with a stream running down the canyon floor, in this case supplied by pumping from the Lewis aquifer, 170 kilometers to the south. Shalbatana was a long series of lazy S's, so that the valley floor looked very picturesque, but the construction of the roof had been complicated.

Nevertheless Nadia had directed the project with only one small part of her attention, the rest being focused on the cascading developments on Earth. She was in daily communication with her group in South Fossa, and with Art and Nirgal in Burroughs, and they kept her informed of all the latest news. She was particularly interested in the activities of the World Court, which was trying to establish itself as an arbitrator in the growing conflict of the Subarashii metanats and the Group of Eleven against Praxis, Switzerland, and the developing China-India alliance—trying to function, as Art had put it, "as a sort of world court." That effort had looked doomed when the fundamentalist riots began and the metanats prepared to defend themselves; and Nadia had concluded unhappily that things on Earth were about to spiral down into chaos again.

But all these crises were immediately cast into insignificance when Sax called to tell her of the collapse of the West Antarctic ice sheet. She had taken his call at her desk in one of the construction trailers, and now she stared at his little face on the screen. "What do you mean, collapsed?"

"It's lifted off the bedrock. There's a volcano erupting. It's being broken up by ocean currents."

The video image he was sending cut to Punta Arena, a Chilean harbor town with its docks gone and its streets awash; then it cut again to Port Elizabeth in Azania, where the situation was much the same.

"How fast is it?" Nadia said. "Is it a tidal wave?"

"No. More like a very high tide. That will never go away."

"So enough time to evacuate," Nadia said, "but not enough time to build anything. And you say six meters!"

"But only over the next few . . . no one is sure how long. I've seen estimates that as much as a quarter of the Terran population will be—affected."

"I believe it. Oh, Sax . . . "

A worldwide stampede to higher ground. Nadia stared at the screen, feeling stunned as the scale of the catastrophe became clearer to her. Coastal cities would be awash. Six meters! She found it very hard to imagine that any possible ice mass could be so large as to raise the sea level of all Earth's oceans by even as much as one meter—but six! It was shocking proof, if one needed it, that the Earth was not so big after all. Or else that the West Antarctic ice sheet was huge. Well, it had covered about a third of a continent, and was, the reports said, some three kilometers thick. That was a lot of ice. Sax was saying something about the East Antarctic ice sheet, which apparently was not threatened. She shook her head to clear it of this nattering, concentrated on the news. Bangladesh would have to be entirely evacuated; that was three hundred million people, not to mention the other coastal cities of India, like Calcutta, Madras, Bombay. Then London, Copenhagen, Istanbul, Amsterdam, New York, Los Angeles, New Orleans, Miami, Rio, Buenos Aires, Sydney, Melbourne, Singapore, Hong Kong, Manila, Djakarta, Tokyo . . . and those were only the big ones. A lot of people lived on the coast, in a world already severely stressed by overpopulation and declining resources. And now all kinds of basic necessities were being drowned by salt water.

"Sax," she said, "we should be helping them. Not just . . . "

"There is not that much we can do. And we can do that best if we're free. First one, then the other."

"You promise?"

"Yes," he said, looking surprised. "I mean—I'll do what I can."

"That's what I'm asking." She thought it over. "You've got everything ready at your end?"

"Yes. We want to start with missile strikes against all surveillance and weapons satellites."

"What about Kasei Vallis?"

"I'm dealing with it."

"When do you want to start?"

"How about tomorrow?"

"Tomorrow!"

"I have to deal with Kasei very soon. Conditions are good right now."

"What are you going to do?"

"Let's try to launch tomorrow. No sense wasting time."

"My God," Nadia said, thinking hard. "We're about to go behind the sun?"

"Yes."

This position vis-à-vis Earth was mostly a symbolic matter these days, as communications were assured by a great number of asteroid relays; but it did mean that it would take months for even the fastest shuttles to get from Earth to Mars.

Nadia took a deep breath, let it out. She said, "Let's go, then."

"I was hoping you would say that. I'll call them in Burroughs and give them the word."

"We'll meet in Underhill?" This was their current rendezvous point in case of emergency; Sax was in a refuge in Da Vinci Crater where a lot of his missile silos were located, so both of them could get to Underhill in a day.

"Yes," he said. "Tomorrow." And he was gone.

And so she had started a revolution.

She found a news program running the satellite photo of Antarctic, and watched it in a kind of daze. Little voices on the screen chattered at speed, one claiming that the disaster was an act of ecotage perpetrated by ecoteurs from Praxis, who supposedly had drilled holes in the ice sheet and set hydrogen bombs down on the Antarctic bedrock. "Still at it!" she cried, disgusted. No other news shows made this assertion, or refuted it—it was just part of the chaos, no doubt, swept away by all the other accounts of the flood. But the metanatricide was still on. And they were part of it.

All existence immediately reduced itself to that, in a way sharply reminiscent of '61. She felt her stomach knotting as of old, tightening past any usual levels of tension, into an iron walnut at the center of her being, painful and constricting. She had been taking medicine recently to prevent ulcers, but it was woefully inadequate to this kind of assault. Come on, she told herself. Be calm. This is the moment. You've expected it, you've worked on it. You've laid the groundwork for it. Now came the chaos. At the heart of any phase change there was a zone of cascading recombinant chaos. But there were methods to read it, to deal with it.

She crossed the little mobile habitat, and glanced briefly down at the idyllic beauty of the canyon floor of Shalbatana, with its pebble-pink stream and the new trees, including strings of cottonwood on the banks and islands. It was possible, if things went drastically wrong, that no one would ever inhabit Shalbatana Vallis, that it would remain an empty bubble world until mudstorms caved the roof in, or something in the mesocosmic ecology went awry. Well—

She shrugged and woke her crew, and told them to get ready to leave for Underhill. She told them why, and as they were all part of the resistance in one way or another, they cheered.

It was just after dawn, on what was looking to be a warm spring day, the kind that had allowed them to work in loose walkers and hoods and facemasks, with only the insulated hard boots to remind Nadia of the bulky clothing of the early years. Friday, Ls 101, 2 July 2, M-year 52, Terran date (she checked her wristpad) October 12, 2127. Somewhere near the hundredth anniversary of their arrival, though it was a date no one seemed to be celebrating. A hundred years! It was a bizarre thought.

Another July revolution, then, and another October revolution too. A decade past the bicentennial of the Bolshevik revolution, she seemed to remember. Which was another strange thought. Well, but they too had tried. All the revolutionaries, all through history. Mostly desperate peasants, fighting for their children's lives. As in her Russia. So many in that bitter twentieth century, risking all to make a better life, and even so it had led to disaster. It was frightening—as if history were a series of human wave assaults on misery, failing time after time.

But the Russian in her, the cerebellum Siberian, decided to take the October date as a good auspice. Or a reminder of what not to do, if nothing else—along with '61. She could, in her Siberian mind, dedicate this time to all of them: to the heroic suffering of the Soviet catastrophe, to all her friends dead in '61, to Arkady and Alex and Sasha and Roald and Janet and Evgenia and Samantha, all of whom still haunted her dreams and her attenuated insomniac memories, spinning like electrons around the iron walnut inside her, warning her not to screw it up, to get it right this time, to redeem the meanings of their lives and their deaths. She remembered someone saying to her, "Next time you have a revolution you'd better try some other way."

And now they were. But there were Marsfirst guerrilla units under Kasei's command, out of contact with the headquarters in Burroughs, as well as a thousand other factors coming to bear, most of them completely out of her control. Cascading recombinant chaos. So how different was it going to be?

She got her crew into rovers and over to the little piste station, some kilometers to the north of them. From there they rode in a freight train, on a mobile piste laid for the Shalbatana job, on to the main Sheffield-Burroughs line. Both those cities were metanat strongholds, and Nadia worried that they would take pains to secure the piste linking them. In that sense Underhill was strategically important, as occupying it would cut the piste. But for that very reason she wanted to get away from Underhill, and off the piste system entirely. She wanted to get into the air, as she had in '61—all the instincts learned in those few months were trying to take over again, as if sixty-six years had not passed. And those instincts told her to hide.

As they glided southwest over the desert, shooting the gap between Ophir and Juventae chasmas, she kept her wristpad linked to Sax's headquarters in Da Vinci Crater. Sax's team of technicians were trying to imitate his dry style, but it was obvious that they were just as excited as her young construction crew. About five of them got on the wrist at once to tell her that they had set off a barrage of the surface-to-space missiles which Sax had arranged to have placed in hidden equatorial silos over the past decade, and this barrage had gone off like a fireworks display, and had knocked out all of the orbiting metanat weapons platforms that they knew of, and many of their communications satellites as well. "We got eighty percent of them in the first wave! —We sent up our own communications satellites! —Now we're dealing with them on a case-by-case basis—"

Nadia interrupted. "Are your satellites working?"

"We think they're fine! We can only tell for sure after a full test, and everyone's kind of busy right now."

"Let's try one out now. And some of you make that a priority, you understand? We need a redundant system, a *very* redundant system."

She clicked off and tapped out one of the frequency and encryption codes Sax had given her. A few seconds later she was talking to Zeyk, who was in Odessa, helping to coordinate activities in the Hellas Basin. Everything there was going according to plan so far, he said; of course they were only a few hours into it, but it looked like Michel and Maya's organizing there had paid off, because all the cell members in Odessa had poured into the streets and told people what was happening, sparking a spontaneous mass work stoppage and demonstration. They were in the process of closing down the train station, and occupying the corniche and most other public spaces, in a strike that looked like it would soon be a takeover. The Transitional Authority personnel in the city were retreating to the train station or the physical plant, as Zeyk had hoped they would. "When most of them are inside we're going to override the plant's AI, and then it'll become a jail holding them. We've got control of the backup life-support systems for the town, so there's very little they can do, except maybe blow themselves up, but we don't think they'll do that. A lot of the UNTA people here are Syrians under Niazi, and I'm talking to Rashid while we try to disable the physical plant from the outside, just to make sure no one in there can decide to become a martyr."

"I don't think there will be too many martyrs to the metanationals," Nadia said.

"I hope not, but you never can tell. So far so good here, though. And elsewhere around Hellas it's been even easier—the security forces were minimal, and most of the population are natives or radicalized emigrants, and they've simply been surrounding security and daring them to do anything violent. It has resulted either in a standoff, or else in the security forces being disarmed. Dao and Harmakhis-Reull have both declared themselves free canyons, and invited anyone who wants to take refuge there if they need it."

"Good!"

Zeyk heard the surprise in her voice, and warned, "I don't think it will be as easy in Burroughs and Sheffield. And we need to shut down the elevator, so they don't start shooting at us from Clarke."

"At least Clarke is stuck over Tharsis."

"True. But it sure would be nice to seize that thing, and not have the elevator come crashing down again."

"I know. I heard the Reds have been working with Sax on a plan for seizure."

"Allah preserve us. I must be off, Nadia. Tell Sax that the programs for the plant worked perfectly. And listen, we should come up and join you in the north, I think. If we can secure Hellas and Elysium quickly, it will help our chances with Burroughs and Sheffield."

So Hellas was going as planned. And just as important, or more, they were still in communication with each other. This was critical; among all the nightmare images of '61, scenes illuminated in her memory by lightning bolts of fear or pain, few were worse than the feeling of sheer helplessness that had struck her when their communication system had crashed. After that nothing they did had mattered, they had been like insects with their antennae ripped off, stumbling around ineffectually. So in the last few years Nadia had repeatedly insisted to Sax that he come up with a plan for hardening their communications; and he had built, and now put in orbit, a whole fleet of very small communications satellites, stealthed and hardened as much as possible. So far they were functioning as planned. And the iron walnut within her, while not gone, was at least not pulling in so hard at her ribs. Calm, she told herself. Thisness. This is the moment and the only moment. Concentrate on it.

Their mobile piste reached the big equatorial line, rerouted the year before to avoid the Chryse ice, and they shunted onto the piste for local trains, and headed west. Their train was only three cars long, and Nadia's whole crew, some thirty people, were all gathered in the first car to watch the incoming reports over the car's screen. These were official news reports from Mangalavid in South Fossa, and they were confused and inconsistent, combining regular weather reports and the like with brief accounts of strikes in many cities. Nadia kept her wristpad in contact with either Da Vinci or the Free Mars safe house in Burroughs, and as they slid on she watched both the car screen and her wrist, taking in simultaneous bursts of information as if listening to polyphonic music, finding she could track the two sources at once without any trouble, and was hungry for more. Praxis was sending up continuous reports on the Terran situation, which was confused, but not incoherent or opaque as it had been in '61; for one thing Praxis was keeping them informed, and for another, much of the current activity on Earth was devoted to moving the coastal populations out of the reach of the floods, which so far were like very high tides, as Sax had said they would be. The metanatricide was still being played out in the form of surgical strikes and decapitation coups, commando raids and counterraids on various corporate compounds and headquarters, combined with legal actions and PR of all sorts—including a number of suits and countersuits finally introduced to the World Court, which Nadia considered encouraging. But these strategic raids and maneuvers were much reduced in the face of the global flood. And even at their worst (video of exploding compounds, airplane crash sites, stretches of road cratered by the bombing of passing limousines) they were still infinitely better than any kind of escalating war, which in biological form could kill millions. As became clear, unfortunately, with a shocking report from Indonesia that came over the car's screen—a radical liberation group from East Timor, modeled on Peru's Shining Path, had poisoned the island of Java with an as yet unidentified plague, so that along with the travails of the flooding there, they were losing hundreds of thousands to disease. On a continent such a plague could become a terminal disaster, and there was no guarantee it wouldn't happen still. But meanwhile, with that one awful exception, the war down there, if that was what one called the chaos of the metanatricide, was proceeding as a fight at the top. A style similar to what they were attempting on Mars, in fact. This was comforting in a way, although if the metanats became adept at the style, they could presumably wage it on Mars as well—if not in this first moment of surprise, then later when they had reorganized. And there was an ominous item in the flow of reports from Praxis Geneva, indicating they might be responding already: a fast shuttle with a large force of "security experts" had left Earth orbit for Mars three months ago, the report said, and was expected to reach the Martian system "in a few days." The news was being released now to encourage security forces beleaguered by rioting and terrorism, according to the UN press release.

Nadia's concentration on the screens was broken by the appearance of one of the big round-the-world trains on the piste beside them. One second they were gliding smoothly over the bumpy plateau of Ophir Planum, and the next a big fifty-car express was whooshing by them. But it didn't slow down, and there was no way of telling who, if anyone, sat behind its darkened windows. Then it was past them, and soon after that over the horizon ahead, and gone.

The news shows continued at their manic pace, the reporters obviously astonished by the developments of the day—riots in Sheffield, work stoppages in South Fossa and Hephaestus—the accounts overlapped each other in such rapid succession that Nadia found it hard to believe they were real.

When they came into Underhill Nadia's feeling of unreality persisted, for the sleepy, semiabandoned old settlement was now abuzz with activity, as in M-year 1. Resistance sympathizers had been pouring in all day from small stations around Ganges Catena and Hebes Chasma, and the north wall of Ophir Chasma. The local Bogdanovists had apparently organized them into a march on the little unit of UNTA security personnel at the train station. This had led to a standoff just outside the station itself, under the tent that covered the old arcade and the original quadrant of barrel vaults, now looking very small and quaint.

So when Nadia's train pulled in, there was a loud argument going on between a man with a bullhorn surrounded by about twenty bodyguards, and the unruly crowd facing them. Nadia got off the train as soon as it stopped, and went over to the edge of the group hemming in the station-master and his troops. She commandeered a bullhorn from a surprised-looking young woman and began shouting through it. "Stationmaster! Stationmaster! Stationmaster!" She repeated this in English and Russian, until everyone had gone quiet to find out who she was. Her construction team had filtered out through the crowd, and when she saw that they were positioned, she walked right up to the cluster of men and women in their flak jackets. The stationmaster appeared to be a Mars old-timer, his face weathered and scarred across the forehead. His young team wore the Transitional Authority insignia, and looked scared. Nadia let the bullhorn fall to her side and said, "I'm Nadia Cherneshevsky. I built this town. And now we're taking control of it. Who do you work for?"

"The United Nations Transitional Authority," the stationmaster said firmly, staring at her as if she had stepped out of the grave.

"But what unit? Which metanational?"

"We're a Mahjari unit."

"Mahjari is working with China now, and China with Praxis, and Praxis with us. We're on the same side, and you don't know it yet. And no matter what you think about that, we've got you outgunned here." She shouted out to the crowd, "Everyone armed raise their hand!"

Everyone in the crowd raised their hand, and all of her crew had stun guns or nail guns or soldering-beam guns in hand.

"We don't want bloodshed," Nadia said to the ever-tighter knot of bodyguards before her. "We don't even want to take you prisoner. There's our train right there; you can take it, and go to Sheffield and join the rest of your team. There you'll find out the new status of things. It's that or else we'll all leave the station here, and blow it up. We're taking over one way or another, and it would be stupid for anyone to get killed when this revolt is already a done deal. So take the train. I'd advise going to Sheffield, where you can get a ride out on the elevator if you want. Or if you want to work for a free Mars, you can join us right now."

She stared calmly at the man, feeling more relaxed than she had all day. Action was such a relief. The man ducked his head to confer with his team, and they talked in whispers for most of five minutes.

The man looked at her again. "We'll take your train."

And so Underhill was the first town freed.

That night Nadia went out to the trailer park, which was near the new tent coping wall. The two habitats that had not been turned into labs were still outfitted with the original living quarters equipment, and after inspecting them, and then going back out and walking around the barrel vaults, and the Alchemists' Quarter, she finally returned to the one she had lived in at the very start, and lay down on one of the floor mattresses, feeling exhausted.

It was strange indeed to lie by herself among all the ghosts, trying to feel again the presence of that distant time in her. Too strange; despite her exhaustion she could not sleep, and near dawn she had a hazy vision, of worrying about uncrating goods from freight rockets, and programming robot bricklayers, and taking a call from Arkady on Phobos. She even slept a while in this state, dozing uneasily, until a tingling in her ghost finger work her up.

And then, rising with a groan, it was just as hard to imagine that she was waking up to a world in turmoil, with millions of people waiting to see what the day would bring. Looking around at the tight confines of her first home on Mars, it suddenly seemed to her that the walls were moving—beating very lightly—a kind of double vision, as if she were standing in the low morning light looking through a temporal stereopticon, which revealed all four dimensions at once with a pulsating, hallucinatory light.

They breakfasted in the barrel vaults, in the large hall where Ann and Sax had once argued the merits of terraforming. Sax had won that argument, but Ann was out there fighting it still, as if it had not been decided long since.

Nadia focused on the present, on her AI screen and the flood of news pouring through it this Saturday morning: the top of the screen given over to Maya's safe house in Burroughs, the bottom to Praxis reports from Earth. Maya was performing heroically as usually, vibrant with apprehension, hectoring everyone in sight to conform to her vision of how things should happen, haggard and yet buzzing with her internal spin. As Nadia listened to her describe the latest developments she chewed breakfast methodically, scarcely noticing Underhill's delicious bread. It was afternoon already in Burroughs, and the day had been busy. Every town on Mars was in turmoil. On Earth all the coastal areas were now flooded, and the mass dislocations were causing chaos inland. The new UN had condemned the rioters on Mars as heartless opportunists who were taking advantage of a time of unprecedented suffering to advance their own selfish cause. "True enough," Nadia said to Sax as he walked in the door, fresh from Da Vinci Crater. "They'll hold that against us later, I bet."

"Not if we help them out."

"Hmm." She offered him bread, regarding him closely. Despite his changed features he was looking more like Sax every day, standing there impassively, blinking as he looked around the old brick chamber. It seemed as though revolution was the last thing on his mind. She said, "Are you ready to fly to Elysium?"

"That's what I was going to ask you."

"Good. Let me go get my bag."

While she was throwing her clothes and AI into her old black backpack, her wrist beeped and there was Kasei, his long gray hair wild around his deeply lined face, which was the strangest mix of John and Hiroko—John's mouth, at the moment stretched into a wide grin; Hiroko's Oriental eyes, now slitted with delight. "Hello, Kasei," Nadia said, unable to conceal her surprise. "I don't think I've ever seen you on my wrist before."

"Special circumstances," he said, unabashed. She was used to thinking of him as a dour man, but the outbreak of the revolution was obviously a great tonic; she understood suddenly by his look that he had been waiting for this all his life. "Look, Coyote and I and a bunch of Reds are up here in Chasma Borealis, and we've secured the reactor and the dam; everyone working here has been cooperative—"

"Encouraging!" someone beside him yelled.

"Yes, there's been a lot of support up here, except for a security team of about a hundred people who are holed up in the reactor. They're threatening to melt it down unless we give them safe passage to Burroughs."

"So?" Nadia said.

"*So?*" Kasei repeated, and laughed. "So Coyote says we should ask you what to do."

Nadia snorted. "Why do I find that hard to believe."

"Hey, no one here believes it either! But that's what Coyote said, and we like to indulge the old bastard when we can."

"So, well, give them safe passage to Burroughs. That's a no-brainer if I've ever seen one. It won't matter if Burroughs has an extra hundred cops, and the fewer reactor meltdowns the better, we're still wading around in the radiation from last time."

Sax came into the room while Kasei was thinking it over. "Okay!" Kasei said. "If you say so! Hey talk to you later, I have to go, ka."

Nadia stared at her blank wrist screen, scowling.

Sax said, "What was that about?"

"You've got me," Nadia said, and described the conversation while trying to call Coyote. She got no answer.

Sax said, "Well, you're the coordinator."

"Shit." Nadia pulled her backpack over one shoulder. "Let's go."

They flew in a new 51B, very small and very fast. They took a great circle route, which headed northwest over the Vastitas ice sea, and avoided the metanat strongholds of Ascraeus, and Echus Overlook. Very soon after takeoff they could see the ice filling Chryse to the north, the shattered dirty bergs dotted with pink snow algae and amethyst melt ponds. The old transponder road to Chasma Borealis was of course long gone, that whole system of bringing water south forgotten, a technical footnote for the history books. Looking down at the ice chaos Nadia suddenly remembered what the land had looked like on that first trip, the endless hills and hollows, the funnel-like alases, the great black barchan dunes, the incredible laminated terrain in the last sands before the polar cap . . . all gone now, overwhelmed by ice. And the polar cap itself was a mess, nothing but a collection of great melt zones and ice streams, slush rivers, ice-covered liquid lakes—every manner of slurry, and all of it crashing downslope off the high round plateau that the polar cap rested on, down into the world-wrapping northern sea.

Landing was therefore out of the question for much of their flight. Nadia watched the instruments nervously, all too aware of the many things that could go wrong in a new machine during a crisis, when maintenance was down and human error up.

Then billows of white and black smoke appeared on the horizon to the southwest, pouring east in what was clearly a high wind. "What's that?" Nadia asked, moving to the left side of the plane to look.

"Kasei Vallis," Sax said from the pilot's seat.

"What's happened to it?"

"It's burning."

Nadia stared at him. "What do you mean?"

"Heavy vegetation there in the valley. And along the foot of the Great Escarpment. Resinated trees and shrubs, for the most part. Also fireseed trees—you know. Species that require fire to propagate. Engineered at Biotique. Thorny resin manzanita, blackthorn, giant sequoia, some others."

"How do you know this?"

"I planted them."

"And now you've set them on fire?"

Sax nodded. He glanced down at the smoke.

"But Sax, isn't the percentage of oxygen in the atmosphere really high now?"

"Forty percent."

She stared at him some more, suddenly suspicious. "You jacked that up too, didn't you! Jesus, Sax—you might have set the whole world on fire!"

She stared down at the bottom of the column of smoke. There in the big trough of Kasei Vallis was a line of flame, the leading edge of the fire, burning brilliant white rather than yellow—it looked like molten magnesium. "Nothing will put that out!" she cried. "You've set the world on fire!"

"The ice," Sax said. "There's nothing downwind but the ice covering Chryse. It should only burn a few thousand square kilometers."

Nadia stared at him, amazed and appalled. Sax was still glancing down at the fire, but most of the time he watched the plane's instruments, his face set in a curious expression: reptilian, stony—utterly inhuman.

The metanat security compounds in the curve of Kasei Vallis came over the horizon. The tents were all burning furiously, like torches of pitch, the craters on the inner bank like beach firepits, spurting white flame into the air. Clearly there was a strong wind pouring down Echus Chasma and funneling through Kasei Vallis, fanning the flames. A firestorm. And Sax stared down at it unblinking, his jaw muscles bunched under the skin.

"Fly north," Nadia ordered him. "Get clear of that."

He banked the plane, and she shook her head. Thousands of square kilometers, burned—all that vegetation, so painstakingly introduced—global oxygen levels raised by a significant percentage. . . . She regarded the strange creature sitting beside her warily.

"Why didn't you tell me about this?"

"I didn't want you to stop it."

As simple as that.

"So I have that power?" she said.

"Yes."

"Meaning I'm kept ignorant of things?"

"Only of this," Sax said. His jaw muscles were bunching and relaxing, in a rhythm that reminded her suddenly of Frank Chalmers. "The prisoners were all moved out into asteroid mining. This was the training site for all their secret police. The ones who would never give up. The torturers." He turned that lizard gaze on her. "We're better off without them." And he returned to his piloting.

Nadia was still looking back at the fierce white line of the firestorm when the plane's radio beeped her code. This time it was Art, cross-eyed with worry. "I need your help," he said. "Ann's people have retaken Sabishii, and a lot of the Sabishiians have come up out of the maze to reoccupy it, and the Reds in control there are telling them to go away."

"What?"

"I know, well, I don't think Ann knows about this yet, and she isn't answering my calls. There are Reds out there that make her look like a Boonean, I swear. But I reached Ivana and Raul, and got them to stop the Reds in Sabishii till they heard from you. That's the best I could do."

"Why *me*?"

"I think Ann told them to listen to you."

"Shit."

"Well, who else is going to do it? Maya's made too many enemies holding things together the last few years."

"I thought you were the big diplomat here."

"I am! But what I got was everyone agreeing to defer to your judgment. That was the best I could do. Sorry, Nadia. I'll help you anyway you want me to."

"You'd damn well better, after setting me up like this!"

He grinned. "It's not my fault everyone trusts you."

Nadia clicked off and tried the various Red radio channels. At first she couldn't find Ann. But while she was running through their channels she heard enough messages to realize that there were young Red radicals whom Ann would certainly condemn, or so she hoped—people who, with the revolt still in the balance, were busy blowing up platforms in Vastitas, slashing tents, breaking pistes, threatening to end their cooperation with the other rebels unless they were joined in their ecotage and all their demands were met, etc., etc.

Finally Ann answered Nadia's call. She looked like an avenging Fury, righteous and slightly mad. "Look," Nadia said to her without preamble, "an independent Mars is the best chance you'll ever have to get what you want. You try holding the revolution hostage to your concerns and people will remember, I'm warning you! You can argue all you want once we've gotten the situation under control, but until then it's just blackmail as far as I'm concerned. It's a stab in the back. You get those Reds in Sabishii to turn the city back over to its residents."

Ann said angrily, "What makes you think I can tell them what to do?"

"Who else if not you?"

"What makes you think I disagree with what they're doing?"

"My impression that you are a sane person, that's what!"

"I don't presume to order people about."

"Reason with them if you can't order them! Tell them stronger revolts than ours have failed because of this kind of stupidity. Tell them to get a grip."

Ann cut the connection without a reply.

"Shit," Nadia said.

Her AI continued to pour out news. The UNTA expeditionary force was coming back up from the southern highlands, and appeared to be on its way to Hellas, or Sabishii. Sheffield was still in the control of Subarashii. Burroughs was an open situation, with security forces seemingly in control; but refugees were pouring into the city from Syrtis and elsewhere, and there was a general strike going on as well. The vids made it look like most of the populace was spending the day out on the boulevards and in the parks, demonstrating against the Transitional Authority, or merely trying to watch what was going on.

"We'll have to do something about Burroughs," Sax said.

"I know."

They flew southward again, past the bump of Hecates Tholus on the northern end of the Elysium massif, to the South Fossa spaceport. Their flight had taken twelve hours, but they had gone west through nine time zones, and crossed the date line at 180° longitude, so it was midday Sunday when their airport bus drove to the rim of South Fossa, and through the roof lock.

South Fossa and the other Elysium towns, Hephaestus and Elysium Fossa, had all come out for Free Mars in a big way. They made a kind of geographical unit; a southern arm of the Vastitas ice now ran between the Elysium massif and the Great Escarpment, and though it had already been spanned by pistes on pontoon bridges, Elysium was in the process of becoming an island continent. In all three of its big towns crowds had poured into the streets, and occupied the city offices and the physical plants. Without the threat of attacks from orbit to back them up, the few Transitional Authority police in the towns had either changed into civilian clothes and melted into the crowds, or else gotten on the train to Burroughs. Elysium was uncontestedly part of Free Mars.

Down at the Mangalavid offices Nadia and Sax found that a large armed group of rebels had taken over the station, and were now busy churning out twenty-four and a half hours a day of video reports on all four channels, all sympathetic to the revolt, with long interviews from people in all the independent towns and stations. The timeslip was going to be devoted to a montage of the previous day's events.

Some outlying mining stations in Elysium's radial cracks, and in the Phlegra Montes, were purely metanat operations, mostly Amexx and Subarashii. These were staffed largely by new emigrants who had holed up in their camps, and either gone silent or else started to threaten anyone who tried to bother them; some even declared their intention to retake the planet, or hold out until reinforcements from Earth arrived. "Ignore them," Nadia advised. "Avoid them and ignore them. Jam their communications systems if you can, and leave them alone."

Reports from elsewhere on Mars were more promising. Senzeni Na was in the hands of people who called themselves Booneans, though they were not associated with Jackie—they were issei, nisei, sansei, and yonsei, who had immediately named their mohole John Boone, and declared Thaumasia a "Dorsa Brevia Peaceful Neutral Place." Korolyov, now a small mining town only, had revolted almost as violently as in '61, and its citizens, many of them descendants of the old prison population, had renamed the town Sergei Pavlovich Korolyov, and declared it an undocumented anarchist free zone; the old prison compounds were to be converted into a giant bazaar and communal living space, with a particular welcome made to refugees from Earth. Nicosia was likewise a free city. Cairo was under the control of Amexx security. Odessa and the rest of the Hellas Basin towns were still holding firm for independence, although the circumHellas piste had been cut in some places. The maglev train system was bad that way; the magnetic systems had to be operating for the pistes to function and the trains to move, and these systems were easy to break. For that reason many trains were running empty or were canceled, as people took to rovers or planes to make sure they didn't get stranded in the outback somewhere, in vehicles that didn't even have wheels.

Nadia and Sax spent the rest of Sunday monitoring developments and making suggestions, if asked, about problem situations. In general it seemed to Nadia that things were going well. But on Monday, bad news came in from Sabishii. The UNTA expeditionary force had arrived there from the southern highlands, and retaken the surface portion of the city after a bitter all-night fight with the Red guerrillas in control of the city. The Reds and the original Sabishiians had retreated into the mound maze or the outlying shelters, and the prospect of continued bloody fighting in the maze was clear. Art predicted that the security force would be unable to penetrate the maze, and so would be forced to abandon Sabishii, and train or fly up to Burroughs, to consolidate with the forces already there. But there was no way to be sure; and poor Sabishii was sadly battered by the assault, and back in security's hands.

Monday evening at dusk Nadia went out with Sax to get something to eat. South Fossa's canyon floor was thick with mature trees, the giant sequoias standing over an understory of pines and junipers and, in the lower stretch of the canyon, aspens and canyon oaks. As they walked down the streamside park, Nadia and Sax were introduced by the Mangalavid people to group after group, most of them natives, all of them unfamiliar faces, but all very happy to meet them, it was clear. It was strange to see so many people obviously, visibly happy; in normal life, Nadia realized, one simply didn't see it—smiles everywhere, strangers talking to each other . . . there was more than one way for things to go when a social order disappeared. Anarchy and chaos, definitely all too possible; but also communion.

They ate in an outdoor restaurant by the central stream, and then returned to the Mangalavid offices. Nadia got back in front of her screen, and went to work talking to as many organizing committees as she could reach. She felt like Frank in '61, working the phones in frantic overdrive; only now they were in communication with all of Mars, and she had the distinct impression that while she was not by any means in control, she at least had a good sense of what was going on. And that was gold, that was. The iron walnut in her stomach began to shift to something more like wood.

After a couple of hours, she began to fall asleep in the seconds between one call and the next; it was the middle of the night back in Underhill and Shalbatana, and she hadn't slept much since the call from Sax about Antarctica. That meant four or five days without sleep—no, wait—she figured it out—three days. Though it already felt like two weeks.

She had just lain down on a couch when there was an outcry, and everyone ran into the hall, then out onto the stone-flagged plaza surrounding the Mangalavid offices. Nadia stumbled blearily after Sax, who grabbed her by the arm and helped her keep her balance.

Apparently there was a hole in the roof tent. People pointed, but Nadia couldn't make it out. "This is where we're better off," Sax said with a satisfied little purse of the mouth. "The pressure under the roof is only a hundred and fifty millibars higher than the pressure outside."

"So roofs don't pop like pricked balloons," Nadia said, remembering with a shudder some of the domed craters of '61.

"And even though some outside air is getting in, it's mostly oxygen and nitrogen. Still too much CO_2, but not so much that we're all poisoned instantly."

"But if the hole were bigger," Nadia said.

"True."

She shook her head. "We need to secure the whole planet, to really be safe."

"True."

Nadia went back inside, yawning. She sat at her screen again, and began watching the four Mangalavid channels, switching among them rapidly. Most of the big cities were either openly for independence or in various kinds of stalemate, with security in control of the physical plants but nothing happening, and much of the population in the streets, waiting to see what would happen next. There were a number of company towns and camps that were still supporting their metanats, but in the case of Bradbury Point and Huo Hsing Vallis, neighboring towns up on the Great Escarpment, their parent metanats Amexx and Mahjari had been fighting each other on Earth. What effect that would have on these northern towns wasn't clear, but Nadia was sure it did not help them to sort out their situation.

There were several important towns still in the grasp of Subarashii and Amexx, and these were serving as magnets for isolated metanat and UNTA security units. Burroughs was obviously chief among these, but it was true also of Cairo, Lasswitz, Sudbury, and Sheffield. In the south, the sanctuaries that had not been abandoned or destroyed by the expeditionary force were coming out of hiding, and Vishniac Bogdanov was building a surface tent over the old robot vehicle parking complex next to its mohole. So the south would no doubt return to its status as a resistance stronghold, for what that was worth; Nadia didn't think it was worth much. And the northern polar cap was in such environmental disarray that it almost didn't matter who held it—with most of its ice draining down into Vastitas, but the polar plateau covered by new snow every winter, it was the most inhospitable region on Mars, and there were almost no permanent settlements left up there.

So the contested zone was basically the temperate and equatorial latitudes, the band around the planet bordered by the Vastitas ice to the north, and the two great basins to the south. And orbital space, of course; but Sax's assault on metanat orbital objects had apparently been a success, and his removal of Deimos from the vicinity was now looking like a happy stroke indeed. The elevator, however, was still in metanat hands. And reinforcements from Earth were due any time. And Sax's team in Da Vinci had apparently used up most of their weaponry in the initial attack.

As for the soletta and the annular mirror, they were so big and fragile that they were impossible to defend; if someone wanted to wreck them, they probably could. But Nadia did not see the reason for it. If it happened, she would immediately suspect Reds on their own side of doing it. And if they did—well, everyone could get by without that extra light, as they had before. She would have to ask Sax what he thought about that. And talk to Ann about it, see what her position was. Or maybe it was better not to put ideas in her head. She would have to see how it went. Now what else. . . .

She fell asleep with her head on the screen. When she woke again she was on the couch, ravenous, and Sax was reading her screen. "It's looking bad in Sabishii," he said when he saw her struggling up. She went to the bathroom, and when she came back she looked over his shoulder and read as he talked. "Security couldn't deal with the maze. So they've left for Burroughs. But look." He had two images on-screen—on top, one of Sabishii, burning as ferociously as Kasei Vallis had; on bottom, troops flooding into the train station in Burroughs, wearing light body armor and carrying automatic weapons, their fists punching the air. Burroughs was filled with groups of these security forces, it seemed, and they had taken over Branch Mesa and Double Decker Butte for their residential quarters. So along with the UNTA troops in the city, there were now security teams from both Subarashii and Mahjari—in fact all the big metanats were represented, which caused Nadia to wonder about what was really going on between them on Earth—whether they hadn't come to some sort of agreement or *ad hoc* alliance, as a result of the crisis. She called up Art in Burroughs, to ask him what he thought.

"Maybe these Martian units are so cut off that they're making their own peace," he said. "They might be completely on their own."

"But if we're still in contact with Praxis . . . "

"Yeah, but we surprised them. They weren't aware of the extent of sympathy for the resistance, and so we got the drop on them. Maya's strategy of lying low paid off in that sense. No, these teams could very well be on their own right now. In which case we could consider Mars to be independent already, and in the midst of a civil war over who has control here. I mean, if those people in Burroughs call us up and say okay, Mars is a world, it's big enough for more than one kind of government, you have yours, and we have Burroughs, don't try to take ours away from us— what are we going to say?"

"I don't think anyone in metanat security is thinking that big," Nadia said. "It's only been three days since things fell apart on them." She pointed to the TV screen. "See, look, there's Derek Hastings, head of the Transitional Authority. He was head of Mission Control in Houston when we flew out, and he's dangerous—smart, and very stubborn. He'll just hold on until those reinforcements land."

"So what do you think we should do?"

"I don't know."

"Can we just leave Burroughs alone?"

"I don't think so. We'd be much better off if we came out from behind the sun with a completed takeover. If there are beleaguered Terran troops, holding out heroically in Burroughs, they're almost sure to come out and save them. Call it a rescue mission and then go for the whole planet."

"It won't be easy to take Burroughs, with all those troops in it."

"I know."

Sax had been asleep on another couch across the room, and now he opened one eye. "The Reds are talking about flooding it."

"What?"

"It's below the level of the Vastitas ice. And there's water under the ice. Without the dike—"

"No," Nadia said. "There's two hundred thousand people in Burroughs, and only a few thousand security troops. What are the people supposed to do? You can't evacuate that many people. It's crazy. It's sixty-one all over again." The more she thought about it, the angrier she got. "What can they be thinking?"

"Maybe it's just a threat," Art said over the screen.

"Threats don't work unless the people you're threatening believe you'll carry them out."

"Maybe they will believe it."

Nadia shook her head. "Hasting's not that stupid. Hell, he could evacuate his troops by way of the spaceport, and let the population drown! And then we become monsters, and Earth would be more certain than ever to come after us! No!"

She got up and went looking for some breakfast; then discovered, looking at the row of pastries in the kitchen, that her appetite was gone. She took a cup of coffee and went back to the office, watching her hands shake.

In 2061 Arkady had been faced with a splinter group, which had sent a small asteroid on a collision course with the Earth. It was meant to be a threat only. But the asteroid had been blown apart, in the biggest human-created explosion in history. And after that the war on Mars had suddenly become deadly in a way that it hadn't been before. And Arkady had been helpless to stop it.

And it could happen again.

She walked back into the office. "We have to go to Burroughs," she said to Sax.

Revolution suspends habit as well as law. But just as nature abhors a vacuum, people abhor anarchy.

So habits made their first incursions into the new terrain, like bacteria into rock, followed by procedures, protocols, a whole fellfield of social discourse, on its way to the climax forest of law. . . . Nadia saw that people (some people) were indeed coming to her to resolve arguments, deferring to her judgment. She might not have been in control, but she was as close to control as they had: the universal solvent, as Art called her, or General Nadia, as Maya said nastily over the wrist. Which only made Nadia shudder, as Maya knew it would. Nadia preferred something she had heard Sax say over the wrist to his faithful gang of techs, all young Saxes in the making: "Nadia is the designated arbitrator, talk to her about it." Thus the power of names; arbitrator rather than general. In charge of negotiating what Art was calling the "phase change." She had heard him use the term in the midst of a long interview on Mangalavid, with that deadpan expression of his that made it very hard to tell if he was joking or not: "Oh I don't think it's really a revolution we're seeing, no. It's a perfectly natural next step here, so it's more a kind of evolutionary or developmental thing, or what in physics they call a phase change."

His subsequent comments indicated to Nadia that he did not in fact know what a phase change was. But she did, and she found the concept intriguing. Vaporization of Terran authority, condensation of local power, the thaw finally come . . . however you wanted to think about it. Melting occurred when the thermal energy of particles was great enough to overcome the intracrystalline forces that held them in position. So if you considered the metanat order as the crystalline structure. . . . But then it made a huge difference whether the forces holding it together were interionic or intermolecular; sodium chloride, interionic, melted at 801°C; methane, intermolecular, at −183°C. What kind of forces, then? And how high the temperature?

At this point the analogy itself melted. But names were powerful in the human mind, no doubt about it. Phase change, integrated pest management, selective disemployment; she preferred them all to the old deadly notion *revolution,* and she was glad they were all in circulation, on Mangalavid and on the streets.

But there were some five thousand heavily armed security troops in Burroughs and Sheffield, she reminded herself, who were still thinking of themselves as police facing armed rioters. And that would have to be dealt with by more than semantics.

For the most part, however, things were going better than she had hoped. It was a matter of demographics, in a way; it appeared that almost every single person who had been born on Mars was now in the streets, or occupying city offices, train stations, spaceports—all of them, to judge by the Mangalavid interviews, completely (and unrealistically, Nadia thought) intolerant of the idea that powers *on another planet* should control them in any way whatsoever. That was nearly half the current Martian population, right there. And a good percentage of the old-timers were on their side too, as well as some of the new emigrants. "Call them immigrants," Art advised over the phone. "Or newcomers. Call them settlers or colonialists, depending on whether they're with us or not. That's something Nirgal has been doing, and I think it helps people to think about things."

On Earth the situation was less clear. The Subarashii metanats were still struggling with the southern metanats, but in the context of the great flood they had become a bitter sideshow. It was hard to tell what Terrans in general thought of the conflict on Mars.

Whatever they thought, a fast shuttle was about to arrive, with reinforcements for security. So resistance groups from all over mobilized to converge on Burroughs. Art did what he could to help this effort from inside Burroughs, locating all the people who had independently thought of coming (it was obvious, after all), telling them their idea was good, and siccing them on people opposed to the plan. He was, Nadia thought, a subtle diplomat—big, mild, unpretentious, unassuming, sympathetic, "undiplomatic"—head lowered as he conferred with people, giving them the impression they were the ones driving the process. Indefatigable, really. And very clever. Soon he had a great number of groups coming, including the Reds and the Marsfirst guerrillas, who still appeared to be thinking of their approach as a kind of assault, or siege. Nadia felt acutely that while the Reds and Marsfirsters she knew—Ivana, Gene, Raul, Kasei—were keeping in touch with her, and agreeing to the use of her as an arbitrator, there were more radical Red and Marsfirst units out there for whom she was irrelevant, or even an obstruction. This made her angry, because she was sure that if Ann was fully supporting her, the more radical elements would come around. She complained bitterly about this to Art, after seeing a Red communiqué arranging the western half of the "convergence" on Burroughs, and Art went to work and got Ann to answer a call, then gave her over in a link to Nadia.

And there she was again, like one of the furies of the French Revolution, as bleak and grim as ever. Their last exchange, over Sabishii, lay heavy between them; the issue had become moot when UNTA retook Sabishii and burned it down, but Ann was obviously still angry, which Nadia found irritating.

Brittle greetings over, their conversation degenerated almost instantly into argument. Ann clearly saw the revolt as a chance to wreck all terraforming efforts and to remove as many cities and people as possible from the planet, by direct assault if necessary. Frightened by this apocalyptic vision, Nadia argued with her bitterly, then furiously. But Ann had gone off into a world of her own. "I'd be just as happy if Burroughs did get wrecked," she declared coldly.

Nadia gritted her teeth. "If you wreck Burroughs you wreck *everything*. Where are the people inside supposed to go? You'll be no better than a murderer, a mass murderer. Simon would be ashamed."

Ann scowled. "Power corrupts, I see. Put Sax on, will you? I'm tired of this hysteria."

Nadia switched the call to Sax and walked away. It was not power that corrupted people, but fools who corrupted power. Well, it could be that she had been too quick to anger, too harsh. But she was frightened of that dark place inside Ann, the part that might do anything; and fear corrupted more than power. Combine the two. . . .

Hopefully she had shocked Ann severely enough to squeeze that dark place back into its corner. Bad psychology, as Michel pointed out gently, when Nadia called him in Burroughs to talk about it. A strategy resulting from fear. But she couldn't help it, she was afraid. Revolution meant shattering one structure and creating another one, but shattering was easier than creating, and so the two parts of the act were not necessarily fated to be equally successful. In that sense, building a revolution was like building an arch; until both columns were there, and the keystone in place, practically any disruption could bring the whole thing crashing down.

So on Wednesday evening, five days after Nadia's call from Sax, about a hundred people left for Burroughs in planes, as the pistes were judged too vulnerable to sabotage. They flew overnight to a rocky landing strip next to a large Bogdanovist refuge in the wall of Du Martheray Crater, which was on the Great Escarpment southeast of Burroughs. They landed at dawn, with the sun rising through mist like a blob of mercury, lighting distant ragged white hills to the north, on the low plain of Isidis: another new ice sea, whose progress south had been stopped only by the arcing line of the dike, curving across the land like a long low earthen dam—which was just what it was.

To get a better view Nadia went up to the top floor of the Du Martheray refuge, where an observation window, disguised as a horizontal crack just under the rim, gave a view down the Great Escarpment to the new dike and the ice pressing against it. For a long time she stared down at the sight, sipping coffee mixed with a dose of kava. To the north was the ice sea, with its clustered seracs and long pressure ridges, and the flat white sheets of giant frozen-topped melt lakes. Directly below her lay the first low hills of the Great Escarpment, dotted with spiky expanses of Acheron cacti, sprawling over the rock like coral reefs. Staircased meadows of black-green tundra moss followed the courses of small frozen streams dropping down the Escarpment; the streams in the distance looked like long algae diatoms, tucked into creases in the redrock.

And then in the middle distance, dividing desert from ice, ran the new dike, like a raw brown scar, suturing two separate realities together.

Nadia spent a long time studying it through binoculars. Its southern end was a regolith mound, running up the apron of Crater Wg and ending right at Wg's rim, which was about half a kilometer above the datum, well

Burroughs Region

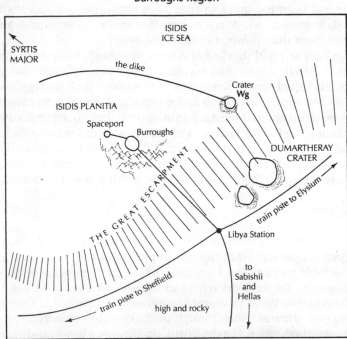

above the expected sea level. The dike ran northwest from Wg, and from her prospect high on the Escarpment Nadia could see about forty kilometers of it before it disappeared over the horizon, just to the west of Crater Xh. Xh was surrounded by ice almost to its rim, so that its round interior was like an odd red sinkhole. Everywhere else the ice had pressed right up against the dike, for as far as Nadia could see. The desert side of the dike appeared to be some two hundred meters high, although it was difficult to judge, as there was a broad trench underneath the dike. On the other side, the ice bulked quite high, halfway up or more.

The dike was about three hundred meters wide at the top. That much displaced regolith—Nadia whistled respectfully—represented several years of work, by a very large team of robot draglines and canal-diggers. But loose regolith! It seemed to her that huge as the dike was on any human scale, it was still not much to contain an ocean of ice. And ice was the easy part— when it became liquid, the waves and currents would tear regolith away like dirt. And the ice was already melting; immense melt pods were said to lie everywhere underneath the dirty white surface, including directly against the dike, seeping into it.

"Aren't they're going to have to replace that whole mound with concrete?" she said to Sax, who had joined her, and was looking through his own binoculars at the sight.

"Face it," he said. Nadia prepared herself for bad news, but he continued by saying, "Face the dike with a diamond coating. That would last fairly long. Perhaps a few million years."

"Hmm," Nadia said. It was probably true. There would be seepage from below, perhaps. But in any case, whatever the particulars, they would have to maintain the system in perpetuity, and with no room for error, as Burroughs was just 20 kilometers south of the dike, and some 150 meters lower than it. A strange place to end up. Nadia trained her binoculars in the direction of the city, but it lay just over her horizon, about 70 kilometers to the northwest. Of course dikes could be effective; Holland's dikes had held for centuries, protecting millions of people and hundreds of square kilometers, right up until the recent flood—and even now those great dikes were holding, and would be broached first by flanking floods through Germany and Belgium. Certainly dikes could be effective. But it was a strange fate nevertheless.

Nadia pointed her binoculars along the ragged rock of the Great Escarpment. What looked like flowers in the distance were actually massive lumps of coral cactus. A stream looked like a staircase made of lily pads. The rough redrock slope made for a very stark, surreal, lovely landscape. . . . Nadia was pierced by an unexpected paroxysm of fear, that something might go wrong and she might suddenly be killed, prevented from witnessing any more of this world and its evolution. It could happen, a missile might burst out of the violet sky at any moment—this refuge was target practice, if some frightened battery commander out at the Burroughs spaceport learned of its presence and decided to deal with the problem preemptively. They could be dead within minutes of such a decision.

But that was life on Mars. They could be dead within minutes of any number of untoward events, as always. She dismissed the thought, and went downstairs with Sax.

She wanted to go into Burroughs and see things, to be on the scene and judge for herself: walk around and observe the citizens of the town, see what they were doing and saying. Late on Thursday she said to Sax, "Let's go in and have a look."

But it seemed to be impossible. "Security is heavy at all the gates," Maya told her over the wrist. "And the trains coming in are checked at the stations very closely. Same with the subway to the spaceport. The city is closed. In effect we're hostages."

"We can see what's happening on-screen," Sax pointed out. "It doesn't matter."

Unhappily Nadia agreed. *Shikata ga nai,* apparently. But she didn't like the situation, which seemed to her to be rapidly approaching a stalemate, at least locally. And she was intensely curious about conditions in Burroughs. "Tell me what it's like," she asked Maya over their phone link.

"Well, they've got control of the infrastructure," Maya said. "Physical plant, gates, and so on. But there aren't enough of them to force people to stay indoors, or go to work of course, or anything else. So they don't seem to know what to do next."

Nadia could understand that, as she too felt at a loss. More security forces were coming into the city every hour, on trains from tent towns they had given up on. These new arrivals joined their fellow troops, and stayed near the physical plant and the city offices, getting around in heavily armed groups, unmolested. They were housed in residential quarters in Branch Mesa, Double Decker Butte, and Black Syrtis Mesa, and their leaders were meeting more or less continuously at the UNTA headquarters in Table Mountain. But the leaders were issuing no orders.

So things were in an uneasy suspension. The Biotique and Praxis offices in Hunt Mesa were still serving as an information center for all of them, disseminating news from Earth and the rest of the Mars, spreading it through the city on bulletin boards and computer postings. These media, along with Mangalavid and other private channels, meant that everyone was well informed concerning the latest developments. On the great boulevards, and in the parks, some big crowds congregated from time to time, but more often people were scattered in scores of small groups, milling around in a kind of active paralysis, something between a general strike and a hostage crisis. Everyone was waiting to see what would happen next.

People seemed in good spirits, many shops and restaurants were still open, and video interviews taped in them were friendly.

Watching them while jamming down a meal, Nadia felt an aching desire to be in there, to talk to people herself. Around ten that night, realizing she was hours from sleep, she called Maya again, and asked her if she would don vidcam glasses, and go on a walk for her around the city. Maya, just as antsy as Nadia if not more so, was happy to oblige.

Soon Maya was out of the safe house, wearing vidspecs and transmitting images of what she looked at to Nadia, who sat apprehensively in a chair before a screen, in the Du Martheray refuge common room. Sax and several others ended up looking over Nadia's shoulders, and together they watched the bouncing image Maya got with her vidcam, and listened to her running commentary.

She walked swiftly down Great Escarpment Boulevard, toward the central valley. Once down among the cart vendors in the upper end of Canal Park, she slowed her pace, and looked around slowly to give Nadia a panning shot of the scene. People were out and about everywhere, talking in groups, enjoying a kind of festival atmosphere. Two women next to Maya struck up an animated conversation about Sheffield. A group of newcomers came right up to Maya and asked her what was going to happen next, apparently confident that she would know, "Simply because I am so old!" Maya noted with disgust when they had left. It almost made Nadia smile. But then some young people recognized Maya as herself, and came over to greet her happily. Nadia watched this encounter from Maya's point of view, noting how starstruck the people seemed. So this is what the world looked like to Maya! No wonder she thought she was so special, with people looking at her like that, as if she were a dangerous goddess, just stepped out of a myth. . . .

It was disturbing in more senses than one. It seemed to Nadia that her old companion was in danger of being arrested by security, and she said as much over the wrist. But the view on-screen waggled from side to side as Maya shook her head. "See how there aren't any cops in sight?" Maya said. "Security is all concentrated around the gates and the train stations, and I stay away from them. Besides, why should they bother to arrest me? In effect they have this whole city arrested."

She tracked an armored vehicle as it drove down the grassy boulevard and passed without slowing down, as if to illustrate her point. "That's so everyone can see the guns," Maya said darkly.

She walked down to Canal Park, then turned around and went up the path toward Table Mountain. It was cold in the city that night; lights reflecting off the canal showed that the water in it was icing over. But if security had hoped to discourage crowds, it hadn't worked; the park was crowded, and becoming more crowded all the time. People were clumped around gazebos, or cafés, or big orange heating coils; and everywhere Maya looked more people were coming down into the park. Some listened to musicians, or people speaking with the help of little shoulder amplifiers; others watched the news on their wrists, or on lectern screens. "Rally at midnight!" someone cried. "Rally in the timeslip!"

"I haven't heard anything about this," Maya said apprehensively. "This must be Jackie's doing."

She looked around so fast that the view on Nadia's screen was dizzying. People everywhere. Sax went to another screen and called the safe house in Hunt Mesa. Art answered there, but other than him, the safe house was nearly empty. Jackie had indeed called for a mass demonstration in the timeslip, and word had gone out over all the city media. Nirgal was out there with her.

Nadia told Maya about this, and Maya cursed viciously. "It's much too volatile for this kind of thing! God*damn* her."

But there was nothing they could do about it now. Thousands of people were pouring down the boulevards into Canal Park and Princess Park, and when Maya looked around, tiny figures could be seen on the rims of the mesas, and crowding the walktube bridges that spanned Canal Park. "The speakers are going to be up in Princess Park," Art said from Sax's screen.

Nadia said to Maya: "You should get up there, Maya, and fast. You might be able to help keep the situation under control."

Maya took off, and as she made her way through the crowd, Nadia kept talking to her, giving her suggestions for what she should say if she got a chance to speak. The words tumbled out of her, and when she paused for thought, Art passed along ideas of his own, until Maya said, "But wait, wait, is any of this true?"

"Don't worry if it's true," Nadia said.

"Don't worry if it's true!" Maya shouted into her wristpad. "Don't worry if what I say to a hundred thousand people, what I say to everyone on two worlds, is true or not?"

"We'll make it true," Nadia said. "Just give it a try."

Maya began to run. Others were walking in the same direction as she was, up through Canal Park, toward the high ground between Ellis Butte and Table Mountain, and her camera gave them bobbing images of the backs of heads and the occasional excited face, turned to look at her as she shouted for clearance. Great roars and cheers were rippling through the crowd ahead, which became denser and denser, until Maya had to slow down, and then to shove and twist through gaps between groups. Most of these people were young, and much taller than Maya, and Nadia went to Sax's screen to watch the Managalavid cameras' images, which were cutting back and forth between a camera on the speakers' platform, set on the rim of an old pingo over Princess Park, and a camera up in one of the walktube bridges. Both angles showed that the crowd was getting immense—maybe eighty thousand people, Sax guessed, his nose a centimeter from the screen, as if he were counting them individually. Art managed to link up to Maya along with Nadia, and he and Nadia continued to talk to her as she fought her way forward through the crowd.

Antar had finished a short incendiary speech in Arabic while Maya was making her final push through the crowd, and Jackie was now up on the speakers' platform before a bank of microphones, making a speech that was amplified through big speakers on the pingo, and then reamplified by radio to auxiliary speakers placed all over Princess Park, and also to shoulder speakers, and lecterns, and wristpads, until her voice was everywhere—and yet, as every phrase echoed a bit off Table Mountain and Ellis Butte, and was welcomed by cheers, she could still only be heard part of the time. " . . . Will not allow Mars to be used as a replacement world . . . an executive ruling class who are primarily responsible for the destruction of Terra . . . rats trying to leave a sinking ship . . . make the same mess of things on Mars if we let them! . . . not going to happen! Because this is now a free Mars! Free Mars! Free Mars!"

And she punched a finger at the sky and the crowd roared the words out, louder and louder with each repetition, falling quickly into a rhythm that allowed them to shout together—"*Free Mars! Free Mars! Free Mars! Free Mars!*"

While the huge and still growing crowd was chanting this, Nirgal made his way up the pingo and onto the platform, and when people saw him, many of them began shouting "*Nir-gal*," either in time with "Free Mars" or in the pauses between, so that it became "*Free Mars (Nir-gal) Free Mars (Nir-gal),*" in an enormous choral counterpoint.

When he reached the microphone, Nirgal waved a hand for quiet. The chanting, however, did not stop, but changed over entirely to "*Nir-gal, Nir-gal, Nir-gal, Nir-gal,*" with an enthusiasm that was palpable, vibrating in the sound of that great collective voice, as if every single person out there was one of his friends, and enormously pleased at his appearance—and, Nadia thought, he had been traveling for so much of his life that this might not be all that far from the truth.

The chanting slowly diminished, until the crowd noise was a general buzz, quite loud, above which Nirgal's amplified greeting could be heard pretty well. As he spoke, Maya continued to make her way through the crowd toward the pingo, and as people stilled, it became easier for her. Then when Nirgal began to speak, she stopped as well and just watched him, sometimes remembering to move forward during the cheers and applause that ended many sentences.

His speaking style was low-key, calm, friendly, slow. It was easier to hear him. "For those of us born on Mars," he said, "this is our home."

He had to pause for most of a minute as the crowd cheered. They were mostly natives, Nadia saw again; Maya was shorter than almost everyone out there.

"Our bodies are made of atoms that until recently were part of the regolith," Nirgal went on. "We are Martian through and through. We are living pieces of Mars. We are human beings who have made a permanent, biological commitment to this planet. It is our home. And we can never go back." More cheers at this very well-known slogan.

"Now, as for those of us who were born on Earth—well, there are all different kinds, aren't there. When people move to a new place, some intend to stay and make it their new home, and we call those settlers. Others come to work for a while and then go back where they came from, and those we call visitors, or colonialists.

"Now natives and settlers are natural allies. After all, natives are no more than the children of earlier settlers. This is home to all of us together. As for visitors—there is room on Mars for them too. When we say that Mars is free, we are not saying Terrans can no longer come here. Not at all! We are all children of Earth, one way or another. It is our mother world, and we are happy to help it in every way we can."

The noise diminished, the crowd seeming somewhat surprised by this assertion.

"But the obvious fact," Nirgal went on, "is that what happens here on Mars should not be decided by colonialists, or by anyone back on Earth." Cheers began, drowning out some of what he said. "—A simple statement of our desire for self-determination . . . our natural right . . . the driving force of human history. We are not a colony, and we won't be treated as one. There is no such thing as a colony anymore. We are a free Mars."

More cheers, louder than ever, flowing into more chanting of *"Free Mars! Free Mars!"*

Nirgal interrupted the chanting. "What we intend to do now, as free Martians, is to welcome every Terran who wants to come to us. Whether to live here for a time and then go back, or else to settle here permanently. And we intend also to do everything we can to help Earth in its current environmental crisis. We have some expertise with flooding" (cheers) "and we can help. But this help, from now on, will no longer come mediated by metanationals, exacting their profits from the exchange. It will come as a free gift. It will benefit the people of Earth more than anything that could be extracted from us as a colony. This is true in the strict literal sense of the amount of resources and work that will be transferred from Mars to Earth. And so we hope and trust that everyone on both worlds will welcome the emergence of a free Mars."

And he stepped back and waved a hand, and the cheering and chanting erupted again. Nirgal stood on the platform, smiling and waving, looking pleased, but somewhat at a loss concerning what to do next.

All through his speech Maya had continued to inch forward during the cheering, and now Nadia could see by her vidcam image that she was at the platform's edge, standing in the first row of people. Her arms blocked the image again and again, and Nirgal caught sight of the waving, and looked at her.

When he saw who she was, he smiled and came right over, and helped boost her onto the platform. He led her over to the microphones, and Nadia caught a final image of a surprised and displeased Jackie Boone before Maya whipped off her vidcam spectacles. The image on Nadia's screen swung wildly, and ended up showing the planks of the platform. Nadia cursed and hurried over to Sax's screen, her heart in her throat.

Sax still had the Mangalavid image, now taken from the camera on the walktube arching from Ellis Butte to Table Mountain. From this angle they could see the sea of people surrounding the pingo, and filling the city's central valley far down into Canal Park; it had to be most of the people in Burroughs, surely. On the makeshift stage Jackie appeared to be shouting into Nirgal's ear. Nirgal did not respond to her, and in the middle of her exhortation he went up to the mikes. Maya looked small and old next to Jackie, but she was drawn up like an eagle, and when Nirgal said into the mikes, "We have Maya Toitovna," the cheers were huge.

Maya made chopping motions as she walked forward, and said into the mikes, "Quiet! Quiet! Thank you! Thank you. *Be quiet!* We have some serious announcements to make here as well."

"Jesus, Maya," Nadia said, clutching the back of Sax's chair.

"Mars is now independent, yes. Quiet! But as Nirgal just said, this does not mean we exist in isolation from Earth. This is impossible. We are claiming sovereignty according to international law, and we appeal to the World Court to confirm this legal status immediately. We have signed preliminary treaties affirming this independence, and establishing diplomatic relations, with Switzerland, India, and China. We have also initiated a nonexclusive economic partnership with the organization Praxis. This, like all arrangements we will make, will be not-for-profit, and designed to maximally benefit both worlds. All these treaties taken together begin the creation of our formal, legal, semiautonomous relationship with the various legal bodies of Earth. We fully expect immediate confirmation and ratification of all these agreements, by the World Court, the United Nations, and all other relevant bodies."

Cheers followed this announcement, and though they were not as loud as they had been for Nirgal, Maya allowed them to go on. When they had died down a bit, she continued.

"As for the situation here on Mars, our intentions are to meet here in Burroughs immediately, and use the Dorsa Brevia Declaration as the starting point for the establishment of a free Martian government."

Cheers again, much more enthusiastic. "Yes yes," Maya said impatiently, trying to cut them off again. "Quiet! Listen! Before any of that, we must address the problem of opposition. As you know, we are meeting here in front of the headquarters of the United Nations Transitional Authority security forces, who are this very moment listening along with the rest of us, there inside Table Mountain." She pointed. "Unless they have come out to join us." Cheers, shouting, chanting. " . . . I want to say to them now that we mean them no harm. It is the Transitional Authority's job, now, to see that the *transition* has taken on a new form. And to order its security forces to stop trying to control us. You cannot control us!" Mad cheers. " . . . mean you no harm. And we assure you that you have free access to the spaceport, where there are planes that can take all of you to Sheffield, and from there up to Clarke, if you do not care to join us in this new endeavor. This is not a siege or a blockade. This is, simply enough—"

And she stopped, and put out both hands: and the crowd told her.

Over the sound of the chanting Nadia tried to get through to Maya, still up on the stage, but it was obviously impossible for her to hear. Finally, however, Maya looked down at her wristpad. The image trembled; her arm was shaking.

"That was great, Maya! I am so proud of you!"

"Yes, well, anyone can make up stories!"

Art said loudly, "See if you can get them to disperse!"

"Right," Maya said.

"Talk to Nirgal," Nadia said. "Get him and Jackie to do it. Tell them to make sure there isn't any rush on Table Mountain, or anything like. Let them do it."

"Ha," Maya exclaimed. "Yes. We will let Jackie do it, won't we."

After that her wristpad's little camera image swung everywhere, and the noise was too great for the linked observers to make anything out. The Mangalavid cameras showed a big clump of people onstage conferring.

Nadia went over and sat down on a chair, feeling as drained as if she had had to make the speech herself. "She was great," she said. "She remembered everything we told her. Now we just have to make it real."

"Just saying it makes it real," Art said. "Hell, everyone on both worlds saw that. Praxis will be on it already. And Switzerland will surely back us. No, we'll make it work."

Sax said, "Transitional Authority might not agree. Here's a message in from Zeyk. Red commandos have come down from Syrtis. They've taken over the western end of the dike. They're moving east along it. They're not that far from the spaceport."

"That's just what we want to avoid!" Nadia cried. "What do they think they're doing!"

Sax shrugged.

"Security isn't going to like that at all," Art said.

"We should talk to them directly," Nadia said, thinking it over. "I used to talk to Hastings when he was Mission Control. I don't remember much about him, but I don't think he was any kind of screaming crazy person."

"Couldn't hurt to find out what he's thinking," Art said.

So she went to a quiet room, and got on a screen, and made a call to UNTA headquarters in Table Mountain, and identified herself. Though it was now about two in the morning, she got through to Hastings in about five minutes.

She recognized him immediately, though she would have said she had long since forgotten his face. A short thin-faced harried technocrat, with a bit of a temper. When he saw her on his screen he grimaced. "You people again. We sent the wrong hundred, I've always said that."

"No doubt."

Nadia studied his face, trying to imagine what kind of man could have headed Mission Control in one century and the Transitional Authority in the next. He had been irritated with them frequently when they were on the *Ares,* haranguing them for every little deviation from the regulations, and getting truly furious when they temporarily stopped sending back video, late in the trip. A rules and regs bureaucrat, the kind of man Arkady had despised. But a man you could reason with.

Or so it seemed to her at first. She argued with him for ten or fifteen minutes, telling him that the demonstration he had just witnessed outside in the park was part of what had happened everywhere on Mars—that the whole planet had turned against them—that they were free to go to the spaceport and leave.

"We're not going to leave," Hastings said.

His UNTA forces controlled the physical plant, he told her, and therefore the city was his. The Reds might take over the dike, but there was no chance they would broach it, because there were two hundred thousand people in the city, who were in effect hostages. Expert reinforcements were due to arrive with the next continuous shuttle, which was going to make its orbital insertion in the next twenty-four hours. So the speeches meant nothing. Posturing only.

He was calm as he told Nadia this—if he hadn't been so disgusted, Nadia might even have called him complacent. It seemed more than likely that he had orders from home, telling him to sit tight in Burroughs and wait for the reinforcements. No doubt the UNTA division in Sheffield had been told the same. And with Burroughs and Sheffield still in their hands, and reinforcements due any minute, it was not surprising they thought they had the upper hand. One might even say they were justified. "When people come to their senses," Hasting said to her sternly, "we'll be in control here again. The only thing that really matters now is the Antarctic flood, anyway. It's crucial to support the Earth in its time of need."

Nadia gave up. Hastings was clearly a stubborn man, and besides, he had a point. Several points. So she ended the conference as politely as she could, asking to get back to him later, in what she hoped was Art's diplomatic style. Then she went back out to the others.

As the night went on, they continued to monitor reports coming in from Burroughs and elsewhere. Too much was happening to allow Nadia to feel comfortable going to bed, and apparently Sax and Steve and Marian and the other Bogdanovists in Du Martheray felt similarly. So they sat slumped in their chairs, sandy-eyed and aching as the hours passed and the images on the screen flickered. Clearly some of the Reds were detaching from the main resistance coalition, following some sort of agenda of their own, escalating their campaign of sabotage and direct assault all over the planet, taking small stations by force and then, as often as not, putting the occupants in cars, and blowing the stations up. Another "Red army" also successfully stormed the physical plant in Cairo, killing many of the security guards inside, and getting the rest to surrender.

This victory had encouraged them, but elsewhere the results were not so good; it appeared from some scattered survivors' calls that a Red attack on the occupied physical plant in Lasswitz had destroyed it, and massively broached the tent, so that those who had not managed to get into secure buildings, or out into cars, had died. "What are they *doing*?" Nadia cried. But no one answered her. These groups were not returning her calls. And neither was Ann.

"I wish they would at least discuss their plans with the rest of us," Nadia said fearfully. "We can't let things spiral out of control, it's too dangerous . . . "

Sax was pursing his lips, looking uneasy. They went to the commons to get some breakfast, and then some rest. Nadia had to force herself to eat. It was exactly a week since Sax's first call, and she couldn't recall anything she had eaten in that week. Indeed, on reflection she found she was ravenous. She began to shovel down scrambled eggs.

When they were almost done eating Sax leaned over and said, "You mentioned discussing plans."

"What," Nadia said, her fork stalled halfway to her face.

"Well, this incoming shuttle, with the security task force on board?"

"What about it?" After the flight over Kasei Vallis, she did not trust Sax to be rational; the fork in her hand began to tremble visibly.

He said, "Well, I have a plan. My group in Da Vinci thought of it, actually."

Nadia tried to steady the fork. "Tell me."

The rest of that day was a blur to Nadia, as she abandoned any attempt to rest, and tried to reach Red groups, and worked with Art drafting messages to Earth, and told Maya and Nirgal and the rest in Burroughs about Sax's latest. It seemed that the pace of events, already accelerated, had caught gears with something spinning madly, and had now accelerated out of anyone's control, leaving no time to eat or sleep or go to the bathroom. But all those things had to be done, and so she staggered down to the women's room and took a long shower, then ate a spartan lunch of bread and cheese, and then stretched out on a couch and caught some sleep; but it was the kind of restless, shallow sleep in which her mind continued to tick over, thinking fuzzy distorted thoughts about the events of the day, incorporating the voices there in the room with her. Nirgal and Jackie were not getting along; was this a problem for the rest of them?

Then she was up again, as exhausted as before. The people in the room were still talking about Jackie and Nirgal. Nadia went off to the bathroom, and then hunted for coffee.

Zeyk and Nazik and a large Arab contingent had arrived at Du Martheray while she was sleeping, and now Zeyk stuck his head into the kitchen: "Sax says the shuttle is about to arrive."

Du Martheray was only six degrees north of the equator, and so they were well situated to see this particular aerobraking, which was going to happen just after sunset. The weather cooperated, and the sky was cloudless and very clear. The sun dropped, the eastern sky darkened, and the arch of colors above Syrtis to the west was a spectrum array, shading through yellow, orange, a narrow pale streak of green, teal blue, and indigo. Then the sun disappeared over the black hills, and the sky colors deepened and turned transparent, as if the dome of the sky had suddenly grown a hundred times larger.

And in the midst of this color, between the two evening stars, a third white star burst into being and shot up the sky, leaving a short straight contrail. This was the usual dramatic appearance that aerobraking continuous shuttles made as they burned into the upper atmosphere, almost as visible by day as by night. It only took about a minute for them to cross the sky from one horizon to the other, slow brilliant shooting stars.

But this time, when it was still high in the west, it got fainter and fainter, until it was no more than a faint star. And was gone.

Du Martheray's observation room was crowded, and many exclaimed at this unprecedented sight, even though they had been warned. When it was completely gone Zeyk asked Sax to explain it for those of them who had not heard the full story. The orbital insertion window for aerobraking shuttles was narrow, Sax told them, just as it had been for the *Ares* back in the beginning. There was very little room for error. So Sax's technical group in Da Vinci Crater had equipped a rocket with a payload of metal bits—like a keg of scrap iron, he said—and they had shot it off a few hours before. The payload had exploded in the approaching shuttle's MOI path just a few minutes before its arrival, casting the metal fragments in a band that was wide horizontally but narrow vertically. Orbital insertions were completely computer-controlled, of course, and so when the shuttle's radar had identified the patch of debris, the AI navigating the shuttle had had very few options. Diving below the debris would have put the shuttle through thicker atmosphere, very likely burning it up; going through the debris would risk holing the heat shield, likewise burning it up. *Shikata ga nai*, then; given the risk levels programmed into it, the AI had had to abort the aerobraking run by flying above the debris, thus skipping back out of the atmosphere. Which meant the shuttle was still moving outward in the solar system at very near its top speed of 40,000 kilometers per hour.

"Do they have any way to slow down except aerobraking?" Zeyk asked Sax.

"Not really. That's why they aerobrake."

"So the shuttle is doomed?"

"Not necessarily. They can use another planet as a gravity handle to swing around, and come back here, or go back to Earth."

"So they're on their way to Jupiter?"

"Well, Jupiter is on the other side of the solar system right now."

Zeyk was grinning. "They're on their way to Saturn?"

"They may be able to pass very close to several asteroids sequentially," Sax was saying, "and redirect their crash—their *course*."

Zeyk laughed, and though Sax went on about course correction strategies, too many other people were talking for anyone to be able to hear him.

So they no longer had to worry about security reinforcements from Earth, at least not immediately. But Nadia thought that this fact might make the UNTA police in Burroughs feel trapped, and thus more dangerous to them. And at the same time, the Reds were continuing to move north of the city, which no doubt added to security's trapped feeling. On the same night as the shuttle's flyby, groups of Reds in armored cars completed their takeover of the dike. That meant they were fairly close to the Burroughs spaceport, which was located just ten kilometers northwest of the city.

Maya appeared on-screen, looking no different than she had before her great speech. "If the Reds take the spaceport," she said to Nadia, "security will be trapped in Burroughs."

"I know. That's just what we don't want. Especially now."

"I know. Can't you keep those people under control?"

"They're not consulting me anymore."

"I thought you were the great leader here."

"I thought it was you," Nadia snapped back.

Maya laughed, harsh and humorless.

Another report came in from Praxis, a package of Terran news programs that had been relayed off Vesta. Most of it was the latest information on the flood, and the disasters in Indonesia and in many other coastal areas, but there was some political news as well, including some instances of nationalization of metanat holdings by the militaries of some client countries in the Southern Club, which the Praxis analysts thought might indicate the beginnings of a revolt by governments against metanats. As for the mass demonstration in Burroughs, it had made the news in many countries, and was certainly a topic in government offices and boardrooms around the world. Switzerland had confirmed that it was establishing diplomatic relations with a Martian government "to be designated later," as Art said with a grin. Praxis had done the same. The World Court had announced that it would consider the suit brought by the Dorsa Brevia Peaceful Neutral Coalition against UNTA—a suit dubbed "Mars vs. Terra" by the Terran media—as soon as possible. And the continuous shuttle had reported its missed insertion; apparently it planned to turn around in the asteroids. But Nadia found it extremely encouraging that none of these events were being treated as first-headline news on Earth, where the chaos caused by the flooding was still paramount in everyone's attention. There were millions of refugees everywhere, and many of them in immediate need. . . .

But this was why they had launched the revolt when they had. On Mars, the independence movements had most of the cities under their control. Sheffield was still a metanational stronghold, but Peter Clayborne was up there, in command of all the insurgents on Pavonis, coordinating their activities in a way that they had not been able to match around Burroughs. Partly this was because many of the most radical elements of the resistance had avoided Tharsis, and partly because the situation in Sheffield was extremely difficult, with little room for maneuvering. The insurgents now controlled Arsia and Ascraeus, and the little scientific station in Crater Zp on Olympus Mons; and they even had control of most of Sheffield town. But the elevator socket, and the whole quarter of the city surrounding it, were firmly in the hands of the security police, and they were heavily armed. So Peter had his hands full on Tharsis, and would not be able to help them around Burroughs. Nadia talked to him briefly, describing the situation in Burroughs and begging him to call Ann and ask her to get the Reds to show some restraint. He promised to do what he could, but did not seem confident that he had his mother's ear.

After that Nadia tried another call to Ann, but did not get through. Then she tried to reach Hastings, and he took her call, but it was not a productive exchange. Hastings was no longer anything like the complacent disgusted figure she had talked to the night before. "This occupation of the dike!" he exclaimed angrily. "What are they trying to prove? Do you think I believe that they'll cut the dike when there's two hundred thousand people in this city, most of them on your side? It's absurd! But you listen to me, there are people in this organization who don't like the danger it puts the population in! I tell you, I can't be responsible for what happens if those people don't get the hell off that dike—off Isidis Planitia entirely! You get them off there!"

And he cut the connection before Nadia could even reply, distracted by someone off-screen who had come in during the middle of his tirade. A frightened man, Nadia thought, feeling the iron walnut tugging inward again. A man who no longer felt in control of the situation. An accurate assessment, no doubt. But she had not liked that last look on his face. She even tried to call back, but no one in Table Mountain would answer anymore.

A couple of hours later Sax woke her up in her chair, and she found out what Hastings had been so worried about. "The UNTA unit that burned Sabishii went out in armored cars and tried to—to take the dike away from the Reds," Sax told her, looking grave. "Apparently there's been a fight over the section of the dike nearest the city. And we've just heard from some Red units up there that the dike has been broached."

"What?"

"Blown up. They had drilled holes and set charges to use as a—as a threat. And in the fighting they ended up setting them off. That's what they said."

"Oh my God." Her drowsiness was gone in a flash, blown away in her own internal explosion, a great blast of adrenaline racing all through her. "Have you got any confirmation?"

"We can see a dustcloud blocking the stars. A big one."

"Oh my God." She went to the nearest screen, her heart thudding in her chest. It was three A.M. "Is there a chance ice will choke the gap, and serve as a dam?"

Sax squinted. "I don't think so. Depends on how big the gap is."

"Can we set counterexplosions and close the gap?"

"I don't think so. Look, here's video sent from some Reds south of the break on the dike." He pointed at a screen, which displayed an IR image with black to the left and blackish green to the right, and a forest-green spill across the middle. "That's the blast zone there in the middle, warmer than the regolith. The explosion appears to have been set next to a pod of liquid water. Or else there was an explosion set to liquefy the ice behind the break. Anyway, that's a lot of water coming through. And that will widen the break. No, we've got a problem."

"Sax," she exclaimed, and held on to his shoulder as she stared at the screen. "The people in Burroughs, what are they supposed to do? God damn it, what could Ann be *thinking?*"

"It might not have been Ann."

"Ann or any of the Reds!"

"They were attacked. It could have been an accident. Or someone on the dike must have thought they were going to get forced away from the explosives. In which case it was a use-it-or-lose-it situation." He shook his head. "Those are always bad."

"*Damn* them." Nadia shook her head hard, trying to clear it. "We have to do something!" She thought frantically. "Are the mesa tops high enough to stay above the flood?"

"For a while. But Burroughs is at about the lowest point in that little depression. That's why it was sited there. Because the sides of the bowl gave it long horizons. No. The mesa tops will get covered too. I can't be sure how long it will take, because I'm not sure of the flow rate. But let's see, the volume to be filled is about . . . " He tapped away madly, but his eyes were blank, and suddenly Nadia saw that there was another part of his mind doing the calculation faster than the AI, a gestalt envisioning of the situation, staring at infinity, shaking his head back and forth like a blind man. "It could be pretty fast," he whispered before he was done typing. "If the melt pod is big enough."

"We have to assume it is."

He nodded.

They sat there beside each other, staring at Sax's AI.

Sax said hesitantly, "When I was working in Da Vinci, I tried to think out the possible scenarios. The shapes of things to come. You know? And I worried that something like this might happen. Broken cities. Tents, I thought it would be. Or fires."

"Yes?" Nadia said, looking at him.

"I thought of an experiment—a *plan.*"

"Tell me," Nadia said evenly.

But Sax was reading what looked like a weather update, which had just appeared over the figures scrolling on his screen. Nadia patiently waited him out, and when he looked up from his AI again, she said, "Well?"

"There's a high-pressure cell, coming down Syrtis from Xanthe. It should be here today. Tomorrow. On Isidis Planitia the air pressure will be about three hundred and forty millibars, with roughly forty-five percent nitrogen, forty percent oxygen, and fifteen percent carbon diox—"

"Sax, I don't care about the weather!"

"It's breathable," he said. He eyed her with that reptile expression of his, like a lizard or a dragon, or some cold posthuman creature, fit to inhabit the vacuum. "Almost breathable. If you filter the CO_2. And we can do that. We manufactured face-masks in Da Vinci. They're made from a zirconium alloy lattice. It's simple. CO_2 molecules are bigger than oxygen or nitrogen molecules, so we made a molecular sieve filter. It's an active filter too, in that there's a piezoelectric layer, and the charge generated when the material bends during inhalation and exhalation—powers an active transfer of oxygen through the filter."

"What about dust?" Nadia said.

"It's a set of filters, graded by size. First it stops dust, then fines, then CO_2." He looked up at Nadia. "I just thought people might—need to get out of a city. So we made half a million of them. Strap the masks on. The edges are sticky polymer, they stick to skin. Then breathe the open air. Very simple."

"So we evacuate Burroughs."

"I don't see any alternative. We can't get that many people out by train or air fast enough. But we can walk."

"But walk to where?"

"To Libya Station."

"Sax, it's about seventy k from Burroughs to Libya Station, isn't it?"

"Seventy-three kilometers."

"That's a hell of a long way to walk!"

"I think most people could manage it if they had to," he said evenly. "And those who can't could be picked up by rovers or dirigibles. Then as people get to Libya Station, they can leave by train. Or dirigible. And the station will hold maybe twenty thousand at a time. If you jam them in."

Nadia thought about it, looking down at Sax's expressionless face. "Where are these masks?"

"They're back at Da Vinci. But they're already stowed in fast planes, and we could get them here in a couple hours."

"Are you sure they work?"

Sax nodded. "We tried them. And I brought a few along. I can show you." He got up and went to his old black bag, opened it, pulled out a stack of white facemasks. He gave Nadia one. It was a mouth-and-nose mask, and looked very much like a conventional dust mask used in construction, only thicker, and with a rim that was sticky to the touch.

Nadia inspected it, put it over her head, tightened the thin strap. She could breathe through it as easily as through a dust mask. No sensation of obstruction at all. The seal seemed good.

"I want to try it outside," she said.

First Sax sent word to Da Vinci to fly the masks over, and then they went down to the refuge lock. Word of the plan and the trial had gotten around, and all the masks Sax had brought were quickly spoken for. Going out along with Nadia and Sax were about ten other people, including Zeyk, and Nazik, and Spencer Jackson, who had arrived at Du Martheray about an hour before.

They all wore the current styles of surface walker, which were jumpsuits made of layered insulated fabrics, including heating filaments, but without any of the old constrictive material that had been needed in the early low-pressure years. "Try leaving your walker heaters off," Nadia told the others. "That way we can see what the cold feels like if you're wearing city clothes."

They put the masks over their faces, and went into the garage lock. The air in it got very cold very fast. And then the outer door opened.

They walked out onto the surface.

It was cold. The shock of it hit Nadia in the forehead, and the eyes. It was hard not to gasp a little. Going from 500 millibars to 340 would no doubt account for that. Her eyes were running, her nose as well. She breathed out, breathed in. Her lungs ached with the cold. Her eyes were right out in the wind—that was the sensation that most struck her, the exposure of her eyes. She shivered as the cold penetrated her walker's fabrics, and the inside of her chest. The chill had a Siberian edge to it, she thought. 260°K, −13° Centigrade—not that bad, really. She just wasn't used to it. Her hands and feet had gotten chilled many a time on Mars, but it had been years and years—over a century in fact!—since her head and lungs had felt the cold like this.

The others were talking loudly to each other, their voices sounding funny in the open air. No helmet intercoms! Her walker's neckring, where the helmet ought to have rested, was extremely cold on her collarbones and the back of her neck. The ancient broken black rock of the Great Escarpment was covered with a thin night frost. She had peripheral vision such as she never had in a helmet—wind—tears running down her cheeks from the cold. She felt no particular emotion. She was surprised by how things looked unobstructed by a faceplate or any other window; they had a sharp-edged hallucinatory clarity, even in starlight. The sky in the east was a rich predawn Prussian blue, with high cirrus clouds already catching the light, like pink mares' tails. The ragged corrugations of the Great Escarpment were gray-on-black in the starlight, lined with black shadows. The wind in her eyes!

People were talking without intercoms, their voices thin and disembodied, their mouths hidden by the masks. There was no mechanical hum, buzz, hiss, or whoosh; after over a century of such noise, the windy silence of the outdoors was strange, a kind of aural hollowness. Nazik looked like she was wearing a Bedouin veil.

"It's cold," she said to Nadia. "My ears are burning. I can feel the wind on my eyes. On my face."

"How long will the filters last?" Nadia said to Sax, speaking loudly to be sure she was heard.

"A hundred hours."

"Too bad people have to breath out through them." That would add a lot more CO_2 to the filter.

"Yes. But I couldn't see a simple way around it."

They were standing on the surface of Mars, bareheaded. Breathing the air with the aid of nothing more than a filter mask. The air was thin, Nadia judged, but she did not feel lightheaded. The high percentage of oxygen was making up for the low atmospheric pressure. It was the partial pressure of oxygen that counted, and so with the percentage of oxygen in the atmosphere so high. . . .

Zeyk said, "Is this is the first time anyone's done this?"

"No," Sax said. "We did it a lot in Da Vinci."

"It feels good! It's not as cold as I thought it would be!"

"And if you walk hard," Sax said, "you'll warm up."

They walked around a bit, careful of their footing in the dark. It was quite cold, no matter what Zeyk said. "We should go back in," Nadia said.

"You should stay out and see the dawn," Sax said. "It's nice without helmets."

Nadia, surprised to hear such a sentiment coming from him, said, "We can see other dawns. Right now we have a lot to talk about. Besides, it's cold."

"It feels good," Sax said. "Look, there's Kerguelen cabbage. And sandwort." He kneeled, brushed a hairy leaf aside to show them a hidden white flower, barely visible in the predawn light.

Nadia stared at him.

"Come on in," she said.

So they went back.

They took their masks off inside the lock, and then they were back in the refuge's changing room, rubbing their eyes and blowing into their gloved hands. "It wasn't so cold!" "The air tasted sweet!"

Nadia pulled off her gloves and felt her nose. The flesh was chilled, but it was not the white cold of incipient frostbite. She looked at Sax, whose eyes were gleaming with a wild expression, very unlike him—a strange and somehow moving sight. They all looked excited for that matter, stuffed to the edge of laughter with a peculiar exhilaration, edged by the dangerous situation down the slope in Burroughs. "I've been trying to get the oxygen levels up for years," Sax was saying to Nazik and Spencer and Steve.

Spencer said, "I thought that was to get your fire in Kasei Vallis to burn hard."

"Oh no. As far as fire goes, once you've got a certain amount of oxygen, it's more a matter of aridity and what materials there are to burn. No, this was to get the partial pressure of oxygen up, so that people and animals could breathe it. If only the carbon dioxide were reduced."

"So have you made animal masks?"

They laughed and went up to the refuge commons, and Zeyk set about making coffee while they talked over the walk, and touched each other on the cheek to compare coldnesses.

"What about getting people out of the city?" Nadia said to Sax suddenly. "What if security keeps the gates closed?"

"Cut the tent," he said. "We should anyway, to get people out faster. But I don't think they'll keep the gates closed."

"They're going out to the spaceport," someone shouted from the comm room. "The security forces are taking the subway out to the spaceport. They're abandoning ship, the bastards. And Michel says the train station—South Station has been wrecked!"

This caused a clamor. Through it Nadia said to Sax, "Let's tell Hunt Mesa the plan, and get down there and meet the masks."

Sax nodded.

Between Mangalavid and the wristpads they were able to make a very rapid dispersal of the plan to the population of Burroughs, while driving down in a big caravan from Du Martheray to a low line of hillocks just southwest of the city. Soon after their arrival, the two planes bringing the CO_2 masks from Da Vinci swooped down over Syrtis, and landed on a swept area of the plains just outside the western apron of the tent wall. On the other side of the city observers on top of Double Decker Butte had already reported sighting the flood, coming in from a bit north of east: dark brown ice-flecked water, pouring down the low crease that inside the city wall was occupied by Canal Park. And the news about South Station had proved true; the piste equipment had been wrecked, by an explosion in the linear induction generator. No one knew for sure who had done it, but it was done, the trains immobilized.

So as Zeyk's Arabs drove the boxes of masks to West, Southwest, and South gates, there were huge crowds already congregating inside each of them, everyone dressed either in walkers with heating filaments, or in the heaviest clothes they had—none too heavy for the job at hand, Nadia judged as she went in Southwest Gate, and passed out facemasks from boxes. These days many people in Burroughs went out on the surface so seldom that they rented walkers to do so. But there were not enough walkers to dress everyone, and they had to go with people's interior coats, which were fairly lightweight, and usually deficient in headgear. The message about the evacuation had been sent out with a warning to dress for 255°K, however, and so most people were layered in several garments, appearing thick-limbed and thick-torsoed.

Each gate lock could pass five hundred people every five minutes—they were big locks—but with thousands of people waiting inside, and the crowds growing as Saturday morning wore on, it was not anywhere near fast enough. The masks had been distributed through the crowds, and it seemed certain to Nadia that at this point everyone had one. It was unlikely that anyone in the city was unaware of the emergency. And so she went around to Zeyk, and Sax, and Maya and Michel, and all the other people she knew that she saw, saying, "We should cut the tent wall and just walk out. I'm going to cut the tent wall now." And no one disagreed.

Finally Nirgal showed up, gliding through the crowd like Mercury on an urgent errand, smiling hugely and greeting acquaintance after acquaintance, people who wanted to hug him or shake his hand or just touch him. "I'm going to cut the tent wall now," Nadia told him. "Everyone has masks, and we need to get out of here faster than the gates will let us."

"Good idea," he said. "Let me just announce what's happening."

And he jumped three meters into the air, grabbing a coping on the gate's concrete arch and hauling himself up so that he was balanced on it, both feet on the same three-centimeter strip. He turned on a small shoulder loudspeaker he was wearing, and said, "Attention, please!—We're going to start cutting the tent wall, right above the coping—there should be a breeze outward, not very strong—after that, people nearest the wall out first, of course—there will be no need to hurry at that point—we'll cut extensively, and everyone should be out of the city in the following half hour. Be ready for the cold—it will be *very invigorating*. Please get your masks on, and check your seal, and the seal of the people around you."

He looked down at Nadia, who had gotten a little laser welder out of her black backpack, and now showed it to Nirgal, holding it overhead so that much of the crowd could see it.

"Is everyone ready?" Nirgal asked over his loudspeaker. Everyone visible in the crowd had a white mask over their lower faces. "You look like bandits," Nirgal told them, and laughed. "Okay!" he said, looking down at Nadia.

And she cut the tent.

Sensible survival behavior is almost as contagious as panic, and the evacuation was quick and orderly. Nadia cut about two hundred meters of tenting, right above the concrete coping, and the higher air pressure inside caused an outflowing wind that held the transparent layers of the tent fabric up and out from the coping, so that people could climb over the waist-high wall without having to deal with it. Others cut the tent near West and South gates, and in about the time it takes to empty a big stadium, the population of Burroughs was out of the city, and into the cold fresh air of an Isidis morning: pressure 350 millibars, temperature 261K°, or −12° Celsius.

Zeyk's Arabs stayed in their rovers and served as escorts, rolling back and forth and guiding people up to the line of hillocks a few kilometers to

the southwest of the city, called the Moeris Hills. Floodwater reached the
eastern side of the city as the last part of the crowd made it onto this line
of low bumps in the plain, and Red observers, ranging wide in rovers of
their own, reported that the flood was now running north and south
around the foot of the city wall, in a surge that at this point was less than
a meter deep.

So it had been a very, very close thing; close enough to make Nadia
shudder. She stood on the top of one of the Moeris hillocks, looking about
trying to gauge the situation. People had done their best, but were insuf-
ficiently dressed, she thought; not everyone had insulated boots, and very
few people had much in the way of headgear. The Arabs were leaning out
of their rovers to show people how to wrap scarves or towels or extra jackets over their heads in improvised burnoose hoods, and that would have
to do. But it was cold out, very cold despite the sun and the lack of wind,
and the citizens of Burroughs who did not work on the surface were looking shocked. Although some were in better shape than others; Nadia could
spot Russian newcomers by their warm hats, brought from home; she
greeted these people in Russian, and almost always they grinned—"This
is nothing," they shouted, "this is good iceskating weather, da?" "Keep
moving," Nadia said to them and to everyone else. "Keep moving." It was
supposed to warm up in the afternoon, perhaps up to freezing.

Inside the doomed city the mesas stood stark and dramatic in the
morning light, like a titanic museum of cathedrals, the banks of windows
inlaid in them like jewels, the foliage on the mesa tops little green gardens
capping the redrock. The city's population stood on the plain, masked like
bandits or hay fever victims, bundled thickly in clothes, some in slim
heated walkers, a few carrying helmets for use later if needed; the whole
pilgrimage standing and looking back at the city: people on the surface of
Mars, their faces exposed to the frigid thin air, standing hands in their
pockets, above them high cirrus clouds like metal shavings plastered
against the dark pink sky. The strangeness of the sight was both exhilarating and terrifying, and Nadia walked up and down the line of knobs
talking with Zeyk, Sax, Nirgal, Jackie, Art. She even sent another message
to Ann, hoping that Ann was receiving them, even though she never answered: "Make sure the security troops have no trouble at the spaceport,"
she said, unable to keep the anger out of her voice. "Keep out of their
way."

About ten minutes later her wrist beeped. "I know," Ann's voice said
curtly. And that was all.

Now that they were out of the city, Maya was feeling buoyant. "Let's
start walking," she cried. "It's a long way to Libya Station, and half the
day is almost gone already!"

"True," Nadia said. And many people had already started, heading
over to the piste that ran out of Burroughs South Station, and following it
south, up the slope of the Great Escarpment.

•   •   •

So they walked away from the city. Nadia often stopped to encourage people, and so quite often she was looking back at Burroughs, at the roof-tops and gardens under the transparent bubble of the tent, in the midday sunlight—down into that green mesocosm that for so long had been the capital of their world. Now rusty black ice-flecked water had run almost all the way around the city wall, and a thick flow of dirty icebergs was coming down from the low crease to the northeast, pouring toward the city in a broadening torrent, filling the air with a roar that raised the hair on the back of her neck, a Marineris rumbling. . . .

The land they walked over was dotted by scattered low plants, mostly tundra moss and alpine flowers, with occasional stands of ice cactus like spiky black fire hydrants. Midges and flies, disturbed by the strange inva-sion, whirred around in the air overhead. It was noticeably warmer than it had been in the morning, the temperatures rising fast; it felt a little above zero. "Two seventy-two!" Nirgal cried when Nadia asked him in passing. He was passing by every few minutes, running up and down the crowd from one end of the line to the other and back again. Nadia checked her wrist: 272°K. The wind was very slight, and from the southwest. The weather reports indicated the high-pressure zone would stay over Isidis for another day at least.

People were walking in small knots, in the process of finding other small knots, so that friends and work groups and acquaintances were greet-ing each other as they moved along, surprised often by familiar voices under masks, familiar eyes between mask and hood or hat. A diffuse frost cloud rose from the crowd, a mass exhalation, burning off quickly in the sun. Rovers from the Red army had driven up from both sides of the city, hurrying to get away from the flood; now they moved along slowly, their outriders passing out flasks of hot drinks. Nadia glared at them, mouthing silent curses inside the privacy of her mask, but one of the Reds saw the curse in her eyes, and said to her irritably, "It wasn't us broke the dike, you know, it was the Marsfirst guerrillas. It was Kasei!"

And he drove on.

A convention was being established whereby ravines to the east of the piste were being used as latrines. They were getting far enough upslope that people often stopped to look back down into the strangely empty city, with its new moat of dark rusty ice-choked water. Groups of natives were chanting bits of the aerophany as they walked, and hearing it, Nadia's heart squeezed inside her; she muttered, "Come back out, damn you, Hi-roko, please—come back out *today*."

She spotted Art, and walked over to his side. He was making a running commentary over the wrist, apparently sending it to a news consortium on Earth. "Oh yes," he said in a quick aside when Nadia asked him about it. "We're live. Real good vid too, I'm sure. And they can relate to the flood scenario."

No doubt. The city with its mesas, surrounded now by black ice-choked water, which was steaming faintly, its surface turbulent, its edges bubbling madly with carbonation, as waves surged down from the north, the noise like waves in a high storm. . . . The air temperature was now just above freezing, and the surging water was staying liquid even when it pooled and went still, even when it was covered with floating brash ice. Nadia had never seen anything that brought home to her more strongly the fact that they had transformed the atmosphere—not the plants, nor the bluing of the sky color, nor even their ability to expose their eyes, and breathe through thin masks. The sight of water freezing during the Marineris deluge—going from black to white in twenty seconds or less—had marked her more deeply than she knew. Now they had open water. The low broad crease holding Burroughs looked like a gargantuan Bay of Fundy, with the tide racing up it.

People were exclaiming, their voices filling the thin air like birdsong, over the low continuo of the flood. Nadia didn't know why; then she saw—there was movement at the spaceport.

The spaceport was located on a broad plateau to the northwest of the city, and at their height on the slope, the population of Burroughs could stand there and watch while the great doors of the spaceport's largest hangar opened, and five giant space planes rolled out one after another: an ominous, somehow military sight. The planes taxied up to the spaceport's main terminal, and jetways extended and latched on to their sides. Again nothing happened, and the refugees walked up toward the first real hills of the Great Escarpment for the better part of an hour, until, despite their increase in elevation, the spaceport runways and the lower halves of the hangars were under the watery horizon. The sun was well in the west now.

Attention turned to the city itself, as the water broached the tent wall on the east side of Burroughs, and ran in over the coping by Southwest Gate, where they had cut the tent. Soon thereafter it was flooding Princess Park and Canal Park and the Niederdorf, dividing the city in two and then slowly rising up the side boulevards, covering the roofs in the lower part of town.

In the midst of this spectacle one of the big jets appeared in the sky over the plateau, looking much too slow to fly, as big planes low to the ground always do. It had taken off southward, so for the spectators on the ground it grew larger and larger without ever seeming to gain speed, until the low rumble of its eight engines reached them, and it plowed overhead with the slow impossible awkwardness of a bumblebee. As it lumbered off to the west the next one appeared over the spaceport, and headed past the water-floored city and over them, off to the west. And so it went for all five planes, each one looking as unaerodynamic as the last, until the last one had trolled past them and disappeared over the western horizon.

Now they began to walk in earnest. The fastest walkers took off, making no attempt to stay back with the slower ones; it was important to begin to train people away from Libya Station as soon as possible, and this was understood by all. Trains were on their way to Libya from all over, but Libya Station was small and had only a few sidings, so the choreography of the evacuation was going to be complex.

It was now five in the afternoon, the sun low over the rise of Syrtis, the temperature plummeting past zero, on its way far down. As the faster walkers, mostly natives and the latest immigrants, pressed on ahead, the crowd became a long column. The people in rovers reported that it was several kilometers long now, and getting longer all the time. These rovers drove up and down the line, picking people up and sometimes letting others out. All available walkers and helmets were being used. Coyote had appeared on the scene, driving up from the direction of the dike, and seeing his boulder car, Nadia instantly suspected he was behind the broaching of the dike; but after greeting her cheerily over the wrist, and asking how things were going, he drove back toward the city. "Get South Fossa to send a dirigible over the city," he suggested, "in case anyone was left behind, and is up on the mesa tops. There must be some people in there who slept through the day, and when they wake up they are in for one very big surprise."

He laughed wildly, but it was a good point, and Art made the call.

Nadia walked along at the back of the column with Maya and Sax and Art, listening to reports as they came in. She got the rovers to drive on the dead piste, to avoid kicking dust into the air. She tried to ignore the fact that she was tired already. It was mostly lack of sleep, rather than muscular exhaustion. But it was going to be a long night. And not only for her. Many people on Mars were entirely city dwellers now, and unused to walking very far at a time. She herself seldom did, though she was often on her feet around construction sites, and did not have a desk job like many of these people. Luckily they were following a piste, and could even walk on its smooth surface if they cared to, between the suspension rails on the edges and the reaction rail running down the middle. Most preferred to stay on the concrete or gravel roads running alongside the piste, however.

Unfortunately, walking out of Isidis Planitia in any direction but north meant walking uphill. Libya Station was about seven hundred meters higher than Burroughs, not an inconsiderable height; but the grade was almost continuous over the seventy kilometers, and there were no steep sections anywhere along the way. "It will help keep us warm," Sax muttered when Nadia mentioned it.

It got later and later, until their shadows were cast far to the east, as if they were giants. Behind them the drowning city, lightless and empty, black-floored, disappeared over their horizon mesa by mesa, until finally Double Decker Butte and Moeris Mesa were submerged by the skysill. The dusky burnt umbers of Isidis took on more and more color, and the sky darkened and darkened, until the fat sun lay burning on the western horizon, and they walked slowly through a ruddy world, strung out like a ragtag army in retreat.

Nadia checked Mangalavid from time to time, and found the news from the rest of the planet mostly comforting. All the major cities but Sheffield had been secured by the independence movement. Sabishii's mound maze had provided refuge for the survivors of the fire, and though the fire was not yet put out everywhere, the maze meant they would be okay. Nadia talked to Nanao and Etsu for a while as she walked. The little wrist image of Nanao revealed his exhaustion, and she said something about how bad she felt—Sabishii burned, Burroughs drowned—the two greatest cities on Mars, destroyed. "No no," Nanao said. "We rebuild. Sabishii is in our mind."

They were sending their few unburned trains to Libya Station, as were many other cities. The nearest were also sending planes and dirigibles. The dirigibles would be able to come to their aid during the night's march, which was useful. Especially important would be any water they could bring with them, as dehydration in the cold and hyperarid night was going to be severe. Nadia's throat was already parched, and she happily took a cupful of warm water from a passing rover handing them out. She lifted her mask and drank swiftly, trying not to breathe as she did. "Last call!" the woman passing out the cups called cheerily. "We'll run out after the next hundred people."

Another kind of call came in from South Fossa. They had heard from several mining camps around Elysium, whose occupants had declared themselves independent of both the metanationals and the Free Mars movement, and were warning everyone to stay away. Some stations occupied by Reds were doing much the same. Nadia snorted. "Tell them fine," she said to the people in South Fossa. "Send them a copy of the Dorsa Brevia Declaration, and tell them to study it for a while. If they'll agree to uphold the human rights section, I don't see why we should bother with them."

• • •

The sun set as they walked. The long twilight slowly ran its course.

While there was still a dark purple twilight suffusing the hazy air, a boulder car drove up from the east and stopped just ahead of Nadia's group, and figures got out and walked over to them, wearing white masks and hoods. By silhouette alone Nadia recognized, all of a sudden, the one in the lead: it was Ann, tall and spare, walking right up to her, picking her out of the rabble at the tail end of the column without hesitation, despite the lack of light. The way the First Hundred knew each other. . . .

Nadia stopped, stared up at her old friend. Ann was blinking at the sudden cold.

"We didn't do it," Ann said brusquely. "The Armscor unit came out in armored cars, and there was a real fight. Kasei was afraid that if they retook the dike they would try to retake everything, everywhere. He was probably right."

"Is he okay?"

"I don't know. A lot of people on the dike were killed. And a lot had to escape the flood by going up onto Syrtis."

She stood there before them, grim, unapologetic—Nadia marveled that one could read so much from a silhouette, a black cutout against the stars. Set of the shoulders, perhaps. Tilt of the head.

"Come on then," Nadia said. There was nothing else she could think to say, at this point. Going out onto the dike in the first place, setting the explosive charges . . . but there was no point, now. "Let's keep walking."

The light leaked away from the land, out of the air, out of the sky. They hiked under the stars, through air as cold as Siberia. Nadia could have gone faster, but she wanted to stay at the back with the slowest group, to do what she could to help. People were giving piggyback rides to some of the smaller children among them, but the fact was there weren't very many children at the end of the column; the smallest ones were already in rovers, and the older ones were up front with the faster walkers. There hadn't been that many children in Burroughs to begin with.

Rover headlight beams cut through the dust they were throwing into the air, and seeing it Nadia wondered if the CO_2 filters would get clogged by fines. She mentioned this aloud, and Ann said, "If you hold the mask to your face and blow out hard, it helps. You can also hold your breath and take it off, and blow compressed air through it, if you have a compressor."

Sax nodded.

"You know these masks?" Nadia said to Ann.

Ann nodded. "I've spent many hours using ones like them."

"Okay, good." Nadia experimented with hers, holding the fabric right against her mouth and blowing out hard. Quickly she felt short of breath. "We still should try walking on the piste and the roads, and cutting down on the dust. And tell the rovers to go slow."

They walked on. Over the next couple of hours they fell into a kind of rhythm. No one passed them, no one fell back. It got colder and colder. Rover headlights partially illuminated the thousands of people ahead of them, all the way up the long gradual slope to the high southern horizon, which was perhaps twelve or fifteen kilometers ahead of them, it was hard to tell in the dark. The column ran all the way to the horizon: a bobbing, fencing collection of headlight beams, flashlight beams, the red glow of taillights . . . a strange sight. Occasionally there was a buzz overhead, as dirigibles from South Fossa arrived, floating like gaudy UFOs with all their running lights on, their engines humming as they wafted down to drop off loads of food and water for the cars to retrieve, and pick up groups from the back of the column. Then they hummed up into the air and away, until they were no more than colorful constellations, disappearing over the horizon to the east.

During the timeslip a crowd of exuberant young natives tried to sing, but it was too cold and dry, and they did not persist for long. Nadia liked the idea, and in her mind she sang some of her old favorites many times: "Hello Central Give Me Dr. Jazz," "Bucket's Got a Hole in It," "On the Sunny Side of the Street." Over and over and over.

The longer the night went on, the better her mood became; it was beginning to seem like the plan was going to work. They were not passing hundreds of prostrate people—although the word from the cars was that a fair number of the young natives appeared to have blown it and gone out too fast, and were now requiring assistance. Everyone had gone from 500 millibars to 340, which was the equivalent of going from 4,000 meters altitude on Earth to 6,500 meters, not an inconsiderable jump even with the higher percentage of oxygen in the Martian air to mitigate the effects; thus people were coming down with altitude sickness. Altitude sickness tended to strike the young a bit more than the old anyway, and many of the natives had taken off very enthusiastically. So some were paying for it now, with headaches and nausea felling quite a few. But the cars reported success so far taking in the ones on the edge of vomiting, and escorting the rest. And the rear of the column was keeping a steady pace.

So Nadia trudged on, sometimes hand in hand with Maya or Art, sometimes in her own world, her mind wandering in the biting cold, remembering odd shards of the past. She remembered some of the other dangerous cold walks she had taken over the surface of this world of hers: out in the great storm with John at Rabe Crater . . . searching for the transponder with Arkady . . . following Frank down into Noctis Labyrinthus, on the night they escaped from the assault on Cairo. . . . On that night too she had fallen into an odd bleak cheerfulness—response to a freeing from responsibility, perhaps, to becoming no more than a foot soldier, following someone else's lead. Sixty-one had been such a disaster. This revolution too could devolve into chaos—indeed it had. No one in control. But there were still voices coming in over her wrist, from everywhere. And no one was going to strafe them from space. The most intransigent elements of the Transitional Authority had probably been killed outright, in Kasei Vallis—an aspect of Art's "integrated pest management" that was no joke. And the rest of UNTA was being overwhelmed by sheer numbers. They were incapable, as anyone would be, of controlling a whole planet of dissidents. Or too intimidated to try.

So they had managed to do it differently this time. Or else conditions on Earth had simply changed, and all the various phenomena of Martian history were only distorted reflections of those changes. Quite possible. A troubling thought, when considering the future. But that was for later. They would face all that when they came to it. Now they only had to worry about getting to Libya Station. The sheer physicality of the problem, and of the solution to the problem, pleased her immensely. Finally something she could get her hands on. Walk. Breathe the frigid air. Try to warm her lungs from the rest of her, from the heart—something like Nirgal's uncanny heat redistribution, if only she could!

It began to seem like she could actually catch little bursts of sleep while still walking. She worried it was CO_2 poisoning, but continued to blink out from time to time. Her throat was very sore. The tail end of the column was slowing down, and rovers were now driving back to it and picking up all the people who were exhausted, and driving them up the slope to Libya Station, where they would drop them off, and return for another load. A lot more people were beginning to suffer altitude sickness, and the Reds were telling victims over the wrist how to pull off their masks and vomit, and then get the masks back on before breathing again. A difficult unpleasant operation at best, and many people were suffering CO_2 poisoning as well as altitude sickness. Still, they were closing on their destination. The wrist images from Libya Station looked like the inside of a Tokyo subway station at rush hour, but trains were arriving and departing on a regular basis, so it looked like there was going to be room for the later arrivals.

A rover rolled up beside them, and asked them if they wanted a lift. Maya said, "Get out of here! What's the matter, can't you see? Go help those people up there, come on, stop wasting our time!"

The driver took off quickly to avoid more castigation. Maya said hoarsely, "To hell with that. I'm a hundred and forty-three years old, and I'll be damned if I don't walk the whole way. Let's pick up the pace a little."

They kept the same pace. They kept at the back of the column, watching the parade of lights bobbing in the haze ahead of them. Nadia's eyes had hurt for several hours, but now they were getting really painful, the numbness of the cold no longer a help, apparently; they were very, very dry, and sandy in their sockets. It stung to blink. Goggles with the masks would have been a good idea.

She stumbled over an unseen rock, and a memory shot into her from her youth: one time she and some coworkers had had their truck break down, in the southern Urals in winter. They had had to walk from the outskirts of the abandoned Chelyabinsk-65 to Chelyabinsk-40, over fifty frozen kilometers of devastated Stalinist industrial wasteland—black abandoned factories, broken smokestacks, downed fences, gutted trucks . . . all in the snowy frigid winter night, under low clouds. Like something out of a dream it had been, even at the time. She told Maya and Art and Sax about it, her voice hoarse. Her throat hurt, but not as badly as her eyes. They had gotten so used to intercoms, it was funny to have to talk through the air separating them. But she wanted to talk. "I don't know how I ever could have forgotten that night. But I haven't thought of it in the longest time. I'd forgotten it. It must have happened, what, a hundred and twenty years ago."

"This is another one you'll remember," Maya said.

They shared brief stories about the coldest they had ever been. The two Russian women could list ten incidents colder than the very coldest experiences Sax or Art could come up with. "How about the hottest?" Art said. "I can win that one. One time I was in a log-cutting contest, in the chainsaw division, and that just comes down to who has the most powerful saw, so I replaced my saw's engine with one off a Harley-Davidson, and cut the log in under ten seconds. But motorcycle engines are air-cooled, you know, and did my hands get hot!"

They laughed. "Doesn't count," Maya declared. "It wasn't your whole body."

Fewer stars were visible than before. At first Nadia put it down to the fines in the air, or the trouble with her sanded eyes. But then she looked at her wristpad, and saw it was almost five A.M. Dawn soon. And Libya Station was only a few kilometers away. It was 256° Kelvin.

They came in at sunrise. People were passing around cups of hot tea that smelled like ambrosia. The station was too crowded to enter, and there were several thousand people waiting outside. But the evacuation had been proceeding smoothly for several hours, organized and run by Vlad and Ursula and a whole crowd of Bogdanovists. Trains were still coming in on all three pistes, from east south and west, and loading up and leaving soon thereafter. And dirigibles were floating in over the horizon. The population of Burroughs was going to be split up immediately—some taken to Elysium, some to Hellas, and farther south to Hiranyagarbha, and Christianopolis—others to the small towns on the way to Sheffield, including Underhill.

•   •   •

So they waited their turn. In the dawn light they could see that everyone's eyes were extremely bloodshot, which, along with the dust-caked masks still over their mouths, gave people a wild and bloody look. Clearly goggles were in order for walks out.

Finally Zeyk and Marina escorted the last group into the station. At this point quite a few of the First Hundred had found each other and clustered against one wall, drawn by the magnetism that always pulled them together in a crisis. Now, with the final group in, there were several of them: Maya and Michel, Nadia and Sax and Ann, Vlad, Ursula, Marina, Spencer, Ivana, the Coyote. . . .

Over by the pistes Jackie and Nirgal were directing people into trains, waving their arms like symphony conductors, and steadying those whose legs were giving out at the last minute. The First Hundred walked out to the platform together. Maya ignored Jackie as she walked past her onto a train. Nadia followed Maya on board, and then came the rest of them. They walked down the central aisle, past all the happy two-toned faces, brown with dust above, clean around the mouth. There were some dirty facemasks on the floor, but most people were holding theirs clutched in their hands.

Screens at the front of each car relayed film that a dirigible was showing of Burroughs, which this morning was a sea of ice-coated water, the ice predominant, although black polynyas were everywhere. Above this new sea stood the nine mesas of the city, now nine cliff-walled islands, not very tall, their top gardens and remaining rows of windows truly strange-looking above the dirty brash ice.

Nadia and the rest of the First Hundred followed Maya through the cars to the last one. Maya turned around and saw them all, filling the final little compartment of the train, and said, "What, is this one going to Underhill?"

"Odessa," Sax told her.

She smiled.

People were getting up and moving forward, so that the old ones could sit together in the final compartment, and they did not decline the courtesy. They thanked them and sat. Soon after that, the compartments ahead of them were full. The aisles began to fill. Vlad said something about the captain being the last to leave a sinking ship.

Nadia found the remark depressing. She was truly weary now, she couldn't remember when she had last slept. She had liked Burroughs, and a huge number of construction hours had been poured into it. . . . She remembered what Nanao had said about Sabishii. Burroughs too was in their minds. Perhaps when the shoreline of the new ocean stabilized, they could build another one, somewhere else.

As for now, Ann was sitting on the other side of the car, and Coyote was coming down the aisle to them, stopping to press his face to the window glass, and give a thumbs-up to Nirgal and Jackie, still outside. Those two got on board the train, several cars ahead of the last one. Michel was laughing at something Maya had said, and Ursula, Marina, Vlad, Spencer— these members of Nadia's family were around her and safe, at least for the moment. And as the moment was all they ever had . . . she felt herself melting into her seat. She would be asleep in minutes, she could feel it in her dry burning eyes. The train began to move.

Sax was inspecting his wristpad, and Nadia said to him drowsily, "What's happening on Earth?"

"Sea level is still rising. It's gone up four meters. It looks like the metanationals have stopped fighting, for the time being. The World Court has brokered a cease-fire. Praxis has put all its resources into flood relief. Some of the other metanats look like they might go the same way. The UN General Assembly has convened in Mexico City. India has agreed that it has a treaty with an independent Martian government."

"That's a devil's bargain," Coyote said from across the compartment. "India and China, they're too big for us to handle. You wait and see."

"So the fighting down there has ended?" Nadia said.

"It's not clear if that's permanent or not," Sax said.

Maya snorted. "No way it's permanent."

Sax shrugged.

"We need to set up a government," Maya said. "We have to set it up fast, and present Earth with a united front. The more established we seem, the less likely they'll be to come hard to root us out."

"They'll come," Coyote said from the window.

"Not if we prove to them that they'll get everything from us they would have gotten on their own," Maya said, irritated at Coyote. "That will slow them down."

"They'll come anyway."

Sax said, "We will never be out of danger until Earth is calm. Is stabilized."

"Earth will never be stabilized," Coyote said.

Sax shrugged.

"It's we who have to stabilize it!" Maya exclaimed, shaking a finger at Coyote. "For our own sakes!"

"Areoforming Earth," Michel said with his ironic smile.

"Sure, why not?" Maya said. "If that's what it takes."

Michel leaned over and gave Maya a kiss on her dusty cheek.

Coyote was shaking his head. "It's moving the world without a fulcrum," he said.

"The fulcrum is in our minds," Maya said, startling Nadia.

Marina also was watching her wrist, and now she said, "Security still has Clarke, and the cable. Peter says they've left all of Sheffield but the Socket. And someone—hey—someone has reported seeing Hiroko in Hiranyagarbha."

They went silent at this, thinking their own thoughts.

"I got into the UNTA records of that first takeover of Sabishii," Coyote said after a while, "and there was no mention at all of Hiroko, or any of her group. I don't think they got them."

Maya said darkly, "What's written down has nothing to do with what happened."

"In Sanskrit," Marina said, "Hiranyagarbha means 'The Golden Embryo.' "

Nadia's heart squeezed. Come out, Hiroko, she thought. Come out, damn you, please, please, damn you, come out. The look on Michel's face was painful to see. His whole family, disappeared. . . .

"We can't be sure we've got Mars together yet," Nadia said, to distract him. She caught his eye. "We couldn't agree in Dorsa Brevia—why should we now?"

"Because we are free," Michel replied, rallying. "It's real now. We are free to try. And you only put your full effort into a thing when there is no going back."

The train slowed to cross the equatorial piste, and they rocked back and forth with it.

"There are Reds blowing up all the pumping stations on Vastitas," Coyote said. "I don't think you're going to get any easy consensus on the terraforming."

"That's for sure," Ann said hoarsely. She cleared her throat. "We want the soletta gone too."

She glared at Sax, but he only shrugged.

"Ecopoesis," he said. "We already have a biosphere. It's all we need. A beautiful world."

Outside the broken landscape flashed by in the cool morning light. The slopes of Tyrrhena were tinted khaki by the presence of millions of small patches of grass and moss and lichen, tucked between the rocks. They looked out at it silently. Nadia felt stunned, trying to think about all of it, trying to keep it from all mixing together, blurring like the rust-and-khaki flow outside. . . .

She looked at the people around her, and some key inside her turned. Her eyes were still dry and raw, but she was no longer sleepy. The tautness in her stomach eased, for the first time since the revolt had begun. She breathed freely. She looked at the faces of her friends—Ann still angry at her, Maya still angry at Coyote, all of them beat, dirty, as red-eyed as the little red people, their irises like round chips of semiprecious stone, vivid in their bloodshot settings. She heard herself say, "Arkady would be pleased."

The others looked surprised. She never talked about him, she realized.

"Simon too," Ann said.

"And Alex." "And Sasha." "And Tatiana—"

"And all our lost ones," Michel said quickly, before the length of the list grew too great.

"But not Frank," Maya said. "Frank would be thoroughly pissed off at something."

They laughed, and Coyote said, "And we have you to carry on the tradition, eh?" And they laughed some more as she shook an angry finger at him.

"And John?" Michel asked, pulling Maya's arm down, directing the question at her.

Maya freed her arm, kept shaking a finger at Coyote. "John wouldn't be crying doom and gloom and kissing off Earth as if we could get by without it! John Boone would be ecstatic at this moment!"

"We should remember that," Michel said quickly. "We should think what he would do."

Coyote grinned. "He would be running up and down this train getting high. Being high. It would be a party all the way to Odessa. Music and dance and everything."

They looked at each other.

"Well?" Michel said.

Coyote gestured forward. "It does not sound as if they are actually needing our help."

"Nevertheless," Michel said.

And they went forward up the train.

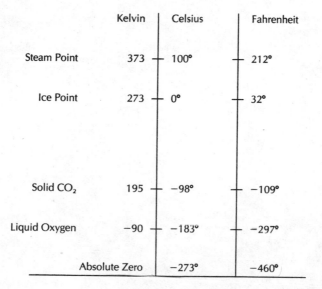

	Kelvin	Celsius	Fahrenheit
Steam Point	373	100°	212°
Ice Point	273	0°	32°
Solid CO_2	195	−98°	−109°
Liquid Oxygen	−90	−183°	−297°
Absolute Zero		−273°	−460°

Temperature Comparisons

Acknowledgments

My thanks to Lou Aronica, Victor R. Baker, Paul Birch, Donald Blankenship, Michael H. Carr, Peter Ceresole, Robert Craddock, Martyn Fogg, Jennifer Hershey, Fredric Jameson, Jane Johnson, Damon Knight, Alexander Korzhenevski, Christopher McKay, Beth Meacham, Rick Miller, Lisa Nowell, Stephen Pyne, Gary Snyder, Lucius Shepard, Ralph Vicinanza, and Tom Whitmore.

A special thanks, again, to Charles Sheffield.